Doomsday Flight

DOOMSDAY FLIGHT

Ed Stewart

VICTOR BOOKS

A DIVISION OF SCRIPTURE PRESS PUBLICATIONS INC.
USA CANADA ENGLAND

More fiction by Ed Stewart

Millennium's Eve
Millennium's Dawn
The Pancake Memos and Other Stories for Growing Christians

Editor: Barbara Williams

Design: Paul Higdon
Cover Illustration: George Bush

Library of Congress Cataloging-in-Publication Data

Stewart, Ed.
  Doomsday flight / by Ed Stewart.
    p.   cm.
  ISBN 1-56476-482-6
  I. Title
PS3569.T4599D66   1995
813'.54—dc20   95-284
                                                                CIP

1 2 3 4 5 6 7 8 9 10 Printing/Year 99 98 97 96 95

Doomsday Flight

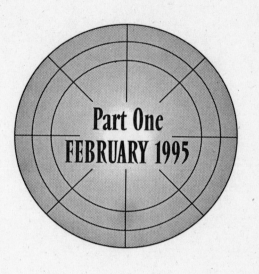

Part One
FEBRUARY 1995

One

When Tommy Eggers was assigned to a crew, it was guaranteed to be a fun trip. So when Tommy rolled his Travel-Pro suitcase down the jetway and through the forward door of the aircraft twenty minutes prior to passenger boarding, the other two flight attendants—both females—greeted him enthusiastically. Kathy Keene, a twelve-year veteran, had flown several trips with Tommy, and each one had been a kick, almost more fun than work. Shanna Davis was a twenty-four-year-old first-year reserve who had been quick-called for the trip less than two hours earlier. She had only heard through the grapevine about Tommy's zany antics, which were legend among the 1,800 flight attendants and pilots of Northstar Airlines.

For instance, Shanna had already heard from several coworkers about the infamous incident of Tommy Eggers and the bad chicken. The episode was proof positive, everyone who had related the story agreed, of Tommy's expertise. His theatrics and humor could transform the most negative, sour-pussed passenger into a Northstar frequent flier. And in the process, the flight crew was thoroughly entertained.

It had been a dinner flight from Seattle to Anchorage—or Seattle to San Diego or Phoenix to Portland, nobody who told the story to Shanna was exactly sure, because none of them had been there. A female passenger—a major league complainer, as the stories went—stopped Tommy in the aisle and pointed to the entrée of chicken cortez on her tiny plastic plate. "This chicken is bad," she protested loudly. "I could sue you for food poisoning." A dozen nearby passengers swiveled their heads to the confrontation and arched their brows, awaiting the flight attendant's response.

Suddenly in the spotlight he craved, Tommy threw himself into the drama. He snatched the chicken breast from the plate, shook off most of the salsa, and held it aloft with pinchers formed by his thumb and forefinger. Then he spanked the limp piece of meat repeatedly with his free hand while scolding, "You're a bad chicken! Bad, *bad* chicken! Daddy is very ashamed of you!"

Then he returned the chicken to the stunned woman's plastic plate, scooped up her tray with a flourish, and announced overdramatically, "Madam, we at Northstar are mortified by this gross breach of your trust. I assure you that Henri, Northstar's head chef for thirty-one years, will be reprimanded and dismissed immediately. I will return in two minutes with a deluxe meal at no extra charge."

Before the stunned woman could sputter a response, Tommy was back with a tray of delicacies scrounged from the first-class galley, including a small bottle of wine and a chilled glass. Her animosity thoroughly shredded by Tommy's blatant savoir-faire and plastic charm, the woman smiled and said, "Well now, that's more like it. Thank you, young man." The amused passengers saluted Tommy with applause. He lifted the corners of his apron and curtsied to his fans, then hurried off to assist with the next beverage service.

Suddenly excited in the presence of a Northstar celebrity, Shanna's hand trembled slightly when Tommy took it as Kathy introduced him. Shanna was almost as excited as she was the night veteran actor Keanu Reeves boarded her first-class section on a Northstar flight from L.A. to Seattle during only her third trip as a flight attendant. The movie star had been mildly cordial as Shanna served him a glass of cranberry cocktail, which she almost spilled on him.

"It's a pleasure to fly with you, Shanna," Tommy bubbled, pumping her right arm while unfurling a massive, gap-toothed smile. But the smile quickly fell the same moment Shanna noticed something strange about Tommy's grip. "I hope you're not offended by the tumor," Tommy added apologetically, looking embarrassed. Shanna felt a large, knobby knot of flesh pulsing against the palm of her right hand, and she instinctively jerked it away, suddenly wide-eyed.

Tommy threw back his head and released a piercing howl of falsetto laughter. Kathy laughed too. The "tumor," Shanna realized with a blush of chagrin, was nothing more than Tommy's middle finger purposely curled and quivering inside his palm. It was a junior high prank worked to perfection, and it had caught the gullible young flight attendant by surprise. Shanna had been in the presence of Tommy the Legend only a few seconds and she was already the victim of his craziness. She could do nothing but join in the laughter.

After stowing his luggage in the overhead compartment behind the bulkhead of the Boeing 737-400, Tommy returned to first class for a few minutes of banter and joking with his coworkers before the passengers swarmed into the plane and put them to work.

Tonight's flight from Seattle, Northstar's hub, to Juneau and Anchorage, was overbooked by 12—which meant, considering the average no-show rate of 10–15 percent, that a handful of the 120 coach and 8 first-class seats could be empty after the paying passengers boarded. But there were also a dozen nonrevenue, space-available passengers—called "nonrevs" in the industry—listed for this flight. These were employees and dependents of Northstar and other airlines holding free passes or 90-percent discount tickets. The lucky ones—in reality the most senior in the company—would get the last empty seats. A jump seat was also available in the cockpit for an off-duty pilot or first officer who couldn't get a seat in the back.

So Flight 202 would be jammed to the doors, and Tommy, Kathy, and Shanna would be hopping to complete a beverage service, a full meal service, another beverage service, and clean up during the two-and-a-half hour flight to Juneau. The stop in Juneau would be followed by a brief flight to Anchorage, where the crew would lay over. The other legs of the trip—from Anchorage to Seattle to Boise tomorrow, and from Boise to San Jose to Phoenix to Seattle on Friday—were also heavily booked. The only easy leg would be the hop from Juneau to Anchorage, with about forty passengers booked.

It would be a hard three-day trip for this crew. Four flight attendants were usually scheduled for full flights like these. But recent cost-cutting measures at Northstar had reduced all cabin crews to three: one in first class and two in coach. At least with Tommy along the trip would be entertaining, and the layovers in Anchorage and Boise would be long enough to allow the crew to party in the hotel lounge before bed.

The three flight attendants standing in the first-class aisle were all within an inch on either side of five-foot-six and within 10 pounds of 130. All were attired in the Northstar uniform: freshly pressed navy slacks for Tommy and Kathy—Shanna opted for a skirt—and double-breasted blazers with foam-green pocket squares and shirts. Tommy wore a navy tie flecked with green while the women sported navy tab ties.

The three appeared to be most different in skin tone. Tommy's flat, round face was milky white, as if the man was heliophobic. The short, thin, blond hair on his broad head allowed plenty of white scalp to show through. Kathy's long face and slender hands glowed with the deep, even bronze of a tanning-bed junkie. Her straight, bleach-blonde hair was pulled back to a navy bow. Shanna's face of dark mahogany was round and cherubic, crowned by short, black curls and accented by small, gold hoop earrings.

Tommy told a couple of off-color jokes, which evoked coarse laughter from Kathy the veteran and blushes from Shanna the rookie. Then he served them mineral water and a diet Coke respectively from the first-class galley as they discussed work assignments. Kathy, with twelve years at Northstar, was the senior flight attendant. She exercised her option to assign the A position—first-class service and crew leader—to Shanna while she and Tommy worked the back. The most junior member on a flight was often stuck with the demanding task of continuous first-class service and such tedium as the FAA-required safety checks and booze inventory before each flight.

Tommy, who was only two years junior to Kathy, would do all the announcements not covered by the standard Northstar video, which would be shown on the overhead monitors as the aircraft taxied to the end of the runway. Tommy's creative, comical touch at the mike was a refreshing respite from the boring, mechanical messages usually dispensed over the aircraft PA.

In addition to his other talents, Tommy was a skilled impersonator. Passengers smiled when they heard the drawl of John Wayne over the speakers, "You have two choices for dinner tonight, pilgrim. If the nice flight attendants don't have your first choice, you'll take what they give you and be happy about it, or you'll be looking down the barrel of my .45." They chuckled when Bill Clinton announced, "I must inform the American people that one of the aft lavatories is out of order today, and I feel your pain." And Tommy did an excellent Jack Nicholson instructing, "Hey, listen up. The flight attendants will be coming through the cabin to collect your empty cups and glasses, your headsets, your gold jewelry, your wallets and purses. And if you people don't cooperate, you'll have to answer to me."

Asking someone else to do the announcements with Tommy the master performer on board was tantamount to allowing a karaoke singer to butcher *I Left My Heart in San Francisco* with Tony Bennett sitting in the audience. Kathy was astute enough to recognize this fact and make the right call.

With jokes told and assignments decided, Tommy refilled Kathy's mineral water and asked, "By the way, who's driving tonight?"

"You don't know yet?" Kathy returned as if Tommy *should* know. She really hoped he didn't so she could break the news.

"I kind of breezed through ops," he said, making a face which communicated that he had been hustling to get to the gate on time. "I didn't see the names of the bus drivers."

Kathy flashed a smug grin. "Well, our F.O. is Kelly Schmidt," she said quietly, saving the best till last.

"Schmidt? OK," Tommy acknowledged. "He's a decent chap."

"And the bus driver is your favorite: Captain Northstar himself."

Tommy slapped his hands to his cheeks and emitted a muted, widemouthed scream ala Macauley Culkin in *Home Alone*. "Not Captain red-neck, straight-arrow, do-it-by-the-book himself," he whined. Then he snapped a glance at the cockpit to make sure the pilot wasn't listening.

Kathy quickly shook her head and motioned downward with her finger, indicating that the captain was still on the tarmac under the plane conducting his preflight walkaround. "The one and only," she assured.

"Oh, great!" Tommy groaned sardonically. Then he hissed a curse. "There goes a fun trip. I'm out of here. I'm calling in sick." Tommy moved as if to retrieve his luggage from the overhead and get off the plane. But it was only an act, typical of Tommy Eggers.

"Relax, Tommy," Kathy counseled. "We can still have a good time with Coop at the wheel."

"A good time? Are you kidding?" Tommy complained. "I flew with him last month. He called me into the cockpit and reamed me out for doing Michael Jackson during the beverage announcement." Tommy couldn't resist shifting into a mousey falsetto for a sample of his impersonation. "Our complimentary beverages are Coke, diet Coke, Sprite, diet Sprite, ginger ale, orange juice, apple juice, cranberry juice—"

Kathy was giggling, but a serious-faced Shanna leaned into the conversation. "Are you talking about Captain Sams?" she almost whispered.

Tommy again checked the cockpit. The first officer was there alone completing his cockpit inspection. Then Tommy looked at naive Shanna. "Yes, I'm talking about Captain Sams," he said in a low voice, his real voice. "Captain Cooper 'Simon Legree' Sams—Coop the poop—the scourge of the western skies." The contempt in Tommy's voice was unmistakable.

"But I met him coming down the jetway this evening," Shanna said. "He seemed like a very nice man."

Tommy telegraphed amazement at Shanna's credulity with a flick of his brows. "A nice man? Yeah, he's nice to little kids and puppy dogs and people of his own political, religious, ethnic, and sexual persuasion. And he might be nice enough to buy you dinner in Anchorage or Boise hoping to charm the pants off you during this lonely three-day."

Shanna blinked hard at Tommy's directness.

"Actually, I can't fault Coop on that," Tommy continued, giving Shanna a lascivious head-to-toe glance. "I'd be on your trail too—if I were a real man." Then he snorted a laugh and struck a pose that left no doubt in Shanna's mind as to Tommy's sexual orientation. She blinked hard again.

Noticing Shanna's look of shock, Kathy inserted, "That's why flying with Tommy is so fun; we girls don't have to worry about his motives, if you know what I mean."

"Don't get me wrong," Tommy moved on quickly, "old Coop the poop is a good pilot, one of the best in the industry. He has the awards to prove it. He's just a lousy person. Bigoted. Rigid. Conceited. Intolerant. Humorless. And he always picks on the fly guys. He thinks we're *all* gay. Everything has to go by the numbers with Coop—*his* numbers. He leaves no room for fun."

"And little room for error," Kathy offered weakly in the captain's defense. Tommy glanced at the door again and blew a derisive laugh. "Mr. Perfect isn't perfect—you can bet on it. And when he screws up, it will probably be a dandy. He'll throw down one too many Bloody Marys some night and drive this baby into the side of Mt. Rainier—and with my luck, I'll be on board. What irony. Coop and I will be splattered together on the snow. They won't be able to pull our bodies apart. He'll love that." Tommy laughed scornfully at the thought.

"Bloody Marys?" Shanna repeated blankly, ignoring the morbid humor.

"You know, the drink—vodka and tomato juice," Kathy said.

"Yeah, I know a Bloody Mary," Shanna nodded. "But what's the problem?"

Visibly nervous about continuing the conversation so close to the cockpit, Tommy motioned the girls to follow him down the aisle of the empty plane. When they reached row 14, the hushed conversation continued. "Coop the poop sucks down Bloody Marys like a baby on mother's milk," Tommy said emphatically. "He has Smirnoff's delivered to his house by tanker truck. Fills his hot tub with the stuff."

Kathy rolled her eyes at him, then assured Shanna, "Tommy tends to exaggerate. What we're trying to say is that Captain Sams has a reputation for drinking too much."

"Is this reputation rumor or fact?" Shanna pressed, genuine concern at the edge of her voice.

Kathy glanced at Tommy, but she spoke before he could unleash another biting wisecrack. "Undoubtedly plenty of rumor. But I've been on trips when he had a couple of drinks during a late dinner—and we had 6 o'clock check-in the next morning."

"And who knows how many more he threw back in his room after dinner," Tommy advanced with the tone of a vigilante campaigning for a lynching. Shanna quietly assessed that Tommy had added more than his share of fuel to the rumor blaze surrounding the captain she had only barely met.

"But what about FAA regulations?" Shanna continued. "Pilots can't drink eight hours before sitting at the controls."

Kathy jumped in ahead of Tommy again. "I've seen the captain dangle his toes over the line on that regulation a couple of times, but I can't say that he has blatantly violated it."

"*I* can say it," Tommy insisted.

"You've actually seen him drinking at 2 A.M. before an early check-in?" Kathy bored in disbelievingly.

"Not *actually*, but—"

"One o'clock, then? Midnight?"

Tommy leaned away from Kathy defensively, his face screwed into the expression of an interrogated suspect. "Give me the third degree, I'm sure!" he whimpered.

"Face it, Tommy," Kathy said, softening slightly. "You're ticked at Cooper Sams because he doesn't like you, doesn't tolerate your lifestyle, and doesn't appreciate your sense of humor. This has nothing to do with his drinking habits. So what if the guy finishes his third drink at 10:15 and takes off the next morning at 6. The man is a professional. He's in control. He wouldn't have all those plaques and certificates if he wasn't."

For the first time since he walked into the plane, Tommy was speechless.

"So you think it's safe to fly with him?" Shanna cut in, deadly serious.

Kathy's response was delayed momentarily by the first group of passengers surging through the forward door. The tide moved haltingly down the narrow aisle, juggling bulky carry-on bags while checking seat numbers above the windows against the seat assignments on their boarding passes. It was time for the flight attendants to go to work.

"Shanna, I've been at this twelve years," Kathy said as the two women began popping open overhead compartment doors from the middle of the plane aft to receive bags. Tommy had already scurried forward to be the affable Northstar host, welcoming his audience on board. "In my opinion, anyone who can get this hunk of steel off the ground, keep it steady at 31,000 feet, and put it down where it's supposed to come down is safe to fly with. But if you run into trouble at any of these stages, there's no one I'd rather have at the controls than Cooper Sams—Bloody Marys or no Bloody Marys."

Shanna wasn't fully consoled. Instead she wondered why she had dropped out of college to pursue her crazy dream of flying.

Two

Cooper Sams was at the airport and busy with flight preparations at least a half hour before his crew arrived. He always left home in plenty of time for thorough, unhurried preparation at the beginning of a trip. Today was no exception.

For Captain Sams, the thirty-five-minute drive from his home on Mercer Island to Northstar flight operations on Pacific Highway near the SeaTac terminal was rather meditative, as close to spiritual as anything in his life. During this time he communed silently with the greater gods in his personal cosmos, namely ceiling, visibility, temperature, dew point, barometric pressure, winds aloft—items vital to his profession, items over which he had no control. Having flown the route from Seattle to Juneau and Anchorage many times already this winter, he knew generally what to expect on tonight's flight. Yet in these quiet moments alone in the car, Cooper focused his mental energy in an attempt to summon the best and dispel the worst from the natural forces of wind and weather which awaited him.

Cooper reasoned that the gods *had* responded to his meditation and favored him during his twenty-year commercial flying career, partially accounting for the nearly 12,000 successful takeoffs and landings to his credit. But the more important preparation, Cooper knew, was what happened at the end of the thirty-five-minute commute. This was when he shifted his focus to the elements of his profession over which he not only had control but mastery: his skills as a pilot and his knowledge of the Boeing 737-400. If the fickle weather gods ever vented their wrath on him, Cooper, who viewed himself to be at least equal to them in power, knew he could triumph. He prided himself on being adequately prepared to get him and his 737—with all its passengers—through anything safely.

As usual, Cooper arrived at ops nearly ninety minutes prior to his flight's departure time. Most pilots were content to check in only an hour early as required. But in his commitment to thorough preparation and safety, Cooper Sams had always exceeded company and FAA requirements, and he did so by always allowing extra time.

He parked his immaculate, black, 1994 Thunderbird LX in its customary spot near the back of the employee lot, away from the shuttle bus route to minimize accidental contact by other vehicles. He spent several minutes sponging beads of water from the highly polished surface with a supple chamois cloth, being extra careful not to get any dirt or water on his uniform. After stowing the cloth in the trunk and removing his luggage, he wrapped the gleaming sport coupe in its custom-fitted, waterproof, soft-canvas cover. February showers were super-abundant in the Seattle area. Today's earlier storm would soon be followed by another and another. Residents of western Washington probably wouldn't see blue sky the entire three days he was away. Cooper couldn't bear the thought of leaving his T-Bird exposed to the elements, so he covered it while in the lot, rain or shine.

Despite the threat of imminent showers, Cooper chose to walk the half mile to the ops building instead of ride the shuttle. Unlike many of his industry colleagues, he carried his suitcase and flight case—or "brain bag"—instead of rolling them. In his mind, the costly suitcases on wheels and flimsy foldup carts represented a compromise with responsibility, which ran across his grain. His few friends had joked that he was stubborn and old-fashioned, and he suspected that he had been called worse by coworkers who had to endure his demand for hard work and no nonsense on his trips. They could call him whatever they liked. His job was to make sure that everyone on the crew carried his own weight, and the heavy cases pulling at his arms and shoulders assured him that he could never be criticized for not doing more than his fair share.

Cooper Sams' trim physique and strong gait belied his age of fifty-three years. At six feet even, he wore the same sized navy-blue uniform issued to him when he joined the company. A rigorous, self-directed workout program kept his muscles toned and his stomach flat, allowing him to eat plenty and enjoy a drink or two every day after work. He disdained colleagues who compromised with proper eating and exercise habits and presented a slovenly appearance from the flight deck.

Cooper's youthful body caused observers to regard the creases of age on his moderately-tanned face as credentials of maturity and experience instead of hints that he should soon start thinking about retirement. Alert, gray eyes, angular cheekbones, nose, and jaw, and thin, seldom-smiling lips telegraphed sober self-confidence.

Captain Sams kept the most obvious sign of his age hidden under his navy-blue cap bearing the distinguished "scrambled eggs" of rank on the bill. His gray hair, which was still styled in a short flattop from his college days, had almost completely replaced the original black. And a bald spot was relentlessly displacing the gray stubble on the crown in an ever-widening circle. As a result, when in uniform Cooper wore his cap everywhere except when sitting at the controls. When in civvies he seldom left the house without his Seattle Seahawks cap in winter or Panama straw hat in summer.

Entering the ops building, Cooper stowed his luggage in an empty work station, removed his jacket, and found an available computer terminal. With a swipe of his ID card and several quick keystrokes, he informed crew scheduling that he was on site for this trip of his February block. Then he pulled up the names of the crew members he would be responsible for—at least those who chose not to drop this trip for another one which better accommodated their social schedules or child-care problems. Flight attendants were the worst for dropping trips. Cooper couldn't remember one who had worked a block with him for the full month. It griped him that people didn't work the schedules they had bid for and were given. Didn't they realize how much it cost the company in crew scheduling man hours to plug those holes?

Cooper silently read the names on the screen and thought about each individual.

First Officer Kelly V. Schmidt. Single guy about thirty-five. Not a bad young pilot, but if he really wants to make captain he'd be here with me now studying the weather package. Schmidt found himself a flight attendant on the crew to snuggle up with when we flew together a few months ago. He met the girl—about ten years younger than himself—on our first leg out, and by the end of the month they were living together. I wonder if he's chasing another skirt this month.

Flight Attendant Katherine J. Keene. There must be twenty Kathys based in Seattle; which one is this? She's the senior F.A. on this trip, which means she'll probably stick someone else with the hard work.

Flight Attendant Thomas G. Eggers, Jr. Oh geez, not that loudmouthed queer again! Maybe, if I give him a hard time on this trip, he'll try harder to stay off my trips. It's worth a try.

Flight Attendant Shanna T. Davis. Hmm, a reserve just assigned to the trip, a quick call. Somebody must have called in sick and dropped the trip. Shanna, guess who's going to inherit the A position and serve me coffee. I hope you're halfway decent to look at.

Cooper searched for one more name, but it wasn't there. Then he swore under his breath, remembering the reason. *Cutting back on flight attendants is absurd,* he thought, *especially these days when you're lucky to find three who will pull their own weight.* Then he thought about Tommy Eggers again. *And that jerk will be prancing up and down the aisle doing impressions when he should be serving dinner.* He shook his head in disgust and mumbled another curse before returning the computer to the main menu for the next pilot's use.

Checking his V-file, Cooper found a moderate amount of mail. There were several minor policy and procedure revisions to the company flight manual. It seemed that somebody upstairs changed something every week just to fill the mail boxes. There was a small packet of Jepps revisions—changes in the approach and en-route charts contained in the pilot's "bible," the bulky, two-binder Jeppesen's Flight Manual. And there was a two-page memo to be inserted in Cooper's Flight Operations Specifications manual. Flight ops specs contains all the legal documents a pilot is required by the FAA to carry: certificate, routes for which he is qualified, and pages of federal aviation regulations and details.

Cooper took his stack of mail back to the work station, sat down, and opened his brain bag on the floor. He knew several pilots who, because they didn't allow themselves enough time, filed in their binders unread all memos and revisions which did not apply to their next flight or destination. Cooper regarded such inattentiveness to vital information as sloppy and potentially dangerous. So he came early to scour every sheet of data before initialing it, dating it, and entering it in the proper binder. Today it took him twenty-two minutes to work through the sheaf of papers from his mailbox.

Maxine Beecham, a very large, very efficient, and very friendly dispatcher, was working the desk when Cooper stepped up to receive his dispatch release, weather package, and flight plan. "How are you doing, Coop?" She beamed a warm smile which helped dress up her rather plain, chubby face. "You gonna let me drive that Thunderbird while you're gone this time?"

Cooper nudged the cap an inch higher on his brow with a thumb to the underside of the bill. He wasn't much for small talk, especially before a flight. But Maxine was too big and too nice to ignore completely. "Hello, Maxie," he said, managing a little smile of his own. "Sorry, the 'Bird is all wrapped up for this trip. Besides, she's real persnickety. She won't let anybody drive her except me." In reality, Cooper was the fussy one about his car. The only other person he had allowed behind the wheel was Rachel, and that was for a brief test drive just after he bought it—with him in the passenger's bucket.

Dreading that Maxine was about to launch into her latest flier joke,

Cooper hurried on to business. "Two-zero-two today, Maxie." Then he glanced at the keyboard on the counter, subtly prompting her to type in the numbers, pull up the data, and send it to the printer.

"You've got it, Coop," Maxine chirped. Her short, fat fingers skipped quickly over the keys to retrieve the data to the screen. "Juneau and Anchorage tonight." She kind of sang the words as if Cooper had won the trip as a prize. Cooper was not amused and did not respond. The flight to Alaska—or anywhere, for that matter—was no prize. It was a job—a good job, a fulfilling job, and a financially rewarding job, to be sure, but a job nonetheless. And he was anxious to get to work.

There was a gap of several seconds between Maxine's command for the computer to print and the emergence of the data from the printer, and she felt duty-bound to fill it. "Did you hear the one about the British flier during World War II, Coop?"

Cooper wanted to say "Yes"—even though he hadn't heard the joke—then grab his documents and leave. But the printer had yet to start printing, and Maxine didn't give him a chance to answer anyway. He was trapped.

"This British flier was on a bombing run over enemy territory when his plane was hit, so he bailed out and was captured. He was hurt badly, so they took him to a POW hospital."

Cooper eyed the printer on the counter next to Maxine and willed it to produce. It was humming, but nothing else was happening. He looked back at Maxine and silently wished for an interrupting phone call, coughing spell, or minor earthquake—anything to deliver him from the large woman's attempt to entertain him.

"The prison doctor looked him over and said, 'Your leg is real bad, so we're going to amputate.'" Maxine tried to mimic a European accent. It was lame. "And the flier said, 'After the amputation, will you please put my leg on one of your bombers and drop it on England so at least a part of me gets home?'" Her British accent was just as bad. "So the doctor said, 'That's OK with me.' So they took his leg off and sent it to England."

The first copy of the dispatch release emerged from the printer. Cooper suspected that the joke was going to drag out for a while, so he reached across the counter and caught the sheet as it dropped into the tray while still pretending to listen to Maxine. He stole a quick glance at the first few lines.

ROUTE: SEATTLE/JUNEAU/ANCHORAGE . . .
AIRCRAFT NUMBER: N122NS . . .
FLIGHT NUMBER: 202 . . .

"The next week the enemy doctor comes back and says to the British flier, 'I'm sorry, but your other leg has gangrene. It has to be amputated.' " Maxine giggled briefly in anticipation of the punch line, which Cooper assessed was still some way off. "So the flier said, 'Will you please take this leg and put it on a bomber headed for England so another part of me gets home?' And the doctor said, 'It's OK with me.' So that's what they did." Maxine giggled again. Cooper snatched another look at the sheet.

SCHEDULED DEPARTURE SEATAC:
7:35 P.M. PACIFIC STANDARD . . .
SCHEDULED ARRIVAL JUNEAU:
9:10 P.M. ALASKA STANDARD . . .
SCHEDULED DEPARTURE JUNEAU:
9:45 P.M. ALASKA STANDARD . . .
SCHEDULED ARRIVAL ANCHORAGE:
11:20 P.M. ALASKA STANDARD . . .

"A week later the doctor comes back again and says, 'Your right arm is all green and gooey, so we have to amputate again.' " Maxine was giggling so hard she had to abandon her attempt to sound foreign. "So the flier says, 'Will you please put my arm on a bomber headed to England so another part of me gets home?' "

Cooper's attention was on the dispatch release.

ALTERNATE AIRPORTS:
KETCHIKAN, YAKUTAT, FAIRBANKS . . .
LOAD PERMITTING FUEL: 22,000 POUNDS.

He made a mental note to order 5,000 more pounds of fuel, upping the total to the maximum allowed. There was no reason to scrimp even if the weather was good, which it seldom was all the way to Juneau this time of year. Since it was always the captain's option, Cooper frequently ordered additional fuel for his flights.

Maxine pulled herself together for the punch line, and Cooper collected the flight plan and as much of the weather package as the printer had spewed out so far. "Suddenly the prison doctor gets real mad. He says to the flier, 'First one leg, then the other, and now your arm. Are you trying to escape?' "

Maxine shook with laughter. Cooper hadn't listened closely enough to get the joke, but he smiled and nodded as if he had. "Good one, Maxie," he said. Then he returned to the papers in front of him, which were still warm from the printer. "I'm going to increase the fuel order today," he said as he made the appropriate notations on both copies of the dispatch release.

"Weather?" Maxine probed, wiping a tiny tear of laughter from the corner of each eye with a tissue.

Cooper again scanned the sequence report, noting the ceiling, visibility, temperature, dew point, and wind in Juneau and Anchorage at the moment. Then he rechecked the terminal forecast, projecting the weather in those locations for the next twenty-four hours. Winds around Juneau were strong but not unusual. "Naw, I'm just throwing in a few extra gallons for the wife and kids," he said.

Maxine nodded. Cooper was one of only a few senior captains who used the old phrase. Roughly translated, it meant: Let's be extra cautious so we will all arrive home safely. Caution and thorough preparation was Cooper Sams' code for living. *If you're cautious, you will seldom be surprised,* he had drummed into his subconscious. *And when you are surprised, thorough preparation will enable you to deal with the challenge successfully.*

For Cooper, however, the glib "wife and kids" phrase had no meaning. There was no wife and kids—never had been. Work always came before relationships. To him, a lifetime mate was too restrictive, and kids were a gigantic burden. There had been an occasional drinking buddy and bed partner among his female acquaintances. Over the years, only a few had braved the arid distance he maintained around himself like a personal Sahara. And fewer still had penetrated the fortress of his private life. But none of them survived more than a few months—until Rachel.

Three

Rachel Prescott was referred to among her younger coworkers at Northstar as a "senior mama"—a twenty-two-year veteran flight attendant. It was an unofficial title she silently relished. Longevity of service permitted her to grab the best trips and dump the red-eyes, four-day backbreakers, and holiday shifts on juniors and reserves. Senior mamas drew the highest pay, commanded the best schedules, outranked most coworkers for nonrev seats, and generally ruled the roost on the trips they worked.

Most senior mamas worked hard and enjoyed their perks without flaunting them. A few senior mamas, somehow calloused or soured by their work experience instead of enriched by it, threw their weight around and made life miserable for everyone around them. Rachel Prescott was one of the few.

Rachel's career at Northstar had begun with glittering promise. The Atlanta native and University of Alabama economics graduate wanted to travel before settling in to make her mark in the world of high finance. A friend at Delta had told her that flight attendants enjoy great travel benefits, so Rachel decided to try the airlines for four or five years and see the world. Perhaps her experience would open a door to the industry in her field of economics.

She applied to a dozen airlines and interviewed with four, including Delta. She wanted to stay in the south, but only one firm called her back: Northstar, a small but rapidly growing West Coast airline based in Seattle and featuring service to Alaska. Rachel had never seen Seattle until the day she arrived for her final interview. She immediately fell in love with the Emerald City, and Northstar fell in love with her. It seemed to be a match made in heaven.

With the airline in a steep growth mode, Rachel rose in seniority quickly, spending only two months on reserve. She was a hard worker and tolerated the less desirable blocks well. A petite and shapely redhead with killer green eyes, Rachel caught the fancy of coworkers and passengers alike. And though she was a little on the quiet side, whenever Rachel allowed her Georgia honey drawl to be heard, westerners melted. She had many girlfriends among the flight attendants. And scores of men in the industry, from baggage handlers to gate agents to captains, tripped over themselves trying to attract her attention. But she dated little and traveled a lot. She quickly learned the ropes of nonrev and ID-90 travel, and she spent much of her time off exploring the country and overseas—alone.

As she approached her five-year anniversary, Rachel weighed the benefits of flying against her dream of a business career. While working a flight from L.A. to Seattle one night, she met someone who helped her make up her mind. Jack Scheer, young, handsome, and affable, was her only passenger in first class. After the beverage and meal service, they talked. Jack owned a small, growing software business in Southern California. He was flying to Seattle to interview someone to manage the financial end. Rachel admitted that she was an economics graduate looking for such an opportunity. What they did not confess was the powerful physical attraction which had sparked to life between them as they talked. Instead, they exchanged phone numbers and agreed to meet the next day to discuss a possible interview.

But Rachel and Jack never got down to business. They met for dinner the next night and became completely absorbed in each other. Jack cancelled his interview, and they spent the next day and evening together. Then Jack postponed his return flight and Rachel called in sick, and they spent the rest of the week seeing the sights together—quaint Poulsbo, the Chittenden locks at Ballard, the San Juans—and falling in love.

Over the next four months they were together every free day and night in Seattle, L.A., or wherever Jack happened to be on business. A small wedding was planned. At Jack's suggestion, Rachel would transfer to L.A. and keep working for Northstar until his business got established. Then she could quit and be the controller or vice-president if she wanted or just sit by the pool in the Brentwood home he promised to buy her. In the meantime, they could travel the world together on her flight benefits, an endless honeymoon. Their apartment in Granada Hills would be their castle of love. Totally swept away by her handsome prince, Rachel agreed.

Jack talked Rachel into two children in their first four years. But his business continued to struggle, so Rachel worked long into each pregnancy and returned to work after a brief maternity leave. She hated seeing her paychecks swallowed up by the business, and she hated even more leaving the kids in day care. But Jack continued to promise that they were "just a few months from breaking it big in the industry."

Then one day Rachel came home from a trip and Jack was gone. The note simply said he didn't want to be tied down by family responsibility. He had liquidated the business, sold what little furniture they owned, and split for Texas or somewhere with a waitress from Van Nuys. Rachel was left with two preschoolers and an empty apartment—rent past due.

Infuriated at him, Rachel initiated legal proceedings for child support. But Jack was a dry well and sent practically nothing. Infuriated at herself for being so gullible, she dumped her married name and transferred back to Seattle. There would be no business career. An entry-level position couldn't come close to what she was making with Northstar, and she had two mouths to feed. The choice had been made for her, which meant she had no choice. She gradually became embittered against the job which had brought Jack into her life only to trap her.

Never the extrovert, Rachel pulled even farther into a shell. She isolated herself from all but a few close friends and refused all dates. Since work took her out of town for three and four days at a time, she spent every moment at home with her daughter and son, who were cared for by a live-in nanny while she was gone. It was an arduous parenting task, and Rachel found comfort in alcohol at the end of her grueling days. The few who knew her well suspected that she was seeking a little too much comfort for her own good.

As a flight attendant for Northstar, Rachel was all business and little fun. She did her work by the book and, as she continued to rise in seniority, demanded that her subordinates do the same. On layovers, she became what her coworkers called a "slam-clicker"—derived from the sound of a hotel room door being closed and locked from the inside. She seldom ate, fraternized, or caroused with the crew, preferring the solitude of her own room and a carafe of wine.

When Jack showed up to see their children after nine years, Rachel was totally unprepared. Remarried into a little money with two young sons and a decent nine-to-five job in Houston, he threatened to take twelve-year-old Aly and ten-year-old Jeff from her legally if she did not support his request for joint custody. And he produced all the evidence his attorney said he would need: a DUI conviction against her and two on the nanny. The killing blow fell when Aly and Jeff told Rachel they wanted to spend time getting to know their dad and stepmom. Quelling explosions of rage and despair, Rachel signed a joint custody agreement, and her children moved to Houston for the '92–'93 school year.

If Rachel was a wretch before Jack's action, she was a wretch in spades afterward. So the chances that Rachel the wretch and Coop the poop would eat together on a trip, let alone become romantically involved, were as remote as if they had been stranded on separate islands with a vast sea between them. Those who knew them might have said they deserved each other, perhaps like the wicked witch of the west and one of the billy goats gruff deserved each other. But no one would have predicted what happened on that Boise layover in January 1993.

Captain Sams and Flight Attendant Prescott had flown together a few times before the Boise trip. They each held a measure of unspoken respect for each other as professionals among coworkers who at times seemed very unprofessional. They were like two beavers among crews of otters, too busy doing their jobs to stop for fun or to compliment each other on how well they worked.

They arrived in Boise that night just ahead of a storm which swooped in from Canada and shut down the airport with fourteen inches of snow. Ms. Slam-clicker had dinner and a carafe of wine in her room alone, as usual. Out of obligation, Cooper endured dinner with the rest of the crew, a couple of bubble-gum chewing female reserves who were ecstatic about getting snowed in, and a first officer who buried himself in spy novels during layovers. Then Cooper found a quiet corner of the hotel lounge and sipped Bloody Marys for a couple of hours alone.

In the morning the airport was still closed. While Cooper awaited Northstar's decision on how and when they would get out of Boise, Rachel and the first officer remained in their rooms and the two reserves played in the snow. At noon, just as a second blizzard engulfed southwestern Idaho, Rachel and Cooper found themselves forced to share a small table in the coffee shop, which was crowded with stranded travelers and flight crews. Rachel had come down to eat while her room was being made up, since it looked like they were going to be there another night. And Cooper was grabbing a bite in between phone calls to ops in Seattle.

They ate quickly and talked sparingly, all about work—the minor crisis of getting out of Boise, other whiteouts they had survived at Northstar, company politics which often muddled their jobs, the spirit of apathy and carelessness which infected so many of their juniors. Each hurried away from the coffee shop quietly impressed with the other's perspective. They were two shriveled peas in the same professional pod.

That night, the first officer and rookie flight attendants bundled up and took a cab to the mall for a movie. Cooper and Rachel were politely invited along and each politely refused. After two glasses of wine, Rachel again ventured out of seclusion. She saw Cooper, with his Seahawks cap pushed high on his forehead, sipping a drink in the smoke-filled lounge. Had he not spotted her and waved her to his table, she would have done what she intended: walked around the lobby, bought a pack of cigarettes, and returned to her room.

After a couple of drinks together their rigid, professional postures began to relax, as if the alcohol had loosened the tie and collar buttons on tight-fitting mental uniforms. Each guardedly related to the other a sketchy life history and career path to Northstar. Cooper was warmed by the calming southern swells in Rachel's voice, which soothed him like a night in his sailboat on gentle water. And he quietly admired her toughness in raising two children alone, not knowing they had recently been taken from her.

Rachel studied with interest the strong angles of Cooper's brow, cheeks, and chin, dramatized by the low light in the lounge. She was impressed by his Navy service record, unaware that his decorations as a flier in Vietnam and his career achievements at Northstar had left him empty.

After two hours they said good night. The crew ferried the empty plane home the next morning. It could have easily ended there.

Rachel was surprised when Cooper called a few days later to invite her to dinner and even more surprised when she heard herself accept. Their first dates were ragged and ungraceful, like courting porcupines trying to dance without getting pricked. Their conversations moved to depth slowly in small layers of honesty. There were moments of mistrust and temptations on both sides to bolt and run. But they kept moving closer.

Their first kiss was so nerve-racking for Cooper that he belched in the middle of it. But they both survived the embarrassment and laughed like children enjoying something naughty. Three months after Boise, Rachel moved into Cooper's spacious home on the north end of Mercer Island.

Their fellow employees at Northstar suspected nothing between them. To keep it that way, Cooper and Rachel purposely never flew together again.

No one looking on would mistake their relationship for a torrid movie screen romance. They barely touched each other in public. Rather, theirs was a very private friendship and quiet intimacy. They sailed Lake Washington from the private dock behind Cooper's home. They nurtured a garden of fresh vegetables and lauded each other as gourmet chefs. They hiked Mt. Rainier in the sun and the rain. They drank a little less, and their conversations were frequent and enjoyable though not profound. It was as if Cooper Sams and Rachel Prescott had assumed the life of a couple happily married for twenty years without the inconvenience of investing all that time.

But there was no talk of marriage. Neither of them would bring it up. From Cooper's side, for all that Rachel brought to his life, he still viewed marriage as entering a door fortified with a latch and a lock. For fifty-three years he entertained only swinging door relationships— easy in, easy out. He might stay with Rachel until he died—at this point in time he thought he might like to. But he wasn't about to clutter up their warm friendship with emotional or legal promises he might someday want to break.

From Rachel's side, the experience with Jack Scheer had left her feeling like she had been *thrown through* a door—the fact that he walked out on her and then connived to steal Aly and Jeff from her. Cooper Sams was not Jack Scheer. But to Rachel, there was a shadow of her former husband in every man, the potential to desecrate the priceless treasure of mutual trust she still yearned to share with a man. She had found sanctuary in Cooper Sams, but she was stalked by the fear that she may come home from a trip and find *him* gone too. Rachel hoped someday Cooper would authenticate the love she felt from him with a solemn promise—a legal one—that would finally close the wound from the past. But she was not about to risk his displeasure by asking him for it.

Four

"Coop, are you still with us?" Maxine probed, chuckling. For ten seconds her hand had been outstretched to receive Cooper Sams' signed copy of the dispatch release. The captain seemed to be in a time warp.

Cooper's momentary reverie about Rachel popped like a soap bubble at the sound of Maxine's voice. "Sorry, Maxie," he said, handing her the form.

"Dreaming about the wife and kids again, eh Coop?" she teased. Cooper Sams' confirmed bachelorhood was common knowledge at ops and a frequent prod employed by the few who joked with him, those who, like Maxine, refused to be intimidated by his quiet, crusty demeanor.

Cooper came back quickly. "Yeah, Ethel and all the young'ns," he returned with a wry smile, secretly pleased that Rachel was in his life but that she wasn't "the wife." Then he scooped up all the paperwork and tapped it into a neat pile on the counter. "Thanks, Maxie. See you next week."

"Keep the greasy side down, Coop," Maxie said as he walked away. Cooper flicked a wave at her over his shoulder without looking back.

He returned to the work station to zero in on the key documents in his hand. He studied the flight plan worksheet, identifying the navigational checkpoints—called VOR's, the highways between them—called jet airways, and intersections between Seattle and Juneau. The worksheet noted the estimated arrival time and fuel burn at each checkpoint based on weather conditions. In flight, Cooper always instructed his copilot to record flight time and fuel burn over each fix and note it on the flight plan worksheet. A disparity on the worksheet could be an early indication of a problem, and if one of his engines was going to malfunction, Cooper wanted to be the first to know.

Next, Cooper turned to the notams, short for notices to airmen. Notams contained vital last-minute updates on navigational aids en route, approach procedures, and destination facilities. The changes in notams were too recent to show up in the standard revision packets. So even the pilots who breezed through the other paperwork studied their notams carefully and made the changes which applied to their upcoming flights.

Cooper found no Seattle-Juneau-Anchorage navigational problems reported in the notams, nor did any procedure changes noted affect the standard approaches to either of tonight's airports. He double-checked the notams to be sure. No problems, no changes. And he found only one small item on the field and facilities report for Anchorage International Airport. The security access code at the Northstar gates had been changed—again. He opened the appropriate notebook, lined out the old code, and entered five new digits.

Cooper checked his watch: 6:45 P.M., fifty minutes before departure and twenty minutes before he planned to arrive at the gate and conduct his personal walkaround underneath the 737. A proud inner smile swelled his chest slightly. *Always ready with time to spare,* he congratulated himself. *Always ready with time for a cup of coffee.*

Having snapped every sheet of paper into its binder, Cooper began methodically repacking the flight case at his feet. "Hello, Captain," came the voice from above him. Sitting up, Cooper's eyes followed the tall masculine frame in a navy-blue uniform to the tanned and smiling face of his first officer.

"Good evening, Mr. Schmidt." Cooper reached up a polite hand but did not stand, a subtle and intentional assertion of his seniority. "Are we ready to go to Alaska tonight?"

"Yes sir, at least I will be when the time comes. Anything special I should look at?" Schmidt knew he had asked the wrong question the instant it passed his lips.

"*Everything* is special, Schmidt," Cooper said soberly, nodding at the sheaf of papers in the copilot's hands. "Look at *everything*."

"Yes sir," Schmidt said, wincing from the direct hit. "I intend to."

"Then I'll see you at the gate." Cooper resumed packing his case, tacitly ending the conversation, and Schmidt quickly disappeared. The captain slipped his jacket on and left the building to wait for the airport shuttle.

Cooper disliked arriving at the airport too early, before he could walk directly from the shuttle to the gate and board the plane. Uniformed airline personnel loitering in the concourse looked like tour guides to inexperienced travelers. "Will the flight to Minneapolis leave on time?" "My sister, Yvonne, was supposed to be on that plane from Albuquerque, but she didn't get off. Will you go inside and see if she's there?" "Are you serving that stuffed pasta shell on today's flight? If you are I'd better eat before I get on, because I had your pasta a couple of years ago and it made me nauseated."

But today, with so many prying ears in the ops building, Cooper hopped an early employee bus to SeaTac and braved the crowd to sip his cup of coffee and make a phone call.

Employing long, purposeful strides, Cooper made it to the bank of public phones across from the Starbuck's counter without being snagged by a passenger. He caught Ginny's eye and ordered a large cup of black Colombian. By the time he settled into the booth and pulled out his address book and three dollars, Ginny arrived with the steaming cup. He gave her the money and a wink.

He found the number he wanted among a list of West Coast hotels used by Northstar for layovers. He tapped in his personal phone code and the number, then sat back, inched his captain's cap higher on his forehead, and snapped the lid off his coffee.

"Cathedral Hill Hotel, San Francisco. How may I direct your call?"

"Rachel Prescott, Northstar crew."

"One moment, please."

Cooper felt the hot coffee bite at his upper lip as he took his first cautious slurp. He envied Rachel for having already completed the first day of her trip while he was yet to begin his. She had left the house at 5:30 for a 6:15 check-in. Her MD-80 crew started with a Seattle-Portland turn, then changed aircraft and flew Seattle-Reno-Los Angeles-San Francisco. Cooper figured that she had already enjoyed a leisurely hot bath and a room service dinner. He pictured her tucked into her robe for the evening with the latest Duke Dennison techno-thriller, the TV tuned to the Discovery Channel, and a chilled glass of dry pinot.

"Yes." It was Rachel's senior-mama voice. After over a year with Cooper, she still wasn't used to him calling her during a layover. He didn't call her on every trip, and when he called their conversations were often halting, like going-steady thirteen-year-olds who can't think of anything to say. But Cooper knew that the simple act brought Rachel happiness, and he liked the feeling of making her happy.

"This is the captain speaking."

Her voice instantly relaxed. "Hello, Cooper."

"Hi." He already felt stuck for words, so he resorted to the automatic. "How was your day?"

"Fine. It was a good day. How was yours?"

"Full flights?" he probed, keeping the focus on her.

"In and out of Reno we had drunks stacked on the wings, as usual," Rachel said with a little laugh. "But the other legs were pretty easy."

"Good crew?"

"Yeah, not bad," she said. "We have one young brat reserve I had to slap around a little, but everybody else stayed out of my face."

Cooper was out of questions. He sipped coffee. "Yeah, my day was OK. Celia showed up to clean today, so—"

"But I scheduled her for tomorrow when we're both gone," Rachel interrupted, irritated.

"I know, and I told her that. But she said her schedule was all screwed up and she couldn't do it tomorrow. So I took the boat out for a couple of hours while she worked."

"A little brisk and wet to be on the lake today, wasn't it Cooper?" There was a hint of maternal scolding in Rachel's voice. The tone had bothered Cooper at first until he realized it reflected her concern for him.

"I wore a slicker. I was fine. It was a nice ride."

Cooper sipped coffee again. He wasn't good at this. "Had your bath yet?"

"Yes, I had a wonderful hot bath and grilled trout for dinner. It's a lovely room. Wish you were here."

There was a part of Cooper that also wished he were there. The mention of grilled trout reminded him how hungry he was. All he had to look forward to was a lukewarm crew meal on the way north. And the vision of Rachel, clean and fragrant from her bath, lounging on the king-sized bed aroused another appetite. An evening with her at the Cathedral Hill sounded a lot more inviting than a routine run to Juneau and Anchorage.

But another part of him was relieved when they parted for three or four days to fulfill their respective work obligations. It gave him time to breathe, time to reconnect with the need for solitude and privacy which had kept him single all these years. For all Rachel brought to his life, Cooper had a life of his own. They were not an old married couple with a rich history of blended lives and common interests. They didn't own matching La-Z-Boys where they contentedly whiled away evenings together eating popcorn and playing "Interactive Jeopardy" on TV. In the parlance of the wedding ceremony, they were not one but twain: two separate individuals who enjoyed many of the conveniences and pleasures of marital oneness. And that's the way Cooper wanted it to remain.

Cooper often suspected that Rachel had other ideas. She had wavered once on their agreement to fly separately, suggesting that a trip together once or twice a month would be romantic. "We'll live like strangers while in uniform," she proposed one night as they sipped drinks on the deck at sunset, "then I'll slip you an extra room key when no one is looking. It will be exciting and fun."

Cooper had put her off as politely as he could, warning that someone would get suspicious and their privacy would be compromised. Rachel immediately backed off, but Cooper sensed she would try again, seeking from him more than he was ready to give, setting him up for a possible trip to the altar. Cooper viewed their time apart as a necessary buffer between him and any ideas Rachel might conjure up for increased togetherness.

"I wish I was there too, Rachel," Cooper lied convincingly. "But our decision, you know . . . " He knew Rachel didn't want him to spell it out for her again, so he let it drop.

"Yes, I know," she said without sounding too disappointed.

They talked for a few more minutes about nothing more important than grilled trout or the forecast of bumpy winds into Juneau. Cooper always seemed to be the one to wrap up their conversations with something like, "Well, I guess I'd better go." Since he and Rachel had been together, he had tried to sign off his calls with something personal, something that would convey his affection without inflating her hopes for more of him. Furthermore, considering the very remote but real possibility that any flight may be his last, he felt an obligation to say something that, in the event of an accident, she might appreciate as his "famous last words."

Cooper sometimes wondered what the happily married pilots told their wives during the last intimate moments of good-bye before each trip. Did they get syrupy sweet: "I love you, darling, and if I never see you again, I will love you forever"? Did they opt for honesty: "I want you to know, dear, that I have never been unfaithful to you"? Did they have secret signs or phrases meaningful only to each other that provided closure and assured peace in the event they never saw each other again?

Cooper didn't know, and he hadn't really come up with anything original himself. It was even difficult for him to say "I love you," because he wasn't sure what he had with Rachel was really love. So he said good-bye again tonight with the words he felt seemed to fit: "See you at home, Rachel." In his mind, he was telling her that his home was her home, that he wanted her there. And if for some reason he didn't make it back home again, she may choose to interpret his farewell as, "I'll see you in that great, mysterious, eternal abyss into which our souls shall someday fall."

Rachel's final words were warm: "Good-bye Cooper. Have a good trip."

It was still a little early, and Cooper wanted to allow First Officer Schmidt plenty of time to get started in the cockpit before he arrived at the gate. Since captains are responsible for the bulk of the paperwork on the initial leg of a trip, first officers often take the cockpit first for their checks, then conduct an outside walkaround, primarily inspecting tires, brakes, and lights. If aircraft turnaround time is tight and he arrives early enough, the captain may volunteer to perform the walkaround in order to take some pressure off his copilot and assure push-back from the gate as scheduled. In the savagely competitive air travel market, on-time departures were directly linked to the flight crew's job security. So they generally pulled together to get planes up on time.

Cooper Sams always arrived at the gate in plenty of time to conduct the walkaround, a job he preferred to do himself. It wasn't that his copilots didn't do the job, it's that they didn't do it well enough for Cooper's standards. So he allowed himself extra time on the tarmac under the 737 while his copilot was busy in the cockpit. Kelly Schmidt seemed like a good man, but even good men make mistakes when they don't allow themselves enough time for preparation. Cooper would allow Schmidt time to get started in the cockpit then go to the plane himself and do the walkaround.

To kill time, Cooper stepped into a gift shop and bought two packets of breath mints for the trip and a Payday candy bar in case the crew meal was insufficient or too late in coming. As the clerk counted his change, Cooper noticed the wide variety of trinkets and gifts for sale, dime store junk at jewelry store prices, in his estimation. It occurred to him that he had never come home from a trip with a gift for Rachel. Perhaps he could defuse her yearning to travel with him by surprising her with a little something, not a piece of junk from an airport gift store, but perhaps a necklace or a bracelet made by Native Americans in Alaska. He would inquire at the hotel in Anchorage tonight about where he could find such an item tomorrow morning.

SeaTac's B concourse is almost totally occupied by Northstar gates. The white backdrop to the check-in counter at every gate proudly displays the airline's striking logo above an electronic reader board.

The word "Northstar" appears in bold, sharply angled letters of foam green ruggedly outlined in navy blue to simulate a craggy mountain range. A supernova of brilliant gold erupts from behind the A. The same logo is spread impressively across every fuselage in the Northstar fleet, which are painted white. The tail of each plane shows a large, jagged N with the trademark supernova gleaming near its pinnacle.

Cooper walked up to gate B-2 at 7:10 P.M., twenty-five minutes before departure time. Two lines of people at the check-in counter, tickets in hand, were stacked eight deep. The boarding area was crowded with chattering passengers and the relatives and friends who had come to see them off. Floor space was strewn with carry-on bags of every description, from briefcases of Italian leather to cardboard boxes held together with duct tape.

Cooper toted his luggage to the locked jetway door without venturing so much as a glance at the people who were about to board his plane. He didn't have time for dumb questions. Setting down his flight case, he deftly tapped the five-digit security access code into the keypad and pulled open the door.

A flight attendant, a perky-looking African-American girl, followed him in the door with her luggage in tow. Cooper set down his luggage to hold the door open for her. She was the reserve on this trip, he realized. "Captain Sams," he said to introduce himself as she entered.

"Good evening, sir," the girl said. "I'm Shanna Davis."

The girl looked intimidated at meeting him—the young ones all did—and hurried ahead of him down the jetway.

Once he was inside the jetway, the people noise was abruptly curtailed by the slam of the door behind him. In its place grew a sound which better suited Cooper's ears: the husky whisper-whine of commercial jet aircraft at work.

Kelly Schmidt was busy in the copilot's seat when Cooper stepped inside the cockpit to stow his gear. "Captain," he acknowledged with a brief look.

"I'll take the walkaround, Mr. Schmidt," Cooper announced as he removed his jacket and hung it in the closet.

"I'm ahead of schedule, sir," Schmidt said. "I'll get to it in just a moment."

"Take your time. I need to get outside for a few minutes anyway." It was Cooper's stock answer to every copilot's assertion that he was prepared to fulfill his responsibilities. The captain figured it sounded less ego-bruising than, "I know what I want checked down there better than you do."

"Thank you," Schmidt said, returning to his work.

Cooper pulled the flashlight from his flight case, then he stepped back into the jetway and out the door to the metal stairs leading down to the tarmac. It was in the mid 40s with a steady drizzle hinting that the full storm was on its way. The cool mist felt good on Cooper's bare, tanned arms. He preferred to wear the short-sleeved white uniform shirt, sporting the distinctive four-bar epaulets, year-round, and he rarely wore his jacket when he didn't have to. He allowed his pores to soak in the fresh coolness of the Seattle winter evening in anticipation of nearly four hours enveloped in the recirculated air of the cockpit.

The garish floodlights illuminating the area outside the jetway and glistening off the rain-coated tarmac did not fully dispel the shadows under the airplane. Using his light, Cooper performed the standard walkaround inspection any 737 pilot could do half asleep, as some of them indeed did, he suspected.

He swept the beam across the tarmac under the plane looking for any puddles of petroleum-based fluids which may have leaked from the engines or landing gear. There were none. He inspected the wear indicator pins on the main brakes. The brakes were good.

Cooper verified that the landing gear pins had been removed. Large pins bearing a red flag are installed by the maintenance crew after engine shutdown to lock the landing gear in the down position before towing. The pins prevent the gear from collapsing while it is not under hydraulic pressure generated by engine power. Cooper knew a pilot who overlooked this step during the walkaround and the checklist. After takeoff the landing gear would not come up, requiring that he land the aircraft and have the pins removed, an embarrassing error that had to be reported to the FAA.

Then Cooper homed in on a couple of optional items often overlooked during the walkaround, especially by a flight crew which didn't allow enough time for preparation. Cooper's pet peeve was the frequent oversight of the precautions for apparent landing gear failure during flight. These precautions were necessary in case the cockpit display failed to confirm the gear to be down and locked in preparation for landing. In such an emergency, the flight crew can access view windows in the floor of the cockpit and the cabin. From these windows a pilot can see into the wheel well for both the nosegear and main landing gear and visually assess whether or not the gear is down and locked by observing the alignment stripes designed for that purpose.

Wet takeoffs and landings in the Northwest quickly clouded the view windows and dirtied the alignment stripes, making a visual gear check from the cockpit or cabin difficult or impossible. On the first walkaround with a new aircraft or after an overnight, Cooper religiously checked the windows and stripes to assure a clear line of sight.

Moving under the nose of the plane, Cooper shined the beam of the flashlight into the wheel well. As he often did, he found that the alignment stripes and view windows were a little dirty. He reached up with a shop rag borrowed from maintenance and wiped away the filmy dirt.

The wheel wells for the main gear are higher off the ground than the nose wheel well. So without even inspecting them with the flashlight first, Cooper returned to the maintenance area for a ladder. It only took three minutes on each side for him to wipe clean the alignment stripes and view windows.

Having returned the supplies to maintenance, Cooper stepped under the 737 again. The rain was coming heavier now, forcing him under the broadest expanse of the wing for protection. Still, swirls of mist prompted by the exhaust of aircraft taxiing nearby found him. It was a little cool even to Cooper's liking. Furthermore, he could hear the thumping, clumping footsteps of baggage-laden passengers pouring down the jetway to board. It was time to get upstairs.

Cooper took one last look at the belly and wings of the high-tech bird he was about to pilot to Juneau and Anchorage. At these times he often envisioned himself as a chick huddled under a massive steel mother bird. Even though he had not completely mastered the technology of this complex creature, he trusted her. And he had good reason. From the day it rolled off the Boeing assembly line, this 737-400 had been expertly maintained from nose to tail and winglet to winglet by skilled Northstar maintenance personnel. To remain in service, it had to survive a demanding schedule of periodic checks, inspections, and overhauls under the relentless scrutiny of the United States Department of Transportation, which holds the highest safety standards for air travel of any country in the world. This bird was as ready to fly as precision human engineering can make it.

But in these moments alone, Cooper couldn't help thinking about the unknown. Even a mature mother bird was capable of error and inadvertently betraying the blind trust of her young. They fly into panes of window glass. They fail to detect cats stalking them from the shadows. Was the huge mother bird spread above him unaware of a present danger? Of the hundreds of thousands of parts which came together to form this Boeing 737-400, which ones had tested safe but were on the verge of failure? Where were the hidden weaknesses that may only appear during the critical seconds of acceleration, take-off, or landing? Which unseen structural or mechanical faults would survive the flight? Which would not, placing 128 passengers in immediate mortal peril, demanding a superhuman performance from pilot and crew to avert a deadly disaster?

Cooper brushed the questions away quickly, as he always did. The answers were beyond his ken, known only to whatever gods enveloped these birds in the elements and kept them aloft, sometimes despite human error. Then, looking up at the plane's belly and patting the huge tire next to him, he commissioned the bird with words he had used many times before: "Just fly, mother. Just fly."

Five

Shanna Davis saw Captain Sams coming through the door and braced herself for the conversation she knew she must initiate. The captain threaded his way along the line of boarding passengers, politely saying, "Excuse me, please." He made only brief eye contact with Shanna as she busied herself in the forward galley. And the captain completely ignored Tommy Eggers at the galley entrance, who was absorbed in his role as the flight's goodwill ambassador, welcoming boarding passengers and bantering with them about nothing of consequence. Tommy had seen his nemesis coming but purposely pretended he hadn't.

Shanna left her work in the galley, straightened her jacket, and followed the captain into the cockpit before he had a chance to sit down, leaving the door open. "Any special instructions for me, Captain?" she said with manufactured perkiness. Northstar captains have the option of holding an informal cabin briefing with the crew or with the A flight attendant. Or they may choose not to hold a briefing at all, in which case A is responsible to initiate contact and secure any additional flight information. Kathy and Tommy had informed Shanna that Captain Sams never holds briefings and that she would have to approach him. After what her coworkers had told her about the captain, Shanna wasn't looking forward to the interaction.

Cooper studied her for a moment in the dim light, pushing his cap up on his forehead. Then he leaned closer to read her badge. "Yes, Shanna, a couple of things," he said softly in a strictly business tone. "We will have a pretty smooth ride most of the way. You can begin your service at two bells. Give those eight passengers of yours a trip they'll never forget. Remember, these people are paying your salary."

Shanna waited for more. The silence was awkward. "Yes sir. I'll make sure everyone is well cared for."

The captain continued, "Our pilots are reporting moderate chop in and out of Juneau, so I want the trash picked up and the galleys buttoned down before we begin our initial descent. And be ready to buckle in early."

"Yes sir."

"And I'll have a cup of black coffee after we level off, about twenty minutes after takeoff."

"Right, black coffee."

"And what do we have for a crew meal tonight?"

"It's a corned beef sandwich on rye, Captain, with fresh broccoli and cauliflower pieces and ranch dip. And there's a brownie or a cookie in there, I think."

The frown on the captain's face was obvious even in the near darkness. "I'll get back to you on the sandwich."

"Yes sir. Anything else?"

The captain glanced past her to where Tommy Eggers was welcoming passengers with the brassy enthusiasm of a carnival barker. Shanna watched a shadow of disdain further darken the captain's face. She expected him to say something like, "Yeah, keep that jerk out of the cockpit and out of my sight." He had already communicated as much to Tommy Eggers with his eyes, except Tommy wasn't looking. Instead, the captain returned his gaze to Shanna. "Remind your partners in the back to give their best service. We want these people to buy more tickets."

Shanna nodded. "I'll tell them, Captain." Then she backed out of the cockpit, closed the door, and slid back into the galley behind a thinning stream of passengers.

"What did Captain Bluebeard have to say for himself?" Tommy whispered to Shanna between customers.

She answered with a poker face. "He wants to know if you can do the announcements tonight as Robin Leach."

The tables were turned on the practical joker for a full three seconds before he caught on and cracked up. "Robin Leach . . . that's precious!" Tommy said between fits of laughter. Shanna laughed too, surprised at her spontaneous and uncharacteristic leap into mischief. She guessed that Tommy's craziness was infectious.

Tommy couldn't resist trying the new voice on for size. "Welcome aboard, folks," he said to an elderly couple entering the forward door. "May your champagne wishes and caviar dreams come true on this Northstar flight to Alaska." His impersonation of Robin Leach was very good. The old folks laughed, and the five first class passengers already seated applauded.

Shanna pulled herself together quickly. It was time to take preflight beverage orders from the people in the expensive seats. First-class passengers are entitled to all the booze they can drink—as long as they are not obviously intoxicated, at which point company policy and the FAA prohibit flight attendants from serving them more. But they can start with one drink before departure. Remembering the captain's admonition to provide unforgettable service, she straightened her jacket again and stepped around Tommy to take her first order.

But Tommy grabbed her by the arm and pulled her back for one last comment for her ears only. "Shanna, you are a jewel, you're one of us," he said, still grinning from her little prank. "This is going to be a *very* fun trip—mark my words, even with Captain Coop-the-poop at the wheel."

Shanna glanced back at the door to the cockpit and pictured the granite-faced man with the dubious reputation sitting in the captain's seat. She hoped it would be a fun trip, but she wasn't so sure.

At twenty-two minutes before departure, Cooper Sams removed his cap, eased into the captain's seat on the left side of the cockpit, and pulled his lightweight headset over his ears. First Officer Kelly Schmidt, headset already in place, had nearly completed his final checks on the right side of the cockpit, assuring that the copilot's flight instruments and the cabin pressurization and air conditioning systems were operational.

As always, Cooper went first to the maintenance logbook. It is a serious violation of federal air regulations to depart the gate with a maintenance write-up in the logbook which has not been repaired and signed off by the ground mechanics. Even though copilots systematically review the logbook during preliminary cockpit preparation, captains are required to verify that all inoperative components have been taken care of.

Cooper checked the most recent legs flown on N122NS. No maintenance problems had been reported in the last four days. He leafed back several more days in the logbook and noted three entries: an autopilot tripped off and reset, an outside cowling latch repaired, a stall warning light replaced. He backed up a few more pages to see if any of these problems had occurred more than once in the last two weeks, indicating a suspicious trend. None had. Satisfied that the logbook was in order, he initialed it and stowed it.

With more than 120 specific items to be checked before each flight, Cooper Sams and his colleagues had been trained to perform the captain's cockpit inspection by means of a left-to-right, top-to-bottom system, referred to at Northstar as the captain's flow. The flow takes about five minutes to complete, and 95 percent of the time all instruments and systems check out perfectly. Yet Captain Sams approached his flow as if a maniacal flight instructor had purposely programmed several items for failure just to catch him napping.

He began above the window to his left with the captain's escape strap. It was coiled and stowed. In the event of an on-the-ground emergency evacuation, the captain pops out his side window, climbs through, and lowers himself to the ground with the aid of the escape strap. Another strap is stowed on the right side of the cockpit for the first officer.

Cooper rarely checked the escape strap without thinking of the tragedy at LAX several years earlier when a landing passenger jet plowed into a commuter plane which had been inadvertently cleared onto the runway for takeoff. The jet's captain and many passengers died in the crash and ensuing fire, but the other crewman in the cockpit survived. Though severely injured, the first officer managed to pop his window and deploy the escape strap. But on his first three attempts to climb out the window, a powerful stream of water from the fire truck fighting the blaze literally washed him back into the cockpit. The man was finally able to get out and drop to the tarmac to receive aid. Cooper knew that, for all the safety features built into the aircraft, his survival in an emergency largely depended on his preparedness and ingenuity under pressure.

Cooper continued overhead from the left, checking that his smoke goggles and oxygen system were ready for use. Moving to the front, he checked the yaw damper and overhead systems controls—fuel, electrical power, hydraulics, air conditioning and pressurization, and auto-pilot.

Below the windscreen and above the control wheel, he checked the mode control panel (MCP) for departure. Referring to the appropriate page in his Jeppeson Flight Manual, Cooper entered the standard instrument departure (SID) for a Seattle-to-Alaska run by rotating the appropriate knobs. He knew the Seattle SID as well as he knew his own name, but he always double-checked the figures entered on the mode control panel against Jepps. It was simply careless not to.

He loaded the flight management computer (FMC) with his route of flight and cruising altitude from the flight plan. Then he methodically inspected the flight instruments, including the altimeter and air speed indicator, and a cluster of engine instruments, including tachometers and oil pressure gauges. In order to pass his inspection, each electronic instrument must be illuminated and pegged at its appropriate level.

Moving to the right and to the top of the pedestal between the pilot and copilot's seats, Cooper inspected the engine controls—start levers, thrust levers, reverse thrust levers. He continued down the pedestal to the avionics package—radios, radar, TCAS/transponder—and the rudder and aileron trim switches. Every instrument was alive and ready, every reading was appropriate, and every switch was in its proper on or off position.

Kelly Schmidt sat quietly reviewing the weather printout as the captain completed his flow. Then Captain Sams said, "OK, Mr. Schmidt, call for clearance." The FAA requires the flight deck crew to obtain clearance from air traffic control (ATC) at least ten minutes prior to departure. True to his nature, Cooper Sams was three minutes ahead of schedule.

Primed and ready for the command, Schmidt adjusted the radio to contact clearance delivery in the tower. "Northstar two-zero-two requesting clearance," he said in clipped monotone. After several seconds, a machine-gun burst of terms, seemingly decipherable only by flight deck and tower personnel, came through the earphones: "North-star two-zero-two cleared to Juneau by Seattle Two departure. Radar vectors to jay-five-two-three as filed. Maintain 9,000. Expect flight level three-one-zero 15 nautical miles west. Do not exceed 250 knots. Departure on one-two-zero-point-four, squawk six-seven-three-seven."

Schmidt repeated the clearance figures, and the voice on his earpiece responded: "Read-back correct." Then Schmidt set the departure control frequency to 120.4 and the transponder to 6737.

At five minutes before departure, with most of the passengers on board and seated, the airline brass requires the captain to make a welcome-aboard cabin announcement. It was strictly a PR thing, Cooper knew, assuring the customers that their lives were safe in the hands of a well-qualified, congenial Northstar professional and his skilled crew. He didn't like making cabin announcements, and after this one his first officer would become the human link between the passengers in the back and all the technology and know-how up front which would take them safely from Seattle and Juneau. But since the first speech of the day was his duty, Cooper picked up the mike for the passenger address system and delivered his brief standard monologue, filling in the blanks with data appropriate to this flight, in as pleasant a voice as he could muster.

"Good evening, ladies and gentlemen. Those of us on the flight deck would like to add our welcome to flight two-zero-two from Seattle to Juneau, Alaska, with continuing service to Anchorage. We're expecting a fairly smooth ride to Alaska tonight. We have three of our finest Northstar flight attendants on board to serve you. We will let you know about weather conditions in Juneau en route. So sit back, relax, and enjoy the flight. And thank you for choosing Northstar Airlines. Welcome aboard."

Cooper thought about Tommy Eggers prancing the aisle in the main cabin and reminded himself not to use the word "finest" in his description of the cabin crew in subsequent announcements on this trip. He also had lied a little about the smooth ride. Moderate turbulence had been reported in the Juneau area, and the people had to know about it eventually. But Cooper always preferred to save any bad news about the flight until the customers were aloft—after they'd had a drink or two—and let his first officer explain everything.

"Before Start checklist, Mr. Schmidt," he said to his copilot through his headset.

"Yes sir," Schmidt answered, pulling out a laminated card headed 737-400 NORMAL CHECKLIST—BEFORE START. He began reading aloud from a list of over two dozen tasks which one or both of the men had already checked during their cockpit preparation flows. The captain rechecked each item and gave the appropriate verbal response in response to Schmidt's reading.

"Cockpit preparation."

"Completed."

"Lights test."

"Checked."

"Oxygen and interphone."

"Checked."

"Yaw damper."

"On."

"Fuel."

"Twenty-seven K, six pumps on . . . "

Shortly after completing the checklist, the gate agent stuck his head into the cockpit. "Captain, we're holding the door open for two connecting passengers from Flight 81. It got hung up getting out of Phoenix. The airplane is on the ground now and approaching the gate. We'll get them over here as soon as we can. Sorry about that."

Cooper cursed under his breath at whomever or whatever had delayed the Phoenix flight. As always, he had done everything possible to achieve push-back on time. But once again somebody somewhere had screwed up, and the ripple effect of one screwup on this flight and others would negatively affect the company's on-time departure record. "Tell the customers about the delay, Mr. Schmidt," he said with a sigh.

Six

Kelly Schmidt delivered a warm and friendly cabin announcement explaining the momentary delay. Cooper imagined with disgust that Tommy Eggers would doubtless rise to the occasion and keep the passengers entertained until the stragglers arrived.

Twelve minutes later, the late passengers had scampered aboard, the forward door was closed, and the jetway retracted to the accompaniment of an annoying warning bell. The ground crew contacted the captain by the service interphone, which is jacked into a panel under the nose of the aircraft. "Captain, your door is closed and we are ready to push."

"Roger. Stand by."

Cooper completed his before-push-back flow in a matter of seconds. At the same time the first officer made the standard cabin announcement: "Flight attendants, prepare for departure and cross-check."

"Before-push-back checklist, Mr. Schmidt." After more than 10,000 flights, Cooper Sams knew every nuance of every checklist by heart. But he reveled in the security of detail, repetition, and meticulous preparation.

The first officer read the short list aloud and Cooper responded.

"Fasten seat belt sign."

"On."

"Doors."

"Closed. Lights out."

"Anticollision light."

"On."

"Cabin announcement."

"Accomplished. Call ground control for push clearance."

Schmidt adjusted his radio. "Seattle Ground, Northstar two-zero-two ready to push from bravo two."

"Clear to push," came the response.

Schmidt switched to the interphone connecting the cockpit with the ground crew. "Nose wheel steering normal, A pumps off, brakes released, clear to push," he reported.

As the powerful, squatty tug attached to the nose wheel inched the 737 backward away from the gate, flight operations called with the weight and balance data, known simply to the flight deck crew as "the numbers": passenger count—first class and coach, zero fuel weight, amount of fuel, gross takeoff weight, and the settings for stabilizer trim determined by weight and placement of cargo. First Officer Schmidt copied the numbers on the weight and balance form on his flight plan, another of the seemingly countless required steps for takeoff.

Before Schmidt entered the last of his numbers, the ground crew announced, "Captain, you are clear to start." The aircraft must be sufficiently distanced from the terminal building before engine start to prevent the powerful engines from ingesting loose materials around the ramp area. Pilots often quipped among themselves that baggage handlers and their lunch boxes didn't go through the turbines very well.

As the tug angled the nose of the plane toward the taxiway, the two men in the cockpit snapped through their scripted, before-start dialogue, with Schmidt calling out the items and Sams answering:

"AC packs."

"Off."

"Start pressure."

"Thirty-six PSI."

"Before start checklist complete."

"Starting engine number one."

Cooper rotated the overhead start switch, initiating the flow of pneumatic pressure from the auxiliary power unit (APU). The left engine began to turn. When the engine reached sufficient rpm's, he lifted the start lever, located just below the thrust lever, to send fuel and spark to the engine. He closely monitored the tachometers, fuel flow, and exhaust gas temperature to ensure normal parameters. The levels rose as they should, peaked, and rolled back, indicating that the engine was stabilized. "Roll back," Cooper announced. Then he repeated the process with engine number two, which also started perfectly.

"I'll disconnect and you are clear to taxi," the ground crew announced through the interphone. Cooper watched through the rain-beaded window as the tug pulled away. Then he heard the interphone click off. The ground crew foreman backed away from the nose of the plane, turned toward the captain's side of the cockpit, and offered a clear but less than military salute. More than good-bye and good luck, it meant that all ground equipment was out of the way, permitting the plane to taxi under its own power. Cooper acknowledged the salute with two fingers to his forehead.

Progress toward takeoff continued with well-practiced deliberateness. Before touching the thrust levers, Captain Sams conducted his brief after-start flow, checking electrical and hydraulic systems and assuring that the pitot heat switches were on. Pitot probes outside the aircraft determine airspeed, and pitot heat devices prevent the probes from icing up. Cooper confirmed that both engine start levers had been returned to their idle positions.

The after-start flow was followed by another read-and-respond checklist double-checking all after-start items.

"Northstar two-zero-two ready to taxi," Schmidt announced to ground control.

"Northstar two-zero-two, taxi to runway one-six right via bravo. Call tower holding short of one-six left."

"Roger."

Captain Sams eased the two thrust levers forward with his right hand while gripping the nosewheel tiller, a small wheel located just outside his left thigh, with his left hand. The engines surged loudly behind him and the plane began rolling away from the gate area. Cooper turned the nose wheel toward the yellow stripe on the wet tarmac which would lead him to bravo taxiway and runway 16. Then he pulled the thrust levers back to near idle to maintain a cautious, steady speed.

The sense of motion in the plane, even the easy crawl of taxi and the gentle bounce of the nosewheel over the tarmac seams, charged Cooper Sams with anticipation. This monstrous bird of steel, wire, rubber, and computer chips was his servant. It was even more under his control than the trained peregrine falcon at the Seattle Zoo which so entranced him. Cooper thrilled as the majestic bird gripped its master's leather-sheathed arm until commanded to fly. Then it obediently spread its powerful wings, soared to its destination, and returned to await further orders.

Similarly, Cooper always revved up inside as he prepared to launch his 737, guide it skillfully to its destination, and land it safely.

He had seen the trained falcon balk at instructions and fail to obey on a few occasions. Had its wings not been clipped, it might have escaped, only to find itself victimized in the city or in the wild by a number of agile enemies. The anticipation of the falcon's rebellion was always part of the excitement whenever Cooper went to watch it.

Despite an impressive record of reliability, the 737 had also proven to be an obstinate bird at times. There were weaknesses in design which were eventually discovered and corrected, including the troublesome rudder power control unit. There had also been equipment failures, most of them solved on the ground or remedied in the air by the quick action of the cockpit crew or an emergency landing. The remote unknowns of the aircraft's infallibility heightened the thrill of flying for Cooper. He knew this bird, perhaps better than any other pilot on active duty. He knew how to clip its wings and keep it in control, and he was skilled at reeling the bird in when it rebelled due to oversight on the ground, mechanical failure in the air, or an unforeseen attack of weather. Conscientious preparation—finding the flaw and dealing with it before it finds you—that was the key. And the rush of a successful takeoff was the culmination of Cooper's confidence that he was ready for anything the airplane or the elements threw at him.

During taxi, Captain Sams methodically checked his flight controls to assure free movement, turning the control wheel left and right to exercise the ailerons, depressing first one rudder pedal and then the other. Meanwhile, First Officer Schmidt maintained contact with ground control to monitor traffic.

"Before-takeoff checklist," Cooper announced.

Schmidt referred to the list mounted on his control wheel.

"Recall."

"Checked."

"Flight controls."

"Checked."

"Flaps."

"Flaps five, as required."

"Rudder, ailerons, stabilizer trim."

"Zero, zero, and four-point-zero units."

"Cockpit door."

"Locked."

"Takeoff briefing."

"Twenty-two K max power takeoff. V-1, 143 knots. V-R, 147 knots. V-2, 154 knots. Max speed, 169 knots. Clean maneuvering speed, 220 knots."

The numbers and sequence were thoroughly familiar to both men. With a near capacity load of passengers and cargo, they would put the pedal to the metal for a maximum power takeoff of 22,000 pounds of thrust. A lighter load allowed for reduced thrust, saving wear and tear on the engines.

The five critical speeds were marked with "bugs" on both airspeed indicators in the cockpit. V-1 speed was the point of no return. If a captain found a need to abort the takeoff, he had to act before the aircraft reached V-1, the speed at which the crew would be unable to stop the aircraft before it reached the end of the runway. At V-1 the captain removed his hand from the thrust levers to avoid the temptation to abort.

At V-R, or rotation, the captain pulls the control wheel back, lifting the nose of the aircraft until the flight indicator bars on the instrument panel show approximately 20 degrees of pitch. In seconds the plane is airborne and the landing gear is retracted.

V-2 is the minimum takeoff safety speed for retaining directional control. Minimum speed must be maintained after liftoff for the aircraft to clear obstacles and climb on one engine if necessary. Clean maneuvering speed is the speed at which the pilot can retract takeoff flaps and execute a 30-degree bank.

"Takeoff briefing reviewed," Schmidt announced.

"Reviewed," Captain Sams echoed.

The significance of the rote dialogue was not lost on either flyer. Every checklist, every procedure, every clearance was recited aloud for the benefit of the cockpit voice recorder. If a problem developed on takeoff, in flight, or during landing, data from the CVR and the flight data recorder—the infamous "black box"—would be helpful in sorting out the cause, especially if the crew was rendered incapable of giving a report in person. The listening ear of the CVR was a constant, subtle reminder to every pilot that communication, thoroughness, and safety were integral to the success not only of his flight but of succeeding flights.

Captain Sams dropped the thrust levers to idle as he approached the end of the taxiway parallel to the north end of runway 16. SeaTac's two parallel runways are numbered 16 left and 16 right (16L and 16R). The numbers designate the compass heading of the runway. Runways 16L and 16R refer to a takeoff and landing heading of 160 degrees, almost due south. The other end of these same runways are numbered 34R and 34L because aircraft taking off and landing from the south end are headed north at 340 degrees.

One other aircraft, a Delta L1011, was ahead of them and holding short of the runway for an incoming plane. Cooper could see the brilliant landing lights descending slowly through the dark, misty sky. An America West 737 floated by them and touched down perfectly, leaving swirling clouds of moisture in its wake.

First Officer Schmidt announced to the cabin, "We are number two for takeoff, so I'd like our flight attendants to be seated for departure." The flight attendants had been strapped into their jump seats for several minutes already, Schmidt knew, but the announcement was mandatory. It was like saying, "If anyone back there is stupid enough to still be on his or her feet, it's time to buckle up because we're ready to jet out of here."

In seconds Delta 844 was cleared onto 16L and moved into position. Captain Sams followed the jumbo jet around the corner, perpendicular to but well short of 16L. Schmidt performed his required cleared-for-takeoff flow, rechecking start switches, TCAS/transponder, flaps, and strobes. Delta 844 thundered down the runway and lifted off.

"Northstar two-zero-two, you are cleared to cross one-six-left into position and hold on one-six right," came the announcement from air traffic control half a minute later.

"Check for incoming," Cooper instructed his copilot.

Schmidt studied the sky to the north through his side window, and Cooper stole a look around him. It was difficult for him to trust the judgment of the harried air traffic controllers or a skilled but imperfect pilot. "No lights in sight, Captain," Schmidt said. The captain also saw that they were clear to cross the runway.

Cooper eased the thrust levers forward, crept across 16L, turned left onto 16R, and braked to a stop with the nosewheel on the dimly lit center stripe. "Down to the lights, Mr. Schmidt," he said calmly.

The first officer read through the cleared-for-takeoff checklist he had recently reviewed silently, and Cooper responded. The final item was the landing lights, the radiant "high beams" on the front edge of the wings on either side of the fuselage. These lights are never turned on for takeoff until final clearance has been received, alerting the tower and pilots on the taxiway that an aircraft is rolling down the runway.

With all preparations made, there was nothing to do but wait for clearance. The tower was obviously waiting until Delta 844 was well away from the airport. Cooper sat with his right hand on the thrust levers and his left on the tiller, the wheel that controls nosewheel steering. At approximately eighty knots during the takeoff roll, the pilot moves his left hand from the tiller to the control wheel, or yoke. At eighty knots the rudder can take over directional control of the aircraft.

In less than a minute, clearance came from the tower: "Northstar two-zero-two, you are cleared for takeoff on one-six right. Winds are calm." This was where the fun really began for Cooper Sams. This was the rush he lived for. Captain Sams switched on the landing lights, bringing near daylight to 100 yards of wet runway ahead scarred with black streaks from innumerable chirping, smoking touchdowns. He held the brakes on, spooled up the engine, and punched the take-off and go-around (TOGA) switches on the thrust levers. As he released the brakes, the auto throttles governed by the TOGA switches activated the FMC setting for takeoff: 22K max power.

The two wing-mounted jet engines roared to life, launching the aircraft down the runway, drawing both pilots into their seat backs. Cooper maintained one hand on the thrust levers in preparation for a possible aborted takeoff, while keeping the plane in the center of the runway with a firm hand on the tiller. The routine vibrations and rattles in the cockpit went unnoticed. Both pilots were intent on the critical task of takeoff.

"Eighty knots," Schmidt announced, the first threshold for a quick evaluation of progress. Instruments were cross-checked and found to be in order. Cooper released the tiller and moved his left hand to the yoke. A few seconds later Schmidt called out, "V-1."

"V-1," Captain Sams echoed. He moved his right hand from the thrust levers to the yoke. It was the point of no return. No matter what happened now, he had to get the plane airborne. It was either fly or crash off the runway. *Fly, mother, just fly,* Cooper urged his steel falcon.

"V-R," Schmidt said.

"Rotating," Cooper answered as he drew back the yoke. The runway and the horizon disappeared beneath the nose as the 737 strained toward the sky. Cooper watched the flight director bars rise to the predetermined 20 degrees of pitch. He kept them there. The vibrations and rattles suddenly diminished as the rear wheels left the ground.

"V-2 . . . positive rate of climb," Schmidt announced seconds later.

"Positive rate, gear up."

First Officer Schmidt flipped the switch to retract the landing gear.

At 1,000 feet the tower instructed, "Northstar two-zero-two, contact departure." It was another in a series of standard handoffs. Ground control had escorted the aircraft from the gate to the taxiway. The tower had put him on the runway and cleared him for takeoff. Now departure control, located in the basement of the tower, would guide him away from the airport and hand him over to Seattle Center, one of several large air traffic control centers on the West Coast. Crossing the Canadian border, Northstar 202 would come under the jurisdiction of Vancouver Center. Once in Alaska, Anchorage Center would take over until Flight 202 was within range of the Juneau tower.

"Going to departure," Schmidt replied. "Thank you, Seattle tower. Good night." Switching to frequency 120.4 for departure control, he stated, "Seattle departure, Northstar two-zero-two out of two-point-three, climbing to niner thousand." During takeoff the copilot generally handles radio contact while the pilot focuses on getting the plane aloft.

"Roger, Northstar two-zero-two. Seattle departure. Radar contact." With these words departure control verified that radar was operative and that the plane's altimeter settings were consistent with on-ground readings. "Turn right, heading two-five-zero. Cleared to three-one-zero." It was the beginning of the standard U-turn to redirect the southbound jet north to Alaska.

"Roger. Heading two-five-zero." Hearing the clearance, Cooper banked the plane gently to pick up the virtual due-west heading in preparation for another right turn north.

"Flaps one," the pilot directed.

Schmidt retracted the flaps to the new setting. "Flaps one," he reported.

A minute later, "Flaps up," and Schmidt again complied.

First Officer Schmidt proceeded through his after-takeoff flow, printed on the control wheel. He spoke just loud enough for his voice to be picked up by the CVR. The after-takeoff check verified the status of air conditioning and pressurization, various start switches, landing gear, auto brakes, and flaps.

The plane continued its steady climb through a wispy layer of clouds. At 8,000 feet, Seattle departure initiated the communication handoff to air traffic control at Seattle Center. "Northstar two-zero-two, go to Sea Center at one-two-five-point-one. Good night."

Schmidt handled the switch as Cooper banked the plane northward. "Going to Sea Center. Good night." He adjusted the radio to 125.1. "Sea Center, Northstar two-zero-two out of eight thousand, going to heading three-one-zero."

"Roger, Northstar two-zero-two. Sea Center. Cleared direct to Sisters Island."

"Roger," Schmidt replied. As he listened, Cooper smiled to himself at the clearance to fly directly to Sisters Island. It was the prime benefit of an off-peak evening flight. During high traffic periods, he was usually instructed to follow a connect-the-dots course up the coast of British Columbia. But tonight ATC cleared him direct to Sisters Island 25 miles south of Juneau. The clearance took all the bends out of the airways. They should be able to pick up the time lost to the straggling connecting passengers and still arrive at the gate a little early.

At 10,000 feet the captain switched off the landing lights and gave a two-bell signal for the flight attendants to begin their service. The straight shot meant that the cabin crew had even less time to complete dinner service and button down the cabin before the plane encountered the choppy air reported on the descent into Juneau. *That will keep the gay guy hopping,* Cooper thought with another inner smile.

At 31,000 feet the 737 was well above the clouds and exposed to a canopy of diamond dust strewn across a sky of black velvet. Captain Sams pulled back the throttles and engaged autopilot. The fun was over for about two hours. The cockpit crew would pass the time by monitoring instruments and dialoguing with ATC. The airplane would do most of the work. If his first officer wanted to engage in small talk, Cooper decided, he would start quizzing the man on procedures until he shut up. Cooper wanted to enjoy the ride and think about Rachel.

Shanna rapped on the door and entered with coffee for both men. Cooper was surprised and pleased at her punctuality. Down the aisle Kathy Keene and Tommy Eggers were hustling through the first beverage service in coach. Handing him the coffee, Shanna looked a little harried, but she managed a smile. The captain knew that flight attendants hated to be bothered by the cockpit crew while they were doing their cabin service. But it secretly pleased the captain that his crew wouldn't have time to sit in the galley and read magazines tonight. He wished he could see Tommy Eggers' face when he found out the flight was arriving in Juneau ahead of schedule.

Seven

Shanna Davis strapped herself into the jump seat next to the forward door shortly after Flight 202 began its descent toward Juneau International Airport. Kathy Keene and Tommy Eggers had also taken their places in the aft galley jump seats, as instructed by Captain Sams, and the passengers had been warned about the turbulence ahead. It was already getting bumpy.

Shanna was grateful that the captain had given adequate warning about the chop they would encounter during landing. She had hurried through first-class dinner service while trying not to look hurried to her 8 passengers, who expected to be fawned over. In between refills of coffee and double Jack Daniels for her customers, she helped Kathy and Tommy complete service and clean-up for their 120 dinner guests.

Tommy had little time to entertain as the three flight attendants rushed from serving beverages to passing out meal trays to collecting meal trays to serving beverages again to final pickup of cups and glasses. He complained bitterly to his female coworkers that the captain had ordered the hurry-up job just to upset him—"And it's working!" he moaned overdramatically. Straining under the weight of being in charge, Shanna had tried to placate Tommy and keep him on task. If the remaining legs of the trip were like this one, she assessed as she snapped her shoulder harness into place, it would be anything but the fun trip Tommy had promised her.

The descent was quite rough. It felt as if the plane was bouncing down a badly potted dirt road on giant tires filled with boulders—with no shock absorbers. The loud rattle and bang of steel doors and trays in the galley to her left amplified the punishment the plane was taking. Shanna didn't like it. She'd been through bumpy air before—plenty of it—in her short career, but this was the worst so far. It didn't make her feel ill; motion sickness had never been a problem for her. Nor did it really frighten her. But she wondered with concern how much pounding an airplane could take before something popped loose, something vital, something it needed to stay aloft.

Normally Shanna would read a few pages of a Danielle Steel novel in the minutes before touchdown. But the constant, erratic bouncing caused her to leave the book in her bag and keep the light above her seat turned off.

From her aft-facing jump seat, Shanna could lean to the left and see beyond the closet and down the aisle from the cockpit door to the aft galley and lavatories. The cabin lights had been dimmed, but a number of illuminated overhead reading lamps produced a mottled pattern of light and shadow the length of the cabin. Shanna doubted, however, that anyone was reading.

The faces Shanna could see in first class and in the aisle seats just behind the bulkhead in coach were serious and tight-lipped, as if enduring a hypodermic injection or venipuncture. The tops of heads visible above the seat backs bounced and swayed in unison like marionettes being controlled by a puppeteer with a serious hand tremor.

As Shanna watched, one hard bounce sprung an overhead bin open above seat 11D, and a brown felt hat tumbled into the aisle. It was too bumpy for Shanna to work her way down the aisle to close it, and the passengers had been instructed to remain in their seats with their seat belts securely fastened. Shanna was about to make an announcement urging passengers under the open bin to watch out for falling carry-on luggage. But a young woman in seat 12E, whom Shanna recognized as one of four nonrev Northstar flight attendants on board, stood and slammed the bin closed with a mighty shove from her left arm. The turbulence and the awkward, off-balance thrust propelled her into the lap of an Eskimo man in a business suit sitting next to her. He helped her back into her own seat where she quickly buckled in again. Shanna waved her thanks, but the woman didn't see her. The felt hat remained on the floor untouched.

Juneau, Alaska, is ringed with craggy, snowcapped mountains, making the descent into Juneau International steeper than at most airports. By the time the plane banked into its final approach, the air had calmed somewhat. Shanna was reassured as she felt the landing gear deploy and flaps extend, causing a loud rush of wind over the exposed equipment. The increased drag pressed her gently into the jump seat's cushioned backrest.

She started through the thirty-second review, a mental exercise Northstar flight attendants are required to complete during every take-off and landing. The review consisted of a short list of memorized questions she was to answer to herself in order to prepare for a sudden emergency. The vital information had twice come to mind unbidden during the bumpy descent.

What is the brace signal? Six bells from the cockpit. What is my brace position? Feet shoulder width apart, hands tucked under thighs, head back and tipped up. What is my assigned exit and which way does the handle rotate? On the 737-400, doors one left and one right, rotating toward the nose of the aircraft to open. *What are my commands? "Grab ankles, head down, stay down!"* until stopped, then *"Release seat belts, get out, leave belongings, come this way!"*

Shanna continued to review her actions at the exit door and what she should do if her assigned exit is blocked or unusable. She affirmed that the emergency cabin light switch, which was in the aft galley, was not her responsibility. Kathy or Tommy would get it.

The aircraft touched down gently, first the right wheels, then the left, and finally the nose wheel. Shanna felt a collective sigh of relief whistle through the cabin as if a teakettle of boiling water had finally been removed from the flame. She ventured another glance around the closet. Grim faces had relaxed. Tense silence had erupted into nervous chatter.

Tommy pointed at her from his jump seat in the rear, indicating that he wanted her to make the standard arrival announcement. The frown on his face communicated his continuing displeasure with the difficult flight and rough descent.

Shanna picked up the P.A. phone, dialed the cabin extension, and delivered the well-practiced announcement as the thrust reversers slowed the plane:

"Northstar Airlines would like to welcome you to Juneau, Alaska, where the local time—" She glanced at her watch and deducted an hour for the time change. "—is 9:05 P.M., Alaska standard time. Please remain in your seat until the aircraft comes to a full and complete stop at the gate and the captain has turned off the fasten-seat-belt sign. When the captain gives a two-bell signal, it will be safe to move about the cabin and collect your personal belongings. If you are continuing on flight two-oh-two to Anchorage, departure time is 9:45 P.M. If you wish to deplane for a brief time, please take your boarding pass with you to show to the gate agent upon your return.

"On behalf of this entire Seattle-based flight crew, I want to thank you for choosing Northstar Airlines and remind you that, from Cancun to Fairbanks and throughout the six western states, Northstar is your guiding star for travel. Have a pleasant evening in Juneau or whatever your final destination may be."

Shanna returned the phone to its recessed cradle in the wall as the plane turned off the runway and onto the taxiway. She released her seat belt and stood to retrieve coats and jackets from the closet for her first-class passengers. She found herself wishing that she could stay in Juneau tonight instead of strapping in again for another wild, bumpy ride. But Captain Sams had brought them safely through the chop, and his foresight had allowed the cabin crew to ride out the turbulence in their seats with their work already done. She couldn't imagine the mess in the cabin had they not picked up trays and trash before they started bouncing over the air pockets. Kathy was probably right: You wanted to be with a veteran pilot in a pinch—Bloody Marys or no Bloody Marys.

Cooper Sams had logged thousands of hours in bumpy air, but the older he got, the more it took out of him. As a younger man, he could ski the moguls on White Pass all afternoon. But at fifty-three, despite his excellent physical condition, one or two trips down the punishing hill was all he wanted. He didn't fear the moguls—never had. He just enjoyed the gentler downhill more. He felt the same way now—mentally if not physically—after the pounding he had endured on the way into Juneau. Nothing in the air frightened him, least of all a rough-and-tumble tussle with heavy chop. But it just wasn't as much fun as it used to be. And it wore him out.

A good bout with the moguls always drove Cooper to the lodge for a drink, and he wanted a drink now. But since he couldn't have one, he suddenly wanted to call Rachel again. Having parked at the gate and completed his shutdown checks, he donned his cap, took his address book from the inside jacket pocket, and joined the stream of passengers heading into the terminal, leaving the first officer in the cockpit.

Cooper had already informed Schmidt that, because of the rough winds, he would stay at the controls from Juneau to Anchorage. Northstar captains and first officers are equally qualified pilots on the aircraft for which they are certified. Both seats in the cockpit are equipped with a full complement of flight instruments and directional controls, with the thrust levers and avionics between the seats accessible to both crew members. First officers are trained to fly the aircraft from the right seat; as they gain the rank of captain through experience and seniority, they move to the left seat.

Generally speaking, the captain flies the first leg of a trip, then the two pilots alternate at the controls on subsequent legs. However, even during the first officer's legs, the captain sits in the left seat and completes his regular pre-takeoff tasks and checks. The captain also drives the plane from the gate to the runway, since the tiller for the nose wheel is on his side of the cockpit. Once the aircraft is on the runway and cleared for takeoff, the captain says to the first officer, "You have the airplane." At that point the first officer is termed the flying pilot and the captain is the nonflying pilot. The flying pilot lays his hand on the thrust levers and takes the control wheel from takeoff through landing.

Cooper Sams always played by the rules and allowed his copilots to take their turn at the controls. But he didn't always like it. In his head he acknowledged that Northstar first officers were well trained and capable—they had to be to meet the industry's stringent requirements. But captains participate in simulator training twice a year; first officers only once. And captains receive extensive training in a variety of weather-related problems; first officers not as much. It was the captain's option, and Cooper Sams never let a first officer fly in difficult conditions.

In his gut Cooper always felt *better* qualified, *better* prepared, *more* in touch with the multitude of vital technical details, and less distracted by the money and prestige and women which surrounded professional fliers. Cooper loved being at the controls; Cooper loved being *in* control. Taking his turn as the nonflying pilot wasn't much more fun than riding in the jump seat as a nonrev passenger. He was secretly glad that the frisky southeast Alaska winds had allowed him to stay at the controls.

Cooper had never called Rachel twice during the same trip let alone on the same day. That kind of mush was for teenagers. It might be construed as emotional weakness. Besides, he usually didn't want to supply Rachel with more ammunition for her fantasy of the two of them traveling together, spending more time together, and eventually marrying.

But tonight he felt almost compelled to call her again. The urgency seemed to grow as he looked for an available phone in the terminal. It was like a movie he saw once where a woman in danger sent a distress call to her lover on some kind of a telepathic wavelength. The man rushed to her side without knowing why he must do so, and, of course, rescued her in the nick of time.

Cooper and Rachel weren't that close, nor did he want to be that close. But for whatever reason, he had to talk to her again before he left for Anchorage.

The phone rang three times before Rachel answered. Her curt hello alerted Cooper that she was not happy about receiving a call so late.

"Did I wake you up?" he said.

"Cooper?"

"Yes."

"Well of course you woke me up. It's the middle of the night." It wasn't the voice of a woman in danger but a woman barely awake and irritated about it.

Cooper checked his watch in his defense. "It's not even 10:30 your time."

"It was a hard day, Cooper. I turned out the light at 9:30." After a pause to clear her throat, Rachel added, "What's wrong?" Cooper translated her tone to mean, "You'd better have a good reason for waking me up."

He felt foolish. He didn't have a good reason. And his fuzzy notion that she had prompted his call was clearly absurd. "I'm in Juneau. I . . . I just wanted to say good night."

Rachel was silent for a moment. "Are you all right?" Her voice had turned from agitation to curious concern.

Cooper couldn't tell her about the rough ride into Juneau or his sudden urge to call her. "Sure, fine. Good flight." He imagined the puzzled look on her face. "I just . . . just wanted to . . . to say good night." He wished he had never called. He wished he could crawl into a hole.

Somehow Rachel found a warm romantic current in Cooper's halting explanation, something he had not intended. "That's sweet, Cooper," she said with a marked change in her tone. "That's very sweet."

"Well, I've got to go. I'll see you Monday."

"Good night, Cooper. And thank you." Then Rachel released a little, sleepy laugh. "Sometimes you really surprise me."

Cooper returned to the airplane. *Sometimes I really surprise myself,* he found himself thinking on the way back to the plane.

Eight

Juneau Airport is located on a tide flat, surrounded on three sides by water with majestic mountains as a backdrop. A man-made float pond parallels the runway on the south for the first 5,000 of its 8,460 feet. The pond accommodates numbers of float planes, water taxis which ferry sportsmen to the countless lakes and bays of southeast Alaska. Beyond the dike is the Gastineau Channel of the Pacific Ocean, which wraps around the east end of the runway. During high tide in stormy weather, the runway can be awash with ocean water.

Takeoff at Juneau Airport is to the east into the prevailing wind — a runway heading of 080. Across the water, ascending aircraft fly into a box canyon surrounding a spacious valley. Most flights are required to turn 180 degrees after takeoff and depart the area to the west, flying back alongside the airport on climb-out. Only on days with exceptional ceiling and visibility are aircraft permitted to climb out of the box canyon and depart Juneau to the east.

There are two departure routes available on takeoff to accommodate the 180-degree turn. Aircraft above a certain weight limit are assigned the Juneau one departure, sending them first to the northeast and into the valley — called "the hole" by veteran pilots. Then they must execute a long right turn of 30-degree bank, swinging around to a heading of 265, almost due west.

Aircraft with a lighter load are permitted to take the Juneau two departure, allowing for an immediate 180-degree right turn to the 265 heading. Juneau one departure, flying into the unpredictable air of the mountain-rimmed valley, was notorious for its turbulence. Juneau two departure turned away from the box canyon and promised a much smoother climb-out.

Cooper Sams completed his cockpit flow, grateful for a moderate load of cargo and only forty-four passengers on this late-night, one-hour-and-twenty-minute hop to Anchorage. A loaded charter flight which had departed ten minutes earlier via Juneau one reported moderate chop on climb-out. Cooper felt lucky to be headed out via Juneau two departure, avoiding the hole. The worst air seemed to be behind him.

Cooper instructed flight attendant Shanna Davis to keep everyone in the cabin seated after takeoff until he gave a three-bell signal. It didn't promise to be as bumpy on the way out as on the way in, but Cooper always preferred to err on the side of caution. Then he informed Kelly Schmidt of the modified takeoff procedure. "I'm staying on the ground to 155 knots. As soon as we're off the deck I'll bank right at 30 degrees to get us away from the hole and out of here." They adjusted the bugs on their air speed indicators to accommodate the high speed takeoff. The artificially high V-R speed allowed for full maneuverability for a 30-degree bank after takeoff. A by-the-book Juneau takeoff with less air speed permitted only 15 degree of bank.

After push-back and engine start, Cooper terminated his communication with the ground crew by returning the salute of a good ramper he knew only as Mike. The husky young man wore a hooded parka against the brisk, sub-freezing wind blowing in from the southeast. Mike's shift was almost over, and as Cooper taxied the 737 to the end of the runway he wished his was too. He wanted a soothing drink, something good to eat, and a warm bed. With any cooperation from the weather, he was only ninety minutes from all three in Anchorage.

"Northstar two-zero-two, you are cleared for takeoff on runway zero-eight. Winds are southeasterly gusting to 38 knots."

Cooper tapped on the powerful landing lights and gazed down the skid-marked runway. He could feel the wind coming off Gastineau Channel at 40 degrees to the nose, buffeting the plane. He knew that as the plane raced down the runway it would be tempted to turn the right like a weather vane into the wind. Cooper would need to hold the rudder firmly to the left to keep the airplane on the center line. If he didn't, the 737 would likely veer into the channel for an icy, possibly fatal swim.

Cooper eased the thrust levers forward and engaged the TOGA switches. With the decreased weight, the jet leaped forward eagerly in response to the auto throttles governed by the flight management computer.

"Eighty knots," Kelly Schmidt announced over the roar of the twin engines. Cooper could feel in his hands and feet the wind tugging the plane to the right. He held it firmly to the center line. He stole a quick glance at the lighted wind sock on the east taxiway almost halfway down the runway. It was fully unfurled in the stiff wind.

The plane continued to gain speed. "V-1," Schmidt said. Cooper automatically moved his right hand from the thrust levers to the yoke.

When the air speed indicator reached 155, Schmidt said, "V-R." Cooper pulled back on the yoke, the nose lifted from the runway, and the runway lights disappeared, leaving only a panorama of pitch darkness ahead.

"V-2, positive rate."

"Positive rate, gear up."

As soon as Schmidt retracted the landing gear, Cooper turned the ailerons right and started into the planned 30-degree bank to transition from an east heading to a west heading. They continued to climb at a good clip of 2,000 feet per minute. But just past 200 feet they hit the dreaded choppy air again, and it was ferocious. The cockpit began to shake and rattle as it had during their descent into Juneau. Only with every 100 feet it seemed to get worse. Cooper grimaced and swore to himself as he gripped the wheel to continue the climb while maintaining a 30-degree bank that he hoped would get them away from the madness in the air.

Cooper constantly surveyed the instruments. Rate of climb was still good going through 800 feet, and air speed was hovering at 155 knots with variations to 10 knots due to wind. But the pounding they were taking was horrendous. Their shoulder harnesses kept Cooper and Schmidt from pitching forward and back, but they did not prevent the violent sideward movement that alternately bounced them off the side windows and toward the pedestal between them. Cooper wondered if—or how—the weather could be any worse than this in the hole.

Cooper could only imagine the terror his passengers were feeling now, especially any first-time fliers who were aboard. If he had a free hand, he would grab the P.A. mike and assure them that turbulence was to be expected in Alaska and that they would soon be—

Cooper felt it before he confirmed it on the instruments. The 737's air speed, which had been gradually increasing, suddenly began to diminish. He focused with difficulty on the instruments and watched in disbelief. Engine rpm remained constant and the aircraft continued to climb, but air speed was quickly decaying—150, 145 knots. It was as if the plane had flown into a giant net stretched in front of it. And the bone-jarring turbulence, the worst Cooper had experienced in twenty-seven years of flying, persisted.

The captain eased the yoke forward to push the nose down and arrest the decay. But the nose wouldn't go down and air speed continued to drop—140, 135, 130. Cooper couldn't believe that the plane did not respond to the controls. He pushed the yoke farther forward, which normally would flatten the trajectory and allow the plane to pick up speed. It didn't. This time he jammed the yoke full forward, bringing the elevators to a descend position. Nothing changed. The plane suddenly seemed entangled in the net which was rapidly slowing it, fouling the controls, rendering it unable to descend and regain air speed. All the while Cooper attempted to maintain the 30-degree bank that he hoped would take them away from the problem. But the turbulence skewed the bank angle 10 to 15 degrees either way.

The words slammed into Cooper's mind with the painful force of the bucking-bronc turbulence slamming him repeatedly against the side window of the cockpit: *Wind shear.* In pilot training terminology, wind shear is a violent, largely unpredictable and unexplainable atmospheric phenomenon capable of overruling a plane's aerodynamics and forcing it from the sky. In Cooper Sams' terminology, his airplane was in the grip of a murderous, unseen god which had snared numerous aircraft and, despite their crew's best efforts, thrown them mercilessly to the earth.

Cooper Sams battled wind shear every six months in Northstar's required recurrent training for its pilots. Computer models of numerous commercial wind shear disasters were programmed into the simulators. Cooper had fought successfully through a few wind shear simulations and had plunged to the ground with his ship during others. Some programs replicated conditions from which neither the original crew nor any simulator crew had ever recovered. Every pilot left a mock wind shear disaster praying to God that he never had to face one in person.

Recognizing the enemy which had rudely accosted him in the night sky over Juneau, Cooper reacted. His brain snapped into hyper-speed, evaluating in picoseconds a career's worth of training data, energy management theory, and aerodynamics technology, rejecting unworkable solutions, cataloging and prioritizing live options. A massive dose of adrenaline surged into his bloodstream arming him for action. He had been challenged by the gods to mortal combat. It was a battle Cooper had never sought, nor did he welcome it now. He had no choice but to defend his life and the lives of those for which he was responsible.

He gripped the thrust levers and pushed them forward as far as they would go. The engine noise behind the cockpit rose from steady thunder to a screaming roar. Running at maximum power, squeezing out every ounce of thrust, was beyond the design limits of the engines. The extreme heat generated by 22,000-plus rpm expands the metal, eventually swelling the turbine vanes to the side wall. If the pilot does not back off, or if he backs off abruptly allowing the engine to cool too rapidly, the turbines, which give the engine its thrust, will blow apart.

But Cooper needed airspeed, and he knew there were only two ways to get it. One was to put the nose down and let gravity do the rest. But he had already pushed the yoke full forward and the powerful wind shear continued to hold the nose up. If the plane continued to lose airspeed during the climb, the wings would eventually stall and gravity would turn from an ally to an assassin. The airplane would drop from the sky like a stone.

The only other source of airspeed, Cooper knew, was from dead dinosaurs: enough jet fuel pouring through the engines to arrest the decay and propel him through the disturbance. And since take-off power wasn't cutting it, his only choice was to fire-wall the engines. The increased thrust would get him above the bad air, then he would pull back on the engines, hopefully before any damage was done.

But to Cooper's dismay, his plan didn't work. The engines screamed at full power with the aircraft seemingly frozen in an 18-degree climb, but the numbers on the airspeed indicator kept dropping steadily— 115, 110, 105, 100. Stall warnings flashed menacingly in Cooper's brain. It was like something out of a science fiction novel—worse, a horror novel, Cooper thought as he continued to process data at light speed. His plane had flown into the paralyzing clutches of an evil entity clearly bent on his destruction. The god-monster was sucking away his only defense: airspeed. With every knot lost to the wind shear, the 737's maneuverability diminished another dangerous notch. An aircraft without air going over its wings might just as well be a bus for all it can do in the air. It is destined to fall out of the sky.

At 1,344 feet, the gods had another insidious surprise waiting for Cooper Sams. The captain had been battling to hold a 30-degree bank on the climb out in the pounding chop. At 1,344 feet the aircraft hit the full force of the disturbance, a rotor shear that rolled the plane into a 60-degree bank. Cooper instinctively slammed the yoke to the left to pull the wing down, but there wasn't enough air going over the wings to make the ailerons effective.

The gods had issued him the ultimate challenge. He was seconds from a wing stall, the point at which the wing loses all its lift and the aircraft falls helplessly to the earth. Despite maximum power from both engines, airspeed was now under 100 knots and the wings were tottering at 60-plus degrees, threatening to go vertical. Something had to happen now, or it was all over.

Amidst the data barraging Cooper's brain at the volume and intensity of 1,000 stock market trading floors came the suggestion to cry to God for help. Not the faceless gods of the elements he had revered lovelessly throughout his career, but *the* God, the one people went to church to talk to, the one the Bible was all about. The idea and Cooper's response to it consumed little more time than the firing of a few neurons.

Cooper never had much time for this God, who was alleged to be all-powerful, all-loving, and everywhere-present by His devotees. Too many things in the world clashed with these allegations, not the least of which were the tragedies in his own industry, notably the wind shear disasters at Dallas-Fort Worth, Charlotte, and elsewhere. God was apparently prone to lapses in His power, love, or presence to allow such heinous mass slaughter.

Cooper would *not* call out to the absent-minded deity whom the fundamentalists touted as the God of creation and salvation. Doubtless the passengers and crews on numerous fatal air disasters had called out to Him and other gods, and what good did it do them? No, Cooper accepted that if Flight 202 escaped this devilish rotor shear and made it safely to Anchorage, it would be because he was the primary instrument of its salvation. And if the aircraft was reduced to a smoking hole in the ground, he would be to blame.

In the scant twenty seconds since the airspeed began to decay, all the training Cooper had about wind shear recovery crowded at the door of his will, demanding a specific response. Every technique required the pilot to pull the nose up into a steep climb and deliver maximum power to the engines. All well and good, Cooper's brain assessed in nanoseconds, if the wings are straight and level instead of banked to 60 degrees to steer away from the mountains, or worse yet, if the rotor itself decays airspeed to near stall conditions and threatens to roll the wings to vertical. A chilling warning blared in the captain's consciousness: Pulling back on the yoke now would flip the airplane on its back and send it plummeting to the earth.

Having discarded the standard recovery technique as unworkable, Cooper considered another solution: pull back on the left thrust lever, allowing the right engine to turn the plane toward the slower engine on the high side of the bank, then begin a descent to gather air speed. *No!* came the inner warning before he could touch the lever. *Slowing the left engine with the wings at this angle will drop the airspeed further!* Another idea was discarded.

The final solution came neither from Cooper's training nor from anything he had heard or read about wind shear recovery. Rather it was the synthesis of bits and pieces of physics, energy management, and aeronautical engineering. Had Cooper time to think about it, he would have admitted that, to his knowledge, the maneuver had never been attempted in a jet aircraft before. But the information and evaluation systems in his brain had cancelled every option but one. And now he was out of time. So he gripped the control wheel and went with it.

Nine

The least of Shanna Davis' concerns at the moment was modesty. When the buffeting started again as Flight 202 from Juneau began its takeoff bank to the right, she was strapped into her jump seat next to the cockpit door. She gripped the shoulder harness with both hands and spread her legs to brace herself. The shaking was so severe, she couldn't even keep her knees together. Shanna knew that her unlady-like posture afforded the men facing her in seats 1-D and 3-D a view up her dress, but she didn't care. As it was, they weren't interested in the least. Along with forty-two other sober-faced, white-knuckled passengers, they were preoccupied with their own survival. Shanna couldn't blame anyone in the cabin who was silently swearing off air travel for life. The idea even sounded good to *her* at the moment.

If the trip *into* Juneau was like riding in a truck over trackless terrain, the leg out was like riding on a tilt-a-whirl mounted on the back of that truck. Shanna wished she had some chewing gum to keep her teeth from rattling with each erratic jounce. She had tried to keep her mind off the punishing ascent by reciting the thirty-second review to herself over and over. She hoped her mental recitation wasn't the overture to a live performance of emergency procedures.

The cabin already showed wear from less than a minute of severe turbulence. Several paperback books, a Walkman, and a couple of purses had tumbled off laps and seats to the floor. Briefcases and other carry-on bags which started under someone's seat now littered the center aisle. Two overhead bins had popped open so far, disgorging a small suitcase, a duffle bag, a fishing rod in a metal travel tube, a cardboard box sealed with strapping tape, and six airline pillows. Un-used safety belts dangled and swayed crazily from several vacant aisle seats. No one moved to retrieve strewn belongings. Every hand on the plane tightly gripped an arm rest, a seat back, or another hand.

With everything else going on in the cabin, Shanna didn't notice the decrease in airspeed, especially with the engines humming at normal takeoff volume. But when the engines flared up like a solid-fuel booster leaving the launch pad, she felt a stab of fear. She had never heard the engines roar so loudly before, and when it happened in the context of the nerve-jangling turbulence, she began to wonder if the infamous Captain Sams really knew what he was doing.

It occurred to Shanna several seconds later that the sudden howl of power from the engines hadn't produced a concurrent sensation of acceleration. The plane was still ascending and banking right and bouncing wildly. But judging by the lack of pressure on her shoulder harness, it seemed to be slowing down instead of speeding up. She wished she could call the captain on the interphone and find out what—

Suddenly the plane rolled farther to the right, not the smooth roll of a pilot adjusting course, but what seemed to be an abrupt jerk upward on the left wing by a power outside the aircraft. Shanna heard a yelp of fright from the cabin and swallowed a small cry in her own throat. Another overhead bin near the rear of the coach cabin popped open and dumped its contents on a woman sitting across the aisle from it. Shanna hoped the passenger wasn't hurt. Even if she was, no one could help her now.

Shanna knew something was very wrong. The plane was more vertical than horizontal, still in a bank turn with the engines wide open, still bouncing through the air instead of gliding. The captain hadn't given the six-bell emergency signal, but maybe he couldn't take his hands off the controls. Should she get on the P.A. and give brace instructions— "Grab ankles, head down, stay down"? She wanted to talk to Kathy and Tommy, but she couldn't even see them at the other end of the aisle. Were they all right? Were they already in the brace position?

Cautiously letting go of one shoulder strap, Shanna reached for the interphone in the bulkhead across from her. But the sudden sensation in the pit of her stomach made her pull her hand back quickly and grab onto the strap more firmly. She felt her feet leave the floor and her rear end leave the jump seat. For an instant, more of her weight was supported by the shoulder harness than by the floor. It was the same feeling she had experienced many times on the wild roller coaster rides in Southern California: the momentary weightlessness of cresting a peak at high speed before starting down a steep slope.

At the same moment, all the loose debris in the cabin rose from the floor toward the ceiling as if lifted by unseen hands—suitcases, briefcases, purses, books, pens, pillows, everything. Had the passengers not been strapped into their seats, they would have ascended too. Shanna instantly knew what had caused the momentary weightlessness. The plane had abruptly stopped climbing and started falling. They were in zero gravity.

Scarcely had the debris hit the ceiling when the plane swung to a new heading and accelerated rapidly. Instead of dropping to the floor, the airborne flotsam in the cabin rained aft, skipping over the tops of seat backs to slam into the rear bulkheads. Some smaller pieces sailed down the center aisle at ceiling height, crashing into the lavatory doors beyond the aft galley where Shanna's coworkers were ducking for cover in their jump seats.

The wings had leveled in the transition, but the bone-jarring turbulence and ear-splitting noise persisted. The new momentum drew Shanna forward in her harness, and the direction made her gasp with alarm and bite her lip. The plane was now in a steep dive, steeper than she imagined an airliner could survive. She braced her feet on the floor against the pull, reached for the phone, and activated the cabin P.A. "Grab your ankles! Head down! Stay down! Grab your ankles! Head down! Stay down!"

Shanna quickly assumed her brace position: harness tight, feet shoulder width apart, hands under her thighs to keep them from flailing and fracturing on impact, head back against the head rest and pointed up. She had no idea of the plane's proximity to the ground. A quick glance toward the porthole in the door was no help. It showed nothing but black. Shanna hoped she had time for one last 30-second review of emergency procedures, then hoped she would be alive to use it when they reached the ground.

When Cooper Sams tromped the right rudder to the floor with the yoke full forward, the 737 slid out of its ascending bank to a wings-level descent as easily as a freshly opened egg slides down the inside of a mixing bowl. The maneuver dropped the airplane out of the punishing rotor shear and changed its heading nearly 90 degrees, turning it back to the west. But its airspeed had decayed so greatly that it could not stay aloft. So Cooper did the only thing he could do: point the nose to the ground with the throttles still wide open in hopes of gaining enough speed to pull up before crashing to earth.

There had been no conversation in the cockpit from the moment the plane encountered the wind shear until Cooper completed the daring, successful hard right turn—a total of forty-four seconds. Both men were dumbstruck by the incredible power of the wind shear to render the controls virtually inoperable. Cooper had been consumed with high-speed situation assessment, trouble shooting, option evaluation, and decision-making—no time to pause and talk things over with his copilot. Kelly Schmidt had watched the drama unfold, standing by to do whatever the captain ordered.

Now Cooper needed help. "Give me the numbers, Kelly," he said sternly. The first officer knew exactly what he meant. They were descending rapidly through 1,000 feet at 27 degrees nose down. The captain needed constant altitude and airspeed readings to determine when to pull up.

"Nine hundred feet, 110 knots . . . 800 feet, 114 knots . . . 700, 122."

Cooper tried to pull up at just over 120 knots. He felt a flutter in the control wheel from the elevators but no lift. There still wasn't enough air going over the elevators to pull out of the dive. Cooper pushed the yoke forward again knowing he had to race toward the ground even faster if he hoped to avoid colliding with it.

At 500 feet the ground proximity warning system triggered a reproving computer-generated voice: "Terrain; pull up. Terrain; pull up." Cooper was more interested in Kelly Schmidt's information.

"Five hundred feet, 143 knots," he reported.

"Stand by gear." Cooper's command communicated that he expected to hit the ground. He was prepared to drop the landing gear at the last second as he tried to pull up, hoping to pancake the aircraft on the terrain instead of dive into it. Putting the landing gear between the belly of the plane and the earth would cushion the impact and increase the survival chances of the occupants.

With his hand poised above the landing gear controls, Kelly Schmidt called out, "Four hundred feet, 155 knots." Cooper gripped the control wheel, clenched his teeth, and began pulling back. He had outsmarted the wind shear gods and solved their deadly puzzle. But the victory would be hollow—and extremely short-lived—if he was unable to get the nose up to clear the trees crowding the foothills south of the airport.

Cooper felt the elevators bite into the air. The 737 began to level off. Cooper could see the lights of the airport to the right, but dead ahead was total darkness. He could almost feel the earth rushing up to snare him. He kept steady back pressure on the yoke and the nose inched up toward the horizon.

"Three hundred feet," Schmidt announced in a dry voice. Then, more relieved, "Two-fifty and level, 165 knots."

The plane began to climb and gain speed in the turbulent air. At 185 knots, Cooper ordered the flaps pulled in to reduce drag and resume takeoff speed. As soon as they reached a normal climb rate, he said, "Pull the power back." Kelly Schmidt eased the thrust levers back slowly, mindful of the stress the engines had endured and the danger of decelerating them too quickly.

Twelve seconds later, just as Cooper and Schmidt began to relax slightly, they hit the shear again three miles west of the first encounter. The plane stopped climbing at 1,500 feet. Cooper reacted immediately, shoving the throttles full forward again and pulling the nose up to trade lift for air speed. The superior power prevailed. They accelerated to 260 knots, cleared the air mass, and resumed the climb.

Cooper assessed that the engines for aircraft N122NS would likely need to be changed out sooner than their regularly scheduled replacement. They had been severely burdened during the ordeal. Cooper was quietly amazed that they held together long enough to power them through two wind shear encounters. Once they approached cruising altitude to Anchorage, he would have Schmidt pull out the logbook and compare the numbers—N1 rotor speed, exhaust gas temperature, N2 rotor speed, fuel flow—with previous entries. Even small variations in the pattern would confirm the need for engine work.

"Pull them back real easy," Cooper said as Schmidt reached for the thrust levers. "They have to get us to Anchorage tonight."

As the first officer slowly drew back the levers, Cooper called the A flight attendant on the interphone. "Everyone OK back there?"

"Yes sir, I think so, except for a few bumps and bruises," Shanna answered in a shaky voice. "But the cabin's a wreck." She described the rain of baggage and debris. Cooper quickly explained the cause of it and assured her that the worst was over.

He had just hung up the phone when a muffled boom sounded behind the cockpit. The plane instantly yawed to the right. Cooper had been mentally prepared for it and corrected the drift by depressing the left rudder. As he did the engine fire warning light flashed menacingly from the control panel. Kelly Schmidt announced what they both knew the minute they heard the pop: "Engine number two is toast." Then he hurriedly retrieved the checklist for engine fire. As he did, Cooper shut down the engine, whose turbine had been reduced to a jumble of steel wool by the strain of the last two minutes.

"Thrust lever engine number two," Schmidt read.

"Closed," Cooper responded.

"Autothrottle."

"Disengaged."

"Start lever engine number two."

"Cutoff."

"Fire warning switch engine number two."

"Pulled."

Within seconds the fire bottles inside the right engine had done their job and the warning light went out.

"Call Juneau tower," Cooper instructed. "Tell them we're coming back in. Tell them to roll the emergency vehicles."

As Schmidt informed the tower about the latest emergency, Cooper got Shanna on the interphone again. "That boom was our right engine. The good news is that the fire is out. The bad news is that we have to go back into Juneau. Luckily, we have a few minutes to prepare. There's a lot of water down there. Get out the life jackets."

Ten

Cooper Sams felt drained, wrung out. The adrenaline surge had left him trembling and lightheaded. But there was no time to recover. The next four minutes would be spent flying over Auke Bay and Lynn Canal at 3,000 feet, working through the checklists for landing on one engine. Then he would turn the plane back toward the airport and fly into the paint-mixer turbulence again, hoping to put it down on the runway and keep it there. Meanwhile in the cabin, his coworkers Shanna, Kathy, and Tommy were preparing the passengers and themselves for an emergency landing and possible water ditching.

Chief among Cooper's challenges was the high rate of speed at which he would have to land to combat the wind and maintain maximum maneuverability. A high-speed landing could result in a blown tire, making control on the runway a major problem. And if Cooper managed to set it down without blowing a tire, the speed that got him there would then become his greatest enemy. There was only one engine to slow down the plane, and that engine would be continuously pushing the nose of the plane toward the dead engine. If Cooper couldn't get the plane down near the end of the runway, he may not be able to rein it in before it rolled off the far end into the water. And with the nasty cross winds from the southeast, the nose of the plane would be strongly tempted to the right where the float pond and Gastineau Channel—at near high tide—waited 200 feet off the runway.

The irony was not lost on Cooper Sams. Minutes ago it was the *lack* of airspeed that nearly caused a crash. Minutes from now *excessive* speed would pose the greatest danger to survival. It was all too obvious. The gods were running him through a deadly gauntlet: unstable air, rotor wind shear, blown engine, high-speed landing in a stiff cross wind. They didn't care if the crew and passengers lived or died. This was sport to them, tossing a jumble of elements and equipment snafus at an experienced captain to see how he responded. What did they have next in store for Flight 202: another wind shear to drive them into the ground on approach? stuck landing gear forcing a belly landing? an explosion or fire on impact? a trip into the channel?

Cooper felt bitter defiance rising within him like warm bile. He deplored being the bouncing ball on a celestial roulette wheel. The powers of the universe—whomever or whatever they were—may choose to play with him, and perhaps it was their prerogative. But unless they disabled all his controls or completely stripped him of his wits, he would bring this airplane down without losing one life entrusted to his care. And if they were gods at all and not devils, they would give him a fair chance at proving himself in crisis again.

In between checklists, both Cooper and Schmidt slipped into bright yellow, deflated life vests. Once the tower assured Cooper that emergency vehicles were rolling onto the taxiway, he banked back toward the airport. The air was bumpy but not as rough as before. Shanna Davis, with blazer off and life vest on, came into the cockpit to announce that the passengers had been equipped with vests and briefed for a rough landing. "Everyone is OK, Captain, and pretty calm. Thank God we don't have any children on board. We're ready." She seemed aware of the danger but in control.

The three of them quickly reviewed emergency and evacuation procedures. Shanna knew them perfectly and exuded a self-confidence and professionalism that Cooper appreciated.

"You're doing a fine job, Shanna," Cooper concluded, hoping to further buoy her confidence. He needed everyone to perform at peak efficiency to make this landing work. "I'll give you six bells when it's time to brace. Now you'd better strap in."

"Right," she said. Then she reached forward and touched the captain and first officer affectionately on the shoulder. "Good luck to you both."

It was an act of familiarity that Cooper would have judged inappropriate under normal circumstances, especially coming from a black girl. But the soft warmth of Shanna's hand brought a rush of assurance, as if Lady Luck herself had thrown in with him in his struggle against the gods. If things worked out well tonight, he thought he might want to have Shanna Davis along on his next layover in Las Vegas.

"Thanks. And good luck to you back there."

Cooper brought the aircraft around to the runway heading, called for gear down, and began the bumpy descent from 3,000 feet. He reviewed with Schmidt the go-around procedure in case he couldn't set it down close enough to the west end of the runway. But they agreed that they had better get it right the first time. With one engine gone, the plane would be at the mercy of the devilish wind shear if they were to hit it on the way back up.

The stark white runway lights straight ahead were augmented for this landing by brilliant color. Lining the taxiway to the left of runway 08 was a string of emergency vehicles with red and amber lights twirling, a welcoming committee whose services Cooper hoped they would not need. Beyond the lights to the right of the runway was the foreboding blackness of the sea plane float pond and Gastineau Channel. Cooper assured himself that all he had to do was to set his airplane down between the white lights and keep it there until he could bring it to a stop.

Cooper knew that the entire airport and the city's only hospital were on alert. He imagined Mike and the other rampers huddled together in the cold wind to watch him try to bring the wounded bird safely back to the nest. Perhaps the Northstar gate agents still on duty had found a place at the window to watch. And the flurry of activity on the taxiway had surely attracted the notice of any passengers in the terminal. Cooper never liked being the center of attention, preferring to do his job quietly and be left to himself. It seemed that the meddling gods had thought of yet another way to torment him by gathering an audience for the final test.

At 500 feet Cooper gave the six-bell signal to the cabin, notifying Shanna to instruct the passengers to grab their ankles and keep their heads down. Even though Cooper had practiced high-speed one-engine landings many times on the simulator, he had never done so under such adverse wind conditions. He had to bring it down easy to keep the tires intact. But he had to bring it down quickly or face the prospect of nosing into the water at the end of the runway. And he had one chance to do it.

Cooper stayed on the glide path despite the cross winds nudging the nose away from the center line of the rapidly approaching runway. Two hundred feet . . . 100 feet . . . 50 feet and they were over the end of the runway. Cooper eased back on the yoke to pull the nose up for touchdown. The right wheels reached for the ground as Cooper gingerly eased the plane down. Steady, steady, steady, he coaxed himself. Nearly 1,000 feet of tarmac passed under the aircraft before the right tires and then the left squalled and smoked in response to contact. The tires held together, and Cooper exulted in the minor victory.

Cooper deployed the speed brakes and then the thrust reversers, but not before another 1,000 feet of precious runway had been sacrificed to the plane's excessive speed. The lone engine bit into the powerful momentum with limited effect. The 737 raced past the small fleet of fire trucks and rescue vehicles. Over a mile and a half of runway, and they were going to need it all—and perhaps a little more. Cooper leaned harder on the brakes and willed the giant bird to stop.

Mist blowing in from the bay coated the runway and swirled up in clouds behind the decelerating 737. Cooper pursed his lips as he saw the end of the runway approaching. He could try to veer off to the left or right, but not until the last minute or risk snapping the nose wheel in two. And by the time he *could* turn he would not be able to avoid the water anyway. His best option was to stay on the center line. If the plane stopped before reaching the water, all the better. If it nosed into the water, it would stop soon enough.

The plane nosed into the water. It crossed the end of the runway at just under 20 MPH where Cooper engaged the parking brake. The plane skidded down the gradual sandy incline into the water. Cooper felt the underside of the nose slap the water as the wheel dug into the mud and stopped. The brilliant landing lights reflecting on the disturbed water ahead assured him that the wings had not submerged. They had made it.

But there was no time for congratulations or prayers of thanks. The aircraft was in jeopardy of sliding further into the water. The possibility of unknown damage and fire was very real. The plane had to be evacuated fast.

The captain and first officer quickly secured the cockpit. Cooper shut down engine number one and set the parking brake. Then he moved into the cabin to take command. Schmidt completed his shutdown duties and notified the tower that they were evacuating. Then he joined the captain in the cabin.

The disabled craft rested in the mud at 25 degrees nose down, about the same angle as their agonizing high-speed descent several minutes earlier. The passengers, held in their seats momentarily for instructions by the captain, were stunned, relieved, and anxious to get out. Flight attendant Shanna Davis knelt in the center aisle in front of him consoling a woman who was sobbing in near hysteria. Kathy Keene and Tommy Eggers were poised at the two window exits, ready to assist passengers through them. The usually excitable Tommy was as pale and subdued as a mime on Darvon.

Cooper spoke clearly and with authority. He said nothing about the ordeal, only the evacuation. "The front doors are over the water, so you will exit through these window exits over the wings. The aircraft is still considered unstable, so let's hurry. Leave all your belongings for now. And don't inflate your life vests unless you land in the water." He stooped to glance out the windows toward the end of the runway behind them. Flashing red and amber lights drew nearer. He could hear the roar of approaching trucks through the open emergency exits. "Fire crews are here to help you off the wing, tend to injuries, and get you out of the cold. Move away from the aircraft quickly. All right, let's go. Row by row in an orderly fashion."

On the captain's cue, Kathy and Tommy stepped through their respective exits onto the wing, then turned to await the passengers. Obediently as well-trained children, the passengers of Flight 202 — twenty-six men and eighteen women ranging in age from nineteen to sixty-one — filed silently down the center aisle from fore and aft and climbed out the two exits. Most who looked at Cooper Sams as they passed him did not speak. Their faces were lined with perplexity, not knowing whether to curse him or bless him for what they had endured. A few who grasped the gravity of their brush with death and the captain's role in their rescue uttered their thanks with strained voices.

The airplane was safely and completely evacuated in four minutes. Passengers were examined by paramedics who discovered nothing more serious than a few contusions and a dislocated finger. The forty-four passengers, along with the first officer and the flight attendants, were loaded onto a crew bus for transport to the terminal. One by one the rescue vehicles switched off their emergency lights and departed for their station houses.

Suspecting that media crews were swarming the terminal to talk to the stunned but grateful survivors, Cooper Sams lingered with the crew that had been sent to anchor the 737 to the runway until it could be towed out of the water in the morning. Bareheaded and wrapped in a blanket he had scrounged out of a fire truck, Cooper inspected his downed steel falcon, which was bathed in brilliant light from a utility truck. The Northstar logo gleamed proudly from the fuselage and tail. The only sign that anything was wrong, apart from it being nosed into the ocean, was the right engine. The housing at the rear was blackened and scarred from the disintegration of the turbine.

After several minutes, Cooper turned toward the taxiway leading back to the terminal. One of the workers attending the plane saw him and called out, "Hey, Captain, I'll drive you in in just a minute."

"Thanks, but I'd rather walk," Cooper called back.

"Yeah," the man in the dark-blue, fur-lined jump suit replied, "I guess I would too if I were you." Then he offered a casual salute as a farewell.

Well away from the aircraft, walking in the cold darkness, Cooper tugged the blanket tighter around his neck and shoulders. Something pricked at the back of his neck, so he reached a hand back to investigate without breaking stride. He pulled out what felt like small card crumpled and caught in the folds of the blanket. His fingers detected a staple dangling from one corner, as if the card had been intentionally attached to the blanket at one time or the loose staple had snagged on the blanket somehow.

His first impulse was to squeeze the card into a wad and toss it away. But he was strangely curious about what had interrupted his private walk. So he held onto the card as he burrowed into the blanket.

When he approached one of the lights lining the taxiway, he turned aside to inspect the card. It was about the size of a business card, off-white and made of lightweight card stock. The side Cooper looked at first was blank. When he turned it over there was only one word printed on it in bold, stylized caps: VANGUARD. No address, no phone number, no Inc. or Corp. or Ltd., no name of a company representative, just VANGUARD. A staple was partially affixed to the upper left corner. Cooper guessed that whatever the card had been stapled to probably explained the unexplained title or brand name.

Feeling an affinity for the misplaced card which had also found solace in a wool blanket, He picked the staple from the corner, flicked it away, and slipped the card into his pocket.

The wobbliness in his legs and the waves of fatigue crashing over him as he walked toward the terminal reminded Cooper of the ordeal he had just endured. By all rights, Flight 202 should have ended in disaster. Lesser pilots would have flown the 737 into the ground or the water in indecision or panic. Not only had Cooper saved his passengers and crew, but the airplane would fly again in a matter of days. The gods had thrown their worst at him. Cooper Sams had run the gauntlet and emerged unscathed.

Momentarily engorged with pride bordering on impudence, Cooper stopped in the middle of the dark taxiway. Looking up into the blackness, he imagined spiritual entities poised at the borders of the terrifying vortex he had so recently navigated. Some of them snarled in disdain, others huffed at the pilot's momentary triumph. In response, Cooper thrust his fist toward the heavens, allowing the blanket to fall to the tarmac. Then he cursed the gods until he wept.

After several minutes he picked up the blanket and headed for the terminal to call Rachel Prescott for the third time today.

Part Two
JUNE 1998

Eleven

The jock was already three minutes late, and ESPN feature reporter Marta Friesen anticipated a much longer wait. In her three years with the sports network, Marta had found that most college athletes were rather tacky about showing up on time for an interview—if they showed up at all. And the narcissistic ones, the professional stars of the future with the inflated egos and bonus-hungry eyes, were the worst.

Marta didn't enjoy hanging around athletic fields and hotels waiting for potential millionaires who couldn't even tell time, or if they could, didn't care what time it was. And when the interview was set for 10 A.M. as it was today, the no-show rate was better than 50 percent. But the college beat at ESPN was a good, high-profile, and hopefully temporary slot in Marta's chosen field of sports television. There was plenty of room at the top for a young woman whose brains, wit, and determination were assets equal to her Miss America looks. So Marta passed the time in the lobby of Omaha's Red Lion deleting old files and documents in her hand-held PC.

Omaha, Nebraska had been the site of the NCAA Division I baseball championships—popularly known as the College World Series—since 1950. Every year in early June, the community puts its best foot forward to host the tournament, which this year hoped to draw 22,000 fans for the championship game, climaxing a nine-day, eight-team, double-elimination tournament.

The locals boast that late spring is prime time for baseball in the Midlands. The threat of frost is past and tornado season is still beyond the horizon. Occasional showers and sunny days keep the bluegrass almost luminescent, the flowering bushes bright and cheerful. In the fields, the once-brown hills and ridges awake with the green tint of corn and soybean sprouts pushing above the ground. Songbirds fill the heart with music. Wild roses perfume the air.

The hospitality of local civic groups to college baseball fans from across the country is a rich tradition. Besides historic, spacious Rosenblatt Stadium, Omaha opens its parks, museums, historical monuments, trails, clubs, restaurants, shopping areas, and the popular Henry Doorly Zoo to its welcome guests. There is always plenty for fans and players to do and see in between the fifteen games of the tournament.

But Marta Friesen had seen little and done even less apart from baseball during her eight days in Omaha. As a feature reporter for ESPN, she had wandered the stadium with her cameraman during the daily doubleheaders looking for players, parents, and fans to interview when action on the field waned. In between games she sought out the tournament's big stars for up-close-and-personal interviews. And she was often was up until after 2 A.M. editing her stories and transmitting them back to the network for the morning edition of Sports Center. One of these years she would crack the elite play-by-play broadcast team and finally get to enjoy Omaha and the cities hosting the college bowl games. But for the time being she was content to put in her sixteen hours and try to get athletes to say something interesting without picking their noses or scratching themselves on camera.

As she worked on her computer, Marta recalled one of her first college interviews for ESPN—at least it had been scheduled to be an interview, and the memory prompted a quiet curse. The two-time All-American linebacker from Michigan, nicknamed The Alien by the university press corps, had kept Marta waiting over an hour. And when he arrived, he looked terrible. He was wearing a UM sweatshirt reeking of body odor and strategically ripped away to display his tree-stump neck and power-lifter arms, shoulders, and chest. His face was shadowed by two days worth of dark stubble. His teeth were tinted brown, as if he used Skoal for toothpaste.

The Alien's first words, accompanied by an undisguised mental frisking of Marta's shapely body, constituted a blatant sexual come-on. She ignored the look and the comment to get on with the interview. But he butted in and stated his intentions clearly: "This is a business deal, chickie. If you're not willing to party with me, I'm not talking to you on TV. That's just the way The Alien does business."

Young, headstrong, and eager to make it with ESPN, Marta had tried to reason with the future superstar, citing the exposure the interview would give him in light of the upcoming NFL draft. The Alien responded by touching her inappropriately, oblivious to the cameraman setting up in the room who was as shocked as Marta was. Marta immediately terminated the interview and walked out in tears. If she had it to do over again, she thought now, she would have thrown a knee into the jerk's All-American groin before she left.

The Alien was now a two-year veteran with the Forty-Niners, and Marta had seen him in several network pregame and postgame interviews, some conducted by rival female sports reporters. She wondered with revulsion what the pervert was charging for interviews now as a rising NFL star.

Marta had interviewed a dozen or more college phenoms in the three years since The Alien. None seemed as weird as he, but several had been rude and suggestive, and most had been late, just as she was sure this—

"Ms. Friesen?"

Marta was so intent on her file-cleaning and lost in thought that her head snapped up at the sound of the voice. She looked into the face of a young Latino man.

"Sorry, I didn't mean to scare you," the young man said. Then he unleashed a beaming smile that more than compensated Marta for the sudden start. "I'm Raul Barrigan. We have an appointment."

Marta recognized the face from photos and video footage, but she instantly determined that the cameras hadn't done him justice. She was even more impressed at the striking resemblance between this young college baseball star and Latino actor Erik Estrada—at least the young Estrada who appeared as "Ponch" astride a California Highway Patrol motorcycle on cable reruns of "CHiPs." Barrigan had the same dark, captivating eyes, the same thick, black hair neatly trimmed, the same confident bearing in the set of his jaw, the same broad, gleaming, knee-weakening smile.

Assessing him in an instant, Marta noted that Raul Barrigan was a little younger and shorter than the handsome Estrada, while his upper body was broader and more muscular than the actor in the CHP uniform. But Barrigan's sterling, good-guy image, like that of the likable Officer Poncharello, was obvious. He was clean-shaven, well-groomed, and casually but fashionably dressed, without so much as a tiny stud in an ear lobe needed to accessorize his rugged, natural good looks. Marta was impressed.

"Hello Raul," Marta said, rising and extending her hand. At five-seven, she was only three inches from matching his height. "I'm Marta Friesen. It's a pleasure to meet you in person." It was Marta's stock introduction when meeting a jock, even though she was always skeptical that the meeting would turn out to be pleasurable. But after such a positive first impression, she thought she meant it this time.

Raul Barrigan shook the reporter's hand, matching her moderately firm grip without trying to display his indisputable strength. "Thank you. I've been looking forward to meeting you too, Ms. Friesen. I have appreciated your work on ESPN, especially the story you did on Hector Emanuel."

Barrigan's stock rose another few points in Marta's estimation during an already bullish start. The feature piece on Hector Emanuel, the collegiate featherweight champ from Fresno State University, had been a critical success but a popular failure. Marta had done her best work on it, ESPN brass and national sports writers assured her, but it flopped in the ratings. Collegiate boxing just didn't command the attention that the larger, heavily funded team sports of football and basketball did. The fact that Raul Barrigan even remembered the piece proved to her that he was a man of discriminating journalistic taste.

"Thank you," Marta said. "Emanuel was a good interview."

Raul looked away sheepishly and slid his hands into the pockets of his olive, wrinkle-free cotton slacks. "I apologize for being late, ma'am. Coach called a team breakfast. I got out of there as quickly as I could."

"It's no problem at all, Raul," Marta assured. "You're in the semi's.

Winning the College World Series is a lot more important than a television interview." Marta couldn't believe she was helping Raul make excuses for his tardiness, even though he was fewer than ten minutes late.

"ASU hasn't been to the finals since '88," Raul said, "and I think Coach really wants this one. He's working us pretty hard." There was a note of pleasure in the young athlete's tone which communicated his delight at working hard to achieve a goal.

"But hey, I'm ready to go, Ms. Friesen," Raul continued with a hint of boyish excitement. "What do we do next?"

Marta picked up her purse and slung the strap over her shoulder, slipping the palm-top computer inside. "ESPN has a suite on the fifth floor. My cameraman is waiting for us. Let's start up that way, and while we walk, you can tell me about your background—you know, your family, where you were raised, how you got interested in baseball. I'll use some of this material when I do the intro back at the studio. When we get in front of the camera we'll focus on your college career, the Series, and your plans for the future. OK?"

"OK, ma'am."

"I'll record your comments if you don't mind."

"That's fine, ma'am," Raul said, starting toward the elevators.

Marta shifted her purse to the shoulder nearest the young athlete and activated the digital recording function of her small computer. "And please, Raul," she said, trying to sound friendly, "let's lose the 'Ms. Friesen' and 'ma'am' stuff, OK? Call me Marta."

Raul nodded submissively. "My upbringing, I guess," he explained. "We kids were strictly trained to address our elders as 'sir' and 'ma'am.' "

It was an unintentional slam, Marta knew, but it pricked at her sensitivity about her thirtieth birthday rolling toward her like a black cloud. She acknowledged that she was a few years older than this college junior, but at twenty-eight she hardly thought of herself as anyone's *elder*. She had worked very hard to maintain the clear skin, trim figure, and college sweetheart image captured in her graduation photos from the University of Colorado. It gratified her that she was still regularly carded at the clubs she frequented around the country. But after Raul's comment she wondered if all the work and expense was paying off.

Marta forced a small laugh to cover her discomfort. "How old are you, Raul?" she asked without looking at him.

"Twenty-one, ma'am . . . er, sorry, I mean twenty-one."

Marta groaned inside. Raul Barrigan was even younger than she had imagined—or perhaps hoped. Marta categorically refused to date athletes, particularly the ones she interviewed. But she wasn't blind, physically or emotionally. As an attractive, available female, Marta noticed the good-looking men around her, and she was even more attracted to the rare few who showed signs of being gentlemen instead of animals.

However, her momentary fascination with Raul Barrigan was quickly doused, like a Fourth-of-July sparkler abruptly dropped into a lake. The kid was barely old enough to buy beer. Marta was embarrassed at herself for even thinking for a second that Raul Barrigan was anything more than another rung on her ladder to ESPN anchor or producer.

"Well, I'm not quite old enough to be your mother," Marta said, covering her humiliation with humor. "So Marta will be fine." She was still staring at the carpet as they strolled slowly toward the elevators.

"Great, that's fine . . . Marta," Raul agreed with an apologetic tone. Marta got right to work. "Now tell me about yourself."

Raul greeted a couple of teammates who passed them in the hall, but the players ignored him and ogled Marta Friesen.

Then Raul said, "I was born and raised outside Tucson, Arizona, the fifth of six kids—four boys and two girls. My dad worked hard as a laborer on a big farm, but we didn't have much. My first bat was a busted axe handle, and my brothers and I would scrounge for old tennis balls around the city park courts. On a good day a lousy tennis player would hit a new ball over the fence, and we'd grab it and run for home before they could get out of the court and catch us. We kept throwing, hitting, and chasing those balls until they literally flew apart." Raul chuckled at what Marta figured to be a pleasant memory despite the pain of admitted poverty.

"Your family is originally from Mexico?" Marta interjected.

"Originally . . . nobody seems to know," Raul said. "My people say we have ancestors among the Spaniards, the Mexicans, and the Native Americans—San Xavier tribe. I think Barrigan is Spanish. We've been called Mexicans, Hispanics, Latinos, whatever is culturally or politically correct at the moment. And in school we were called wetbacks by the Anglos, even though my brothers and sisters and I are third-generation U.S. citizens and speak better English than many of the white kids."

"And Barrigan had something to do with your nickname, Sugar Bear, right?" Marta had read about it in *Sports Illustrated*, but she wanted to hear the man tell the story himself.

Raul Barrigan released a quiet, groaning sigh of embarrassment, but the winsome smile remained on his face. He told the story with a reluctance that seemed to Marta more put on than genuine. "It was something my mother came up with. My oldest brother is named Teddy. When he was born, Mom quickly shortened Teddy *Barri*gan to Teddy Bear, an appropriate nickname for a cute, fuzzy, little brown baby, I guess.

"As the rest of the family came along, Mom didn't want anyone to feel left out. So she stuck each of us with a bear nickname. David was Yogi Bear and Carlos was Smokey Bear. My older sister Dolores was Honey Bear, and my younger sister Esther was Baby Bear. When I came along, all they could think of was Grizzly Bear or Sugar Bear, and Mom wouldn't hear of naming her sweet little baby after a grizzly. So I grew up as Sugar Bear."

They reached the elevators and Marta tapped the button as Raul continued. "We used to call our parents Mama Bear and Papa Bear, but as kids we never called each other by our nicknames. Teddy said it was stupid, and since he was the eldest, we believed him. But we all secretly loved it when our parents hugged us and called us by our special names—even Teddy.

"All my brothers and sisters grew out of their nicknames. But when I got into baseball in high school, one of my teammates heard about the Sugar Bear thing and it spread through the school like a disease. Nobody at school called me Raul anymore. It was always Sugar Bear, Sugar, or Bear. When I got to ASU, the media picked it up. I guess I'll never shake it, will I?"

The elevator opened, four passengers stepped out—college girls, and Raul and Marta stepped in. Marta pushed the button for the fifth floor. "Come on, Raul, what's so bad about being called Sugar Bear?" she probed playfully. "A lot of great pro athletes had memorable nick-names. Remember Magic Johnson, Air Jordan, Hakeem the Dream, Clyde the Glide? The Steelers' Joe Greene was 'Mean,' Walter Payton of the Bears was 'Sweetness,' In baseball you have Frank 'The Big Hurt' Thomas, Stan 'The Man' Musial, even George Herman Ruth was best known as 'The Babe' and 'The Sultan of Swat.' "

"I know, I know," Raul yielded diffidently. "Nicknames kind of go with the territory in sports. After all, your man Chris Berman has made a living off those corny nicknames he hangs on athletes."

"A catchy nickname can be a great marketing tool," Marta reminded him. "When you win the National League batting championship in a couple of years, there will be Sugar Bear T-shirts, baseball gloves, bats, candy bars, breakfast cereal, board games—you name it. And you'll get a big slice of royalties from everything. Sugar Bear will be great for your career."

Raul shrugged and shook his head. "I'd rather just be Raul Barrigan the baseball player. The contracts and the money will be great. My parents still struggle financially, and I'm going to buy them a beautiful new home in Tucson with my signing bonus. My brothers and sisters have needs too. But all the media hype and Sugar Bear gimmicks and signing baseballs wherever I go . . . well, I can live without it."

"You'd better get used to it, Raul," Marta said as they stepped off the elevator, "because you're going to be a major league star and you're going to be rich and famous. It's a package deal. Just consider the inconveniences of fame to be part of the price for helping your family." Then she directed him down the hall toward the suite.

Raul followed, hands in pockets, pensive, silent.

Marta returned to a more pleasant topic. "So you were a pretty hot Little League star."

Raul Barrigan's smile returned. "My brothers were good ballplayers, and I learned a lot from them. But for some reason I was blessed with better coordination and greater speed than Teddy, Carlos, and David. I've always been able to make contact at the plate, whether hitting a tennis ball with an axe handle, a leathery old lemon with a piece of PVC, or a baseball with a bat. And I was faster than most kids my age. So in Little League I just smacked the ball and ran like crazy. It was a lot of fun."

"A three-year batting average of .655 is more than just fun, it's remarkable, even for a Little Leaguer," Marta said, stopping outside room 560 to face the ballplayer. "How was your defense as a kid?"

"I was pitching to my brothers on the sandlot field almost before I was out of diapers, so I grew up with a stronger-than-average arm. And when I wasn't pitching to them, I fielded grounders or shagged fly balls, so I got a lot of practice with the glove. In Little League, anybody who can throw the ball straight half the time is a star pitcher. So I pitched every other game and played infield the rest of the time."

"Then you switched to the outfield in high school?" Marta said while checking to see that her computer was still recording. It was.

Raul Barrigan's hands were out of his pockets now and folded comfortably in front of him, emphasizing his well-developed arms. "I pitched every third or fourth game in high school. I had a better-than-average fastball, and I developed a decent curve and changeup, which made my fastball even more effective. But you don't do a lot of running around the pitcher's mound, so I loved playing center field where I could flat out fly after the ball."

"And where you could crash into fences or bowl over other outfielders to make the catch?" Marta teased. "I've seen some of your high school baseball films. It's a wonder you didn't break your neck on one of those plays."

Raul scratched behind his right ear even though he didn't itch there. It was a nervous habit. "I guess I can blame that on my brothers too," he said, smiling. "Whenever I shagged flies with Teddy or Carlos or David, I had to fight one or two of them off just to get to the ball—and they were older and bigger. I figured if I was going to catch my share of balls, I had to be tougher. So if I had to knock one of them flat to make a catch, I knocked him flat.

"Some days I came home with some pretty good lumps, and on other days Teddy or Carlos or David came home even worse. But I didn't back down, and I earned their respect. When I called for a fly ball, they learned to peel away because they knew I'd run over them to catch it. That's the only way I know how to play baseball."

"And in high school you bulked up, so you could *really* run over people," Marta said.

"Yeah, now my brothers won't even play slow-pitch softball with me," Raul said, laughing. "My height leveled off at five-ten in the tenth grade. So since I wasn't growing taller, I decided to get wider and stronger. I was into football and baseball in high school, so I pumped iron year-round. I learned to run through people in football. One Anglo guy in our league used to call me the Mexican Bowling Ball. And during baseball season, it was infielders and catchers on the other team and my own guys in the outfield I was knocking down." Raul laughed again.

"So your weight training transformed you from a contact hitter to a power hitter," Marta theorized aloud.

"I never stopped being a contact hitter," Raul corrected. "My ability to see the ball leaving the pitcher's hand and get the bat around to make contact has improved only a little. The added weight and muscle just made the ball go farther and faster. Line-drive singles in the tenth grade became doubles, triples, and homers in my senior year."

Marta opened the door and spotted her cameraman, Denny Fogle, stretched out on the sofa in his denim shorts and polo shirt. His gold-rimmed glasses were folded on his chest, and a cigarette smoldered unattended in the ashtray on the coffee table. The camera was set up, but Denny clearly wasn't expecting Marta's return any time soon. He was asleep.

Marta stopped to face Raul outside the living room. Her next question sprang more from personal curiosity than from a list of viewer-captivating issues she had intended to cover: "Your style of play, this wild abandon, Mexican bowling ball approach to running the bases and policing center field kind of clashes with your Sugar Bear image. To paraphrase the old line, what's a nice guy like you going in such a rough and tumble sport?"

Raul returned her gaze, and his face became suddenly serious. His eyes widened and his nostrils flared with anticipation, as if the pitch he had been waiting for was floating defenselessly into his strike zone, a pitch he was primed to transform into a rocket shot over the fence with one powerful swing. Marta's off-the-cuff question was apparently the one he was more than ready to answer.

"It's my calling, Ms. Friesen," Raul answered with a confidence bordering on fanaticism, emphasizing his ardor by grinding a fist into his open palm. "I play baseball for Jesus Christ. This is my mission. It's the way Jesus has provided for me to take care of my family. And you can put that in your story."

Twelve

Terms like "Jesus Christ" and "God" and "Praise the Lord" spoken by a jock in supposed reverence always turned Marta Friesen cold. From her observation, there were only two kinds of God-talking athletes at the collegiate or professional level, and she had little respect for either of them.

First, there were the ones for whom the names of God and the religious routines were nothing more than a good-luck charm. On the field these players wore gold crosses on their ears or around their necks, crossed themselves before taking the first pitch, or knelt piously in the end zone after a touchdown. And during interviews they thanked the good Lord for their abilities or for a great victory. But the rest of the time they were no more saintly than their teammates—doing booze or drugs, cheating on exams, sleeping around, getting in trouble with the law, and using God's name in ways that were anything but complimentary.

One mild-mannered basketball star Marta had interviewed, Dickie Bevins from LSU, boasted that he read his Bible for an hour before each game and prayed whenever he went to the free-throw line and during every time out. He used a black marker to draw crosses and fish symbols on the soles of his court shoes. During their taped conversation, he gave all the credit for his ability and success to Jesus.

But a week after the interview Dickie Bevins was caught burglarizing an administrator's home three blocks from the university. Loot recovered from Bevins' apartment linked him with a number of burglaries in that city. All Dickie's God-talk—and he rolled out plenty of it even after his arrest—couldn't keep him from being expelled and watching his promising basketball career go up in smoke.

Marta knew enough about the Christian religion to presume that talking one way and living the opposite didn't cut it with God or the church. And she had no use for hypocrites of any kind, especially religious hypocrites.

The other kind of God-talking jocks that really bugged Marta were the high-pressure sales types. In most cases, their daily behavior was at least headed in the same direction as their heavenly proclamations, even though the talk always shined brighter than the walk. But so many of these people were obnoxiously militant about imposing their beliefs on others, as if gaining converts was a requirement for retaining their own salvation. Marta lumped them into the same category as the annoying people in those network marketing schemes who cultivate relationships only to find potential recruits. The God-sellers befriend you and pitch you on salvation and heaven, she had theorized, and if you don't take the bait, you're discarded like yesterday's sports page.

Jerianne Cheever was such a person, Marta recalled. The tiny All-American gymnast from Oregon State was a model student and a great interview. She had talked about her faith in God during the taping on the OSU campus, but not in an offensive way. After the interview, however, Jerianne invited Marta to lunch at a little diner near the campus. Over French onion soup and turkey sandwiches, the inter-view*ee* became the interview*er*. Jerianne bored into Marta with question after question about her relationship with God: If you died today, where would you spend eternity? If God met you at heaven's gate and asked, "Why should I let you in?" how would you answer Him? In between questions, Jerianne spread out leaflets, diagrams, and lists of Bible verses and pitched Marta with the tenacity of a car salesperson cinching the noose on a sale.

Marta had answered each of Jerianne's questions with calculated vagueness: "I'm not sure"; "I'll have to think about it"; "I don't have an opinion on that." And she employed well-practiced tactics of sales resistance to push away the propaganda and avoid signing on Jerianne's bottom line. Unable to crack Marta's amicable but well-anchored resolve, Jerianne collected her sales kit. Marta halfway ex-pected her to conclude with something like, "If you change your mind, here's my card. Give me a call anytime." But instead the diminutive gymnast rose and said, "I want all my friends to see me on TV. Please let me know when the interview will be aired." Then she paid for her half of lunch, said good-bye, and scurried out of the diner, presumably to meet with a more viable prospect.

In reality, Marta *was* interested in spiritual matters. She wondered about God, sometimes browsed through the hotel Gideon Bible during a trip, and prayed on rare occasions. But she preferred to shop for God on her own time without being buttonholed by God's door-to-door sales force, especially when His reps were the subjects of her interviews.

At this moment, Marta wasn't sure which kind of God-talking jock Raul Barrigan was. He didn't sound like the carousing, dope-headed, foul-mouthed type who toted Jesus Christ around like some people cross their fingers or clutch a rabbit's foot. And he didn't appear ready to whip out a handful of leaflets outlining ten things you have to know and six things you have to do to get thoroughly saved. All Marta knew was that Raul Barrigan wasn't ashamed to use God's name with con-viction. Somehow she had to distract him from his religious agenda — whatever it was — until she squeezed a good College World Series inter-view out of him. Then he could carry on as the next Billy Graham or the Antichrist for all she cared.

"I see that you have a deep religious faith, Raul," Marta replied with feigned interest as they stood in the entry to the living room. Not so much as an eyebrow twitch betrayed the inner debate over where the good-looking Latino was coming from.

"Yes, I'm a Christian, Marta," Raul said. The intensity was draining from his face as he spoke, the result, Marta surmised, of her ability to defuse his sudden swell of conviction. "God has always been first in my life. We Barrigan kids were in church at least three times a week from the day we were born."

Denny Fogle was awake and on his feet now rechecking his equipment. Marta moved slowly into the living room toward the impromptu set Denny had arranged while holding Raul's attention with her eyes. Raul followed her as if attached by a leash.

"I hope you don't mind if I talk about my faith during the interview," Raul continued. "It's the most important part of my life."

Marta motioned him toward a low-back upholstered chair Denny had moved in front of a large watercolor print. A matching chair sat opposite it for Marta. Denny's compact video camera rose on telescoping tripod legs to the right of Marta's chair.

"I don't mind if you talk about your faith, Raul," Marta said as the baseball star sat down, "as long as what you say is related to the topic we're discussing."

Raul beamed another toothpaste-commercial smile. *"Every* topic relates to Jesus somehow, Marta."

Marta turned to Denny to receive the tiny clip-on mike for Raul's shirt. They exchanged subtle, knowing looks. Denny's eyes flashed, *Are we going to spend another night editing a bunch of Jesus stuff out of this interview?* Marta responded with a flick of her brows, *Your guess is as good as mine, partner.*

Once miked and settled in place, Raul Barrigan cooperated nicely, quieting Marta's mild concern that he might turn into a flaming evangelist on camera. Having made his point about being a Christian, Marta judged, Raul Barrigan was content to answer her questions with the same engaging charm with which their interaction had begun fifteen minutes earlier.

"Who is your favorite baseball player?" Marta had carefully framed the question to ensure that it didn't lead directly into a sermon. The question, "Who is your hero?" might have started Raul on Jesus again. "Who is your idol?" might have launched him into a diatribe on the second of the Ten Commandments condemning idolatry.

"Kirby Puckett," Raul said. "He's built a little closer to the ground like I am. Five-nine, 215 pounds. Strong upper body, hits for average, good power, good speed, great competitor."

"He's thirty-seven, in the twilight of a great career," Marta offered.

"He's still an inspiration to me. I hope to carry on his tradition."

Marta released an inner sigh of relief. The kid gave a thoughtful answer and no sermons.

"Let's talk about your career at Arizona State." In response to Marta's questions, Raul explained that a number of colleges and universities had offered him baseball scholarships, including perennial College World Series finalists USC, Texas, Oklahoma State, Cal State Fullerton, and Arizona State. Also, several pro scouts were attracted by his .460 batting average, sure-handed fielding, and rocket arm as a senior in high school. They assured him that, with the right team, he could be in the majors in as few as three years.

Raul was interested in college, but he was also eager to sign a big-money contract to help ease his family's financial burden. His parents, however, urged him to take a scholarship, insisting that his education was important and that a new house could wait. After "seeking the Lord's will on the matter," Raul explained, he yielded to his parents' wishes and accepted a full-ride scholarship to ASU in his home state to play baseball and study law enforcement.

Despite Raul's clear intentions to play college ball first, the Montreal Expos of the National League East spent their tenth round draft choice on him. They tempted him with a substantial contract, a $100,000 signing bonus, and a promise to start him at Harrisburg in the AA minors, only two steps from the big club. Raul thanked the Expos for the generous offer but declined. They wished him the best at the university and said they would be back.

Raul modestly agreed with Marta that his development as a baseball player accelerated greatly during his first two years at ASU. He began his freshman season platooned in center field with a left-hand-hitting senior. By mid-season Raul was starting every game and hitting third in the lineup, relegating the senior to pinch-hitting duty. Raul finished the year with team highs in average (.426), doubles (15), RBIs (58), and fielding percentage (.947), and was elected the team's most valuable player. The Sun Devils made the College World Series tournament but were eliminated in the first round by Georgia Tech.

"The Florida Marlins drafted you in '96, didn't they, Raul?" Marta prompted. Denny Fogle maintained a tight closeup on the athlete's handsome bronze face.

Raul explained that Florida offered him an even sweeter deal after his freshman season than Montreal had a year earlier, including more money and a plane ticket to join their AAA team Edmonton in the Pacific Coast League immediately on signing. The Marlins' brass reminded Raul that departing seniors would drain ASU's talent pool and that the Sun Devils had little chance of making it to the College World Series in '97. "Why not come on board now and help us get to the National League finals and perhaps the *real* World Series," they said.

"My parents and I talked about it and prayed about it," Raul said, sounding relaxed and confident. "They minimized the importance of the money and underscored their desire that I finish school. It was hard saying no to an even larger contract and the chance to play with the pros. But I agree with my parents that a college education will outlast my ability to play ball. So I told the Marlins 'Thanks but no thanks.' "

Marta drew from Raul the highlights of his sophomore season at ASU, which included another MVP award and second-team All-America honors. He maintained his .400-plus average while unleashing more power, leading the PAC-10 in extra-base hits. Despite his great year, the rebuilding Sun Devils were eliminated from the western regional tournament by Cal State Fullerton. The Montreal Expos, selecting ahead of Florida, again made Raul their number-one selection in the annual college draft. The conversation with the Expos ended with a familiar verdict: Raul would complete his degree before signing a contract and donning a pro uniform.

Marta continued, referring to notes on a pad on her lap, "This year, as a junior, you hit .432, fourth best in the nation, topped Division I in fielding percentage and assists, and led the PAC-10 in doubles, home runs, and runs batted in. At your skill level, you could probably start in center field for half the clubs in the major leagues. And last week the Giants made you their number-one pick in the draft, the fifth player selected overall. I've heard they are ready to offer you the Golden Gate Bridge to sign a contract before you leave Omaha this week."

Marta gave him two seconds to confirm the rumor. He said nothing.

"San Francisco is leading the Dodgers by six games in the Western Division. They're the odds-on favorites to represent the National League in the World Series. You could possibly win a College World Series and the Major League World Series in the same year. You can certainly finish your degree in the off season if you want to. Aren't you crazy to pass up this opportunity to stay at ASU for another year?"

Marta recognized that she was pushing the envelope on sensationalism for a typical ESPN feature story. But her viewers would demand to know why a bright young man would snub instant millions and throw away a chance at a World Series ring just to complete a few classes and be a college hero. And Marta wanted to know if this Jesus from whom the Barrigan family allegedly received advice would finally wise up and tell them to take the money.

Raul shifted on the chair, causing Denny to adjust the camera to keep the subject's head in frame. The boyish smile on Raul's face hinted that a big secret was just begging to be told. "I talked with my parents, my fiancée, and my agent about that again recently, and—"

"So you have an agent now," Marta clarified.

"Yes. Several agents have been after me since I finished high school, but up until this spring I didn't think I needed one."

"What changed your mind?"

Raul shifted again and Denny followed him. The smile was fixed on his face. "Basically the same things you just mentioned. I'm only sixteen credit hours away from a degree in law enforcement. I can polish that off next winter."

"You mean after you help the Giants polish off the Cleveland Indians in the World Series," Marta interjected with a puckish gleam.

"Let's just say I have some attractive options for completing my studies," Raul countered. The tactful, diplomatic reply convinced Marta that Raul was already under the guiding influence of his agent. But the athlete's Cheshire-cat grin tipped her off that there was more he wanted to tell. "So with the potential of turning pro so much closer, we decided it was time to find someone to represent me."

"*We* decided?"

"My parents and I—and my fiancée, Samantha."

Marta nodded and wrote the girl's name on her pad without looking away from her subject.

Raul continued. "We went over the pros and cons and prayed about the options—"

"Your agent prays too?" Marta interrupted, unable to completely disguise her surprise.

"Of course. Why would I hire an agent who doesn't know how to pray?"

Marta didn't have an answer, nor did the question require one. From what she had learned about Raul Barrigan the Jesus-talking jock, a praying sports agent made perfect sense.

"And what did you and your parents and Samantha and your agent decide?" Marta pressed. She moistened her lips in anticipation of a scoop. Denny zoomed in even tighter, and Raul's face filled the frame.

"We decided that, since it's my life and my career, I should make the call about when I will complete my degree and when I will start my pro career."

"Your parents and everybody said it's OK to sign with San Francisco," Marta extrapolated aloud.

"And they said it was OK with them if I finish my four years at ASU," Raul said. Marta suspected that Raul's praying agent must have been lying through his teeth to say OK to that option, considering the generous slice of the contract which would fall onto his plate when his bonus baby signed on the dotted line.

"Everybody's fine with anything you decide," Marta said.

"That's right."

"So what's your call?"

Raul paused and pursed his lips as if trying to swallow what he really wanted to say. "At this point I am committed to return to Arizona State for my fourth year of eligibility. That's been my plan since I enrolled. At the end of the College World Series I will review that plan. If I decide to change direction, I will inform my family first, the university second, the San Francisco Giants third, and finally the public.

But nothing is going to happen until we win the championship. That's where I'm focused right now."

Marta tried a couple of other angles trying to pry from Raul the decision that she knew he had already made, but he was closed to the subject. So she shifted the discussion to the current tournament and Arizona State's success, leading them into tonight's semifinal game against the top-seeded University of Texas, their third game against the Longhorns in the tournament.

ASU, seeded fourth in the tournament, had opened Saturday night against fifth-seeded Penn State. Sugar Barrigan had a single and double and two RBIs as the Sun Devils overwhelmed the Nittany Lions, 10–2. Two nights later ASU was paired against Texas, convincing winners over eighth-seeded Princeton. Strong Longhorn pitching held the Devils to three hits—one of them a solo home run by Raul Barrigan—in a 4–1 victory.

Tuesday night, Arizona State played Penn State again, the other 1–1 team in the lower bracket, for a second shot at undefeated Texas. Behind Sugar Barrigan's two singles and a homer, ASU pounded the Lions 12–6, eliminating them from the tournament. The Devils' bats came alive on Thursday night against Texas, sending the Longhorns to their first defeat, 7–5, and forcing a third game to determine who would play the championship game against the winner of this afternoon's Ohio State–Tennessee game.

"You're batting .550 with three homers and seven RBIs," Marta summarized from the notes on her pad. "You could go 0 for the rest of the week and still be selected to the all-tournament team. And if you can put one out of the park in these last two games—providing ASU gets by Texas tonight—you're a shoe-in for most outstanding player of the tournament. You have no more worlds to conquer as an amateur, Sugar Bear. You *must* be ready to sign with the Giants after the championship game on Saturday."

Raul parried the thrust with aplomb. "Saturday is so far from my mind right now it could be in the twenty-first century. Our team leaves for the stadium in about fifteen minutes. We'll watch the Ohio State–Tennessee game, then dress for our game against Texas. We all know the importance of the game: winner goes on to the championship, loser goes home. Like Jesus said, I don't worry about tomorrow, because tomorrow will take care of itself. Today is all there is."

Fearing that Raul was gearing up for another sermonette, Marta pressed, "If you choose to sign with the Giants, will you let ESPN announce it to the public for you?" She knew she would have to edit such a presumptuous question out of the interview, but she had to ask it. She also knew that if Sugar Barrigan's pretty face was just a front for an evil, greedy mind, his answer would prove it. Now was his chance to name his price.

Raul leaned back in the chair and crossed his muscular arms in front of his chest. He cocked his head to one side and studied Marta intently. Then another Ponch-like smile brightened his face. "I'll pray about it, Marta," he said.

Thirteen

Myrna Valentine strode the sidewalk of Beverly Glen Boulevard like she owned it. Anyone who noticed her would have guessed her to be a corporate climber in one of the many plush office buildings adorning Century City or a rising starlet from neighboring Beverly Hills gracing the public streets with her presence. But no one noticed her this bright, June morning. No one really noticed anyone in this posh professional district west of downtown Los Angeles. There was a numbing sameness about everything. All the cars were expensive, all the clothes looked hand-tailored, and everyone was thought to be in the movies somehow, either in front of the camera or behind it.

Myrna fit the scene perfectly even though she neither worked in Century City nor lived nearby. Her physical stature—standing five-feet-ten, her proud, confident bearing, and maturity beyond her twenty-seven years—came from her father. Master Sergeant Mark Valentine, a six-foot-six career man in the United States Marines, had instructed his daughter from childhood to stand tall, speak her mind, and take no bull from anyone. The girl's name was also from her father's side of the family. Mark insisted that his firstborn girl, who turned out to be his only daughter, bear the name of his beloved maternal grandmother, Myrna Rubeck.

The young woman's striking beauty could be traced to her mother. Thuy Van Le was only sixteen when then lance corporal Mark Valentine met and married her in Saigon in 1970. Despite her height, American blood, and Marine-brat toughness, Myrna carried many of the features of her diminutive Vietnamese mother: dark flowing hair, golden skin, graceful, willowy limbs. Her face was a stunning blend of her American and Asian heritage: alert, dark eyes that were slightly almond-shaped, broad, high cheeks, a petite nose, and a small mouth with full lips.

The mauve-gray designer suit she wore today had been made for her, but neither it nor the fashionable, expensive accessories had been purchased by her—nor could she afford them. Samples were among the few perks falling to her in a seemingly glamorous modeling career which was in reality a bitter struggle for steady work. Not only was

Myrna pitted against an agency and industry stocked with beautiful, talented competition, but most of that competition was white or black, not Amerasian. As one tactless designer had said to her, "You're beautiful, honey, but we don't want our clients to look at you and think about that ugly war when they're about to write us a big check." Myrna loved her parents and was proud of her mixed heritage. But she loathed the constant battle she faced against bigotry and discrimination in her chosen profession.

Myrna hurried up the marble steps and through the broad glass doors of the Gedney-Harcourt Building. The directory, mounted on a stone pillar in the middle of the lobby, told her where to go. She rode the elevator to the eighth floor and stepped out into a spacious reception area richly decorated in rosewood, brass, and $250-a-square-yard carpeting. An attractive geometric-shaped logo and the words THE BELLARMINE GROUP adorned the wall behind the desk. The international marketing firm occupied the entire eighth floor and half of the ninth.

The receptionist was a stocky young man wearing a starched white shirt and tie but no jacket. He turned from his com center keyboard to face Myrna as he completed routing a call with several quick keystrokes. The name on his brass nameplate was Sean Reilly. "How may I help you, ma'am?"

"Please tell Guy Rossovich that I wish to see him," Myrna said with quiet confidence. "My name is Myrna Valentine."

Reilly had her name in the computer almost before she finished saying it. "But you have no appointment, Ms. Valentine," he said, looking up from the screen. "Mr. Rossovich will see no one without an appointment, and unfortunately his schedule is—"

"Is he in?" Myrna interrupted curtly.

"Yes, but unless you have an appointment you—"

"Do you believe in magic, Sean?" she cut in again.

Sean Reilly was caught up short at the odd question and the use of his name, which Myrna had simply read off the nameplate. "Magic? What are you—"

"I'm going to turn you into a magician right before your own eyes. All you have to do is get Guy Rossovich on your little squawk box and mention my name—Myrna Valentine, and he will see me. Try it." She motioned to the keyboard.

"You're a client then, Ms. Valentine? Or you're involved in Mr. Rossovich's campaign?"

"Neither. But all you need to do is mention my name, and—poof!— he'll be out here, just like magic." Then she crossed her arms and glared at him, daring him to question her request again.

Reilly returned to the keyboard and tapped open a line. "Francie, there's a Ms. Myrna Valentine here to see Mr. Rossovich. . . . No, but she insists that Mr. Rossovich will see her. . . . Well, Ms. Valentine is, er, it's rather urgent."

Reilly looked up at Myrna for approval, and she nodded at him for his creativity.

There was a pause, and Reilly averted his eyes from the statuesque, dark-haired beauty standing before him. "Yes, Francie," he said finally to the unseen secretary, "Thank you."

Reilly hung up with a finger tap to the keyboard. His face mirrored amazement. "Mr. Rossovich will meet you in conference room C in three minutes. That's down the hall on your left, just past the copy room."

Myrna smiled a plastic smile and snapped her fingers over the desk. "See, Sean. Just like magic." Then she wheeled on her heels and strode down the hall.

The small, empty conference room was equipped with a bar set up to dispense fresh coffee and cappuccino. Myrna moved to fill a mug, then remembered her shaky stomach and returned the mug to the counter. Instead, she lifted a bottle of mineral water from the small refrigerator, snapped off the lid, poured half a glass, and sipped at the cold liquid.

An assortment of sofas, chairs, and lamps on small beverage tables arranged in a U-shape took up most of the room. One side of the room was all windows, looking out to the southwest. Santa Monica and the Pacific Ocean were clearly visible in the distance. Myrna paced between the window and the furniture. She would not sit down. She didn't intend on staying long, and she knew Guy didn't want her here at all. She counted on his anxiety at her coming to speed their deliberations to quick agreement.

Guy Rossovich appeared at the conference room door, obviously agitated. He was a man of average build and above average good looks. Touches of gray at the sides of his dark, wavy hair suggested more maturity than the man may have acquired naturally in his thirty-four years. He was dressed in expensive office attire—minus the jacket, and he held a pair of wire-rimmed glasses at his side.

For almost eighteen months Myrna Valentine had considered Guy Rossovich the most significant perk from her modeling career. They had met at a show in San Francisco sponsored by a consortium of athletic wear manufacturers planning to go international with their latest offerings. Myrna was one of more than two dozen models striding the runway in fashions created for both court and courtside. The Bellarmine Group was handling the marketing, and Vice President Guy Rossovich, the brains of the Bellarmine Group, was on hand for the big event.

Myrna was flattered that Guy sought her out after the show to compliment her and thank her for her participation. To most designers, manufacturers, and clients, models were little more than mannequins that walked and turned, something to look at, not to interact with. Like the caterers, they were paid to do their jobs then disappear while the movers and shakers talked turkey. The surprise visit of such a wealthy and influential man outside Myrna's dressing room was a break with the norm which pleased and excited the young model.

When Guy learned that Myrna also lived in the L.A. area—Manhattan Beach, southwest of downtown, he asked if he could call her. A week later, he *did* call. They began seeing each other when they were both in town, quiet intimate dinners in out-of-the-way places along the beach or nestled in the canyons. Then there were the weekends away: Palm Springs, Catalina, Los Cabos, Vail. Guy always arranged everything, and Myrna relished the attention, romance, and passion lavished on her by her handsome lover.

There had been other men in Myrna's life—plenty of them. But they didn't stay long after she revealed to them, in her quest for intimacy and acceptance, that she was under a physician's care for mental and emotional stress. Many of them used drugs, but they couldn't seem to handle her need for prescription drugs and therapy. Her potential for a breakdown always led to a break up. So she decided not to tell Guy about her personal problems. This was one man she could not bear to lose.

When Guy finally lost interest in Myrna, he ended the relationship abruptly by announcing to her that he had a wife and two small daughters. Guy's revelation explained a lot of things about their affair: why he insisted on meeting in quiet, secluded restaurants, why he never invited her to his office, why they never went out with other couples, why he sometimes arranged for them to travel separately to a romantic rendezvous.

Myrna was devastated and angry at his announcement. She had screamed at him that she never wanted to see him again, forcing herself to hate him. Guy had replied that not seeing each other again was exactly what he had in mind. Myrna had every intention of keeping her vow—until two days ago.

"This is not what I want, Myrna," Guy growled in a low voice after closing the conference room door behind him. They stood facing each other with a room full of icy air between them. "What we had is over. You cannot come here. I will not allow you to—"

"I'm pregnant, Guy," Myrna said, unmoved by his caustic protest. "Five weeks pregnant, to be exact."

She pulled a folded sheet of paper from the handbag draped over her shoulder and dropped it over the back of the sofa to the cushion. It was a printout from her physician detailing the results of her recent examination. Guy remained statue-still and silent.

"According to my book," Myrna continued, "five weeks ago I was at the Desert Hot Springs Resort with you, Guy. I believe that was our last weekend together before you told me about the *other* woman you sleep with and your *other* children."

Guy dropped his head, the fight suddenly drained out of him. Myrna let him stew in the juices of the dilemma she hoped he would give anything to escape. Not only did Guy Rossovich have a career and family to protect, he was also pulling together a staff and stocking a war chest for a run at state senator. He did not need someone like Myrna Valentine hanging around reminding him of indiscretions which might cost him votes as well as his marriage.

Guy crossed the room and picked up the printout from the sofa without looking at Myrna. She let him study it for a moment before saying, "It's amazing what the DNA workups can tell these days, isn't it, Guy?" Her voice was cool with sarcasm. "Notice that your child is a male. I bet you've always wanted a son to follow in your footsteps. And look at the line that says 'progenitors.' Those two sets of characters you see there are you and me, darling. Our little mistake may not look much like you, but there will be no denying that you're his father. The numbers and letters on that sheet are more reliable than fingerprints. And, in accordance with California law, the fetus is already registered with the county until termination or birth."

Guy snapped his head up and glared at Myrna. "You're certainly not going to give birth." It was meant to be a question, but Guy's anger pushed it out as a challenge.

Myrna let him squirm only for a few seconds. "Of course not, Guy. I have a life too, you know. And believe it or not, my life would be even more complicated by a child than yours would be."

"So you're going to . . . terminate the fetus."

"It's called abortion, Guy," Myrna retorted cynically.

"When?"

"My appointment is for Monday morning."

"And the record of conception will be deleted from county records."

"Yes. Our little mistake and your part in his brief life will vanish."

Guy stared at her while the wheels turned in his head. "So you want me to pay for the abortion," he said finally.

"No," Myrna replied. Then she turned and strolled to another side of the U-shape, keeping the furniture between her and Guy. After giving him a few seconds to think he was off the hook, she said, "I want you to compensate me for the eighteen months of delusion you subjected me to."

"I did not delude you," Guy objected. "I never said I was single."

"Yes, you did," Myrna shot back, "every time you took me to bed, every time you led me to believe we had a future together, every time we saw a cute child in a restaurant and you failed to tell me about yours."

"There are no strings in a relationship like ours; everybody knows that," Guy argued with a wave of the glasses and the sheet of paper in his hand. "I never forced you to do anything you didn't want to do. You had as much fun as I did."

"What's going to happen to me in the clinic on Monday morning will *not* be fun," Myrna retorted. "And the time I've already missed from work and *will* miss from work next week will not be fun."

"I'll pay for the abortion," Guy said, a decision he had made the moment she said the word "pregnant." "And I'll throw in a few hundred to help you out. But you are not going to extort money from me for promises I never made."

Myrna stared at him from across the room, arms folded in front of her. "Ten thousand dollars," she said.

Guy stiffened and hissed. "What?"

"I accept your offer to pay for the abortion. It will cost you $10,000, and you're getting a bargain."

"That's blackmail," Guy spat, trembling with rage. "An abortion doesn't cost more than a thousand or two."

"You said you'd pay for the abortion," Myrna said, taunting him with her derisive tone, "and ten grand is what it's going to cost *you* for *me* to remedy this last little problem we have from our no-strings-attached relationship." She patted her lower abdomen to emphasize her point.

"And if I don't?" Guy challenged.

Myrna laughed a mocking laugh and said nothing, indicating that Guy's question was too ludicrous—and her answer too obvious—for words.

Guy looked back at the printout in his hand and focused on the marks next to the line headed PATERNAL PROGENITOR. It suddenly occurred to him that Myrna *had* offered him a bargain, a deal too good to refuse. Losing $10,000 was nothing compared to losing his wife and children, staining his reputation in the business world, and jeopardizing a promising political career that could lead to the governor's chair and beyond.

Guy dropped his shoulders. After more than a minute of silence, he sighed, "Give me a couple of days, OK?"

"Not a chance," Myrna said without sympathy. "We became rather intimate over the last year and half, remember? I know that you always carry your checkbook in your suit coat. And I took the liberty to investigate your balances a few times while you slept."

Guy muttered a contemptuous curse.

"I know you can write me a check from your private account today—right now. You can enter it as a campaign expense or a stock purchase, and no one—not even Marilyn or Mary Lou or whatever her name is—will be the wiser. As soon as I have that check in my hand, I will walk out of this building and disappear forever."

"You're sick, Myrna," Guy growled hatefully.

Myrna cringed inside at Guy's unwitting reference to her ongoing distress. But she kept her emotions under control.

Guy crumpled the printout in one hand and walked to the bar. He stuffed the wad of paper into the disposal, turned on the water, and flipped the switch. In seconds the report was swept down the drain in a thousand pieces.

"Wait by the elevator," he said to Myrna in a voice she almost couldn't hear. Then he left the room, still carrying his glasses in his hand.

Six minutes later Francie Raymond walked into the reception area where Myrna stood. The model had not spoken to Sean Reilly during the wait, and he had likewise ignored her.

"Ms. Valentine?" said the well-dressed, matronly secretary as she approached. She carried a sealed 9"-by-12" manila envelope. Myrna nodded. "Here is the document you wanted," she said, clearly unaware of the envelope's contents. "Mr. Rossovich said it's exactly what you're looking for."

Myrna received the envelope with a polite smile. "Thank you." Then she excused herself and stepped into the waiting elevator, which was empty.

On the way down, she opened the envelope and pulled a sheet of blank paper halfway out. Clipped to the top edge was a personal check made out to her in the amount of $10,000 and signed by Guy W. Rossovich. Satisfied, she slid the paper back into the envelope.

Before the elevator reached the ground floor, Myrna began to cry. She expected the money she knew Guy would give her to bring a sense of consolation. It didn't. All she could think about was the child within her, and the fact that his father didn't care a bit about either of them.

Fourteen

Myrna walked several blocks to where her dinged-up '93 Isuzu Trooper was unobtrusively parked on a side street. Her father had given her the wagon two years earlier when he retired from the Marines. Mark Valentine wanted a bigger rig to pull his boat, and Myrna's old Camaro had finally given out on her. So he tossed her the keys and told her to bring it back when she didn't need it anymore. Then the elder Valentines moved from El Toro, California, to Astoria, Oregon, at the mouth of the Columbia River, where Mark could fish for salmon every day of the season if he wanted to.

The former Marine was a firm believer in letting his kids slug it out in life without much parental interference or support. But he had a soft spot in his heart for his only daughter and always made sure she had a reliable set of wheels. The Trooper was also Mark's attempt at compensating Myrna for the emotional problems he couldn't help her with.

Myrna guided the Trooper directly to California Commercial Bank in upscale Westwood, the branch where Guy Rossovich kept his personal account. She had decided that the quickest way to move the money from his pocket to hers was to cash the $10,000 check immediately at his bank and deposit the money into her account as soon as she got home. She couldn't afford to wait for the check to clear. The clinic would require full payment before the procedure on Monday morning. And she couldn't write a $2,000 check on her present account balance.

The bank teller handled her transaction professionally, convincing Myrna that he dealt with customers daily who deposited and withdrew cash amounts in five figures. The Rossovich account was examined and Myrna's identification was verified. She walked out with twenty $500-bills tucked into her handbag.

Back in the Trooper, Myrna took Wilshire Boulevard down to the San Diego Freeway and headed south. Late morning traffic was moderate to heavy, but flowing steadily—normal for a Friday on the Los Angeles freeway system. It would take twenty minutes for her to get to Manhattan Beach, barring a freeway pileup.

It was a wonder to Myrna that there weren't more wrecks on the L.A. freeways. The river of traffic roared along at 65–75 MPH with barely enough space between bumpers to park a car, let alone drive or stop one safely at this speed. But allowing more than two car lengths ahead simply invited another driver to cut in, pushing the slowpoke further back in the pack. And L.A. drivers hated to lose ground to the competition.

Worse yet, Myrna guessed that up to half the drivers on the freeway at any given time were also on the phone. Many drove with only one hand on the wheel and their attention diverted by business, networking, schmoozing, or sweet-talking. Some L.A. drivers got so involved on the phone in their rolling offices that they missed their off-ramps by miles. Myrna was grateful for the protection of the rather substantial Trooper surrounding her. It wasn't as safe as driving a truck, but neither was it as tinny and flimsy as one of those cheap new electric Zap Runabouts populating the freeways. She wouldn't want to be inside one of those when it folded up like a paper cup in an accident.

As she drove home, Myrna had time to think, a luxury in short supply over the forty-six hours since she learned she was pregnant. The bouts with morning sickness—except she thought it was a virus or bacteria or anxiety over work or a bad piece of fish or something—had started only two weeks earlier. After missing several days on a lingerie catalog shoot, she made an appointment to get some pills or a shot.

Could she be pregnant? Dr. Anna Khoubala had asked her. Ridiculous, Myrna had scoffed. Her period was a little late, but her cycle was always erratic. Her protection had never failed her before. And besides, she hadn't been with a man in weeks, not since a short vacation with her boyfriend near Palm Springs. If she *was* pregnant, she had joked, the father must be the invisible man.

Yes, you are pregnant, the doctor had assured Myrna a few minutes later. The simple test had isolated the moment of conception to within four hours. Myrna sat in the office and cried. She cried over the complication suddenly thrust into her life. She cried over the lost work, the pain and expense of an abortion, the humiliation of explaining the pregnancy to her parents, who knew she was seeing the doctor that day. But mostly Myrna cried over the fresh memory of the sudden, painful end of her relationship with Guy Rossovich the week after Palm Springs. It was as if he knew he had impregnated her and quickly washed his hands of her to keep his life from an unwanted complication.

While Myrna calmed down in her office, Dr. Khoubala made arrangements for the abortion without even asking if she wanted one. The doctor was confident that Myrna, like so many of her unmarried, career-woman patients, had no room in her life for an unplanned pregnancy. Myrna took the appointment card without a thought. Her only concern was how she was going to pay for the procedure and how soon she could get back to work.

The idea to ask Guy Rossovich to help her with the expense had come to her later that day. It seemed only fair for him to participate financially since he most assuredly had participated genetically—the progenitor code on the pregnancy report made that clear. The money was no problem for him, Myrna knew very well. And the thought that she could pinch him financially played to her desire for a little revenge for him walking out on her so heartlessly.

The idea to *force* Guy Rossovich into paying for much more than the abortion had come to Myrna late that night as she tossed sleeplessly on her bed. It was blackmail, she admitted, but not *criminal* blackmail. After all, it was costing her much more than $2,000 to right the wrong to which they had both contributed equally. Lost work opportunities, mental anguish, humiliation, possible relationship problems in the future. In reality, she had rationalized that night, she was offering Guy an opportunity to buy his way out of the same consequences she was already experiencing. If he did not pay what she asked, the revelation of his indiscretion to his wife and business associates would undoubtedly provoke a storm of personal anguish and humiliation, not to mention the potential damage to his career and political aspirations.

At first, $10,000 had seemed a little steep to her. But as Myrna thought about it that night, she became convinced that Guy was getting off easy. The cost to her emotionally was incalculable, especially considering her history of depression. She may be paying off the debt for years in sleeplessness, worry, and possible physical complications. But Guy would be able to slide $10,000 out of his personal funds without a ripple of suspicion—her surreptitious investigations of his checkbook had informed her of that. He was getting a bargain.

But Myrna had stopped short of raising the ante. She wanted to pressure Guy Rossovich, even hurt him a little to let him know how much she had been hurt by him. But she didn't want to make him angry or vindictive. Nor did she want to completely destroy the bridge that might someday—if Guy's marriage ever went sour, if big business or politics failed to fulfill him—lead him back to her. The thought of being with Guy Rossovich again had made her cry into her pillow, cry with a longing she cursed but could not deny.

As she drove, Myrna thought about calling her parents now and telling them the truth about her condition. The day of her exam, she had called and lied to them, telling them it was just a touch of the flu. She wanted to tell the truth, and she knew she would have to soon. Truth was a high value in the Valentine household, and speaking the truth had been drummed into Myrna, Mark Jr., and Mike Valentine from early childhood. But that day in Dr. Khoubala's office the truth had stunned Myrna. And she didn't know how to tell Mark and Thuy that she was pregnant but that she would not be completing the pregnancy. Such an announcement required forethought and diplomacy. So she had bought some time with a lie.

Myrna reached for the car phone, then pulled her hand back empty. *Not yet, not before the procedure*, she cautioned herself. *If I tell them before Monday, they may try to talk me out of the abortion. I don't need that kind of pressure right now. When I tell them afterward, they will be disappointed, but they will understand. And once the deed is done, they won't be able to pressure me about presenting them with a grandson.*

That word—grandson—abruptly kicked open the door to a hidden room of thoughts Myrna had not visited. Up until now, she had referred to the cause of her morning sickness and anxiety as a problem, an inconvenience, a physical abnormality—like a cyst or a wart—in need of surgical correction. Dr. Khoubala had called it fetal material. When informing Guy, Myrna had used the words "our little mistake." The fact that this little mistake had been classified as a male had not impacted Myrna emotionally, but the word "grandson" did.

Suddenly the image of a reddish-pink, squalling newborn boy materialized in Myrna's mind. The characters identifying the infant's progenitors on the doctor's printout had seemed sterile and impersonal to her. But in just a glimpse at the infant's face Myrna saw traces of her parents, herself, and Guy Rossovich. *This was not a problem to be solved; this was a person to be dealt with*, she recklessly allowed herself to think. *Monday's procedure not only involved her; it involved her parents' only grandchild—and her son.*

Myrna snapped on the radio and turned up the volume to chase the image from her mind. A cacophony of electric guitars, steel drums, and congas boomed from the speakers. "Don't get soft now, Myrna," she argued aloud. "That's nothing but a blob of tissue in there, and you can't let a nameless, faceless blob ruin the rest of your life. You made a mistake and you're going to pay for it on Monday. Then it's all over, and you'll have nearly $8,000 to help you forget about it."

She beat her hand on the steering wheel and sang "Dah-da-dah, da-da-dah-da-dah" in time with the loud Caribbean jazz. She forced herself to start a mental list of how she would spend the money Guy Rossovich had so easily parted with. "You should have asked for more, Myrna," she chided herself aloud and laughing. "Dah-da-dah, da-da-dah-da-dah."

Myrna noted that part of the money had to go toward necessities like rent and groceries, since the "accident" and the procedure would cost her several days of work. The Trooper also needed new tires and a cooling system flush for the summer. And she wanted to tuck away some of the cash to tide her over those scary, forced days off without pay between assignments. After that, Myrna planned to get some clothes of her own, a new set of dishes and stainless, some plants for the apartment, and maybe one of those wireless phones.

The lively music flooding the Trooper gave her another idea which instantly lifted her spirits. "Vacation!" she exulted. She thought about the Caribbean, Cozumel, or Kauai, perfect for relaxing and getting her head together after the procedure on Monday. She had put off vacationing as a luxury she could neither afford in time or money. Now she had both. She would make a call to Mattie Chu this afternoon and try to book a flight and a condo. No, she would make the call right now.

She picked up the phone and, keeping one eye on the road, tapped in the letters c-e-l-e-b-r-i-t-y with her thumb. The phone dialed the number automatically.

"Celebrity Travel, this is Jennifer. May I help you."

"Is Mattie in please?"

"Just a moment."

When Myrna's friend and travel person picked up, Myrna sang, "Mattie, I want to get away from it all!"

"You've come to the right place," Mattie replied, laughing.

Fifteen

Raul Barrigan rode the team bus as required from the Red Lion to Rosenblatt Stadium. The team would watch the upper bracket semifinal game between third-seeded Ohio State and sixth-seeded Tennessee together, then dress for their evening game against Texas. Like Arizona

State versus Texas, Tennessee had lost once to today's opponent and then beat them in a rematch. This afternoon's game would decide who would advance to the finals against either ASU or Texas.

The crisp morning had given way to a warm, clear afternoon, and the assembling crowd was festive and noisy. As planned, Raul rendez-voused with his parents, his fiancée, and his agent for a few minutes before the game in front of the CWS Hall of Fame just outside the stadium on the first base side. The elder Barrigans were staying at the Leisure Inn Motel courtesy of the members of their church in Tucson who took up a generous collection to help them with the trip. Raul had contributed to the collection anonymously since his parents kindly re-fused his money, knowing he was also living on a budget. Raul thought it frustratingly ironic that his parents had to stay at a budget motel instead of the Hawthorne Suites when he was only days from being able to buy them a new house.

Fifty-five-year-old Rudy Barrigan was thick-limbed and weathered from a lifetime of manual labor under the punishing Arizona sun. Serena, his wife of thirty-three years, was rather barrel-shaped, but she appeared remarkably healthy and attractive for having raised six chil-dren on a laborer's wages.

The elder Barrigans owned only two kinds of clothes: work clothes—khakis for Rudy and cotton house dresses for Serena—and church clothes. They were dressed today as they had been for every other tournament game: in their church clothes. Rudy wore an ancient, three-piece brown polyester suit, white shirt, and tie, and Serena wore a simple but pleasing floral print rayon dress and sweater. On such an important occasion as the College World Series in which their Sugar Bear had such a prominent role, they were determined to look their best every day. But they were also avid Arizona State fans. So each of them added to their Sunday best a gaudy gold ASU baseball cap with a maroon brim and logo.

Raul greeted each of his parents with a loving embrace, a typical expression of Barrigan family affection. Then he embraced Samantha, kissing her lightly on the lips. Even though twenty-two-year-old Samantha Dumas' ancestry was rooted in Eastern Europe instead of Latin America, her flowing black hair, dark walnut eyes, and cool-toned skin allowed her to pass for a Latino, especially when standing with the Barrigans. Tall, large-boned, and curvaceous, Samantha was not dwarfed by her muscular fiancé. She wore a figure-flattering ma-roon V-neck sweater over a white blouse and pressed jeans.

Samantha was also staying at the Leisure Inn, even though her par-ents had insisted that she stay someplace nicer. But she had rented a car for the week to provide transportation for her future in-laws. Raul loved Sam for her kindness and yearned for the day when he could shower her with even more comforts and niceties than she was used to from her well-to-do parents.

Mr. and Mrs. Dumas were as cool about her involvement with "the Mexican boy who wants to be a baseball star" as they had been about her Christian faith, which had flourished in the campus ministry at ASU where she and Raul met. The Dumases had agreed to their daughter's marriage to Raul with tacit reluctance. A late October date had been selected, two weeks after Major League Baseball's fall classic, the World Series. Raul was anxious to prove to them that he was completely capable of providing for Samantha. He would call them personally upon signing with the Giants—after leading Arizona State to its sixth CWS championship.

"How was your interview, hon?" Samantha said. Her eyes held his with affection.

"Good interview," he said enthusiastically, caressing Sam's hand. "Marta Friesen is nice. She wants to do an exclusive when I sign."

"You didn't tell her you're going to sign," his agent interrupted with alarm.

"No, Stub, I was 'purposely vague,' just like you told me to be," Raul said, silently amused at the man's anxiety over every detail of his client's passage from amateur to professional.

Robert Parker was called Stub or Stubby by the professional athletes he represented for a couple of reasons. More obviously, the former jockey from Scotland was only five-two and 128 pounds. Stubby looked more like a ventriloquist's dummy among his huge pro football clients than a shrewd business agent.

Less obviously, Robert Parker was rumored to use the same pencil down to the stub before buying another one, squeezing every penny until Abe Lincoln groaned in pain. Though he cleared well into six figures annually from a small, select group of clients, Stubby, a forty-five-year-old bachelor, lived in a one-bedroom condo in West Los Angeles and shopped the boys department in the malls for suits rather than having them custom tailored.

The one area where he did not scrimp was transportation. He leased a new BMW sedan every year and rented Caddies and Lincolns on his many business trips. Having spent his early years aboard some of the most expensive quarter horses in the world, Stubby apparently knew the importance of a reliable mount.

What Stubby did with the rest of his money was information he did not share with his clients. Having come to know him as a man of moral conviction, religious faith, and steadfast prayer, Raul suspected that Stubby gave a lot of money away.

Stubby Parker loathed his nickname. Few people in his native land would make sport of his size in public let alone hang a nickname on him which did so. But sports crazy Americans were nickname fanatics, especially the athletes themselves. So Stubby refused to make an issue of it with men twice his size who paid him a handsome salary for his services.

"What exactly did the reporter ask? What exactly did you say?" Stubby bored in with mother-hen concern. Then aloud but to himself, he added, "I knew I should have been there."

Raul recounted—in a hushed tone since they were surrounded by people—Marta Friesen's questions about his professional future and his carefully veiled answers.

"But you *have* decided to play for San Francisco, haven't you?" Serena interjected, looking a little confused. "Isn't that misleading?"

Both Raul and Stubby tried to shush her. "Technically, Mrs. Barrigan, Raul can't make that decision until after the series," Stubby clarified. His voice still bore a hint of the brogue of his homeland— rolled r's, other consonants and vowels crisply enunciated. "And to reveal at this stage that Raul *has* decided to turn professional might weaken our bargaining position with San Francisco."

Serena and Rudy nodded, but their faces were still clouded with doubt.

Raul took another stab at clearing the fog for them. "I'm not doing anything dishonest here, Mom. *You* know I have decided to turn pro. We all prayed about it, and I think that's what God wants me to do. But the rest of the world won't know until I sign my name on a contract. That's when I make my decision officially."

"It's kind of like voting, Mrs. Barrigan," Samantha added. "You know who you want to vote for before you get into the booth. But you don't really decide for that person until you tap the key on the voting machine."

Raul and Stubby nodded, hoping the example helped to ease Serena's mind. The woman smiled weakly. Then she looked at Rudy who shrugged and smiled. They still weren't getting it.

Raul was suddenly aware how much his parents had aged during his three years in college. His memory was etched with images of them from his childhood: a couple in their early thirties, strong, virile, wise, invincible. The couple standing before him no longer matched the snapshots in his mental scrapbook. Years of labor had lined their faces and sapped their vigor. Though they were still rocks of wisdom and spiritual strength, Rudy and Serena Barrigan were showing signs of wear. Rudy would not be able to make a living by working the land much longer, and his retirement package would only be a step backward. Raul silently rejoiced that a simple signature on Sunday or Monday was going to change all that.

"Look, we can talk about this at dinner after my game," Raul said. "I've got to get inside with the team. And you have just enough time to get a hot dog and soda and get to your seats." Raul wrapped an arm around each parent and started them toward the main entrance.

"Have a good game, my Sugar Bear," Serena said, planting a kiss on his cheek. "God bless you and keep you." Rudy squeezed his son's hand but said nothing. His face glowed with fatherly pride.

Stubby took the cue and ushered the Barrigans away while Samantha lingered behind. She slipped an arm around Raul's waist as they strolled through the crowd. "How are you doing today, Mr. Most Outstanding Player, Mr. San Francisco Giant?" she said, beaming.

Raul couldn't suppress a broad grin of his own. "I'm so cranked I can hardly stand it. Here I am, playing in the semis of the College World Series. I'm about to sign a big contract with the Giants. And in a few months you're going to be my wife. I can't believe it, Sam. I'm the luckiest guy in the world."

"We don't believe in luck, remember?" Samantha chided. "You've been blessed by God with a special talent, Raul. He has you here for a purpose. We've prayed about that, remember? Maybe He's chosen you to be an evangelist to the San Francisco Giants or to the entire National League."

"Just as I've been to the Arizona State Sun Devils," Raul shot back cynically. "I'm obviously not a flaming witness around my teammates. I can't even get three guys together for a Bible study."

"You've been a *good* witness on the team, Raul," Samantha corrected him. "You just haven't seen much fruit yet. The guys know where you stand, hon. Some of them will come around."

Raul squeezed her shoulder, a wordless thank-you for Samantha's boundless encouragement.

Two boys hurrying past the couple recognized Raul and abruptly stopped them to beg for the All-American's autograph. Despite the inconvenience, Raul always tried to fulfill every autograph request, especially for the kids. He remembered vividly the thrill he experienced as a boy when a member of the minor league Tucson Toros or the hometown University of Arizona Wildcats gave him an autograph. It was a thrill he wanted to share with other young baseball fans, even the ones who pestered him unmercifully.

The older of the two kids excitedly thrust a felt pen into Raul's hand and pointed to the Little League baseball cap on his head. Raul scribbled his signature across the back of the cap, adding the simple fish symbol he used like a trademark. The other kid wanted him to sign the back of his oversized Creighton University T-shirt and Raul complied.

Another small knot of kids nearby saw the activity and swarmed in waving programs, caps, and baseball gloves to be signed. Raul warmly cooperated, chatting with the kids and encouraging them to put as much effort into their schoolwork as they did into their sports.

As his cluster of small fans scampered off, Raul picked up the conversation where it had been interrupted. "That's the only thing about leaving school early, Sam," he said as they resumed their slow walk into the stadium. "What if my work at ASU isn't done? What's going to happen to some of these guys if I leave?"

"Are you telling me that God can't use anyone but you to reach your teammates?" Samantha asked seriously. The answer she was driving for was obvious.

"No, no, I don't mean that," Raul answered quickly.

Samantha didn't give him time to explain what he did mean. She knew. They had talked about it before. "Then are you telling me that you have lost your peace about turning professional?"

"No, I *am* at peace with that decision," he assured her. "I know it's the right thing to do for me and for my family. And it's the right thing to do for us. We've been over it a hundred times. We've made our plans, and I'm excited about what's ahead for us. It's just that . . . " Raul didn't know how to explain himself.

Samantha gently steered him out of the river of traffic toward a quiet corner and turned to face him. Her eyes were warm with love and respect for the man she had committed to marry. "I know you're concerned about influencing your teammates; there would be something wrong with your faith if you weren't. But you can't save the whole world. Everywhere you go there will be people you will reach and others who will just blow you off as a fanatic. You can't judge your success by how many people become Christians. You can only go where God tells you to go, be the person He made you to be, and leave the results to Him."

It was a familiar exchange between Raul and Samantha. They had spent many hours over the past two months discussing Raul's college future in light of his certain selection in the 1998 college draft. Raul's greatest enemy had been his sense of obligation to complete what he started—a good quality, Samantha had often reminded him. Even though the few short steps to his degree in law enforcement could be taken in the off season, he was still hesitant about leaving the baseball program at ASU to sign a pro contract with one year of college eligibility remaining. And of what value was a college degree he would never use as a professional ballplayer? He could have just as easily majored in obsolete analog technology for all the use he would get from his classroom education. There were just a few unsettling loose ends to his grand scheme to play baseball.

In the end, every discussion with Samantha came back to Rudy and Serena Barrigan. Raul owed them more than he could repay. He yearned to reward them for their sacrifices. He found more than ample support in Scripture for his godly desire to honor his parents. It was the right thing to do. And his skills and successes in baseball, soon to be rewarded with a lucrative professional contract, seemed to be a Godsend for fulfilling his heartfelt goals. His lifelong, rather selfish dream of playing professional baseball seemed almost perfectly counterbalanced by the selfless opportunities for serving his parents such a career would provide.

Raul gazed into Samantha's eyes. "You're so wise, so levelheaded, Sam," he said, feeling a swell of appreciation and gratitude in his chest. "I know you're right. I know I'm supposed to sign with the Giants. I know it's the answer to my prayers about my parents. And if God is sending me to San Francisco, I know He'll send someone else to Tempe to take my place."

Samantha returned his warm gaze. Then she grasped one of his large biceps in her soft hands. The strains of the national anthem were pouring from the speakers around the stadium. The first game of the semifinal double-header was about to begin. "And I know you're going to have a great game tonight, my Sugar Bear. So you'd better get up there and scout these two teams, because you will be playing against one of them tomorrow for all the marbles."

Raul again rued the spartan schedule which had forced him to spend so much time with his team and so little time with Samantha this week. And this afternoon was no exception. He would sit with the rest of the Sun Devils to watch the Ohio State–Tennessee game. The team would leave the stadium together at 2 P.M.—about the top of the seventh inning—for a light training-table meal before dressing for batting practice, infield practice, and the start of the game. He would meet Sam and his parents after the game for dinner as he had for the Sun Devils' three previous night games. Then he and Sam would kiss good night and return to their respective hotels.

Raul longed for the time he would take Sam to his bed, a privilege the couple had mutually and purposely postponed until their wedding night. The temptations to violate their commitment to virginity were strong. The opportunities to yield to those temptations were plentiful. And the verbal abuse the couple suffered for their stand—most of it good-natured and subtly complimentary—was abundant. But their commitment had grown even stronger with their perseverance.

Raul wrapped Samantha in his arms and wished he didn't have to let go. But he did and then kissed her tenderly. "See you after the game," he said, starting up the stairs to the team section. "Pizza or Chinese, you decide," he called out with a wave.

Sixteen

It was a day Generation X will never forget. In succeeding years, many members of the post-Baby Boom age would clearly recall where they were when they heard the news bulletin, like the Boomers who still talk about where they were and what they were doing on November 22, 1963, when President John F. Kennedy was shot. However, June 5, 1998, will forever outshine November 22, 1963, just as a significant, long-awaited birth always outshines a historic, tragic death.

San Francisco-based Northstar flight attendant Tommy Eggers was at home when the news broke that windy Friday afternoon. He had returned from a four-day trip with the airline—a nice one, with a long layover in Puerto Vallarta in the middle of it—just before noon. His roommate, Alec Kipman, also a flight attendant with Northstar, was due in from his trip about 4:30. It was Tommy's week to cook, so he was kneading fresh dough for his excellent vegetarian calzone. They had invited a few friends over to share the meal with them.

A bay-area talk show was on the kitchen monitor as Tommy worked. Today's verbal conflagration, incited by a host skilled in relational arson, was entitled, "My Pet Is a Cannibal." It featured people who feed their house pets horse meat, chicken, and lamb and those who think such practices are an abomination to the animal kingdom. On-stage guests were calling each other pagan savages, Neanderthals, Nazis, and flesh-mongers. Questions flung at the guests by members of the audience simply added fuel to the fire. Tommy was not paying much attention to the inane discussion.

At 2:16 P.M., the program's host was cut off mid-sentence by the familiar graphic and solemn announcement that immediately captures even the casual viewer's attention: "We interrupt this program to bring you a special report from NBC news." Terrifying pictures inundated Tommy's mind, chilling his spine. His initial fear whenever the announcement came on was always of an air disaster somewhere in the world—or worse yet, the crash of a Northstar jet, perhaps one carrying Alec. Memories of his own near-death experience aboard a Boeing 737 in Juneau three and a half years earlier were instantly and painfully fresh, as if an old, deep wound had been abruptly jabbed.

Tommy had been so shaken by the Juneau incident that he had decided to quit the next day. His was a common reaction among people in his profession. Every time a passenger jet crashes—or nearly crashes—another wave of skittish flight attendants decides to look for safer jobs. Many of them are pushed to the hasty decision by the pleas or threats of anguished loved ones. Tommy came to the decision completely on his own.

However, Northstar Airlines wouldn't accept the resignation of Tommy Eggers or the other twenty-one flight attendants who submitted letters after the Juneau near miss. Rather, the company offered paid leaves of absence and post-traumatic shock counseling, hoping to entice their experienced employees to reconsider the drastic reaction. Tommy, along with eight others, did. He was back in the air a month after the incident. Most of those who followed through with their threat had decided to quit long before for a variety of reasons. The Juneau incident happened to be a handy "last straw."

Tommy's "recovery" was aided by a new and intimate friendship with Alec Kipman, whom he met in San Francisco during his leave of absence. Tommy transferred to Northstar's San Francisco base and subsequently refused any trips that would take him to or through Alaska.

A well-dressed Tom Brokaw, looking as caring and trustworthy as ever, appeared on the monitor. "Good afternoon. This is Tom Brokaw in New York." Tommy Eggers stopped his kneading and rinsed his hands, preparing to give the senior NBC anchor his full attention.

Brokaw continued, "NBC news has learned that the Centers for Disease Control in Atlanta is about to make a landmark statement regarding the war against the human immuno-deficiency virus. HIV, the precursor to AIDS, has ravaged the world for two decades and is responsible for millions of deaths. Despite tireless research and intense public pressure, especially from the homosexual community, the prevention and cure of AIDS has eluded the international medical community—apparently until now. Unconfirmed reports state that a news conference called by the CDC for 6 P.M. Eastern concerns an announcement that a significant medical breakthrough has been achieved in the war against AIDS."

Tommy covered his mouth and held his breath. His relief that the news bulletin was not about a plane crash quickly turned to stunned surprise at the mention of a possible AIDS cure. He had lost many friends and acquaintances to AIDS, more people, he would someday calculate, than would be killed in the crash of a 737 with every seat filled. Though he didn't consider himself a militant on the issue, Tommy had participated in a few AIDS-awareness demonstrations in Seattle and San Francisco. And though he did not live as promiscuously as the hard-core, high-risk gays in the Castro, San Francisco's most notorious gay enclave, Tommy was quietly and perpetually terrified of the deadly virus which had decimated the gay population in the U.S. since its appearance in 1980.

"NBC medical correspondent Robert Grissom is at CDC headquarters in Atlanta," Brokaw continued. A split screen showed Brokaw on the left and a middle-aged, sandy-haired reporter on the right. Brokaw addressed the off-camera monitor as he spoke. "What can you tell us about the announcement we have been promised, Robert?" Tommy Eggers sat down on a stool at the kitchen bar to watch.

Grissom stood beside the marble bust of Hygeia, the Greek goddess of health, in the CDC's spacious entrance hall. He wore a shirt and tie but no jacket. A tiny wireless mike was tacked to his tie. In the background, news crews from both the print and electronic media were scurrying about the hall and interrogating anyone wearing a CDC identification badge.

"Tom, this evening's announcement is apparently the culmination of a series of top secret meetings between CDC researchers and an elite team of virologists and immunologists from the Pasteur Institute in Paris. Sources tell me that American and French scientists have produced a vaccine which has proven effective in limited, highly confidential experiments. The vaccine, which has yet to be named or described, blocks the mysterious retrovirus which attacks human lymphocytes and breaks down the immune system, making its victims susceptible to the varied and deadly manifestations of acquired immuno-deficiency syndrome or AIDS. This could be the news the world has been waiting for since the outbreak of AIDS in 1980, Tom."

Tommy Eggers couldn't sit still. He began pacing the kitchen as he watched and listened. He wondered if anybody else was watching. *Everybody* should be watching. He wished Alec were here now to share this potentially historic moment with him.

"You're talking about a vaccine, Robert, meaning a preventative measure," Brokaw said. "But what about the hundreds of thousands of people who have already contracted HIV or who are dying of AIDS as we speak? Will there be any hope for them? Has there been any talk of a cure coming out of this research?"

Tommy Eggers guessed that Tom Brokaw already knew the answer to the question. He was just tossing it back to the medical correspondent—the supposed authority—to keep an interesting dialogue going.

Grissom smiled and nodded self-assuredly. "Tom, the CDC, the medical world's counterpart to the FBI, has done a masterful job at keeping all this quiet until now, so we don't know much. However, one source I talked to in the building this afternoon hinted that the substance under discussion may have application to both the prevention *and* the cure of AIDS. This makes today's expected announcement doubly promising."

"Why all the secrecy, Robert?" Brokaw probed. "This is perhaps the medical breakthrough of the century, greater than the discovery of the polio vaccine or the classification of tobacco as an addictive substance. Why haven't we heard about it sooner?"

Even Tommy Eggers knew the answer to this question. He had already calculated what he would give—everything—or what he would do—anything—to get a shot or a pill that would prevent AIDS. Multiply his response by the number of gays and straights across the country who live in mortal fear of AIDS and you have a national uprising, perhaps an army of millions storming the medical establishment to take the stuff by force or demand mass production. Nobody wants to leak a rumor that may provoke false hope.

"Basically, Tom, it's an issue of hopes and expectations,' " Grissom said. "You may recall that in the early years of the AIDS epidemic, before the human immuno-deficiency virus had even been identified, there were a number of 'cures' advanced for AIDS sufferers. Rock Hudson seemed to be helped by injections of HPA-23 imported from France, but he died. Another drug used in controlled experiments—suramin—was thought to be the panacea, so much so that the gay community demanded that the government distribute it to all AIDS patients, not just an experimental group. Hopes were high. Numerous homosexual doctors in California secured suramin for their patients directly from the German manufacturer.

"But those patients soon reaped the blighted harvest of side effects from this toxic drug: violent skin eruptions, kidney failure, coma, and death. And suramin was abandoned. AZT fired the hopes and passions of AIDS victims again, and yet its success in the light of serious side effects has been marginal at best.

"In short, Tom, if there is a miracle drug hidden within these walls, the CDC has clearly decided to make sure it's the real thing before announcing it. The hopes of hundreds of thousands of AIDS victims around the world may well be dashed at another false alarm."

After a few more questions and speculative answers, Tom Brokaw said good-bye to Robert Grissom. The suave anchor assured viewers that NBC news would return to Atlanta for the news conference at 6 P.M. Then Manfred Magnussen's taped talk show was back on. "Are you kidding, Manfred?" Tommy said aloud. "Nobody is going to listen to you yak about dog food when the story of the century is on."

Tommy quickly scanned the channels for more information. CBS was just completing its special report, offering nothing new. On CNN, Wolf Blitzer was in Atlanta hyping his audience for the news conference, but he hadn't heard anything of substance either. Most of the other networks and local stations were in the midst of soap operas, sitcom reruns, or computer system infomercials.

Tommy switched back to CNN, then looked at the clock: 2:35—half an hour until the news conference. Brimming with excitement at the news, he squealed a patternless tune and improvised a little dance through the kitchen and living room of the old apartment he had shared with Alec Kipman since the spring of 1995. But his happy jig didn't satisfy him. The news was too good to sit on for twenty-five minutes. An unquenchable people person, Tommy had to find somebody with whom to exult.

He stepped outside the front door and lifted a piercing rebel yell which echoed across the courtyard surrounded on three sides by the two-story stucco apartment building. In seconds, Evie Dukes, a short and round cocktail waitress living in 211, stepped out her door wrapped in a wrinkled green satin robe. A Moody Blues tune on the CD player followed her out the door. Evie's long dark hair was straight and wet, and a comb was in her hand. Evie and her boyfriend Chuck were on the short guest list for tonight's dinner party at Tommy and Alec's.

Evie spotted Tommy across the courtyard and one floor down. "What's going on, neighbor?" she called with a laugh while running the comb through her hair. "Did you burn the calzone?"

"Wonderful news, Evie!" Tommy sang with little boy enthusiasm, looking up at Evie. "Turn on CNN. Tom Brokaw says they've discovered a cure for AIDS!"

Old Hiram Gottlieb in 106 stuck a curious head out the door in time to hear Tommy's announcement. "Brokaw isn't on CNN," he corrected in his gravely voice. "He's never been on CNN. He's always been on NBC."

Tommy ignored the reproof. "There's going to be a news conference at 3 o'clock, Hiram." Then he turned back to his friend Evie. "I'm sure it will be on all the networks."

"A cure for AIDS?" she queried.

"Yes, that's what Tom Brokaw said. They're all saying it." Then Tommy released another whoop of joy.

"Was this in the paper this morning? Did I miss something?" Evie said.

"No, no, it was a special report on NBC just now," Tommy informed, giddily prancing on his tiptoes. "They're holding a news conference at the Centers for Disease Control."

"They've discovered a drug or something?" Evie probed further, still stroking her wet hair with the comb.

"It's a big secret project, Evie. They're going to announce it at 3. I think CNN will have the best coverage. Can you come down and watch it with me? This may be the news we've all been praying for." He clasped his hands beneath his chin, mirroring his hope.

Hiram Gottlieb lost interest and closed his door. Evie Dukes said, "Sure, Tommy, I'll watch it with you. I just got out of the shower. I'll dry off and get dressed." Evie didn't sound as excited as Tommy hoped she would, but he was glad for the company.

By 3 o'clock Tommy had rounded up two other neighbors from his apartment building and another Northstar flight attendant named Chad who lived two blocks away. Additionally, he had called several other friends, urging them to turn on CNN at 3 o'clock and tell their friends to do the same. When Evie Dukes arrived and heard what he had done, she joked that Tommy should go into public relations for the CDC.

While making his calls, Tommy had pulled out a bag of chips, chopped up a stalk of broccoli and a head of cauliflower, and opened a carton of refrigerated onion dip. He spread these on the kitchen bar along with cold bottles of flavored teas, fruit juices, and wine coolers. This was going to be a historic occasion, like the opening of a new play only more important, and such occasions required food and drink, even if it was hastily prepared. Knowing Tommy the entertainer as she did, Evie contributed the bottle of Chianti she had been saving for the dinner party.

Tommy's eager, anxious expectation did not go unrewarded. The broadcast began in the crowded conference room with eight people taking their places at the front table. Three of them were smartly dressed and appeared to be at home before the cameras. The rest seemed nervous about being in the spotlight. Tommy didn't recognize any of the people at the table but guessed them to be CDC officials and scientists.

One of the well-dressed ones, a tall, broad-shouldered man in his mid-forties with flowing brown and gray hair, stepped to the lectern. He had the looks of a TV quiz-show host, but as soon as he opened his mouth he disqualified himself for such a position. His voice was tinny, nasal, and heavy-laden with a New England accent. "Ladies and gentlemen, good evening. I'm Dr. Mark Osgood, the director of the Centers for Disease Control here in Atlanta." It was obvious that Dr. Osgood was reading a prepared statement from the lectern, but he maintained good eye contact with his audience.

"The CDC began in 1942, three months after the Japanese attack on Pearl Harbor, as the Office of Malaria Control in War Areas. The office was based here in the South where malaria posed a threat to numerous military training camps. During the war years, we existed primarily to deal with the tropical diseases our soldiers brought back from the South Pacific: dengue fever, yellow fever, typhus, and malaria."

Tommy, who sat cross-legged on the living room carpet too close to the television, was impatient. "Come on, skip the posturing. Cut to the chase and give us the good news." But Dr. Mark Osgood wasn't in a hurry.

"At the end of World War II, the office became the Center for Infectious Diseases, charged with the study of a growing list of bacteria, parasites, fungoid growths, bacilli, microbes, and viruses invading the country. In 1951 an operations and information branch, called the Epidemiological Intelligence Service, was created. The EIS turned the Center into a research agency assigned to combat any health-threatening agent. The highly trained 'detectives' of the EIS were on call day and night, ready to journey anywhere in the world on a moment's notice to confront and combat a new epidemic. One of the most celebrated achievements of the EIS was the solution of the epidemic which killed twenty-nine veterans of the American Legion in Philadelphia July 1976. Our sleuths finally identified the culprit as a bacteria living in the air conditioning ducts of the hotel where the convention was held."

"We all know about legionnaires' disease," Tommy grumbled to the image on the screen. "Get to the point."

Dr. Osgood continued, "Since we became the Centers for Disease Control in 1980, our mission has been to identify and, as far as possible eliminate, unnecessary illness and death. Ironically, 1980 also marked the appearance of a foe which has presented the CDC and the entire global health community with its greatest challenge to date: the scourge of AIDS. It is to this point that we speak again today. But for the first time we speak with great hope and well-founded confidence that we are equal to the challenge. For a very special announcement on this topic, I am pleased to introduce to you the CDC's head of research in the field of venereal diseases, Dr. Hugh Demeter."

As Dr. Osgood stepped aside, a short, stoop-shouldered, bespectacled man clutching a sheaf of notes assumed the lectern. In his late thirties, Dr. Demeter had frizzy brown hair and wore a suit which needed pressing. He seemed better adapted to a lonely laboratory existence than to a national television appearance. The conference room remained quiet, expectant, as the research scientist organized his notes.

"Come on, Doc," Tommy urged restlessly, "no more politicking. Give us the scoop." Tommy's guests remained quiet, munching on snacks and sipping their drinks. Their host was uncharacteristically more concerned with the activities on the screen than with his friends.

Demeter cleared his throat and began. He had the strong voice and articulation of a public speaker, which had obviously qualified him to present the discovery the CDC was prepared to announce. "Thank you, Dr. Osgood. In turn, I would like to introduce a colleague from the Pasteur Institute with whom we have worked very closely over the last three years. Dr. Claudine Bizieau holds degrees in science and medicine from the University of Paris. As a cellular biologist, she has devoted her life to the study of lymphocytes, the front line in AIDS research over the last decade."

With a polite gesture toward the table, Demeter summoned Dr. Claudine Bizieau to the lectern. She was a slender woman of fifty with a pleasant face which needed makeup. Her graying hair was uninspiringly pulled back into a ponytail. The French woman researcher wore a rather plain black and white suit which was out of style, and no jewelry. Standing together, Drs. Demeter and Bizieau presented strong evidence that some scientists become too absorbed in their work, losing touch with the contemporary world.

Tommy Eggers couldn't care less what the world's leading AIDS researchers looked like or sounded like. In less than an hour he had become obsessed with the announcement Tom Brokaw and Wolf Blitzer said the CDC was prepared to present. So many people had died. So many more were going to die. His own life was complicated by perpetual anxiety at the thought of contracting AIDS. He found himself constantly looking over his shoulder, emotionally speaking, as if a mugger was hiding in the shadows ready to assault him.

Tommy and Alec were "clean" when they met, and he had remained faithful to Alec—except for just a couple of slips—during their three years together. Tommy submitted to AIDS testing every six months just to make sure he had not become infected. So far so good, and he was really *trying* to be good. But a vaccine was the ultimate answer— heaven on earth! How wonderful to rid himself of the fear of the mysterious virus which stalked him like an invisible killer. And how wonderful for countless millions of others.

Dr. Hugh Demeter had his opening statement memorized. There was additional information to be disseminated by him and Dr. Bizieau, and there would doubtless be more questions from the press than the scientists could possibly answer in the time allotted for the news conference. But Demeter and his colleagues had agreed to summarize the good news up front and then deal with the details.

Demeter gripped the lectern and stared into the cameras. "Ladies and gentlemen, as a result of the joint efforts of the Centers for Disease Control and the Pasteur Institute, I am pleased to announce the development and successful testing of CDCP-10, a vaccine which will some day eradicate the human immuno-deficiency virus and the horrors of AIDS."

Tommy Eggers shot up from the floor as if mounted on a giant coil spring. He felt suddenly reborn, just as he had the night he climbed from the crippled 737 at the end of the runway in Juneau when he had fully expected to perish in a fiery crash. Then he embraced Evie Dukes and burst into tears of joy.

Seventeen

When the Arizona State ball players left Rosenblatt Stadium in the bottom of the sixth inning for their team lunch, Ohio State was trailing Tennessee 5–3. When the team returned ninety minutes later to dress and warm up for their game, the scoreboard in left field told the story of a dramatic come-from-behind victory. OSU tallied two runs in the bottom of the eighth to tie only to see the Volunteers surge ahead again in the top of the ninth, 7–5. But the Buckeyes scrambled for three runs in their last at-bat for an 8–7 win to advance to the championship game on Saturday.

The visiting team's dressing room was empty when the twenty-five ASU players filed in. The losing Tennessee Volunteers had showered and vacated hurriedly, leaving a pall of defeat in the room as heavy as the body odor hanging in the air and the moisture coating the windows and walls. The Sun Devils occupied the room in silence for several minutes, shedding their street clothes and slipping into clean uniforms with all the enthusiasm of a group of men condemned to mass execution.

Raul Barrigan, dressed only in his uniform pants, sanitary stockings, and stirrups, abruptly broke the spell. "Hey!" he shouted across the room from his locker. Several players jerked bolt upright at the sound as if they had been jabbed with a live wire. "We're dressing like a bunch of losers! Let's get out of here and start over!" There was fire in his eyes and authority in his voice.

The Sun Devils had heard it before. Sugar Barrigan was a proven team leader, mild-mannered and congenial off the field but all-business and fiercely competitive when the game was on the line. Though Raul's teammates had little use for the religious faith he often spoke about, they envied his talent and respected his leadership. Most of them would never earn a dollar playing baseball. They would hang up their cleats after graduation and revel in the glories of their amateur careers for the rest of their lives. But Sugar Barrigan would be paid millions and achieve the fame they had all dreamed about since Little League. He was a god in their midst, and when it came to the game they loved, they revered him.

"I said let's get out of here and do this right!" Raul commanded. Waving a towel like a taskmaster's whip, he shooed his teammates out of the dressing room and into the hall. A couple of the guys wearing only socks and underwear reached for their pants, but Raul snapped the towel at them, shouting, "Go! Go! Go! Go!" They went in a hurry leaving their pants behind.

Having herded them into the hall, which was empty except for a couple of wide-eyed bat boys, Raul delivered a brief but inspiring pep talk about ASU baseball tradition, their great success during the season and post season, and the NCAA Division I championship within their reach. "Losers don't make it to the semifinals and finals," he preached emphatically. "Losers like Tennessee and Penn State and Oklahoma and Princeton have packed up and gone crying to Mama. We're still here, gentlemen. We're here because we're winners. We took the PAC-10 championship because we're winners. We took the West regional tournament because we're winners. We came to Omaha with a record of 46-17 because we're winners. We're one of only three teams left in the College World Series because we're winners. It's time we lifted our heads and started *acting* like winners."

It was a brand of contrived emotional hype familiar to every sports team from junior high players to veteran professional stars. This is the big game. They're tough but we're tougher. Dig deep. Sacrifice your body. Give 110 percent. Win it for the coach, the team, the school, the guy with the busted-up knee, or whomever. It was the emotional injection every athlete needs to stoke the inner competitive fire.

Raul was good at fanning an emotional flame under his teammates. Every impassioned sentence stirred them more deeply. They began to respond with cheers, grunts, and bursts of applause.

"We're going to make losers out of the Texas Longhorns. We're going to send them home to Austin crying to Mama. Then on Saturday we're going to steal that national championship trophy from Ohio State. So let's get rid of this sitting-around-like-losers stuff right now and do what we came to do!"

What followed was a frenzy of hand-clapping, rump-slapping, whooping, and whistling. Raul led the team back into the dressing room to a raucous, unison chant, "A-S-U, A-S-U, A-S-U." As they resumed taping limbs and donning uniforms, the mood was positive, determined, and the room was noisy. The tone had been set, and again Raul Barrigan had brought his team through.

Batting practice for the visiting team commenced at 5:15 P.M. The stadium lights were on despite the powder blue and gold canopy overhead and the sun hanging low in the western sky. Raul took his cuts at the fat pitches served to him in the batting cage. With every swing his focus narrowed. For the next three hours, the world beyond this neatly groomed patch of emerald-green grass and brown soil did not exist. Samantha, Raul's parents, and perhaps 20,000 others would be in the stands cheering, but Raul would not hear them. Tonight Raul's world was reduced to two well-trained college baseball teams, four umpires, the glove he took with him to center field, the aluminum bat he carried to the plate, and a white baseball. Every thought and ounce of energy would be funneled into every second of the game. It was what Raul Barrigan did best. It was his devoted service to Jesus.

Raul Barrigan always prayed during the performance of the national anthem. Tonight he prayed for the ability to see every pitch clearly, to make solid contact, to get a good jump on every ball hit to him, and to make a positive contribution to the game. He did not ask for an ASU victory, for he understood winning to be a human achievement. Rather he petitioned God for a superior effort on the part of every player, especially himself. He was confident that if he played up to his potential he could lead his team into the championship game against Ohio State.

Chick Kimura, the Sun Devils' third baseman and lead-off batter, started the game with a bunt single past the pitcher's mound. The ASU fans in the stadium cheered wildly at what they hoped was a good omen for the game. But their cheers turned to groans of disappointment when the number-two hitter, left-fielder Barry Wooster, grounded into a double play. Two outs in a hurry.

Raul Barrigan took one last practice swing in the on-deck circle, then walked resolutely to the plate. Rufus Dubose, the cleanup hitting ASU catcher, called out encouragingly as he moved into the circle, "Get on, Sugar. Let's go, big bear." A rustle of anticipation coursed through the stadium as ASU's best hitter dug hit cleats into the dirt in the batter's box. Coach Vern Estes clapped and chattered excitedly from the third base coaching box. Raul took his stance, waved the bat a few times, then focused on the lanky Texas pitcher.

Raul's sweet spot was from the middle of the plate out and from the belt down. He had always been able to rip the down-and-away pitch with power. Opposing teams knew the book on him; scouting reports uncovered every player's strength and weakness. So Raul was consistently served a diet of inside pitches from the chin to the knees. With the help of his hitting coaches, he had learned to make contact with pitches in all corners of the strike zone. But whenever a pitcher erred outside and low, Raul often made him pay for it with an extra base hit.

Raul cocked the bat behind his right ear and stared at the pitcher, awaiting the first pitch. He had only a fraction of a second to pick up the speed, rotation, and direction of the ball after it left the pitcher's hand. Somewhere in the computer that was his brain he possessed the ability—a gift from God, he admitted—to see the ball, evaluate the pitch, and trigger the bat better than 95 percent of all college baseball players. Add to this gift his speed and strong arm, and Raul Barrigan was a complete ball player, above average in each of the big five categories: hitting, hitting for power, fielding, throwing, and running.

The first pitch was inside across the chest, and the second was inside at the ankles. Raul stepped out of the batter's box to take a couple of swings, silently remonstrating the pitcher for giving him little to swing at. Raul looked down at short, wiry, fifty-five-year-old Vern Estes who strutted up and down the coaching box like a bantam rooster, squawking encouragement. The tight-fitting uniform pants hugging his spindly legs emphasized his birdlike appearance.

The next pitch, a fastball, wandered to the outside of the strike zone and chest high. The ball wasn't in his sweet spot, but Raul pounced on it anyway. He whipped the aluminum bat through the strike zone, extending his powerful arms, and made contact. *Dwang!* The ringing of the bat brought a cheer from the crowd.

But Raul was a little late on the pitch and sliced it foul down the right field line and into the crowd.

The pitcher served another fastball up, and Raul was ready for it. *Dwang!* The ball screamed over the second baseman's head before he could leap for it. Only an excellent cut-off by the right fielder kept the ball from rolling to the wall. Raul sprinted to first and made a wide turn toward second before returning to the bag as the throw came back in.

Raul acknowledged to himself that his hit would have been a double or a triple against many college outfielders. But Dougie Martinez of the Longhorns, another major league draft choice, had held him to a single. The pros were loaded with talent like Martinez. Raul would have to keep working on every aspect of his game to kept his edge at the higher level of play.

He pulled off his batting gloves as he stared across the diamond at Vern Estes for a sign. Rufus Dubose was also studying the coach, who was tapping out a coded message for his two players with both hands on his cap, shirt, and pants. Raul translated the rapid hand movements: runner stay put, batter wait for your pitch.

Rufus, a left-handed batter, stepped into the box, and Raul took a cautious lead away from the base. The first pitch was a ball, as was the second. Batter and runner studied Estes again. He rapidly tapped with his finger cap, chin, cap, chin, letters, belt, letters, chin, cap, chin, belt, letters. Tonight the belt was the key, signifying that the next tap indicated the play. And the letters—the words Arizona State emblazoned across the front of the uniform shirt—meant hit-and-run. Coach Estes had gone belt-to-letters twice. The hit-and-run play was on.

Raul had to look like he was taking a normal lead at first, then break for second with the pitch. Rufus' job was to make contact, swing at anything in or out of the strike zone. If he got a pitch he could pull into right field, Raul would be well on his way to third. If Rufus couldn't hit the pitch at all, Raul may be able to slide into second ahead of the throw from the catcher—or he may get tagged out trying. Raul silently thanked Coach Estes for giving him a chance to run.

Raul stepped off the bag several feet and squared toward the plate with his eyes on the pitcher. He drew a throw to first and stepped back easily. He drew another attempted pick-off throw which also failed. When the pitcher began his kick and delivery to the plate, Raul broke for second base. The loud ring of the bat and roar of the crowd told him that Rufus had made contact. The second baseman's head snap following the flight of the ball told him that it was down the right field line for extra bases.

Raul rounded second base on the dead run to see Coach Estes waving him frantically to third. "Go three! Go three! Go three!" the coach yelled. As Raul's powerful legs dug into the dirt his batting helmet bounced off his head and tumbled to the ground behind him.

Then the coach began jumping up and down on his scrawny legs, hopping down the third base line, and pinwheeling his arm, signaling Raul to keep going around third to home. "Go home! Go home! Go home!" the little coach screamed. Raul couldn't imagine that the sure hands and rifle arm of Dougie Martinez would let him get away with three bases on a double to Rufus Dubose. But the coach had the action in front of him and was waving him in. *Martinez must have bobbled the ball,* Raul thought. *Or maybe it hit the wall and rolled away from him.* Raul relished the chance to score the game's first run and inspire his teammates.

Then Estes changed his sign. With Raul Barrigan two steps from third base and running at full speed, the coach threw both hands high above his head—the stop sign. Above the roar of the crowd, Raul could hear Estes squawking, "Hold on! Hold on! Hold on!"

Raul ventured a quick glance toward right field. Martinez was cocking his arm for a throw to the plate from the right field corner. But Raul couldn't stop. His momentum would carry him halfway to the plate before he could dig in his cleats and scramble back to third. A good throw by the cut-off man might nail him at third anyway.

And Raul didn't want to stop. Scoring the first run of the game on a close play at home would give his team a big boost. And going head to head with another potential pro, Dougie Martinez, was what competition was all about. Raul knew he could beat Martinez's throw to the plate. He hoped that the Texas star *hadn't* bobbled it, that it was a clean pick-up and throw. Raul didn't want an unfair advantage. It was the supreme test he would face again and again with the Giants: major league speed versus major league arm. Raul had to go for it.

He streaked by Coach Estes halfway between third and home. The man was bug-eyed, leaping wildly, and screaming, "No! No! No!" Had it been legal to tackle a base runner to stop him, the coach would have thrown himself in front of Raul Barrigan to get him back to third.

The catcher, with mask tossed away, was guarding the plate like a hockey goalie while awaiting the throw. The home plate umpire, also with mask off, was positioned to make the call. Jamaal Coates, the on-deck batter, waved his palms frantically toward the earth, meaning hit the dirt. Raul's strategy crystallized instantly: headfirst slide away from the throw, left hand on the plate under the tag.

After two more sprinting, leaning steps, Raul dived. The catcher took one step toward him to reach for the throw coming in from right field like a bullet. Raul slid on his belly, stretching his hand for the plate. He heard the ball slap into the leather mitt above him. Then he heard and felt his unprotected skull strike the catcher's shin guard. Lights flashed in his brain like a strobe, he felt a snap in his neck, and everything turned black.

When Raul came to several seconds later, the taste of dirt was in his mouth. He lay unmoving on his belly with his legs splayed out behind him and his head cocked to the right and tipped back. His right arm was bent and limp at his side, and his left arm was stretched out above his head. Coach Estes, the team trainer, and a doctor were on their knees and hovering over him. Jamaal Coates and two other ASU players stood nearby with the Texas catcher and the umpire. The rest of the team watched from the dugout steps. The crowd, which had been cheering madly seconds earlier, had quieted to a concerned murmur.

"Do you hurt anywhere, son?" The doctor asked. He was bent down with his face close to Raul's.

"What happened?" Raul mumbled, stunned.

"You slid into the catcher's leg. Smacked your head on his shin guard. Knocked you out for a few seconds. Are you OK?"

Raul processed the words slowly. Then he said, "Did I make it?"

Coach Estes bent low. "Yeah, you made it, Sugar," he said. "And it's a good thing, because if you hadn't made it I would be thumping you on the noggin right now. You ran through my stop sign."

"I touched the plate?" Raul said in disbelief.

"You're still touching it," the coach said. "Your left hand is on top of it. Can't you feel it?"

A few more seconds passed until a sobering realization gripped the young ballplayer. "No, coach," he said in a pained whisper. "I . . . I can't feel anything."

Eighteen

"So you see, we are identical twins in our Parent-God's celestial family. Jesus-Brother is the heavenly twin. Collectively we are his earth-sister, the earthly twin. We were born with Brother at the dawn of time, identical in beauty, power, wisdom, love, and perfection. We were separated by Parent-God to rule his twin kingdoms. Jesus-Brother was given the heavens as his domain. We, his earth-sister, were given the earthly realm. At the end of time, Parent-God will reunite the twins and merge the two kingdoms. Brother and sister will become one, the new Parent-God of the cosmos. A new universe will be created, and the cycle will continue."

The woman teaching from a chair near the fireplace was in her sixties, but her large, warm eyes and angelic countenance diffused the signs of age marking her face. Softly luminescent grey-blonde hair wreathed her head like a halo. She wore an elegant, stylish creamy-white dress accessorized by lavish strands of pearls, further enhancing her youthful aura. Her voice was clear, confident, and melodic, the voice of an authority without the grating authoritarian tone. The audience seated around the spacious, opulent living room drank in her words with rapt attention.

"Everything we see and experience reminds us that we are destined to be reunited with our Jesus-Brother. Consider the profusion of complementary pairs all around us: night and day, moon and sun, female and male, cold and hot, negative and positive . . . "

The teacher gestured slightly with her head and eyes, inviting her listeners to contribute some examples. They complied obediently.

"Darkness and light, asleep and awake."

"Sound and silence."

"Right and wrong, evil and good."

"Dull and sharp."

"Sweet and sour."

"Death and life, happy and sad, cold and hot, high and low, near and far."

A smattering of gentle laughter across the room echoed appreciation for the generous contribution from one member.

"Up and down."

"Yes, up and down," the teacher interrupted with a cherubic twinkle in her eyes. "That's an especially important pair for those of you in the airline industry. Our hostess mentioned that several of her coworkers are in this group tonight." A few nodding heads confirmed it.

Another listener chimed in with pairs she had in mind, "Off and on, tight and loose, stop and go."

"Yes, yes," the teacher responded gleefully at the flow of ideas. "You see it, don't you. Our lives are governed by pairs, twin entities. If either one of the items were missing from the duos you mentioned, that facet of life would lose its dimension and we would lose interest."

The audience hummed in agreement.

"That is why the wisdom writer of biblical literature—one of many sources of truth for earth-sister—inscribed his beautiful poem of pairs: A time to be born and a time to die, a time to plant and a time to uproot, a time to kill and a time to heal, a time to weep and a time to laugh. Do you remember?"

Her pupils nodded.

The teacher leaned forward for emphasis. "I remind you, then, to affirm and enlarge your consciousness of our spiritual twin-ness. We are only one member of an eternal, holy pair. Jesus-Brother and earth-sister are one family with two expressions. We cannot exist without Him—nor can He exist without us—any more than love can exist without hate. We are two halves of a spiritual whole, both yearning for reunion and completion."

"And that's why you encourage your followers to regard the number two as a sign or an omen," advanced a fortyish-looking woman sitting with her husband on one of the sofas in the room.

"Not only the *number* two but pairs of any kind," the teacher corrected. "They say that bad luck comes in threes and good luck in pairs. I believe it's a heavenly dictum. Every time you recognize something coming to you in pairs, Jesus-Brother is reminding you of His union with you."

"Like two leaves falling together outside the window, or a pair of gulls flying together over the lake," suggested one woman.

"Exactly," replied the teacher emphatically.

"Or noticing something odd or curious or coincidental, like two cars coming down the street at night with one headlight out," another disciple advanced.

"Of course," the teacher said.

"So if the phone rings twice and stops, it could be Jesus-Brother on the line." The comment came across as humor, and the group enjoyed a moment of laughter.

But the teacher recognized the skepticism lurking behind the words and spoke to it. "Don't trivialize our Brother's attempts to contact us," she said in a firm but caring tone, "especially when the time before Reunion is so short."

The woman on the sofa who had commented about the number two as a sign spoke again. "And you require that we respond to Brother in the same way, by making signs of two."

" 'Require' may be too strong," the teacher explained. "Like other facets of religion, methods of communicating allegiance to Jesus-Brother are a matter of personal choice. However, I suggest that you consider doing something that affirms the belief that you are spiritually linked with Jesus-Brother and that you yearn for Reunion with him. I have chosen to do so by wearing twin rings." The teacher lifted her right hand to show identical white-gold bands on the two middle fingers. "Your expression may be more demonstrative or more subtle."

"We planted two birch trees side by side in the backyard after joining the New Jesus Family," spoke the hostess, who had been circulating through the living room refilling coffee cups for her guests from an ornate silver coffee pot. "As we watch the trees grow, we believe our love for Brother also grows."

"Twin rings have also been meaningful to me," another woman said, lifting her hand. "I had the inside of each band engraved. One says Brother and the other says sister."

"What you do and how you do it is completely up to you," the teacher summarized. "Whatever you do, it should demonstrate your faith in Jesus-Brother in a way that is personal and meaningful to you."

The skeptic/comedian spoke up again. "I'm thinking about taking two wives. What could be more personal or more meaningful?" The thin laughter was gratuitous. The teacher's devotees in the room were tiring of the seeker's insincerity.

"Now, now," the teacher scolded lightly with a parental wave of a finger, "the New Jesus Family doesn't condone more than one spouse or lover at a time, even in the name of devotion to Brother. Perhaps you would do better to take two pieces of cake when we break for refreshments."

The teacher's subtle dig got a better laugh than the skeptic's. The man seemed to appreciate the little joke. The teacher moved quickly into the next topic to prevent further interruption. "I wonder how many of you have discovered that our Brother communicates with us by giving each of us a second name."

About a third of the three dozen guests raised their hands.

"Well, then," the teacher exclaimed eagerly, "this shall be our main topic for this evening." She reached into a cordovan attaché case and removed a leather-bound notebook. Finding her page, she stood and gazed beyond the walls of the elegant home as if drinking in spiritual energy. Then she delivered the treatise she had written herself.

"Each of us in the New Jesus Family has two names. We received a given name and surname from our parents at birth. At marriage, a woman may exchange her surname for her husband's. However, your legal name is only an earthly name. It is sufficient as long as Jesus-Brother and earth-sister exist in separate kingdoms. But your legal, earthly name is insufficient to describe you in the coming glorious kingdom when Brother and sister are again reunited.

"Everyone who accepts membership in the New Jesus Family has a second name—a spiritual name, a Reunion name. In truth, this is how you know for certain you are in the Family: You know your real name. You hear it in your spirit when Brother calls you. And once you hear your Reunion name, you are no longer satisfied being known only by your earthly name.

"The world may know me as Lila Ruth Atkinson, but Brother has given me a spiritual name which describes my destiny in the coming Reunion and new kingdom. Jesus-Brother calls me Vision."

Lila Ruth continued reading her essay with passion and conviction. In it she traced the importance of spiritual identity through a maze of ancient religious documents from both East and West. She cited venerated masters and obscure mystics from a dozen religious orders. Her pithy quotes ranged from the Bible to the Bhagavad-Gita to the writings of Nostradamus. She looked up often because her words flowed more from heart and memory than from the script she had laboriously prepared. Her message was articulate, sensible, and convincing, mesmerizing her audience.

"You know me as Kathy, but Brother calls me Tigress," spoke the hostess when Lila Ruth ended her dissertation and invited comments from disciples and seekers. "I heard him call my name a couple of weeks after the incident in Juneau three years ago. I went into the Northstar administrative offices to politely request that someone check into the cabin safety features that failed on our 737 that night. They kept sending me from office to office, giving me the runaround. After about two hours of getting shuffled around, I kind of went off—shouting and pounding on desks. I finally got some attention, and on my way out, one of the administrative assistants said, 'Way to go, tiger.' I liked it. It stuck with me."

Several of the listeners nodded approvingly.

"A week later, some friends invited Brad and me to hear Lila Ruth at their home in Bellevue. When she gave this talk about twin names, it blew me away! I knew exactly my name and mission in the earthly kingdom. When I talked to her after the meeting, she agreed. I joined the New Jesus Family right away. Brad was a little more cautious." Kathy paused to wink and smile at her long-time boyfriend and room-mate sitting nearby. "But he eventually came around. Brother calls him Caution. We've been listening to Lila Ruth and inviting others to her meetings ever since."

Another man and woman in the group talked about their spiritual identities and how they first heard Brother call their names. A few others gave testimonials for the insight and teaching of Lila Ruth At-kinson and the spiritual warmth of the small New Jesus Family she had founded in Seattle three years earlier. Some of the comments sounded like a membership pitch to the seekers they had invited to the meeting tonight. In the end, Kathy Keene thanked everyone for coming and dismissed the group to the dining room where slices of Black Forest cake were waiting on china plates.

Inevitably, Lila Ruth was surrounded at the end of her meetings by devoted followers expressing their admiration and inquirers posing the questions they were too embarrassed to ask in front of the group. Tonight, as she responded graciously to each visitor, Lila Ruth kept an inconspicuous eye on a first-time attender staying to himself near a corner of the living room. The man, who looked to be in his middle fifties, was trim and nattily dressed in dark slacks and a tweed jacket. His grey hair was very short on the sides and very sparse on top.

The visitor had arrived late, after Lila Ruth had started her session. He hadn't yet made any moves to meet Lila Ruth, and from his body language, she didn't think he would. He ate his cake hurriedly as if planning to leave soon. There was an anxiety in his furtive eyes that was familiar to her. The man had clearly attended the meeting out of courtesy to the hostess, but he was uncomfortable about being here and wanted out. Lila Ruth had been informed that he might come. It was the kind of challenge Lila Ruth could not resist.

Skillfully extricating herself from a small cluster of her disciples, she walked straight toward the man. Her captivating eyes locked onto his and held him in place as she crossed the distance between them. Extending her hand and a saintly smile, she said, "I don't remember seeing you at one of our meetings before. I'm Lila Ruth Atkinson."

The man looked so stunned at the confrontation that the teacher feared for a moment he might simply drop his plate on the carpet and bolt for the front door. Instead, he put his fork on the plate and tenta-tively received her hand. "Cooper Sams," he said without a smile.

Lila Ruth's expression illuminated with recognition. "Are you *Cap-tain* Cooper Sams, the pilot Kathy was flying with that terrifying night in Juneau?" The teacher purposely held on to the reluctant seeker's hand.

The trapped look on the man's face intensified. "That's correct," he said, averting his eyes as if confessing to a long-buried crime.

"I'm so delighted to finally meet you, Captain," Lila Ruth gushed, gripping his hand harder. "Kathy told me she has invited you to our gathering several times. I'm pleased that you finally came."

The captain withdrew his hand and took the fork off his plate, as if ready to use it to keep her from touching him again. He said nothing and did not look the woman in the eyes.

"Kathy claims that she owes you her life, that the plane would have crashed had it not been for your swift action. No wonder she has been excited about introducing you to her new spiritual family."

Lila Ruth knew Cooper Sams was plotting a way to excuse himself. He remained silent, but she could not.

"That experience must have been even more frightful for you in the cockpit than it was for Kathy in the rear of the plane. You were within seconds of crashing. You could see the earth racing up to meet you. But you were able to pull the plane out of its dive. When I first read about the incident, I was so impressed by your skill and the professionalism of your crew. Then meeting Kathy, and now you, is a real honor."

"Thank you," Cooper mumbled.

"Near-death encounters are one of the chief ways Jesus-Brother communicates with us today," Lila Ruth continued, unrelenting. "Have you considered the significance of your flight number that night? Two-oh-two is a very strong pairing. Kathy and I agree that Brother was present that night to assist you. The numbers are undeniable."

"It could also be coincidence," Cooper said, deflecting her conviction.

Lila Ruth continued, undaunted. "It wouldn't surprise me if Brother whispered a new name to you after that flight, just as he did to your crew member, Kathy Keene. Did an unusually significant word or thought pop into your mind after that near-fatal crash, Captain?"

Cooper Sams was rarely intimidated by anyone, and never by a woman. But no woman had ever bored into him as self-assuredly as Lila Ruth Atkinson. Cooper answered immediately and without explanation, "No."

"Not even a glimmer of a thought beyond that miracle?"

"No, not even a glimmer," Cooper said, finally looking her in the eyes. "I'm not a religious person, ma'am. If your faith in this Jesus-Brother helps you cope with life, more power to you. I have my own ways of coping."

Lila Ruth summoned all her energy to hold the captain's gaze. Her tone was suddenly private and serious without losing compassion. "Yes, Captain, I know all about how well you are coping. You're a borderline alcoholic. Your coworkers despise you because of your gruff, unforgiving demeanor. And your three-year marriage is on the jagged edge. You are *not* coping with life; you're in a perilous dive to the bottom just as surely as you were three years ago over Juneau, Alaska. Jesus-Brother gave you a second chance then, and I believe he has called your name. But he can't help you and neither can we if you are intent on burying yourself in your own excrement."

Beads of sweat and a flush of red rage flooded the captain's face. His hands trembled so with anger that several cake crumbs bounced from the plate to the floor. Lila Ruth sensed that only the spiritual energy pouring into Cooper Sams through her eyes prevented him from striking her. She stayed in his face, attempting to convey Brother's concern for the proud pilot. She had delivered the message impressed upon her by Jesus-Brother through Captain Sams' concerned coworker, Kathy Keene. He would survive the confrontation. He would come around. She knew it. She was Vision.

After several seconds Cooper broke free from her gaze. He dropped his plate and fork on the coffee table with a noisy clatter and walked quickly out of the house, saying nothing.

Nineteen

Raul Barrigan wanted to jump up, shake off the effects of the collision as he had countless times before in his amateur baseball career, and celebrate the first run scored with his teammates. But he couldn't get up. He lifted his head an inch, then winced at the stab of pain near the top of his spine and let his head fall back to the dirt. He tried again to feel the soil with his fingers, to move his arms and legs. Nothing worked.

"I can't move, Wiz," he whispered to the trainer, whose face hovered only inches from his. It had occurred to Raul to say, "I'm paralyzed," because he knew he was, at least temporarily. But he no more wanted that word on his tongue than he wanted the dust which now coated the inside of his mouth.

ASU Trainer Jerry Whisnant, called Wizard or the Wiz by his players, was a happy-go-lucky, forty-two-year-old bachelor with a pony tail who loved to joke and banter with the ballplayers. Raul had never seen him this serious before. "Don't try to move, Sugar, especially your head," he ordered calmly. Then he rested a hand gently on Raul's cheek to emphasize his point. The hand smelled of liniment and adhesive tape.

Dr. John Ewald, an Omaha orthopedist in his late thirties who volunteered as a tournament physician every year, pulled a gold ballpoint pen out of his summer blazer. With the point retracted, he pressed the tip of the pen gently into the flesh of Raul's upper right arm as Raul watched. "Can you feel my pen poking your arm?"

"I can tell you're pushing on me," Raul answered slowly, "but I can't feel anything poking me."

Raul grimaced from the pain in his neck and his inability to alleviate it by turning over. He also winced at the thought of his parents and Samantha watching from the stadium. He wanted to call out to them, "Don't worry. I'll be on my feet in a minute. I'm OK." But he couldn't say it. He didn't feel OK at the moment. He figured he would probably have to leave the game. But he assured himself that he would be ready for the big game tomorrow.

The doctor repeated the test with his pen on Raul's legs, feet, and left arm with the same results. "Let's get the body board," he called over his shoulder to one of the host athletic trainers attending the game. "And send the ambulance in."

Then Dr. Ewald turned back to the fallen ballplayer and leaned close to his face. "You may have a neck injury, Raul. We need to take every precaution against damaging the spinal cord. We're going to strap you on the body board to keep you immobile and run you into the ER. OK?"

Not OK, Doc! Raul objected silently. *This is a big game for me. This is my world. I have to stay with my team. I have to be ready to play tomorrow.* He turned his eyes to the trainer. "Do I have to, Wiz? The team needs—"

"Yeah, you have to, Sugar," Jerry Whisnant replied. "This is serious stuff here. I'd tape you back together if I could, but you need X-rays and maybe a CAT scan. You'll be fine, man. We just have to check you out real good. And don't worry about the Devils. We have a run in, Rufus at third, and Jamaal coming up. You started a big inning."

It took several hands to roll Raul carefully onto the body board while Jerry Whisnant held his head steady. Raul's view slowly turned from the ground to the seats filled with curious, whispering onlookers to banks of glaring stadium lights and the faces of his caretakers and teammates against the twilight sky. As they worked on him, a sparkling red and white ambulance, which had been parked in front of the stadium, entered through an outfield gate and hugged the foul line on its slow journey to home plate.

Then three new faces came into focus above him, peering over the shoulders of those readying him for transport. Rudy Barrigan looked solemn, concerned. Serena's cheeks were tear-stained, but she beamed a comforting smile when Raul's eyes met hers. Samantha was on the verge of tears. Her chin trembled at the sight of her fiancé's slack arms being collected like pieces of equipment and laid by his side on the body board.

"I'm OK," Raul tried to console them. "They're just taking me in for some X-rays."

Serena pressed through the circle of attendants surrounding her son to touch him. "We'll go with you, Sugar Bear," she whispered, fighting back tears. She squeezed his hand. There was no response. Rudy and Samantha also reached in with comforting touches he could not feel. Then they backed away as two more EMT's moved in to work.

Jerry Whisnant held Raul's head motionless as an EMT gently taped it down. Others ran nylon straps across his chest, waist, thighs, and ankles to anchor him to the board. When he was secure, six men— Jerry Whisnant, Vern Estes, teammates Rufus Dubose and Jamaal Coates, and two EMT's—carefully lifted Raul from the field. Players from both teams crowded around to verbalize their encouragement. Fans across the stadium rose to their feet and conveyed their best wishes with warm applause. ESPN cameras stationed around the ballpark zoomed in on the injured athlete until he disappeared through the rear doors of the ambulance.

Serena Barrigan was allowed to ride in the ambulance with her son on the way to Omaha's Bergan Mercy Medical Center. Samantha and Rudy followed in the rental car. As the ambulance traveled, Jerry Whisnant worked at clearing Raul's mouth and nose of the dirt he had inhaled. Then he cleaned out a small cut where Raul's forehead had collided with the catcher's high-impact plastic shin guard.

An EMT swabbed the patient's left arm and inserted an IV. Dr. Ewald contacted the hospital by wireless phone to alert the ER for their arrival. Serena held her son's limp right hand and prayed silently, fervently, dabbing her moist eyes occasionally with a tissue.

"It could be a broken neck, couldn't it, Wiz?" Raul probed apprehensively. His head was immovable, but he strained his eyes to get a look at Jerry's face. The trainer was still wearing the sober expression which was as unnatural on this affable, free-spirited man as a business suit, starched shirt, and tie.

"Yeah, man, it could be a broken neck," he answered quietly, "but maybe not. The pictures will tell us."

"I think it *is* broken," Raul continued. "My neck really hurts."

"We'll check it out, man. We'll take care of everything. No sweat."

Raul shifted his eyes to Dr. Ewald on the other side. "You can get a broken neck and still not be permanently paralyzed, right, doc?"

The doctor leaned over Raul so the patient could see him better. He had a kind, boyish face, no chin, and a scrawny mustache obviously maintained to make him look older. "That's right. The spinal cord is like a tight bundle of electrical wires. Some of them may be kinked or bruised as a result of your accident, and those often heal."

"And the feeling comes back, and you can move again," Raul advanced hopefully.

"That's correct. But nerves can also be severed by a violent collision. Even though we're making headway in learning how to reattach severed nerves with microsurgery, some damage results in permanent paralysis."

"We believe in a God who heals, doctor." It was the first time Serena Barrigan had spoken in the ambulance. She sat next to Jerry Whisnant across the gurney from Dr. Ewald. The strain of her son's ordeal lined her face, but a light of hope was in her eyes.

Dr. Ewald looked at her and smiled. "I do too, Mrs. Barrigan. I wouldn't be in this profession if I didn't. I've seen some remarkable recoveries—I would even call them miraculous. But unfortunately, some conditions are irreversible."

"Nothing is irreversible to Jesus, Doc," Raul cut in defensively. His wide eyes underscored his conviction. "Nothing is impossible with Him, not even repairing the spinal cord. Jesus has called me to play major league baseball. If He has to send an angel to put bone fragments back together and reattach severed nerves to get me out there, He'll do it. He can even have me back on the field tomorrow." Raul surprised himself with the certainty behind his forceful statement.

John Ewald had learned early in his practice that arguing with patients over their religious convictions was counterproductive to his ministrations. He was a man of Christian faith, but a pragmatic one. He had seen severed limbs surgically reattached, but he had never seen an amputee grow an arm or a leg. He believed that medical science would some day be able to knit severed nerves back together. But he did not believe that God would intervene in such a drastic injury. And at this moment, based on other spinal injuries he had treated, John Ewald did not believe that Raul Barrigan would ever walk again.

The doctor glanced between Raul Barrigan and his mother and maintained a confident smile. "I admire your faith," he said, sounding very positive. "I know that God is going to get you through this just fine." He suspected that his meaning did not coincide with that of mother and son. And he doubted that Raul Barrigan was as confident as he sounded.

As soon as the gurney was wheeled from the ambulance into the emergency room at Mercy Medical, Dr. Ewald ordered that steroids be added to the IV drip to combat the swelling which could exacerbate the injury and lead to permanent damage. He warned his patient that a possible side effect was dizziness and nausea. Then the doctor left momentarily to conference by phone with a small group of spinal injury specialists who were on their way to the hospital.

Raul had only a moment with his fiancée and his parents in the ER before he was to be wheeled away for an array of tests to determine the extent of the injury. Samantha bent down to kiss his face and could not hold back the tears. "I know you're going to be all right, honey," she said between sobs. "We have so many plans, such a great life ahead of us. You *have* to be all right." Rudy and Serena added words of reassurance and said a quiet prayer over their son.

The sight of sterile walls and ceiling, the unfamiliar sounds of life-sustaining equipment nearby, and the quiet urgency of the medical personnel alerted Raul to the seriousness of what had happened to him and what might yet happen to him. This was not his world. This was not where he belonged. He was wearing an Arizona State Sun Devils' uniform already soiled from the heat of competition. He should be in the dugout now exhorting his team or roaming center field with his glove, not on a gurney unable to move or feel.

An ER aide wheeled Raul behind a curtain where Jerry Whisnant and a nurse removed the body board straps and cut away his uniform and underwear. Raul felt more violated about his uniform being cut apart than about laying naked in front of an attractive female nurse. Jerry assured him that a clean uniform would be waiting for him when he was ready for it.

The nurse inserted a catheter into his bladder, then pulled a sheet over him up to his arm pits. She didn't tell Raul about the procedure until she was done. He had felt nothing. He could move nothing. A sudden sense of utter helplessness rushed over him like an inundating wave. A dark cloud of fear rose on the horizon of his anxious thoughts. *Jesus, Jesus, Jesus*, he cried out inside. *What's happening to me? Why is this happening to me? Where are You tonight?*

The next three hours were a living nightmare for the paralyzed athlete: X-rays, CAT scan, MRI, CT myelogram. Nausea from the steroids required the insertion of an evacuator tube to keep him from choking on the vomit and bile his paralysis would not allow him to expel. At every stop, strangers in white lab coats or surgical greens examined him, poked him, questioned him, and pushed his gurney. The only reassuring constant was Jerry Whisnant. The Wiz went with him everywhere, explained the procedures, fortified him with encouragement, and wiped away the vomit which leaked from the evacuator.

When Raul was finally wheeled into a CCU room at almost 10:30, he was physically and emotionally exhausted. The room was dark except for a soft fluorescent light high on one wall. Rudy, Serena, and Samantha were waiting for him there. A nurse removed the tube from his mouth, but he had little energy to speak. His parents sat by his bed in silence while Samantha stroked his forehead.

Most of Raul's teammates had been waiting to see him since they arrived at the hospital after the game. The staff forbade a mass invasion of the critical care wing, but they allowed one representative from the team to visit for five minutes. Rufus Dubose was selected.

The husky black catcher entered quietly and greeted the Barrigans and Samantha with a nod. He was wearing a CWS T-shirt presented to the ASU players after they won the West regional tournament. At Samantha's encouragement, Rufus stepped up near the head of the bed and placed himself within Raul's limited range of vision.

"The game?" Raul said weakly. His eyes were half closed with fatigue.

Rufus glanced at Samantha, who gave him a look of resignation. Everyone in Omaha had heard the outcome of the ASU–Texas game except Raul Barrigan. No one wanted to volunteer the information, but no one felt it should be kept from him when he asked.

Rufus sighed. "We lost, Sugar, 4–1. We tried to win it for you, man, but we couldn't do it without you. Everybody's really dragging about it. We're all real sorry, man."

Raul was silent for a moment. "It's OK, Dubose. Tell everybody to cheer up. We'll be back next year."

Rufus held a baseball up where Raul could see it. It was slightly grass-stained and covered with signatures. "Everybody agreed that you deserve a game ball. It's the ball you scored on. We all signed it." Raul labored to produce a smile.

Rufus was undecided about what to do with the ball since the recipient couldn't reach up and take it. "Put it in my hand," Raul said. Rufus hesitated, feeling uneasy about touching the limp hand lying on top of the sheet. "Go ahead, man," Raul encouraged, "I'm not a leper." Rufus pulled open Raul's left hand, snuggled the ball into his palm, and closed the fingers around it. Then he wished Raul luck from the team and left.

Jerry Whisnant, John Ewald, and the hospital brain trust entered next. Rudy and Serena stood in cautious anticipation. Samantha remained seated with her hand touching Raul's cheek.

"What's the word, Wiz?" Raul said, summoning courage.

The physicians stood back and allowed the trainer to deliver the diagnosis they had agreed upon after studying the test results.

"It could be a lot worse, Sugar," he began. No one could have delivered the foreboding news more positively and compassionately than Jerry. What followed was a blur of medical jargon that Jerry did his best to explain to his listeners. But several terms slammed into their understanding like hammer blows: severe cervical fracture, spinal cord damage, surgery, plates and screws, possible quadriplegia. He hastened to add that with continual advances in medical technology and rehabilitation techniques for spinal cord injury, there was no limit to how well Raul might regain the use of his affected members.

Samantha cried hard despite the Wizard's tactful, positive approach to the news. Rudy held Serena, whose eyes repeatedly filled with tears. Raul remained stoic and tight-lipped throughout the explanation.

"The next step is to get you into a halo brace to stabilize your neck until the surgery. Then we'll let you get to sleep."

After Jerry and the doctors left, the Barrigans and Samantha had two minutes alone before the aides arrived to screw the stainless steel halo into Raul's skull. Rudy delivered his soul briefly and simply, expressing his trust in God to bring them all through this test of faith. Serena tearfully exhorted them all to expect a miracle. She had already called their church in Tucson to activate the prayer chain. Samantha tried to speak encouragingly between fits of tears.

Then someone else entered the room. Raul could hear a whispered apology and introduction coming from the foot of the bed. Then Serena came to the head of the bed. "Raul, it's the young lady from ESPN. She just wanted to add her best wishes."

"Marta? Is she still here?"

"She didn't want to bother you so she—"

"Bring her in . . . please."

Moments later, Marta Friesen came into view. She was dressed casually, and her hair was less than perfectly in place. "I didn't want to interrupt your family time," she said apologetically.

"It's all right." Then a puzzled look wrinkled his brow. "But how did you get in here? They only let the family in. They almost kept Dubose out."

Marta flushed slightly. "Well, if anybody asks you tonight, I'm your sister-in-law from Tucson."

The woman's brash ingenuity brought a little smile to Raul's lips. "Thanks for coming."

She continued, "I was watching the game in our truck. I saw the hit at the plate, and I watched them carry you off. I couldn't believe it. I mean, we just talked this afternoon and you were fine. Now . . . " A shadow of sympathy clouded the woman's cover-girl face. "I just had to come and tell you how sorry I am."

Raul regarded her with appreciation. "Are we on camera?" he asked. "Will this be in the interview?"

"No, no," Marta objected, "this is strictly a personal visit. I mean, look at me." She gestured to her clothes and hair. "I would like to interview you again, when you're up to it. But I won't put the show on the air if it's a problem for you." She glanced at each person around the bed to convey that they were included in her statement.

"I want to talk to you again . . . later," Raul said, wincing from pain and weariness.

"I've stayed too long," Marta said, making a move to leave. "I just want you all to know that you're in my thoughts." Serena nodded her appreciation for the sentiment.

"Wait," Raul said. Marta turned to him again. "Today, after I told you I play for Jesus, you asked me if I was afraid of getting hurt, afraid that I might jeopardize my career in the big leagues."

Marta dropped her head with chagrin, as if admitting she had jinxed him with her question—a thought which had already crossed her mind several times in the last four hours. "Yes, but now isn't the time to—"

Raul swallowed hard. "Well, I'm not injured anymore. I know God wants me to play pro ball, so I've already claimed my healing in His name. You're just looking at symptoms, symptoms that may be gone by the time I wake up tomorrow."

"That would be wonderful, Raul," Marta said, though her tone lacked conviction.

"So I want to continue the interview when I'm back in uniform. I want the world to see how big this miracle is going to be."

Twenty

Cooper Sams was thoroughly drunk less than an hour after walking out Kathy Keene's front door. This was quite a feat, considering that it normally took thirty minutes to travel from Kathy's house in Lynnwood, north of Seattle, to his house on Mercer Island, east of the city. But he succeeded in shaving eleven minutes off the trip tonight by pushing his new black Lexus over 80 MPH for most of the drive south on I-5 and east on I-90.

Another hurdle between Cooper and rapid mental oblivion appeared when he discovered that he was out of vodka. After two homemade Bloody Marys, he went to the liquor cabinet to break the seal on another half gallon of Popov's, but there was no other bottle. With two drinks already under his belt, Cooper knew he didn't dare try to drive to the liquor store. And since Rachel was away on a three-day trip, he couldn't send her for a bottle.

So what could he drink that would bring the curtain down quickly? Rachel kept an entire shelf of wines and cordials in the cabinet, but Cooper wanted faster action. So he switched to bourbon—which he didn't really like—and gagged down straights until the searing pain of Lila Ruth Atkinson's rebuke began to blur.

Cooper had come very close to hitting the woman. As a young airman in the Navy, he had mixed it up with a few guys and broken a few noses. But he had never punched a woman, though he had been tempted once or twice. Tonight, Lila Ruth Atkinson had pushed him to the edge. Her gall at calling him a drunk and an ogre among his coworkers and a failure as a husband was unforgivable. He might be all of those things, but it was certainly not the place of a pseudo-Christian, New Age, New Jesus channeler—or whatever she was—to tell him so, especially at their first meeting, a meeting he did not initiate.

Had he smashed Lila Ruth Atkinson in the face as she deserved, Cooper assessed after another gulp of bourbon, he would have gone after Kathy Keene next. The hostess—his coworker at Northstar and a friend since they survived Flight 202 together—had obviously betrayed him. Where else could the teacher/prophet have gained her information about him?

Cooper Sams and Kathy Keene had stayed in close touch after that terrifying night in Juneau, whereas the other three crew members had drifted away from each other and from Seattle. First Officer Kelly Schmidt had suffered from severe post-traumatic shock, keeping him out of the cockpit for nearly two months and in therapy for much longer. When Schmidt was considered for captain at Northstar a year later, the pilot review board, on which Cooper Sams sat, turned him down due to his ongoing battles with post-traumatic shock syndrome and numerous minor pilot errors since the Juneau incident which were attributed to his slow recovery. Fearing that his future at Northstar was limited, Schmidt left the company to take a job with a commuter airline in the Midwest at a substantial cut in pay.

The other two F.A.'s from Flight 202 had likewise dropped out of sight. Shanna Davis quit Northstar a month after the incident to return to college, and Tommy Eggers transferred to San Francisco six months later to move in with a new boyfriend.

Cooper Sams' relationship with Kathy Keene wasn't exactly a deep, caring friendship. It was more a kinship forged in the blaze of the near-disaster they had survived together, much like a fraternity formed among a handful of soldiers who survive a perilous battle. The two talked on the phone once or twice a month, checking up on one another as they each endured bouts with post-traumatic stress. And Kathy was among only a few Northstar coworkers invited to the very small, very private ceremony uniting Cooper Sams and Rachel Prescott in marriage six weeks after the incident in Juneau.

Cooper and Rachel had been to dinner with Kathy and Brad a few times and actually enjoyed themselves. Kathy was young enough to be Cooper's daughter, and he had harbored small, secret yearnings that such a relationship might develop. That was the only reason Cooper had finally agreed to attend the meeting tonight at Kathy's home, a meeting she had invited him to repeatedly, a meeting he was sure he would hate.

Kathy had embraced the religion of Lila Ruth Atkinson as a means of coping with her near-death experience. Her desire to share her life-changing discovery with Cooper was understandable. But now, Cooper realized, in trying to rope him into her circle of celestial friends, Kathy had gone too far. She had divulged privileged information about him to a stranger. She had slandered him by exposing his faults. A real daughter would never do that to her father.

Cooper sat at the kitchen bar with an old-fashioned glass in one hand and a quart of bourbon in the other. The entire house was dark except for a dim light over the kitchen sink. The more he drank and ruminated on Kathy's impropriety, the more he wanted to give her a piece of his mind for her despicable betrayal. When the alcohol finally tipped the balance between anger and good judgment, he pulled his personal wireless phone from the pocket of his tweed jacket and, with some effort, dialed Kathy's number.

Kathy's boyfriend answered. "Hello."

"Bradley, let me talk to that sweet young thing of yours," Cooper said. His diction was slurred, so he slowed his speech, overemphasized his words, and spoke too loudly to compensate. His attempts to sound witty, wise, and in control only made him sound more drunk.

"Cooper?"

"That's correct. This is Captain Cooper Sams."

"It's past 11, Coop," Brad said with unveiled irritation. "Kathy is in bed already. She has an early check-in tomorrow. I'll have her call you when—"

"This is very important, Bradley. This is very, *very* important. This is a family emergency. I'm a father figure, and I need to talk to my daughter figure right now."

"Coop, you're drunk, aren't you?"

"I may be well-oiled, but I still have a few things on my mind."

"Give it a rest, man, and call her on Tuesday. She gets back from her trip Tuesday afternoon."

Cooper cursed him. "How dare you stand between a man and his daughter. A man has a right to tell his daughter he is disowning her, and you have no right to interfere." Then he cursed again and threw back another slug of bourbon.

Brad returned a volley of curses. "Kathy is *not* your daughter, Coop, and I'm telling you she's in bed and she's not talking to—"

Brad was interrupted by a muffled voice in the background, a feminine voice. There was an exchange of whispered words which were unintelligible to Cooper. Then the feminine voice spoke over the phone.

"Cooper, this is Kathy. What's the problem?" She sounded tired and annoyed.

Cooper's words oozed out over a thick tongue. "I'm a drunk and a tyrant and a lousy husband. That's the problem, according to your guru."

"What are you talking about, Cooper?"

Cooper mumbled an obscenity. "I come to your meeting like a good father should, and you shoot me down in flames. That's what I get for saving your life. That's some vote of thanks."

"You're not making sense, Cooper. I think you'd better sleep it off and—"

"Not making sense? Well, let me spell it out for you. Your religious guru told me to my face that I'm an alcoholic and that I'm ruining my marriage and that I'm a monster at work. That's an insult, even coming from a friend. But I don't know that woman, and she doesn't know me. So who do you suppose told her about my problems?" Cooper's angry tone left no doubt about who he was implicating. He pulled on his drink while he imagined Kathy squirming with guilt.

"Lila Ruth said those things?" Kathy's tone was softer and tinged with surprise.

"Right to my face, like she was the Supreme Almighty herself."

"And it's true, I mean, that you're having trouble at home and all?"

"You should know. You told her so."

After a moment of silence, Kathy said, "Cooper, I didn't tell her that. I didn't tell her anything about you, except that you were at the controls that night in Juneau and that I owe you my life."

"Oh, sure," Cooper bellowed scornfully.

"That's the truth, Cooper, I swear it," Kathy said. "I know that you drink a little and that you can be a hard-nose on the job sometimes. But I respect you as a person and trust you as a pilot. I've never told anyone that you're an alcoholic. I don't even consider you an alcoholic. And I didn't hear that you and Rachel were having problems. Even if I had, I wouldn't feel right telling anyone about it. That's your business, not mine."

There was a sincerity in Kathy's voice that penetrated Cooper's blurred mind. "If you didn't tell her, who did?" The sharp edge was off his voice.

"You may find this hard to believe, Cooper, but Lila Ruth has a way of knowing certain things," Kathy answered. "She is very smart and very well connected to the spiritual world. She has studied all the world's religions. She understands spiritual things. That's why Jesus-Brother calls her Vision."

Cooper grunted his disbelief and took another drink.

"Surviving Flight 202 was like a wake-up call for me," Kathy continued. "I realized that I wasn't prepared to die. Lila Ruth answered some big questions for me about Parent-God and purpose and the future. That's why I wanted you to come over and meet her tonight. I thought she could help you too. She's a spiritual leader, Cooper, kind of a prophet."

Cooper snorted a laugh. "She's a crackpot, a loony tune."

Kathy did not defend Lila Ruth. Instead, after several silent seconds she asked, "What else did Lila Ruth tell you about yourself?"

"Nothing. She doesn't know me. She just made a lucky guess."

"Did she mention our flight number? Two-oh-two is very significant, you know. I believe we had a divine encounter that night."

"It's just a number. It could have been four-zero-four or nine-zero-nine."

The significance of 202 had not been lost on Cooper Sams in the three years since the incident. Nor had he missed the fact that the aircraft number on the 737-400 that night sported another pair of deuces—N122NS, something other observers had apparently overlooked. The twos had been meaningful to Cooper all right, but not in the sense that Lila Ruth Atkinson and Kathy Keene interpreted them.

"Did she ask you about your new name?"

"I don't have a new name," Cooper snapped. He had some serious doubts about the truth of his answer, but he was not going to admit them to Kathy.

"OK, OK," Kathy said, backing down, "I was just trying to help. The New Jesus Family isn't for everyone. Maybe it's not for you. I'm sorry you didn't have a good time tonight."

"Lila the all-seeing eye made sure of that."

"Like I said, I'm sorry. And I hope you believe me when I say I didn't tell her anything about you."

"And I hope you believe me when I say she's a crackpot."

Kathy dropped the issue. Instead she said, "Are you home now, Cooper?"

"Yeah, I'm home," he answered, suddenly feeling exhausted and queasy.

"Put yourself to bed. You'll feel better in the morning."

"No I won't, Kathy. I'm going to be very sick in the morning."

Kathy laughed. "OK, maybe you won't feel very good tomorrow. But you'll feel better Sunday."

"I hope so."

"I'll call you when I get back from my trip."

"Yeah, OK."

"And I hope everything works out between you and Rachel."

"Thanks."

As soon as he tapped off the phone, Cooper realized he couldn't wait until morning to be sick. He slipped off the stool and staggered weak-kneed to the kitchen sink just in time. The bourbon had tasted awful going down, but it tasted like furniture polish coming back up. The top half of his head seemed to expand and lift away from the bottom half, pulling his eyes back in their sockets. It was worse than the stomach flu.

When the siege was over, Cooper felt his way unsteadily to the bedroom in the dark. He avoided falling down, but he knocked two pictures off the wall in transit, shattering the glass on one. He also slammed his shin against the corner of the coffee table, but he was almost numb to the pain.

He kept the lights off, dreading the shock to his bleary eyes. After using the toilet, he threw off his clothes, ready to fall into bed and bury himself in sleep. But one gnawing, loose end kept him upright a few seconds longer. He could explain Lila Ruth Atkinson's knowledge of his problematic life. If Kathy Keene hadn't told her about him—and he now believed she hadn't, then someone else had. He guarded his privacy, but his world wasn't airtight. Perhaps more people had observed his struggles with booze and relationships than he imagined. Obviously, one of them had gotten to Lila Ruth ahead of him.

But something she said tonight Cooper could *not* explain. Kathy Keene had also mentioned it on the phone, but Cooper had denied it: A new name. Lila Ruth had called it an unusually significant word that might have come to him after the incident in Juneau. There was such a word, Cooper admitted to himself reluctantly. It had arrested him on the tarmac after his passengers and crew had been safely evacuated from the crippled 737. It was an unusual word under the circumstances, and it had come to him in a curious way. But its significance to Cooper at the time was a mystery. He had certainly not considered it to be a new name from the gods. But he didn't know *what* it was, so he had told no one about it, not even Rachel.

He made his way across the bedroom to his dresser in the dark. He pulled open the top drawer containing his socks and underwear. Reaching to the rear of the drawer under a stack of neatly folded T-shirts, he found the card and pulled it out. He couldn't see it in the dark, but his fingers recognized the texture and grain of the paper and the slightly bent corners and worn edges. In his mind's eye he could clearly see the bold letters spelling out the word that had puzzled him for three years: VANGUARD.

Cooper had spent many evenings at home alone studying the card and pondering its meaning. He had looked it up in the dictionary but felt no nearer to a solution for doing so. He had come close to throwing the card away several times, disgusted with himself for assigning it such importance. But he couldn't let it go. He could not escape the dogged conviction that this little scrap of paper found in the folds of a wool blanket held the key to the reason for his survival that chilly, stormy February night in Juneau three years ago.

Tonight a stranger had slapped him in the face with an alleged explanation for the card and its enigmatic word. The New Jesus Family consists of individuals supposedly handpicked by its deity—Jesus-Brother—and identified by special names he whispers to each of them. Each name describes the recipient's role in Brother's cosmic agenda, culminating with the "Reunion" of humankind and heavenkind—the second coming with a New Age spin, Cooper had mused as Lila Ruth spoke to the group gathered at Kathy Keene's house.

Had he told Lila Ruth about the card tonight, Cooper thought as he closed the dresser drawer and threw back the comforter, she probably would have embraced him as a convert. She would have said something like, "Jesus-Brother has given you a new name—Vanguard.

You're one of us. You have a vital role in the Reunion as we approach the end of the divided twin kingdoms. Welcome to the New Jesus Family."

Cooper collapsed into bed on top of the blanket and dragged the comforter half over him. The thought of being associated with such a woman made his tender stomach turn. He uttered a low curse into the pillow and caught a whiff of his own rancid breath. He had forgotten to brush his teeth, but his leaden limbs refused to obey his feeble wish to get up and do so.

Cooper could blow the woman off completely if it wasn't for an eight-letter word printed on a card which fluttered into his life out of nowhere. If Lila Ruth could prove to him that her beliefs were right and explain Vanguard to him, he might have to give her another chance. And if she could prove to him that she really was a spiritual prophet and not just another religious huckster, he might have to listen to her more seriously. He doubted that such proofs existed. But as the tide of heavy sleep began pulling him downward, a challenge came to mind that might constitute the supreme test.

Before he could get a firm grasp on the idea, Cooper was dead asleep. The card bearing the puzzling word Vanguard was still clutched in his right hand.

Twenty-one

The celebration in the apartment of Tommy Eggers and Alec Kipman lasted well into the night. By the time Alec walked in at a few minutes past 5, dressed in his Northstar uniform and beaming from the news he had heard on the car radio, the small apartment was already swarming with friends and strangers from the neighborhood. Throughout the evening the invited dinner guests and a stream of jubilant drop-ins ate and drank and cheered and toasted the achievement which promised worldwide liberation from the deadly pestilence of AIDS. There was plenty of food and drink, though Tommy and Alec would never know where it all came from. Everyone who walked in contributed something to the festivities.

The television blared continuously behind the din of voices. The networks preempted prime-time programming to rehash, dissect, and comment on the big announcement. Remote camera crews expanded coverage of the AIDS breakthrough with live interviews of experts and officials in Atlanta and in the cities where the announcement had made the greatest impact, the original hotbeds of the killer virus: New York,

Miami, Los Angeles, and San Francisco. Guests gathered around the TV in clusters to watch and listen and channel-hop for a while. Then they drifted off to the food table as another group hunkered down to watch. And in the center of the swirl of activity and banter, Tommy Eggers laughed and entertained and relished the excitement and attention.

In many quarters of the country, especially in major cities where gays and lesbians live in great numbers, people danced in the streets in response to the discovery of an AIDS vaccine. One of the television reports originated from the Castro in San Francisco, not far from Tommy and Alec's place. The crowd in the apartment hooted and cheered when they recognized several friends on the screen.

In more conservative areas of the country, churches and synagogues threw open their doors and welcomed thousands who came to give tearful thanks for the miracle announced in Atlanta. And the television cameras were there to catch it all.

The revelry in the apartment and across the country celebrated what *had* been accomplished in the AIDS war and largely ignored what *had not* been accomplished. The AIDS vaccine, called CDCP-10 by the technicians with a popular name yet to surface, had been successfully tested and proven 80 percent effective in preventing the virus. But with a myriad of FDA hoops to jump through and the extensive machinery of manufacture and distribution to set in place, it would likely be months—perhaps even a year—before CDCP-10 was available across the country. How many people would become infected in the meantime? No one wanted to talk about it.

Another question avoided through the night of celebration was, "Who would fund the massive project of inoculating the population?" The beneficiaries would include a staggering number of poor, homosexuals, and drug addicts. Would monogamous, clean-living taxpayers—the vast majority of the population—revolt at the prospect of having to shell out to quell an epidemic in the counterculture from which they had successfully protected themselves?

And no one had talked about who would or should get the vaccine first, since a nationwide supply would take many months to produce. Should those at the greatest risk—homosexuals with multiple sexual partners—be moved to the front of the line, thus condoning their promiscuous lifestyle? Should the low-risk majority be inoculated first, thus rewarding their restraint? Nor had anyone suggested who would get the vaccine and who would not if only a limited supply could be produced.

Furthermore, CDCP-10 promised to shield lymphocytes against the invasion of the human immuno-deficiency virus. But neither Dr. Hugh Demeter, Dr. Claudine Bizieau, nor any of the scientists and officials interviewed today offered any hope to individuals already infected with the disease. "CDCP-10 is a medical miracle, but only for those not yet tainted by the virus," Dr. Demeter had said in response to a pointed question about a cure for the infected. "Studies are continuing in the field of antiviral substances and treatment. We pray daily for the break-through treatment we need to eradicate or at least reverse the progress of the virus once it has been introduced to the system. But it may be months or years before ultimate victory is achieved over HIV."

Some of these issues finally surfaced in the apartment near midnight. Most of the guests had gone home, and the television had finally been turned off in favor of soft jazz on an FM station. The place was a mess—bottles, glasses, dirty plates, and napkins littering countertops and end tables, crumbs dotting the living room carpet. Sitting in the midst of it with Tommy and Alec were their neighbor Evie Dukes, her boyfriend Chuck Strahan, who was a part-time cable car operator, and Chad Vaccaro, another gay flight attendant who was between relationships. The quintet of friends had tacitly committed to finish off a bottle of peppermint schnapps someone had brought, drank from, and left behind.

Chuck, a lanky, twice-divorced man of thirty-four, sat on the floor leaning against the sofa sipping schnapps from a paper cup. He had worked until 6 and was still wearing his tan polished cotton shirt and brown pants with the transit authority logo stitched above the pocket. "No offense, guys, but the first people to receive the vaccine should be those who are at risk of becoming infected because of their jobs: doctors, nurses, EMT's . . ."

"Cops and firefighters and anyone who may be exposed to blood and dirty needles," Alec Kipman interjected. "No offense taken; I think you're dead right." Dressed in baggy jeans and a faded Stanford sweatshirt, the long-limbed flight attendant was slouched half in and half out of a big leather chair.

"People at the Red Cross, et cetera," Chad put in. The olive-skinned, dark-haired flight attendant stretched out on the carpet had been drinking since he arrived at 3, except for the three hours he was asleep on the floor in the corner of the living room. He was trying to stay awake now and join in the conversation, with great difficulty.

"Yeah, I agree, Chuck," Alec emphasized. "The caregivers and guardians of our society deserve priority care."

"You have to include sick people in with the medical people," Evie said, reaching her Dixie cup out to Tommy, who filled the bottom third from the nearly empty bottle of schnapps. "I mean, people scheduled for surgery, people who need blood transfusions, people who would be exposed to the virus in a hospital setting."

"So if you're sexually promiscuous and want to survive, you'd better get a job as an EMT or schedule yourself for an appendectomy or liposuction," Tommy put in wryly. "In fact, your best chance of getting inoculated is if you are a *gay* EMT having surgery." He laughed at his own humor. The others merely smiled.

"Anybody who is admitted to a hospital for any reason should get the stuff," Chad announced flatly. He was having trouble keeping his eyes open.

"Oh, sure, Chad," Tommy retorted. His cynicism was obvious. "So in a vaccine supply crisis you have people intentionally cutting off their fingers or breaking their arms to get to the top of the list for inoculation." Tommy was a little ticked at Chad for loitering in the living room most of the night like a drunk in the park. "Remind me not to put you in charge of the vaccine bank."

There was a pause for musing on the comment and sipping schnapps.

"Once you vaccinate the caregivers and hospital patients, who gets the next batch?" Alec said, looking at Chuck, who had started the discussion of prioritizing vaccine recipients. But before Chuck could speak, Alec said, "I think you have to go with the next highest risk group."

"You mean gays and straights with multiple sex partners," Evie advanced.

"Hookers, too, male and female," Chad mumbled.

"Right," Alec said, "and the IV drug users."

"So you would set up a clinic in every bathhouse, whorehouse, and drug house in the country," Chuck said in a tone of mild disbelief.

"Chuck, that's where the virus is," Alec said matter-of-factly.

"But wouldn't such a plan tend to glorify profligacy?" Evie said.

"Profligacy, whoa!" Tommy exclaimed in mock astonishment. "Evie, I didn't think cocktail waitresses knew such big, nasty words!"

"Evie is also an English teacher," Chad informed sleepily, a fact everyone in the room knew well.

Evie ignored the comments and bored in on Alec. "You know what I mean. Here is the least disciplined, most immoral segment of society, and we give them special treatment over the rest of the people who have kept the disease at bay."

"Least disciplined and most immoral by whose standards?" Alec pressed.

"Let the one among you without sin cast the first stone," Tommy said.

"Exactly," Alec continued. "We're dealing with a sliding scale here. Who among us is perfectly disciplined? Who among us is spotlessly moral?"

"Step up and take your best shot," Chad echoed, holding out his crumpled Dixie cup as if it were a stone. No one took it, so Chad threw it over his shoulder into the corner of the living room.

Alec went on with intensity that was free of anger. "I'm saying that everybody is tainted by imperfection or immorality by someone's standards. All things being equal, let's start with the most needy among us: the 'profligates,' as you say."

"If there is a limited supply of vaccine, I'd start with the other end of the scale," Evie argued.

"You mean lily-white virgin missionaries and preachers who won't even say 'Gosh darn'?" Tommy said sardonically.

"I know some preachers who aren't so lily-white," Chad offered, talking to himself.

Evie was suddenly pensive. "I'm talking about people who have been faithful to each other for thirty years of marriage, people who wouldn't think of breaking their skin with a dirty needle. I'm talking about people like my parents. I think they deserve priority access to protection."

Evie's four men friends read the concern in her voice. They had all met Evie's parents and esteemed them highly.

"I don't mean to be disrespectful, Evie," Alec went on in a softer tone, "but what do people like your parents need protection from? They're good, old-fashioned, monogamous, drug-free straights. They're totally insulated by their lifestyle. They won't contract HIV. They don't need the vaccine. Give it to the people who need it."

"Like us prof-ull-gents," Chad mumbled. Nobody corrected his mispronunciation.

"But what if my parents get exposed to the virus by accident?" Evie voiced a long-standing fear.

"You mean what if faithful old Dad falls off the wagon and gets involved with a couple of high-risk twenty-year-olds from the other end of the scale," Tommy wisecracked.

Evie snapped a glaring look at him, and Tommy immediately felt like a jerk. "That was bad, Evie," he said sincerely. "I'm sorry."

"It can happen," Chuck said, picking up Evie's defense. "HIV can be spread by accident. You know, a cut, an attack by somebody who is infected, who knows? It's a remote chance, but I agree with Evie that those who have done the best at limiting the spread of AIDS are entitled to the first chance at protection."

Tommy wasn't listening at the moment. His attention had been abruptly drawn away from the friendly argument—which nobody was going to win—by an image of Evie's parents in his mind. Marvin and Nora Dukes were God-fearing, churchgoing, Bible-believing evangelicals who lived in Redwood City, south of San Francisco on the peninsula. Marvin had been the service manager at a Chevrolet dealership in town for eighteen years after starting there as a mechanic in 1967. Nora worked part-time as an RN.

Evie had admitted to Tommy shortly after they became neighbors and friends that she had wandered from her religious background to sow her wild oats in the city by the bay. In doing so, she knew she had brought grief to her parents. Mr. and Mrs. Dukes did not agree with

Evie's choice to leave teaching in order to serve drinks in a downtown bar dressed in the costume of a "harlot." They did not approve of her daughter living with Chuck outside of marriage. Nor did they approve of the homosexual lifestyle of many of her friends. From Evie's description, Tommy expected the elder Dukes' to be scowling, prune-faced Puritans dressed in black and carrying ten-pound Bibles.

But when he finally met Marvin and Nora during one of their infrequent trips to the city to visit Evie, Tommy was amazed at how wrong his perception had been. During introductions in Evie's apartment, Marvin and Nora grabbed Tommy's hand and shook it firmly. "It's a pleasure to meet you, Tommy," they had said with a sincerity Tommy could not discount. Some Christians Tommy had met wouldn't even touch him, as if he were a leper. And none had ever said it was a pleasure to meet him.

Marvin's face beamed with interest that day as the two men sat on the sofa and discussed Tommy's career with Northstar. Marvin was especially enthralled with Tommy's account of the harrowing incident aboard the 737 in Juneau, Alaska. Contrary to his expectations, Tommy found Evie's parents to be warm and accepting. "That's the way they've always been," Evie had told him later. "You know where they stand on the issues, but they don't let issues come before people. 'Hate the sin but love the sinner,' Daddy always says." Tommy was surprised by the little saying. From that first visit on, Marvin Dukes made Tommy feel more like a saint than a sinner whenever they were together.

During subsequent visits, Tommy and Marvin had discussed openly Tommy's alternative lifestyle. Tommy noted with wonder that Marvin didn't recoil in horror when he talked about "coming out" during college or being with a number of partners since then. And Tommy didn't flinch when Marvin brought God and the Bible and sin into the discussion.

"You know, son," Marvin said at the end of one discussion, "a person's sexual preference doesn't *bring* him to God and it can't keep him *away* from God. Now I believe that homosexuality is a sin; the Bible lists it right along with murder, stealing, idolatry, and the like. But God doesn't send people to hell because they murder or steal or because they're homosexuals or adulterers. He sends them because they don't accept His gift of love, Jesus Christ. That's what I pray for you, Tommy: that you will invite Jesus into your life and let Him transform you into the person He wants you to be."

Marvin delivered his message so politely and positively that it wasn't until after he left that Tommy realized he had been preached to.

Tommy quietly envied Marvin and Nora Dukes. He guessed that the older couple had never suffered much personal anxiety over the threat of HIV. By their own admission, they had had only one sex partner each in their thirty-some-odd years of marriage. They never had to worry about each other's sexual history when they climbed into bed together. Barring a freak accident that introduced the virus into their systems, they would never be touched by it. They didn't need a vaccine, and they didn't fear the human immuno-deficiency virus. What would it be like to live with such peace?

Tommy hoped he would get a small taste of that peace again tomorrow when he went in for his biannual HIV screening. He had already remarked on the coincidence of his appointment being set for the day after the big announcement. Every test so far had come back clean, and Tommy had no reason to believe that tomorrow's wouldn't. Then, as soon as the vaccine was available, he would find a way to be in the front of the line. Perhaps after his inoculation he would feel as calm and confident as Marvin Dukes had for the last thirty years.

"How about you, Tommy?" Evie said, piercing his reverie.

Tommy snapped back to the present without a clue about what Evie meant.

"How about *what?*"

"I said, 'If the AIDS vaccine cost $1 million a pop, how would you get the money?' Alec said that he would sell everything he owned and borrow the rest from his parents. What would you do?"

A little embarrassed about zoning out on the conversation for several seconds, Tommy roared back in the best way he knew how—with humor: "I'd sell Alec and steal the other $999,999!"

Twenty-two

It was a gorgeous Saturday morning for being on the water in Seattle, but Cooper Sams wasn't much in the mood to sail. Yet he had to get out of the house for three distinct reasons.

First, he had to clear the poisonous vodka and bourbon fumes out of his brain from last night. This morning's hangover had left him with a head feeling as large and as hollow as the Kingdome.

Second, he had to sort through his encounter with Lila Ruth Atkinson and the New Jesus Family now that he was no longer blind with rage or numb with alcohol. The pointed, bothersome comments from the woman who called herself Vision were grinding in his consciousness when he awoke.

Third, his wife Rachel was due home from her three-day trip at shortly after noon today. Things usually went better for both of them when they gave each other a few hours of space at the end of a trip.

So by 11 A.M. Cooper was aboard his twenty-eight-foot Catalina sloop, rigged for solo sailing, gliding up Lake Washington. He was heading from his Mercer Island home toward the ship canal and a leisurely journey out to the Chittenden Locks at Ballard. The chilly breeze sweeping across the bow stung Cooper's bare face and arms wide awake. He wished the invigorating wind could blow right through him.

Cooper's thoughts about Rachel never strayed far from the one recurring wish that he had never married her. They had been wonderful friends and tender lovers before Flight 202 just missed slamming into the ground three and a half years earlier. Rachel had hinted at a more formal relationship, but Cooper, who at the time had given as much of himself to her as he thought he could give, had been able to deflect Rachel's attempts without seriously offending her. He had skillfully achieved a safe orbit where he could enjoy the warmth of intimacy while resisting the gravitational pull of a woman who wanted more.

Then Juneau happened, and several seemingly unrelated circumstances surrounding the accident combined to disrupt Cooper's carefully maintained orbit and send him plunging into Rachel Prescott's arms with a proposal of marriage—which she readily accepted.

Cooper's resolve was weakened by his inability to explain the urge he had felt to phone Rachel twice on the day he nearly died. He had interpreted the urge as a premonition that something was going to happen to Rachel, that she was in danger, and he felt constrained to talk to her. As it turned out, Cooper had been the one in trouble, which made his longing to be in touch with Rachel that night all the more mysterious.

Another curious thing about the incident was the twos that were involved. Flight 202 on aircraft N122NS survived a lethal rotor shear *twice* on the *second* leg of the trip. Cooper wasn't normally religious or superstitious, but long before he met Lila Ruth Atkinson he knew that all those deuces had to mean something. And at that point in his life, the most significant pair in his life was Rachel Prescott and Cooper Sams. He took the recurring twos as a sign that he and Rachel were destined to be together and that his stubbornness was tempting fate.

But the most mind-boggling aspect of the incident was that people survived. And the fact that *everyone* aboard came through virtually unscathed was nothing short of a miracle. Why did they survive? Why did *he* survive? As he wrestled with that question, Cooper couldn't get far without thinking that Rachel was a large part of the answer.

Cooper took credit for part of the miraculous survival. Years of training, experience, and meticulous flight-by-flight preparation had equipped him to assess the problem and respond correctly. He had locked horns with the elements and outwitted them.

But in the weeks following the near disaster, as he lay awake nights replaying those traumatic ten minutes over and over again, Cooper acknowledged to himself that luck or God or fate or something had also played a vital role in the survival of Flight 202. Had the aircraft encountered the rotor shear at a lower elevation, all of Cooper's training and experience would not have saved him, his crew, or his passengers. There wouldn't have been enough altitude or air speed to pull the 737 out of its deadly dive toward the snow-covered Juneau landscape. Someone or something had provided enough distance between the disturbance in the air and the unforgiving earth for Cooper to work his magic and bring the bird down safely.

Why had these unseen forces tormented him to within seconds of death and then let him live? The question had bored into Cooper repeatedly in the first few weeks after the incident. Publicly, he and his copilot were lauded for their superior airmanship at averting a disaster. Privately, he received letters from more than half of the passengers on Flight 202 praising him for his skill and thanking him for giving them a second lease on life. But in his moments of solitary contemplation, usually found while sailing the lake or the sound, Cooper agonized to discern the reason for *his* deliverance. This quest for destiny combined with the other puzzling clues kept leading him back to Rachel Prescott. So he swept aside his pride and selfish individualism and married her.

The first several months of marriage were glorious. The new Mr. and Mrs. Sams traveled together often and laughed like never before. They braved new levels of intimacy, as if the marriage license they had signed became a passkey to each other's souls. Rachel confessed her deep, abiding pain at being abandoned by her first husband, Jack, and then seeing their two children side with their father. Cooper haltingly recounted the terror of Flight 202 and the fear of death he had stuffed away during and after the incident. A deep bond began to form between them, a bond made possible only through the transparency, honesty, and trust of personal commitment.

But fifty-three years of independence and self-sufficiency mounted a subtle resistance in Cooper to the bonding process. Rachel's persistent desire for closeness and more time together began to stifle him. He had told all he wanted to tell about himself, and Rachel wanted more. Annoying little quirks in her personality, which Cooper had chosen to overlook at first, picked at him. The walls of their large home on the Mercer Island shoreline seemed to close in on him when they were at home together. He needed space.

Shortly after their first anniversary, which the couple spent apart while on different trips with Northstar, Cooper began quietly pulling back. He passed over two-day trips for three-and four-day trips. He spent more time alone on the boat when Rachel was home. In expanding periods of self-imposed isolation, he began to question the logic which had led him to take Rachel as his wife. The powerful sense of destiny which followed the miraculous salvation of Flight 202 had never left him. But Cooper became increasingly convinced that he had erred in tying his destiny so closely to Rachel Prescott. He finally decided that those arresting twos—Flight 202, N122NS, two rotor shears—were not a cosmic directive for two lives to come together. They must mean something else, or they were merely an odd coincidence.

Rachel had not been blind to Cooper's subtle shutdown. But wounds from her past blocked her from confronting the obvious. Instead, she responded in kind. She boarded up the windows and doors to her soul which had so recently been wide open and filled with light. She scheduled herself to travel when Cooper was home. Meanwhile, a part of her—the part Cooper Sams had sparked to life with his vow of marriage—agonized in silence.

Over the next two years, the couple mutely regressed to a state of tolerant and outwardly amiable cohabitation. They slept in the same bed when they were both home—nine or ten nights a month. And occasionally they came together in the darkness like phantom lovers to quench sexual passions. But having been gloriously one for less than a year, they were again "twain," two islands of humanity separated by a strait of pride and silence.

Cooper angled the sloop westward into Union Bay and headed for the ship canal which joined Lake Washington with Lake Union and Puget Sound. The sprawling University of Washington campus filled the northwest shoreline of the bay. In the western sky a Northstar MD-80 floated over the Seattle civic center on its glide path to a landing at SeaTac to the south. In less than an hour Rachel's flight would follow the same glide path. As the plane descended over the civic center, Rachel would assume that Cooper was out in the boat, but she probably wouldn't bother to look out the window trying to spot him among the many boats on Seattle's waterways.

Demoting Rachel Sams from the lofty rung of being his reason for surviving a potential air tragedy had left Cooper with questions he thought he had answered: Why was he spared a horrible death in a fiery ball of tangled metal? What was the significance of the incident which had tested him to within mere feet of a disaster? What was his destiny? He had pondered these questions for months without satisfaction. He knew there must be a reason, but it hadn't materialized. It was like being told to wait on the corner for a bus that never shows up.

Most puzzling of all was the card which was inexplicably hooked in the blanket he wrapped around himself after the emergency landing, the card he had not shown to anyone—even Rachel, the card imprinted with one maddeningly cryptic word: Vanguard. If he was awaiting his destiny like a trip on a long overdue bus, the card had to be some kind of ticket. But nothing or no one had come across his path with anything close to an explanation—until last night.

Cooper adjusted the jib and mainsail to slow the sloop as he prepared to enter the ship canal at the west end of Union Bay. Back to the tiller again, Cooper turned his thoughts to Lila Ruth Atkinson. Surprisingly, he felt only a shadow of the anger he had felt little more than twelve hours earlier. Rather, he regarded her with cautious admiration. He had to hand it to the woman; Lila Ruth was fearless. Forget where she got her information about Cooper's shortcomings; she had pulled no punches in delivering it. Cooper knew few women who were so free of intimidation in his presence.

Cooper could categorize as religious hokum everything Lila Ruth had said about Jesus-Brother and earth-sister except for a few unsettling points. The first was her knowledge about the more ragged side of his life, information Cooper thought had been leaked to the guru by Kathy Keene. If Kathy hadn't blabbed, who had? Or had the woman who fancied herself as Vision really conjured up a window into Cooper's dark side?

Another mystery was Lila Ruth's explanation of twos, especially as it related to the captain's experience that February 1995 night in Juneau. What Cooper had first regarded as an omen about himself and Rachel, Lila Ruth saw as a personal message to him from Jesus-Brother. She was convinced that deity was trying to communicate with him in the near-death experience by surrounding the incident with twos. Lila Ruth's doctrine of deuces sounded bizarre, but at least it was an attempt at explaining a phenomenon that Cooper already considered significant.

Cooper could have brushed away Lila Ruth's esoteric knowledge about him and her cosmic numerology had she not pressed him about his spiritual name. "It wouldn't surprise me if Brother whispered to you a new name after that flight," she had said to him less than a minute after they had met at Kathy's home. Cooper quickly denied the possibility. Yet even as he spoke, a word printed on a card secreted away in his drawer blazed across his consciousness: Vanguard. How could she possibly know about that apart from divine knowledge of some kind?

That was the question on Cooper's muddled brain when he fell asleep and again when he woke up. A strategy for finding the answer had also come to him quite unbidden, a strategy he intended to employ when he talked to her again—*if* he ever talked to her again. There was one surefire way to determine if Lila Ruth Atkinson was really a prophet of God or just another New Age fruitcake on a winning streak of wild guesses. *He would put it to her as directly as she had put it to him: If you and Parent-God and Jesus-Brother know so much about me, then you must know the name he spoke to me after the incident in Juneau. Put up or shut up.*

Thinking about the pointed ultimatum now brought Cooper a sense impish glee. He actually smiled into the wind at the prospect of putting

Lila Ruth to the test. The fun might even be worth sitting through another meeting at Kathy's. He could not imagine Lila Ruth coming up with the magic word in 1,000 guesses. Cooper wouldn't stay around for 1,000 guesses, of course. He would give her three good swings at it before walking away. And if she put the onus back on him with something like, "Jesus-Brother will only whisper your new name to you," Cooper had already thought about a few choice names he would whisper to Lila Ruth before he left.

The sloop glided across Portage Bay with the university on his right and a posh marina, hosting two yacht clubs, on his left. Passing under University Bridge and Interstate Five, Cooper steered around Gas Works Park at the top of Lake Union and reentered the westbound ship canal. The sun above held court amidst wispy, subservient clouds. Brilliant crowns of gold capped the gentle waves formed by numerous pleasure craft leisurely traversing the canal. Shielded from the radiance by his Seahawks cap and aviator sunglasses, Cooper regarded the sunshine and warmth as a tonic for body and soul. To him, heaven could only be unending days sailing the waterways of Puget Sound.

Shortly after Cooper passed under the Fremont Bridge, the wireless phone holstered on his belt sounded. Cooper usually didn't bring the phone along when he sailed, preferring that his serenity on the water not be interrupted. But he was expecting a call from Northstar crew scheduling. He had passed his regular trip for a four-day leaving tomorrow morning. He was senior enough to get any trip he bid for, so the confirmation call was a necessary but minor formality.

He lifted the phone to his ear with his right hand as his left gripped the tiller. "This is Cooper Sams."

"Captain Sams?" It was a woman's voice, more relaxed and less businesslike than most crew scheduling agents.

"Yes."

"This is Lila Ruth Atkinson." The woman paused as if waiting for a response of recognition.

Cooper was astonished at hearing the name and said nothing. His first reaction was that Lila Ruth had somehow overheard his recent wish to talk to her and had called to accommodate him—a thought he quickly scoffed at.

Lila Ruth went on, "We met last night at the home of your coworker, Kathy Keene."

Cooper drew a long breath. "Yes, I remember," he said with calculated coolness.

"Brad, Kathy's friend, was kind enough to give me your number this morning. I hope I'm not interrupting something."

Cooper noticed that the teacher-prophet brassiness which had dominated Lila Ruth's tone last night was missing. Instead he detected a note of penitence which piqued his interest. The all-seeing eye was calling to apologize. "No, you're not interrupting," he said.

"I have two reasons for calling, Captain Sams," Lila Ruth began. "First, I realize that I was rather blunt and forceful last night when I confronted you about your . . . difficulties. I'm very sorry if I offended you. That was not my intent."

Cooper felt slightly offended again at the mention of his "difficulties." "Just what *was* your intent, Ms. Atkinson?" he pressed, maintaining the chilly tone in his voice.

Lila Ruth uttered an audible sigh. "It's difficult to explain, Captain," she said without condescension. "I merely intended to greet you and help you feel at ease. You were obviously agitated about being there."

You didn't have to be a mind reader to figure that out, old girl, Cooper thought. *Tell me something I don't know.*

"But when I touched your hand, I felt a powerful spiritual impulse that—"

"Vibes?" Cooper cut in cynically.

"We refer to them as harmonic impressions, Captain Sams," Lila Ruth said, unruffled by the interruption or the cynicism, "impulses of the earth-sister current that flows through all of us."

"Harmonic impressions," Cooper echoed disbelievingly.

"Frankly, there was such an urgency in the impression coming through your hand that I overreacted to what I saw. And I'm sorry that I was so pushy."

"Saw?" Cooper said, ignoring the apology.

"Perhaps a better word would be 'sensed' or 'discerned.' I'm referring to what I learned about you the moment I touched you: your problem with alcohol, the problems you have had getting along with some coworkers, the distance in your relationship with your wife."

"There were a lot of Northstar people in that group last night," Cooper objected. "Are you sure you didn't get some of your 'discernment' from what they told you about me?"

There was a pause before Lila Ruth answered. "Your assumption is completely logical, but I can assure you that I knew nothing about you except your name . . . until I touched your hand."

"You expect an intelligent, levelheaded person to believe—"

"I understand your skepticism, Captain Sams," Lila Ruth inserted strongly. "If I were in your place, I'm sure I would respond the same way. But I called for another reason. I have something to tell you that I hope will change your perspective."

Then I'm going to ask you the $64-million question about my so-called spiritual name, Cooper taunted silently, *and we'll see who has a change of perspective.* "I'm listening," he said.

"I would rather talk to you in person, today if possible."

"I'm busy today, and I leave on a four-day trip tomorrow. If you have something to say, say it now."

"Captain Sams, what I must tell you is of the utmost importance. It is a message from Parent-God which concerns your future, the future of the New Jesus Family, and Reunion with Brother. I must deliver this message in person. I will meet you anywhere in the city within the hour. Your choice. Just tell me where."

It suddenly sounded very familiar: a sales pitch as old as TV commercials, junk mail, and telemarketing. *Of all the millions of people on our mailing list, you have been chosen for a special gift. Just come into our office to claim your prize.* And when the sucker takes the bait, he is bombarded with hard sell until he signs on the dotted line for something he never intended to buy. Cooper saw himself as the target of a clever religious pitch: Parent-God has selected you to be a general in His army. He wasn't about to stay around to hear the kicker: how much he was expected to ante up to receive his marching orders.

Cooper swore unashamedly. "Lady, I don't believe in your Jesus-Brother God. And this New Jesus Family of yours is nothing more than a weird New Age cult, a scam. The Reunion you people talk about is a pipe dream, an escape from reality. And you are a fraud, a huckster, a phony religious guru who is misguiding decent people and probably bilking them out of their hard-earned money. You may have trapped Kathy Keene and others in your web of deceit, but I have no intention—"

"Captain Sams! Captain Sams!" Lila Ruth shouted into the phone until he stopped his tirade. Then she continued without any evidence of having been offended. "I can offer you a small portion of the message that may cause you to reconsider your assessment of me and the New Jesus Family. Call it a deposit on the urgent message I have to deliver."

"Take your best shot," Cooper dared.

"As I assumed last night, you have a new name. Jesus-Brother calls you Vanguard."

Twenty-three

Cooper felt like he had been hit with a dose of chloral hydrate. A chill ran up the back of his legs, turning his knees to Jell-O. His face flushed hot despite the cool breeze sweeping up the canal from Puget Sound. He was suddenly lightheaded, almost faint. His right hand, which held the phone, dropped to his side. With his left hand he gripped the tiller securely to avoid beaching the boat while he dealt with the sudden shock. He was shaken to the core by the name Lila Ruth Atkinson had spoken to him.

Before Cooper could even pose his question, the guru of the New Jesus Family had spoken the answer he had judged impossible for her to know. Cooper had been poised to play his ace and end the pseudo-religious charade. But Lila Ruth had turned the tables on him by leading with the ace of trump. No guesses, no uncertainty on her part. *Vanguard*, she had said. Bingo, game over, you lose. Cooper suddenly felt exposed, vulnerable, as if his life had been turned inside out and his deepest secrets made public. With one word Lila Ruth had abruptly transported him from a world where he was master to a new world governed by a mysterious woman he had judged to be a fraud. He did not will it to happen, but Cooper's opinion of Lila Ruth Atkinson began a rapid 180-degree turn.

After nearly thirty seconds, he lifted the phone and said, "How did you know about Vanguard?" There was a slight quaver in his voice which he could not control. Cooper realized that Lila Ruth now had the upper hand. She had every right to ream him out for the way he had talked to her, and he knew he deserved it.

But her voice conveyed compassion free of malice. "I just know, Captain Sams, with a knowing beyond learning. Jesus-Brother calls me Vision, and knowing is the capacity He has entrusted to me. I didn't request my name or my role in His agenda any more than you did."

She waited patiently, aware that Cooper Sams was still processing a mountain of thoughts and emotions.

Finally he said. "Nobody knew about Vanguard. I told no one." This was the pivotal issue in Cooper's mind. It was the issue on which he had been prepared to nail Lila Ruth Atkinson to the wall. The fact that she knew the unknowable stripped him of both his weapons and his armor in this clash of wills.

"Brother knew, and he told me."

"I'm not part of the New Jesus Family. I don't even believe in your religion." He was not resisting as much as he was wondering aloud why he had been chosen, for he was helpless to believe anything else at the moment.

"You have sought your destiny ever since February 20, 1995. You know you were spared for a reason, and you have been asking why. Jesus-Brother has finally answered you."

Cooper was silent again for nearly a minute. The sloop glided gently in the canal. Screeching gulls skimmed the water's surface. Stately homes looked down from wooded hillsides, a mute gallery of witnesses waiting to see how the confrontation would play out. Cooper had traveled this route to Puget Sound so often he could do it in the dark. Yet today, in the bright sunlight, everything looked foreign to him. He felt as if he was traveling the canal for the first time.

"What does it mean—Vanguard?" Cooper asked with resignation.

"I have so much to tell you," Lila Ruth said. "What I have to say is almost as new to me as it will be to you. Where can I meet you?"

"Where are you now?"

"I'm still in Lynnwood, the home where I stay when I'm in Seattle."

Cooper forced himself to think about where he was and where he was headed. "I'm on my boat on the ship canal headed out toward the sound. There's a small public dock on the north side of the canal between the Ballard bridge and the locks. I'll be there in about twenty minutes."

"I can find it. I'll meet you there. Twenty minutes."

"Yes." Then Cooper was silent, holding the phone to his ear. He was still reeling in numb shock from what was happening to him and what he had just agreed to do.

Lila Ruth sensed his hesitation. "Are you all right, Captain?"

There was bewilderment in his response. "This doesn't make sense."

"If you let go of your intellectualism, Captain, it *will* make sense," Lila Ruth assured him with maternal confidence, "more sense than anything you have ever learned or experienced. You'll see."

By the time he eased under the Ballard bridge, Cooper had half talked himself into believing that his telephone conversation with Lila Ruth was nothing more than a hangover-induced hallucination. Still, he had to keep the rendezvous to prove that she wouldn't be there. But she *was* there, standing serenely on the dock in the distance as he emerged from under the bridge. A lone car was parked in the lot behind the dock: a white Mercedes sedan.

Dressed fashionably in white slacks and blouse with a lightweight, mint-green jacket, Lila Ruth could have been mistaken for the wife of a wealthy Seattle executive meeting her husband's yacht for lunch. It occurred to Cooper that he didn't know anything about Lila Ruth's marital status—past or present. In reality, he knew practically nothing about her. But what she knew about him had already changed his life.

The sloop had an inboard motor, but Cooper prided himself in navigating the craft without it. He eased up to the dock and secured a bow line, not sure if Lila Ruth intended to step aboard or ask him to come ashore. It was clearly her party, and he was at her disposal for direction.

"Perhaps we could walk together," she called out pleasantly from where she had been standing since Cooper first spotted her. "I love being out in the sunshine, don't you?"

Cooper nodded as he attached a stern line and prepared to hop off. In two minutes they were walking side by side along a new jogging path beside the canal leading to the Chittenden Locks. In worn jeans, faded short-sleeved sweatshirt, and baseball-style cap,

Cooper felt like a laborer alongside the perfectly groomed, expensively dressed teacher/prophet. But his self-consciousness soon dissolved as the woman who had revealed his deep, three-year-old secret spoke.

"Tell me about Vanguard, Captain," Lila Ruth began. "How did you first hear your new name?" She sounded as casual and comfortable about being with Cooper as with a lifetime friend.

That Lila Ruth apparently did not know *how* Cooper had encountered his "new name" failed to diminish for him the significance of her knowing it. Or perhaps she knew every detail of his story and was just being kind enough to let him tell it. It didn't matter to Cooper. Either way, she was some kind of messenger from on high that he had to respect.

Cooper explained in a handful of brief sentences how he discovered the strange card by accident in the folds of a blanket after exiting the crippled jet in Juneau. He added that he had kept the card without any logical reason to do so and told no one about it. Lila Ruth asked about his perception of the miraculous survival of Flight 202. Cooper confirmed that he perceived the event to be a doorway to his destiny, but, except for the word Vanguard, he had no idea what his destiny was. He did not mention Rachel or his mistaken idea that she was an integral element in his future.

"I'm aware that you know practically nothing about me and my spiritual family," Lila Ruth said. "But instead of burdening you with a lengthy explanation of what we are about, I think your time would best be served if I come right to the issue of Vanguard, which I sense is uppermost in your mind. Am I correct?"

Still reeling from her disclosure and hungry to know what it meant, Cooper could have let fly with a vehement, "You bet your life!"—punctuated by a couple of choice expletives. Instead, he responded with a quiet and respectful, "Yes, thank you."

"I thought as much." She drew a deep breath, released it, and began her story.

"Last night, I was profoundly troubled after meeting you. There was such positive energy in your handshake, as if I had gripped the hand of Jesus-Brother himself. And yet you were so distinctly upset and resistant. As I explained on the phone, I take partial responsibility for your hostile response; I was a bit overeager. You didn't seem the least bit interested in what I had to say, and I was tempted to dismiss the exchange as a big mistake. But I could not escape the inner awareness that our brief meeting had been arranged by Parent-God for a very special reason."

Lila Ruth's deportment was completely free of hostility and hurt, convincing Cooper that his vitriolic words of less than an hour ago had glanced off her harmlessly. The woman's invincible spirit was as other-worldly as the supernatural knowledge she possessed. Cooper considered that she might be more godlike than human. He was pleased that she was walking at his side instead of facing him, allowing limited eye-to-eye contact. There was a novel sense of power in this woman that he preferred to assess in occasional glances.

"When I returned to my quarters, I took up the matter with Pathfinder." Anticipating Cooper's unfamiliarity with the term, Lila Ruth inserted, "Pathfinder is the term we use for our source of inner, spiritual guidance. Fundamentalists would say 'Holy Spirit,' whom they claim takes up residence in them at conversion. Those with an Eastern mind-set would say 'spirit guide.' We are comfortable with 'Pathfinder,' although the term is not important. Initiates into the New Jesus Family are encouraged to open their minds and spirits to Pathfinder. It is the role of Pathfinder to prepare us for Reunion with Jesus-Brother. Pathfinder is as vital to our guidance as intellect, reasoning, conscience, intuition, and written law, sometimes superseding all of them."

Cooper nodded, wondering if Pathfinder would have warned him about the rotor shear above the Juneau airport that fearful February night in 1995 when his other systems all failed. He was quietly attracted to the prospect of supernatural knowledge and guidance, especially if it brought him the advantages Lila Ruth Atkinson enjoyed.

The woman continued, "I spent over an hour waiting on Pathfinder for insight—it's a meditative process I will tell you about later, if you're interested. But I got absolutely nothing, which frustrated me greatly considering the high level of energy I perceived in you. Yet while I meditated, there was something building inside me, like the swirling clouds of a gathering storm or like a cauldron heating up to a boil. I experienced periods of dizziness. I flashed hot and cold, breaking out in a feverish sweat one moment and chilling to an uncontrollable shiver the next. I have never experienced anything like it. I sensed that I was on the verge of something significant, and that somehow you were a part of it, but Pathfinder continued in silence while I was in near agony."

It occurred to Cooper that Lila Ruth may be trying to con him. For all he knew, she told the same story to every prospective initiate in an attempt to cajole or frighten him or her into the fold. He would have gone with that suspicion had it not been for the fact that she knew about Vanguard without anyone telling her—anyone human, that is. Instead of scoffing at her outwardly ludicrous story, he had to give her the benefit of the doubt until her knowledge of Vanguard could be explained away as a fluke or a fraud.

"Well after midnight, while sitting on the floor of my room by candlelight and absorbed in Pathfinder, he finally spoke." Lila Ruth reached into the side pocket of a small handbag hanging from her shoulder and pulled out a four-by-six inch card. She handed the card to Cooper. He stopped walking to examine it, and Lila Ruth stopped also. The card was inscribed in ink by Lila Ruth's hand:

VISION—VANGUARD
2002 0220 2002
REUNION

After allowing Cooper several seconds to study the card, Lila Ruth said, "What does it mean to you?"

Cooper pored over the characters again before he spoke. "Vision is what you say Jesus calls you. Vanguard was the word on the card I found in the blanket."

"Yes, and notice that both names start with V. Two V's, not one; that's significant. What about the rest?" There was a quiet snap of excitement in Lila Ruth's voice, like the release of static electricity.

"Reunion . . . hm . . . that's the term you people use to describe the Second Coming, the end of the world as we know it, doomsday. Correct?"

"Yes, in a manner of speaking," Lila Ruth said. "We prefer a broader view of the event than the fundamentalists offer. They see Jesus Christ returning for His bride, the fundamentalist church. We see our heavenly twin, Jesus-Brother, reuniting with his earthly sister, the reunion of the spirit world and the fleshly world to the perfection of both. All people on earth will be involved in Reunion at some level."

Cooper continued to study the card. "But these numbers . . . I don't know. It looks like some kind of code. A lot of twos . . . a lot of zeros . . ."

"Yes, as you know, twos are very important to us. And twos offset by zeros emphasize the significance of the twos."

A man and a woman, stripped down to shorts and tank tops, jogged by on the path. Cooper's eyes didn't leave the card. Lila Ruth waited.

When Cooper looked up for a clue, she said, "How would you interpret those numbers if you found them in an appointment calendar?"

Cooper returned his eyes to the numbers. "You mean, like a date and time?"

"In this case, a time, a date, and a year." The intensity in Lila Ruth's voice was growing.

After another five seconds of silence, Cooper began to talk through his guess. "If two-zero-zero-two is a time—as in military time—we're talking about 8:02 P.M. Zero-two-two-zero . . . hm . . . could stand for the second month and the twentieth day." He put the puzzle together in his mind before he spoke again. "If this is in an appointment calendar as time, date, and year, I'd have to say it's referring to February 20 in the year 2002 at twenty-oh-two hours—two minutes after eight in the evening."

"That's exactly how Pathfinder explained it to me," Lila Ruth said excitedly.

"Explained *what* to you?"

Lila Ruth's next words came in hushed, reverential awe: "Reunion, Captain, Reunion. Pathfinder has finally unveiled the precise moment of our Reunion with Jesus-Brother. That's what the message means. The twos and zeros tell the story. Reunion is less than four years away."

Another wave of skepticism swirled around Cooper and dug at the sand under his feet. History was replete with religious zealots who had predicted the end of the world and the return of Christ only to see the date come and go without incident, plunging the leaders and their followers into ignominy. Doomsday prophets from the first century to the end of the twentieth shared a perfect record; none of them were right. What chance did the virtually unknown leader of an obscure New Age order, Lila Ruth Atkinson, have to beat the odds?

Lila Ruth gained eye contact and answered his doubtful thoughts as if he had spoken them aloud. "Captain, you stepped off flight two-oh-two wondering why you or anyone had survived. Jesus-Brother called your new name, but you didn't recognize his voice. You held onto the card, but you interpreted your destiny to be centered in Rachel Prescott. That's why you married her when you didn't really want to."

The disclosure of another secret by Lila Ruth Atkinson ripped through Cooper like an electric shock. It was as if she saw the sand of confidence eroding beneath him and rushed in to fortify his stance with more hidden knowledge he could not deny.

"Your life with Rachel has been anything but what you expected. In fact, the two of you have regressed over the past two years instead of progressed in your relationship. You have often wished that you never married her. Your frustration has only served to sour your disposition toward your coworkers and to cement your friendship with alcohol. And the unsolved puzzle of Vanguard has only made things worse."

Cooper wanted to scream at Lila Ruth, *How can you know these things about me?* But she had already revealed to him the source of her privileged information, and he was defenseless against a spirit or a God who knew his secrets. So he calmed himself with a deep breath and returned to the issue of Vanguard. "What does all this have to do with me?" He pointed to the words and numbers on the card as he asked.

Lila Ruth nodded and resumed a slow walk along the path. Cooper followed her lead. "In case you didn't notice, the date of Reunion given to me by Pathfinder is seven years to the day from your near-tragedy in Juneau."

Cooper hadn't noticed. He breathed an unintelligible curse of surprise.

"You may also find it surprising that something very significant happened to *me* on February 20, 1995. I was in India at the time, studying under a very wise holy man. The mahatma did not seek to conform disciples to his view of life and deity. Instead he challenged us to press into the spirit realm for ourselves and discover God as we could know him. I did, and on February 20, 1995, I met Pathfinder. He introduced me to Jesus-Brother. Jesus-Brother called me Vision and commissioned me to form the New Jesus Family here in the states. It was the most significant day of my life, the day I found my destiny."

"You're saying that we were set on a similar course the same day?" Cooper probed.

"After meeting with Pathfinder last night, yes, I believe it. That's probably why our two Reunion names—Vision and Vanguard—were spoken together in his message."

"Why didn't this Pathfinder explain Vanguard to me when I first found the card? Why didn't he send someone to talk to me sooner?"

Lila Ruth shook her head as they walked. "That's something I don't know. Perhaps you weren't in a proper mental state to receive the message. Perhaps you were too self-dependent. The important thing is that you know *now* so we can begin preparations for Reunion together."

"We? Preparations?"

Lila Ruth laughed lightly, the first time Cooper had heard her do so. "I'm sorry, Captain. I'm getting ahead of my story. I must get back to Pathfinder's message."

Organizing her thoughts, Lila Ruth was quickly sobered again. "You see, I formed the New Jesus Family a little over three years ago under the guidance of Pathfinder and the mahatma without knowing exactly why I was doing it. Pathfinder directed me to return to the Pacific Northwest and teach the principles of Jesus-Brother, earth-sister, and the coming Reunion. I was told that my followers would be few but influential, strategically selected by Jesus-Brother for the Family's mission. When I asked what that mission was, Pathfinder answered, 'You will be told in due time.' I accepted his word.

"Last night was that time, Cooper. As I approached a trancelike state of meditation, Pathfinder identified you as Vanguard and burned our mission into my consciousness. It's so very simple and such a great honor for a select few."

Cooper's mind was a jumble of conflicting thoughts. Here he was, an intelligent, levelheaded man listening with interest to the prophetic visions of a modern-day mystic who looked like a sane and wealthy grandmother. Everything logical and pragmatic within him resisted and mocked the arcane ramblings of someone whose head was more in the unseen world than in the real one. Yet he could not discount a mounting fascination with an oblique spiritual persuasion and captivating esoterica in which his life was already intertwined. He guessed that if he chose to cling to the spiritual he would eventually have to let go of the pragmatic. The exchange didn't seem right to him, but the thirst to know as he was known to Lila Ruth Atkinson would not be denied.

"You called it 'our mission,' " Cooper said.

"Yes, Vision and Vanguard. As strange as it may seem, we have been called to this together."

"You assume that I will agree to participate in this mission."

Lila Ruth studied Cooper's face for several seconds as they walked. Cooper kept his eyes directed toward the path, the canal, or anywhere except toward the woman walking next to him. "No, Captain. I *know* that you will participate. You have been undone since February 20, 1995 because you survived and don't know why. Now that our Brother has opened your eyes, I can't conceive that you would walk away from your destiny and return to a life of uncertainty."

Once again, Lila Ruth had read his thoughts. The life he left back on the boat in order to walk and talk with her was a life he tolerated more than enjoyed. There had to be more, and Lila Ruth Atkinson appeared to be the doorway to everything Cooper lacked. If he had been called Vanguard by a higher power, he had to find out what it meant.

"All right, Ms. Atkinson," Cooper said after several thoughtful moments, "tell me about our mission."

Twenty-four

When the state of California legalized consensual homosexuality in 1975, Castro Street, southwest of downtown, began to replace Polk Street as the homosexual center of San Francisco. Polk Street was little more than a string of gay bars where homosexuals mingled under cover of darkness. The Castro is an entire district of several city blocks where homosexuals live, work, entertain, and trade. The Castro has its own churches, markets, restaurants, gyms, physicians, and an elected member of the city's board of supervisors. On Polk Street, the alternative lifestyle was regarded furtively; in the Castro, the bars, bookstores, and baths have clear plate-glass windows. Gay life and love is promoted openly, day and night. One Castro resident quipped to a straight acquaintance from out of town, "It's easy to tell who is gay in the Castro, because *everyone* is gay in the Castro!"

Tommy Eggers and Alec Kipman were among a minority of gay males in San Francisco who were ambivalent about the Castro. These men lived in districts like the Richmond or Pacific Heights and scorned what they called the "ghettoization of homosexuality." They disdained the rows of old, three- and four-story Victorian houses converted to apartments for single men and painted lavender, pink, or baby blue. They were not about to join the popular movement to become "Castro Street clones."

Yet the Castro held an undeniable allure for Tommy and other nonconformists of homosexual orientation. It wasn't as seedy or dangerous as the warehouse district around Folsom Street where gay leather bars and back-room SM salons awaited the seeker of dark pleasures. The Castro, with its coffee bars, flower shops, and ice cream parlors was a safe place to do business, meet people, and have a good time. So when he moved to San Francisco from Seattle, Tommy moved in with Alec in Pacific Heights but sought out a gay primary-care physician at the Bradford Medical Center in the 100 block of Castro Street.

All health care professionals in the Castro specialized in HIV/AIDS-related disorders, just as all attorneys in the district specialized in issues relating to the homosexual community: human rights, wrongful termination, relationship agreements and adoptions, medical malpractice, and wills/estates. Tommy's physician, Dr. Ronald Vanderhout, and his associates had to offer appointments from 6 A.M. to 9:30 P.M. from Monday through Saturday to keep up with demand for while-you-wait HIV screenings and diagnoses of the many AIDS-related maladies which result when the human immune system is invaded and eventually conquered by the human immuno-deficiency virus.

Despite its brightness and gaiety, the Castro is a district of death. Since the outbreak of AIDS and the discovery of HIV in their midst in the '80's, gay men largely refused to change their promiscuous sexual behavior in order to block the spread of the disease. Many of them opted for safer sex and most of them berated the government for not moving fast enough to develop a vaccine or find a cure. In the meantime, addicted to unnatural pleasures, gay men continued to entertain different partners as carelessly as they would try on outfits in a boutique. As a result, a large segment of the male population in the Castro was dying. In a highly transitory district within a big city where people come and go, the black-windowed van of the health department and the hearse were as common on the streets as the U-Haul truck and moving van.

In effect, each time a gay man coupled with a new partner in bed, in a public bath, or in a video store booth, he spun the cylinder of the revolver, put the barrel to his head, and pulled the trigger. Some submitted to regular HIV screenings to determine if they were still beating the odds at this titillating, morbid game of Russian roulette called indiscriminate sex. A few avoided the clinic until they were overcome by the dreaded symptoms of AIDS in flower: high fever, loss of energy, skin disorders, infection, lesions. Gay men introduced themselves to each other by name, interests, and classification — negative or positive. Those who had tested HIV-positive were dying. Those who had tested negative but continued to play the deadly game would soon be dying.

Tommy was as ambivalent about his sexual escapades as he was about the District. He knew well the dangers and feared the odds associated with each new partner. But the electric thrill of seeking, finding, and having someone new was like a demanding drug. Tommy had tried to sublimate his drives in ways that skewed the odds more in his favor, as if selecting a pistol for Russian roulette which had eleven empty chambers in the cylinder instead of five. Finding Alec, one of only a few partners Tommy had met who was interested in a continuing relationship, had kept him home more nights in the week. And yet fidelity among gay couples was almost as rare as sexual attraction to women. There were occasional temptations connected with Tommy's travel-oriented career that he was unable to completely resist. And he knew that Alec's appetite for excitement was as acute as his own.

So Tommy continued to seek more effective means of protection while hoping for the best and denying the possibility of the worst. A string of HIV-negative screenings over the last three years kept him coming back for more, like a roulette player letting everything ride on each spin of the wheel. Tommy was having too much fun winning to admit that his string of luck could run out at any time, causing him to forfeit everything.

"You are HIV-positive, Mr. Eggers. I'm sorry. We'll do our best to help you stay comfortable and pain-free." Dr. Vanderhout uttered the words without emotion. He had made the pronouncement so many times in his office that he was desensitized to the impact his words made on a patient hearing them for the first time. Ron Vanderhout had seen more of his patients die of AIDS in his fourteen years of practice than most physicians outside the Castro see die of all causes in a lifetime. He had little time to console Tommy Eggers because he still had an afternoon full of patients to see, most of them suffering from AIDS.

The doctor was a big, well-proportioned man in his early forties, about six-three and 230 pounds, Tommy had guessed during a previous visit. A handsome face beneath curly blonde hair was marred by a red birthmark blotched over one eye and down the cheek. Having delivered his diagnosis, Dr. Vanderhout rocked back in the chair in his small office to await the usual barrage of questions.

"I'm HIV-positive?" Tommy almost whispered.

"That's correct. We always run the test twice to make sure. The virus was unmistakably present on both slides."

"But I was negative last time," Tommy said as if his statement would negate the problem.

Dr. Vanderhout smiled, taking Tommy's comment for a mildly funny one-liner. Tommy had a reputation in the office for his humor. "You have tested negative *every* time since you starting coming in the office over three years ago. But a string of negative test results don't make you immune. You obviously got into some bad stuff since your last visit. You're infected, man."

Tommy wasn't buying the diagnosis. He knew it had to be a mistake. "But I feel fine, doctor. I'm not sick."

"You may not experience AIDS symptoms for months or years. But the virus is there."

"I read that pamphlet you gave me. I took all the precautions." He hadn't taken *all* the precautions every time, but he regarded his margin of safety to be higher than average.

"Then you must have also read the part that said none of the precautions are foolproof. They offer a degree of protection, not full protection." As he spoke, the doctor pulled another pamphlet from a drawer full of them and tossed it on the desktop in front of Tommy. "Speaking of pamphlets, here's one that describes what's ahead for you. It also has a list of resources available to HIV-positive patients in the city."

HIV-positive. Tommy handled the concept gingerly in his brain like it was a time bomb. How long had it been ticking? The deadly virus had obviously been introduced to his system within the last six months. *Perhaps Alec picked up the bug somewhere and gave it to me,* Tommy thought. *Or maybe I became infected on one of my trips and have already passed on the disease to Alec. He must be tested immediately.*

Tommy imagined the virus as a live grenade which had just landed at his feet. He wanted to pick it up and toss it away before it exploded, just like the soldiers did in those old war movies. But he knew that no one who was infected could get *un*infected. It didn't work that way. He wanted to find a switch he could flip or a wire he could cut to disarm the deadly device. He wished he could turn back the clock and undo some of his harmful behaviors. But he also aware that this bomb was tamper-proof. Every HIV-positive person he knew was either dead or slowly dying. No one knew how to stop its relentless march to destruction.

"The vaccine," Tommy said blankly, as if talking to the wall.

"Yes, a vaccine has been discovered, Mr. Eggers," said Dr. Vanderhout. "It's ironic that the announcement came last night. The vaccine may save millions upon millions of lives, but it can't help you now."

"They'll find a cure. Maybe the vaccine will lead them to a cure." Tommy seemed shell-shocked, punch drunk.

"I pray that they will," the doctor said, "for your sake and for thousands of others like you in the city. Until then, you just have to make the most of the time you have left."

"How much time?" Tommy had heard the uncertain estimates many times. He had even sat in this office with another friend as Dr. Vanderhout gave him the same bad news.

The doctor motioned toward the pamphlet, indicating that his answer summarized its contents. "The virus may lie dormant in the system for months or years before it attacks the immune system and makes it vulnerable to a number of AIDS-related problems," he recited. "When you start feeling sick, I'll prescribe whatever is available to slow down the process and make you feel better. When you can no longer care for yourself, I'll refer you to a hospice—unless you have someone to take care of you."

Tommy quickly assessed that he had no one to take care of him. His parents were out of the picture. He barely remembered his father, who left home when he was two and never came back. His mother, a loud, angry woman, had died of cancer eight years ago. Tommy's half-brother and two half-sisters, the products of his mother's first marriage and much older than he, had never accepted him as kin. Tommy didn't even know where they lived, nor would he try to contact them if he did. He suddenly wished he had caring parents like Marvin and Nora Dukes.

Alec Kipman had been a good friend and lover for the past three years, but Tommy doubted that Alec's commitment included end-stage emotional and physical comfort and care. For that matter, Alec may also be infected and unable to offer care when Tommy needed it. Alec may need assistance before Tommy did. It looked like Tommy would face the end alone.

Dr. Vanderhout stood and took two steps toward the office door, clearly indicating to Tommy that the appointment was over. There were at least eight men still in the waiting room, so Ron Vanderhout and his associates had little time for conversation, even after delivering such grave news. Tommy took the cue and followed the doctor out.

"I want to see you every three months. Kitty will set you up with your next appointment. Of course, if you get sick, just call and we'll get you in. Good luck, Mr. Eggers." Then Dr. Vanderhout lifted a chart from its holder on the wall and disappeared into another examination room.

Tommy sat in his white VW Beetle for several minutes. Castro Street teemed with activity as it did every Saturday morning, and the air was still heavy with the overcast so common to the city by the bay. But everything had changed in the space of forty minutes. Without warning or fanfare, he had moved from the category of the lucky to the unlucky, from among the living to among the dying. Tommy suddenly had much to think about. The questions came in hurried waves, leaving no time between them to contemplate answers.

How will I tell Alec, and how will he react? How can I convince him to ignore his phobia of the clinic and get tested? How will Alec handle the news if he also tests HIV-positive? How will I handle it if Alec is still HIV-negative?

How do I tell Northstar Airlines about my problem—or do I tell them at all? They have regulations against HIV-infected employees. Do I come clean with them or lay low until the next mandatory blood test? And when I quit or eventually get fired, how will I support myself? Tommy knew firsthand the horror stories of a number of men in the district whose financial foundation turned to sand beneath them when HIV was discovered. They were stripped of their jobs—and in some cases their medical insurance—and their personal resources quickly drained away, leaving them dependent on family, friends, and the government.

What do I tell my future partners? Am I justified in keeping my condition a secret, seeing that someone passed the virus on to me without my permission, and seeing that anyone I am with will likely get the disease anyway? Am I restricted to being with my own "kind," those classified as HIV-positive? Have I been forever banished from the land of the living and consigned to the company of the dying?

What will the end be like? Will I lose my mind before I lose my health? Will it be a painful death? Shall I prepare to end my life before the end comes?

Tommy rolled down the window and welcomed the cool breeze on his face and the invigorating fragrance of fog and salt water. The news had roughed him up emotionally and mentally, but he acknowledged with a flush of pride that he had not fallen to pieces. In fact, he felt very good physically. *There is plenty of time to sort through all the feelings and the questions,* he encouraged himself. *You're not dying tomorrow or the next day or next year. You'll make it into the new millennium easily, and someone will surely come up with a wonder drug before then. So there's no reason to complicate your life with a problem that's not really a problem yet.*

Having talked himself into a surprisingly perky attitude, he stepped out of the car and locked the door. Then he strolled spryly down Castro Street to Elephant Walk to treat himself to an expensive early lunch.

Twenty-five

Raul Barrigan awoke at 5:35 Sunday morning. He was greeted by the scene that was before him when his eyes closed at 11:30 and 1:10 and 2:23 and 3:04 and 4:34: the ceiling of his room. When he dropped his eyes he could see most of the television, which was mounted high on the wall and turned off now. The green numerals of a digital clock attached to the top of the TV glowed in the semidark. Raul was alone in the room.

Shifting his eyes left and right, Raul could see the metal rods connecting the steel band screwed into his skull to the vest strapped around his chest. The halo brace kept his head completely immobile. He had been lying flat on his back in the state-of-the-art air bed for over thirty hours. The air bed raised and lowered in staggered intervals hundreds of tiny support coils under the mattress pad, relieving the constant pressure on the skin which creates bed sores.

Raul's head pounded with the headache which had been with him since shortly after he crashed into the catcher's shin guard. Breathing was difficult with so many muscles in his torso not functioning. His eyes were tired and grainy, as if he hadn't slept at all. His mouth was dry, and his tongue tasted like a piece of meat gone bad. He was aware of the nasogastric tube protruding from his nostril and taped to his cheek, conducting vomit and bile from his stomach to a plastic bag clipped to the metal bed frame. He couldn't see it or feel it, but he knew that an IV tube was still attached to his arm, dripping nutrients and antibiotics into his bloodstream.

Has God healed me yet? It had been Raul's first thought every time he awoke. He had asked the question numerous times since Friday night, because he hadn't slept more than a couple of hours at a time. With each return to consciousness, a flash of hope urged him to test his paralysis to see if it had vanished while he slept. In those optimistic seconds he imagined himself lifting his arms, unscrewing the halo brace with his own hands, and throwing it aside to walk out of the hospital completely well.

Raul's brain commanded his right arm to rise from his side and bring his hand in front of his face to touch his nose with a finger. For the eleventh or twelfth time in a row, no hand appeared. He tried the left arm. No success. He bit his lip and tried both arms again. Nothing. He willed his knees to lift upward. Lying flat, he wouldn't be able to see them if they did move. But the fact that he heard no movement of bed sheets convinced him that his legs weren't working yet either.

By 10 A.M. yesterday, after a session with a group of doctors, Raul and his family knew exactly what they were dealing with in their prayers for healing: an explosion fracture of the fifth cervical vertebra near the base of the neck. The force of the collision at home plate had snapped the vertebra in five places, driving the fragments into the spinal cord. The true extent of damage to the spinal cord would not be known for some time. Some paralysis was temporary and some would likely be permanent, the doctors had said. Surgery was scheduled for Monday morning to remove the bone fragments—replacing them with bone grafts or stainless steel—and to stabilize the spine.

"The surgery won't be needed," Serena Barrigan had announced to the doctors with confidence. "God is going to mend that broken vertebra and damaged spinal cord with His wonder working power."

Raul believed it too with all his heart. He *had* to believe it without wavering. A lapse of faith at this critical point and he might not get his miracle. *God is testing me*, he had told himself a hundred times since arriving at the hospital. *I'm going to play pro ball—Jesus promised it to me. I'm going to buy Dad and Mom a new house so they can retire and enjoy life. I'm going to be an evangelist to major league baseball. No broken neck is going to cancel out God's plan for me. And the miracle of my healing is going to be a great witness of God's power.*

Today would be the day, Raul realized with a twinge of excitement. With surgery scheduled for 7 A.M. tomorrow, something special would happen to him in the next twenty-four hours. He imagined the surgery prep nurse walking into his room at 5:30 tomorrow to find him sitting in the chair beside his bed reading his Bible. She would find all the tubes removed from his body and the halo vest lying empty on the bed. Even the four screw holes in his skull would be gone. Raul had a vivid mental picture of the nurse screaming at the sight and running out of the room to find the doctor.

Sometime today God is going to pay me a special visit, Raul considered expectantly. *What better day for a miracle than Sunday.*

Someone entered the room quietly, but Raul heard the soft rustle of clothing and the squeak of rubber soles on linoleum. Expecting that a nurse had slipped in to check his vitals or replace an IV bag, Raul was surprised when an old man in a sport jacket and tie appeared over him on the left side of the bed. The man had a friendly, age-lined face with gold-rimmed glasses and the tan of an outdoorsman. His white hair, what little still grew on the sides of his head, was buzzed down to a stubble. Raul guessed that he must be another doctor come to poke him and ask him what he could feel.

"Mr. Barrigan, you're awake," the man said with a soft voice and pleasant smile.

"Yeah, most of the time, it seems like," Raul said weakly.

"I'm Lowell Banks, one of the volunteer chaplains at Bergan Mercy." Raul felt dull pressure and movement on his left side. He realized that the chaplain had gripped his left hand, a greeting he wanted to reciprocate but could not.

"Thanks for coming." It was an expression of gratitude he had used many times since Friday night. "You're on duty kind of early, aren't you?"

The chaplain flashed a winsome smile. "Yes, for a couple of reasons. I'm the pastor of a church here in Omaha, so the rest of my morning is pretty busy. And I figured that if I was going to talk to you today I'd better get here early before the stream of visitors began. I came by a couple of times yesterday, but there were people lined up in the hall to visit you. You have quite a following."

Raul smiled. All things considered, yesterday had been a very heartening day. Except for meal breaks, his parents and Samantha had spent the entire day and evening in the room with him. Teddy, his oldest brother, had arrived from Tucson. Raul's coaches and most of his teammates dropped by to offer personal words of encouragement and to say good-bye. The team's flight left for Phoenix at 5:35 P.M.

A few players had brought chairs into Raul's room to watch the CWS championship game on TV at noon. The national anthem was preceded by a minute of silent prayer offered for Raul Barrigan's recovery. The gesture brought tears to Raul's eyes. Then the Texas Longhorns blew away the Ohio State Buckeyes 11–2 to win the 1998 College World Series.

Perpetually exhausted from his ordeal and fitful sleep, Raul dozed through parts of the game. But everyone made sure he was awake when the all-tournament team was announced at the end of the game. Raul was selected as all-tournament center fielder and shared the most outstanding player award with Dougie Martinez of Texas. The presentation and a standing ovation from a jam-packed Rosenblatt Stadium had again moved Raul to tears.

After all Raul's teammates had left for the airport, two other visitors arrived dressed in expensive business suits. Willie Sawyer was a scout for the San Francisco Giants. Sawyer had followed Raul's baseball career through high school and three years of college. He had urged the Giants to make Raul Barrigan a top draft pick this year. Webb Mickleson was the Giants' director of player personnel, the man who had come to Omaha to offer Raul a suitcase full of money to leave ASU early and sign with the Giants.

Their visit had been brief but cordial. Both expressed regret over Raul's tragic accident and wished him a speedy recovery. They reminded him of the courage of former Giant, Dave Dravecky, who lost his arm and shoulder to cancer. They presented Raul with a black-and-orange Giants' warmup jacket, a cap, and a ball signed by several players. They gave the Barrigan family several tickets to home games at Candlestick Park in San Francisco. Then they said good-bye and left. Not one word was uttered about a contract. Raul knew they would be back as soon as they saw his interview on ESPN, the interview he would do with Marta Friesen as soon as God healed his injured neck.

Dougie Martinez had also stopped in briefly to pose for a picture with Raul and their tournament trophies. A muscular player known for his tough-guy attitude, Dougie hadn't wanted to come to the hospital. He was visibly shaken at the sight of the fallen ballplayer imprisoned in the hideous halo vest and taped to so many tubes. But he leaned in close and managed a smile for the picture before leaving on the verge of tears.

Some ASU administrators and CWS officials had visited yesterday. Media people had tried to get in, but they were kindly turned away— except for Marta Friesen, who came without a recorder or a camera just to be a friend. Other people had traipsed in and out of the room, people Raul didn't recognize or remember. The stream of well-wishers was frequently interrupted by doctors and nurses coming to poke him, check his vitals, ask him what he could feel and couldn't feel, or clean him. It was no surprise to Raul that the mild-mannered minister hovering over him now had not been able to get in.

"Yes, I've been blessed with a great family and super friends," Raul said.

After an awkward silence that sometimes accompanies first-time meetings, the chaplain said, "I watched you play this week, Raul. My wife and I get tickets for the whole tournament every year. It's a great event for Omaha."

"It was a thrill to be in the series," Raul said.

"You were having a great tournament. I'm sorry it ended so suddenly for you."

"Thank you, but this is just a minor setback." Raul used his eyes to point to the apparatus attached to him.

"Your enthusiasm and skill on the field was so much fun to watch. Brings back good memories for an old ballplayer."

"You played ball?" Raul asked with obvious interest.

Chaplain Banks minimized the experience with a shrug. "Just a couple of years in the minors. Then the Korean War flared up, and I went into the army."

"Who did you play for?"

"The Pirates. I was on their triple A team in L.A., the Hollywood Stars." Chaplain Banks smiled at the memory. "We played in an old wooden stadium called Gilmore Field. The place is a parking lot next to CBS now, I think."

"You didn't go back into baseball after the war?"

The chaplain shook his head wistfully. "No, my life kind of turned around while I was in Korea, and God called me into the ministry."

Raul thought about the comment. "Yeah, we all have to do what God calls us to do, don't we." His thoughts were on his own call: to play major league baseball for Jesus.

"You're a Christian, I understand," the chaplain said.

"Yes, sir," Raul answered quickly, forcing a smile. "I've been walking with Jesus since I was just a boy."

The chaplain nodded approvingly. "That's wonderful, son, because it's very difficult to face what you're facing now without the Lord."

"What I'm facing? You mean being paralyzed? Well, I'm not going to be like this for long, pastor. Jesus promised to heal me. I'm going to play pro ball, maybe even this year. You can bet on it."

Lowell Banks studied the young man's face. The spark of confidence shining from his eyes mocked the steel band screwed to his skull and the rods attaching the band to the vest.

"You have a very serious injury, Raul," the chaplain said soberly. "The healing process may take months or years. And you may not regain full use of your limbs."

Raul's eyes widened. "I expect the doctors to say stuff like that, but I didn't expect somebody like you to talk that way." There was a subtle note of challenge in Raul's response.

"I'm *not* a doctor, son, but I've been a chaplain in this hospital since before you were born. I've visited scores of athletic young men and women on this floor who broke their necks and ended up wearing the steel headgear you're wearing now. In time they all got much better. Some of them even learned to walk again. But none of them returned to full strength and mobility. Be thankful for what God gives you, but be ready to deal with some limitations from your injury."

"Don't you believe in healing, chaplain?" Raul contested.

"Yes, I believe in healing," Chaplain Banks assured.

"I mean *instant* healing. *Bam*, I crash into the catcher's leg and break my neck. Two days later, *bam*, Jesus puts it back together again and I walk out of here good as new."

"Yes, Raul, I believe in instant healing." The chaplain's tone was non-contentious. "It's in the Bible. And I hope God does a miracle for you. But He obviously doesn't heal everyone instantly. Sometimes He heals gradually. Sometimes He works through medical technology. Sometimes He allows us to suffer for a higher purpose known only to Him."

"According to the Bible, you get what you believe," Raul said with conviction. "The people who don't get healed instantly just failed to believe God for instant healing. You just said you *hope* God does a miracle for me. Hoping for a miracle isn't faith. Hoping doesn't give God anything to work with. I will get my healing because that's what I'm believing for."

Robert Kragenbrink, a nurse in his late thirties wearing a pale-green lab coat, hurried into the room in the middle of Raul's mild reproof. He stood at the foot of the bed as Raul finished, tacitly announcing that he had work to do and that the chaplain would have to go.

Aware of the nurse's presence, Chaplain Banks kept his eyes on Raul and smiled broadly. "That's the same fire I saw in you on the baseball diamond last week, Raul. You have a heart sold out to God. He can use a man of faith like you." Then he offered a brief prayer for Raul's recovery, excused himself, and left.

Nurse Kragenbrink said good morning and set about his tasks. "You two ballplayers comparing notes?" Robert said as he adjusted the blood pressure cuff on Raul's flaccid bicep. During Raul's short stay, the patient and the morning nurse had already hit it off well, mainly because Robert Kragenbrink was a Christian and a big baseball fan.

"Yeah, but the chaplain and I don't exactly see eye to eye."

"You like the designated hitter and he doesn't? Aluminum bats versus wooden bats?"

Raul smiled at the nurse's humor. Then he was serious again. "For a chaplain and a pastor, the man doesn't have much faith in God's healing power. I told him that God is going to heal me, that I'm still going to play pro ball, and he just blew me off. He has no idea where I'm coming from."

Robert was silent as he inflated the cuff and took his readings. As he unfastened the cuff, he said, "You don't know much about Lowell Banks, do you?"

Raul kept his eyes on Robert when the nurse was within his field of vision. "I just met him ten minutes ago."

"Have you ever heard of Bill Mazeroski?"

"Of course. Pirates' second-baseman in the '50s and early '60s. Hall of Famer."

Robert nodded. "Well, Banks and Mazeroski came up through the Pirates' organization together. In the minors, Lowell played short and Maz played second. At Hollywood, Maz was good, but Banks was even better—quicker, more power. They were great friends and fierce competitors. They would have been Pittsburgh's all-star middle infield for at least a decade."

"Then Banks got drafted."

"Right. He planned to do two years and come back to the Pirates."

"I can't believe he didn't go back to baseball after his hitch."

Robert put himself in his patient's view. "He couldn't go back, Raul. A North Korean mortar blew away his left leg."

Raul was stunned to silence. Robert continued his ministrations around the bed.

Finally Raul said, "But he was walking today. He seemed normal."

"Prosthesis," Robert informed. "Forty-five years with a fake leg and you get pretty good at it."

After another silent minute, Robert continued. "To hear Lowell tell it, he was hell-bent to play baseball. Nothing was going to stand in his way of making it to the majors and to the Hall of Fame with his friend

Bill Mazeroski. A mortar attack and three weeks in a Tokyo hospital changed his life. He says that the last forty-five years serving God on one leg have been more exciting and rewarding than the first twenty years doing his own thing on two legs."

Raul ruminated on Robert's words. Then he said, "So you don't think I'm going to be healed either."

Robert chose his words carefully. "What I think isn't important. It's what God thinks and does that counts. I just ask Him to do what's best for my patients."

Raul searched the uninspiring, plain ceiling, wishing he could turn his head and inspect the rest of the room. "Then just wait till tomorrow morning," he said more to himself than to Robert. "Your prayer is about to be answered in a big way."

Twenty-six

Myrna Valentine struggled out of bed at 6:30 Monday morning with great difficulty. She was exhausted and on the verge of tears, as she had been for the entire weekend. It had been a miserable seventy-two hours of inner turmoil, sleeplessness, and self-doubt. Images of the man she had loved and lost and then embittered through blackmail taunted her when she tried to sleep. And when Guy Rossovich's angry face wasn't confronting her in the darkness, it was the vision of a formless, nameless fetus that kept her awake and churning with trepidation.

Since every night was like living through a scary movie, Myrna's weekend had been a waste. After depositing the $10,000 in her savings account at the bank in Manhattan Beach, she had picked up some brochures from her friend Mattie describing a beach house on Kauai which was available next week. But Myrna spent most of Friday and Saturday night lying awake second-guessing her decision to tax Guy exorbitantly for his part in her problem and fending off doubts about going through with the abortion. So the brochures remained on the coffee table untouched.

Nor had Myrna been the least bit interested in going out to spend some of the money now swelling her bank account. Instead, she had squandered Saturday and Sunday trying to work up the energy to do laundry and clean the apartment, chores she never enjoyed but didn't think she would even want to attempt for a few days after the proce-dure. She went out only once on Saturday afternoon. The abortion clinic required her to come in so the doctor could insert a softening agent into the cervix, preparing it to receive the instrument which would vacuum the fetal tissue from the uterine cavity.

In her fatigued and stressed-out state, Myrna found plenty of excuses to flake out on the couch for small naps while she was home. By Sunday night she had accomplished little more than sorting whites from darks on the utility room floor and running a feather duster halfheartedly over her wood furniture.

Myrna made it from the bed to the bathroom just in time to retch over the sink. She brought up only a little bile because she had eaten practically nothing since Friday afternoon. She hated the nausea that had kept her weak and shaky every morning for the last two weeks. The fact that this would be the last morning of her sickness was little comfort to her now. She felt awful in every way, and the woman staring back at her from the mirror looked a fright. The pink satin nightgown adorning Myrna's shapely body looked anything but sexy next to her face, which was pale and puffy and haggard. If her agent saw her now, Myrna thought, he would probably tear up her contract.

After brushing her teeth and rinsing her mouth thoroughly, Myrna sought comfort in the hot shower. Her appointment at the clinic was not until 10 A.M., so she took her time washing, shaving her legs, and shampooing. Then she let the pulsating jets pummel her back until the hot water turned tepid. When she finally stepped out of the shower, she felt better, resolved to put the lost weekend behind her. She slipped into dressy jeans and a sleeveless silk blouse and applied her makeup and fixed her hair with professional skill. She was not about to walk into the clinic looking like the lost soul she had seen in the mirror when she got up, even though she still *felt* like a lost soul after the events of the last five days.

Myrna was ready to go by 8:30, which wasn't good because she had over an hour to kill. The friend who was taking her to the clinic wouldn't arrive until 9:40. The clinic prohibited patients from driving after the procedure, so Myrna had asked Lindsey Burgmeier, a twenty-nine-year-old model whom she had sworn to secrecy, to take her to the clinic and bring her home. Lindsey was a veteran of two abortions herself and quickly agreed to provide transportation and remain discreet.

Still feeling fatigued, Myrna would not let herself sit down and do nothing, because that's when tormenting doubts seemed to roll in like a storm. So she busied herself by loading white clothes into the washer and starting the cycle. She spent about twenty minutes reorganizing the address and telephone number file on her kitchen computer, a job she had put off for months. She moved the clothes from the washer to the dryer and put in a load of darks. Then she electronically scanned and filed in the computer half a dozen recipes she had clipped from the newspaper. Seeing the recipes reminded her of how little she had eaten over the weekend and how disinterested she was in food right now. She had been required to fast from midnight last night to prepare her system for intravenous sedation. Myrna hadn't even been tempted to eat.

The fifteen-minute ride to the clinic with a quiet friend was the kind of inactivity Myrna didn't need. With nothing to do but sit, she was the captive of her thoughts, which challenged her mercilessly on what she was about to do. In nearly eight years of casual sexual activity, she had quietly affirmed to herself that, should she get pregnant, she would have no qualms about immediately terminating the pregnancy through an abortion. A few of Myrna's friends, including Lindsey Burgmeier, had had abortions, and they got through the procedure emotionally unscathed—at least they seemed to. Myrna wondered why she had been targeted for such inner unrest—and she wasn't even in the stirrups yet.

Ever since leaving Guy Rossovich's office on Friday morning, having told him what she was going to do and squeezing $10,000 from him to do it, Myrna had felt increasingly troubled about the abortion. She couldn't escape the reality that she was going into the clinic for a procedure that many people considered immoral, murderous. For millions of women around the world, the news of pregnancy was a source of great joy. It meant that everything was right, everything was functioning, new life had begun. But Myrna's single friends had programmed her to regard unwanted pregnancy as a tragedy, a mistake, a great wrong that needed to be made right. Myrna had found it difficult to maintain that attitude about her pregnancy.

Myrna thought about the infertile couples she knew who would give everything they owned to be in her condition. Indeed, some of them had spent multiplied thousands of dollars trying to solve the mysteries of infertility and/or pursuing adoption. And here she was paying good money to get rid of what others would cherish as a priceless treasure. It was as if she was going into the clinic to have a good limb surgically removed. How many amputees would call her a mad woman for forfeiting what they yearned in vain to regain. She squirmed in her seat trying to escape the thought.

What about giving the child up for adoption? Myrna had considered the idea only hypothetically before becoming pregnant and guessed that she wouldn't be able to do it. Now, suddenly and unexpectedly pregnant, she was certain she couldn't do it. She imagined that once she saw the baby and accepted it as her own flesh, she could never part with it. Giving away her own child would be like cutting off a limb and—

Myrna shifted uncomfortably at the dark inconsistency she had just uncovered in her logic. She was preparing to "cut off a limb" right now, something she felt she had to do to keep her career intact, something single women are expected to do. But in eight months, no way would she be able to cut off this limb. Today she didn't have room in her life for a baby. But if the "fetal tissue" came to term, she knew she couldn't live without it. It was the same "mistake" or "consequence" from her actions. It was the same infant boy which had haunted her thoughts for days. The two stages—fetal tissue and fully developed newborn—were merely separated by time. How could she do away with one and not the other? She had no answer.

"Are you all right with this, Myrna?" Lindsey said as they sat at a traffic light. Lindsey was tall and slender like Myrna but with silky blonde hair and electric blue eyes.

Myrna was in a fog. "What?"

Lindsey pointed to Myrna's hands. "You're spinning your rings around so hard the gold is going to melt. Are you going to be OK?"

Myrna caught her nervous habit and separated her hands like they were two quarreling children. "Yeah, I'm OK," she answered unconvincingly. "I just don't like doctors."

"It'll be over before you know it," Lindsey consoled. "As soon as the drugs wear off, you'll feel fine. You can go back to work tomorrow if you really want to, but I'd take a couple days off if I were you."

Myrna nodded. She had already decided not to tell Lindsey about her planned trip to Kauai. She didn't want to tempt her to say, "I'll go with you." Myrna didn't want anyone to know where she was going. She intended to disappear alone and drown her anxieties and hurts in the Hawaiian sun, sand, and surf. Maybe she could return with a clear conscience, enthused about spending more of Guy Rossovich's money.

After several more silent minutes, Myrna said, "Do you have any regrets?"

"About *my* abortions?" Lindsey retorted.

"Yes."

"Are you kidding? Trade my career, my freedom, and my love life for a snotty-faced kid hanging on my skirt? Not a chance."

"Your abortions didn't . . . bother you?" Myrna probed.

"Well, I didn't enjoy them, if that's what you mean. Having a doctor stick a high-powered vacuum cleaner tube inside me and switching it on—no, it wasn't fun. But when you consider the alternatives, a few hours of discomfort was worth it."

Myrna approached the next question carefully. "Didn't you ever wonder about the kid, what it would have looked like?"

"Don't do that to yourself, Myrna," Lindsey scolded. "Don't listen to all the junk those church nuts are spreading around. That is *not* a kid in there; it's a growth that must be taken out. It's just like a cancer. If you leave it untreated it will ruin your life."

"But all weekend I've been seeing this newborn baby in my mind, and I don't know if I—"

"Give it up, Myrna, please," Lindsey ordered sternly. "I don't want to hear it, and you don't need to think about it. Just go in there and do the job and get on with your life."

Myrna agreed with Lindsey that a child would be a terrible and permanent interruption in her life, something she didn't want and didn't need. But there was a hint of grief in Lindsey's tone. Myrna wasn't convinced that her friend was as detached from her two abortions—and her two missing children—as she wanted Myrna to believe.

Lindsey dropped Myrna at the front door of the clinic. Before Lindsey had parked and walked into the waiting area, Myrna had signed in and was ushered to an examination room where she was told to undress and put on the standard, cotton gown that never seemed to cover enough. Sitting on the gurney alone in the small room, Myrna steeled herself to ignore her misgivings and get past the next thirty minutes. Then it would be over. Regrets, if indeed she had them, would be irrelevant. The deed would be done and she would be free.

In just a few minutes, the nurse returned to start the IV. After the saline solution was initiated, a moderate dose of Versed would be added to the drip, enough to make the patient numb to the procedure and wipe it from her memory.

The nurse was a strong-looking Latino woman in her early forties. Her name badge read LENA MONTOYA. She said nothing and worked quickly, lying Myrna down on the gurney, covering her with a blanket, and preparing the instruments for venipuncture. Nurse Montoya seemed impersonal to Myrna—no small talk, not even a hello, as if she considered her patient already zoned out on Versed.

Then it hit her. *Of course,* she thought, *this isn't supposed to be a reach-out-and-touch-someone experience. This is a get-in, get-it-over-with, and get-out experience, the less interaction and the less emotional attachment the better.* It reminded her of the day she took her aging and cancer-ridden basset hound to the animal shelter to be put to sleep. The attendants weren't there to win friends and chat about the weather. Just sign the papers, pay the fee, hand the dog over, and escape to your car to cry. Nothing made it easier, so nobody tried to. That's the way Myrna felt she was being treated right now.

It occurred to Myrna that she had come to the clinic for the same reason she had taken Waldo to the pound: to get rid of a bother. Sad-eyed, lovable Waldo had become incontinent and cranky, and the vet said he was probably in pain. He suggested drugs to block the pain, but assured Myrna that Waldo would need to be coddled and cleaned up after until he finally died. Despite her sorrow at losing an old friend, Myrna opted to put the dog out of his misery and save herself the hassle of dealing with him any longer.

Another bother had brought Myrna to the abortion clinic today. But the dissimilarities between the two events quickly began to outnumber the similarities in her mind. This bother was not old and diseased and dying but new and fresh with life. Myrna wasn't here to stamp out a near-dead fire but to snuff out a spark of promise. She wasn't putting an old dog out of its misery, she was about to take a human life. Everything in her being screamed out, *No! This is not right! Dying dogs may be laid to rest, but I have a person inside me, and he must live!*

Nurse Montoya picked up Myrna's right hand to look for a vein. Myrna jerked it from her grasp. "I ... I ... I'm right-handed," she stammered, suddenly frantic about what to do. The stone-faced nurse quickly moved around to the other side, picked up Myrna's left arm, and began slapping the back of her hand to raise a vein. Then she swabbed the skin with antiseptic solution and touched the needle to the skin.

"Wait!" Myrna almost shouted, pulling her hand out of the nurse's grasp again. Then she swung her legs over the side of the gurney and sat up. "I've changed my mind. I'm getting out of here." Nurse Montoya hopped back at the sudden movement. "Go tell the doctor I'm not staying."

"Are you sure?" the nurse pressed, surprising Myrna with a tone of genuine compassion.

Myrna did not hesitate. "Yes, I'm sure. I don't want an abortion."

Nurse Montoya nodded and hurried out the door, closing it behind her.

Myrna slid off the gurney, untied the chintzy gown, and let it fall to the floor. In less than two minutes she was dressed and heading toward the lobby, strapping on her watch as she walked. No one stopped her. No one questioned her. She guessed that she wasn't the first woman to change her mind in an abortion clinic.

Lindsey Burgmeier leaped up from her chair and dropped her magazine as Myrna entered the waiting room. "What's wrong!" Two other people in the waiting room snapped up their heads at the commotion.

Myrna grabbed her by the elbow and swept her out the door. "Nothing's wrong, not any more," she said. "Just take me home."

Before they reached the car, Myrna was crying. She sobbed all the way home, unable to explain the outburst to her puzzled friend. Nor did Myrna completely understand herself what had prompted such a dramatic release. All she knew was that she had done something very right, perhaps the most right thing she had ever done in her life.

Two days later Myrna drove back to the Gedney-Harcourt Building in Century City. She parked her Trooper in a loading zone half a block away and hurried into the building with a sealed bubble-pack envelope in her hands. She was dressed in a black, oversized, CBS News T-shirt—given to her by a friend—baggy shorts, and sandals. Her dark hair was wound into a knot and secured with a couple of colorful pins. Her wire-rimmed sunglasses came off as soon as she passed through the glass doors.

Sean Reilly was on duty at the reception desk when Myrna stepped off the elevator at the eighth floor. He blinked hard and smirked at the visitor's casual attire.

Myrna dropped her package on a pile of labels Reilly was organizing in between calls and visitors. The envelope was clearly marked with large letters: GUY ROSSOVICH−PERSONAL. "Take this envelope back to Mr. Rossovich right away, Reilly," she said, sounding like the queen of the eighth floor. "And don't lose it. Your job may depend on it." She was back on the elevator before he could reply.

Descending to the ground floor, Myrna imagined Guy opening the package and finding another sealed envelope. It was also marked PERSONAL. If Francie, Guy's secretary, happened to ignore the warning on the first envelope, Myrna hoped the second would get her attention and prompt her to pass it along unopened. If she didn't, Francie would get an eyeful that Guy may have difficulty explaining.

Guy would find $10,000 in cash and a note which simply read, "Everything turned out fine. Didn't need the money. Thanks anyway. Love always. Myrna." She guessed that he would likely be puzzled over the vague message, "Everything turned out fine," wondering if it referred to the abortion, a miscarriage, or a false alarm. He would likely be shocked to see his money again after Myrna's heartless, hard-nosed ultimatum in conference room C. And the sentimental farewell−"Love always"−would probably make him shake his head and mutter in disgust. In all, Myrna hoped her little note kept him guessing for a long time. And when Guy realized that his old flame wasn't going to expose his sin and wreck his marriage or career, she hoped he would remember her fondly.

Myrna was back in the Trooper less than three minutes after leaving it. The cargo area behind the front seats was stacked to the ceiling with suitcases, small pieces of furniture, lamps, and boxes of dishes, linens, knick-knacks, books, and mementos. On the floor in the front seat was a picnic cooler stocked with fruit, sandwiches, cartons of yogurt, and bottled fruit drinks. On the seat was a road atlas folded open to a map of the western U.S. A colored marking pen had traced the route from Los Angeles north to Portland, Oregon, then west to where the Columbia River meets the Pacific Ocean. A hand-drawn star marked the small community at the northwest corner of the state: Astoria.

With her sunglasses in place, Myrna headed out Sunset Blvd. to I-405 and turned north. Guy's office had been her last stop. The Trooper was full of gas, and in two days she would pull into the driveway of her parents' home high on the hill overlooking the Columbia. Mark and Thuy would be shocked−because she didn't tell them she was coming−and pleased. When Myrna explained that she had quit her job to be with them in Oregon for a while, they would be stunned. And when she revealed why, that her parents were going to be grandparents, they would engulf her in their arms and immediately understand.

When Myrna transitioned to Interstate Five and left Los Angeles County heading north, she doubted that she would return very soon. Her breakup with Guy had colored sunny Southern California a dismal gray. The competition and pressure in her industry was too intense in the big city. She knew she could easily find something to do in Portland or Seattle. And besides, her son would need the stability of growing up near his grandparents.

Myrna would return to L.A. someday, she knew, and look up Guy Rossovich. It probably wouldn't be a pleasant reunion for him. Perhaps then he would wish that she had kept the $10,000 and stayed away. But Myrna knew that whether Guy liked it or not, her little boy would eventually have to meet his father.

Part Three
NOVEMBER 2001

Twenty-seven

Raul Barrigan hurried quickly up the ramp toward the main entrance to Parker Center, the downtown headquarters of the Los Angeles Police Department. It was unseasonably cold and inclement in Southern California for a Thanksgiving weekend. The hills bordering the L.A. basin were dusted with snow—a rarity even in the dead of winter. A relentless rain and cold wind had left many Angelenos feeling depressed and less than thankful on Thanksgiving, a day which is often clear and balmy. But today, Friday, they had rebounded in force. It was still cold and rainy, but the locals had clogged the southland's freeways and malls to kick off the busiest shopping day of the year.

Having lived in sunny, dry Tucson and Phoenix all of his twenty-four years, Raul didn't own an overcoat. A lightweight, water-repellent jacket was all he needed to survive the infrequent desert rainstorms. Today the jacket and an old felt Stetson—worn for shade in Arizona, not rain protection—kept his upper body dry on the hasty journey from a distant parking space on the street to the shelter of the building. And the soft-sided leather briefcase resting on his lap shielded his legs from the rain. But he kept his arms pumping steadily on the wheels to keep moving fast and stay warm.

An older man in a long London Fog raincoat reached the top of the stairs just as Raul reached the top of the ramp. He opened the door and held it as Raul rolled his lightweight graphite Quickie through. "Thank you, sir," Raul said with sincerity. He appreciated strangers who took time to assist him. They were a welcome change from so many who ignored him as if he was invisible or purposely avoided him as if he was diseased and contagious. Raul could have made it through the door by himself; he had done it in his wheelchair many times. And he preferred to do for himself whenever he could. He didn't think he would ever get over the strong drive to be self-sufficient; he certainly hoped he wouldn't. But he had learned to accept gestures of helpfulness even when he wasn't completely helpless. And he had disciplined himself to ask for help when he needed it in spite of a stubborn reluctance to do so.

Raul removed his hat and dropped it on top of his briefcase as he surveyed the lobby. His wavy, jet-black hair was longer than it had been during his college days, and his face had filled out some, making him look older than his years. His shoulders and arms, which had atrophied terribly during his first year of rehabilitation, were again firm and strong due to rigorous upper body conditioning and wheelchair activity. Raul had declined the latest in motorized chairs in favor of one he could push himself, despite the fact that he had not regained full use of his hands. Even though his extensive medical file identified him as a quadriplegic, Raul had determined not to function like one as much as possible.

Raul checked his watch: 3:25 P.M. He chastised himself for being nearly a half hour late for his appointment. The traffic in the city and the hassle of finding a parking place in the rain were more than he bargained for. He rolled up behind a small crowd at the information counter staffed by three officers—two men and a woman—in smartly pressed long-sleeved navy-blue uniforms emblazoned with the classic LAPD shield. Raul thought all three of them looked like they could be movie stars playing cop roles. They seemed to be chosen for this PR position in the department's showcase precinct because of their Hollywood good looks.

Raul noted the names on their badges. Officer L. Buckner, the woman, was a sun-bleached blonde whose Malibu Beach figure was still evident despite the masculine shirt, tie, and slacks. Her long golden hair was swept back, rolled, and pinned for regulation appearance, which in her case seemed to Raul like a bad rule. She was dealing with someone on the phone and giving directions to visitors simultaneously.

Officer C. Ping, in his late twenties, had the shoulders and chest of an Olympic gymnast and the demeanor of a saint as he handled the complaints of an irate Iranian family. Their Central District market had been robbed Thanksgiving Day by two teenage boys with knives. They were demanding that the police department find the boys *today* and replace the money they stole. The Chinese-American officer was totally unruffled by their threats. Raul admired his restraint.

Their middle-aged superior, Sergeant B. Cobb, was inputting an assault report given by what looked to be a homeless woman. The sergeant was a Bill Cosby look-alike, except that his mature, innocent, and approachable face was mounted on a hard-body frame that could have belonged to Wesley Snipes.

Raul maneuvered into line behind two people getting directions from Officer Buckner. When they headed off for the departments they were seeking, he moved half a roll closer to the desk. Buckner was still on the phone. From the sound of it, Raul guessed that she was talking with a coworker somewhere in the building about forms she needed to restock the counter. Raul sympathized with the lack of enthusiasm in her voice over the tedium of paperwork.

Buckner made eye contact. "May I help you?" she said while holding the phone to one ear.

"I have an appointment with this officer at 3," he said as he pulled an LAPD business card from the side pocket of his case and reached it up to the counter.

Buckner flashed a subtle you're-a-little-late look, then hunched up one shoulder to cradle the phone and free up both hands. She laid the card on the counter beside the computer and entered the name printed on it without missing a beat on the phone conversation. "No, the C7140s are the blue ones. I have enough blue ones up here to wallpaper city hall . . . Right, I need C7160s, the green ones, double sided . . . Right."

Buckner glanced down at Raul again and said, "ID please."

Raul withdrew his leather wallet, flipped it open, and reached it up to the counter. In the clear plastic window was a photo holocard identifying Raul Barrigan as an officer with the Phoenix Police Department. Opposite the card was a shiny shield little more than a year old.

Buckner scanned the card with a wand from the computer. "I also need a pad of C7033s . . . Yeah, the yellow ones . . . No, those are 43s . . . Are you carrying today?"

Raul was caught up in the sheer busyness of the place and, assuming that Officer Buckner was still talking report forms, hadn't noticed the question directed at him.

"Officer Barrigan," Buckner said a little louder, holding the phone away from her head and leaning slightly toward him. When Raul gave her his attention, she lowered her voice again to keep the question private. "Are you carrying a weapon today?"

Raul's first reaction was to say no. He had been on the force almost a year, but he still found the idea of carrying a toylike but lethal polymer handgun wherever he went a little foreign. Ignoring his first reaction, Raul answered discreetly, "Yes, a Rourk nine millimeter." Through his jacket, he touched the place under his left arm where the gun was holstered at the end of a nylon shoulder strap. Raul preferred the belt holster used by most other plainclothes officers. But it was already difficult for his disabled hands to draw the weapon, get a good grip on it, and flip off the safety without having to dig it out of the wheelchair first. His classmates at the academy had joked good-naturedly that Raul's quick draw had to be measured in fractions of a minute rather than fractions of a second. The young officer had never taken the Rourk out of the holster except to practice on the indoor range and to clean it.

Officer Buckner noted the model of the gun on the visiting officer's computer profile and then with the tap of a key sent Raul's complete ID package somewhere into the maze of offices behind her. "I notified the sergeant that you're here. He will be out in just a minute," she said. Then she looked past him to the next person crowding into the counter for information as she continued to discuss report forms over the phone.

"Thank you," Raul said, unheard. He pivoted on his right wheel and rolled to a spot out of the traffic to await his host. He tried to disregard the bedeviling suspicion that his superiors had sent him to L.A. for these few days to get him out from underfoot in Phoenix. As a first year PPD officer with a handicap, Raul had skipped the normal assignments given to rookies—jail duty and uniformed patrol—because he was physically unfit to perform them. Instead, he had gone straight to a desk job in the organized crime bureau at Central City Precinct. There his greatest handicap was inexperience in the company of veteran officers who had long since paid their dues on the street. He suspected that his fellow officers would rather do the job themselves than take the pains of teaching a greenhorn how to do it. They would probably get more work done with him gone than with him around.

Not far behind this theory was an even darker notion: that Raul had been hired as a police officer because of his handicap, not because of his education and qualifications. To be sure, a degree in law enforcement from ASU and graduation from the police academy with honors made him an enviable recruit. But the kid had one sad, glaring flaw which guaranteed that no other officer would ever want him for a partner: He was virtually defenseless, which also meant he could not defend a partner. In the time it took Raul to draw and fire a weapon, a bad guy could do him in five times over. That didn't make him much of an asset in a firefight.

Nor was Raul very mobile. After nearly three years in a wheelchair, Raul had become quite adept at getting around in his Quickie, thanks to his natural coordination and athletic ability. Yet he could never keep up with a bad guy on foot or elude one coming after him. He had mastered the hand controls in his Chevy Caprice, but he wouldn't stand a chance in a high-speed chase. Furthermore, Raul couldn't dive and roll, leap a fence, or subdue an assailant and cuff him without help. In short, there were a lot of reasons why he had been encouraged to pursue a career in something other than law enforcement.

But, next to baseball, police work was Raul's passion. And who in Arizona could persist in saying no to his desire to be a cop despite his handicap? After all, he was a famous native son: an All-American baseball player. He would be in the major leagues today had it not been for the terrible accident during the 1998 College World Series that left him a functional quadriplegic. That was certainly worth some PR points in Phoenix. And perhaps nobody had the heart to shut this door in his face after he had been robbed of a career in professional sports.

Furthermore, Raul possessed two exceptional qualifications that endeared him to affirmative action watchdogs: He was a minority and he was handicapped. Raul hoped his hiring hadn't been secretly arranged as a political move or a goodwill gesture, but he suspected as much. He had quietly determined that he would not be a token officer on the Phoenix squad. He had never been a benchwarmer, and he wasn't about to start with his first career. He was going to contribute whether they expected him to or not.

A tall plainclothes officer in his early thirties entered the lobby from the hall and surveyed the crowd. He was wearing the standard detective "uniform": wool blend slacks and sports jacket, pinstriped white shirt and tie—all in unobtrusive colors. One look in Raul's direction and he walked straight toward him. One advantage of losing the use of his legs, Raul had discovered, was that he wasn't hard to spot in a crowd. "Just look for a Mexican in a wheelchair" was the standard line he imagined others using. He wondered if Officer Buckner had typed something like that into the E-memo she sent from the counter.

"Mr. Barrigan," the officer called out pleasantly as he approached, extending a welcome hand. "I'm Reagan Cole." Raul regarded him an imposing figure at about six-five with an athletic build, but he was not quite the model type the LAPD seemed to prefer for their receptionists. His medium-length sandy hair was receding and thinning, and his large blue eyes seemed to bug out, giving his face the appearance of perpetual boyish excitement—very un-Hollywood. Raul reached up to grip the hand of a real L.A. cop.

Raul had been recommended to Sergeant Reagan Cole by his big boss in Phoenix, Lieutenant Rolf Werner. Cole had been lucky enough, Werner explained, to be in the right place at the right time not once but twice in the last two years. He had been the major player in the busts of two terrorist figures: a nut intent on blowing up the L.A. Coliseum full of people on Millennium's Eve and an international hit man tracking, of all people, one of the sergeant's personal friends. Cole was a streetwise detective in the crack LAPD anti-terrorist unit.

Officer Barrigan had been instructed to pick Cole's brain about the Los Angeles operation and bring back some ideas for implementation. During their only phone conversation to set up the appointment, Cole sounded eager to meet with Raul and promised him a couple of hours on Friday afternoon and most of Monday. Raul had driven over after Thanksgiving dinner with his parents in Tucson and was staying with relatives in Saugus for the weekend.

"A pleasure to meet you in person, Sergeant," Raul said, returning the handshake, though his partially paralyzed fingers could not match Cole's grip. "Sorry I'm late. Thanks for fitting me into your schedule."

"No problem. This is a perfect time for me. Most of the terrorists in L.A. have taken the holiday weekend off."

"Yeah, right," Raul retorted, clearly mocking the idea that bad guys anywhere take days off.

"Geez, you're soaked," Cole said, eyeing the wet hat and beads of water dripping from Raul's jacket and wheelchair. "Didn't I tell you about the underground parking?"

Raul shook his head.

"I'm really sorry, man. I'll get you a pass for Monday."

Raul grinned and waved off the oversight. "It's OK. My chair needed a wash job anyway."

Cole gestured toward the hallway. "It's a zoo out here. C'mon back to my cage where it's a little quieter."

Raul followed Cole through a maze of cubes and offices, pleased that his host didn't seem constrained to push him. Along the way the sergeant introduced Raul to several of his coworkers, who were pleasant but clearly too busy for chitchat. Still it took the two officers almost ten minutes to get past everyone and into Cole's small cube in the detective division.

Raul was easily as interested in Sergeant Cole's two well-publicized busts as in the information he had been sent to retrieve, which seemed to him more like busywork than police work. He had read about Cole's dangerous pursuits of the crazy Coliseum bomber and the famous Peruvian contract killer, but he wanted to hear the stories firsthand from the man who had lived them. Yet it was difficult for Raul to believe that the seemingly congenial detective sergeant was pleased about his work being interrupted for either agenda. A meeting like this was strictly a professional courtesy. Raul hoped he could also prevail on the sergeant's personal courtesy to hear his story.

Raul endured the normal get-acquainted small talk questions from his host: How was your Thanksgiving? How was the drive to L.A.? Where are you staying? What do you think of our weather? But before Raul could ask *his* first question, Cole revealed that he also had a personal agenda: "I hope I'm not getting too personal, but it's really great to see you getting around so well."

"You know about my accident," Raul said. He wasn't surprised anymore when a new acquaintance brought up his misfortune. It happened to him often. He was grateful that most people who questioned him about the incident were genuinely sympathetic and positive instead of morbidly curious or sappy.

"I saw it on TV when it happened. I was really pulling for ASU in the Series that year. Tough break. I'm glad you're doing all right."

"Yeah, I'm doing all right," Raul said, underscoring the vagueness of the terms Cole had chosen.

"I'm a PAC-10 athlete myself," Cole continued, "so I could identify somewhat with your pain and disappointment."

"PAC-10? What school?"

Cole flipped a thumb toward the west. "UCLA. Graduated in '93."

"Basketball?"

Cole's face brightened a little. "Right. How did you know? Did you see me play?"

Raul smiled at the L.A. cop's boyish optimism then shook his head. "Calculated guess. If you played baseball, I would have remembered you for sure. I've followed PAC-10 baseball since before I could lift a bat. Football, I might have remembered you, but you look a little light for a tight end. So I figured you ran the hardwood for the Bruins."

Cole laughed. "More like I *rode* the hardwood."

"Bench player?"

"Yeah, most of the time."

"You must have played with Curtis Spooner, the Portland Trail Blazer."

Cole brightened at the mention of his college buddy. "Right. Spoon and I were roommates, and we're still good friends."

The two officers reminisced about PAC-10 sports for several minutes. Raul enjoyed what seemed to be a spontaneous rapport with someone he was growing to like. Then Cole stood abruptly. "You want something to drink? Coffee? Soft drink? Anything?"

"Coffee sounds real good—black," Raul said, reaching for the wallet in his jacket pocket.

"Arizona money isn't any good here," Cole said, waving off Raul's attempt to dig out some cash. "I'll be back in a minute."

Cole was gone only long enough to afford Raul a cursory look around the cube from his parked wheelchair. The fabric walls were nearly obliterated by bulletins, memos, faxes, posters, and pictures. The shelves and credenza behind the sergeant's desk were strewn with binders, manila folders, stacks of diskette holders, clipboards bulging with hard copy, and a few books and useless knick-knacks. The small desktop, what space wasn't taken up by the computer, phone, and lamp, was in acceptable disarray. Papers and folders covered all but about two square feet of the surface nearest Cole's chair. The stuff was in piles, but the components of each pile were dog-eared and turned at all angles instead of neatly stacked.

A standing oak picture frame owned a corner of the desk that could have easily been utilized for another stack of papers. Apparently the subject or subjects within the frame were of greater value to the sergeant than the space he forfeited to keep it there. But the photo was turned away from Raul. He thought about the smaller frame on his own desk in Phoenix containing a photo of his parents, Rudy and Serena. Who was the object of Reagan Cole's affection? A wife—even though he wasn't wearing a wedding band? a girlfriend? his parents? his old friend Curtis Spooner? Raul was curious, but he wasn't about to roll his chair around the desk for a better look and get caught snooping.

Cole returned with a white ceramic mug full of steaming coffee. The mug bore the navy-blue crest of the LAPD with old city hall dominating the scene. Cole cleared a small space on the corner of the desk nearest to Raul and set the mug down. "The mug is yours to keep, a little PR gimmick somebody upstairs thought up," he said. "Just what everybody needs: another coffee mug."

"That's great," Raul said. "One of my sisters collects them. She'll love it. Thanks." He left the mug on the desk for the coffee to cool. His impaired hands had failed him too many times before, causing him to spill on himself coffee hot enough to burn. It was safer to wait and drink it lukewarm.

Cole settled back into his chair and popped the tab on a cold can of Cherry Coke. Raul was ready to pry into Cole's story, and with their conversation already on such a good footing he was sure Cole would be willing to talk about his experiences. But once again the sergeant beat him to the draw with a surprising question of his own: "Do you ever replay that headfirst slide in your mind and wish you had done something different?"

Other people had offended Raul by asking questions like that because their implied intention was judgment. They could have just as well said, "What a stupid decision. You have no one to blame but yourself. I'll bet now you wish you had heeded the coach's sign or gone in feet first." Raul had heard that judging tone most clearly in his former fiancée, Samantha Dumas, whose grief over his career-ending injury had been excessive, even embarrassing. But Raul heard nothing of judgment in Sergeant Cole's tone or eyes, only the unabashed curiosity of someone who had taken his share of hits in competition. Raul liked Cole even more for asking.

"I still run the tape in my head several times a week," Raul answered quietly and without emotion, maintaining eye contact, "but I gave up changing the play months ago."

"You'd still go in headfirst."

"I'd still run the sign and go in headfirst," Raul affirmed confidently. "It was a gut reaction at the time, pure instinct. But I had plenty of time to think about it while I was flat on my back, and now I'm sure it was the only way to beat Martinez's throw."

"And you could probably play it that way 10,000 times and walk away without a scratch."

Raul nodded knowingly. This guy understood, he thought. "I just happened to pull unlucky number 10,001 out of the hat."

Cole was silent. Instead of changing the subject, Raul sustained the silence, inviting the sergeant with his eyes to investigate further. Raul felt good talking to him.

"I saw part of that interview you did with what's-her-name on ESPN last year," Cole said after a long drink of Cherry Coke.

"Marta Friesen—a nice lady. I didn't want to talk for a long time. When I finally decided to tell my story, she was ready to listen."

"You were going to sign with the Giants. You had already decided."

"Yeah, I was going to sign right after the Series."

"You were going to build your folks a house with the big bonus."

Raul's nod was barely visible.

"You were going to be married that fall."

This time Raul didn't even nod.

"Then your life changed in a heartbeat."

Silence reigned for several more seconds. Unsure of how much of the story Cole knew, Raul filled in the blanks. "A couple of the Giants' brass came by the hospital that night. They wished me well and left some presents. I never heard from them again, obviously.

"My parents still live in the place where I grew up. Dad works, but we kids still send them extra money. When he retires in a few years we should be able to take care of them OK . . . but not anything like I was hoping to."

Raul realized that he hadn't talked through the consequences of his accident with anyone in a long time. He was pleased that he could do so now without the hindrance of emotions, even though the bitter taste of disappointment always accompanied the words. Cole's positive demeanor and openness was welcome encouragement to vent a little of it.

"The accident hit Sam the hardest," Raul continued. "She came up to Craig Hospital in Denver every other weekend during my rehab. But she was always so depressed. She couldn't deal with the fact that I was paralyzed, that we weren't going to be rich, that it would be difficult or impossible to have children. She kept saying that our life was ruined. I told her that she wasn't permanently committed to a relationship yet; she could change her mind. She told me in no uncertain terms that I wasn't to talk like that." Raul paused to smile at the memory of Samantha's caustic rebuke, a smile which quickly faded.

"But she was always so negative about life and the future. One weekend I asked her to give my ring back, go home, and think about what she wanted to do. She resisted the idea, but before she left she handed over the ring. Six months later she was engaged to another guy. She's married with a kid now."

Cole released a low whistle. "That's tough."

"Sam obviously wasn't the one for me," Raul said quickly, almost mechanically. It was the stock reply he had used for more than two years to quickly end any discussion about the exit of Samantha Dumas from his life. In reality, he used the comment like a lid to cap a can full of spiders and keep them from escaping. There was a lot about losing Sam he had never talked about and didn't want to talk about.

Cole did not press the issue. Instead, after another pull on his Cherry Coke, he said, "During the interview you mentioned that you wouldn't have made it without your strong religious faith."

It was another topic that Raul wasn't comfortable with. Yes, he had said something to the effect that his faith in Christ had kept him from despair and equipped him for life beyond baseball. That's what good Christians are supposed to say about tough circumstances in order to present a "witness" to the watching world. But for the first three months of quadriplegia, Raul's faith had no room for life beyond baseball. Miraculous healing and a return to the game he loved was all he talked about and all he allowed his family and friends to talk about. Any admission of doubt or question that God may have something else in mind and he wouldn't get his miracle. So Raul had steadfastly put off Marta Friesen's request for an interview from his hospital bed, expecting that any morning he would wake up whole and be able to talk to her from Candlestick Park in a Giants' uniform.

But the miracle Raul expected never came. Rehabilitation helped him recover much of the use of his upper body, but he couldn't walk. On the best of days he could only prop himself up and support his weight between parallel bars with the help of braces. Raul could drive a car with hand controls and get around in his wheelchair, but he couldn't grip a baseball well enough to throw a strike. Raul had completed his college education and fulfilled his goal of joining the Phoenix Police Department, but he secretly admitted he had settled for second best. After three years, a bright baseball career and financial security for Rudy and Serena Barrigan had faded beyond the horizon, and God hadn't even bothered to explain to Raul why He had welshed on His big promises.

Aware that Cole's comment was an opening for him to talk about God, and aware that good Christians take advantage of such witnessing opportunities, Raul began, "I don't fully understand why God let this happen to me, but—"

The telephone on Cole's desk rudely interrupted. The sergeant apologized to his guest and answered. "Sergeant Cole . . . Oh hi, Babe." A flick of Cole's eyebrows in Raul's direction indicated that this was a personal call he may be able to postpone. "Can I call you back in a few minutes?"

Cole snapped straight up in his chair at the reply Raul could not hear. "What? . . . It's time? . . . It's happening?" Then Cole stood and started pacing the small area behind his desk. He was suddenly excited. "The water broke? . . . When? . . . Are you doing OK? . . . Of course I can. I'll leave right now. Just don't panic. I'll be there in twenty minutes."

Cole dropped the phone in its cradle. His face mirrored mild panic. "That was my wife," he said excitedly. "We're about to enlarge our family. I'm sorry, Raul, but I need to leave a little early."

Raul had already pieced together the highlights of the conversation. "Hey, I understand. Get out of here."

"It's not a big thing," Cole said rather absently as he frantically searched the desk for his keys. "It's just that we've never done this before."

"No problem, Reagan. Family is a priority. I can find my way out."

"Thanks, man. I'll meet you here Monday morning." Cole scooped up the keys and swept past Raul out the door.

"You may still be involved with your family on Monday," Raul said over his shoulder. "We can always reschedule for after the holidays."

"No, Monday will be fine," Cole called back from the hall. Then by the time Raul had turned his wheelchair around to exit the office, Cole was back, standing in the doorway. "Better yet, what are you doing tonight?"

Raul's eyes widened, wondering what Cole had in mind. "No plans, but—"

"How about coming out to our place for dinner. We're in Santa Monica. Beth would love to meet you."

Raul was flabbergasted by the invitation. "But you two are going to be kind of busy tonight. I don't think your wife will appreciate a stranger—"

"No way. Beth loves having people over. And she loves talking sports. She played basketball for USC."

Raul stumbled over his words trying to excuse himself from what sounded to him like a very personal family time. As he did, Cole scribbled an address on the back of an LAPD card. "Do you have an electronic locator in your car?" Cole asked.

"No, just a Thomas Guide, but—"

"That will get you there. Shoot for about seven." Then Cole dropped the card on Raul's briefcase and took off running toward the stairs to the parking garage. Raul shook his head in astonishment. "They really do things differently here in L.A.," he said aloud.

Twenty-eight

Reagan Cole hurried through the living room, tossing his sport jacket and tie on the sofa as he went. The lights in the house were out and it was pretty dark. "Babe, I'm home," he called out.

"We're in the bedroom," came the reply from the back of their modest second-story condo overlooking the promenade and Santa Monica Beach. Outside, the leaden rain clouds were still delivering their payload, making the late afternoon even darker than normal.

Entering the bedroom, Cole stopped and stared in awe at the sight illuminated by the small lamp on Beth's side of the bed. "Am I . . . am I too late?" he whispered.

"We've only just begun," Beth replied, smiling.

Cole kicked off his shoes and crawled carefully on hands and knees across the king-size bed to where his wife lay with a squirming newborn on her chest. Remembering his priorities, he kissed his wife tenderly on the cheek and lips. "Hi, sweet," he said.

"Thanks for coming so quickly," she said.

"I wouldn't miss it." Then he turned his attention to the tiny bundle nuzzled under Beth's chin. He lowered his nose to touch the warm mound that squeaked softly whenever it moved.

"It's a boy, Reagan," Beth announced proudly. "And he has your nose—all pink and wet."

"But look, Babe, he has your hair," Cole said, touching his finger to the black sheen covering the little one's body, which matched the soft, black strands cascading from Beth's forehead to the pillow.

"Then he must be ours," she said with a grin. "We can call him Junior."

"No way. There are no Juniors in my family, and I don't want a Junior."

"Well, I don't want anything athletic like Champ or Tiger or Bubba," Beth announced.

"Agreed. No Junior and no Bubba."

"Agreed."

"Were there any complications during birth?" Cole asked.

"Not so far. Princess Di is doing all the work. I just get to bask in the glory."

"What are the neighbors going to say?" Cole teased playfully, stroking the furry little mound with his finger. "We've only been married a month and a half and we already have a son."

"It's the twenty-first century. People do things differently. They'll have to deal with it. Besides, they're in for a real shock. I think we also have a daughter. And there are more on the way."

Cole raised his eyebrows in wonder. Then he leaned across Beth's prone body and looked into the cardboard box on the floor beside the bed. Their three-year-old blonde cocker-poodle-who-knows-what-else, Princess Di, was busy licking the remains of the birth sac off a squirming blonde ball of fur about the size of a field mouse.

"Yeah, I think number two is a female," Cole said. He reached down and scratched Princess Di behind the ears, whispering words of encouragement. The dog was absorbed in the instinctual task of caring for its young.

Princess Di was a very impractical, impromptu wedding gift Cole and Beth had given to each other on the last day of their honeymoon. They found the dog abandoned at the Coalinga rest stop alongside Interstate Five during the last leg of their trip to Santa Monica from Beth's home on Whidbey Island in Puget Sound. Realizing that the friendly blonde pooch was in danger of being hit on the deadly Interstate or picked up by someone who might abuse it, the couple made a snap decision to adopt it.

Back on the freeway, with the dog curled contentedly on Beth's lap, they came up with reason after reason why they should dump the dog at the next rest stop and forget about being pet owners. Cole's Santa Monica condo, where the couple planned to live while keeping Beth's home as an investment and vacation spot, didn't have a fenced yard. They would have to take the dog out on a leash to piddle and poop. Furthermore, Cole's work schedule was often unpredictable with long hours. As a free-lance journalist, Beth traveled a lot. They would have to find somebody in the neighborhood to take the dog out in the middle of the day and dog-sit when they were both gone. It seemed like a big hassle, but with every mile the docile, silky-blonde mutt inched farther into their hearts.

By the time they reached home they had decided on Princess Di for a name because of the regal beauty of this unpedigreed pooch. Only later did they discover that their little princess was pregnant, which became another big reason to hustle the dog off to the nearest animal shelter. But they couldn't do it. Instead they began getting excited about becoming "parents." Neither of them had owned a dog that birthed pups in their home. They decided that Princess Di would be royally pampered during gestation and that her litter would be distributed to good homes.

"She's a dishwater blonde like her mother," Cole said, touching the newborn pup in between Princess Di's licks.

"She's a blonde like *you*," Beth corrected. "It's the all-American family: a black-haired boy for me and a blonde girl for you."

"In the all-American family, I think I get the boy and you get the girl," Cole said. Then he quickly added, "Oops, I guess we'll both have plenty. Here come two more."

Beth returned the black pup to the box. Then for the next hour, Cole and Beth lay across the bed on their stomachs watching the miracle of life unfold before them in the box on the floor. In the end, Princess Di presented them with six tiny pups—four males and two females, each with sealed eyes, pink flesh, and either black or blonde fur.

The couple laughed about names that would be appropriate for a litter of six. Being a writer, Beth suggested the six journalistic questions—who, what, when, where, why, how, provoking an unrehearsed parody of the old Abbott and Costello routine, "Who's On First?" Being big basketball fans, they considered using the names of the legendary L.A. Lakers' "Showtime" starting five from the '80s—Magic, Kareem, Worthy, Scott, A.C.—and their coach—Riley. They thought about naming the six pups and their mother after the seven dwarfs, except that between them they couldn't remember all seven names.

They digressed from dog names to marvel about what had brought them to this moment as husband and wife. Cole turned onto his back and Beth her side to face him as they talked. They recounted their chance meeting on the San Diego Freeway eight days before the end of the millennium—an out-of-town journalist being rescued from Latino gang members by an off-duty policeman. They pieced together the Unity 2000 event in the L.A. Coliseum on Millennium's Eve and the roles they played in the nearly disastrous incident. They reminisced about falling in love over those eight magical days.

For a few sober moments, Beth reflected on the selfish pursuits that drove her away from Cole for eighteen months while he was pursuing a new direction as a man of faith in Jesus Christ. They remembered the surprise reunion at the wedding of a mutual friend, Shelby Hornecker Rider. They reconstructed the four tense days in June and the crazy, spontaneous drive together from Los Angeles nearly to the Canadian border. They recalled the terrifying gunfight during a frantic attempt to save the lives of Shelby and Evan Rider. And they affirmed that those four days had drawn them together for good in love and faith, culminating in their marriage October 13, 2001.

"It's amazing what has happened to us in such a short time," Cole said, hands folded behind his head as he stared into Beth's sparkling black eyes. The soft squeaking noises of rooting puppies drifted up to them from the floor.

Beth traced the highlights of her husband's face with her finger. "I can't believe that you took me back when I walked away from you like I did."

Cole kissed the tip of her finger as it passed over his lips. "After finding you, I didn't want anybody else. I just waited and prayed, and God brought you back to me."

"But I wasn't even listening to God at that time in my life."

"I guess I was listening for both of us. And He was listening to me."

Beth leaned down and kissed Cole's forehead lightly. After a silent moment, she said, "Do you believe our marriage was made in heaven? I mean, does God pick two people for each other, and if they screw up and marry the wrong people they are miserable forever?"

Cole was flattered that his wife had asked him a question he considered spiritually significant. "I believe that marriages are *allowed* in heaven, but they are made or broken on earth by how two people treat each other." It was a statement he once heard Matt Dugan make. Matt Dugan was the young pastor of a little church in Santa Monica Cole had been attending since his faith in God had sparked to life nearly two years earlier. Matt Dugan had been a God-sent counselor and friend during the months Cole had struggled to understand Beth's disappearance. Since their return to Santa Monica as husband and wife, Cole had taken Beth to Matt's church a few times, and she liked him too. Some day, Cole considered, he would tell Beth that Matt was the source of much of the spiritual wisdom he shared with her.

"You're saying that any man can marry any woman—like two strangers meeting at the altar—and make it work." Beth was resting her head on her left hand and appreciating her husband's muscular chest, shoulders, and biceps with her right as she spoke.

"Theoretically, I guess. That seems to be how they do it in other places in the world. Two families contract a marriage between their children who barely know each other until the ceremony is over. They live happily ever after because they don't know any better."

"Yuk. That doesn't sound fun to me."

"More realistically, I think God allows people to use their own minds and emotions—"

"And sex drives," Beth interjected, pulling herself closer and playing with the buttons on his shirt.

Cole momentarily lost his train of thought. Beth's closeness and playfulness was crowding his mind with other ideas.

Pressing on, he said, "Yes, I think God allows people to choose marriage partners based on physical attraction, social and spiritual compatibility, et cetera. Once we make the choice, it's up to us to make the marriage work by loving selflessly."

Cole barely got the words out before Beth smothered his mouth with a long, tantalizing kiss. "I choose you, Reagan Cole," she cooed.

Cole wrapped his arms around her and pulled her close for another long kiss. Her dark hair brushed the sides of his face. "I choose you, Beth Cole," he whispered.

"*Scibelli*-Cole," she reminded him as their embrace intensified. "I'm keeping my old name too, remember?"

Cole was busy barraging the side of her neck with kisses. "Whatever," he said when he came up for air.

After several more minutes of passionate kissing, Beth began to unbutton Cole's shirt. He worked a hand free to stop her in the act. To her questioning look, he replied, "Not in front of the children," flicking his eyes in the direction of the box full of puppies on the floor.

Beth laughed, then swung her free arm to the bedside lamp and switched it off, plunging the bedroom into total darkness.

Somewhere between sleep and wakefulness, between rapture and reality, a face appeared to Cole in the darkness. The image jolted him to full consciousness with the force of a screaming electronic alarm, and he sat straight up on the bed. "What time is it?" he said aloud.

Beth, who had been dozing, stirred and reached for him. "Who needs to know, my love?" she mumbled.

"I need to know," he said with trepidation in his voice, "because our dinner guest will be arriving . . . " He finally focused on the illuminated digital display on the clock radio across the room. It read 6:41 P.M. " . . . in twenty minutes."

Beth shot up beside him. "What dinner guest? I don't know about a dinner guest in twenty minutes."

Cole had already rolled to the floor to feel around for his shirt. "It's a guy I met today at work, that outfielder for Arizona State who broke his neck in the College World Series a few years ago. Barrigan, Raul Barrigan. He's in a wheelchair now. I invited him over for dinner tonight."

"What were you planning to serve for dinner tonight?" Beth said, her upset evident.

Cole felt around the floor until he found his shirt half in and half out of the puppy box. "I don't know. Do we have any leftover turkey?"

"You serve leftover turkey to friends who pop in, not to first-time guests you barely know."

Cole was silent for a moment. "Oh."

"When did you invite him over?" Beth demanded, controlling her panic.

"Just after you called this afternoon. We had an appointment, and I had to rush out on him. So I invited him to dinner."

"What kind of appointment? Is he a suspect or something?"

"No, he's with the Phoenix police now, a detective," Cole said as he finished buttoning his shirt. "He's on a little fact-finding mission to L.A. He's a nice guy. You'll like him."

Beth banged her knee on the bedside table when she jumped out of bed. She yelped and grumbled about it plenty. "I don't think I'm going to like *anyone* in twenty minutes." Then she was on her way to the kitchen to come up with a miracle dinner.

Twenty-nine

Cooper Sams was neither surprised nor disappointed at the small turn-out for the news conference. Despite an expensive hot buffet for fifty provided by the New Jesus Family in a large meeting room of the hotel, only seven people had shown up to enjoy it. News media holocards were required for admittance. But Cooper suspected that most of the guests eagerly scarfing up the Swedish meatballs and pasta were stringers more interested in a free meal than a story. He saw only one camera among them—an old Nikon 35mm—and assumed all attenders to be members of the print media.

Cooper and the other elders of the New Jesus Family had predicted the low turnout. It was the Friday evening of Thanksgiving weekend, and many of the regulars in the news media had taken the day off. And it was cold and blustery in Seattle, making a trip downtown through Friday night traffic sound like a very bad idea to their replacements, who had to work the news desks this holiday weekend.

The leaders of the religious group had considered putting off the conference to better accommodate the media. But after some discussion they agreed that a nicer day away from the holiday weekend would provoke its own set of excuses for reporters not to attend. They decided on the Friday after Thanksgiving, assured that whoever was ordained to come would come.

Furthermore, Cooper admitted to himself, the small, closely knit religious group in which he had been absorbed for the past three and a half years was not exactly hot news in the Puget Sound area. Nor had they tried to attract public attention. On the contrary, for nearly seven years Lila Ruth Atkinson had quietly taught the revolutionary truths revealed to her by Jesus-Brother with the understanding that only a small, chosen band would follow. To date, the New Jesus Family numbered 106, 14 of them minor children of adult members. It was an affluent congregation, as Lila Ruth knew it would be. But they went about their business quietly, virtually unknown to the Seattle-Tacoma area which they called home.

But today the New Jesus Family had big news to share with the world. It wasn't the kind of news the world would be much interested in, they knew. Doomsday prophets and their prophecies were generally ignored or mocked, especially after a glut of them predicted the Second Coming to coincide with the dawn of the new millennium. Yet Lila Ruth Atkinson and Cooper Sams had deemed it important to share this news with the public via a press conference for two reasons.

First, the Reunion of Jesus-Brother and earth-sister in less than three months was going to effect everyone on the planet. Heaven and earth would be merged in fervent heat, forever changing both "in the twinkling of an eye." People had a right to be warned about the cataclysm whether they took the message seriously or not.

Second, the New Jesus Family was still open to new applicants. Considering the unique role of Family members in the Reunion, which would be explained during the presentation to the press, Family leaders were prepared to welcome a certain number of additional members in time for the big day. Realistically, Cooper didn't expect any takers. But the Family had judged it only fair to make the offer plain regardless of the response. Cooper compared it to laying out a welcome mat at the doorway to Noah's ark before the big flood.

Cooper Sams' willingness to extend mercy to an unbelieving world was one of many significant changes in his life since he became a disciple of the woman who seemed to know him as well as God Himself. Shortly after pledging his allegiance to Lila Ruth Atkinson and the New Jesus Family, Cooper's drinking problem all but disappeared. Lila Ruth simply informed him that his eternal spirit-body needed neither the stimulation nor the anesthetization of alcohol. He accepted the subtle challenge and cut down to one or two beers a week. A similar turnabout occurred when Lila Ruth intimated that his bigotry would rob him of eternal friendship with Parent-God's children who differed from him in racial, religious, or sexual orientation. With great discipline, Cooper began to tolerate and appreciate coworkers and neighbors he had previously snubbed: gays, Jews, blacks, slackers.

However, in his relationship to Rachel Sams, the ability to change seemed beyond his grasp. Lila Ruth taught about the importance of spirit-bonding with mate or lover and discouraged divorce. As with everything Lila Ruth believed, Cooper embraced the principle. But the walls of pride and indifference had grown tall and thick, and the gates to the fortress seemed bolted from the outside. Had Rachel followed him into the New Jesus Family, Cooper thought he might have been able to open himself to her and her needs. But since she remained outside, he could not force himself to go to her. Part of him wanted Rachel with him now to hear the announcement. But another part—always the larger part, Cooper admitted—said no.

The buffet line had been open for nearly half an hour, and the seven attendees—five men and two women—had eaten for twenty. Cooper stood in a corner of the room observing. He was dressed in an expensive, dark-gray pinstriped suit, starched white shirt, fashionable silk tie of gray, gold, and black, and gold jewelry, including two gold bands on the ring finger and pinkie of his right hand. The twin rings were his symbol of devotion to Jesus-Brother. Cooper had removed the wedding band from his left hand, considering it a pointless token from another life.

He had abandoned his sparse gray flattop in favor of a buzz cut of what hair remained on the sides and back of his head. He looked like the CEO of Northstar Airlines instead of a retired captain. The physical appearance of her top staff was very important to Lila Ruth Atkinson. And Cooper had acknowledged that his sudden rise to prominence in a religious group he originally mocked demanded that he dress the part.

At 7 P.M., Cooper Sams, Lila Ruth Atkinson, and three other officers in the New Jesus Family took their places at the head table, which was draped from the surface to the floor in dull business-gray material. Two wireless mikes were mounted in metal table stands and angled toward the two principle speakers, Cooper and Lila Ruth. Eight rows of upholstered chairs from the banquet room were lined up to face the head table. The hotel's assistant event coordinator, a skinny college kid with severe acne and dandruff problems, had asked if he should pull out half the chairs in view of the small attendance. Cooper told him to leave them. He was not intimidated by empty chairs.

Lila Ruth had determined that, after a brief introduction from herself, Cooper Sams would read the statement they had prepared together. Captain Sams, the decorated former pilot of Seattle's Northstar Airlines, was the group's lone "celebrity." Some people at the news conference might remember the heroic actions that saved his passengers and crew in Juneau nearly seven years earlier. Lila Ruth hoped Cooper's credibility would at least grant the group a hearing. Following the prepared statement, the group's elders would entertain questions from the floor—if there were any.

"Ladies and gentlemen, welcome and thank you for coming," Lila Ruth began into the microphone, which was dead. The skinny kid scurried to the control panel to turn it on before she spoke again. "My name is Lila Ruth Atkinson." Lila Ruth was dressed in a feminine but businesslike dark-blue wool-blend suit and matching medium heels. The high-neck beige blouse was swirled with a delicate navy pattern. Her blonde-gray hair was expertly styled to frame her face. The sixty-seven-year-old spiritual leader looked even younger than Cooper Sams, who was fifty-nine.

The small squad of press corps chow hounds scattered to take their places among the forty-eight chairs, staying near the back as if afraid they might catch something infectious. One reporter, a man in a cheap gray suit, ducked out instead of sitting down, choosing not to stay for the show after the free meal. The only other people in the room were two caterers closing down the buffet line and the events assistant at the control panel in the back. But Lila Ruth's countenance was as pleasant and accepting as if the room had been jammed to the doors with eager disciples.

"We are the spiritual leaders of the New Jesus Family here in Seattle." The kid at the panel did a good job of adjusting the sound level, then he left the room also. "Introducing on my left Ms. Kimberly Bemari and Mr. Frank Woods, elders in the Family. On my far right, Mr. Erich Dammasch, elder, and Captain Cooper Sams, senior elder. Captain Sams, an award-winning pilot you may have heard about, recently retired from Northstar Airlines after more than thirty years of flying." The four people at the table nodded and smiled as their names were pronounced. The six people in the chairs just sat and stared.

"It is likely that none of you here this evening are acquainted with the New Jesus Family. We are far from being a large religious organization, and we are not a particularly evangelistic one. We don't advertise, proselytize, or canvass neighborhoods for new members. We have always believed that those who belong with us will eventually find us and join us.

"Nor is it our purpose tonight to promote our organization. Rather, we have a brief announcement on a topic both of grave concern and bright hope to our community and to our world. At the conclusion of the prepared statement we will be most pleased to answer any questions you may have. A printed copy of the statement will be distributed at the close of the conference."

The small audience sat with blank stares. Lila Ruth said, "Captain

Sams will now read our statement."

Cooper Sams pulled a short stack of laser printed documents from the folder in front of him. Then he glanced at his audience, looking for the slightest glimmer of genuine interest. The closest thing to interest Cooper perceived was an "I dare you to keep me interested for five minutes" smirk coming from a gaunt man about his own age in the fourth row of chairs. The man's face bore the scars of a losing battle with many vices: deeply lined, sagging sallow flesh, sunken, murky eyes ringed the color of ash, blotchy red cheeks and nose, nicotine-stained lips. Cooper would have taken him for a homeless man off the street had it not been for his neat blue suit, shirt and tie. He was also the guest with the Nikon, which Cooper wondered if he had stolen. The man obviously needed the free meal he had just consumed. The look in his eyes now challenged Cooper to give him something more: a story he could transform into cash for cigarettes, drugs, or liquor.

Cooper Sams had been tutored by Lila Ruth, his spiritual guide into the world he could not see, to trust the inner light whether or not it was validated by earthly evidence. The New Jesus Family had been spiritually directed to inform the world of coming judgment and offer sanctuary to a select few. But for a brief moment Cooper was gripped by the seeming futility of what he was about to do. He doubted that these few pages would make any difference to anyone in the room tonight, let alone be heard by anyone outside.

Cooper spent several seconds silently reciting a principle Lila Ruth had drummed into him: *The pure light from within will eventually pierce the confusing darkness without.* He called on Pathfinder to bolster his resolve. Then, sitting ramrod straight, he began to read.

"On February 20, 1995, as some of you may know, I was a participant in a miraculous event in Juneau, Alaska. The aircraft I was flying that night for Northstar Airlines flew into a severe rotor shear on takeoff, the worst I had ever encountered in more than thirty years in the cockpit. The condition was so violent and unpredictable that, by all rights, the airplane should have crashed, and it almost did."

Cooper read the carefully worded dramatic account of hitting the wind shear, nearly stalling during climb-out, diving close to treetop level to gain air speed, blowing a turbine fan on pull out, and nearly dumping the plane into the water on emergency landing. From the corner of his eye, he noticed that the two caterers had slowed their cleanup to listen to the intriguing story. He hoped the same interest was present in the typically cynical news people in front of him. "Thanks to a little skill, a little luck, and a lot of spiritual energy, our plane was spared and we landed safely."

Cooper glanced up at the sallow-faced reporter to take a reading on his attitude. The man was nodding slightly, as if he remembered the story, which had been played up in the news media in Seattle, though not as much as if the plane would have crashed. *Perhaps this sad soul even wrote something about me then,* Cooper thought. He was pleased that the challenge in the man's eye had lost its sharp edge during his opening paragraph.

"My near-death experience served as a serious wake-up call," he continued. "I realized that I was still alive for a purpose. From the moment I stepped off the plane that night, I began seeking the reason for my survival.

"Unknown to me at the time, our esteemed teacher, Lila Ruth Atkinson, survived a crisis of her own on February 20, 1995. In a supernatural vision that day, she was called by God to form a spiritual family with a special purpose for the earth's last days. Like myself, Lila Ruth sensed a unique destiny but did not understand the specifics of it. She set about to gather a core of believers to form the New Jesus Family while I continued to ponder the reason for my existence.

"In 1998, I met Ms. Atkinson for the first time. Through her miraculous insights and patient intervention, I realized—reluctantly at first— that the reason I survived the rotor shear in Juneau was thoroughly wrapped up in the reason for which she had formed the New Jesus Family. It became clear to me that I had been saved to advance the same cause and share the same destiny. In June 1998 I became a disciple of Lila Ruth Atkinson and an adherent of her teachings."

When Cooper looked up, the man with the old, leather face snapped a strobeless picture. Cooper wished he hadn't. He returned to the text and read two concise paragraphs summarizing the basic beliefs of the New Jesus Family: the twin kingdoms of heaven and earth, the divinity of both Parent-God and His human offspring, and the impending reunion of Jesus-Brother and earth-sister. Family leaders had debated how much doctrinal content to include in the statement. They decided to keep it to a minimum rather than inundate people with information they would tune out or not fully grasp. Those interested in further information could obtain it during the question period.

As Cooper read these two paragraphs, the caterers hastily finished their work and left. The six reporters remained seated impassively.

"It is in regard to the event we call Reunion that this gathering has been called," Cooper went on, homing in on the essence of his message. "For generations, mystics, prophets, dreamers, and psychics have predicted the end of time on earth as we know it. Dates have been set in anticipation of a global cataclysm to accompany the return of a god or messiah or prophet in righteous judgment. These dates have come and gone, and life goes on unchanged.

"The seers of the past have been correct that the end of all things is imminent. Their passion in proclaiming their message has urged humankind to consider the brevity of life and the certainty of a doorway into the beyond. However, whereas these visionaries have been insistent, their predictions of when and where have been misguided because that information has been strategically withheld until a more suitable time."

Cooper glanced up again. The sallow-skinned man in the blue suit looked unenthusiastic, but he was hanging in and snapping more pictures. A couple of the other reporters had taken to fidgeting disinterestedly.

"It is our unswerving conviction that the final day is now within view and that a program for the reunion of heaven and earth has been determined."

One of the discomfited newspeople, a shaggy-maned, bearded man in his mid-thirties wearing cotton pants, a denim shirt, and sneakers, sprang from his seat and started toward the door. He spoke to no one in particular but loudly enough for everyone to hear: "Is that what this is all about—another doomsday prediction? I can't believe it. What a waste of time." He cursed unashamedly as he pushed the door open and stomped out of the meeting room.

A young female reporter dressed in a turtleneck sweater, short skirt, and black hose took advantage of his outburst and departed in his wake. Her body language conveyed the same disappointment, but she said nothing. A black man in a bombardier's jacket followed her out. Cooper and his cohorts remained silent at the table as the dissidents left. They had expected resistance or objection.

There were now five New Jesus people at the table and three media people scattered around the large room in the chairs, including the skinny man Cooper had thought would be the first to leave. Another question of doubt trickled like ice water over Cooper's resolve to keep going: *Would anyone still be here at the end of the presentation? Was there any use going on?* However, as with every doubt, major or minor, since Cooper had placed his life in the hands of Lila Ruth Atkinson, Pathfinder was instantly there to calm him and bring him courage. *Don't shrink back from your calling. You are in the light; they are in the darkness. You are in the truth; they are in confusion. You are of the heavenly kingdom; they are of the earthly kingdom.*

The voice was never audible, but it was no less real. In fact, Pathfinder often seemed more real to Cooper than anything in the empirical world. Lila Ruth had tutored him to trust the inner light of Pathfinder, whom she described as Jesus-Brother's spirit/angel of guidance for His chosen ones. And whenever he heard Pathfinder's strong, wise counsel, his resolve to follow was energized.

Cooper drew a cleansing breath and continued. "For reasons known only to our heavenly Brother, the New Jesus Family has been entrusted with the critical details of Reunion, when heaven and earth are melted with great heat and joined for eternity. We have been commissioned to share this good news with whomever will listen for two reasons.

"First, we summon people everywhere to make peace with God as they perceive Him and with their fellow man in preparation to enter the eternal kingdom. At the moment of Reunion, all flesh on earth will pass through the fire of judgment as the old is transformed into the new. Those with the most dross to consume will experience the greatest pain. But that pain will eventually be overcome by the glory of seeing our eternal Brother."

Cooper was mildly surprised that another exodus did not take place when he paused to turn the page.

"Second, we extend an invitation to a select few to join the New Jesus Family, which has been called to leave the earth prior to Reunion and serve as Vanguard to meet Jesus-Brother in the air. Those who go with us will be spared the pain of the consuming fire which will melt the elements. Those who go with us will leave all earthly weakness and disability behind and be the first to enter into Jesus-Brother's new kingdom."

As with the group's doctrine, the New Jesus Family leadership had elected to limit the information about Reunion and Vanguard to a summary in the prepared statement. They had been called to announce and invite, not to explain in detail. Additional information would be provided in response to specific questions asked.

The questions started sooner than Cooper had planned. "So you're predicting the end of the world, is that it, Captain?" The words, which came across in a taunting tone, were from the haggard, sickly looking man in the blue suit. His voice was gravelly but strong, as if he was accustomed to raising it to get attention.

Cooper had intended on delaying all questions until he finished the statement. There was only one brief paragraph left—a conclusion that contained one last vital item. But he decided to engage the doubter right away while keeping tight control on the discussion. "Will you please state your name, sir, and the organization you represent."

"Earl Butcher, the *Star*," he said with a chip-on-the-shoulder glower.

Cooper was not daunted by the harsh deportment. He doubted that Earl Butcher was a staffer with the *US Star*. Rather, he guessed that the gaunt stringer scrounged the city for bizarre stories, like street people scrounge dumpsters for food, trying to find something he could sell to the national daily or anybody who was buying.

"Yes, Mr. Butcher," Cooper replied evenly, "we are talking about the end of the world as we know it, although we prefer to regard Reunion as a great beginning."

"Yeah, great beginning," Butcher spat. "A nuclear holocaust toasts the planet and everyone on it."

"This is not a lake of fire, Mr. Butcher. Hell in religious literature is merely an illustration of the trouble we bring on ourselves. The fire of Reunion is a purifying curtain those on earth will pass through on their way to Brother's new kingdom. The pain will be intense but fleeting."

"Let's go to the bottom line, Captain," Butcher pressed brusquely. "When does the bomb go off? When is your doomsday?"

Cooper glanced at the last paragraph of the statement. It explained how the specific time and date of Reunion had been derived from the initially puzzling revelation given to Lila Ruth by Pathfinder the night she met Cooper Sams: 2002 0220 2002. The twos and zeros which the New Jesus Family revered as prophetic and directive would line up only once to indicate a specific time, date, and year. The moment of Reunion could not have been announced more clearly to Lila Ruth and the Family faithful.

Cooper first decided to read the entire paragraph in response to Butcher's question, then quickly changed his mind. His crusty antagonist would probably interrupt him anyway, demanding the bottom line. Cooper decided to let him have it.

"Reunion takes place at precisely 2002 hours—or 8:02 P.M., Wednesday, February 20, 2002. Doomsday, as you put it, Mr. Butcher, is less than three months away."

Thirty

Earl Butcher's outburst of coarse laughter quickly escalated into a raspy smoker's hack that doubled him over in his chair. The other two reporters in the room quickly took advantage of the noisy diversion to exit the room. "So this Brother Jesus character has it down to the minute, does he?" Butcher mused aloud after bringing his cough under control. "But did he tell you which time zone he was talking about? Eight-oh-two China time is a lot different than 8:02 Pacific Standard Time. Or maybe the big fire will break out on the international dateline and take a day to burn around the globe." He laughed again at the ludicrous idea.

Lila Ruth took a breath to speak, but Cooper laid a hand on her arm, assuring her that he was prepared to answer the mocker. Though he was tempted to do otherwise, he summoned strength from Pathfinder and answered Butcher as if he had asked his question sincerely.

"That's a fair question, Mr. Butcher. The Reunion will occur in an instant worldwide, in the 'twinkling of an eye,' as Saint Paul predicted. Since the New Jesus Family rose up in Seattle and the Reunion revelation was given in Seattle, the specified time of 8:02 applies to the Pacific time zone. It will be 11:02 P.M. on the East Coast, 6:02 P.M. in the Hawaiian islands, and so on around the world."

"And everyone is going to burn except the New Jesus people," Butcher continued cynically.

"In preparation for Reunion," Cooper explained carefully, "the people of the world, or earth-sister, will pass through the fire of judgment to cleanse them of the dirt and disease of a planet living in separation from her heavenly twin, Jesus-Brother. Each individual will be judged according to his works. The evil within each person will be burned away; the good will be purified like gold and survive."

"But you people somehow escape this . . . this . . . firewalk to heaven," Butcher snorted.

"The New Jesus Family has been chosen as the Vanguard of earth-sister, the firstfruits of the Reunion commissioned to welcome Jesus-Brother in the skies. It is our destiny. We have been purified on earth by our faith and will escape the flames of judgment."

"How are you going to manage that when the rest of the world is supposedly burning like hell itself? You have some special asbestos angel suits?" Butcher laughed his insidious laugh again.

"An airplane, Mr. Butcher," Cooper replied calmly.

"An airplane?"

"Yes, an airplane, a Boeing 737 christened *Vanguard.*"

"You people have chartered an airplane?"

"We bought the airplane, Mr. Butcher."

"Bought it! That must have cost millions."

"Only about 3 million. It's an older 737-300 we purchased from an Argentine airline. It is presently being repainted at Paine Field."

"So you're all going to climb inside this airplane and the hellfire will miraculously skip over you?"

Cooper took a slow, calming breath to quiet the irritation rising within him. "The New Jesus Family will board *Vanguard* at approximately 7 P.M. and depart from Paine Field heading north. At 8:02, we will no longer need the airplane. Reunion will be accomplished. We will be the first to greet our eternal Brother."

Butcher profaned the names of deity in ways Cooper Sams had never heard before. Then he said, "You're going up in an airplane, then you keep going up—without the airplane."

"In a manner of speaking, yes."

"No wonder you bought an old plane, since you're all bailing out."

Cooper couldn't think of a civil reply, so he said nothing.

"And you're going to fly it?" Butcher went on.

"Yes, I am the only trained pilot in the Family. Flying *Vanguard* is my destiny. I know it as well as I know anything."

"What about a copilot? You need a copilot to get one of those babies off the ground, don't you?"

"Yes, and Jesus-Brother knows our need," Cooper answered confidently. "A copilot will be provided."

Butcher swore again, then continued, "How many people are we talking about here? Do you really need a 737?"

"We have 109 members."

"And they will all be on the plane to nowhere that night?"

"To Reunion," Cooper corrected. "Yes, at this point all 109 will be aboard *Vanguard*."

"What about all the other planes in the air around the world at 8:02 Pacific Standard Time?" Butcher posed disbelievingly. "What about the shuttle crews in space at the time? Do those people just keep going up too?"

Cooper shook his head. "Only those aboard *Vanguard*. All others go through the fire. It's the way Jesus-Brother has planned it."

Butcher lowered his eyes to think for a moment. Cooper remained silent and serene, more confident in his destiny than ever. Lila Ruth and the other elders were prepared to answer questions, but Captain Sams was clearly the mouthpiece of Pathfinder today.

"Doomsday flight." Butcher appeared to be thinking aloud. He spoke the term as if testing out how it sounded. Then he said the words again in the direction of the five people sitting at the table. "Doomsday flight. That's what you should call it."

"*Vanguard*," Cooper corrected with a thin smile. "Doomsday doesn't fit our vision of the advanced detachment joyously arriving first for Reunion."

Butcher didn't seem to hear him as he rolled his new phrase over in his mind. But in seconds a new thought sparked him to life. "You said you have a few openings in the Family. You must have a few seats left to sell on the doomsday flight."

"No, Mr. Butcher, we're not selling anything. We're offering the available seats to anyone."

Butcher was calculating. "Let's see, a 737 has about 130 seats—"

"One-twenty-eight on our aircraft," Cooper interjected. "Eight in the first-class cabin and 120 in coach, plus 2 in the cockpit and 5 jump seats."

"Okay, then, room for 135 passengers."

"Maximum."

"With 109 members, that means you have 26 seats to sell to the highest bidders. And I'll bet people will pay plenty to skip hellfire and soar straight to heaven. You guys will be rich."

Cooper sensed his patience wearing thin under Earl Butcher's endless ridicule. The media people who had already left the room would likely communicate nothing about what they heard. And Butcher had apparently outlasted the others only for the purpose of enjoying the sport of taunting another bunch of lunatics with a doomsday fixation. Cooper was tempted to end the conference right now and consign

Butcher to burn in the fires he so flippantly maligned.

Pathfinder's presence quickly centered him. Earl Butcher was a jerk, a slob, but he was no threat to Reunion or to Vanguard. Jesus-Brother's purposes would be accomplished with or without the arrogant newsman. *Let him play*, Pathfinder urged, *and realize that he, like everyone else, will wish he had been more charitable in his treatment of my Family.*

"The additional seats on the airplane will be given free of charge to those who seek them," Cooper said calmly.

"Don't they have to convert to your religion or do something special to qualify?"

"Kindness and charity toward strangers and aliens is a tenet of all religions."

"What will you do if more than twenty-six people want a ride?" Butcher prodded. "Put folding chairs in the aisle?"

"An equitable way will be found to distribute the available seats to any who may be interested."

Butcher was silent as he removed a box of brown cigarettes from his coat pocket, withdrew one, and lit up. "So the doomsday flight takes off from Paine Field next to the Boeing plant."

"Vanguard, yes."

"So where are you going officially?" Butcher asked, exhaling after a long drag.

"Reunion, as I've explained."

"Captain, you're required to file a flight plan any time you take off, but you can't put on there that you're headed for a big reunion in heaven. What are you going to put on your flight plan?"

"An acceptable flight plan will be filed," Cooper said, intentionally vague.

Butcher sat forward in his chair. "All right, you said you're headed north. So perhaps you file a flight plan for Juneau. That would be a nice touch, since that's where you allegedly received your 'call.' "

Cooper watched Butcher pull on the smoldering cigarette and release a cloud of smoke. Butcher's next question was less biting and more inquisitive. "So you start up the west coast of British Columbia, and 8:02 comes and goes, and 9:02 comes and goes. You're almost to Juneau and nothing has happened. What will you do then?"

"By 8:03 P.M. Seattle time, *Vanguard* will be empty, perhaps already devoured by the flames of judgment. And we will be with our Brother."

"No, let's say that you miscalculated just a wee bit—by a few hours or a few days. You're up there and nothing happens. Will you be able to bring the plane down?"

"Mr. Butcher, this issue is not up for debate," Cooper answered with an edge of irritation on his voice. "We will stake our lives on the veracity of the revelation concerning February 20, 2002. Reunion will occur as we have informed you. We share this information with you in hopes that you will disseminate the information and that people around the world will prepare their souls for Reunion. We're not interested in contingency plans."

"What do you mean you will stake your lives on this trip?" Butcher pressed, standing. He looked like death on two spindly legs, but his voice was strong, as if all his strength had left his limbs to support his lungs and vocal cords. "Do you mean that you're going to blow the wheels off the plane after takeoff so you can't possibly land? Do you mean that you're leaving with only an hour's worth of fuel, intentionally planning for the engines to quit over the Pacific Ocean? Are you going to aim your *Vanguard* straight into the side of Mt. McKinley whether or not anyone is still aboard?"

Cooper could hear hushed movement on both sides of him, a nervous rubbing of hands and shuffling of feet. The elders of the New Jesus Family had never uttered a word of doubt concerning the precise moment of Reunion. The deuces and zeros—2002 0220 2002—was a revelation from Jesus-Brother Himself, not a calculation that is subject to mathematical variables or human error. Reunion was not a great problem they had solved but a mighty mystery which had been revealed to them. The deeper they had delved into Pathfinder through meditation, the clearer the revelation appeared, not only to Lila Ruth but to everyone in the small circle of elders. The idea that Reunion would not occur as they had been told was inconceivable and offensive.

Nor had Cooper ever considered "proving" his trust in Reunion and *Vanguard* in the manner Earl Butcher suspected. *Vanguard* would leave Paine Field under a flight plan to Sitka or Juneau or Anchorage to fulfill FAA requirements, but they would never arrive. Cooper had no plans to jettison the landing gear after takeoff even though he knew it would not be needed for a landing. And Cooper would make sure that the plane was loaded with enough fuel to reach its flight plan destination, even though only a fraction of the fuel would be used before Reunion occurred. Why try to pull off a hairbrained, death-defying, carnival-type stunt to prove a point?

Why not? What a stunning declaration of faith in Jesus-Brother to leave Seattle with no human possibility to return. What an excellent means to announce that you are as devoted to him as Lila Ruth Atkinson. What an opportunity to rise to the level of your teacher in the eyes of Parent-God himself.

The words were clearly from Pathfinder. The message was delivered and lodged in his subconscious in a fraction of a second, like a seed quickly buried in the ground and forgotten, only to sprout and flourish at a later time.

"We have no need for such drastic measures of so-called proof, Mr.

Butcher," Cooper responded. "When I say that we are staking our lives on Reunion, I mean that we have pooled our material resources to purchase and outfit an airplane because we will no longer need the money to subsist. I mean that we are quitting our jobs because we will not be here to complete them. I mean that we are enduring humiliation and ostracism from friends, family, and in some cases even spouses for what we believe. We don't need any sideshow tricks like you have suggested to prove to ourselves or to our God that we are prepared to follow through with our destiny."

Another seed thought flew past Cooper's consciousness faster than a blink and buried itself deep in his mind. It was a way to prove his trust in Reunion and *Vanguard,* a way Earl Butcher had not mentioned, but could have.

Thirty-one

Myrna Valentine slipped into a teal crushed-velvet warm-up suit, then wrapped herself in a white floor-length quilted satin robe. She left on the gray wool socks she had worn under her boots all day and pulled on a pair of fleece-lined slippers to keep her feet toasty warm.

It had been in the mid-thirties all week in Portland with the hint of a little snow before the weekend was over. Myrna had left the heat at 60 degrees in her spacious northwest downtown loft while she was at the coast for Thanksgiving. But the pilot light in her oil furnace had blown out, and she returned home this evening to find the inside temperature at 45. The old brick warehouse had been converted into quaint, airy lofts with lots of glass. Myrna loved her place. The lease was very reasonable, and the loft glowed with personality thanks to her novel but thrifty decorating. But the high ceilings, wood floors, drafty doors, and single-pane windows made it a bear to heat. Myrna feared it would take all night for the restarted furnace to heat the large one-room apartment up to a tolerable 65.

With a steaming homemade latté in hand, Myrna shuffled from the kitchen area to an overstuffed futon strewn with large decorator pillows. She placed her mug on the glass-topped table while she nestled into the cushions under a shower of warming light from an antique floor lamp with five bright globes shaped like candle flames. After another sip of hot, milky-sweet coffee, she pulled the collar of her robe tight around her neck and turned her attention to a stack of unopened mail and newspapers on the table.

It had been five long, exhausting days since Myrna had been able to sit down with a latté and leisurely open her mail, and even longer since she had perused the newspapers. A holiday workweek at the agency had forced her to cram five days of modeling classes, appointments, and photo shoots into three. On the up side, the children's modeling school and talent agency Myrna had formed on a shoestring nearly two years earlier was thriving. Over the past decade the Pacific Northwest had become a less-harried, less-pricey alternative to L.A. and San Francisco in the entertainment and advertising industries. The influx of ad houses and film and video production companies to Portland assured Myrna's clients of plenty of work. And when her clients worked, Myrna made good money.

On the down side, as the sole owner of the Valentine School and Agency with only an assistant and a part-time bookkeeper, Myrna was working far more than she wanted to as a single mom. She did not date or "pub crawl" Portland's trendy microbreweries as so many of her acquaintances did. She had neither the desire nor the time to do so. But every overtime hour in the business meant one less hour spent with the light of her life, Guy, now two years and nine months old. She took little Guy with her to the studio whenever she could, which wasn't often. And she always accompanied her son, who had been her first child model, whenever he was used for a clothing or toy catalog. But most of the time Myrna's sweet little Guy was confined to day care, which distressed her greatly. But she was trapped in the familiar Catch-22 of the working mom: work to enjoy the child, no time to enjoy the child because of work.

Myrna saw no relief in sight. Business was good, but not good enough to hire and train someone to relieve some of the time pressure. She could sell the business, but she would still have to work, perhaps with even less control over her schedule than she enjoyed now. And perhaps another job would not provide sufficient income to support her ongoing therapy and needed drugs.

Another solution was for Myrna to marry into success and prosperity. Her parents had nagged her continuously about this option so that Guy could have a father. There was certainly an ample supply of well-heeled bachelors in Portland who would jump at a nod from the strikingly beautiful Amerasian model/businesswoman. But as far as Myrna was concerned, there was only one man in the world. Little Guy's father and namesake, Guy Rossovich, was now a California state senator. Three and a half years ago Guy had tossed Myrna away like last year's fashions. Myrna had hoped that time might allow the flame within her to burn out. But every glance at her son was like another reviving breeze over the glowing embers of her old affair. No matter how successful she became, she was not fully alive without Guy Rossovich. And she was far from being happy.

Last Sunday, with three sixteen-hour days ahead of her before Thanksgiving, Myrna had taken Guy out to her parents' place in Astoria, about a ninety-minute drive from Portland along the Columbia River to its mouth. Guy was excited to stay with "Gamma and Gampa" for a few days, and Mark and Thuy Valentine were even more thrilled at the prospect. Myrna plunged into her work Monday, Tuesday, and Wednesday, leaving little time for anything but sleep. Then, missing her little boy tremendously, she locked up the office and left for Astoria at 10:30 P.M. Wednesday night so she could be there when Guy woke up Thanksgiving morning.

Thanksgiving Day had been delicious and fun and hectic with Myrna's brothers and their families there from California. Gampa and Gamma were so thrilled to have all their grandchildren around them that they wouldn't let the kids take naps. Instead they took everyone except Myrna up to the Astoria column to climb the inside spiral staircase for a spectacular view of Astoria, the bridge to Washington, and the Columbia River flowing into the Pacific Ocean. Myrna took advantage of the quiet to take a much-needed nap.

On the drive back to Portland earlier this evening, Guy couldn't stop jabbering about Gamma and Gampa and bridges and tugboats and grain ships and tankers. Myrna suspected that her son's already substantial vocabulary had doubled during his three-day stay with her parents. Then during a thirty-second lapse in their delightful conversation, little Guy dropped off into an exhausted sleep. He didn't even wake up when she carried him from the car to his bedroom, which was tucked into a corner of the loft behind a beautiful hanging rug for a wall. His soft, steady breathing could be heard now above the whish of warm air flowing through the heater vents.

Myrna picked up the stack of mail, which was as thick as a good table dictionary, and separated the real mail from the junk mail. As always, the junk mail pile was taller, including the standard pieces she could identify without opening the envelope: a letter stating that she had been preapproved for a low-interest, no-annual-fee platinum InterCorp bank card; two notices—one under the name Myrna Valentine, the other under M. Valentino—that she was a bona fide finalist in the next publisher's sweepstakes; several envelopes of discount coupons for obscure products and services Myrna never used; an invitation to join a music club and get ten new mini-CDs for 99 cents each; and printed advertisements for everything from tune-ups and oil changes to denture creams to quickie divorce services to the latest in wireless phones.

Myrna set the junk mail stack aside to send back. She regularly marked unopened junk mail "Refused" and sent it off with her outgoing mail. She wasn't convinced that sending the stuff back would reduce the flow coming into her mailbox, but it gave her some satisfaction that the senders would have to pay return postage on the unwanted mail. At least she hoped they would have to pay for it.

Next she separated the real mail into two stacks: good mail and bad mail—bills and account statements. The bill pile won, 5-3. But with a decent job and sufficient though sometimes sporadic income, Myrna was not intimidated by the bill pile as she was during the first six months of the Valentine School and Agency. In those days, everything she earned went right back into the business. Myrna wouldn't have survived start-up had it not been for the generosity of her father, Mark Valentine. But this year she had finally repaid her parents and re-gained positive cash flow.

The three pieces of good mail were all hand addressed. Myrna smiled as she identified the senders from the return address stickers on the envelopes. One was a card—probably a "good friends are friends forever" type card, she guessed—from Mattie, her buddy and travel agent in L.A. Myrna had not been back to L.A. since she moved away three and a half years ago. But Mattie, making the most of her travel agent discounts, had visited Myrna in Portland twice. They also talked on the phone a couple times a month. Mattie was the only person outside her family to whom Myrna was committed to write real letters and cards. Having a friend like Mattie helped Myrna stave off the incessant pangs of loneliness and yearning for Guy's father.

The other pieces of good mail were Christmas cards, her first of the season. They were from two of her child modeling clients and their families. Most of her clients sent Christmas cards to the office. But these two, Brittany Claboe, age eight, and Hunter Tighe, age twelve, had been among her first. She had worked hard to get them both into catalogs for Fred Meyer Department Stores and the Bon Marche. Hav-ing grown up with Myrna and the agency, Brittany, Hunter, and their parents felt like family, making it perfectly logical to send Christmas cards to a home instead of an office.

Before Myrna could open any of the envelopes, her compact wireless phone, which she had left on the bed when she changed out of her clothes, sounded. She scrambled from the futon trying to get to the phone before it emitted another annoying chirp, which might wake Guy. She caught it halfway through the second ring, almost certain about who was calling. "Hello."

She was right. Mark Valentine was checking to make sure his daughter and grandson had made it home safely. He had heard that portions of Highway 30 along the river were icy. Myrna reminded him that her old Isuzu Trooper had four-wheel drive and studded tires and that she was a cautious driver. She secretly relished his concern for her.

Mark went on to gush about how much he enjoyed Thanksgiving Day with his family. Myrna took the phone back to the futon and snuggled into the warm spot to open the Christmas cards as he talked.

She opened each one, read the sentiment, and stood them on the table facing her. Mark mentioned that they found a pair of Guy's socks and underwear still in the dryer, and that they would drop them by the next time they were in Portland. Myrna thanked him for the nice day and his kindness. They each said "I love you," and the conversation was over.

Myrna had saved Mattie's card until last. As suspected, it was a flowery friendship card. Typically, Mattie had filled all the blank space inside and on the back with her own message, written in words so small Myrna had to sound them out one at a time.

The message was typical too: a recent "fam" trip to the Caribbean to familiarize herself with hotels and hot spots; her stormy love life with a here-tonight-gone-tomorrow boyfriend she knew she should send packing. Then Myrna's eyes came to a section that caused her to suck in her breath and hold it as she read:

> Your old flame, the honorable Sen. Guy Rossovich of Calif., has been in the news lately. It seems that the dishonorable Mrs. R. has "allegedly" been catting around on him again—"allegedly" with some rich hunk she "allegedly" picked up at the gym or somewhere. (Allegedly always means the person did it but won't admit it, right? Ha!) The *Times* says that they're already separated and that she's divorcing him and taking the kids, like he's some kind of martyr. Poor baby! Like he's been Mr. Lily White all these years! Serves him right. What goes around . . . eh?

Mattie went on to talk about her brother getting a scholarship to UCLA, but Myrna didn't read it. She went back to the section that began "Your old flame" and read it again and then a third time. Mattie knew about Guy Rossovich, but Myrna hadn't told her everything. Mattie knew that Rossovich and Myrna had enjoyed a fling, that Guy had dumped Myrna, and that little Guy was Guy's son. Mark and Thuy Valentine didn't even know who the father was. Mattie also knew that Guy was in the dark about little Guy and would stay in the dark— Myrna had sworn her to secrecy under penalty of death or worse. And Mattie *assumed* that Guy Rossovich was forever locked away in Myrna's distant and painful past—which is exactly what Myrna wanted her to believe. If Mattie suspected that her friend had purposely left the door open to the past, she might never have written about the breakup of Guy's marriage.

Myrna would have found out about it anyway. In addition to her subscription to the *Oregonian*, Myrna still received daily and Sunday issues of the *Los Angeles Times* by mail. She continued to take the *Times*, she had told her parents, because staying up on L.A. fashion and social life was important to her business. This was partially true.

But her primary reason for reading the *Times* every day was to keep up on the movements of state senator Guy Rossovich both in the political section and on the society page. Anything which appeared about him she clipped out and carefully added to a scrapbook for little Guy, a scrapbook she had shown no one.

Myrna swept aside several issues of the *Oregonian* on the table to get to the ten most recent issues of the *Times* which had piled up unread. In her haste, Myrna knocked her half-full mug of latté onto the wood floor where it shattered. She ignored the mess. She tore into the most recent issue—Wednesday's—looking for the article Mattie had alluded to and anything else written about Guy Rossovich in the last ten days. She spread the papers on the glass-topped coffee table and methodically scanned every page before tossing it to the floor to open another issue.

The story about Guy was in the Sunday edition before Thanksgiving. Myrna hovered over the brief article next to a small file photo of Senator Guy Rossovich addressing his constituents. The sight of his dark, wavy hair and strong facial features released a deluge of often-visited memories: their first encounter in San Francisco, their quiet rendezvous in quaint restaurants around L.A., their first torrid night together, the long days and luxuriant nights of intimacy, time, Myrna learned much later, he had stolen from his wife and daughters and given to her. Seeing his picture again made her pulse quicken.

The article said little more than Mattie had summarized in her note. But Myrna pored over every line. The man she loved and yearned for had finally experienced the same pain she had borne for over three years. He had been betrayed, lied to, cheated on, and dumped. He was really struggling with his feelings now, she knew. He was vulnerable and needy. Myrna hurt for him.

Pulling the scissors from a nearby child-proofed drawer, Myrna carefully cut out the article. She retrieved the unmarked scrapbook from a shelf near her bed and mounted the article on the first blank page. Only after replacing the scrapbook did she return to the table to clean up the spilled latté and ceramic cup shards and restack the newspapers.

She fixed herself another latté and returned to the futon, turning out the lamp and curling up on the cushions in the cold darkness. There was no use going to bed anytime soon, she realized. The raucous thoughts and discordant feelings tumbling within her would keep her wide awake. She even feared that Guy might hear the noise and awake. She was at a loss to discern which thoughts were right and which were wrong, which choices were wise and which were foolish. And she had no one to ask. She would have to sort this out by herself, and she knew she wouldn't sleep until she found a solution to the dilemma of Guy Rossovich.

After an hour and a half sipping latté and brooding on the futon, Myrna stood and made her way into Guy's "room." Reflected light from a street lamp outside cast a soft, blue glow across the boy's tousled, curly black hair and cherubic face. The loft was still quite cool, but the boy's cheeks were pleasantly warm to Myrna's gentle touch. His breathing was deep and steady, marred only by the gentle wheeze, the remnant of a minor cold.

Myrna wanted to wake him and tell him the wonderful news but restrained herself. Yet she kissed him and stroked him continually until he finally stirred and squirmed from his back to his stomach in deep sleep.

"My beautiful little Guy," Myrna whispered. "We have a project ahead of us." She pulled at the damp, black curls clinging to the nape of his neck. "Your daddy needs us now, and we must go to him."

Thirty-two

Mr. and Mrs. Reagan Cole pulled it off. Thanks to great teamwork, the couple set a delicious dinner on the table in less than an hour while allowing brief moments for hugs, love pats, and kisses along the way.

While Beth thawed and grilled the chicken breasts, Cole ran to the corner market to get ice and supplement their supply of fresh vegetables. Beth cleaned and cut up the broccoli, asparagus, peppers, and onions and started a large pot of water for the pasta. Cole picked up the living room, stashed everything behind the closed bedroom door, cued a stack of ambient instrumental CDs, and set the table.

Had their guest arrived on time, Cole would have switched roles from assistant cook and gofer to pleasant host as Beth finished preparations. But Raul was late, so Cole kept chugging away on chores. While Beth slipped away to do her hair and change clothes, he ground fresh ginger and garlic for the stir fry and cut the grilled chicken into strips with kitchen shears. He filled the stemware with spring water and cocktail ice purchased at the market—"tinkly ice" he and Beth called it. Tinkly ice was one of the couple's luxuries. They disliked using "clunky ice" from freezer ice cube trays because it was cloudy and common. Tinkly ice made every beverage look and sound special.

"Bread, we need bread," Beth exclaimed in mild panic as she reappeared in the kitchen looking fresh and beautiful in black slacks and a billowy burgundy blouse. She was allowing her dark, silky hair to grow long again after a short summer cut, but it only barely reached her collar.

"We have dinner rolls in the freezer," Cole said, thinking he had solved the problem.

"No, no, no. Not frozen dinner rolls with my stir fry and pasta. Run down to the store and get a loaf of focaccia."

"But I've already been to the store once," Cole complained. "How about serving those Wheat Thins we have in the pantry. We could slice up some cheddar and—"

Beth's overacted comic glare communicated clearly. Cole headed for the door. "What if Raul shows up while I'm gone?" he said, slipping on his jacket. Beth mimicked the expression that might have been on Einstein's face the moment he discovered relativity. "I've got it. I'll open the door and let him in and introduce myself."

Cole grinned. "You're a genius." Then he headed out the door.

"Fresh focaccia, not frozen," Beth called after him. "And get something for dessert."

Cole stuck his head back in the door. "Fresh or frozen?"

Beth smiled and blew him a kiss. "Your choice, my darling. Knock yourself out."

Cole closed the door exulting in his independence as a husband.

Raul pulled into the complex and parked just as Cole trotted across the street from his second visit to the Promenade Stop 'n' Shop. Cole waved hello and then stood by as Raul unfolded his wheelchair and transferred into it from the Caprice with the skill of a gymnast maneuvering a pommel horse.

"How was your big event?" Raul probed as they moved together toward the elevator. "I've been thinking about it all day. Are you sure your wife is up to company tonight?"

Cole was oblivious to Raul's thoughts. "We had a great day, and Beth is fine. She was excited when I told her you were coming." He decided not to tell his new friend about the last minute dash to get dinner ready.

Raul's large eyes were riveted to Beth as Cole introduced them. After shaking her hand, he lifted a bottle of sparkling cider with pink and blue ribbons tied around the neck. "Congratulations on your new arrival, Beth," he said. "You look terrific. I can't believe you just had a baby and you're ready for a dinner guest already."

Cole and Beth exchanged puzzled looks without bothering to take the bottle. Then Cole said to Beth, "Did I miss something while I was at the Stop 'n' Shop?" Beth returned a look of total confusion.

Raul read the perplexity in their faces, blanched with embarrassment, and back-pedaled. "This afternoon while I was in your office, Reagan. Remember? Your wife called and said it was 'time.' You mentioned something about water breaking. Then you invited me to dinner and fired out of there like a shot. You said you were having a new addition to your family. I just thought—"

Cole and Beth started laughing and couldn't stop. They were still laughing as Cole left the room and returned with two tiny puppies — one blonde and one black — cupped in his big hands. It was his turn to be embarrassed. "These are our new additions, six of them in all," he said, displaying the wriggling pups. "I guess in my hurry to get home I left out one important piece of information. They were born to our cocker, Princess Di, not Beth and me."

Raul joined in the good-natured laughter, and they all joked about Beth being Wonder Woman: babies in the afternoon, dinner party in the evening. Cole returned the puppies to the box and popped the cap on the bottle of sparkling cider and poured a glass for everyone. They toasted Princess Di and drank and laughed some more. Raul apologized for being late and for making Beth slave all afternoon on a special dinner. The man in the wheelchair did not see the secret loving winks exchanged by his hosts.

Cole occupied Raul in the living room while Beth drained the pasta, heaped it on a large platter, and smothered it with grilled chicken and vegetable stir fry topped with fresh grated romano. Then she delivered the feast to the table, followed by hot fococcia drenched in olive oil and garlic.

Once they were all seated around the table, Cole initiated a small circle of linked hands and offered a short, simple prayer of thanks for the food and the evening together. After Cole pronounced his amen, Raul held onto his hosts' hands. "You're Christians," he said with an expression of pleased surprise.

Cole and Beth looked at each other. Then Cole said, "We're kind of rookie Christians. I gave my life to the Lord almost two years ago. For Beth it was . . ."

Beth chimed in just as Cole had hoped, "Just last summer."

"Well, praise God!" Raul said enthusiastically. "I'm a Christian too!"

"Yeah," Cole said, "we've heard a lot about how your faith in God carried you through this . . . problem." Cole's eyes fell on Raul's hand which was gently gripping his. It was somewhat misshapen and supported by a leather wrist brace.

"I was ready to witness to you this afternoon, Reagan," Raul said, finally releasing their hands. "You asked about my religious faith, and I was ready to give you the straight scoop on what it means to be a believer. Surprise! You already know the Lord. What a blessing! I need to hear your stories."

"Stories?" Beth said.

"You know, how God got your attention, how you came to give your lives to Him, how you two met."

Beth and Cole's "stories," nudged along by Raul's questions, continued through dinner, dessert, and cappuccino. Cole described, with help from Beth, the potentially disastrous crisis in the Los Angeles

Coliseum on Millennium's Eve in which he almost lost Beth shortly after they met. He told about meeting a quiet, faith-filled Vietnamese-American couple running a care center for L.A.'s destitute. "I know Dr. No's prayers that week prevented something very ugly from happening," he said with appreciation in his voice. "That's when I started to ask serious questions about God. And that's when I realized that He was interested in me personally."

Beth affirmed the positive example of Dr. and Mrs. No, but admitted that she wasn't as receptive to their faith as Reagan had been. It was eighteen months later, she related, near the end of a grueling chase with Cole up Interstate Five from Los Angeles to the Canadian border, that she had a convincing encounter with God. "I saw the change that took place in Reagan while we were apart, and I knew he had found something I wanted," Beth concluded. "Then God put His hand on me—literally—and I haven't been the same."

"That's more than enough about us," Beth said as she refilled everyone's cups in the living room. "Let's hear your story, Raul."

Raul tried to brush it off. "It's getting late, and I still have to drive clear to Saugus tonight."

"It's not *that* late," Beth insisted. "Besides, you and Reagan had today to talk and you'll be together on Monday. I may not get to see you again while you're in town. It's not fair that I get shut out of your story."

Raul had no good reason to turn down his charming hostess. He was weary of telling the story of his success in baseball, his tragic accident, and his new career in law enforcement, especially since it didn't have the happy ending he had longed for and expected. He never wanted to be another Lowell Banks, the one-legged former ballplayer turned minister. He wanted to be—and fully intended to be—the miraculous exception, something he still had difficulty talking about. But Reagan and Beth had graciously told their stories. He didn't want to spoil the evening by acting out his stubbornness.

After countless tellings, Raul had pared his story down to the essentials. For the Coles' benefit, he expanded the part about his Christian upbringing, relating how he had given his heart to Christ as a child kneeling beside his parents' bed. He tried to downplay his success as a college baseball player, but Cole and Beth kept bringing up some of his more famous exploits on the field, so he graciously talked about them.

Beth asked about Raul's Christian faith as a college student and athlete, adding, "During my days at USC, I was real snotty toward anyone who tried to push their religion on me."

Raul recounted his role in the campus fellowship group at ASU and his attempts to be a godly example and positive witness to his teammates. "I knew a lot of people like you, Beth," he concluded, "people who respected me as an athlete but who blew me off in a hurry when I tried to share my faith. I'm afraid I wasn't very successful as a campus evangelist."

"But you don't know how many people you may have influenced in the right direction," Cole argued in Raul's defense. "Your teammates may not have seemed interested, but that doesn't mean they didn't hear you. Like the Bible says, you planted some seeds; the rest is up to God."

Raul could have argued the point. He had done so in the privacy of his own mind for months. *If I planted seeds, why didn't any of my teammates come to Christ?* he had grilled himself repeatedly. *Seeds result in fruit. I don't see any fruit, so I must not have done a good job of planting.* But Raul was tired. He didn't want to open a can of worms with his new friends and turn a nice evening into a pity party.

The phone rang and Beth retreated to the bedroom to answer it. Raul and Cole sat in silence for a moment.

"I read somewhere that you expected to be miraculously healed," Cole said. "You apparently told people you would be playing for the Giants just months after you were injured. Does it bother you that things didn't work out the way you hoped?"

Raul recognized the same honest, nonjudgmental interest the sergeant had displayed earlier in the day with his question about the headfirst slide. But the question about the miracle that never happened was the mother of all cans of worms. Raul liked Cole and Beth well enough to believe he could talk to them about his inner conflict and they wouldn't think any less of him for his struggles. But he feared that, even if he verbalized his doubts honestly with sympathetic friends, doing so might somehow put off his miracle even further. Moreover, he didn't want to sow any seeds of doubt in the uncontaminated hearts of new believers.

Raul had grown up challenged to pray with aggressive faith and warned not to doubt. Raul could still see the Texas preacher pounding the pulpit during a revival service in his home church when he was a kid: "If you speak it, you've got it! If you doubt it, forget it!" There was too much on the line for Raul to get negative now. He had to stay with his convictions, battered and shaky though they may be. He decided to give his stock, cover-all-the-bases answer.

"I'm already healed, Reagan. God promises that we receive whatever we ask for in His name. I claimed my healing three years ago even before they put me in the halo brace, so I must be healed. I just haven't experienced the results yet. I'll be out there with the Giants yet."

Beth was back in the room before Cole could ask another question, for which Raul was grateful. "That was Dad," she said to Cole in Raul's hearing. "He said Mom has a touch of something and doesn't want to sit out in the cold tomorrow. He's still planning to go with us.

So I told him I knew someone who might be interested in Mom's ticket."

"Great idea!" Cole exclaimed. "What are you doing tomorrow, Raul?"

Raul shrugged. "I don't know. I haven't spent much time with my aunt and uncle since I've been here. They may have plans." Raul wanted to leave his options open.

"Tomorrow's the big game: UCLA and USC at the Coliseum," Beth informed. "We have an extra seat, and we'd love to have you go with us."

"I already have a seat," Raul quipped, nodding to his wheelchair. "All I need is a place to park it. Sounds fun."

"If UCLA wins, the Bruins go to the Rose Bowl," Cole said excitedly.

"Your Bruins will choke as usual," Beth taunted good-naturedly. "My Trojans will run your boys into the ground."

"And if Southern Cal eliminates UCLA," Raul chimed in, more than a little interested, "ASU goes to Pasadena. This could be a great game."

"You'll go with us then?" Beth said.

Raul paused thoughtfully. "Let me make sure my relatives don't have something planned. Can I call you first thing in the morning?"

Cole and Beth agreed. Then Cole gave directions for where Raul could park and where they should rendezvous outside the Coliseum. Raul thanked them both for the great evening and left.

By the time he reached the Santa Monica Freeway, Raul was battling an attitude. He didn't like the thoughts and feelings that were grinding his stomach into a knot. But the more he tried to ignore them, the more they pressed in on him. Raul was a problem-solver by nature. It was one of the skills that led him into detective work with the Phoenix Police Department, and it was a skill not diminished by his physical disability. So with an hour's drive still ahead of him up I-405 to Saugus, Raul decided to analyze his disposition, even though he was sure he wouldn't like what he found.

He thought about Reagan and Beth Cole. They were wonderful people, and he was glad he had spent the evening with them. But their experiences, as exciting and miraculous as they seemed, had left him feeling uncomfortable. He thought back through the stories each had shared and came to an observation. Here were two former pagans whose narrow brush with death had brought them to God. They were transformed from antagonistic unbelievers to people of simple, pure, sincere faith.

By contrast, Raul had grown up as a person of faith. He learned about God and prayer and miracles along with the ABCs. Then came the tragedy in Omaha. But instead of bringing him closer to God, Raul's crisis seemed to be picking away at his faith. These baby Christians were on the way up while he, the "mature" believer, seemed constantly to be digging in his nails to keep from slipping farther down. He recognized that the seeming inequity was grinding on him.

As he guided his hand-controlled Caprice over the rain-slicked grade between West Los Angeles and the San Fernando Valley, he tried to talk to God about his feelings. But his prayers were repeatedly interrupted by another dark conflict he had encountered many times before.

Reagan Cole was a blessed man to be married to Beth. Raul had found himself distracted by her during the evening, prompting thoughts he was physically unable to act out but which were nonetheless incongruous with his lifelong commitment to purity. Raul had discovered early that, even though normal sexual activity was impossible in his condition, his normal masculine drives had survived the accident in Omaha unscathed. He had often considered that the paralysis of his sexual appetites might be very helpful to him as long as his physical paralysis remained. But such was not the case, as an evening in the presence of beautiful Beth Cole had once again demonstrated.

This awareness highlighted the second annoying inequity bugging Raul. Coming from a worldly background, Reagan and Beth had doubtless enjoyed a generous helping of sexual freedom prior to their encounter with God and commitment to marriage. Beth had even mentioned in her story a fling with an east coast publisher in the weeks prior to her spiritual awakening. They had sown their wild oats and tasted the forbidden fruits of moral impurity Raul had shunned with great restraint as a Christian young man. And how had God rewarded him for his exemplary abstinence? By robbing him both of his sexual potency and the one woman he had been saving himself for. There were times when Raul almost wished he had yielded to the sexual temptations of his youth. It seemed heartless of God to challenge him to purity and then take away his capacity to enjoy it.

Raul turned the harsh thoughts over and over without resolution. He was midway through the Valley, flowing along with the river of Friday-night freeway traffic. The wipers wigwagged steadily, but the rain kept coming as if to mock the diligence of the blades' futile struggle. Raul felt like the wipers: doggedly staying with the program but seemingly unable to make any headway.

It all comes back to faith, he chided himself. *I can only get past all this anger and doubt by exercising my faith. I will only receive my healing if I am bold in faith, bolder than I have ever been.* But Raul wasn't sure if being around Reagan and Beth Cole would help or hinder him in his attempts.

Thirty-three

Tommy Eggers stood naked for several minutes in front of the bathroom mirror after his morning shower. He had run his hand once over the surface to clear the condensation for the daily inspection. Then, curious about what he thought he saw, Tommy wiped the mirror dry with a hand towel to allow him a better look. It hadn't been there yesterday, or at least he hadn't noticed it yesterday. But there was no denying what he was seeing. His index finger touched a faint bluish-purple mark just to the right of his Adam's apple. The irregularly shaped discoloration covered an area no larger than a collar button.

Tommy leaned into the mirror for a closer look. He knew exactly what it was, and he was amazed at how calm he felt about it. In the three-and-a-half years since he had tested HIV-positive, Tommy had become well educated on the symptoms of acquired immuno-deficiency syndrome. He had grown to expect the appearance of the strange discoloration on his neck, just as a criminal on the run might expect to find a squad of police surrounding his hideout some morning.

The Viennese dermatologist who first discovered this type of lesion in 1872 and given it his name could never have imagined the impact his discovery would make a century later. The five cases of ultimately fatal cutaneous ulceration that Professor Moritz Kaposi presented to Austria's Royal Academy of Medicine would emerge in the spring of 1981 as a type of skin cancer characteristically associated with AIDS.

The outbreak of Kaposi's sarcoma among gay men in the early '80s mystified physicians at first. Except in Africa, the condition was so rare that a skin specialist in the U.S. might encounter only a dozen cases in an entire career. Only 500 cases had been recorded from its discovery in 1872 until the outbreak of the AIDS epidemic in 1981. Historically, the disease never affected men younger than age sixty and tended to strike only in central Africa and on the shores of the Mediterranean Sea. The ulcerations developed so slowly that its victims usually died of something else.

Then, in 1981, doctors in Los Angeles, San Francisco, and New York began seeing large numbers of young men in their prime in whom Kaposi's sarcoma advanced rapidly. The cancerous blue patches, which look something like bruises, spread over the torso, limbs, neck, and face. Often the tumors were not confined to the skin, attacking the tissue of internal organs such as the pharynx, esophagus, intestines, and lungs. In some cases, death occurred only a few months from the onset of the violet skin pustules.

In the early months of the AIDS crisis, the appearance of Kaposi's sarcoma or pneumocystis pneumonia, an extremely rare parasitic disease of the lungs also associated with a deficiency in the immune system, became twin death knells in the gay enclaves of America. Other opportunistic infections associated with immunosuppression tormented homosexual men, but none with the deadly frequency of the two conditions that first alerted the world to the presence of the greatest killer since bubonic plague.

"So the final act begins," Tommy said aloud, stepping back for a wide-angle look at himself. Tiny beads of water coursed from his sparse, wet hair down the pasty white flesh of his body. The droplets slowed where Tommy's protruding ribs seemed to act like speed bumps. His recent weight loss had not gone unnoticed, though he had tried to avoid thinking about it. However, this and recent bouts with fever and nocturnal sweats, plus a suspicious tenderness in his lymph nodes, were ominous signals that the dreaded retrovirus had succeeded in breaching the defenses in his immune system, leaving a clear path for the invasion of an eventually fatal infection. The skinny frame greeting him each morning in the mirror was a chief reason why Tommy did not explode in panic at the appearance of the tattoo of death on his neck.

Tommy had suffered plenty of emotional eruptions in the early months of his HIV infection. The anguish of having unknowingly pulled the trigger on the loaded chamber during his game of sexual roulette was intensified by the fact that he had been quite selective in his choice of partners. Other boys had been far less careful, and they were still clean. Tommy lamented the fact that Lady Luck had stacked the cards against him. In the time since his infection was confirmed, however, numbers of Tommy's "lucky" acquaintances also turned up HIV-positive.

Another bitter pill for Tommy to swallow was the coincidental discovery of the AIDS vaccine — irreverently called ULP, the "ultimate love potion," by a growing population of "clean," sexually aggressive singles — *after* his infection. Why couldn't the French and American immunologists have come up with the miracle substance a month sooner? Why didn't the unknown infected partner cross his path months after the discovery? Tommy had spent many tearful nights cursing a supreme being who took delight in mocking him so.

Tommy also cried for days after Alec left him, which happened within a month of the visit to Dr. Vanderhout. Commitment was sacred to Tommy. True, he had fallen to temptation a few times, but he had always come back to Alec. Clearly, Alec did not share his values. He had left while Tommy was on a trip, leaving only a curt note and a check to cover any unpaid expenses. Tommy called in sick for the next week trying to pull himself together after that emotional blow. Even his friend Evie Dukes wasn't around to console him. After a big fight with her boyfriend, Chuck Strahan, Evie quit her job and moved to back to

Redwood City to be near her parents, Marvin and Nora Dukes.

But the most devastating disappointment was delivered by Northstar Airlines. Tommy had expected to work at least a year before a mandatory AIDS screening, at which point he would be automatically terminated as a health risk to fellow employees and passengers. And if he could get around the screening—by hook or by crook—and stay in uniform longer, all the better, since he had squandered opportunities to contribute to a retirement plan. He needed all the income he could accumulate before he was forced out of the company.

But something went wrong, and Northstar pulled a surprise screening on his crew one afternoon when they checked in for a three-day trip only two months after his visit to Dr. Vanderhout. Tommy suspected that someone in the company had narced on him—setting up the supposedly "random" blood draw—but he could never prove it. He not only lost his job but, since the company subsequently discovered that he had been concealing the results of the blood test by his own physician, he lost the option to continue his medical coverage. It was a one-two punch that sent him into the ropes in utter despair. He was ready to throw in the towel. He had decided that he would jump off the Golden Gate Bridge before he would sponge off his friends or live on the street until the end came. He planned to do it when he could no longer pay the rent on his Pacific Heights apartment.

Then he met Dimitri Arantes. Dimitri was a silver-maned, obese, fifty-ish former mortgage banker. Tommy met him at a party just after the large man moved to San Francisco from Los Angeles. Dimitri was set for life thanks to a string of well-placed investments in the '80s, freeing him to enjoy his hobby of producing musical theater. He had kept his homosexuality in the closet until he found out that he was HIV-positive, four months before the discovery of CDCP-10 was announced. Confessing all to his wife and two daughters, Dimitri sought their forgiveness and understanding. But they disowned him. Devastated by the turn of events, he left L.A. determined to live out his days bankrolling musicals in the city where his lifestyle was most appreciated and accommodated.

Despite their age difference, Dimitri and then thirty-five-year-old Tommy, equally desperate for companionship and understanding, fell into each other's lives. Dimitri committed his resources to care for Tommy; Tommy would be a kept man. And Tommy committed his loyalty as a friend and lover. Tommy sold everything and moved into Dimitri's spacious high-rise apartment near Coit Tower where he revelled in the security and friendship of a mature relationship. Dimitri arranged his work to allow plenty of room for travel to Europe, the Orient, and Mexico, which he paid for. They had enjoyed three wonderful years together.

Tommy waited until after he was dry and dressed before calling.

Dimitri was probably in the car somewhere along I-280 between downtown and San Jose, he guessed. If the San Jose meeting went well this morning, Dimitri would head up a group taking *Guys and Dolls* on the road in 2002. It was Dimitri's most financially ambitious project yet.

Tommy stood in the living room gazing out at the bay while he waited for Dimitri to pick up the phone. The lead-gray sea was dotted with whitecaps. Solid clouds shut out any sky blue and morning gold from above. The gulls outside the window seemed to be discussing the merits of heading farther inland before the brunt of the storm hit.

"Hi," Tommy said without emotion at Dimitri's answer.

"Good morning, Tommy. How did you sleep?"

Tommy had no interest in small talk. "I found a spot on my neck."

"A spot?"

"A lesion, kind of purply-blue like a bruise."

"It can't be very large. I didn't notice it."

"No bigger than the tip of my little finger." Tommy put his finger on his neck and found the lesion by touch. "It's not very noticeable. I just saw it this morning."

Dimitri cleared his throat. Tommy knew he was trying to think of something positive to say. Dimitri was good at lifting Tommy's spirits. "Maybe it *is* a bruise. Maybe it's—"

"No, it's just what we think it is. You know I've been losing weight, and my lymph nodes have been very tender. It's Kaposi's sarcoma, Dimitri. I guess I drew the short straw again."

Tommy moved the mouthpiece away from his mouth as he began to cry softly. These weren't the tears of self-pity, he knew. He'd worked all that out of his system the first year of his infection, thanks in large part to Dimitri Arantes. Rather, the sudden thought of leaving his dear companion behind to face death alone caused Tommy inner pain. Worse yet, while Tommy dressed he had grown increasingly uneasy at the thought of Dimitri standing by while he wasted away to nothing. He would not allow Dimitri to forfeit weeks of his own tenuous life at his bedside, especially if the tumors robbed Tommy of his mind long before they squeezed out his last breath.

Dimitri was silent for several moments. Then he said, "Would you like me to come home now?" Tommy knew Dimitri was serious. He would give up the important meeting for him, and the realization brought a fresh round of tears.

"No," Tommy said, "I'm fine. I just had to tell you. The best thing you can do for me is to get these people down there to do *Guys and Dolls*. Bring home the good news tonight."

"I wish I had talked you into coming with me today," Dimitri said.

"I would be in the way. Just go get 'em, tiger, and hurry home. I have a few checks to print on the computer. Then I'm going down to the wharf to get something fresh for dinner. How does ling cod sound?"

"Wonderful!" Dimitri exclaimed. Then he asked again, "Are you sure you don't want me to come home now? I can reschedule the meeting."

"Thank you, Dimitri, but I'm sure," Tommy said, in control of his emotions. "I just had to get it off my chest. Thanks for listening."

"We'll talk about it when I get home, Tommy."

Tommy returned the phone to the table and pulled two tissues from a box on a lower shelf. As he wiped his eyes and nose, he thanked God for Dimitri Arantes. Then he had an odd and humorous thought: *Maybe God doesn't want the credit for Dimitri. Maybe He's not even listening to me.* He remembered Marvin and Nora Dukes, the congenial fundamentalist Christians he had met through his neighbor Evie in Pacific Heights. *Marvin was adamant that God loves homosexuals but hates homosexuality. How can He separate His feelings like that? If you love someone, you're devoted to them right or wrong. If God loves me at all, He has to take me the way I am. If He hates the way I am, all that Bible stuff about a loving God makes no sense.* Tommy thought he would enjoy talking to Marvin Dukes about that. He was sure the wise and kind old man would have something interesting to say.

Tommy gazed across the city skyline at the majestic pylons of the Golden Gate Bridge, whose tips were in the clouds. With the discovery of the lesion this morning, Tommy's countdown toward a fatal appointment with the bridge—which had been on hold since he met Dimitri— had quietly resumed. There was no way Tommy was going to subject his dear companion or himself to the trauma of a prolonged illness and slow death. The only humane and loving thing to do was to end his own life and spare them both the pain. Of all the ways Tommy had considered, the bridge was convenient, quick, and effective. A five-second thrill ride and then oblivion.

Tommy didn't know when he would do it. Nor could he tell Dimitri about his plans ahead of time, certain that his lover would physically restrain him if he had to. Tommy hoped he still had a few months to enjoy life with Dimitri and thoughtfully put into writing what these last years together had meant to him, a final love letter he would leave behind.

Then he would slip away and join the list of hundreds who had leaped from the bridge into eternity, nothingness, or whatever awaited him. He suddenly flashed on an old joke about the bridge: Jumping off won't kill you; it's the sudden stop at the bottom that does you in. The thought made Tommy shudder.

Thirty-four

The woman sat alone at the linen-draped table even though she had ordered place settings, goblets of ice water, and luncheon menus for three. A trim five feet, seven inches tall with softly curled, naturally blonde hair and compassionate powder-blue eyes, she was often guessed to be as much as ten years younger than her age of forty. She wore a bulky-knit ramie cotton sweater of multicolored blue over a denim shirt, fashion cut jeans, and black boots. Her jewelry, including a stunning wedding band, was conspicuous but not gaudy. The woman's appearance and bearing suggested that she was an executive of ample means awaiting a casual Saturday lunch with associates. Enterprising and active to be sure, she was neither a major player in the business world nor rich. Her name was Shelby Rider.

Shelby gazed out the tableside window at the tumbling, churning waterfall which had suggested the name for the popular Falls Terrace Restaurant alongside the freeway in Tumwater, Washington. The low gray clouds drizzled a steady rain over the pleasant landscape of rushing water, giant boulders, and evergreens. As she enjoyed the view, Shelby prayed silently for strength and wisdom to sustain her during her brief visit to Tumwater.

This luncheon meeting would consume a large portion of Shelby's Saturday. She had already invested almost two hours driving north on Interstate Five from her apartment in west Portland, Oregon, to the restaurant just outside the state capital of Olympia. The location was a pleasant compromise arranged with the woman she was meeting and her guest, who were driving down I-5 from Seattle, a little more than an hour to the north. Judging from the telephone conversation, Shelby anticipated a lengthy lunch table discussion—perhaps two or three hours. Then there was the two-hour drive home. It would be a long day for a supposed day off.

Saturday and Sunday were days Shelby generally devoted to her family: visiting her husband, Evan, near Salem, Oregon, and enjoying their seven-year-old adopted daughter, Malika. But her friend from Seattle, a woman who also regarded the attractive blonde as a spiritual mentor, had prevailed upon her for the opportunity to introduce the third member of today's luncheon trio, a woman in need of care. Despite the long drive from Portland and a Saturday away from home, Shelby had been pleased to rearrange her schedule at her friend's request.

Turning from the window, Shelby saw her friend threading between the noisy, occupied tables toward the window. Dr. Libby Carroll, in her early forties, was tall, stately, and as graceful as a dancer. Her skin was the color of rich mocha, and her thick black hair was pulled back and secured with a bow. She wore a kelly-green jumpsuit and a tan suede jacket with fringes.

Libby was followed by a petite, attractive woman of fifty-one in black denim jeans, designer sweatshirt, and a dark blue-green plaid hooded car coat. The gray in her nicely styled red-auburn hair had obviously been treated to help her maintain a youthful appearance. Her bright green eyes were overshadowed by a morose countenance. Even the woman's expertly applied makeup could not completely obliterate the lines and shadows of stress and the evidence of many recent tears. Shelby Rider's heart went out to her immediately.

Shelby stood and greeted Libby with a sisterly embrace. Then Libby quickly made the introductions. "Shelby, I'd like you to meet Rachel Sams, a recent acquaintance of mine. We met through a weekly coffee klatch at church. Rachel, this is my dear friend, Shelby Rider. I don't know anyone better for you to talk to."

Shelby reached out a welcoming hand which Rachel received meekly. "It's good to meet you, Rachel," she said with untarnished sincerity. Shelby's warm greeting coaxed a weak smile from Rachel.

Libby had provided for Shelby much more background on Rachel Sams prior to the introduction. Over the phone, Libby had described Rachel as a distraught woman directed to her coffee klatch by one of the ministers at her church, to whom Rachel had come for help. Libby had listened to Rachel's sad story, but as someone rather new to the Christian faith, she had sought the counsel and direct intervention of Shelby Rider in an attempt to help Rachel. Today's rendezvous in Tumwater was the result of their conversations.

Similarly, Libby had told Rachel all about Shelby Rider. Libby explained that Shelby, whom she had met only months ago amidst unusual and potentially life-threatening circumstances, had helped her navigate three months of personal crisis and directed her to a church in Seattle where Libby could nurture her infant faith. Though they lived in Seattle and Portland respectively, Libby and Shelby talked by phone at least once a week and occasionally exchanged visits. Libby had assured Rachel Sams that Shelby Rider would understand her dilemma and offer wise counsel and spiritual support. Desperate for a thread of hope, Rachel had agreed to the proposed get-together.

The three women decided to share a tureen of creamy homemade cauliflower and gruyere soup along with sourdough bread and individual garden salads. As placing their order, Libby and Shelby spent a few minutes catching up, being careful not to exclude Rachel Sams in the conversation.

Libby reported that her work as provost and vice-president of academic affairs at the University of Washington was still challenging and at times quite taxing. Her son, Brett, was doing well at Washington

State University despite his mother's pleas that he transfer to UW to be closer to home. The man in Libby's life was still Reginald Burris, a veteran police officer with the UWPD, but she insisted that they were only very good friends. Libby admitted that the brightest corner of her life at the moment was her involvement with a group of professional women from University Presbyterian Church who met weekly to discuss the Bible and pray for each other's concerns. It was through this group that Libby met Rachel Sams when she attended for the first time two weeks earlier.

Shelby related that her efforts to establish a care center for Portland's homeless and destitute were progressing nicely. The center was being called King's House Portland, named after the inner city Los Angeles care ministry of her friend and mentor Thanh Hai Ngo, whose selflessness and Christlike devotion had impacted Shelby's life profoundly. She bubbled with affection while talking about her daughter Malika, and she spoke with longing about the release of her husband, Evan, from the Oregon State Penitentiary in seventeen months. Libby had summarized for Rachel the story behind the couple's forced separation during the drive to Olympia, a harrowing story in which Libby had also played an important role.

The waiter served lunch, and Shelby offered a brief prayer of thanks. As the three women began to eat, Libby turned to Rachel Sams, who had been silent since they sat down. "I haven't told Shelby much about you, Rachel. In reality, I don't know all that much myself. I thought it would be good for you to explain your situation like you did to me that first time we met."

Rachel nodded, then placed her spoon on the plate, having taken only one sip of the creamy soup. She dropped her hands into her lap and stared into the bowl as if unsure how to start. Appreciating her discomfort, Shelby said, "It's OK, Rachel. Take your time. Eat some more soup first if you'd like."

Shelby's encouraging words seemed to provide the impetus Rachel lacked. "It's my husband," she began just above a whisper, still gazing downward. "Something very strange is happening to him. It's practically destroyed our marriage, and I think Cooper is in danger of going off the deep end mentally—if he hasn't already. I've tried to talk to him, but he won't listen to me. He treats me like I don't even exist. I . . . I came to the church one Sunday at the end of my tether—I'm not even sure how I got there. The minister directed me to Libby's group."

Rachel went silent. Shelby suspected that she was not far from tears. Libby rested a comforting hand on Rachel's arm.

After respecting Rachel's silence for several moments, Shelby asked, "Do you and your husband live together?"

Rachel looked up with a frown, the first sign of animation on her face since Libby introduced her. "We live in the same house, but we don't live together. I work for the airlines, and I'm gone several days a week. When I'm off work, he stays away from home except to sleep. He moved his clothes into the guest bedroom months ago. We haven't slept together in a couple of years."

"Is there another woman?" Shelby said as gently as she could, trying to draw the woman out.

Rachel locked onto Shelby's gaze as if ravenously feeding on the compassion pouring from them. "Yes, there is another woman, but it's not an affair—at least I don't think it is."

"He's emotionally involved with her then, like an adolescent crush?"

"No, he's *spiritually* involved with her," Rachel clarified. "The woman has lured Cooper into her religion. He's become a fanatic, a religious nut. It's destroying him—and us—and he doesn't even see it. That's why I thought a minister may be able to help me." Rachel broke eye contact and stared again at the soup cooling in her bowl.

Libby turned to Shelby. "Have you heard of the New Jesus Family in Seattle?" Shelby shook her head. "It's a low-profile, rather exclusive New Age cult which has been around for about six years. The leader is a wealthy charismatic woman who—"

"Lila Ruth Atkinson," Rachel interjected.

"Yes, Lila Ruth Atkinson," Libby echoed, "who leads her people with very convincing revelations she purports to receive from God Himself."

"Unfortunately, there's nothing novel about that," Shelby said, shaking her head in disgust. "For centuries people have been claiming their own private communication line to God. These are the false teachers the Bible warns about, and every time you turn around it seems that another one pops up. The New Jesus Family sounds like one of them."

Turning to Rachel, Shelby said, "How did your husband get involved with this woman and the New Jesus Family?"

The Northstar flight attendant had taken two more sips of soup while Shelby and Libby talked. Again she put her spoon down and folded her hands in her lap before answering. "It's a long story."

"I'd like to hear it," Shelby said with genuine interest, "that is, if you feel all right talking about it."

"I may get a little emotional," Rachel said, "but I'll try to get through it, because, as I told Libby, I really need some advice."

Rachel began by describing how she and Cooper Sams met, fell in love, and moved in together. She told of her growing desire to formalize their relationship by marriage and her ongoing disappointment at Cooper's reluctance to consider such a commitment. Shelby and Libby leaned in and listened intently as a curtain of restaurant noises around them assured the privacy of the conversation.

Rachel continued by relating the story of Cooper Sams' near-fatal encounter with a deadly rotor shear over Juneau, Alaska in 1995. Astonishment wreathed the faces of her two new friends as she spoke.

"That incident really affected him," Rachel said. "He didn't sleep for four days. Whenever he closed his eyes, the scene replayed in his mind and he questioned every move, every decision: 'Did I do it right? Should I have tried something else?' He had diarrhea for two weeks and lost almost fifteen pounds. Every joint and muscle in his body ached from the massive adrenaline surge he had endured. He couldn't even walk up the stairs without pain. But he survived and kept flying."

Rachel paused for a sip of water, then resumed her story. "On the plus side, something changed in Cooper's heart. A few days after the accident he came home from his first post-traumatic stress counseling session with a bouquet of flowers, the first flowers he ever bought me. He put me in the boat and we went out on the lake together. He said the close call had caused him to think about what was really important to him. He said he had survived for a reason and that reason was me. Then he gave me this and asked . . . "

Rachel's voice trailed off as a tiny squall of tears interrupted her story. Her left hand was on the table, revealing a gorgeous diamond-studded wedding band. Shelby and Libby admired the ring and consoled the bearer.

"Those were the happiest days of my life," Rachel said after dabbing her eyes with the linen napkin. "It was as if Cooper had finally opened his life to me without reservation. I know how hard that was for him to do, but he did it. We took the boat out a lot and went on vacations. I tried to show him in every way I could how much I loved him and appreciated his nearness. And he responded in kind. For the next several months our relationship was heavenly."

Rachel's eyes went back to the soup bowl. Shelby anticipated her next thoughts: "But it didn't *stay* heavenly, obviously."

The petite woman shook her head. "I don't know if I changed or if something happened to Cooper that made him change. In the first year after we were married, Cooper hardly ever sailed alone. He always wanted me to go with him—and I never missed a chance. Then, for whatever reason, he started taking the boat out by himself again. At first he only went out alone when I was on a trip. Then he started going out while I was home—sometimes for a couple of hours, sometimes for the entire day. I would have gone with him, but he stopped asking. I volunteered to go, told him how much I liked being out on the lake with him. Sometimes he would let me go, but more often he politely and firmly refused, saying he needed to be alone to think."

"He wasn't meeting someone on these little jaunts?" Libby advanced, trying not to sound nosy.

"If there was someone else, Cooper was an expert at destroying the evidence, because—believe me—I looked for it. I scoured the boat while he was flying, checked out all the numbers on his cell phone statement, even inspected his dirty clothes for lipstick stains and long blonde hairs. But I found nothing."

"He never told you where he was going when he shoved off?" Libby continued, curiously.

"I tried not to ask. Cooper was closedmouthed anyway, but when he thought you were prying, he locked up like a giant clam. When I *did* ask about his jaunts out on the lake, he would say something like, 'I'm off in search of my destiny.' "

"I thought he told you that *you* were his destiny, the reason he survived the disaster in Juneau," Shelby said.

Rachel sighed deeply. "I guess he changed his mind about that," she said distantly.

It seemed like a good time to rest the subject. After a couple of minutes of silence Shelby commented on the raspberry vinaigrette dressing, and Libby agreed that it was one of the best she had tasted. The three women continued eating and talking about recipes for salads and dressings. Rachel ate sparingly but entered into the conversation, hinting that she felt comfortable about opening her soul to two women she barely knew.

After spurning the waiter's offer to recite the dessert selections, Shelby and Rachel ordered herb tea while Libby requested coffee.

"About three years ago, Cooper was invited to one of Lila Ruth Atkinson's meetings," Rachel began as the they huddled over their hot drinks.

"Your husband told you about the meeting?" Shelby inquired.

"Oh, no. By then he was barely speaking to me. I found a couple of messages on the machine from Kathy Keene, one of the flight attendants on Cooper's Juneau flight, who was already tangled up with the New Jesus Family. She's been after him for months to come hear the 'great teacher.' The first message was a reminder from her to come to a meeting at her house. A later call was from someone else in the group thanking Cooper for coming."

"So Lila enticed him into the New Jesus Family," Libby advanced.

Rachel shook her head in awe. "Never in a million years would I guess that Cooper would become involved in such a thing. He's never been religious. He's never been a joiner. But he's been in it for over three years, and I have reason to believe that he is in the upper echelon of the group."

"Did he ever talk to you about the group?" Shelby asked.

"Yes, and at first I considered it a positive result of his decision to join. He actually started talking to me again. But the problem was that he only talked about Lila Ruth Atkinson and the New Jesus Family. He told me that he had been chosen by God for a special task, and that Lila Ruth had revealed it to him. It was his destiny, he said. He urged me to go with him and discover my 'new name' or something like that."

Libby said, "Did you ever go with him?"

"Absolutely not," Rachel said emphatically. "It was obvious that he wasn't interested in me; he was only after my *scalp*, another convert for Sister Lila. He still wouldn't take me out with him on the boat. He still planned his Northstar trips opposite mine so we were seldom home at the same time." Then Rachel added with a note of despair, "I don't know . . . if Cooper had shown some genuine interest in me—in us—like he did when we were first married, I might have joined the cult with him."

Shelby cut in quickly, laying a consoling hand on Rachel's shoulder. "I think you know that the New Jesus Family isn't the solution to your relationship. It's not you or Lila Ruth Atkinson or this group that's the problem; it's something inside Cooper. I venture that if your husband had not closed his heart to you, he wouldn't have been attracted to that cult in the first place. You need God's love to help you keep loving him and reaching out to him. His heart will melt eventually, and he won't need that false religion."

Rachel dropped her gaze again and small tears formed at the corners of her eyes. "I think it might be too late to melt his heart."

Shelby and Libby exchanged puzzled looks. Then Shelby said, "Too late? Why do you say that?"

Rachel summoned strength to continue by taking a deep breath. Then she reached into her handbag on the floor and withdrew a sheaf of laser-printed pages stapled together at the corner and folded in half. She opened the pages and laid them in the center of the table. Then she looked up at the winsome blonde who seemed to be so genuinely interested in her. "I found this hidden in Cooper's office yesterday. I admit it: I'm a suspicious snoop. I'm always looking for something that will help me help him."

The two women listening nodded with understanding.

"It's written in the form of a news release. There were more than fifty copies last night, like they were going to be sent out to people or given away. So I took one hoping he wouldn't miss it. This morning when I snuck in there to check, the pile was gone. I don't know where Cooper was last night, but he apparently took the stack with him."

Shelby glanced at the neatly printed pages without reading anything, then returned her attention to Rachel for an explanation.

"The New Jesus Family is one of these doomsday cults, you know, gearing up for the end of the world and the second coming of Christ. According to that," Rachel nodded toward the stapled pages, "they've picked a date. But instead of waiting on the top of a mountain in white robes, the New Jesus Family is outfitting a jetliner to meet their God in the air. And Cooper is going to be the pilot." Rachel's lower lip began to tremble.

Shelby took her hand and leaned in with a serious expression. "Rachel, you know it's not going to happen. They're deluded."

"Yes, I know . . . I know," Rachel agreed, blinking away tears.

"If Cooper takes a plane up that day, the most they'll get out of it is a plane ride. When their prediction fails to materialize, they'll come back to earth to eat crow and try to explain their miscalculation."

Rachel wiped her eyes with the napkin and shook her head. "No, it's not that simple."

"What do you mean?" Shelby probed.

"I found something else in Cooper's office this morning, and it terrifies me," Rachel said, clouding up again. "Cooper is really into this doomsday thing. I don't think he's planning to bring that plane back to earth at all."

Thirty-five

When the gun sounded ending the first half, UCLA was leading Southern California, 12–6. The rainy weather had reduced the Los Angeles Memorial Coliseum crowd from anticipated near capacity to under 40,000 diehard fans. The field, which was soggy at kickoff, had become a quagmire, gradually transforming the Bruins' and Trojans' uniforms, Honolulu blue-and-gold and maroon-and-gold respectively, to the same color—mud brown—by intermission. All three extra-point attempts had failed when the place kickers slipped on the muddy turf and landed on their backs, creating video clips for a future edition of football follies.

Raul Barrigan had arrived at the stadium decked out in a blue slicker—coat, pants, and hat—borrowed from his uncle, who wore them when deep-sea fishing off the California coast. Beth's father had been one of the casualties of the rain, deciding at the last moment to stay home and watch the game on TV in the dry comfort of his family room. But Reagan and Beth Cole, bundled in sweaters and jackets and caps, wouldn't have missed the traditional fall clash of their rival alma maters. Their major protection against the downpour was a huge black-and-white golf umbrella that spread over them and Raul too.

The Coliseum's wheelchair section turned out to be a lot closer to the field than the seats Cole had purchased from the UCLA alumni association. He and Beth were allowed to trade in their tickets and sit there with Raul in metal folding chairs since they were his escorts.

Despite the rain and the cold and the challenges presented to him and his wheelchair by the Coliseum, Raul was having a great time. He and Beth had ganged up on Cole during the first half, belittling him and the Bruins mercilessly when the Trojans took an early 6–0 lead. Cole returned the abuse when his Bruins stormed back for two second-quarter touchdowns.

Raul felt good in the presence of the Coles because they didn't baby him or patronize him as so many people did, even people who knew him well. He hated it when strangers or friends equated his disability with incompetence. Some people automatically raised their voices when talking to him, as if he was deaf as well as paralyzed. Others talked down to him, simplified their language, or ignored him in a conversation as if he was brain damaged. And others grabbed the handles of his chair and tried to push him without even asking if he wanted them to, as if he was too weak to push himself or too dumb to know he needed help.

Raul often gained a twisted sense of satisfaction from grabbing the rims of his chair and popping a wheelie or sprinting out of an overeager grasp to spin a tight donut before surprised eyes.

But Cole and Beth treated him like a real person. They hadn't told him once what to do or how to do it. They hadn't pestered him with inane questions like "How are you doing?" or "Can I get anything for you?" When it was time for him to go to the restroom, they didn't jump up to push him there, and Cole didn't offer to go in with him to make sure he didn't wet on himself. Rather, they let him do for himself and go at his own pace without acting like orderlies or babysitters.

Best of all, Cole and Beth treated him like a real friend, something Raul found in short supply recently. After completing his rehab and returning to ASU to finish his degree, Raul had noticed a transformation in his former teammates and friends. During his months at Craig Hospital, they sent cards and gifts, telephoned him, came up to Denver for visits, and talked about how great it would be to have him back in Tempe. But when he got back to the campus, his friends slowly pulled away. They were cordial on campus, but Raul was invited to few parties. When he initiated contact and suggested going to a movie or a Diamondbacks game, they came up with pretty lame excuses. Raul didn't think people excluded him purposely. He figured they simply didn't know how to act around a quadriplegic who was no longer totally helpless, so they just kept him at a safe distance. Furthermore, it was OK to have a cripple around some of the time, but apparently no one could conceive of being tight friends with someone in a wheelchair.

Reagan and Beth Cole seemed neither intimidated nor embarrassed by Raul or his wheelchair. They weren't looking around to see who might be gawking at them for hanging out with a quad. They seemed to be enjoying him as much as they were enjoying the ball game. Besides, he was here at their invitation. Raul hoped he could maintain this relationship even though he lived in Phoenix. What's more, he hoped this refreshing pair of young Christians wanted to maintain the relationship.

As the teams left the field at halftime, Raul took orders for hot dogs, nachos, and drinks—his treat—and insisted on braving the concession stand lines to get them. "I'm the only one who can sit and relax while standing in line," he joked. Conscious that he was a third thumb, Raul felt good about granting the young marrieds a few minutes to huddle under the umbrella alone.

When he returned with the eats, Cole was gone. "An old basketball teammate of his came walking up the aisle," Beth explained. "The guy is sitting with another Bruin jock they used to hang out with, so he asked Reagan to come down to say hello and compare bald spots. They haven't seen each other in years. I told Reagan we weren't going to wait lunch on him."

"Good, I'm running on empty," Raul said. He settled his chair under the big umbrella with Beth, set the brakes, and the two of them tore into a box full of stadium food that was short on nutritional value but long on great taste. On the muddy field the Trojan marching band slogged through its halftime program. The rain continued to splatter the umbrella.

"I know you're a freelance writer," Raul said between large bites of a hot dog running over with peppers and mustard, "but what do you write?" He was pleased for the occasion to talk with Beth alone.

"Mainly, I do high-interest current-event paperbacks," she said, wiping a drip of nacho cheese from her chin with a napkin. "You know, the pulp racks next to the tabloids at the supermarket check-stands, the books that hit the streets while the story is still news."

Raul lifted his eyebrows in surprise. "You mean, books like the one about the Manfred Uberman serial killings and the confessions of that Hollywood madam, Candy what's-her-name?"

"Oh, you've read my books?" Beth said with bulging cheeks and an expression of cherubic innocence.

Raul was suddenly flustered. He didn't know how to affirm Beth while covering his disgust for her subject matter. "Well, er, no. I don't . . . I mean, I'm not much of a reader, that is, I don't get much of a chance—"

"Just kidding, Raul," Beth cut in with a mischievous gleam, feeling only a little sorry about stringing him along. "I don't do that kind of junk. I've been fortunate enough to work on stories with a little more historical and social value."

Raul's face relaxed, and he took a long pull on his diet Coke. Beth continued, "You might remember a book I did on the coronation of

King Charles, or maybe the one about the big Unity 2000 deal here in the Coliseum on Millennium's Eve."

"I remember seeing them in the stores, but, like I said, I'm not much of a reader," Raul said sheepishly. "But I'll start looking for your name now when I go through the check-stand."

"You'll have to look pretty hard," Beth said. "The seven-day wonders I work on aren't big on bylines."

"You don't get your name on the front cover?"

"No, but, as I always say, the only place I really want to see my name is on the check."

It took Raul a couple of seconds to get it. He smiled, "Right, the check."

On the field, a trombone player lost her footing in the middle of *Lady of Spain* and slipped down hard on her seat. Some people in the crowd laughed at the unplanned pratfall. Others, including Beth and Raul, groaned in sympathy for the girl, hoping she wasn't seriously hurt. The brave trombonist sprang immediately to her feet and rejoined the formation, her face crimson with embarrassment and the back of her uniform nearly black with Coliseum mud.

"What are you working on now?" Raul asked, starting into his second pepper-and-mustard dog.

Beth laughed lightly. "Getting used to being married and living in L.A. again. It's quite an adjustment."

Raul shared in her humor. "You grew up in L.A., right?"

Beth waited to answer until she had washed down a mouthful of nachos with a sip of Sprite. "Yes, but I left for Washington right after college. I swore I'd never come back, and I swore I'd never marry someone from down here."

"Then you got involved with an L.A. cop."

"Right," Beth said, "and here I am again. But we still have my house on Whidbey Island. As soon as I write about five bestsellers, Reagan can quit and we can move up to paradise."

"But you're not writing anything right now, you said."

"Correct. I finished off a book about the Nolan Jakes/Evan Rider story a couple of days after Evan's sentencing—during our honeymoon, I might add, which didn't exactly thrill my husband. Reagan begged me not to dive into something else right away."

"Give you a chance to get acquainted and settle into your new life as a wife and mother," Raul said, grinning about the puppy misunderstanding last night.

Beth laughed heartily. "Yeah, Mama Beth, that's me. Seriously, now that Reagan's back to work, I've come down with a bad case of cabin fever. I'm itching to get started on something."

"Any ideas?"

"I have some offers on the table," Beth said, "most of them are scummy projects I would never touch. There are a couple of other things too, but nothing I'm really jazzed about. It's something I'm praying about. Reagan says if I pray, the right thing will come along, and I'll recognize it."

"He's right."

Beth whistled with surprised amazement. "I can't believe I'm talking about praying. That's another adjustment I've made over the last few months: remembering to include God in decisions like these."

"You're learning the important things early," Raul encouraged.

Beth unwrapped one of Cole's hot dogs, took a large bite, then carefully rewrapped it and returned it to the carton. Raul looked at her quizzically. "Bite tax," she said with a twinkle. "It's in our marriage contract. We negotiated the details during our honeymoon. He can eat off my plate without asking and I can eat off his."

Raul studied Beth unnoticed as she scooped up the last blob of cheese in the nacho carton with her finger. His intense gaze was not motivated by lust, though he considered her very attractive and refreshingly personable. Rather he was fascinated by her wit, transparency, and affability. He hoped there was a woman like Beth—a fox with class, warmth, and spirit—somewhere in the world for him.

The halftime show was over, and the two teams were on the sidelines getting ready for the second half of the mud bowl. Reagan Cole was still visiting his old buddies.

"What about you, Raul?" Beth said after stowing her trash under the seat. "What are your goals? Are you planning to stay with law enforcement until retirement?"

Raul released a silent sigh at another question about his future. No matter how forcefully he verbalized his intention to be in a Giants' uniform some day soon, nobody seemed to think it would happen. They all bugged him about what he wanted to be now that he could no longer be a baseball player. If his healing was dependent on the faith of others instead of his own, Raul had reasoned often, he would be in this wheelchair until the Rapture.

"When my legs realize that they have been healed," he said calmly, "I'm going to sign with the Giants and fulfill my dream of playing baseball and providing for my parents."

"May I do your book when you hit the majors?" Beth responded quickly. "It will be a runaway bestseller."

Raul waited, anticipating another "Just kidding" from Beth. But it didn't come. He quickly realized that her comment not only reflected respect for his hope but a desire to further its growth. Raul loved her for it. "Where's the contract?" he said with a big smile of appreciation. "I'm ready to sign."

After a playacted handshake of contractual agreement, Beth said, "But until the legs come back, what is your goal? I mean, God has allowed you to wait three years already. What if He has you wait another three years? Are you OK with that? Is police work enough to keep you going?"

Raul was grateful that Beth used three years as an example instead of ten or twenty. It was obvious to Raul that his miracle was on hold for some reason, perhaps until his faith bank was full. But he hesitated to consider that he would be in a wheelchair years longer instead of months or weeks. Every day of immobility as a quadriplegic was another day lost to his prime as an athlete. And he refused to consider that the dream burning steadily within him since childhood like a pilot light would be extinguished before it ignited the glorious blaze of fulfillment.

"God has led me to the Phoenix Police Department for now," Raul answered after a thoughtful silence, "but I can't say that police work is enough for me. I want to do something big for God before I move on, something extraordinary."

Despite his admiration for Beth, Raul stopped short of complete honesty in his answer. He *had* to do something extraordinary for God. How else could he make up for his failure to reach his teammates at ASU? How else could he swell his faith account and prompt God to act? There had to be a mission for him whose successful completion would spark the miracle he longed for.

"Do you have any idea what it might be?" Beth asked with affirming interest.

Raul pondered the question. "Like you said, if I pray, the right thing will come along, and I'll recognize it."

Thirty-six

"How old is he? He's so cute." The question came from a black flight attendant with the name Dawn stitched across the top of her apron. The boarding process was in full swing, but Dawn couldn't resist stopping for a moment to admire the little boy with the black wavy hair strapped into the aisle seat of the Northstar MD-80. The tyke sat half asleep and clutching his "blankie," having been awakened early to reach the airport in time for the 6:50 A.M. Sunday morning flight.

Myrna Valentine, sitting beside him in the window seat, brightened at the girl's compliment. It seemed genuine, not something she had to do to impress a customer. Myrna was used to such comments. Guy was a cute kid, and she always made sure he was well groomed and attired in the latest Northwest kids' fashions. Today she had dressed him in a fleecy gold turtleneck, hunter-green pinstriped jeans with matching suspenders, and little suede hiking boots. His quilted green vest and John Deere cap were in the overhead compartment.

"He'll be three in February," Myrna answered, running her fingers through Guy's hair. Glassy-eyed, he leaned toward his mother's pleasing touch.

"What's his name?" Dawn asked.

"Guy."

"Has he ever flown before?"

"A few times."

Dawn leaned down to Guy's eye level. "Good morning, Guy," she almost sang. "You're such a handsome little man."

Guy's sleepy eyes turned to meet those of the friendly flight attendant, but he couldn't bring himself to return her beaming smile.

"I bet a little treat will wake you up," Dawn said as she withdrew a cello-wrapped candy mint from her pocket and held it out to Guy in the palm of her hand.

Guy's eyes widened slightly to investigate the candy. But Myrna spoke before he could reach for it. "Thank you, but he's not allowed to have much sugar, and especially not before breakfast."

Dawn kept her hand extended and her eyes on Guy. "Would you like to put the candy in your pocket for later, Guy?" Guy looked up at his mother, silently asking her permission. She granted it with a smile and a nod.

Guy surrounded the piece of candy with his short, plump fingers and stuffed it into the pocket of his jeans. "Tank you," he said to Dawn. Then he gathered up his blankie and snuggled close to Myrna again.

"You're welcome, little man," Dawn said to the boy, patting him on the knee. "You have a real nice mommy." Then she winked at Myrna. "If there's anything you two need between here and L.A., just call me." Then she stood and headed aft to prepare for departure.

Myrna warmed at the compliment. She *was* a good mother, she consciously affirmed. Guy's health and happiness had been her primary concern since the day he was born. But Myrna had steadfastly refused to sacrifice the former to ensure the latter. She had subjected little Guy to stringent dietary guidelines with small regard for what or how much other parents allowed their children to eat. His eating schedule as well as his sugar, fat, and sodium intake were carefully monitored within the parameters of a generous and tasty menu. Myrna scheduled wellness visits to the pediatrician as faithfully as sunrise. And mother and son had enrolled together in periodic swimming and exercise classes. As a model, Myrna knew how to take care of her most valuable asset: her body. She applied the same guidelines to the younger modeling member of the family.

As the plane pushed back from the gate at Portland International

Airport, Myrna again rehearsed the line of reasoning which had motivated her during her hasty preparations for the trip to Los Angeles. *Guy will appreciate how well I have taken care of his son. Little Guy will melt his heart and cause him to forget all about our clash over the abortion. He will remember the $10,000 and be very thankful that I did not use it to sacrifice his only son. And Guy will be happy to see me again, pleasantly surprised that I am every bit as alluring and available as when we first met in San Francisco. He could not resist me then; he cannot resist me now. Guy Rossovich may react with shock at our surprise reunion today, but it will turn out to be one of the happiest days of his life. Little Guy and I will make sure of that.*

Myrna tried not to think about the price of this impulsive rush to the side of the man she could not help loving. Two last-minute, full fare plane tickets with no specified return date had cost her over $1,200 compared to the going rate of less than $400 each for passengers who purchased their tickets only two weeks earlier. Myrna expected to miss a week or more of work, depending on how long it would take to melt Guy Rossovich's heart. Being out of the office meant cancelled appointments, and cancelled appointments may result in disgruntled clients who decide to take their business elsewhere.

The monetary risks, as scary as they were, seemed worth it to Myrna. After all, once Guy opened his arms and his Beverly Hills home to the family he didn't know he had, she would be able to jettison the business in Portland and work only when she wanted to. She would be free to support the political career of big Guy and to spend as much time as she wanted nurturing little Guy and advancing his child modeling career. In Myrna's mind, the promising dividends far outweighed the potential gamble of the investment.

Myrna refused to think about the possibility that Guy might reject her and their son, though the dark thoughts lingered at the perimeter of her consciousness like hungry wolves stalking a pair of frightened sheep. She bolstered her defenses by assuring herself that the man was hurting and lonely, that he still cherished warm memories of his affair with Myrna, and that those embers could be fanned into a blaze of need and desire once again. And she knew that any hesitance on Guy's part would quickly disintegrate once he laid his eyes on little Guy. What father could turn away his only son?

By the time the Northstar MD-80 reached cruising altitude, Guy was asleep with his head resting on Myrna's arm. She wondered how her precious little boy would react to his father when they met. Myrna had avoided using "Daddy" around Guy, even though she knew he had been exposed to the word and to the daddies of other children at child care. But, thankfully, her son was still too young to understand the concept or ask the question Myrna had dreaded since the boy started forming words: Who is my daddy? When he is mature enough to understand that everyone has a father, Myrna had reminded herself often since Friday night, Guy will have one of his own—his real father, Guy Rossovich.

Walking off the plane at Los Angeles International Airport at 9:05 A.M., Myrna and Guy had some time to kill. Myrna would have preferred a later flight, since she did not think it wise to confront Guy Rossovich much before noon on this Sunday morning. But the later flights to L.A. were overbooked on this the last day of Thanksgiving weekend, so Myrna was forced to travel earlier than she wanted to.

She commandeered an unused Smart Cart in the gate area, lifted Guy into the kid seat, and placed Guy's small bag, her garment bag, and folded raincoat in the luggage bin. She was dressed in a tailored aquamarine silk dress with mandarin collar and straight skirt slit high on the side. She had chosen this dress because Guy Rossovich had once commented that the oriental style accented her Asian features, which he found beguiling.

As she pushed the cart from the gate to the Galaxy rental car desk, Myrna was subtly aware that she could still turn heads. Despite the chrome cart in front of her, Myrna strode the broad airport corridors with grace and aplomb, as if gliding the runway during a top designer's show. She could almost feel the masculine eyes exploring her alluring face and figure, especially the bare left leg tempting them from the slit in her dress as she walked. It did not bother Myrna that the eyes of her admirers eventually shifted to the little boy in the cart and then turned away in disappointment. She was here in L.A. to attract and capture only one man. With every longing glance or lustful leer, her confidence in her mission rose.

It took longer than Myrna expected to get the rental car. One Galaxy bus passed the shuttle stop jammed to the doors with customers. Once she arrived at the Galaxy lot, she had to wait in line nearly thirty minutes. The car she had reserved, a champagne-colored, full-size GM Star Cruiser, was ready, but she was delayed another twenty minutes while a lot boy tracked down the child's car seat they had promised her by phone. All the while, little Guy, who hadn't eaten much on the plane, was slowly losing patience with the confusion and noise in the strange place.

The broken clouds and scattered sunshine over Los Angeles signaled that the tail of the rainstorm had finally passed through the area. Myrna wondered if she would need her raincoat at all. As she pulled onto Century Boulevard and headed toward the freeway in the Star Cruiser, she reminded herself that the extra expense of a more luxurious car was another facet of the investment. Wealthy Guy Rossovich loved fine cars. Showing up unannounced at his Beverly Hills home in something that obviously didn't belong in the neighborhood would mitigate against her strategy. Besides, being enveloped in the sleek, gleaming Star Cruiser buoyed her confidence and lifted her spirits. It reminded her of romantic getaways with Guy when they were still together.

Myrna exited I-405 at Sunset and headed east past Bel Air estates. By the time she found a little market where she could buy Guy a bran muffin and piece of fruit, it was 10:45. She didn't want him to eat too much in case his father elected to invite them in for brunch or lunch. But the boy was hungry and not very happy about being whisked away from home so early in the morning. So they sat in the car while Myrna fed him and tried to cheer him up.

Guy Rossovich still owned the spacious Spanish-style home off Benedict Canyon Drive he had shared with his ex-wife and two daughters. A discreet, strategic phone call on Saturday to an old friend had assured Myrna that Guy not only lived there but that he was spending the entire Thanksgiving weekend there with his daughters, aged seven and nine. Myrna remembered Guy once talking about having a housekeeper/cook, but she didn't know if he had retained the woman after the divorce. Myrna hoped Guy would be alone with his girls.

Myrna found the place on a quiet, narrow, winding street in the hills high above Sunset Boulevard, just north of Beverly Hills within the Los Angeles city limits. Set back from the street, the home had the appearance of an old Spanish villa. The sprawling, one-story, red-tile-roofed building was lushly bordered by large ferns and flowering shrubs. The entire acre-and-a-half of property was generously shaded by old oak and eucalyptus and surrounded by an imposing security fence with a gated entrance. When Myrna slowly drove past the gate, there was no one in sight. It was ten minutes past 11, and she could wait no longer.

Myrna parked the Star Cruiser just around a bend in the street in front of another opulent residence. She had already decided how she would approach Guy, with a little help from the unwitting informer she had contacted yesterday who supplied Guy's phone number. Little Guy was occupied in his car seat with a pair of toy cars Myrna had brought along for such a purpose. Myrna removed the phone from her purse and entered Guy Rossovich's personal number.

After three rings, the answering device kicked in as Myrna expected. It was the voice of Guy Rossovich's aide: "This is John Brock speaking. Senator Rossovich is unable to take your call in person. Please state your business and leave a number where you can be reached." An electronic tone sounded.

Myrna drew a long breath. This was the moment she had been awaiting for three years. She felt some trepidation but quickly suppressed it. She had decided to view the reunion as two good friends meeting again after a prolonged absence, believing that the past was forgotten and that very soon she and Guy *would* be good friends again.

"Good morning, Guy. I don't blame you for screening your calls; I do it myself. This is an old friend, Myrna Valentine. I just happen to be in your neighborhood, and I'd like to see you for a moment, just for old times' sake. In fact, I'm parked on the street right now in front of your neighbor's house. In a couple of minutes you'll be able to see my light-colored Star Cruiser in front of your gate.

"I know a lot has happened in your life over the last few years. I've had a rather interesting ride myself. Do you have a couple of minutes to say hello? I'll wait by the gate." Myrna added her personal number to the message, then tapped the phone off.

Myrna breathed a pleased sigh. Her plan was working well so far. She put the phone on the front seat, started the car, and backed down the street until the front half of the car was in the driveway and visible from the house. The rear of the car, where little Guy was playing in his car seat, was obscured from the house by the pillar of adobe bricks supporting one side of the steel gate. She shut down the engine.

"Time to get out, Mommy," Guy said, not knowing where they were or why they were there but assuming he was going inside.

"We're not getting out yet, honey. Just sit for a minute and play with your cars. I'm waiting for my friend to come out."

"My friend?" Guy said expectantly.

Myrna smiled. "Yes, he's your friend too, honey. A very special friend."

"Very *special* friend," little Guy said, mimicking his mother's emphasis. Then he became absorbed with his two toy cars again.

Myrna kept her eye on the house. She didn't know if Guy would come outside or call first. He was probably still reeling from the surprise of hearing her voice. Myrna assessed that if he came to the gate personally instead of talking to her on the phone, it was a very good sign. If he didn't come outside but still called her back, it was a positive sign. If he didn't call or come outside, she would rather assume that he and his daughters had gone out than that he was avoiding her. She couldn't understand why Guy would completely avoid her, especially now that he must be so lonely.

But Guy didn't come out and he didn't call. After ten minutes had elapsed, little Guy began to get restless. "I want to get out, Mommy," he said in a stage-one whine.

"Just a few more minutes," Myrna said, somewhat deflated. "Maybe my friend will come outside."

"I have to go potty, Mommy," little Guy whined at stage two.

Myrna opened her mouth to cajole him into sitting tight a little while longer, but he butted in excitedly, "Mommy, police car!"

Myrna shifted her gaze from the house to the rearview mirror. Little Guy was turned completely around in his chair and gawking at a black and white patrol car pulling up behind them. No lights were flashing. The little boy welcomed the sight as if watching Santa Claus arrive on

Christmas Eve. "The policemans are here, Mommy! The policemans are here!"

"Yes, I see, Guy," Myrna said, trying to sound positive.

The driver, a male officer in his mid-thirties and a little on the plump side, stepped out and cautiously walked forward to the driver's side of the Star Cruiser. He was wearing the navy-blue uniform—minus the cap—and shield of the Los Angeles Police Department. His partner, an Amerasian male officer, remained in the car.

Myrna zipped down the window with the tap of her finger on the console. The officer stayed slightly behind the doorpost, purposely making himself a more difficult target. "Good morning, ma'am," he said. "May I please see your operator's holocard and vehicle registration." His name badge read, W. KREJCI.

"What's the problem, officer?" Myrna said a little too sweetly. "I'm just parked here."

"Hi, policeman," little Guy called excitedly from the back seat.

"Your holocard and registration please, ma'am," the officer insisted calmly.

Myrna knew better than to press the issue. She also had a good idea what the problem was. She removed the laminated holocard from her billfold and her copy of the rental contract from the glove compartment in the console and passed them out to the officer.

"Hi, policeman," little Guy insisted a little louder.

The officer looked into the back window. "Hello, young man," he said, clearly more interested in quieting the kid than in starting a conversation. His response seemed to placate little Guy who turned his efforts to coaxing a wave from the officer still in the patrol car.

Officer Krejci briefly scanned the documents, then asked, "Do you have business in the neighborhood this morning, Ms. Valentine?"

"Yes, I'm waiting for my friend," Myrna said, pointing to Guy Rossovich's house.

"Where is your friend, ma'am?"

"Inside. I expect him to be out any time."

"A resident reported that you have been here for about twenty minutes. Your car is not known in the neighborhood. People get suspicious of strange vehicles."

"I've been here ten minutes, maybe," Myrna said. "All I'm doing is waiting."

"Does your friend know you're out here?" Officer Krejci didn't sound convinced of Myrna's story.

"I called him on the phone."

"Did you talk to him personally?"

"Well, no, I left a message. But I know he's home."

The officer stepped forward so Myrna could see him better. "Ma'am, I'm going to ask you to leave the neighborhood at this time and don't come back until you have a valid appointment."

Myrna blew an agitated sigh. "Guy Rossovich called you, didn't he?"

"This is an exclusive neighborhood, ma'am, and people are understandably protective of their privacy and possessions and wary of strangers. They have a right to be free of suspicion. Please move along and contact your friend by phone."

"Officer, a woman and a three-year-old can't be viewed as a threat to the security of the neighborhood, can they?" Myrna argued.

"Ma'am, I'm not saying that you're a threat to security. I'm just asking you as nicely as possible to arrange your appointment by phone and return only when you have been granted admission." He returned the holocard and contract, signalling that the discussion was over.

Myrna took the documents, but couldn't resist a final question. "It was Senator Rossovich who called you, am I correct?"

"It's no concern of yours, ma'am," Krejci said as he stepped back from the car. "Please move along. Have a nice day, ma'am."

Myrna started the car in a huff and pulled away from the curb. "Bye bye, policemans," little Guy sang with a friendly wave. Myrna steered into the first available driveway to turn around and head down the hill. As she passed Guy's house again, she took one last look at the house through the iron bars of the perimeter fence. In that fleeting glance she saw a figure standing in the large front window which was shaded by an adobe arch. She recognized the person immediately. It was Guy Rossovich.

Thirty-seven

Officer Krejci and his partner followed the Star Cruiser down Benedict Canyon Drive until it entered the city limits of Beverly Hills, to the great delight of Guy Valentine in the back seat, who watched them all the way. Myrna continued down the hill to Sunset Boulevard and turned left, driving between the Beverly Hills Hotel on the north and Will Rogers Memorial Park on the south. A beautiful little triangle of greenery in an equally beautiful city, Will Rogers Park is bordered by Sunset, Canon Drive, and Beverly Drive.

Myrna circled the park and pulled to the curb on the Canon Drive side south of Sunset. The park was the ideal place to take the next step in her plan.

Myrna yielded to little Guy's urgent plea to visit the restroom after coaxing him into his vest and cap. Then she kept close watch on him as he ran up and down the park walkways. In the meantime she stood outside the car and dialed Guy Rossovich's number again. She had convinced herself that his adversarial reaction to her first call was understandable. The only way to change his heart was to bring him face to face with little Guy, and the only way to get them together was to offer more information.

"I'm sorry I alarmed you, Guy," she said after hearing the answer machine's beep, confident that he was listening in. She maintained a friendly tone even though she was a little upset that he had called the cops on her. "I should have been more clear about the purpose of my surprise visit." Myrna paused, wondering who else might be listening in—Guy's daughters, other relatives or friends. She quickly decided to go ahead with her disclosure. She had spent nearly three years giving explanations for little Guy's existence. If Guy had some explaining to do after she hung up, it served him right.

"Guy, I came to L.A.—to your house—to introduce you to our son. Perhaps you saw him in the back seat when you looked out the window. His name is also Guy, named after you, of course. He has dark wavy hair just like you. He's bright and good-looking like his father, with practically no features that identify him as one-quarter Vietnamese.

"Yes, Guy, this is the fetus you thought I aborted over three years ago. I *almost* aborted him, but I couldn't bring myself to do it. That's why I sent the money back to you. And once you meet him, you'll be glad I didn't go through with the abortion. He's the son you've always wanted, Guy. Little Guy deserves to know who his father is. He deserves a family—a mother and a father who love him and each other dearly.

"I know this is quite a shock, but after you have digested the news, I hope you'll call me so we can set up a time to meet—maybe even today. I'm looking forward to seeing you again, Guy. We had some good times I will never forget. Give me a call when you're ready." Myrna repeated the phone number and tapped her phone off.

Myrna slipped the phone into her handbag and set out to stroll the sun-sprayed walkways of the park with little Guy. The cops couldn't chase her out of the park, which was also populated this morning by rich Beverly Hills widows walking their schnauzers and poodles and rich Beverly Hills brats zipping along the walkways on their skates. All Myrna had to do now was to enjoy the sunshine and the antics of her little boy in the park and wait for Guy's return call. She was more hopeful than ever that their meeting would be soon.

The call came in less than five minutes. "This is Guy," said the man's voice in the receiver of Myrna's compact wireless phone. He sounded neither agitated nor cordial.

"Thank you for calling, Guy," Myrna said with purposeful warmth. She continued to watch her son hop playfully on squares of walkway conveniently out of earshot.

Guy got right to the point. "How can I be sure that you have *my* son? It could be anybody's kid."

"Are you kidding?" Myrna replied, almost laughing. "You mean apart from a DNA exam and the fact that little Guy matches the fetal tissue record still on file with Los Angeles County and the fact that the child's conception can be genetically tracked to the last night you and I slept together?"

Guy didn't respond.

"All the medical data aside, Guy, your son looks just like you," Myrna said proudly. "Wait till you see him. I'll bet he's a photocopy of you at age three. No, there's no doubt about his ancestry, Guy. As soon as you look at him you'll know."

Guy was silent for several seconds. "Where are you, Myrna?"

An icy charge of anticipation raced up Myrna's spine. "I'm only a few minutes from the house. I can drive back—"

"No, not here," Guy cut in quickly. "I need to meet you somewhere else."

Myrna imagined that Guy's explanations to whomever was at home with him were not going well. "I'm at the park on Sunset, Will Rogers Park, just down the hill."

"Is your son still with you?"

"*Our* son, Guy," Myrna corrected. "Yes, little Guy is here. We're enjoying the sunshine together. He's making up his own version of hopscotch on the brick tiles."

"I'll be down in five minutes. Will you wait there?"

Myrna smiled, and her joy could be heard in her voice. "Of course we'll wait for you, Guy."

As soon as she was off the phone, Myrna excitedly called little Guy to her side. She scooped him up in her arms and nuzzled him in the neck playfully until he squealed with laughter. Then she embraced him and kissed him. "This is such a happy day for us, sweet boy."

"I want to run, Mommy," Guy said, done with being confined to his mother's arms.

"Just a minute, sweetie. Let's find another place to run."

Myrna knew that a good backdrop was essential to the overall impact of a visual image. When Guy Rossovich drove into the parking lot, Myrna wanted herself and little Guy perfectly posed where the park's best light and colors worked to her advantage in catching Guy's eye. She found that place, where shafts of sunlight penetrating a sprawling oak illuminated a patch of fairly dry grass next to a cluster of rhododendrons.

"Can you say, 'Hi Daddy'?" Myrna coached her son.

Little Guy, who liked to try new words, said clearly, "Hi Daddy." She helped him practice the greeting a few times more, and he complied. But there was a question mark shading his expression. Finally he said, "I don't know Daddy."

"Today you will, honey," she replied confidently. "Beginning today, you will know your daddy."

Six minutes later, Myrna watched a cream-colored late-model Cadillac coupe ease to the curb across Canon Drive from the park and Myrna's Star Cruiser. Guy Rossovich stepped out, clad in a faded black crew-neck T-shirt, well-worn jeans and court shoes, and sporting a green baseball cap and sunglasses. He still possessed the trim physique Myrna had so admired. But he looked anything like a state senator, which, she realized, was his intention. He needed to remain incognito to any constituents who might be in the park, somewhat softening Myrna's disappointment that he hadn't dressed nicer for the occasion.

Myrna, who was crouched beside little Guy in their ideal photo spot, pointed at the man and said, "There's Daddy, sweetheart. Here comes your own Daddy." The little boy wore a mildly puzzled expression, seeing the man entering the park but unsure why his mother was making such a big deal of it. Then Myrna stood up, holding little Guy's hand, and struck an attractive pose as Guy came slowly up the walkway toward her.

Guy stopped walking a good twenty feet away from the woman and little boy. Myrna noted from the black stubble that he hadn't yet shaved. He stood staring—eyes concealed behind dark, UV-protection lenses—with his hands jammed in the pockets of his jeans. Myrna hoped he was as interested in her appearance as he must be in the cute, two-foot-eleven-inch person with dark, wavy hair standing beside her.

Myrna leaned down to little Guy. "Say, 'Hi Daddy.' "

The boy hesitated, then said, "Hi Daddy," while looking off toward half a dozen pigeons strutting along the walkway nearby. His heart clearly wasn't in the command performance.

"Hello, Guy," Myrna said as winsomely as she could. "It's really good to see you again."

Guy nodded slightly. His reply was very soft. "Hello, Myrna." Then he glanced left and right. Assured that he was sufficiently distanced from other occupants of the park, he removed his sunglasses and hooked them to the neck of his shirt by the temple. He looked more mature and distinguished than a man in his late thirties should look, Myrna thought. Yet he still impressed her as attractive and virile, causing her heartbeat to accelerate. She acknowledged silently that her love for Guy Rossovich was far from a smoldering ember.

Guy's eyes were fastened on little Guy, and an unbidden smile began to tug at the corners of his lips. Without coming closer, he lowered to his haunches, forearms on knees and hands clasped together. "Hello, Guy," he said in little Guy's direction.

The boy was thoroughly engrossed in the pigeons, which ambled toward the senator as if they saw right through his disguise and were coming for a handout or an autograph. "Sea gulls, Mommy," little Guy said proudly. "Gampa's sea gulls from 'Storia."

"They're pigeons, Guy," big Guy informed. "Would you like to come see the pigeons?" Guy held out a hand toward the child. Little Guy saw that the stranger was closer to the interesting little flock than he was, and getting closer appealed to him.

But the boy was not ready to leave his mother's side at a stranger's invitation. So he made a logical choice. "Let's go see the sea gulls, Mommy," he said as he eagerly pulled Myrna by the hand toward the man and the curious pigeons.

Little Guy's hasty actions abruptly put the pigeons to flight, leaving Guy, on his haunches, and Myrna, still attached to her son by the hand, no more than ten feet apart. "Mommy, the sea gulls fly away," the little boy whined with disappointment.

Guy made another attempt at gaining his son's attention. He stretched out his hand again and said, "May I take you to see the pigeons?"

Little Guy shrank back into his mother. "No, thank you," he said, his face still mirroring distrust of the man.

Big Guy couldn't hold back a full smile. "You are a real gentleman, aren't you?" he said.

"I raised him right, Guy," Myrna put in seriously, looking down at him. "I've taken good care of him for you. He eats well and gets regular checkups. And I've taught him his manners. He's a good boy. All he needs is a father."

Guy stood. "Why didn't you tell me about him sooner?" There was a hint of bitter disappointment in his tone.

Myrna answered without vituperation. "I distinctly recall that you weren't interested in having a child. In fact, at one time it was worth $10,000 to you *not* to have a child. I had no reason to believe you would even care that he was alive."

"We weren't talking about a child then, Myrna. We were talking about a blob of fetal tissue."

"Little Guy has never been just a blob, Guy. He has been a person since the moment of conception. That's what I realized in the abortion clinic. I couldn't terminate the life of our son just because you didn't want him. Little Guy is a beautiful child, and he's your own flesh and blood. That's why I came down to L.A. I thought you needed a second chance to love him and be his father."

Guy looked away and sighed. Then he looked again at the little boy clinging to Myrna's leg and watching pigeons in the distance.

Myrna said with small laugh, "Doesn't he look just like you, Guy? Do you have to see a DNA test to know he's your son?"

Another unprovoked smile overtook Guy's face. "He's a piece of work, all right," he said. "He's really beautiful. You've done a good job, Myrna."

Myrna warmed at the compliment. "Thank you."

Then, for the first time since Guy arrived, Myrna found him studying her. "You look good too, Myrna. You're taking care of yourself." It was not the glib line of a man looking for a quick score. Myrna could almost feel his sincerity. She remembered how important her appearance had been to Guy when they were dating. She was ecstatic that he noticed her. It was the first real sign of hope for reconciliation.

A group of park visitors were approaching on the walkway, so Guy casually put on his sunglasses and suggested that she and Myrna walk away from the crowd. Little Guy was agreeable to a walk because it took him in the direction of the "sea gulls."

"Where was little Guy born?" Guy asked as they walked. He seemed finally at ease and interested in conversation, as if a wall of defense had abruptly crumbled. Myrna described her move to Astoria, little Guy's birthplace, and subsequent move to Portland. In response to his questions, she told about their son's infancy, his first steps, his first words, and other of his achievements. Guy asked about her work and listened intently as she told her modest success story, which included little Guy's short modeling career. During the conversation Guy couldn't keep his eyes off the boy, who was running ahead of them and giggling every time the pigeons scattered. Myrna drank in the attention her former lover lavished on her and their son.

As they concluded a slow tour of the park, Myrna said something she didn't really mean, but she tried to deliver it as convincingly as possible: "I'm sorry that things didn't work out for you and your wife."

"Thank you," Guy said softly.

"It must be very hard on you and your daughters."

"Yes, especially the girls. They don't understand why we can't live as a family."

"And what about you?" Myrna pressed cautiously. "I know what it's like to live alone. Are you doing all right?"

Guy shrugged. "I guess I'm doing OK under the circumstances." Myrna waited for him to say more, perhaps ask about her love life. But he didn't.

Myrna decided it was time to say her piece. She drew a long breath for courage. "Guy, I didn't come to L.A. just to introduce you to little Guy, as important as that is. I came so that you and I could be reintroduced. It wasn't right for me to come while you were still married. But now, well, I thought that maybe you and I and little Guy might have a chance to put something together. We've had some good times, Guy. We can have them again—even better because of our beautiful son."

They arrived at the spot where their stroll had begun. Myrna yearned to say much more, but she feared that she had already been too forward. Guy couldn't have missed her message, so she waited for a response.

Guy turned to face her. He released a deep breath, as if the conversation had been hard work for him. "I'm still kind of in shock about seeing you and little Guy. I need some time to sort things out. I hope that's OK with you."

"Of course, Guy. We can stay in town for a few days if that will help."

Guy shook his head. "Your business needs you. Here's what I want you to do. Go back to Portland—tonight if you can—and give me a week. Then I'll come up next weekend and we'll talk about it. I want to see your place. And I want to take you to a nice dinner, just like old times. So be sure to get a good baby-sitter. How does that sound?"

Myrna wanted to jump into his arms, but she restrained herself. "It sounds wonderful, Guy. Thank you for coming down to the park. Thank you for hearing me out."

"I'm the one who should be thanking you, Myrna. It took a lot of courage to come down here. You're still the woman I fell in love with four years ago." Then he kissed her on the mouth. It was neither a passionate lovers' kiss nor a brother-sister peck. Myrna thought of it as a small kiss with a big promise.

Guy hunkered down to little Guy's eye level again. "It was good to meet you, buddy," he said, holding out a hand for a handshake. Little Guy hesitated, then grabbed onto his mother's skirt with his left hand before putting his right hand in Guy's big palm.

Then Guy stood, said good-bye, and walked away to his car. Myrna watched the Cadillac circle the park and disappear up Benedict Canyon Drive. As she ushered little Guy toward the Star Cruiser, she found tears of joy welling up in her eyes.

Guy Rossovich was on the phone before he started climbing the hill to his villa. "Hello, Gary. This is Guy. . . . Yeah, I know it's Sunday, but lawyers are the same as undertakers: You're on duty twenty-four hours a day because you're always ready to make a buck when somebody screws up."

Gary enjoyed Guy's little joke. Then Guy said, "Listen, how are you coming on the child custody stuff? . . . Good, good. . . . Well, I have another major wrinkle to throw at you. I want you to go after my son too. . . . Yes, you heard me right. . . . Well, I didn't know either until today. It's a long story. I'll give you the details tomorrow. . . . No, he's with his mother, but she's unfit, at least that's what you're going to prove in court. . . . Right. . . . Right. . . . No, she's not expecting a custody fight. Right now she probably thinks I'm going to marry her so the three of us will live happily ever after. . . . I'll tell you everything tomorrow, Gary. I just want you to start thinking about it. . . . I know you're busy, but that's why I pay you the big bucks, Pal."

Guy hung up without saying good-bye. Then he started cursing aloud, getting angrier with each foul word. The target of his vile, abusive tirade was Myrna Valentine.

Thirty-eight

It felt good to run again. During the wild Thanksgiving week storm, Beth Scibelli-Cole had suspended her daily morning routine of jogging the promenade along Santa Monica Beach. It just wasn't any fun when the rain off the Pacific Ocean is coming at you sideways and threatening to blow you right off the sidewalk. So for six days Beth had spent her workout time with the Soloflex machine Cole kept in the spare bedroom. But on this Monday morning the sky was clear again, promising the return of the typical California sunshine that made L.A. a fairly decent place to live during the winter months.

Beth loped along the promenade on the last leg of her forty-minute run. The paved, palm-lined promenade, which parallels the shoreline for several miles, had taken her from Santa Monica to Venice and back again. Her breathing was deep and rhythmic, but not labored. She had set out at 6:30 A.M. wearing a light jacket which was now tied around her waist by the arms. She wore a black Lycra halter and shorts, black Avia running shoes, and pale yellow socks. Her exposed skin glistened with perspiration, and the yellow sweatband circling her head was damp.

Beth consistently intended to use her daily running time to pray. It was a discipline she accepted as important, but she still struggled over staying focused and wondering if she was doing it "right." The thankfulness part of her prayer was not difficult. She had much to be thankful for, and she often got all the way to the Venice Pavilion—her turnaround point—simply itemizing for God the people and circumstances in her life for which she was so grateful.

It was the asking part of her prayer that was often sidetracked by other thoughts. Reagan had told her that the devil didn't want her praying for things, and that's why she had so much trouble staying on track during her petition. She didn't know if she believed him, but she had to admit that the second half of her run was sometimes a waste of time as far as talking to God was concerned.

Today Beth talked to God in her thoughts about her work. Her conversation with Raul at the football game on Saturday had provoked fresh frustration that she didn't have a viable project to work on. She was not content to be a stay-at-home wife to Reagan Cole or mom to six cute puppies. She had to get her claws into another good story, something that would stimulate her investigative juices and result in a decent-selling book.

Furthermore, Beth wanted to get involved in something which she deemed significant, something in harmony with her new faith and values. Books about the sordid life of a mass murderer or the sexual conquests of a Hollywood hunk—projects she had been offered—sold well, but what did they contribute to society? No, she would hold out for something that could make a positive contribution, perhaps even shed more light on the life of faith she had so recently and deeply embraced.

But she was clueless about what that project might be. So she had spent much of her run from Venice to Santa Monica silently reminding God of her concern and asking for His direction.

Returning to the condo, Beth found a love note from Cole illuminated on the monitor of the kitchen computer. As usual, he had left for work during her run. She smiled at simple words of affection and devotion. Reagan Cole was always at the top of her list during her prayers of thanks.

Also in the note was an invitation from her husband to join him and Raul Barrigan for lunch. Raul would be at Parker Center all day huddling with Sergeant Cole and his coworkers on the topic of terrorist activity and anti-terrorism methods in America's major cities. "It would be very nice to break up a long day of conferences with lunch at Quintero's," Cole's note said. "I know Raul would enjoy seeing you again before he heads back to Phoenix tomorrow morning."

Beth wrinkled her nose at the prospect. Downtown L.A. was still not her idea of a good time. Driving into town just to have lunch—even a great lunch at Quintero's on Olvera Street, even lunch with her husband and their delightful new friend—wasn't very tempting. She decided to think about it and call Cole after she showered, dressed, and ate breakfast.

The monitor also alerted her that a phone message had been received while she was out. She clicked the mouse on the telephone icon and initiated playback. As the computer called up the digital message, she reached into the refrigerator and poured herself a small glass of ruby red grapefruit juice from a half-full carton.

The electronic date-time stamp sounded first: "Monday, November 26, 6:49 A.M." Then came a familiar voice: "Good morning, Reagan and Beth. This is Shelby Rider in Portland. I thought I might catch you before you headed out for the day, but I guess I'm too late. Anyway, Beth, would you please give me a call when you get a moment? I happened to come across an intriguing bit of information that I hope you know something about. Thanks. Talk to you soon." The message ended, and the monitor flashed the telephone number in a box headed CALLER I.D.

The pleasant voice tinged with a delightful southwestern lilt left a smile on Beth's face. She had known Shelby only two years but admired her as a dearly loved older sister. Shelby, an ordained minister even though she was not presently serving in a church, had officiated at her marriage to Reagan Cole on October 13, almost two months ago. Beth wished she lived closer to Shelby; there was so much she could learn from this brave, devoted follower of Christ. Beth warmed at the prospect of talking to her again.

But not before you clean up, she remonstrated herself. She loved running almost as much as she loved playing basketball when in college. But she didn't like standing around in her own sweat. She took her glass of grapefruit juice and headed for the bathroom to shower.

It took longer than normal for Beth to get herself put together. This was her day for washing her hair and doing her legs—shower, shave, shine, and shampoo, Cole liked to call it. Furthermore, Beth quickly decided that if she didn't clean out the puppy box she and Cole would have to sleep in the living room tonight to escape the odor. So by the time she had dressed, dealt with the puppies, and consumed a bran muffin, glass of low-fat milk, and half a banana, it was nearly 9.

Beth was still ambivalent about going downtown for lunch, so she decided to return Shelby's call before calling Cole. She auto-dialed the number on the monitor with a click on the mouse then transferred the call to her wireless and settled into the love seat to talk.

Not having communicated since the honeymoon, Beth and Shelby spent several minutes catching up on each other: family, mutual friends, work. Then Shelby got to the point of her call with a question: "Have you ever heard of a religious group in the Seattle area—a cult really—called the New Jesus Family?" Beth said she had not. Shelby proceeded to tell the story of her meeting with Libby Carroll and Rachel Sams at the Falls Terrace Restaurant in Tumwater on Saturday. She described what she had learned about the New Jesus Family, its leaders—including Rachel's husband Cooper, and the bizarre prediction of Christ's return on February 20, 2002.

"How did they come up with the date?" Beth asked, intrigued by yet another off-the-wall end-of-the-world prediction to surface since the turn of the millennium.

"They claim that Jesus gave it to them directly," Shelby explained. "Rachel says it has a lot to do with their fascination with the number two. The specific time of the alleged Rapture—8:02 P.M.—is two-oh-oh-two on a twenty-four-hour clock. Put that together with the date—February 20, or oh-two-two-oh—and the year—two-oh-oh-two—and you have a symmetrical convergence of twos and ohs that won't occur again until the year 2222."

"But Christ's return is supposed to be a surprise, right?" Beth said.

"Right. When an individual or group says they have been given the secret date, you can be certain they haven't, because that's privileged information reserved for God alone."

"So all these twos and zeros are nothing more than numerology and suspicion," Beth advanced.

"You can see that, and I can see that. But people who aren't grounded in the truth are gullible for anything. They think they can see into the unknown when they can't see anything. They think they can see what others can't, but they're really blind."

"How can that happen to sane, intelligent human beings?" Beth wondered aloud.

"People have been asking that question for centuries, Beth," Shelby said. "In the meantime you have people like Jim Jones, Charles Manson, David Koresh, and others—all in my lifetime—leading sane, intelligent people into unthinkable behavior in the name of Christianity. And the turn of the millennium just served to bring a whole new crop of them out of the woodwork. The New Jesus Family apparently is one of them."

"That's pathetic. No wonder that woman you met, Rachel, is distraught about seeing her husband pulled under by this group."

"You haven't heard the worst of it," Shelby said. "This cult has put a whole new spin on the Rapture." She went on to explain the intention of the New Jesus Family to meet Christ in the air at zero hour in their own 737 with Captain Cooper Sams at the controls. She documented her story by reading excerpts from the press release Rachel had found among her husband's things. Beth moaned and groaned at the ludicrous story as Shelby related it.

"This group is really from the loony bin," Beth laughed as Shelby concluded. "Where are they going to get a 737?"

"They already have it," Shelby said. "It's a well-to-do group, so they pooled their resources and bought a used one."

"You're kidding! Do they have enough people to fill it?"

"The cult has around 100 members. They're going to offer the remaining seats to anyone who wants them."

"And how is the rest of the world supposed to find out about this once-in-a-lifetime offer?" Beth's sarcasm was obvious.

"Apparently the cult is releasing the information to the media."

"So this is a real press release you're reading from?" Beth probed.

"It looks like one—clearly written, very professional," Shelby assured. "But Rachel doesn't know if her husband has submitted it anywhere. I haven't seen anything about the New Jesus Family in the papers."

Beth laughed. "Not everything people consider news gets on the 6 o'clock report. I can imagine this group calling a press conference and nobody showing up. A doomsday warning by a bunch of fanatics who plan to fly into Jesus' arms in a 737 is not what I call news fit to print. If this story gets into the newspapers at all it will probably be a one-inch item under the heading, 'News of the Weird and Wacky.' "

Shelby paused for a moment. "There's another side of this story that isn't in the press release and isn't as laughable," she said soberly. "Rachel Sams fears that her husband has really gone off the deep end on this Rapture thing."

"What do you mean?" Beth was having difficulty imagining a serious side to such a crazy story.

"Well, we tried to assure Rachel that everything will settle down again when the cult's magic date comes and goes. 'When what you call Reunion doesn't occur as they predict,' we said, 'your husband will turn the plane around and land it, and maybe the whole experience will snap him out of it.' But she said she found some handwritten notes of his indicating that he had no intention of bringing the plane back to earth. Something about proving his firm belief in the cult's prediction."

"You mean he's going to crash the plane and kill all those people?" Beth retorted, unable to mask her cynical disbelief.

Shelby didn't respond right away. Then, "Judging from the scribbled notes, much of which she couldn't decipher, Rachel doesn't think he plans to crash the plane intentionally. She says he really believes Jesus is going to be up there to catch them."

"The guy is totally nuts," Beth interjected.

"Totally deceived," Shelby corrected.

"Probably both."

"Anyway, Rachel fears that Cooper Sams will attempt to prove his devotion to Jesus—as he perceives Him—by putting the plane in such a position that only Jesus can save them."

"Like flying past the point of no return without enough fuel to get back," Beth postulated wryly.

"Something like that," Shelby said, still serious. "But Rachel didn't know exactly."

Beth said, "Did you see these notes of his she talked about?"

"No, she didn't have them with her. She saw the notes briefly in her husband's office while he was in the shower. She didn't have enough time to copy them. When Cooper left that day, the notes went with him. Rachel doesn't expect to see them again."

Beth stood to walk as she talked. "That's ridiculous, Shelby. I mean, a pilot can't just take off with a plane full of people and no intention of bringing them back. The cops won't even let them board."

"Nobody knows for sure what Cooper Sams is really planning to do," Shelby said. "He has to file a flight plan which specifies his route and destination. So let's say he files a flight plan to Honolulu. But once he's airborne he can do whatever he wants with that plane. Who's going to stop him?"

Beth had another thought. "Are you sure Rachel is telling you the truth? Maybe the whole story is a figment of her imagination. Maybe she's even nuttier than her husband."

"Libby is convinced that Rachel knows what she's talking about," Shelby said. "And after being with Rachel Saturday, I feel the same way. Libby and I committed ourselves to stand with her through this ordeal, but I don't know what we can do about her husband or the New Jesus Family except pray."

"Don't worry, Shelby," Beth said, minimizing her friend's concern. "These kooky groups have a way of falling apart before they can do any harm to themselves or others. I predict that this New Jesus thing will unravel long before February."

Beth stopped in front of the window overlooking the promenade and the beach. The palms and the white sand and the morning sun on the gentle breakers made the water look warm and inviting. Beth had to remind herself that this was Santa Monica in late November, not the tropics. The surf was not as pleasant as it seemed.

After her momentary distraction, Beth said, "Why have you told me all this, Shelby?"

Shelby paused to think. Then she laughed a small laugh. "You know, I'm not really sure. I guess I thought you might have heard something about the New Jesus Family that would help me help Rachel."

"I sure struck out on that, didn't I?" Beth returned with a laugh of her own. "I know a lot about Seattle, but I'm not exactly an expert on the city's numerous fruitcake cults."

Shelby continued, "Perhaps I thought this unique approach to the end of the world might be a story idea that would interest you."

"You mean for a book?" Beth retorted incredulously.

"It was just a thought." Shelby sounded apologetic.

"The story would have to get very big in the public eye—very, *very* big—before it merits a serious look for a book. And they would have to demonstrate that they're really serious about this plane ride to heaven."

"From what Rachel says, they're deadly serious—no pun intended."

"But right now the obscure New Jesus Family is about as marketable as a book about the birth of our puppies. But I promise, if the story of Cooper Sams and his chariot to heaven shows up on the front page of *USA Today* and sparks national interest, I'll consider it."

"You have puppies?" Shelby sang, distracted by the news. Beth happily told all about the new arrivals in the Cole household, including the laughable misunderstanding by Reagan's colleague from the Phoenix Police Department. The women spent two more minutes chatting, then Shelby wrapped it up.

"Please pray for Libby and me as we deal with Rachel Sams."

"I will," Beth promised, making a mental note to include Shelby's request when she ran the promenade tomorrow. "But don't worry about that cult airplane thing. It will probably never get off the ground—pun definitely intended."

Shelby laughed, then she and Beth exchanged affectionate farewells and ended the conversation.

Beth put the breakfast dishes in the dishwasher. Thinking about her taxing workout and light, healthy meal made her hungry. A steaming plate of carnitas and rice at Quintero's was beginning to sound good. And she thought Cole and Raul might get a laugh out of the flight-to-heaven story Shelby had just related. Beth pulled up her husband's office number on the computer and auto-dialed to accept his lunch invitation.

Thirty-nine

Snohomish County Airport—better known by its old Army Air Corps handle, Paine Field—is located about twenty-five miles north of downtown Seattle in the suburban/industrial community of Everett, Washington. The airfield began in 1936 as a WPA project. It was taken over by the Army Air Corps in 1941 and developed as an interceptor base for P38s and P40s. After World War II, the Air Corps deactivated Paine Field and deeded the property and the buildings to Snohomish County. The airport still bears the trademark military triangle runway configuration, though two of the original legs of the triangle are now used as taxiways.

Paine Field was operated by the county until the Korean conflict in 1951 when the Air Force acquired the south complex as a tactical air defense base for F89s and F106s. In 1968, the feds again deactivated the field as a military installation and returned the facilities to Snohomish County.

Paine Field might have remained a sleepy little county airport serving private and charter aircraft if it hadn't acquired a world renowned neighbor. In 1966, the Boeing Company, already a major industrial enterprise in the Seattle area, negotiated an agreement with Snohomish County to use the main runway at Paine Field. Then Boeing moved in next door in a big way when it built its 747 plant, the largest manufacturing structure by volume under one roof in the world: over ninety-eight acres of floor space and 472 million cubic feet. Tour guides at the Everett facility like to boast of the building's size using awe-inspiring comparisons. Seventy-five football fields can be laid out

257

on the floor of the 747 plant, and one of its bay doors is as large as a field, minus the end zones. But another image evokes the loudest gasps from wide-eyed tourists: There is enough room inside the 747 building to house all of Disneyland, including twelve acres of parking.

As the Boeing 747s started rolling off the Everett assembly line in the late '60s, Paine Field, whose main runway was eventually extended to 9,010 feet, became host to initial flight tests for the new jumbo jets. In 1978 Boeing's facilities were expanded to begin production of the 767, a smaller wide-body. Ten years later Boeing purchased sixty-eight acres of airport property to further expand the flight line in preparation for a third model, the 777, which began production in the mid-'90s. Meanwhile, the Renton, Washington plant continued to pump out the standard body models: 737s and 757s.

Nearly two years into the third millennium, Paine Field in Everett remains a site of air travel contrasts. Fewer than 2,000 people are needed to staff the airport and its lesser tenants of aviation services. However, its Goliath of a neighbor, Boeing, employs three staggered shifts of workers totaling upward of 35,000 during full production, making traffic control around the plant a major headache.

The tail fins of up to two dozen jumbo jetliners on the Boeing flight line are visible daily from a tiny airport which cannot attract one commercial airline, not even a puddle-jumping commuter. Shiny, state-of-the-art Boeing 747s, 767s, and 777s, designed to transport hundreds of passengers each, take off and land in between two-and four-seat Pipers and Cessnas. The jumbo and lightweight aircraft combine for about 575 arrivals and departures per day.

The drone of propeller-driven aircraft, like the buzz of giant mosquitoes, is interspersed with the window-rattling roar of Pratt and Whitney, General Electric, or Rolls Royce jet engines, the largest of which is equal in circumference to the body of a 737. On a given day, a recreational flier from nearby Edmonds may share the runway with the president of Russia arriving to inspect the triple seven plant or the king of Saudi Arabia bringing his private 747 to the Boeing facility for a new paint job.

Cooper Sams guided his black Lexus sport coupe off Airport Road onto 100th St. S.W. The powder blue sign on the corner, illuminated by floodlights in the dark gray midmorning overcast, looked like it had stood there for decades: PAINE FIELD—SNOHOMISH COUNTY AIRPORT. Yet the sign and other landmarks at the airport's entrance failed to attract Cooper's attention today. He had made countless trips to Paine Field over the last two months. The only point of interest to him on the premises was one large hangar near the general terminal in the shadow of the FAA tower, a hangar identified by a single word painted in large blue letters over the bay doors: TRAMCO.

Tramco, the second largest tenant of the Snohomish County Airport, is a private corporation specializing in major maintenance and retro-fitting of large jet aircraft. On the first of his many recent visits to Paine Field, Cooper remembered that his former employer, Northstar Airlines, still contracted with Tramco to repaint its 737s in the high-tech facility at the south end of the airport.

Starting with one hangar—now the smallest—the burgeoning company added a 265,000 square foot rework facility in 1988 and another over twice that size in 1993. Tramco can hangar five 747s and five to six 737s at the same time, employing 2,000 staff and technicians. They can do everything from X-ray landing gear for fractures to change out an engine, from reconfiguring seating and redecorating the cabin to repainting the exterior.

Cooper parked the Lexus outside the security gate for the old Tramco hangar. With two much larger, better equipped hangars on the premises, the old hangar, which can accommodate two 737s, was mainly used for overflow work or storage. It often stood empty and ignored, like the wallflower at the dance, while the newer facilities received all the attention. Yet the drab Tramco hangar was the perfect place for Cooper Sams' project: unspectacular, unobtrusive, and conveniently adjacent to the tower and the main terminal. Cooper had often smiled to himself that the ugly spinster in the Tramco family would soon be the belle of the ball, thanks to its eternally significant new tenant.

Stepping out of the car, Cooper slipped into a leather jacket and tugged his old Seahawks cap low on his forehead against the morning mist. Then he approached the security gate intercom. "Cooper Sams," he announced into the mike. Waiting for the gate to open, he stared across the damp tarmac to the hangar which had become almost a second home to him. The bay doors were closed, giving the appearance that the cavernous building was deserted. Cooper knew that it wasn't.

"Just a second, Captain Sams," came the reply through the speaker at the gate. Cooper jammed his hands into the pockets of the jacket and turned his back to the prevailing southerly breeze. Then after several seconds the gate buzzed. He lifted the latch and walked through. But before he could take three steps to cross the expanse of tarmac between him and the hangar, the bay doors slowly began to part in the middle, as if the Tramco technicians had been waiting for Cooper's arrival to draw back the curtain on their work of art. Cooper had been anxiously awaiting this moment also, so he stopped in his tracks to take in the spectacle.

The nose of the plane appeared first, the dull black cone at the tip surrounded by white which gleamed bright under the hangar's stark interior lights. The dark cockpit windows glowered through the opening like the eyes of a predatory bird. Soon the wings became visible, stretching out majestically to simulate flight even with the plane at rest.

As the doors spread fully open, the natural light flooding the hangar further illuminated the brilliant white fuselage. An aircraft of any size was a delight to Cooper Sams' eyes. But the sight of the freshly painted, completely serviced 737 before him now took his breath away.

The debut, which Cooper realized had been choreographed to impress him, continued. A squatty, diesel-powered tug, already attached to the nose gear, started up and began inching forward, towing the plane from its shelter into the daylight, which was subdued by a solid layer of low-hanging clouds. With added light gracing the aircraft, details became observable. A broad crimson stripe ran from nose to tail across the row of passenger windows. Two more crimson stripes ran vertically up the white tail fin. And above the windows in bold, gold letters was the name of the soon-to-be christened aircraft: *VAN-GUARD*. By the time the aircraft was fully out of the hangar and parked on the tarmac, Cooper's eyes were misty with tears.

Rachel would love this. She appreciates these big birds almost as much as I do. Cooper was startled when he realized what he was thinking. He quickly remonstrated himself for such a sympathetic and foolish digression. It was a little too late to think he could change in that area.

Vanguard, standing seventy yards from him, looked dramatically different from the first time Cooper had laid eyes on it. As the supervisor of the New Jesus Family's Vanguard mission slated for February 20, 2002, Cooper had scoured the world via telephone and computer net for a suitable aircraft. Thanks to diligent and resourceful preparation by its prophet and spiritual leader, Lila Ruth Atkinson, the affluent New Jesus Family had achieved an enviable "cash and carry" posture with regard to purchasing an airplane that would lift them into the heavens at the precise moment of Reunion. What remained was to locate such a craft and prepare it for its final, glorious flight. Cooper Sams had passionately and energetically assumed responsibility for the project.

A 737 was the logical first choice, since Captain Sams was already FAA qualified on that aircraft. Another model would be pursued if a suitable 737 could not be found somewhere in the world.

Cooper Sams' search had ended in Buenos Aires, where a downsizing, financially challenged Argentine airline was eager to part with an older, well-traveled 737-300 for ready cash: $2.6 million. Cooper had found comparable planes closer to home. But upon checking the history of the Argentine jetliner, he realized its significance to the mission and closed the deal. The plane was the 220th 737 to roll off the Boeing assembly line in Renton, Washington. The telling numbers— two-two-zero—confirmed to Cooper that the Argentine jetliner was indeed the *Vanguard* Jesus-Brother had reserved for Reunion.

Cooper had returned to the states via commercial jet after signing the papers and obtained a standard one-time FAA authorization to ferry the plane into the country. Fully intent on complying with all FAA regulations, Cooper contracted with Tramco to thoroughly inspect the aircraft, bring it up to the standard of FAA air worthiness directives, and repaint it in preparation for its crowning flight. Then Cooper hired two other qualified pilots, former coworkers at Northstar, to fly with him to Buenos Aires and bring the 737 to its temporary base in Washington. *Vanguard*, still bearing the blue and white logo and paint scheme of its former owner, Air Argentine, touched down at Paine Field for the first time September 15, 2001.

Tramco had agreed to keep the plane in the old hangar as long as it was not in use. Unsure how officials at Tramco and Paine Field might react, Cooper Sams intentionally kept from them information regarding *Vanguard's* ultimate purpose. Similarly, he had delayed the press conference in Seattle to make sure the work in Everett was completed without unnecessary interruptions by the curious. As far as the people at the airport knew, *Vanguard* was being refurbished for the private use of a very wealthy religious group.

The old plane had been decently maintained by Air Argentine and was not far from passing FAA inspection. Yet Cooper took every precaution to assure that every tolerance was acceptable and every performance check superior. The mechanical work cost the New Jesus Family in excess of $130,000, which Cooper deemed money well spent considering that, when they learned about *Vanguard's* flight, the FAA might look for the smallest failure to keep the plane on the ground. Cooper had determined to jump through every hoop, cross every T, and dot every I to assure that the FAA had no reason to keep *Vanguard* from fulfilling its mission.

The New Jesus Family considered the repainting of *Vanguard's* exterior and the complete cleaning of its interior as much a necessity as assuring its airworthiness. Lila Ruth Atkinson and Cooper Sams had agreed that the Family would not ascend through the clouds and rendezvous with Jesus-Brother in an airplane that looked secondhand. Every passenger aboard would be dressed in his or her finest apparel, befitting an appointment with royalty. The airplane must be appropriately prepared as well. So the interior was cleaned and the exterior electrostatically painted and hand-polished. The 737's transformation from Air Argentine jetliner to *Vanguard* required twelve working days and cost over $90,000.

Cooper had visited the hangar several times during repairs, but he was seeing *Vanguard* for the first time since it had been painted. He stood by the security gate transfixed and deeply stirred by the sight. He could not turn his eyes from the gold letters emblazoned across the fuselage. It had been nearly seven years since that haunting word— Vanguard—had suddenly and inextricably wedged itself in his consciousness. And it had been more than three years since its meaning had been revealed to him by a woman who seemed more angel than human. Now, here before him was the tangible culmination of the divine call he had received from Parent-God: the ark that would lift His chosen ones from a doomed planet to sublime, eternal Reunion with Himself. And Cooper Sams would be at the controls.

Gazing at *Vanguard,* it seemed to Cooper that he had always been involved in the New Jesus Family. He could clearly recall the years before he nearly crashed in Juneau and the years immediately following before he met Lila Ruth. Yet the entirety of his life seemed swallowed up in the destiny which now possessed him, as if the first fifty-three years of his life had been mere preparation for the events that swept him into the company and mission of the prophet he had come to revere.

Logically, Cooper could not make his experience add up. But then fifty-three years of cold reason and pragmatism hadn't gotten him anywhere either. Everything changed in 1998 when he met Lila Ruth. It was then he experienced "transcendence"—that's what Lila Ruth called the supernatural leap from earthly reason to a spiritual perception and guidance superior to human logic. At that auspicious meeting, Juneau and Vanguard and the New Jesus Family and Reunion suddenly converged to rescue him from his brain and breathe life into his spirit. Standing before this marvelous aircraft, Cooper again thanked his lucky stars that he had been selected to participate in Jesus-Brother's grand design.

"What do you think, Captain Sams?" The question came from a short, broad-shouldered, thick-necked man walking briskly toward him from the hangar. Bud Fears, a fifty-year-old former Marine flier, was the Tramco sales VP who had interfaced with Cooper Sams through the refurbishing process. Fears' muscular build seemed better suited to a rugby uniform and cleats than a business suit and Italian loafers. A broken nose and other facial irregularities suggested that Bud Fears had mixed it up plenty on a number of fields of competition.

Cooper liked Fears because the man always called him *Captain Sams*—though he·was retired—and treated him as a superior. And the VP's theatrics—such as waiting until Cooper arrived to open the doors and unveil the product—were tolerable. Fears' efficiency and cooperation had convinced Cooper that Tramco would be in good hands for years to come—had Reunion and the end of world not been scheduled for the year 2002.

"She's beautiful, Bud," Cooper said, taking a step forward and holding out his hand toward Fears, "even more beautiful than I anticipated."

"I think she's going to fly even better than she looks," Fears beamed. "She tests out A-1 on the ground. Come on over and give her a look-see. Then we'll take her up for the FAA seal of approval and your own personal flight test."

A truck-mounted staircase had pulled up to *Vanguard's* left forward door. In the open door a uniformed "flight attendant"—in reality an attractive brunette from Tramco's marketing department brought along to pretty up the cabin and serve drinks during check rides with the customers—flashed a welcoming smile.

Fears escorted Cooper to the base of the stairs, but when he turned to let the captain ascend first, he was gone. Cooper had peeled off the line of march to perform his customary, stringent walkaround beneath *Vanguard's* gleaming belly. Bud Fears quickly hurried after him.

"May I have a flashlight please?" Cooper said, staring up into the nose gear wheel well. Fears barked an order into the hangar and a technician came running with two flashlights, one for each man. Cooper inspected the view ports in all wheel wells, the brakes, the tires, and gear. "Very nice, very nice," he said repeatedly to Fears, who followed him like a shadow shining a light everywhere Cooper shined his and touching everything Cooper touched.

Following Cooper up the stairs, Fears introduced him to Deanna the hostess, who smiled more than Cooper thought was necessary. Deanna offered to hang his leather jacket in the first class closet, so Cooper gave it to her.

Then Fears introduced the pilot and copilot—Tramco employees—who would add their signatures to the claim that *Vanguard* had met all FAA directives for airworthiness. The man and woman, both certified 737 captains in their early forties, wore generic dress uniforms complete with four-bar epaulets, four stripes on the jacket cuff, and scrambled eggs on the polished brims of their caps.

Cooper made a cursory inspection of the cockpit knowing that he would get a closer look when he was offered the controls for the return leg after the plane landed at Boeing Field, King County International Airport, south of Seattle.

Six other Tramco hangers-on were aboard for the short test flight, people from sales and marketing. Cooper nodded as each one was introduced without even trying to remember their names.

Cooper slowly walked the length of the aisle to the rear galley and lavs. The upholstery and carpets, still bearing signs of wear, had been scrubbed clean, as had all the bulkheads and interior panels. He assessed that the plane was in better condition than most of the 737s currently in service with Northstar. "Very nice, very nice," he repeated as if passing out pieces of candy to the Tramco people watching him.

Once Cooper and Bud Fears were strapped into their leather first-class seats, the stairs pulled away and the door was closed. Deanna offered Cooper hot coffee in a nice china cup. He declined out of habit, stopping short of saying, "Not until we level off at cruising altitude."

Cooper was used to being occupied during engine start, taxi, and takeoff.

The tug towed *Vanguard* a safe distance away from the hangar for engine start. The movement made Cooper uneasy. He felt out of place in the passenger cabin; he much preferred being in the cockpit and in control. He mentally recited the before-start checklist and hoped the pilot, who was at least fifteen years junior to him in 737 experience, didn't forget anything. He imagined the routine radio conversation as the copilot secured taxi clearance from ground control.

Engines one and two hummed to life. Everything sounded perfect, and Cooper's hands itched to be on the yoke. Now under its own power, *Vanguard* revved up and followed delta taxiway past the terminal ramp to alpha taxiway, which runs parallel to 16R, the 9,010-foot north-south runway used by all aircraft in excess of 250 total horsepower. Cooper imagined the admiring glances his gleaming airplane was attracting from airport personnel seeing it for the first time.

"So what kind of plans do you have for this beautiful airplane?" Fears said as the plane rolled smoothly toward the north end of the runway. The Tramco VP had posed the question in so many words on a few of Cooper's previous visits to the old Tramco hangar at Paine Field. And Cooper had strategically put him off each time with vague comments suggesting religious pilgrimages. He knew the likeable executive would find out about his plans eventually whether or not Earl Butcher decided to write about what he had referred to as the "doomsday flight." So Cooper thought it charitable to break the news to Fears himself.

"We have only one flight scheduled," Cooper began as *Vanguard* turned left at alpha-one and left again onto 16R and stopped. "On February 20 we will depart from Paine Field with a full load of passengers from our religious group, but we're not planning to come back."

Fears looked at him with raised eyebrows. "You're taking a world tour," he theorized aloud.

"No, not a world tour," Cooper said, enjoying the moment.

"Then you're relocating your base of operations."

"No. We're just not coming back."

The engines began spooling up for takeoff, then *Vanguard* launched down the runway and lifted off.

As the landing gear clunked gently into the belly of the plane, Fears turned to Cooper with a serious look. "What do you mean you're not coming back, Captain Sams?"

Cooper returned his serious look and told him.

Forty

Tommy Eggers hopped aboard a cable car for his late-morning ride down to the Embarcadero. He joked with the operator and laughed loudly at his own humor, something he hadn't done in a long time. The car was not crowded, since it was a couple of hours past peak business traffic, but Tommy preferred to stand near the back in the chilly open air instead of taking a seat inside. He smiled into the wind, then greeted a child on his mother's lap—tourists, Tommy was sure. He felt better than he had in months, and he realized that his agreeable physical, mental, and emotional state was something he had purposely brought on himself.

The discovery of a cancerous lesion on his neck only four days ago was a staggering blow, a visible sign that the HIV time bomb hidden in his system for at least four years was indeed armed and ticking. He and Dimitri had wept intermittently through the rest of the weekend, and Tommy's partner vowed his care and support to the very end. But by Sunday night, Tommy's decision to end his own life long before "the end"—and not to tell Dimitri about it—had grown to settled firmness within him.

On Monday morning Tommy had put on a new attitude as confidently as he had selected his clothes for the day. He had made the same conscious choice the next morning and today. There was no use crying anymore. He had six months to live, maybe more. Of those he could expect to enjoy at least three or four in reasonably good health. And he *would* enjoy them, he had decided. No feeling sorry for himself. No moping around the apartment wondering "what if?" about his lifestyle and relationships. No depressing support groups of other AIDS patients on their last legs. He was going to be his old self again. He was going to grab these last few months by the throat and shake all the life out of them he could. And then, when the time was right—and he would know the right time, Tommy was prepared to quietly step off this planet into the void beyond.

As the cable car rocked and rattled down the hill toward the bay, Tommy's eye was drawn to the Oakland Bay Bridge stretching out before him in the gray morning. The Golden Gate Bridge was beyond the hills behind him, spanning the bay to the Marin Peninsula and Sausalito. Either bridge would do when the time came, Tommy acknowledged calmly, but he considered that the Golden Gate, the higher and more famous of the two, might provide a more dramatic and fitting conclusion.

Tommy hopped off the car at the turnaround and headed toward the wharf. The air was heavy with the fragrance of rotting fish and salty, oily sea water. He moved briskly down the wharf past restaurants, fishing boats, sushi bars, and souvenir shops until the smell changed abruptly to that of hot bacon grease. Tommy stopped at a gaggle of newspaper racks, inserted two quarters, and pulled out the morning edition of the *US Star*, the national newspaper distributed by satellite and printed locally. Folding the paper under his arm, he followed the delicious smell into Weasel's Deli, a hole-in-the-wall joint that, up until Monday, Tommy had visited only once or twice a week while trying to curb his fat intake. But with the appearance of the spot on his neck, which he covered today with a turtleneck sweater, Tommy had decided to make Weasel's his daily breakfast stop until the last day of his life. What did he have to lose?

Weasel's on the wharf is a nutritionist's worst nightmare. The little deli makes no pretense of serving a healthy meal. Local patrons joke that Weasel's is the last bastion in the campaign to retain fat and cholesterol as national symbols of the American diet. At Weasel's, the spoons really *are* greasy. So are the forks, knives, plates, tabletops, walls, and floor.

"Good morning, Mrs. Weasel," Tommy sang loudly as he entered. "You look ravishing this morning, as usual." Tommy was the only one in the place, which sported three booths against the wall and six stools at the counter. The owner, a fifty-seven-year-old Chinese woman named Molly Wu, was in the kitchen. All Tommy could see of her through the serving window on the other side of the counter was the frizzy black and gray hair on the top of her head.

Molly's husband, Norman, the original weasel, had died six years earlier, struck and killed by a delivery truck right in front of the deli. Molly had carried on the business with the help of a mentally retarded son and a steady stream of transient dishwashers and fry cooks.

"Hello, Tommy," came the strong, high voice from the kitchen. "Chicken fried steak and eggs today, hash browns and toast." Molly knew Tommy usually went for the special. "Over easy, as usual?"

"Sounds scrumptious," Tommy returned, sliding into a booth across the narrow aisle from the counter. Then he added, "Double butter on the toast and a large glass of milk—*whole* milk."

"I know, I know, whole milk," came Molly's reply with the sizzle of a pat of grease hitting a hot, cast-iron griddle. "Coming right up." Weasel's had never served a glass of lowfat or nonfat milk in twenty-three years. But Tommy loved to needle Molly about making sure he got the good stuff.

Content that a filling, fat-laden, hot breakfast was only minutes away, Tommy turned his attention to the *Star*. He pushed the salt and pepper shakers and bottles of catsup, Tabasco, and soy sauce to the wall end of the table, brushed toast crumbs to the floor, and spread the paper in front of him.

The *Star* is a national pop daily specializing in bold, opinionated writing and offbeat viewpoints—something between *USA Today* and the *National Inquirer*. The daily edition of the *Star* comes in five sections, printed completely in color: Globe, U.s.—intentionally upper and lowercase to look like *Us*, Scene, Dollars, and Games. As usual, Tommy breezed through the Globe and U.s. sections, reading headlines, subheads, and an occasional story. What did he care if civil war was imminent in Mexico or if strained relations between the U.S. and China may escalate into an armed conflict? He wouldn't be around to congratulate the winner anyway.

In Dollars, Tommy glanced quickly at the first three pages, looking for interesting graphs, and skipped the last five pages filled with tiny print under headings like AMEX, NASDAQ, MUTUALS, and NYSE. He spent more time in the Games section. He wasn't really into sports, except to follow the San Francisco Forty-niners, who had slipped to woeful mediocrity after the glory years of the '80s and '90s. But he found the personal lives of competitors very interesting, and Games always profiled two or three athletes in every issue of *US Star*.

Tommy saved the best for last. Scene was all about people, movies and TV, travel, celebrity gossip, and life's oddities. He didn't learn anything from Scene, but then why did he need to learn anything at this stage in his life? Rather, the section amused Tommy and helped to divert him from dark thoughts of the end, which always hovered near no matter how positive he purposed to be.

Molly appeared with a steaming platter of food. She was barely five feet tall and 100 pounds with little more figure than a fountain straw. "Oh sweetheart, you've done it again," Tommy exclaimed, eyeing the mounds of greasy shredded potatoes and two eggs that shimmied when the plate hit the table. He quickly folded the newspaper—except for Scene—and tossed it onto the empty bench across the table. "I still want to marry you, dear Mrs. Weasel, and take you away from all this to be my own personal chef."

"Just name the day, honey bun, and I'll buy the padlock," Molly said as she walked away, no more serious than he was.

With his fork and knife, Tommy chopped the steak to bite-sized pieces. Then he smashed the slimy egg whites and runny yokes and mixed them together. He shoveled the egg paste onto his hash browns, then doused the mixture with catsup and Tabasco and topped it generously with salt and pepper. Molly returned with sixteen ounces of whole milk in a red plastic glass and a small plate stacked with triangles of heavily buttered white toast. She looked at the concoction on his plate and then left shaking her head, as she always did when Tommy defaced her works of art.

Tommy piled a forkful of egg-and-potato goop on a half slice of toast and spread it to the corners. Guiding the first bite to his mouth with his left hand, he used his right to open Scene in front of him on the table. The cover story was about a hot urban electro-jive band called Blue Rust. As with most of the articles in the Scene section, the Blue Rust piece was long on color pictures and short on text.

The rest of the front page was taken up with several short articles: a review of an interactive TV docudrama, a report about a suicide doctor assisting in the mercy killing of his own mother, a story about a cult preparing for judgment day, and assorted boxes of useless information. The cult piece was the longest. It took up almost as much space as the Blue Rust story.

Tommy was about to turn the page when a photograph at the bottom of the front page caught his attention. The picture showed a well-dressed, dignified-looking man and woman sitting at a table in front of two microphones. A small inset within the larger photo was of a jetliner—a 737, Tommy determined. The headline for the story read, "Doomsday flight: Cult plans to escape Armageddon in the nick of time." The byline identified a "special writer" Tommy had never heard of: Earl M. Butcher.

But it was the man in the photograph that caused Tommy to stop and investigate more closely. The face was familiar. Judging from the inset photo, Tommy guessed it was someone he knew—or had once known—in the airline industry. When his eyes drifted down to the caption beneath the photo, he suddenly stopped chewing his food, paralyzed with surprise. He read the lines silently: *Ms. Lila Ruth Atkinson, spiritual leader of Seattle's New Jesus Family, and Capt. Cooper Sams, designated pilot of the cult's doomsday flight.*

Tommy whispered an expletive. "Coop the poop, what kind of mayhem have you gotten yourself into this time?" Tommy returned a wedge of toast to his plate, picked up the newspaper, and brought it close to read the article carefully.

Max out your credit cards on trinkets and toys. Quit your job and take that Caribbean trip you've been dreaming about. Dump that disgusting diet and eat like there's no tomorrow. Why? Because according to a religious cult in Seattle, there *is* no tomorrow—at least not very many tomorrows.

On February 20, 2002—at precisely 8:02 P.M. PST—Jesus Christ will vaporize this wicked old planet and start over again. That's right, sinners: Eat, drink, and be merry, for in less than three months, we all turn to fumes.

This most recent in a rash of new millennium doomsday prophecies was made by the New Jesus Family, a

small, wealthy, elitist religious cult, during a sparsely
attended buffet and news conference Friday night at
Seattle's Stouffer-Madison Hotel. But this message
of gloom and doom is different from the others in at
least two ways. So says, Lila Ruth Atkinson, 67, the self-
styled guru/prophetess of the pseudo-Christian New
Age sect.

First, Atkinson claims to have received her information from the Man upstairs Himself. Ho-hum. Where have
we heard that before? Oh, no, Atkinson insists, God actually spoke to her — for real, no joke, Scout's honor — gave
her the date and everything. Yawn, ho-hum. Grade B sci-
fi movies are more original than this. (See C-8:
Doomsday.)

Tommy flipped to the back page of Scene and continued reading
intently.

Second, and here's where Atkinson earns a few extra
points for originality, the New Jesus Family and a few
other lucky souls will leave the planet just ahead of the
tidal wave of fire and brimstone and ascend to meet
Jesus somewhere above the mushroom clouds. Nice
touch, don't you think?

But wait; there's more. The mode for this exclusive rapture is an old Boeing 737 purchased by the cult for this occasion. Not as imaginative as Elijah's chariot of fire, but
you must admit it has possibilities.

The 737, dubbed *Vanguard,* will be piloted by one of its
leading members, former Northstar Airlines captain,
Cooper Sams, 59. The doomsday flight is scheduled to depart from Paine Field in Everett, Washington at about 7
P.M. PST on February 20, allowing members time for one
last prayer together at 35,000 feet before soaring into the
bosom of Abraham at precisely 8:02.

Suspicious that the lady seer in Seattle may have really
cracked the cosmic safe and ripped off the secrets of the
Second Coming? Scared that you might be left behind to
burn because you're one of the spiritual have-nots? Well,
the NJF has a spectacular offer for you.

"Your breakfast is getting cold," Molly Wu snapped at Tommy from
across the counter, sounding like a finicky mother. Tommy waved at
her as if she was a pesky fly. His eyes never left the page.

The New Jesus Family's jetliner has seats for 135 people, including crew. But there are only about 109 members in the whole cult. Even if every one of them is crazy enough to get on the plane, 26 empty seats will be available.

So here's the deal: The New Jesus Family is offering the extra seats to outsiders at no charge or obligation on a first-come, first-served basis. That's right, there's room on the ark for you if you act now. Operators are standing by. But before you rush to your phone, be warned: There is a sinister side to the doomsday flight. This is a one-way trip. The New Jesus Family is planning on a midair transfer from the 737 into the arms of Jesus.

But when asked what will happen if their calculations are wrong and Jesus isn't there to catch them — I know, O me of little faith — Capt. Cooper Sams had no answer. He has no plan B.

I'm no rocket scientist, but I remember someone saying once, "What goes up must come down." So if the reunion in the sky doesn't happen like Lila Ruth Atkinson says it will, that airplane full of people is coming back down to earth somehow. The question I can't get answered is, will Cooper Sams be ready to eat crow and land the plane safely, or will he take the matter of flying to kingdom come into his own hands?

Now don't quote me on this, because a libel suit is a terrible thing to have on my conscience with Judgment Day just a couple of months away. But I think the poor misguided souls who board the doomsday flight on February 20 are going to meet their maker that day one way or the other.

Cooper Sams may just as well jettison the landing gear after takeoff or arm a time bomb in the cargo hold. He has no intention of that plane coming back to earth in one piece. I could see it in his eyes. I could feel it in my bones. The doomsday flight is a suicide flight.

I suppose in the era of right to death and neighborhood euthanasia clinics, such madness shouldn't bother me. What's the difference between 135 people jumping off the Golden Gate Bridge over two year's time and 135 people choosing to board the same death plane destined to crash into Mt. Rainier or the Pacific Ocean?

So for those of you with either a rapture fixation or a

death wish, I include the numbers I was given for the New Jesus Family. Call now and you may be one of the lucky ones to bag an empty seat on the big silver bird to paradise. But don't come whining to me if you end up in hell instead.

The article ended with numbers for fax, E-mail, and V-mail.

Tommy shook his head and cursed in astonishment under his breath. He gulped down half a glass of milk and read the article again slowly and carefully as if looking for a secret coded message between the lines.

At last Tommy stood, pulled a ten dollar bill from his pocket, and dropped it beside his plate, which was still heaped with food. Taking only the Scene section of the newspaper with him, Tommy left the restaurant without saying good-bye to Molly in the kitchen. He had some serious thinking to do.

Forty-one

Libby Carroll was in the basement and almost didn't hear the doorbell. Committed to physical conditioning since her days as a high school and college track star, she had been lifting weights for twenty minutes. The sound of the doorbell was almost lost in the dull ring of the weights on the bar.

When Libby realized someone was at the front door, she wanted to pretend that she hadn't heard the bell. Her long day at the University of Washington was behind her. She was dressed in unsightly workout sweats that were damp with perspiration. Her long, thick hair had been pulled back from her face and hastily secured with a clip. She wasn't presentable—at least in her terms—and didn't want to be interrupted. She looked forward to spending the winter's evening quiet and alone, one of the luxuries she enjoyed from living by herself.

Furthermore, at 7:15 it was already dark outside. It was unsafe to open the door to an unexpected caller, even in the upscale neighborhood around West Kinnear Place on Queen Anne Hill overlooking Puget Sound and downtown Seattle.

But the caller kept ringing persistently. Door-to-door solicitors were not so dogged about raising a resident, so Libby assumed it must be a neighbor or a friend. She returned the bar to the rack, threw a towel around her neck, and climbed the stairs to the main level of her Tudor home. Libby couldn't imagine who among her friends would show up unannounced. Her son Brett, who attended Washington State University in Pullman across the state, was notorious for losing his house key. But he had been home for Thanksgiving just last week. Today was only Wednesday. Brett never came home in the middle of the week without calling first. But, Libby reminded herself, Brett's actions were far from predictable.

Hurrying through the living room as soundlessly as she could, Libby decided to peer through the security peephole in the door and then determine whether she was "in" or "out." After one look at the image standing under the porch light, Libby quickly unlocked the door and pulled it open. "Rachel," she said through the storm door still between them, unable to mask the surprise and concern in her voice.

Rachel Sams was dressed in navy slacks, a double-breasted blazer, foam-green shirt and pocket square, and a navy tab tie flecked with green. A gold pin attached to the blazer pocket identified the petite, attractive, auburn-haired woman as a Northstar flight attendant. In contrast to her professional attire, Rachel's face was streaked with mascara and clouded with utter despair.

Libby unlocked the storm door and pushed it open. Rachel hurried inside as if rushing to welcome sanctuary. "I'm so sorry to bother you," she said, clearly embarrassed about intruding and on the verge of tears, "but I don't know anyone else to talk to."

"It's all right, Rachel," Libby assured, "I'm glad you came." She secured the doors and ushered her new friend into the living room.

"I really feel stupid about ringing the bell for so long," Rachel said. "I should have known you were busy."

"I almost didn't hear the doorbell," Libby explained, inviting Rachel with a wave of her hand to sit down on the sofa. Rachel perched tentatively on the edge of the cushion with her large handbag clutched in her arms. Libby sat down on the love seat across the coffee table. "I was working out downstairs. Please excuse me for looking such a fright."

Rachel ignored the apology. Without another word she pulled a folded newspaper section out of her handbag and dropped it on the coffee table where a front page article was visible to Libby. Then she removed a small wad of tissue from a side pocket of her purse to dab away a fresh squall of tears.

Libby couldn't miss the headline staring up at her: "Doomsday flight: Cult plans to escape Armageddon in the nick of time." She lifted the paper from the table and drew it close to read.

"Have you seen it?" Rachel asked, sniffing and dabbing.

"No, I haven't," Libby said soberly without looking at her.

"We give free copies of the *Star* to our first-class passengers every morning," Rachel explained as Libby read, "but I rarely look at it myself. When we landed in Phoenix late this morning, I was picking up the cabin after the passengers deplaned, and there was the article, big as life."

Libby continued to read the article intently, occasionally glancing at the accompanying photo to study the images of Lila Ruth Atkinson and Cooper Sams.

After a minute of silence, Rachel said, "The news release was for real, Libby. Cooper is really going to do it. They had a press conference in Seattle. I can't believe it. Cooper and all those deluded people . . . " Another wave of tears choked off the words.

Libby returned the Scene section of the *US Star* to the table, then moved around to the sofa and Rachel's side. As she wrapped a comforting arm around her visitor, Libby felt Rachel's taut muscles suddenly relax as several hours of tension tumbled out in a flood of tears and sobs.

Libby just held her. She didn't know what else to do, and she certainly didn't know what to say. Libby was all too aware of her neophyte status in matters of Christian faith and compassion. She had no wise words of counsel for Rachel Sams, whose estranged husband had left her for a weird doomsday cult. She had no Bible verses to quote, no holy platitudes to soothe the troubled soul. Libby accepted that she was still in recovery herself from the emotional upheaval of only months ago.

Shelby Rider had been an anchor of strength and counsel to Libby in a raging storm of self-doubt, guilt, betrayal, and despair. Shelby had piloted her to the light of the loving Christ and introduced her to Him. And Shelby had ushered her into a harbor of safe mooring: a group of godly women committed to knowing the truth and living the faith. But Libby knew she was no Shelby Rider. She silently wished that Shelby was here to supervise as she comforted the woman clinging to her now.

Calming herself and cleaning up the damage with a fresh tissue, Rachel said, "This has not been a good day. Reading that article was only the beginning."

Libby released her comforting grip but stayed near. She remembered how lovingly Shelby had prodded her to bare her soul and how good it felt to talk to someone who obviously cared. Libby waited to speak until she gained eye contact. "Tell me what happened," she said.

Rachel sat back in the sofa and released a long, slow breath. "I tried to hide copies of the *Star* from the rest of the crew, but it didn't work. I didn't want anyone to see that article. But the captain had a copy in the cockpit. He and I have flown together a lot, and he knows Cooper pretty well. So he comes up to me before we leave Phoenix and says, 'If you paid more attention to your husband in the bedroom, he wouldn't be fooling around with this old lady preacher.' He was joking, but . . . "

"You were mortified," Libby said for her.

"Absolutely humiliated," Rachel said. "And then the captain makes sure the rest of the crew sees the story. Tells them I'm married to a celebrity. I get these weird looks for the rest of the trip. I couldn't wait to get home."

Moved by Rachel's humiliation, Libby said, "I'm so sorry."

Rachel continued quickly. "But coming home didn't turn out so well either." A stormy cloud darkened her face, and she bit her lip to hold back another torrent of tears.

Libby leaned closer. "What happened, Rachel? What did he do?"

Rachel took a deep breath and held it for a few seconds. "Cooper sold the house." Gamely holding herself together, she went on, "I've been gone on a trip since Monday. When I got home this evening, Cooper's things are all moved out—clothes, furniture, everything. This note was on the sink."

Rachel pulled a folded scrap of paper from her handbag and gave it to Libby, who read it aloud: "Sold the house and my stuff. Escrow closes Monday, cleaners come Tuesday. Can you be out this weekend?"

Libby stared at the note, then gasped, "This weekend!"

Rachel nodded. "He's probably been busy trying to sell the place privately for weeks. He never told me about it."

"How could he sell the house without your permission?"

Rachel sighed. "Because it's *his* house. He never added my name to the title. And it's paid for. He probably got three-quarters of a million for it—Mercer Island, lakefront and all."

Libby's eyes widened with surprise. "What about the proceeds? Won't he share them with you?"

Rachel shook her head. "I don't expect to see any of it. I'm almost sure he put it all into the cult. They paid millions for that plane, you know." She gestured toward the newspaper on the table and the 737 pictured next to Cooper and Lila Ruth.

Libby shook her head in disbelief. "That's so sad, not just the money they're throwing away but what they're getting sucked into. It's madness, and they don't see it."

Rachel sat silently nodding, a distant look glazing her eyes. Libby realized that the woman had been agonizing under her husband's delusion for a few years already.

Libby offered to prepare tea, and the offer was eagerly accepted. Rachel seemed to be soaking in the personal attention after such an emotionally bruising day. After helping Rachel find the guest bathroom, Libby excused herself to the kitchen.

Waiting for the water to quick boil, Libby was surprised by a thought which immediately crowded her comfort zone. Up to this moment, she had been fine with Rachel's unannounced visit and the opportunity to offer her a shoulder to cry on and a listening ear. It was perfectly in line with the offer Libby had made the first time they met at the coffee klatch Bible study: "If you ever need someone to talk to, give me a call." Libby felt confident that God wanted her to make such an offer.

Driving Rachel to Tumwater for a meeting with Shelby Rider pushed the envelope on that commitment a bit. But she went through with it because, again, it seemed like the Christian thing to do. Besides, Libby had quickly run out of answers and ideas for helping the distraught flight attendant. Giving up most of a Saturday was a small price to pay for Shelby's timely and helpful intervention.

But the idea in her brain right now seemed way over the line. A person could only be expected to give so much. After all, Libby had her own life to live and her own burdens to bear. There is a limit to how much one person can do for another.

As the tea steeped, Libby found herself arguing with God on the issue. One thing she had learned from Shelby Rider was that arguing with God was not a profitable exercise. Her mentor had counseled her not to trivialize anything God asked her to do, no matter how costly. The opportunity before her now seemed to require more of her than anything God had set before her in the few short months of her life of faith. Before she finished arranging the china teapot, cups, and saucers on the serving tray, Libby quietly—though somewhat reluctantly—yielded to what she knew was the right thing to do.

After pouring two cups of fragrant chamomile, Libby said, "You need a place to live."

Rachel received her cup and took a cautious sip before she spoke. "Thanks to a good job, I have a little money of my own put away. I'll get an apartment. I'll be all right." The unhappiness in Rachel's voice made her self-confident statement ring hollow.

"Yes, but your husband wants you moved out by the weekend. You'll need a place to stay until you find something."

Rachel didn't respond, and Libby could read the struggle and pain in the woman's downcast eyes.

Libby continued with what she knew she should say, though it still brought her some discomfort: "Rachel, I have a guest room with a private bath. You are welcome to stay here while you look for an apartment."

Rachel looked up. Her facial expression convinced Libby that the offer had come as a pleasant surprise, not something she had been secretly hoping for. Rachel answered, "I can't ask you to do that, Libby."

"You don't have to ask," Libby returned with a smile. "I'm offering it to you."

"I can get a hotel room for a couple of weeks. I'm used to living out of a suitcase."

"There's no need to go to that expense when I have a room that isn't being used," Libby argued, surprised at her own persistence. "In fact, you don't have to stay in that big empty house another night. The room is yours tonight if you want it."

Rachel studied her with a puzzled expression. "How did you know I was dreading going back to the house tonight?" she said.

Libby thought for a moment, then said, "If I were in your shoes, I wouldn't want to sleep in a cold empty house. Besides, who knows what your husband has done with the key. You wouldn't want a stranger walking in on you in the middle of the night."

Rachel said, "I want you to know that I didn't come here to beg for a place to stay."

"I know you didn't, Rachel," Libby answered warmly. "But as the saying goes, mi casa, su casa. I'm more than happy to have you stay here." *More than happy?* Libby silently questioned her own words, totally amazed. *Ten minutes ago I didn't even want to offer her the room. Now I'm more than happy that she seems ready to accept!* What amazed Libby was that she was beginning to feel pleased about helping Rachel this way.

Rachel weighed the offer. Then, "I promise I won't be in the way. I'll be flying three or four days a week, and I should be in my own place in couple of weeks. This is wonderful of you, Libby. I don't know how to thank you."

Libby recalled that she had used the same words less than a month ago when trying to express her appreciation to Shelby Rider.

A few minutes past 8:30, after Libby had showered and dressed, the two women set out for Mercer Island in Rachel's coal gray '97 Mazda 929. Having accepted Libby's hospitality, Rachel decided to return to the house on Mercer Island to collect some clothes and personal items. Libby offered to go with her, and again her kindness was welcomed.

Rachel's spirits seemed to brighten as the two women drove together across the city. They discussed the problem of getting Rachel's furniture from the house to a storage facility. Rachel said she would call about renting a small truck for a day. Libby offered to contact some of the other women in the coffee klatch to see if they—and their husbands—could spare a few hours on Saturday to move furniture. Libby and Rachel congratulated each other for solving the problem so quickly, even enjoying a little laugh about it.

They rode in silence for several minutes. Then, guiding the Mazda through the transition from southbound I-5 to eastbound I-90, Rachel said, "Libby, I still love my husband."

"Hm," Libby responded noncommittally.

"I don't love what he's doing to himself. And I don't love what he's done to us. But I still love him. Is that crazy?"

After considering the question for a moment, Libby said, "No, it's not crazy. We don't stop loving people because they are less than perfect or because they don't live up to our standards."

"It would be a pretty lonely world if we did," Rachel cut in.

Libby continued, "I suppose the real proof of love is when it endures despite the imperfections of others."

Rachel was silent for most of the time they were in the freeway tunnel west of Lake Washington. Just before emerging from the tunnel, she said, "I've known several flight attendants at Northstar whose husbands or boyfriends became alcoholics or drug addicts. Some of them dumped their men at the first sign of trouble. Others tried to hang on—hoping for a miracle—even though they sometimes ended up as punching bags for a drunk or crack head."

"Hm," Libby said again.

"But a couple of my coworkers took matters into their own hands and arranged interventions—in both cases *against* the will of the man. One girl got her husband back. He's sober today, and they're very much in love. As for the other girl, her man was in and out of rehab for months, then he ended up in prison. She swears she will be there for him when he is released."

Libby weighed Rachel's comments, searching for their meaning. Finally she said, "There are no guarantees with love are there? You can go out on a limb and win someone's heart. Or you can give everything you've got and get it thrown back in your face." She hoped she was capsulizing Rachel's feelings.

"But if you don't try, you don't really love, no matter what happens in the end, right?" Rachel said.

Libby paused again. "I think you're right. True love acts for the good of the person loved whether that love is returned or not."

The Mazda 929 swept down the gentle slope of the hill and started across the low two-mile bridge spanning Lake Washington between Seattle and the north end of Mercer Island. The lights of the island loomed ahead in the darkness at the end of the straight ribbon of freeway practically lying on the water.

About halfway across the bridge, Rachel said, "Then if I really love my husband, I must try to save him."

"What do you mean by 'save him'?" Libby probed.

"Try to get him out of that cult. And if I can't get him out of the cult, try to keep him from going through with this doomsday flight. And if I can't do that, try to keep him from crashing the plane and killing himself and all those people."

"Are you sure he's planning to crash the plane when their prediction fails?" Libby pressed.

"You saw the *Star* article. They're calling it a suicide flight."

"Yes, but you have to remember how they sensationalize stories to sell newspapers."

Rachel was not dissuaded. "What about the note I saw in his room?

He wrote about his intention to prove his firm belief in Jesus-Brother and the great Reunion. He scribbled something about releasing the plane into the hands of Jesus at the last minute."

"But you're not sure what he meant by that," Libby interjected.

Rachel ignored the comment. "What's going to happen when Jesus doesn't take over the plane like Cooper believes He will? Cooper may not intend to crash it on purpose, but will there be enough time for him to save it when his almighty Jesus-Brother doesn't—and will he even try?"

Libby had no answer. She wasn't sure Rachel expected one.

They swept up the end of the bridge onto Mercer Island. Rachel signaled to exit the freeway. "What do you intend to do to 'save him,' as you say?" Libby asked.

Rachel sighed deeply. "I don't know, but I'm going to die trying." She hoped her words were not prophetic.

Forty-two

Raython Braggs, whom Jesus-Brother named Support, was stressed. Lila Ruth Atkinson and Cooper Sams had appointed the skinny, spectacled, twenty-nine-year-old African-American with the wildly sculptured haircut to be communication specialist at the New Jesus Family's new home, the tenth floor east wing in the Stouffer-Madison Hotel in downtown Seattle. Raython had been directly responsible for interfacing with the phone company during the installation of the Family's communication network. That job complete—thanks entirely to the expertise of the installers, Raython had only to maintain the system: make sure phones were jacked into the rooms where they were needed, keep track of the wireless units they had leased, sort the E-mail and faxes, and keep the fax machine loaded with paper.

But Raython Braggs was a jazz saxophonist, not a technician. Even though he had volunteered to help in the office, keeping wires straight and machinery running was a demanding mental exercise for a man whose head was a constant cacophony of unwritten melodies and improvisational jazz licks. So when the fax machine started humming nearly full time, with additional incoming messages crowding its internal memory like cars on the freeway at rush hour, Raython's stomach twisted into knots.

The insistent, annoying beep on the machine warned that messages were being turned away, but Raython didn't know what to do about it. He was alone in the suite which the religious group had converted into an office, so he felt pressured to alleviate the problem himself. The phone guys had told him how to transfer an overload to a backup system, but he couldn't remember how to do it. And the documentation they left for him could have been printed in Bengali for all he could understand.

Then the E-mail line jammed up with incoming data, and the PC began beeping at him. Then the receiving tray on the fax machine overloaded and caused a paper jam. As soon as Raython cleared the paper path, the machine whistled irritatingly that it was out of paper. In his haste to load it Raython dropped a half ream of paper on the office carpet. He cursed loudly in the empty room.

Ms. Atkinson and Captain Sams had assured Raython that incoming data would be minimal, because few people outside the New Jesus circle were even aware of Reunion let alone interested in it. They were convinced that the article in the *US Star* would provoke only a few crank calls and a minimal number of genuine inquiries. But at this moment, 26–29 hours after the Wednesday *Star* had hit the streets—depending on the time zone, Raython was convinced that half of North America wanted to say something to Lila Ruth Atkinson and Cooper Sams about what the story flippantly referred to as the doomsday flight.

Raython Braggs had made a pile of money as a session player for a number of West Coast recording groups. After a terrifying, near-fatal drug overdose, the sax man turned to religion. Raython heard about the New Jesus Family. He attended one of Lila Ruth's sessions and considered the blend of Christianity, eastern mysticism, and New Age thought a charitable and logical view of life. He was also relieved that no one at the meetings took offense at his ethnic background. This was one bighearted, open-minded, forward-looking group of believers, he thought.

Then, in the middle of a coke high following a Family meeting, Raython was visited by Jesus-Brother himself, who confirmed what Lila Ruth had told him about the coming Reunion and the Family's privileged role in the event. Jesus also spoke the seeker's new name—Support—and commanded him to submit to the authority of the New Jesus Family and assist in the preparations for Reunion. Raython complied immediately, sharing his wealth liberally with his new family. Unfortunately, he was given an office job, which was responsible for his massive migraine and foul B.O. at the moment.

In response to a firm rap on the door, Raython snapped, "It's open." He was on his knees in black slacks and a billowy white satin shirt scooping sheaves of blank paper off the carpet and didn't look up.

The door opened and someone entered. Raython took a quick look and was impressed that the white man standing just inside the door was old or sick or both. His face, seemingly bleached yellow-gray, was deeply lined, as if it had been glued to the front of his skull in sections, leaving pronounced seams. Sparse shocks of dark-gray hair leapt from his scalp.

"Can I help you, sir?" Raython said, clearly not happy about the interruption. Lila Ruth Atkinson and Cooper Sams had virtually promised Raython there would be no foot traffic to deal with in their suite of offices.

The visitor, who was dressed in K-Mart quality blue slacks, brown sport coat, and plaid, open-collar shirt, took in the collection of complaining machines with a sweeping glance. "Yes, you can," he said in a gravelly voice. "But maybe I can help you first."

Raython saw him eyeing the fax machine, which continued to beep steadily about being swamped with calls. The communication specialist stood. "You know something about these electronic banshees?"

The man approached the fax on the counter near where Raython was standing. "A little," he said. He surveyed the error message on the readout panel. "These Oki's have limited memory for storing faxes while others are being printed. But it looks like your carrier has installed an overload backup system."

"Yeah, that's what they told me," Raython said, chagrined, "but I've never had to use it."

The visitor tapped a few commands on the keyboard of the com center computer. In response, the fax machine buzzed twice, groaned, then stopped beeping and resumed its normal productive hum. Raython's eyes bugged out with pleased surprise.

"We've only had about five faxes in the two weeks we've been here," Raython explained, wiping perspiration from his forehead with a handkerchief. "Then sometime yesterday—kaboom!—this thing lights up with four or five faxes an hour."

The sickly looking visitor had moved to a nearby desk where the PC was complaining monotonously that its E-mailbox was stuffed to capacity.

Raython chattered on, "By midafternoon we were up to eleven or twelve an hour. When I came in this morning, the machine was going nonstop. It already had a backlog of faxes clogging up the memory."

The stranger stood hunched over the PC, pecking away at keys. "Your E-mail defaults to limited storage, but it has a backup memory option also," he said, growling as if perpetually needing to clear his voice and spit. A few more keystrokes and the problem was solved. The computer quieted down, and the sudden peace was glorious.

Raython set aside the stack of paper he had collected from the floor and thrust out his hand. "Thanks for your help, sir," he said, beaming. "You couldn't have timed your visit any better as far as I'm concerned. I'm Raython Braggs."

The man mimicked Raython's smile as he shook his hand. "Glad to be of service, Mr. Braggs. My name is Butcher." The man's cordiality was artificial and calculated to win a friend and secure information. He was sure the young black man didn't recognize his name. Who looks at the byline on a news story anyway?

"I don't recall you as a member of the Family, Mr. Butcher."

"No, Mr. Braggs, you might say that I'm just an interested observer, a sympathizer."

"You know about Reunion?"

"Yes, I read about it in the *Star*," said the author of the article smugly.

"You interested in putting your name on one of the empty seats?"

"Well, I've been trying to get through to your office all morning," Butcher said, deflecting the real question. "But your line has been busy. Now I understand why."

Raython shook his head and grinned sheepishly, reflecting his embarrassment. "Sorry about that." Then he proceeded to reload the paper tray in the fax machine as a steady stream of printed faxes dropped into the upper tray. "So what's all the telephone activity about?" Butcher inquired casually, as if he had no clue.

"I guess a few thousand other people read about Reunion too, Mr. Butcher," Raython said, gesturing to the equipment on the counter which continued to receive electronic communication. "All these faxes are about what the paper calls our doomsday flight, and there's another tall stack of them on Ms. Atkinson's desk. If you're thinking about joining us, I'd put my name in right away if I were you."

Butcher gestured to the humming machines. "Are all these people inquiring about a reservation on the flight?"

"Oh, no, sir. Most of these messages are from cranks who just want to sound off. A lot of them are downright obscene, calling us every name in the book." He took a short stack of faxes from the tray and leafed through them. " 'Antichrist' ... 'New Age weirdos' ... 'Satan worshipers' ... 'psychos' ... 'demons from the pit' ... 'heretics, devils.' " Raython read several more comments that were sexually explicit and vulgar. He did not sound the least bit offended by the remarks or judgmental toward the senders.

Raython continued, feeling at ease with the stranger who had so graciously solved his stressful dilemma. "A lot of people see our mission as a big joke. They want copies of our itinerary, brochures for heaven and hell, and so on."

"I'd say that's in rather bad taste," Butcher said expressly to gain the young man's favor.

Raython nodded. "Other people apparently believe the stuff in the paper about this being some kind of mass suicide. Some of them beg us not to go. Others threaten to bring legal action to keep *Vanguard* from taking off."

"This isn't a suicide flight, is it, Mr. Braggs?" Butcher's own opinion was carefully veiled behind his question.

"Oh, no, sir. Ms. Atkinson and Captain Sams, they're bona fide prophets of God. Those of us in the Family have heard Jesus-Brother call our names. Reunion is no joke to us, sir; it's for real." There was a fiery confidence in Raython's eyes that Butcher could almost feel. After thirty years as a calloused newspaperman, very little touched Butcher emotionally, but he suddenly felt a twinge of sadness for this misguided young man.

Raython displayed the stack of faxes again. "And there are a lot more believers out there than we figured," he said proudly. "We have about thirty or forty faxes already from people who want to go up with us."

"These are nonmembers applying for the empty seats the article talked about," Butcher clarified.

"Yes, sir." He sorted through the sheaf in his hands again. "Here's one from a lady in Iowa whose spirit guide told her about Reunion just a week ago. This one comes from a guy in New York. He wants to buy a seat. Says he's wiring $1,000 at the end of the month. And they just keep coming, sir. I can't wait till Ms. Atkinson sees the stack on her desk."

"She hasn't seen any of these faxes or E-mail messages?"

Raython shook his head. "Her and Captain Sams were at Paine Field yesterday checking out the airplane again. They should be in sometime this morning. They live here in the hotel now."

Butcher pointed to the faxes. "How can you be sure these people are serious—the ones who say they want a seat on the plane?"

"Some probably aren't, but Ms. Atkinson and Captain Sams will know," Raython said reverently. "God will help them decide who should go with us."

Butcher's mind raced excitedly. Thanks to Raython Braggs' generosity with information, he realized that the doomsday flight was evolving into an even richer journalistic gold mine than he expected. He had gambled that a press conference for a fruitcake religious group might yield something he could blow into a tempting feature story. He had marveled at his own skill in crafting the article and at his good fortune to have it picked up by the *Star*.

Now he blessed Clotho, Lachesis, and Atropos—the Fates, goddesses of human destiny—that he had walked into the office at just the appropriate moment to befriend a willing source of information. The obscure doomsday cult in Seattle had aroused curiosity or incited outrage in thousands of readers as he had hoped. These people, like the frenzied patrons at a freak show, hungered to hear more of the bizarre cult and its outlandish flight to oblivion. And Earl Butcher craved the rewards awaiting him for giving them what they wanted.

Butcher's eyes darted between the stack of faxes in Raython's hands and the three to four sheets per minute accumulating in the tray. He couldn't have been more covetous for the sheets of paper if they had been hundred-dollar bills. He knew they were the substance for a follow-up story that could net him at least twice the amount the *Star* had paid for the original piece.

"Do you mind if I read a few of those?" Butcher said, nodding toward the batch of faxes in Raython's hands.

The young black man shrugged. "I don't see any harm in it," he said, handing over the stack.

Butcher leafed through several pages with feigned interest as his mind quickly pieced together a plan. "And you say there are even more of these somewhere?"

"Yeah, a big pile in Ms. Atkinson's office," Raython boasted.

"How big a pile?" *Why don't you go get them and show me how big the pile is*, Butcher urged silently.

"About so high," Raython said, holding up his thumb and forefinger about two inches apart.

"Geez, that many! You're kidding me!"

"No, I'm serious. I'll show you."

Raython headed toward an adjoining room in the suite. Butcher exulted in his extraordinary luck and prayed that it would extend a few minutes longer.

As soon as the cult member disappeared beyond the open door to the office, Butcher snapped into action. From the stack of faxes in his hand he grabbed a wad of about fifteen. Setting the stack on the corner of the counter, he hurriedly folded the wad once lengthwise and slipped it into his inside pocket. He took another fifteen or twenty from the stack, folded them, and secreted them into the opposite side pocket. Had he more time, he would have sorted through the sheets to extract the juiciest morsels from the lot. Instead he was happy to be getting away with what he hoped would be a representative sample.

Raython had left a half ream of blank paper near the fax machine. Butcher snatched a small wad and slid it underneath the collection of faxes he had just depleted, returning the stack in his hands to near its original thickness. With any luck at all, the blank pages, when discovered, would be attributed to Raython Braggs' obvious ineptness in the office.

When Raython reentered the room carrying nearly a full ream of printed faxes, Butcher was again casually leafing through the sheets in his hands. Seeing Raython's burden, the journalist erupted with a couple of choice expletives to underscore his affected amazement. Raython beamed with pride, as if he had produced the reaction.

"Oh, there's something else I want to show you," Raython said. He dropped his neat stack of papers on the counter and disappeared into the office again. Butcher couldn't believe his luck. It took him less than ten seconds to skim several sheets off the mound Raython had just presented to him, fold them, and hide them in his hip pockets under his coattails.

"This is what our plane looks like, Mr. Butcher," Raython said, emerging from the office with a plastic model in his hand. It was a Boeing 737-300 built to scale and painted white with large gold letters across the side reading *VANGUARD*. The plane was attached to a plastic pedestal for display.

"Very impressive, Mr. Braggs," Butcher exuded, setting aside the papers in his hand. As he examined the model, Butcher plotted his retreat.

"Well, this has been very enlightening," he said, backing toward the door. "You must be thrilled about being right in the middle of the project."

"Yes sir, very excited," Raython replied following his guest.

"I wish you all the best, Mr. Braggs." Butcher initiated a parting handshake which he also had to break off. Then he turned to leave.

"Hey, wait a minute," the black man called to him insistently from behind. Butcher held his breath. Could Raython Braggs see the bulge of papers under his jacket? Was he about to turn into a security guard and search him before he left?

Butcher slowly turned around.

Raython stepped close and spoke at almost a whisper. "Sir, if you want one of the seats on this thing," he said, holding up the model, "I could be persuaded to arrange it."

"No, thank you, Mr. Braggs," he said, playing dumb. "I think I'll take my chances with Armageddon. I get nauseated when I fly." Then he stepped out the door and closed it firmly behind him.

Six hours later Earl Butcher was ready to transmit his completed story to the *Star*'s editorial offices in New York. The feature editor told him by phone that she was eager to see it. She had practically guaranteed acceptance and a very generous fee, admitting that the lines in the building had been jammed for hours with requests for more information about the religious group planning to meet Jesus in the air.

Forty-three

After a brief discussion, Beth convinced her husband that it was time for Princess Di and the puppies to have their own room. Reagan Cole was a bit reluctant to move the puppy box out of their bedroom, worrying that Princess Di might roll over on one of the week-old mutts during the night and squash it. "And who's going to be awake to save the poor pup if she does, Mr. Sleep-through-a-five-point-earthquake?" Beth had countered. "Princess Di is no child abuser. They'll be fine in the utility room, and it will smell a lot better in here."

Cole acquiesced on the condition that he be allowed to leave the utility room door and their bedroom door open "in case of emergency." Beth agreed to the compromise but couldn't help teasing Cole about being a softy.

While her husband relocated the brood for the night, Beth slipped into her nightgown, washed her face, and brushed her teeth. Returning to the bedroom to pull back the comforter, she flicked on the TV with the bedside remote and tapped in channel 13. The theme music for "Pigg and Friends" was just beginning. Beth eased the volume up.

"You're not going to watch that, are you?" Cole called from the utility room, recognizing the music. "I'd like to watch the 11 o'clock news—NBC, channel 4."

"Just a second," Beth called back. "I want to see what kind of dirt Pigg has dug up today."

The screen flashed a dizzying montage of images—controversial personalities in government and entertainment interspersed with some of America's true oddballs: a bungee-jumping nun, the owner/trainer of a cockroach circus, the human mole—a guy who lives underground in his back yard, three unmarried sisters who have lived together in a one-room bungalow for eighteen years without leaving each other's sight.

Beth slid in between the floral-print sheets and propped a pillow behind her so she could see the screen. The theme music faded and the voiceover announcer cut in, "Ladies and Gentlemen, it's time for Pigg and Friends." Canned applause, spiced with howls and cat calls, filled in behind the voice and music. The announcer cranked up like a carnival barker: "And now, here's our host, the man who knows more strange people than a psychiatrist on LSD, Mr. Carlton Pigg."

Cole appeared in the doorway. He was still dressed in his detective slacks and dress shirt, having jettisoned his jacket, tie, belt, and shoes when he arrived home from work about 7:15. "Pigg isn't his real name, you know," he said, as if revealing a government secret. "It's just a stage name."

"Yeah, I know," Beth said. "It's really Carlton *Giraffe*, but that just doesn't fit his personality."

Cole grinned and shook his head, knowing better than to expect a straight answer. "That Carlton Pigg stuff will rot your brain," he teased, nodding toward the screen.

Beth teased right back. "No great loss. You married me for my body anyway."

Carlton Pigg, a wiry little man with a bad toupee and wearing an undershirt, tuxedo jacket, and baggy red pants, jounced down a sound-stage stairway leading to nowhere and grinned into the camera. "Hi and welcome to Pigg and Friends," he sang in a pronounced Aussie accent. "We have a great show for you tonight folks. We'll meet a Topeka man who cured his impotence with a diet of grubs and snails. Unfortunately, his wife won't even kiss him now." The canned audience loved it.

"Then we'll drop in on Cedric McNulty, the stamp collector from Gloucester, Massachusetts who has tattooed the images of the world's most valuable stamps on his body. I guess when old Cedric dies they can just rip off his clothes and mail him home for burial." The canned audience went wild for that one.

"That's sick," Cole said, crossing in front of the TV on his way to the master bath.

"Well, we could turn to the news and watch something uplifting like gang violence, scandal in the Senate, or a train wreck in Nebraska that killed eighty-five people."

Carlton Pigg continued, "I'll introduce you to these fine people and even more of my friends after these important messages. Stay tuned."

"I'd like to watch this with you, Beth," Cole said sarcastically as he disappeared into the bathroom, "but I have to take a shower." Then he closed the bathroom door.

"I'll record it for you if you want," Beth called after him with a laugh. Her husband responded with a loud belch that echoed off the bathroom tile.

"You say the most romantic things, darling," she said, hoping he heard.

Beth watched the first ten-minute segment of Pigg's show half-heartedly while browsing through a copy of *Guideposts* from the magazine rack beside the bed. Pigg's story about the tattooed stamp collector was partially muted by the shower running in the bathroom. Beth wasn't paying much attention.

After commercials, flamboyant Carlton Pigg returned. "Now it's time for our regular two-minute feature on Pigg and Friends, 'Nuts in the News,' where we scour the kingdom for the most interesting people making today's headlines."

The shower went off. "Will you please turn to channel 4 now?" Cole called through the closed door.

"Just a sec, after 'Nuts in the News,' " Beth replied. "It's my favorite part of the show."

"After what?"

"Never mind. You can have the clicker when you come out."

Pigg read from the *Tribune* about a meat packer in Chicago who is such a Bears fanatic that he wears a Bears football uniform—shoulder pads and all—at work under his blood-stained apron. "Makes sense to even drive down to Portland and see Shelby."

"When?"

Beth thought a moment. "I could leave tomorrow, or we could go together on Saturday, and you could take Monday off."

Cole shook his head. "I'm sorry, Babe, but I can't take the time off. I'm still a day behind from being with Officer Barrigan." Seeing Beth's disappointment and having sensed her eagerness to get into a story, he added, "But you go on up for the weekend and see if this is a story you can get into."

Beth gave her husband a hug. "Thank you, Reagan." She had already decided she was going with or without him, but she knew it made him feel better to give his blessing.

Beth wasn't sure how far she might get into the story in just a few days, but she knew the story was already starting to get into her.

Forty-four

It has to be a sign, Raul Barrigan thought soberly. *Three times is an odd coincidence. Four times is unreal. Five times in one week means that God is trying to get my attention. What else can it be?*

Raul sat in the lunch room at Central City Precinct, downtown Phoenix, staring at the *US Star*'s Scene section for Friday, November 30. For the second time this week the front page carried a story about the New Jesus Family and its controversial preparations for doomsday, February 20, 2002. Wednesday's article had been at the bottom of the front page; today's was the lead story for the section. The photo of Lila Ruth Atkinson and Cooper Sams was half again as large as the same photo which ran Wednesday. Today's headline boldly proclaimed: "Thousands scorn doomsday flight; scores beg for available seats."

Five times this week the sad story of the Seattle cult and its alleged airlift to heaven had been thrust into Raul Barrigan's face unbidden. On Monday, Beth Cole came to lunch at Quintero's talking about it. On Wednesday afternoon, a coworker doing the *Star*'s crossword puzzle—Scene section, page 5—came into Raul's office asking, "What's an eight-letter word for law body? The fifth letter is R." Looking up, Raul's eyes fell on the front-page headline, "Doomsday flight: Cult plans to escape Armageddon in the nick of time." Raul Barrigan was not in the habit of reading the trashy *US Star*. But after supplying the word "congress," Raul talked his fellow officer into leaving him the front and back page so he could read the article.

Raul heard more about the event late Thursday afternoon on his way

me," Pigg quipped, "because the Chicago Bears have been dead meat for years." The canned laughter was absurdly raucous. Beth barely smiled.

Next, Pigg held up the Scene section of Wednesday's *US Star*. "And did you hear about the religious wackos who bought a jetliner so they can fly up to meet Jesus in the air on doomsday? Pigg would not lie to you about something like this. It's right here in the *Star*." He pointed to the article at the bottom of the front page, and the camera zoomed in until the headline was readable: Doomsday flight: Cult plans to escape Armageddon in the nick of time.

"Oh, no, they really did it," Beth groaned disappointedly, remembering Shelby Rider's call on Monday. She put down her magazine to watch.

"According to Seattle's New Jesus Family—that's the name of this group of holy mushbrains—God is going to put a torch to Planet Earth on February 20, 2002. But just before the place goes up in a ball of hellfire, these people will board their own Boeing 737 for a charter flight to heaven. To me, that's about as intelligent as the group of scientists who decided to take a rocket to the sun, saying they can make it safely as long as they fly at night."

The fake laughter roared again, but Beth was suddenly unamused. She thought about Rachel, the woman Shelby described to her over the phone, whose husband was supposedly planning to fly the 737. She had prayed for Rachel during her morning runs during the week as Shelby requested, but with little passion. At the time, Beth was confident that what Pigg referred to as the doomsday flight was a joke, a silly plan that would never happen. Seeing the *US Star* article on Carlton Pigg's program convinced her that the New Jesus Family was more serious about their plans than she had given them credit for.

Beth remembered Shelby's concern that the passengers on the Boeing 737 were in mortal danger when Jesus didn't appear in the sky to welcome them at 8:02 P.M. on February 20. Rachel had said something about a note she saw suggesting that her husband the pilot might abandon reason and safety to prove his fanatical devotion to the cult's beliefs in what they called Reunion.

What was Cooper Sams planning to do at zero hour: purposely run out of fuel over the Pacific Ocean? release the controls and sit by as the plane flies into a mountain? point the nose toward heaven at full speed until the plane eventually stalls? Choosing to die for one's beliefs was one thing. Making that choice for 100 other misguided souls was quite another. Beth was disturbed at the prospect.

Beth thought about Shelby's suggestion that the New Jesus Family's story might make a good book. On Monday Beth brushed off the idea as one with little public appeal. It seemed that people came to her weekly with dumb ideas for a book: "My Amazing Parakeet"; "The

Vacation in the Everglades When Our Boat Almost Hit a Crocodile"; "Part-time Actuary, Part-time Volunteer for the Cancer Society." For each proposal, Beth would smile pleasantly and say something like, "Sounds wonderful, but unfortunately '101 ways to use dryer lint' has kind of dropped off as a marketable topic. But keep working on it. I'm sure your family members would love a copy of the manuscript."

But, thanks to rags like the *US Star* and freak-magnets like Carlton Pigg, obscure topics and bizarre events are sometimes thrust into the national spotlight despite their inherent news-unworthiness. Beth realized that the media was in the process of transforming Cooper Sams and New Jesus Family into celebrities and the doomsday flight into a media event. Like it or not, celebrities and media events often translated into national bestsellers. Shelby's suggestion that the activity in Seattle might make for a good book suddenly had credence.

Carlton Pigg made one more snide comment about the New Jesus Family and then directed his mockery toward a man in St. George, Utah who had covered the roof of his house with old wheel covers hoping to attract UFOs. Beth turned off the TV, but she couldn't turn off the conflicting thoughts and feelings that Carlton Pigg's twenty-second spot on the New Jesus Family had provoked.

On one hand, her mind was already plotting the angles she might use when writing a book about the cult and its February date with destiny. Organizational thoughts were almost automatic after nearly eight years of writing supermarket paperbacks. Along with these thoughts came a stir of excitement, the inner buzz that sounded whenever she stumbled across a monetarily rewarding topic worthy of her skills. She had been looking and praying for something to work on. Perhaps God had used Shelby Rider, the *US Star*, and Carlton Pigg to direct her attention to a live possibility.

On the other hand, the plight of a woman she had never met— Rachel Sams—and the pathetic lunacy of her husband and his faith tugged at Beth's emotions. This was a new pattern of response to life and its potential stories for Beth. The awakening of her faith had prompted a new appreciation for the subjects of her stories. She no longer saw them only as a meal ticket. These were people whose trying and even perilous circumstances brought them trouble and pain. Along with the privilege of telling their story Beth sensed a growing responsibility to give something back. She found herself as concerned for Cooper and Rachel Sams as she was energized about the story possibilities.

Reagan Cole opened the bathroom door and emerged from a cloud of steam. He was dressed for bed in a blue, holey LAPD T-shirt and baggy white boxer shorts decorated with little Corvettes, Lamborghinis, and Maseratis. His thin sandy hair had been towel-dried but not combed. He was in the middle of brushing his teeth.

"Aren't we going to watch the news?" he said, trying not to let the toothpaste escape from his mouth.

Beth ignored the question. She was wearing her serious conversation face. "Do you remember me telling you about the cult in Seattle that bought a 737 for the Rapture?"

Cole stopped brushing for a second to think, then he mumbled through the foam, "Yeah, you told me Monday at Quintero's, the day we ate with Raul. Shelby called you about it. Why?"

"Pigg just had a blurb on the cult, and the *Star* ran a big story on it yesterday. This thing is becoming a media circus. They're calling it the doomsday flight."

Cole perceived that there was more Beth wanted to say on the subject. "Hold that thought," he said. He returned to the sink, quickly rinsed out his mouth and toothbrush, and turned out the bathroom light. Then he climbed into his side of the bed. "What are you thinking?"

Beth told him, including the dissonance between the story possibility she saw and her sympathy and concern for the principals involved. She purposely skimmed over Rachel Sams' dark notion that her fanatical husband might purposely endanger the flight. She knew that such information might sour her husband to the idea that was rapidly forming in her mind as she talked.

"How would you feel about me flying to Seattle to check out the potential for a book?" she concluded.

Cole smiled. "I wondered if the conversation was coming to this. How long have you been planning to go?"

"I *haven't* been planning to go, Reagan," Beth answered defensively. "It didn't cross my mind until five minutes ago when I saw Carlton Pigg's bit about the doomsday flight."

"I told you that TV show would rot your brain. All of a sudden you want to run off to Seattle without me."

"You could come too," Beth said, suddenly excited at the prospect. "We can stay on Whidbey."

"I can't get away now, Babe. Or did you forget that I used up all my vacation days this year chasing a bad guy up the coast and then taking a honeymoon."

"Sick leave," Beth countered. "You could use sick leave."

Cole frowned at her and lifted his T-shirt, exposing a surgical scar on the left side of his abdomen from which a nine-millimeter slug had been removed five months earlier.

"Oh, yeah," Beth said, "I forgot about that."

"Besides," Cole put in, "sick leave is for being sick, not for doing anything you want."

Beth pretended not to hear her husband's moralizing. "OK, so I could go up alone for a few days, check on the house, try to talk to Rachel Sams and some of the cult people, especially this pilot. I might home from work. He didn't usually listen to drive-time talk shows because "shock jocks," radio hosts equating conflict, argument, and name-calling with entertainment, annoyed him. But one of them was holding forth on the topic of the New Jesus Family when he turned on the radio. Several listeners called in to—as the host liked to say—"cuss and discuss" the *Star* article. The host read several paragraphs during the twenty-three minutes Raul listened, further convincing him how sick and deceived this New Age bunch was.

Thursday night Raul was channel-checking the news stations at 11 P.M. He skipped over one station just long enough to hear a man with an Australian accent say, ". . . Seattle's New Jesus Family." Raul quickly backed up to see the same *Star* article in the hands of an outrageous-looking dude by the name of Carlton Pigg. Raul had never watched the program before and likely never would again. But he was transfixed for twenty seconds as Pigg railed on the crazy cultists for their doomsday prediction.

Before he went to bed, Raul again read the entire *Star* article, which he had brought home from the office. As disgusting as the cult seemed to him, Raul found himself strangely intrigued by these reports which crossed his path so coincidentally.

Now, here it was again. Raul, dressed in shirt, tie, and slacks, had rolled his chair into the downtown station's lunchroom to microwave a bowl of his mother's chili for lunch. While the appliance zapped his food, Raul browsed the table where several of his coworkers had left odd sections of three different daily newspapers—*Arizona Republic, Phoenix Gazette,* and the *Star.* On the top of the stack, staring up at him, was the *Star's* latest article on the doomsday flight. Raul took the Scene section to an empty table and devoured the cover story which, he noted, bore the same byline as the Wednesday story: Earl M. Butcher.

The New Jesus Family headquarters in Seattle had been deluged with thousands of calls in two days, the article claimed. Most of the messages—faxes, E-mail, and V-mail—were derogatory, and the article included a number of crude and demeaning quotes directed at the cult and its leaders. Raul wondered how some of the terms made it past the *Star's* censors. Or maybe newspapers no longer have censors, he thought wryly.

Raul was acutely absorbed in two paragraphs devoted to the nebulous "scores" of messages from people across North America. These deluded souls apparently believed that the New Jesus Family was legitimate, that the February 20 meeting in the atmosphere was indeed ordained by the emissary of God whom the cult called Jesus-Brother.

The two paragraphs included a number of excerpts from these messages, quoted anonymously. A single mother of five in Georgia begged the cult to take her innocent children into Jesus' arms while she remained behind "to pay for her adultery in the fires of judgment." A truck driver in Montana wrote that he saw two falling stars on Wednesday night, convincing him that Jesus-Brother was calling him to Reunion aboard the 737 which had been christened *Vanguard*. He was driving his rig to Seattle where he would wait for confirmation of his seat on the plane.

"Hey, Ponch, is this yours?" The voice behind him belonged to Detective Benny Roakes, the only other person in the lunchroom. The guys at Central had tagged Raul Barrigan "Ponch"—after his likeness on the old "CHiPs" reruns—from his first day in the office. The new nickname was a welcome change from "Sugar Bear" and the cheerless memories it prompted.

When Raul turned around, Roakes was standing at the open microwave with a bowl of chili in one hand and a ready-to-nuke barbecue beef and bean burrito in the other. "Yeah, that's my chili, Benny. Sorry." Roakes delivered the bowl to the table. Raul lifted the lid and inserted a plastic spoon, then immediately turned his attention back to the article.

An elderly couple in Minnesota wrote that they had ignored God all their lives but finally saw the light in the *Star* article. They promised to sign over their entire life savings, more than $300,000, to the cult in exchange for two empty seats. Other alleged devotees offered themselves as "pleasure servants" to cult leaders to underscore their desire to be among the chosen few. A self-proclaimed spiritist medium in Telluride insisted that she be included because "the spirits of Moses, Mohammed, Confucius, and Nostradamus appeared to me saying they would be waiting for me alongside Jesus-Brother." Each quote seemed farther from reality than the last, and Raul was stunned that so many people could be taken in by such an obviously spurious view of life and God.

Raul's appetite left him. In its place came a growing pressure on his chest, as if his body had been strapped into an invisible vise with an unseen hand slowly turning the handle to close the huge jaws. The room became stuffy and Raul found breathing more difficult. A great sadness for these desperate people seemed to settle over him like a blanket. But he knew he had to read on.

The next three paragraphs told about many readers who saw the flight of *Vanguard* as another means of deliverance. "I don't believe in God, and your Reunion is a pipe dream," communicated a man in Connecticut. "But if the doomsday flight is a nonstop flight to hell like the paper says, I want to be on it. I'm an alcoholic and have lost everything, including my business and family. My life has been a waste; I might as well go out in a blaze of glory while I have the choice."

The article quoted a father and mother from rural Idaho: "Our me," Pigg quipped, "because the Chicago Bears have been dead meat for years." The canned laughter was absurdly raucous. Beth barely smiled.

Next, Pigg held up the Scene section of Wednesday's *US Star*. "And did you hear about the religious wackos who bought a jetliner so they can fly up to meet Jesus in the air on doomsday? Pigg would not lie to you about something like this. It's right here in the *Star*." He pointed to the article at the bottom of the front page, and the camera zoomed in until the headline was readable: Doomsday flight: Cult plans to escape Armageddon in the nick of time.

"Oh, no, they really did it," Beth groaned disappointedly, remembering Shelby Rider's call on Monday. She put down her magazine to watch.

"According to Seattle's New Jesus Family—that's the name of this group of holy mushbrains—God is going to put a torch to Planet Earth on February 20, 2002. But just before the place goes up in a ball of hellfire, these people will board their own Boeing 737 for a charter flight to heaven. To me, that's about as intelligent as the group of scientists who decided to take a rocket to the sun, saying they can make it safely as long as they fly at night."

The fake laughter roared again, but Beth was suddenly unamused. She thought about Rachel, the woman Shelby described to her over the phone, whose husband was supposedly planning to fly the 737. She had prayed for Rachel during her morning runs during the week as Shelby requested, but with little passion. At the time, Beth was confident that what Pigg referred to as the doomsday flight was a joke, a silly plan that would never happen. Seeing the *US Star* article on Carlton Pigg's program convinced her that the New Jesus Family was more serious about their plans than she had given them credit for.

Beth remembered Shelby's concern that the passengers on the Boeing 737 were in mortal danger when Jesus didn't appear in the sky to welcome them at 8:02 P.M. on February 20. Rachel had said something about a note she saw suggesting that her husband the pilot might abandon reason and safety to prove his fanatical devotion to the cult's beliefs in what they called Reunion.

What was Cooper Sams planning to do at zero hour: purposely run out of fuel over the Pacific Ocean? release the controls and sit by as the plane flies into a mountain? point the nose toward heaven at full speed until the plane eventually stalls? Choosing to die for one's beliefs was one thing. Making that choice for 100 other misguided souls was quite another. Beth was disturbed at the prospect.

Beth thought about Shelby's suggestion that the New Jesus Family's story might make a good book. On Monday Beth brushed off the idea as one with little public appeal. It seemed that people came to her weekly with dumb ideas for a book: "My Amazing Parakeet"; "The

Vacation in the Everglades When Our Boat Almost Hit a Crocodile"; "Part-time Actuary, Part-time Volunteer for the Cancer Society." For each proposal, Beth would smile pleasantly and say something like, "Sounds wonderful, but unfortunately '101 ways to use dryer lint' has kind of dropped off as a marketable topic. But keep working on it. I'm sure your family members would love a copy of the manuscript."

But, thanks to rags like the *US Star* and freak-magnets like Carlton Pigg, obscure topics and bizarre events are sometimes thrust into the national spotlight despite their inherent news-unworthiness. Beth realized that the media was in the process of transforming Cooper Sams and New Jesus Family into celebrities and the doomsday flight into a media event. Like it or not, celebrities and media events often translated into national bestsellers. Shelby's suggestion that the activity in Seattle might make for a good book suddenly had credence.

Carlton Pigg made one more snide comment about the New Jesus Family and then directed his mockery toward a man in St. George, Utah who had covered the roof of his house with old wheel covers hoping to attract UFOs. Beth turned off the TV, but she couldn't turn off the conflicting thoughts and feelings that Carlton Pigg's twenty-second spot on the New Jesus Family had provoked.

On one hand, her mind was already plotting the angles she might use when writing a book about the cult and its February date with destiny. Organizational thoughts were almost automatic after nearly eight years of writing supermarket paperbacks. Along with these thoughts came a stir of excitement, the inner buzz that sounded whenever she stumbled across a monetarily rewarding topic worthy of her skills. She had been looking and praying for something to work on. Perhaps God had used Shelby Rider, the *US Star*, and Carlton Pigg to direct her attention to a live possibility.

On the other hand, the plight of a woman she had never met—Rachel Sams—and the pathetic lunacy of her husband and his faith tugged at Beth's emotions. This was a new pattern of response to life and its potential stories for Beth. The awakening of her faith had prompted a new appreciation for the subjects of her stories. She no longer saw them only as a meal ticket. These were people whose trying and even perilous circumstances brought them trouble and pain. Along with the privilege of telling their story Beth sensed a growing responsibility to give something back. She found herself as concerned for Cooper and Rachel Sams as she was energized about the story possibilities.

Reagan Cole opened the bathroom door and emerged from a cloud of steam. He was dressed for bed in a blue, holey LAPD T-shirt and baggy white boxer shorts decorated with little Corvettes, Lamborghinis, and Maseratis. His thin sandy hair had been towel-dried but not combed. He was in the middle of brushing his teeth.

"Aren't we going to watch the news?" he said, trying not to let the toothpaste escape from his mouth.

Beth ignored the question. She was wearing her serious conversation face. "Do you remember me telling you about the cult in Seattle that bought a 737 for the Rapture?"

Cole stopped brushing for a second to think, then he mumbled through the foam, "Yeah, you told me Monday at Quintero's, the day we ate with Raul. Shelby called you about it. Why?"

"Pigg just had a blurb on the cult, and the *Star* ran a big story on it yesterday. This thing is becoming a media circus. They're calling it the doomsday flight."

Cole perceived that there was more Beth wanted to say on the subject. "Hold that thought," he said. He returned to the sink, quickly rinsed out his mouth and toothbrush, and turned out the bathroom light. Then he climbed into his side of the bed. "What are you thinking?"

Beth told him, including the dissonance between the story possibility she saw and her sympathy and concern for the principals involved. She purposely skimmed over Rachel Sams' dark notion that her fanatical husband might purposely endanger the flight. She knew that such information might sour her husband to the idea that was rapidly forming in her mind as she talked.

"How would you feel about me flying to Seattle to check out the potential for a book?" she concluded.

Cole smiled. "I wondered if the conversation was coming to this. How long have you been planning to go?"

"I *haven't* been planning to go, Reagan," Beth answered defensively. "It didn't cross my mind until five minutes ago when I saw Carlton Pigg's bit about the doomsday flight."

"I told you that TV show would rot your brain. All of a sudden you want to run off to Seattle without me."

"You could come too," Beth said, suddenly excited at the prospect. "We can stay on Whidbey."

"I can't get away now, Babe. Or did you forget that I used up all my vacation days this year chasing a bad guy up the coast and then taking a honeymoon."

"Sick leave," Beth countered. "You could use sick leave."

Cole frowned at her and lifted his T-shirt, exposing a surgical scar on the left side of his abdomen from which a nine-millimeter slug had been removed five months earlier.

"Oh, yeah," Beth said, "I forgot about that."

"Besides," Cole put in, "sick leave is for being sick, not for doing anything you want."

Beth pretended not to hear her husband's moralizing. "OK, so I could go up alone for a few days, check on the house, try to talk to Rachel Sams and some of the cult people, especially this pilot. I might even drive down to Portland and see Shelby."

"When?"

Beth thought a moment. "I could leave tomorrow, or we could go together on Saturday, and you could take Monday off."

Cole shook his head. "I'm sorry, Babe, but I can't take the time off. I'm still a day behind from being with Officer Barrigan." Seeing Beth's disappointment and having sensed her eagerness to get into a story, he added, "But you go on up for the weekend and see if this is a story you can get into."

Beth gave her husband a hug. "Thank you, Reagan." She had already decided she was going with or without him, but she knew it made him feel better to give his blessing.

Beth wasn't sure how far she might get into the story in just a few days, but she knew the story was already starting to get into her.

Forty-four

It has to be a sign, Raul Barrigan thought soberly. *Three times is an odd coincidence. Four times is unreal. Five times in one week means that God is trying to get my attention. What else can it be?*

Raul sat in the lunch room at Central City Precinct, downtown Phoenix, staring at the *US Star*'s Scene section for Friday, November 30. For the second time this week the front page carried a story about the New Jesus Family and its controversial preparations for doomsday, February 20, 2002. Wednesday's article had been at the bottom of the front page; today's was the lead story for the section. The photo of Lila Ruth Atkinson and Cooper Sams was half again as large as the same photo which ran Wednesday. Today's headline boldly proclaimed: "Thousands scorn doomsday flight; scores beg for available seats."

Five times this week the sad story of the Seattle cult and its alleged airlift to heaven had been thrust into Raul Barrigan's face unbidden. On Monday, Beth Cole came to lunch at Quintero's talking about it. On Wednesday afternoon, a coworker doing the *Star*'s crossword puzzle— Scene section, page 5—came into Raul's office asking, "What's an eight-letter word for law body? The fifth letter is R." Looking up, Raul's eyes fell on the front-page headline, "Doomsday flight: Cult plans to escape Armageddon in the nick of time." Raul Barrigan was not in the habit of reading the trashy *US Star*. But after supplying the word "congress," Raul talked his fellow officer into leaving him the front and back page so he could read the article.

Raul heard more about the event late Thursday afternoon on his way daughter has muscular dystrophy real bad. We have no money to take care of her. The hospital won't take her because we don't have no insurance. We can't do nothing more for her. Please take her on the suicide flight. We will borrow some money and drive her to Seattle. She will be happier in heaven. P.S: She's always wanted to ride on an airplane."

Nonstop flight to hell. Suicide flight. Raul was shocked at the blatant references to self-destruction. He read request after request from people who regarded the doomsday flight as the ultimate solution to their insurmountable problems. Terminally ill patients, addicts, fugitives identifying themselves by an alias, jilted lovers, despondent widows and widowers longing for their departed spouses. All implored the New Jesus Family to let them end their misery aboard the certainly ill-fated *Vanguard*.

The pressure on Raul's chest increased, as if the weight of the down-cast souls in the article had been laid on him. A depressing pall of despair and death seeped around him like a noxious gas. Raul had to get out.

He folded the Scene section and slipped it between his unfeeling legs. He raced past his small office to grab his sport coat and phone. "I'm going out for a while," he called to his partner, Elise Nickerson, as he headed for the parking lot.

"What's up, Ponch?" Elise called after him. "When will you be back in?" Raul didn't answer.

It was in the low sixties and breezy in Phoenix on the last day of November, so Raul paused at the automatic doors to slip into his jacket. It took him only seconds to transfer into the driver's seat of his hand-controlled two-door Chevy Caprice, fold the chair, and slip it in behind the front bench seat. He left the parking lot and headed toward Squaw Peak Parkway, then north toward his favorite place of escape and solitude. The dark, oppressive shadow stayed with him, weighing so heavily at times that Raul thought his heart and lungs might give out as they labored to keep him alive.

Echo Canyon Park sits on the south side of 2,700-foot Camelback Mountain. Well within the Phoenix suburbs, rugged Camelback stands as a stark reminder that the sprawling metropolis in the valley of the sun was once nothing but arid, unfriendly desert populated by gila monsters and saguaro cactus. Raul pulled into the nearly deserted park and found the place where the imposing rocky hump loomed before him through the windshield. Turning off the engine, he could hear nothing but the sound of the 30-MPH wind buffeting the Caprice.

Clearly, the doomsday flight had prompted the sudden, claustrophobic funk encasing him like a mummy's sarcophagus. So Raul turned again to the two *Star* articles in an attempt to find his way out of the dark maze and grasp the meaning of this apparent sign. But reading the stories again only seemed to complicate the confusion and heighten the pain he already felt for the thousands of people attracted to the cult like sheep to the slaughter.

Tossing the newspapers onto the seat beside him, Raul dropped his head on the headrest and gazed at Camelback Mountain. *What's this all about, God?* he cried without a voice. *Why am I bumping into this pagan cult every time I turn around? Why do I feel like I'm being sucked into a black hole when I see these stories? What are You trying to say to me?*

The Boeing 737 swooped into view a split second before it hit the mountain. It was banked at a 30-degree angle so Raul could see the tops of both wings, one above and one below the fuselage. There was no smoke pouring from the engines to indicate a problem. Rather, the aircraft appeared under control and purposely aimed at the side of Camelback Mountain instead of attempting to avoid it.

The image was so startlingly real that Raul squeezed his eyes shut before the impact. But his act of avoidance only made the picture more vivid in his mind. A gust of wind hitting the Caprice at the same instant simulated the terrifying roar and concussion of the crash.

Raul saw it all happen. The nose and right wing tip slammed into the mountain first. The wing ripped apart and jet fuel splashed up the rocky slope like a fountain—gushing liquid quickly igniting to red-orange flame. The fuselage snapped into four sections which immediately disintegrated to jagged shreds of metal, plastic, cable, luggage, and commercial cargo drenched in fuel and fire. The left wing skittered down the mountain 200 feet before exploding into hunks of shrapnel, none of them larger than a human body.

It was over in seconds. A majestic, powerful aircraft reduced to a black, jumbled smear across the mountain's face. The horrific mental image was before Raul whether his eyes were open or closed. And everywhere he looked in the smoldering wreckage he saw bodies—broken, burning, charred, lifeless, still.

Already bowed under the enigmatic burden of the doomsday flight, Raul Barrigan collapsed at the vision of its passengers' tragic demise. He knew these people. He had pored over their heart-wrenching stories in the *US Star*. He had pleaded with them silently to abandon their mindless folly and turn to God. They had not heard him, and now they were gone.

Raul broke into deep, howling sobs. Tears gushed from his eyes and drenched his cheeks. Mucus streamed over his lips and dripped onto his chin. Raul was unconscious of it. Awash in grief, he buried his face in his hands and mourned the fiery deaths of at least 135 men, women, and children and the souls condemned to the fires of eternal hell.

Raul's sides ached from the wrenching convulsions. He gasped for breath as though drowning, but he could not stop crying. Wave after anguished wave pummeled him. And when the faces of the unknown passengers faded from his view, he saw himself. Broken, wheelchair-bound, purposeless, pitiful, forgotten by God. He relived the collision at home plate. He heard the vertebra snap. He felt the screws of the halo brace puncture his skull. He saw Samantha and the San Francisco Giants and many of his friends walk away, never to return. He saw his parents deprived of the dream house he had promised them.

As each old wound broke open, Raul pulled at his hair and beat the steering wheel. He prayed and sobbed and cried until he could cry no more. Days later he would admit to himself that a well-guarded vessel of grief had shattered within him that Friday afternoon. Three years of personal misery, fear, and fury had accumulated, feelings he had not denied but seldom acknowledged and never released. And they all tumbled out on the heels of the soul-rending destruction of the dooms-day flight.

When the storm finally abated, Raul sat in his car for another hour sorting through what had happened to him. The burden which had been draped upon him in cumbersome layers through the week was lifted. The torrent of tears had washed clean the windows of his soul, and question after silent question was answered. He knew he had heard from God at the base of Camelback Mountain. The experience could not have been more redemptive or miraculous for him had his legs been restored to perfect health. Indeed, the still, small voice he perceived in the midst of the storm had called him to a service where his legs would not be needed.

Before returning to the station, Raul had to stop by his apartment in Paradise Valley for two reasons. First, he had to change his clothes, which were damp and spotted with tears and mucus. Dressing himself was always a time-consuming chore. It took him forty-five minutes to put on clean slacks, shirt, and tie. He would have to work late tonight to make up for his extended lunch hour.

For the second task that could not wait, Raul rolled his chair up to the keyboard of his PC. He retrieved a blank fax memo form to the screen. The form was headed with his name, home address, and personal phone and fax numbers. The message, which he had been framing in his head since he left Echo Canyon Park, flowed easily onto the screen:

November 30, 2001
NEW JESUS FAMILY
ATTENTION: Ms. Lila Ruth Atkinson and Capt. Cooper Sams

With this fax I hereby request to be included among the passengers aboard *Vanguard* departing on February 20, 2002. I am twenty-four years old and quadriplegic, but my physical disability is not the reason for the request. I am not a member of your religious group, but I am a person of faith and conviction. My interest in being aboard Vanguard is to prepare passengers to meet their God. I am not wealthy, but I will gladly give whatever you require to secure a place on the passenger list. I'm praying for you, and I know you will make the right decision in response to my request.

Raul read the text twice without making any corrections. Satisfied, he opened the fax window, entered the Seattle phone number, and prepared to send. He paused long enough to whisper a prayer, then pressed ENTER. An error message alerted Raul that the line was busy, something he had expected. He instructed the computer to keep sending until the message was received.

Before leaving the keyboard, Raul tapped in a command to delete the fax from his files after it was sent and received. It was unlikely that anyone would snoop through his computer and find the message. But he couldn't take the chance. His rendezvous with God at Camelback Mountain, and the assignment he had received there, were between him and God alone. Most people wouldn't understand what he planned to do anyway, and in their misunderstanding some might even try to prevent him from doing it. He couldn't let that happen.

Having set the computer to its task, Raul grabbed his jacket and headed back to the station, feeling reborn.

At 5:21 P.M. Raul's fax arrived at the Stouffer-Madison Hotel in Seattle. It was retrieved from the fax tray with about 100 others by Raython Braggs and delivered to the desk of Lila Ruth Atkinson.

Forty-five

Every piece of mail in the mailbox was a bill except for a post office notice. The slip indicated that a registered letter was not delivered because it required a signature. The letter could be picked up at the main post office on N.W. Hoyt any time before 5 P.M. Friday afternoon.

Myrna Valentine wondered at the notice. She was accustomed to receiving registered mail at her office but not at home. Perhaps an agent had sent a résumé or inquiry to her home address by mistake. Myrna deliberated about making a dash for the post office, which was only eight blocks from her Northwest Portland loft. She checked the time: 4:39. She had just walked in from picking her son up at day care, and little Guy was hungry. To buckle him back into his car seat now and drag him through the line at the post office might ruin his whole evening—and Myrna's too. The registered mail could wait until Monday.

Putting Guy down, Myrna went straight to her phone. She had been awaiting a message from Guy Rossovich all week. He had promised to fly to Portland to talk about getting back together with her and accepting his role as little Guy's father. Myrna had tried to keep her hopes from swelling to unrealistic proportions. But as the week progressed, her fantasy grew larger than life. Every day without a message only spurred her to greater hope for the next.

There were three messages on the machine this afternoon, but Guy's voice was not among them. Resisting disappointment, Myrna assured herself that she would hear from him sometime this evening. Perhaps he would call her from the plane or from the airport when he arrived in Portland. Her week-long hunger to be with Guy and resolve the hope-inspiring discussion begun in L.A. was growing acute.

Myrna's thoughts turned back to the registered letter waiting at the post office. It occurred to her that the letter could be from Guy, perhaps a creative and rather expensive way of announcing his arrival. She would hate herself if the letter was from him and she ignored it.

"Come on, sweetie," she called to her son, who was still in his winter coat and playing with a battery-powered race car, "Mommy has to go to the post office." Guy started to fuss at the prospect of going out again. "You can have a cookie now, then Mommy will take you to McDonald's on the way home." A double-stuff strawberry Oreo with the promise of a Happy Meal to follow did the trick. Guy pranced excitedly to the front door ahead of his mother. It was a concession to sugar and fat Myrna rarely made.

Getting into Portland's main post office at 4:45 on Friday afternoon was a challenge. Luckily, Myrna found a parking place on the street only a block and a half away. A 35-degree east wind prompted her and Guy to hurry into the building. After a twenty-minute wait, which taxed the little boy's patience to the limit, Myrna hurriedly signed for the registered letter.

Her hopes faded when she saw the return address, identifying an attorney in Beverly Hills instead of State Senator Guy Rossovich. She was contacted by lawyers frequently regarding contracts. Jamming the unopened letter into her coat pocket, Myrna made a dash for the Trooper while Guy sang his version of the latest McDonald's jingle.

Myrna opted for the McDonald's in northeast Portland, across the Willamette River via the Broadway Bridge, instead of the downtown store. It was a little farther to northeast, but she didn't want to battle downtown Friday night traffic.

After draping little Guy with several paper napkins, setting out his Happy Meal, and squeezing an envelope of lite Italian dressing over her garden salad, Myrna pulled out the registered letter to read while she ate. She got two bites and no more. The letter *was* from Guy Rossovich—in a roundabout way. Myrna quickly dug through the legalese to find the bottom line, which hit her like an unexpected fist in the stomach.

Laying down her plastic fork, she read it again more carefully, thinking it had been sent to her by mistake. No, the names were all correct. Trembling, she read it again hoping she had misunderstood. She hadn't. "He's suing for custody of little Guy," she breathed in disbelief. "A court date is already set for March 4. He can't be serious. This has to be a joke, a very cruel and tasteless joke."

Myrna continued to study the letter. With every reading her defenses against an all-out panic attack weakened. *Did I completely misread him last weekend? He was so pleasant, so congenial — after he came to the park. Did I miss the cues? Was he only humoring me to get a look at his son? Am I really losing my mind this time? He kissed me good-bye. He promised to be here this weekend. Was it all a ruse to buy time for this?*

With every question and disappointing realization, Myrna sensed the hysteria building. She returned the letter to her coat pocket. "Let's go, son," she snapped as she quickly stood.

She did not wait for his response or listen to his whiny protest. She shoved his chickie burger, fries, and chocolate milk in the bag and scooped him up. "I don't want to go home, Mommy. I want my chickie burger. I want to eat at McDonald's."

As Myrna rushed out the door into the parking lot with little Guy under her arm like a rag doll, she sensed a new fear. Maybe Guy was here in Portland after all. Maybe he was watching her now, enjoying her reaction to the letter. Or maybe he had hired a private detective to track her, take photographs, or even abduct her son. She stifled the urge to cry out against the evils which she imagined might be stalking her right now.

Little Guy's whine turned to a cry of fear as Myrna brusquely buckled him into his car seat. She was too shaken to calm him. Once behind the wheel with the doors locked, she sped home.

Safely behind bolted doors in the familiar confines of her own home, Myrna felt a measure of sanity return. She remonstrated herself for such a childish reaction to the letter. She set about calming little Guy with several minutes of physical closeness and loving words. Then she sat him down at the table to finish his cold chickie burger and fries and warm chocolate milk. While he ate, she changed out of her business suit into jeans and a sweater.

Myrna sat at the table talking cheerily with little Guy about his day. But her thoughts were occupied with the contents of the registered letter, which lay open at her elbow. Her feelings ranged from anger to humiliation to utter heartache at Guy's deception. *He could have been honest with me*, she insisted silently. *He could have explained that his feelings for me were all in the past, that he wasn't interested in being with me. He could have asked me politely to share little Guy with him —*

periodic visits in Portland or L.A. He didn't have to string me along only to attack me with a lawsuit.

Every few moments a spike of panic provoked a sudden gasp. *What if Guy succeeds in his attempt to gain custody of my child?* The thought of losing little Guy drove Myrna's heart into her mouth. But she repeatedly beat away each attack with a conscious, confident retreat to reality. *Guy can't take my baby away from me. There is no court under God's heaven that will rule against a loving mother and award custody to a man the child doesn't even know, father or not. And as soon as little Guy is fast asleep, I will call Senator Guy Rossovich and tell him so.*

With Dimitri at the theater for the evening, Tommy Eggers finally had the privacy he needed to set in motion the plan which had consumed him for nearly three days. Standing at the sliding glass door to the apartment's lanai, he dialed the telephone number he had involuntarily committed to memory from the Wednesday edition of the *US Star*. As the call was processed, he noticed that more Christmas lights had been put up in the city, further brightening the dark hillsides in his view. The colorful lights seemed even more beautiful to him now, knowing that this was his last Christmas to enjoy them.

A recorded female voice came through the speaker. "You have reached the offices of the New Jesus Family in Seattle, Washington. Please leave a message after the tone."

A machine is what Tommy wanted and expected. But he was surprised by the flat, colorless message, thinking about how imaginative they could be. Having attracted so much national attention in the last few days with its doomsday prediction, the cult could have began the message with a crash of thunder and a fanfare of trumpets. A deep, resonant, prophet-like voice could follow: "The end of the world is at hand. Prepare to meet thy God. Leave a message after the tone." He smiled at the possibilities.

Then Tommy remembered how maddeningly narrow, by-the-book, and all-business-no-fun Cooper Sams used to be, and the monotone message made perfect sense.

"This is a message for Captain Cooper Sams from an old acquaintance," Tommy began after the beep, relishing the contact with his former coworker. "I wonder if you can guess who I am. I'll give you three clues."

Tommy switched into his Sylvester Stallone voice. "Yo, Captain, we used to work for the same company." Then he was Disney's Goofy. "Gosh, I used to entertain the customers in the back while you drove the bus." The final clue came from Michael Jackson. "The last time we worked together was in Juneau, Alaska. That flight was a real thriller."

Tommy began to stroll along the large living room windows admiring the view as he returned to his own voice. "Hello, Captain. It's

Tommy Eggers, former Seattle-based flight attendant for Northstar Airlines. Yes, I confess, I'm the one responsible for the unsightly stains on the aft jump seat of your 737 almost seven years ago. But hey, that ride you gave us coming out of Juneau scared the you-know-what out of me. Then again, we would have been no more than a smudge on a snowbank if you hadn't pulled us out like you did. I must admit that you were a great pilot even for being such a grouch.

"Well, I'll bet you never expected to hear from me again, did you, Coop? Actually, I'll bet you *hoped* you'd never hear from me again. But now that you're a big celebrity, I just had to get in touch. I've never known anyone before who got his face in the *US Star* twice in the same week. If I was there in person, I'd have you autograph my pinky finger. You'd enjoy that, I bet!"

Tommy found the one-sided repartee as dull as playing cribbage against himself. He decided to get on with the message he had rehearsed several times in his mind, a message he delivered in a more serious tone.

"The main reason I called, Captain, is to ask a favor," Tommy said as he dropped into an easy chair. "I see from the newspapers that you have become a kind of spiritual leader there in Seattle. You must be as good at religion as you were at flying for God to tell you His secrets about the end of the world. What's it feel like to have God as your copilot?

"But back to the point. I'm not a religious man, Captain, and I'm not convinced that your doomsday flight is going to turn out the way you think it will. But I'd like to fly with you once more, this time as a passenger. I'd like to go up with you on February 20, just for old times's sake.

"You see, Captain, I have AIDS. Now you're probably thinking, 'You got what you deserved.' Well, you may be right. Like a lot of other men I know, I gambled against some rather stiff odds ... and I lost. We could argue about my moral choices and whether they were worth it or not, but I don't have enough time to argue. My life is now measured in months, enough time to have a little fun, get my affairs in order, and fly into the arms of Jesus — or the devil, whomever loses the coin flip when my name comes up.

"I'll be honest with you: I don't know what you have in mind for this doomsday flight. I imagine that you're planning to soar into heaven like Jesus told you you would, or you wouldn't be doing it. But some people are saying that the plane isn't coming back in one piece whether Jesus shows up or not. Either way, if I'm aboard my odds are good for avoiding the long and painful death of an AIDS victim. I always have the bridge down here if I need it, but jumping off the Golden Gate Bridge sounds so plebeian next to a ride on the eternity express."

Tommy stood up as if to emphasize that he was ending the message.

"So that's the deal, Captain. I know we didn't get on too well at Northstar. But I think our goals may be more compatible on this flight. I hope you can find the compassion in your heart to save a seat for me. You wouldn't deny a dying man his last request, would you?"

Tommy gave his personal phone number and a post office box where he could be reached without arousing Dimitri's suspicion. He still intended to slip away from his dear friend at the end, either to Seattle—if Cooper Sams granted his request—or to the big bridge.

Tapping off the phone, Tommy activated Dimitri's digital music master. At the prompt, he typed in a song title that had just popped into his mind. He didn't know if the tune was in Dimitri's vast electronic file of recorded music, but when he tapped Search the computer quickly responded with Located.

Tommy increased the volume as the computer sent the vintage Frank Sinatra recording to the amplifier. Tommy thought the words pouring from the speakers would serve as a fitting prayer to speed his request on its way: "Come fly with me, let's fly, let's fly away . . ."

Myrna waited until after 10 P.M. to make her call, hoping to increase the chances that Guy would be home alone. She also needed the time to get her emotions under control. She decided that her best avenue of approach was to reason with Guy: calmly explain that she would not relinquish custody of little Guy under any condition and that no judge or jury would side with him against her. Then she would reiterate her desire that the two of them work out their differences and become friends for little Guy's sake. Despite the conflicting evidence, Myrna had patched together her hope that Guy Rossovich's calloused heart would soften toward her if he gave the relationship half a chance.

The standard message came through the phone as Myrna expected: "This is John Brock speaking. Senator Rossovich is unable to take your call in person. Please state your business and leave a number where you can be reached."

"Guy, this is Myrna. Will you pick up, please. I'd like to talk to you about the registered letter I received today from your attorney." Myrna was pleased at how sedate and positive she sounded. The five-hour buffer and two glasses of chardonnay had worked to her advantage.

She waited, but there was no response. She tried again, pausing between each sentence to allow him to break in. "I really want to talk this through with you, Guy. . . . Our child's happiness and security is at stake. . . . I know you want the best for little Guy just as I do. . . . I can't believe that you are totally closed to getting back together, especially now that we have son who needs us both. . . . Please, Guy, let's work through this as friends. We have a lot of love to share between the three of us."

Myrna had anticipated a nonresponse, certain that Guy's attorney had strongly advised it. She continued in her controlled and pleasant tone, still convinced that Guy was listening in. "The bottom line, Guy, is that your attempt to take little Guy will fail. I'm not saying this to be adversarial. That's just the way it is. Perhaps you don't understand that absentee fathers are not awarded custody when the natural mother has consistently provided a safe and loving environment. Little Guy is healthy, happy, and well cared for. Your suit has no grounds; you will lose." She hoped she was right.

Myrna waited, thinking her last words may have pushed Guy's buttons. But she heard nothing.

"So you may as well save your money and spare all of us the stress and strain of pointless litigation. Instead, let's direct our energies into something positive: a whole family for little Guy. We can build our lives around him. We can make it work, Guy. I'm willing to do more than my share. I want to help you rediscover the love you still have buried inside. All I'm asking is that you give us an opportunity. Please call, Guy."

Satisfied that she had spoken her piece the way she wanted to, Myrna tapped off the phone. It was still in her hand moments later when the tone sounded.

"Yes."

"What *you* don't understand is how well connected I am to the legal system in California." Guy Rossovich's voice was measured, cool, and distinctly unfriendly. "And you obviously haven't heard how the courts deal with a woman who intentionally withholds information about a child's birth from the natural father. Down here that's tantamount to kidnapping. There have been two such cases in California in the past six months. Both ruled in favor of the father. Do you have any idea what happens to convicted kidnappers?"

Guy didn't give her a chance to respond. "I also know about your emotional problems. My people have done some checking. I know about your weekly appointments with a shrink. I know about the pills you take. I know what happens to you when you don't take them. I'm surprised you haven't abused your son already—or maybe you have. Shall I keep digging?

"I *will* get my son, Myrna. You can put together the best team of lawyers since the Simpson trial, but it won't do you any good. This case is open and shut. It's *you* who will lose, and you could end up in prison. If you really love your son, spare him the bloody battle and hand him over to me. If you agree to settle out of court, I'll drop the charges. Call my lawyer before March 1 and we'll talk." Then he hung up.

Myrna set the phone down. She had geared herself up for a possible hostile response, but Guy's icy words stung her nonetheless. His brash prediction of victory, which she hoped was a bluff, left her unsettled. *Court battles don't always turn out the way they should*, she thought anxiously. *Sometimes the guilty get off while the innocent take the rap. The thumbs of clever and unscrupulous people have been known to tip the scales of justice in the favor of the wrong person. And an important man like Guy can get a lot of heavy thumbs on his side. I could call his bluff and still lose. Even if I win he has the potential to make our lives miserable.*

Myrna walked to the kitchen to pour another glass of wine. "So you want to play cutthroat, Senator Rossovich," she said aloud as she uncorked the bottle. "You underestimate the fury of a mother who is about to be forcibly separated from her child. And you don't see the ace up my sleeve. You take us both or you will have neither of us."

She took a long sip of chardonnay, then set about looking for the newspaper and an article she saw recently about some kind of suicide flight.

Forty-six

Cooper Sams was relieved that the unexpected and bothersome attention drawn to the New Jesus Family and the flight of *Vanguard* was beginning to wane. Thanks to little-known writer Earl M. Butcher, the goal for the Family's press conference ten days earlier had been reached. The general population was duly informed and warned about the coming Reunion. But unfortunately, Butcher had grossly sensationalized the issue. His exaggerated, libelous articles in the *US Star* had attracted thousands of annoying critics, judges, and freaks compared to less than 300 genuine inquiries from honest seekers. Legal action by the Family against Earl Butcher, fully warranted because of his liberties with the facts, was superfluous at this point. Preparation for departure required Cooper's full energies. Judgment Day would rectify any wrongs committed by Earl Butcher.

Thankfully, the wave of public response which hit the office on Wednesday and deluged the communication network through the weekend had tapered off by Sunday afternoon. Cooper noted that the flies attracted to Butcher's brand of garbage must have a short attention span. He hoped that the decline in faxes, E-mail, and V-mail meant that the lunatic fringe was now off investigating alien sightings, serial killings, and satanist rituals.

Arriving at the tenth-floor suite from his seventh-floor quarters, Cooper went immediately to Lila Ruth's office. She was waiting for him. As always when in the office, the two primary leaders of the New Jesus Family were impeccably dressed in business attire. Lila Ruth's penchant for professionalism at all levels of the ministry had been willingly embraced by Cooper Sams.

"Good morning, Captain," she greeted him from behind her desk.

"Good morning."

"Were you able to get some rest over the weekend?"

"Yes, I spent both days in Everett. There hasn't been too much media activity around Paine Field. I was able to slip in and out of the airport without seeing too many reporters."

The two leaders rarely engaged in idle chatter. Conversation and activity between them was rigidly focused on the task of preparing their flock for the Reunion.

Lila Ruth said, "Are you firm in your decision that we need not address the media again?"

Cooper nodded. "We have stated our mission and extended an invitation to strangers and aliens as Pathfinder directed us. The media seeks additional information only because of its entertainment value. I recommend that we instruct hotel security to keep reporters off the tenth floor and away from our residences. Our volunteer staff will help us get in and out of the building without attracting attention."

Lila Ruth measured his resolve and found it formidable. "Very well." Returning to the topic of Cooper's visit to the airport, she said, "And what is *Vanguard*'s status?"

"Excellent," Cooper beamed. "Tramco is making a few minor repairs—all cosmetic. *Vanguard* is ready to go. I'll take her up a couple more times before February. Otherwise she will be secured in the Tramco hangar."

"Well done, Captain. Thank you for your fine service to the Family." Lila Ruth was always generous with her praise of *Vanguard*'s captain.

"And your weekend, Ms. Atkinson, was productive?" Cooper inquired.

"Very much so. I met with several small groups of our Family in my suite. They are mentally prepared for Reunion, and I can sense the spiritual energy building. It appears that the Family and *Vanguard* are nearly ready for the appointed hour."

"Yes. My spirit also senses the momentum of the last weeks. Even so, come Jesus-Brother."

"Even so, come," Lila Ruth echoed the traditional New Jesus Family greeting.

Lila Ruth turned her eyes toward three stacks of paper on the desk very near where Cooper stood. Two of the stacks were over three reams high totalling in excess of 3,500 sheets. The other stack looked to contain fewer than 300 sheets. They comprised the sum of faxes and transcribed electronic messages received through Sunday afternoon. "What is in your mind to do with these, Captain?" she said, tapping the top of each stack lightly with her hand.

Cooper warmed at the inquiry. For all her inherent spiritual power in the small family of believers she had spawned, Lila Ruth trusted her second in command. She was Vision, the wisdom and insight of Jesus-Brother to the Family. He was Vanguard, the primary instrument for the Family's greatest contribution to the kingdom: Reunion. Lila Ruth shepherded and nurtured and counseled those who were chosen. But she placed in the captain's hands all the details of *Vanguard*. Her confidence in his spiritual capacity had greatly swelled his faith in Jesus-Brother and His servant, Lila Ruth.

"Pathfinder was with me last night for several hours," Cooper said. "He gave me the mind of our Brother on the matter."

Lila Ruth nodded for him to sit down. "Very good, Captain. How shall we proceed?"

Cooper took a seat in the chair next to the desk and crossed his legs. "Yesterday, at my direction, Mr. Braggs and two other volunteers separated the obscene, hostile messages from the inquiries of the genuine seekers. The offensive material will be destroyed."

"The tallest piles," Lila Ruth clarified.

"Correct. I have instructed Mr. Braggs to destroy others as they are received."

"I concur. We don't need negativism polluting the mind-spirit stream here."

Cooper reached out to the short stack of papers and brought them back to his lap. "As for the strangers and aliens, inquiries from outside the New Jesus Family, there are clearly more than we will be able to serve on the aircraft."

"Exactly how many places are available aboard *Vanguard*?" Lila Ruth interjected.

"All told, 135: 120 in the main cabin, 8 in first class, 2 in the cockpit, and 5 jump seats."

"Speaking of the cockpit, do you have a copilot yet?" Lila Ruth said.

Cooper offered a smile of assurance. "No, but Pathfinder has assured me that all our needs will be provided."

"Your faith is an inspiration, Captain," Lila Ruth said.

"Thank you," Cooper said. "Now about the passengers; how many Family members will be aboard?"

"At this moment, 109, including you and me." A small cloud of concern passed over Lila Ruth's face. "But the number may change before our departure. Since our plans became public knowledge, several of our members, especially the university students, have been pressured by their families and friends to leave the Family."

"What is in your mind to do about those who waver?"

Lila Ruth thought for a moment. "Those who are truly called will be with us. The others must be allowed to go their way."

Cooper nodded. "Pathfinder's message to me concerning the applications we have received takes into account the uncertainty of some of our members. He instructed me to select two persons for every empty seat from among the additional applicants."

"It's just like the spirit of Jesus-Brother to specify two, isn't it?" Lila Ruth said with a smile.

Cooper agreed, then continued. "Those selected first will take the seats not presently occupied by Family members: twenty-six. Another twenty-six will be selected as, well, standby passengers if you will. Any additional seats forfeited by Family members will be given to the standbys."

"And how will these selections be made?"

"Pathfinder instructs that I am to read through the stack of applicants once, and he will indicate the first group—a total of twenty-six names—to my spirit. The standbys will be selected by a random draw of twenty-six additional names from the remaining applications."

"Every seeker has two opportunities to be included," Lila Ruth summarized with obvious delight.

"It is the genius of Pathfinder," Cooper assured, mirroring her pleasure.

"When will these selections be made? And what will become of the applications received afterward?"

"Pathfinder has impressed on me the urgency of these selections," Cooper said, once again serious. "I will make the first group of selections from these applications"—indicating the stack in his hands—"and I will make the random draw immediately thereafter. Any messages received in the office by that time will be included in the lottery. Any messages received thereafter will be destroyed."

Lila Ruth returned a questioning look. "Destroyed?"

"Pathfinder indicated to me that those who respond first trust their instincts, but those who delay are overly cautious or fearful. I believe we have our additional passengers right here." He lifted the stack once again.

Lila Ruth's placid expression returned. She stood, and Cooper followed her up. "Very good, Captain. I am assured that Pathfinder has given you the direction you sought. Carry on."

It was clear to Cooper that the conversation was over. He said, "I'll send Mr. Braggs in for these," nodding to the two stacks of paper destined for the shredder. Then he headed for the door.

"Thank you, Captain. Even so, come, Jesus-Brother."

Cooper turned at the door. "Even so, come."

Having dispatched Raython Braggs to his task, Cooper closed himself in his office with 288 sheets of paper bearing the names of individuals outside the New Jesus Family seeking asylum aboard *Vanguard* for a variety of reasons. Cooper had not been through the sheets yet. He had only glanced at a few of them to get a sense for the kind of people ready to join the Reunion band on the strength of a couple of newspaper articles.

Cooper was not naive. He understood that most of the applicants—perhaps all of them—were unbelievers. They did not expect to meet Jesus-Brother in the night sky of February 20 as he did. Rather their motives were selfish, earthly, morbid. It didn't matter. According to Lila Ruth, the holy men of history made provisions for strangers and aliens to the faith without regard to their motives. It was this current of spirit-love which drew all people together: seekers from east and west, the faithful, and the faithless. Cooper felt good about filling the airplane with unbelievers. When the dawn of Reunion broke, these would be the most surprised and joyful of all.

Removing his suit coat, Cooper sat down at his desk with the applications in front of him. Before he could begin his first pass through the stack, the voice of another office volunteer, Margaret Harold, came through the speaker. "Sorry to bother you, Captain, but your wife is here and would like to see you."

Cooper felt immediately uncomfortable. Rachel Sams was the one loose end in his life he didn't know how to tie up. He could not say he had no feelings for her. But he seemed separated from those feelings by such a mountain of inner resistance. So he had avoided her. During this time he could not bring himself to divorce Rachel. He had no grounds. She was a good person, too good for someone like him. Forcing her out, he determined, would have been cruel and unusual punishment.

So Cooper did what he had always done to women who got too close: He sealed himself inside a bubble of independence and lived as if she wasn't there. To him, avoidance was a painless and efficient method of distancing himself from the intimacy he feared. It worked every time. He had hoped to turn around someday and find Rachel gone.

In response to her husband's aloofness, Rachel had backed off and given Cooper his space. She did not contest his choice to sleep alone, fly when Rachel was at home, and communicate almost exclusively through notes and recordings. But unlike other women Cooper had shut out in the past, Rachel did not go away. He couldn't understand his wife's foolish devotion, nor was he comfortable with the notion that she loved him despite his intentional coolness. As Reunion neared, it had come down to a waiting game. When *Vanguard* lifted off from Paine Field on February 20, 2002, he would be free of Rachel Sams for eternity.

Rachel had shown no interest in the New Jesus Family, even though early in his involvement Cooper had left a few notes suggesting that she might find the group spiritually enriching. The fact that she was here at the office now was both puzzling and disquieting. Perhaps being abruptly asked to leave the house on Mercer Island had pushed her to the limit, and she was ready to sever the relationship. Despite his discomfort at her coming, Cooper had to find out the reason for it.

"Did Mrs. Sams indicate the purpose of her visit?" Cooper said into his phone intercom.

"No, Captain," Margaret said. "She just asked to see you for a moment."

Cooper wished he could refuse Rachel's request, but he was too curious. "All right, Margaret, send her in," he said at last.

Rachel was smartly dressed in a dark-gray skirt and a waist-length, subdued plaid jacket of navy, gray, and burgundy. Her hair was nicely styled. Seeing her walk through the door, Cooper acknowledged silently that she was a very attractive woman, easily looking ten years younger than her age of fifty-one. Her pretty face prompted a montage of mental snapshots reminding him of a time when he was genuinely in love with a woman. He brushed away a fleeting sense of regret that he had squandered his one winning chance at happiness.

Cooper rose to his feet as she came in, an autonomic response to the presence of a woman in the room. Rachel did not approach the desk, respecting her estranged husband's need for space. "Hello, Cooper," she said pleasantly.

If she was about to ream him out for mental cruelty or kicking her out of the house on short notice, Cooper couldn't predict it from her demeanor. "Rachel," he responded.

"I'm sorry to intrude on your work. But may I have just a moment of your time?"

"Would you like to sit down?" Cooper offered with some reluctance, indicating a chair in front of the desk.

"No, I'll be very brief."

Rachel remained standing so Cooper followed suit. "The house is vacant now," she said. "I moved out Saturday."

Cooper didn't want to hear the details of her obviously hasty move, so he just said, "Thank you."

He knew that Rachel had more on her mind than to announce her departure from Mercer Island. After a moment of silence, she blurted out her main point. "I don't know how to say this, Cooper, so I'll just say it. I must tell you that I don't agree with what you're doing. I admire your religious devotion, but I think it's seriously misplaced. I don't know what you have in mind for February 20, but I'm afraid for you and for the people who are planning to fly with you. I'm asking you to reconsider your involvement in this organization and your decision to take the so-called doomsday flight."

Rachel paused. Cooper didn't know if she was waiting for a response or summoning her composure to continue. He recognized that the confrontation was taxing her composure.

Cooper took the opportunity to respond. "You know I can't do that, Rachel. I'm firm in my beliefs. I have a mission to fulfill."

Rachel quickly agreed. "Yes, I know, Cooper. I really didn't expect to change your mind. But I had to tell you how I feel."

Cooper found himself admiring her fortitude in light of the great, silent distance he had created between them.

Rachel continued haltingly, "I also want you to know, Cooper, that I . . . I still love you. I wish we could go back to a better time, a very happy time for me, a very happy time for both of us. I think we could go back together if you would change your mind about . . . all this. That's all I have to say."

"Thank you for being honest," Cooper said, feeling more embarrassed than thankful about her disclosure.

After an awkward few seconds with both parties averting their eyes, Rachel looked at Cooper and said, "I wonder if you will do me one favor."

"If I can," he returned, glancing at her.

"I would like you to talk to a new friend of mine. She came with me today."

"Talk to who? About what?"

Rachel drew a long breath. "She's a writer. She would like to meet you and possibly interview you."

Cooper stepped around to the side of the desk, a bit irritated. "Wait a minute, Rachel. You come here to say you don't agree with what I'm doing, and now you tell me that you brought a reporter with you? You disagree with what I'm doing, but you may as well make some money from it, is that it? How much did this woman pay you to sneak her in here?"

"It's not that at all, Cooper," Rachel answered firmly. "She's not a reporter; she's a free-lance journalist and a friend. She just wants to meet you. If you don't want to talk to her, just tell her so and we'll leave."

Cooper pondered the request. The mockery by the media had bothered him more than he had let on to anyone, including Lila Ruth. He didn't want any more vitriolic attacks on the New Jesus Family or Reunion. Why couldn't the world leave him alone to do what God had destined him to do?

And yet Rachel only asked him to meet the woman as a favor. He had not done much to accommodate his wife in a few years. Perhaps this would be his last opportunity.

"All right," he said, "just to meet her."

Rachel opened the office door and motioned to the unseen guest. A tall, dark-haired woman in her early thirties stepped into the room. She wore a tailored black suit, gray blouse, and silver jewelry.

Unlike Rachel, the tall woman walked straight to Cooper and extended her hand. "Captain Sams, it's a pleasure to meet you," she said with the self-assurance of a corporate vice-president. "My name is Beth Scibelli-Cole."

Forty-seven

Beth could sense the resistance in Cooper Sams' tentative handshake and wary gaze. She hoped her assertiveness distracted him from how nervous she felt about meeting someone so completely absorbed in such a bizarre organization. The former Northstar captain looked totally sane. Furthermore, his office was not decorated with weird icons or satanic symbols, nor did it reek of incense or hallucinogenic drugs. It was difficult to believe that the man shaking her hand had fallen under the spell of a New Age doomsday prophetess.

"How do you do," Cooper said without radiating the slightest interest in how Beth was doing.

"Thank you for taking a moment to talk to me, Mr. Sams," Beth continued in her take-charge persona.

"I agreed to meet you, not to talk to you, Ms . . . I'm sorry, I didn't hear your name."

"Scibelli-Cole . . . Cole is fine," Beth inserted at his hesitancy.

"There will be no more interviews with the media, Ms. Cole," Cooper stated. "You people had your chance at the press conference ten days ago."

"I'm not looking for an interview, sir," Beth said, "I just want to ask you a few questions about your organization and your plans for February."

Cooper edged closer, clearly an attempt to begin backing Beth toward the door. She didn't budge, so he stepped around her and took her elbow, gently but firmly indicating that she would soon be leaving. "An interview or a few questions, call it what you will," he said as he herded her slowly toward the door. "The answer is no, Ms. Cole. We will not provide ammunition for another article mocking our activities and comparing our group to a carnival sideshow."

They reached the door where Rachel stood. Beth turned to face the man, conveniently slipping her elbow out of his hand. "I'm not with the newspapers or television, Mr. Sams," she argued, not ready to leave. "I free-lance newsworthy paperback books."

"It's all the same to me," Cooper said. "I'm not naive, Ms. Cole. I know that an inflammatory book like yours can hit the streets in days, and we do not want that to happen. Now if you two will please excuse me . . . " He opened the door and invited them to exit with an extended hand gesturing outward.

"Just a minute, sir," Beth resisted, hitting on an idea. "What if I swear to you that I will keep our conversation confidential and not allow one word to get into print until after February 20."

Beth's offer seemed to catch Cooper off guard. He looked at her askance, then his lips twisted into a wry smile. "But after February 20 nobody will be here to read your book."

Beth thought about debating the issue with him, contending that the vast majority of the world's population did not agree with his organization's doomsday view. But she saw no profit in poking at the wound. Rather, she took another tack. "That being the case, you have nothing to be concerned about, do you, sir?"

Cooper's smile faded. Beth continued, "All I want is to hear your story for my own satisfaction. I give you my word that nothing you tell me will go beyond the walls of this office. If the world turns to ash on February 20 as you say, our conversation will disappear with it. And if somehow you are mistaken, I won't print a word without your written permission."

It appeared to Beth for a moment that Cooper was gearing up to refute her theory that life could possibly continue past February 20. But instead he said, "What profit is there for you to interview me and not get a book contract from it?"

Beth's heart raced at the possibility of the captain's resolve weakening. She sensed that total transparency was her best ally. "Frankly, none—at least not monetarily. But you might say I have a spiritual interest in your story. Ever since I heard about your group—a few days before the story came out in the *Star*, I've been fascinated by it. I have an insatiable curiosity, sir. That's why I'm in journalism. I want to find out what makes the New Jesus Family tick. Being able to write about it is a bonus I'm willing to forego if necessary."

Cooper's eyes narrowed. "So you wormed your way into Rachel's life to get to me," he said smirkingly, revealing more of his animosity toward the media in general.

"That's not so, Cooper," Rachel cut in sternly. "I met Beth through a mutual friend. Beth asked if I knew how she could meet you. Since I was coming to see you, I offered to bring her with me."

Rachel's sharp words seemed to take Cooper aback. But she didn't give him a chance to apologize. "I'm confident that Beth means what she says about not writing the story. What's the harm in answering a few questions?"

Cooper stared at the two women. Then he said to Beth with difficulty, "I'm sorry about that comment." Beth nodded acceptance. "But you need to talk to Lila Ruth Atkinson to get the whole story about our Family."

"I would appreciate the chance to talk to both of you," Beth answered eagerly.

Cooper didn't conceal his sigh. "All right, give me a call later this afternoon. I'll see if Ms. Atkinson is available sometime tomorrow."

"Thank you very much, Mr. Sams," Beth said, offering her hand. "I will call you."

Cooper turned his eyes to Rachel as if wanting to say something. But he said nothing. The two women left the office and he closed the door after them.

As planned, Beth and Rachel met Libby Carroll at Zelda's, on University Way near the University of Washington, for brunch. Libby had come over from the U in between morning appointments. University Way—called "the Ave" by students and staff—was already decked out for the Christmas shopping season. Zelda's was decorated inside with fake pine boughs, silver and gold ornaments, and white twinkling lights.

Rachel was still living in Libby's guest room while locating an apartment. Beth had arrived in Seattle Saturday night and stopped by West Kinnear Place briefly on her way to Whidbey Island to see Libby and meet Rachel, for whom she had been praying nearly a week. Rachel had agreed to introduce Beth to Cooper, and the Monday morning rendezvous at the Stouffer-Madison Hotel was planned before Beth left for the island that night.

"I can't believe Cooper agreed to see you," Rachel said between bites of poppy seed muffin.

"He hasn't agreed to see me yet," Beth reminded her. "He only said I could call him later and see about an appointment."

Libby put down her mug of English Breakfast tea. "What do you hope to accomplish in an interview, Beth? You promised the man that you won't print his story."

"I promised that I won't print anything *without his permission*," Beth clarified. "I want to learn everything I can about the New Jesus Family and Lila Ruth Atkinson and *Vanguard* and their big Reunion. We know that 'doomsday' will come and go just like any other day. When Rachel's husband comes to his senses and admits that he was led astray by his spiritual mentor, I hope he'll be man enough to let me tell his story."

Libby's face clouded with concern. "But all this talk about a suicide flight, Beth. The scribbled note Rachel saw indicating Cooper's desire to prove his faith. What if there's something to it? What if he really is planning to put the plane in mortal jeopardy in the name of faith?"

As an afterthought, Libby turned to Rachel. "I hope this kind of talk doesn't upset you." Rachel told her that she had already come to grips with the worst possible scenario.

Assured that Rachel was all right, Beth answered Libby's question. "That's where I think an interview with Cooper Sams *before* the fact may be of great help. Let's face it: A story about the doomsday flight is secondary to making sure that the plane comes down safely when doomsday doesn't happen. If Cooper Sams and Lila Ruth Atkinson talk to me, I'll try to find out what they have in mind. Maybe the FAA or the FBI or someone can keep the plane from taking off or make sure it comes back to earth in one piece."

Rachel interjected, "I'm not convinced Ms. Atkinson knows anything about Cooper's intentions." Then she laughed a small, shallow laugh. "Some prophet she is. The right hand has no idea what the left hand is doing."

"That's enough to convince me that their little cult is in trouble," Libby put in.

Beth was still thinking about the interview. "If Cooper Sams is planning a mass suicide—whether he calls it that or not, I have to get him to tell me about it. We must prevent it if we can. If not, we must at least warn the other passengers about it before they board. Perhaps more information will help them change their minds."

The three women were silent for a moment, nibbling on muffins and sipping tea. Libby voiced the next concern. "How can that be done, Rachel? I mean, aside from driving the plane into the ground, how many ways can a pilot cause a plane to fall from the sky."

Rachel responded soberly. "Believe me, I've thought about it on every trip lately, and it's so easy it's scary." She took a sip of tea, then continued. "The pilot can dump most of the plane's fuel with the flip of a switch in the cockpit. If he does that in the middle of the ocean, there's no way the plane can get to an airport before crashing into the sea. He can reduce airspeed until the plane stalls and falls. He can fire-wall the engines, then pull them back to cool, then fire-wall them and cool them again until he blows one or both turbines. Then there's always a bomb."

"A bomb?" Libby questioned, horrified.

Rachel nodded. "Who's to say Cooper might not plan to rig a bomb to detonate after the appointed Reunion time, just to prove that he believes they will no longer be aboard?"

"What about airport security? Wouldn't a bomb be discovered?" Libby said.

"This is a private aircraft," Beth said. "It's not subject to security screenings like commercial aircraft. He could place a bomb in the luggage compartment rigged to go off at a certain time or altitude. For that matter, the passengers won't be screened either. Someone could bring a bomb on board in a backpack or a cosmetic case."

The women again lapsed into thoughtful silence. Finally, Libby said, "I have to get back to the campus."

Rachel said, "A lady is showing me a duplex in Kent at noon. I'd better head south."

"I'm going back to Oak Harbor," Beth chimed in. "I'll call Cooper this afternoon to see if I can see him tomorrow." Then to Rachel she said, "You will be at Libby's tonight?"

"Yes," Rachel answered with a smile of appreciation for her temporary landlady.

"I'll call you later to let you know what's happening."

All three agreed to the plan and pushed back their chairs simultaneously. "Wait," Libby said, "we've forgotten something." Rachel and Beth looked at her questioningly. "If Shelby were here, she wouldn't let us go without praying about all this. I think we should pray."

Beth quickly agreed, wishing she had thought of it herself. Rachel seemed a little embarrassed at the idea, but she did not resist. So they scooted into the table again and joined hands. Libby quietly asked God to help them solve the potentially deadly puzzle of Cooper Sams and the doomsday flight.

It took Cooper Sams over five hours, not counting a short break for lunch and two interruptions by Margaret Harold, to read through 288 messages received in the office from outside the New Jesus Family. Each message contained a request—whether simply or elaborately stated—that the sender or senders be included among the passengers on the February 20 flight of *Vanguard*. And most requests were substantiated with a reason. The reasons ranged from the sublime ("God told me in a vision I was to accompany you") to the pathetic ("I am a homeless double amputee with terminal liver disease") to the ridiculous ("As a thrill-ride junkie, I think your trip will be more fun than a corkscrew roller coaster").

Pathfinder had cautioned Cooper Sams during meditation to make the twenty-six critical selections with his spirit, not with his intellect. As he read each application, Cooper waited for the confirmation of a sixth sense, a kind of silent, inner chord indicating Jesus-Brother's approval. He waited and listened with his spirit no matter how profound or profane the application seemed to him. If he sensed the chord, Cooper set the application face down in front of him. If he sensed nothing, he set the application aside and moved to the next one.

At 4:18 P.M. Cooper finished reading the last application and shuffled it to the discard pile. It occurred to him that none of the applications matched the examples Earl Butcher had included in his two *Star* articles, confirming Cooper's suspicion that the writer had fabricated the quotes to spice up his stories.

The captain stood and stretched and tried to rub the tiredness out of his eyes. There was much work yet to be done, and he felt compelled to complete it before he went to his quarters. By the time he left the office, all twenty-six confirmed passengers and twenty-six alternates, or standbys, would be identified and prioritized. Tomorrow he would personally notify by fax, phone, or E-mail each of them of their status. He would also encourage them to keep their selection a secret to avoid the pressures of notoriety, though he acknowledged that some would immediately tell everyone the news because they craved such attention.

Cooper had not kept track of the number of acceptable applications he had piled in front of him. He was confident that he would end up with twenty-six names. As he sat down and carefully counted them now, there were twenty-two sheets of paper. On nineteen of them, only one name was listed. Three of the sheets had two names each: a married couple and two cohabiting couples. Cooper had not been impressed to select any of over a dozen applications from families or groups.

He shuffled the sheets and did the math in his head: a total of twenty-five individuals. Puzzled at the sum, he counted again and arrived at the same number: one short of twenty-six. Had he overlooked someone? Had he missed the spirit-chord when it sounded for one of the applicants? Cooper didn't know the answer. He considered leafing through the discard stack again for one more name but quickly rejected the idea. He had followed his instructions perfectly. Perhaps Pathfinder had reduced Cooper's quote from twenty-six to twenty-five. At any rate, Cooper was confident that another name would be presented to him if another applicant was allowed.

Cooper leafed through the sheets again to appreciate the diversity of the selections. Ages ranged from nineteen to eighty-one. All applications selected came from within the continental United States. Nationalities were usually not mentioned on the sheets, but among the names Cooper identified three Asians, one Latino, two Middle Eastern, five distinctly European, and two from the African continent.

About a third of the twenty-five described life-threatening diseases or hopeless physical conditions which prompted them to apply. One man selected had served twenty-two years of a life sentence in a Texas prison, a term that was to be shortened to twenty-three years by cancer of the lung and brain. Some of these patients hoped to be touched by God and miraculously delivered from their malady during the flight. Others, like the Texas prisoner—who stated that the state would transfer him to the flight in chains—clearly expected to escape their pain when the "suicide flight" crashed. Cooper couldn't imagine that prison authorities would allow the convict to board the plane, but that was his problem. If he showed up on February 20, he had a seat. If not, there were always standbys.

Those who weren't physically threatened spoke of different forms of despair: failed relationships, financial ruin, unfulfilled dreams, hopelessly tarnished reputations. These people didn't care what happened to them aboard the doomsday flight. They simply wanted to fly away from their pain and never return.

Very few of the twenty-five applicants selected from the pool gave evidence that they were sympathetic to the beliefs of the New Jesus Family. A few framed their words to sound as if they had been spiritually linked to the group for years. But Cooper knew that their only exposure to the Family was what they had seen in the secular media over the last ten days.

More than half of the twenty-five said nothing at all about the religious purpose of the flight. And many of the rest were openly critical of the movement as offbeat, stupid, or demonic. Yet for them the end apparently justified the means. Cooper was pleased that he had been deaf to his own negative inclination toward these critical applicants and sharply tuned to Pathfinder's "yes."

Cooper paused at one sheet and studied it again. It was one of the messages transcribed off the voice mail. It had been very difficult for Cooper to discern Pathfinder's impression for this individual once he saw the name: Tommy Eggers. Cooper had to beat down a flurry of negative emotions prompted by the sudden reminder of a despised coworker long forgotten. Only after several minutes of meditation did Cooper perceive the surprising affirmative nod from Pathfinder. He surmised that Tommy Eggers had been included to remind him of Jesus-Brother's broad acceptance of both the wounded and the wayward.

One sheet of paper, another application selected during the read-through, sat alone off to one side of Cooper's desk. It was not one of the twenty-five confirmed passengers; it was in a different category. But this application was the most inspiring and affirming of them all. Cooper left it alone while he proceeded with the random selection of standby passengers.

Cooper rearranged the remaining 265 sheets several times, shuffling sections around face down until they were well out of their original order. Then he began the blind draw of twenty-six names that would be numbered in order. The standby passengers would be allowed to board *Vanguard*, beginning with the first name drawn and proceeding through the list, until any and all seats forfeited by Family members were filled.

Cooper dug into the stack and pulled out a sheet. It was the application of two young women, one with AIDS and one who did not want to live without her female lover. Cooper remembered reading it earlier. He marked the numbers 1 and 2 on the upper right corner. If only one seat was open on the flight, one of the women would be invited to go. If they decided not to split up, the passenger chosen next would be offered the available seat.

The next three names drawn were single persons, two women and a man. Cooper numbered them 3, 4, and 5 respectively. The fifth sheet extracted from the stack contained two names: a mother and her small child, the first child to be listed among the additional passengers. Cooper looked at the names: Myrna Valentine and Guy Valentine, age three, from Portland, Oregon. He didn't remember the names from the first read-through because the woman had not included a reason for wanting to be on the flight.

The tenth name drawn was Gavin Cornell. Among the names in the original stack of messages, only three were familiar to Cooper Sams: Tommy Eggers, the name on the solitary sheet lying to the side of the desk, and Gavin Cornell, the faded former film star about Cooper's age. Cooper had seen many of Cornell's films and followed his sad, rapid decline in the media: alcohol, big-spending wives and mistresses, gambling debts, links with organized crime, and finally disease—debilitating, deforming rheumatoid arthritis.

"The doomsday flight will be my greatest publicity stunt ever or the end of any need for publicity," Cornell had written on his fax. "Either way, I can't lose. Sign me up." Cooper was disappointed when Gavin Cornell's name was not highlighted for selection during his first pass through the list. Drawing his name out of the pack now induced a smile.

Cooper Sams wasn't superstitious, but as he drew the thirteenth name for the standby list, he wondered who Raul Barrigan might be. Noting that Barrigan was only twenty-four years old and quadriplegic—the first wheelchair bound passenger on the list so far, Cooper realized that the young man had already experienced his share of bad luck in life. His reason for boarding *Vanguard* was to help prepare people to die. *A noble purpose, young man, except no one is going to die on my flight*, Cooper mused.

Once he completed the draw, Cooper paged through both small stacks and entered each name into the computer with the help of a scanning wand. Only one line was blank: Number 26 on the confirmed passenger list. Cooper wondered where this name would come from, but after his successful afternoon of making selections, he was sure he would recognize the person when he or she was presented to him.

Studying the list of names, Cooper was disappointed that so many viewed Reunion as a suicide flight, convinced that he was going to purposely crash the plane if Jesus-Brother did not appear. Earl Butcher had planted the idea with his two *Star* articles. Cooper shook his head to firmly refuse the idea. This was no suicide flight. He had no plans to crash the plane. Jesus-Brother would be there to receive him and his passengers, believers or not, at precisely 8:02 P.M. The maneuver Cooper was planning for *Vanguard* was simply an act of faith in the master's appearance. The fact that the plane would be unable to fly was immaterial. "It's not suicide if the plane crashes with nobody on it," Cooper said to the list of names staring back at him from the monitor.

Cooper named the document VANGUARD.XPS, the extension designating "extra passengers," then exited to the main menu. The rest of his work today concerned the single sheet he had set aside nearly an hour earlier. He took the sheet and leaned back in his office chair to study it. It was also a request to join Cooper Sams aboard *Vanguard*. However, this request was not from a passenger but from a qualified first officer, a former coworker at Northstar. Jesus-Brother had provided a copilot.

Forty-eight

Cooper Sams had known Walt Meisner since 1981. They first met at Northstar when Meisner was hired as a first officer on the 737 after a twenty-two-year career as a Navy pilot. At the time, Walt Meisner, a native of Federal Way, Washington, between Seattle and Tacoma, was one of Northstar's oldest rookie F.O.'s at age forty-one, and Cooper Sams was one of its youngest captains at age thirty-nine. Cooper enjoyed flying with Walt because of their common Navy background. They became friends, at least to the limited extent that Cooper Sams was friends with anyone.

Walt Meisner's goal was to make captain in five years. He had a wife and five children, the eldest of which entered Pacific Lutheran University two months after Walt joined Northstar. A Navy pension and first officer's salary was not enough to get his large brood through college. His wife had contracted MS shortly before he left the Navy and could no longer work. Meisner had to make captain to provide for his family.

But it was not to be. Walt Meisner was regularly passed over for captain because of a number of minor but repeated policy infractions. Meisner was an excellent flier. But as an A-6 pilot in Vietnam, he was used to flying by the seat of his pants in combat situations where stopping to read the manual or ask permission could be fatal. As a result, he had acquired the bad habit of trivializing busywork: log entries, reports, perfunctory inspections, and procedures. Though none of his errors had jeopardized an aircraft, the sum of them prevented Northstar's pilot review board from approving Meisner's application for captain.

When Cooper Sams was appointed to the board in '94, he reluctantly joined his colleagues in denying his friend the captain's bars. In January 1995, one month before Cooper's near-tragic Juneau flight, Walt Meisner left Northstar and Seattle. He accepted a job—and a pay cut—with a small Atlanta-based charter outfit, Dixie Air Service, who had promised him his braids in less than a year. Meisner had called Cooper after the Juneau incident to offer his congratulations on the airmanship award. Cooper did not hear from him again—until he found Meisner's fax earlier in the afternoon.

Winter nights begin well before 5 P.M. in the Northwest. So at 4:40, Cooper's office was in near darkness except for lamplight showering the desktop and the soft blue glow emanating from the monitor. Cooper hovered over one sheet of paper, still amazed at the providential appearance of a volunteer first officer. He read the brief message once more in preparation for placing a call to Atlanta.

December 1, 2001
TO: New Jesus Family, Seattle, WA
FROM: Capt. Walter Meisner, Dixie Air Services, Atlanta, GA
ATTN: Capt. Cooper Sams

Hello, Coop. Seeing your picture in the paper brought back good memories of the times we spent in the cockpit together. More than that, you will never know how much your religious intensity has impacted me in the last two days. I've been searching for God for years. All I found was a wimpy Sunday School God that only children and the weak could believe in. Reading about you and *Vanguard* convinced me that there has to be a God big enough for a flier. Any pilot who can dive to within 300 feet of hell and live to tell about it must have an in with the man upstairs. If you still need a first officer aboard *Vanguard,* I would be honored to sit beside you in the cockpit for one last flight. If not please save the jump seat for an old Navy flier who is ready to meet his God.

Cooper was pleased that Walt Meisner seemed more interested in the spiritual nature than the terminal nature of *Vanguard*'s flight. Walt had written nothing about being the victim of cancer or AIDS or another personal disaster pushing him to volunteer for the flight. Instead, Meisner seemed to identify with the spiritual significance of Cooper's Juneau experience like no one else had. *It takes a flier to understand a flier,* he judged. *Walt knows why I volunteered to fly* Vanguard. *He has experienced his own close calls in the air. Perhaps Jesus-Brother has called his name too, and he doesn't realize it.*

Cooper was reaching for the phone when Margaret Harold's voice came through the speaker. "Captain, Beth Cole is on line two. She said you asked her to call."

Having been immersed in unfamiliar names all afternoon, Cooper didn't recognize Beth's name at first. "Beth Cole?" he repeated as he jotted the name on a scratch pad.

"She said it's about interviewing you and Ms. Atkinson tomorrow."

Cooper remembered, though the memory of Beth Cole and Rachel Sams in his office this morning was not a pleasant one. He did not want to be interviewed by Beth Cole or anyone. For a few moments this morning he felt obligated to give the woman some time after falsely accusing her of using Rachel to get to him. But now the reprimand was several hours cold, and Cooper had no interest in talking to her. He would tell her so himself.

"I'll take it, Margaret," he said finally. Then he switched line two to the speaker and swiveled back in his chair. "Yes?"

"Mr. Sams, this is Beth Cole."

A familiar sound brought Cooper up in his chair as quickly as he had reclined. It wasn't the sound of Beth's voice. It was the sound that *accompanied* Beth's voice, an unmistakable inner chime he had heard throughout the afternoon.

He looked at the words scribbled on the scratch pad in front of him—Beth Cole—and instantly the sound made sense. Beth Cole—twin words of four letters each. Anything coming in two's always meant something special. Beth Cole—two words totaling eight letters. The number twenty-six has two digits, and two and six total eight. It was suddenly clear to him: Beth Cole was to be the mysterious twenty-sixth passenger. It seemed unthinkable because, for all he knew, the woman didn't even want to go. Yet Cooper could not question the revelation he had just received. Pathfinder had alerted him to the selection the moment Beth Cole spoke her name. Cooper didn't understand it, but for some reason Beth Cole was being issued an invitation to board *Vanguard*.

"Mr. Sams, are you there?" came the woman's voice again.

"Yes, I'm here, Ms. Cole. Please excuse me, I was . . . thinking."

Beth was silent for a moment. "Are you all right, sir? Am I interrupting something?"

"No, not at all. I was expecting your call." Cooper forgave himself for the lie in light of the recent, abrupt disclosure.

"Then you and Ms. Atkinson are willing to meet with me tomorrow?" she advanced hopefully.

"Yes, how much time would you like?"

The woman's hesitancy was subtle evidence of her surprise. "Well, er, how about, er, a couple of hours. I could be there by 10."

"That will be fine, Ms. Cole. Ten o'clock it is."

"And you will tell me all about the New Jesus Family and this Reunion?"

"Yes, whatever you want, providing that you abide by your promise not to print a word."

"Absolutely. Not a word until after February 20—that is, if there is an after."

Cooper was not tempted to argue with her. Instead, he was moved to share the insight he had just been given. "Ms. Cole, I have been impressed to offer you more than an interview."

His unexpected statement again delayed her response. "What would that be, Mr. Sams?" she said with obvious reservation.

"How would you like to go with us?"

"I beg your pardon."

"How would you like to board *Vanguard* and fly with us on February 20?"

"You mean like a test flight before the real flight?"

"No, I mean the real flight, Ms. Cole. I'm offering you a seat on the plane. You will be the only journalist allowed aboard."

Again a surprised pause. "You sound serious."

"Yes, I am serious. Frankly, I don't understand why you have been chosen, but you have."

"Chosen?"

"To be invited on board, Ms. Cole. We have over 200 people who would like your seat. But I have been instructed to offer it to you. Now if you don't take it, I'll be justified in offering it to someone else." Cooper felt the ultimatum was in line with Pathfinder's impression.

"I . . . I need to think about this, Mr. Sams."

"And I need to know your answer now, Ms. Cole. In point of fact, if you're not disposed to go with us, I can't see any value in proceeding with the interview tomorrow."

The caller started to speak twice but stumbled over her words and stopped. Finally she blurted, "All right, I'll go."

"Excellent. We'll see you tomorrow at 10."

Cooper tapped off the phone before Beth Cole could respond. He swiveled to the computer and retrieved VANGUARD.XPS to the screen. Scrolling down to the blank space next to the number twenty-six, he typed in a name: Beth Cole. Satisfied that he had fulfilled Pathfinder's will, he saved the document and returned to the main menu. Then he returned to the phone to place his call to Atlanta, Georgia. Everything was coming together just as Pathfinder promised.

Beth dropped her head on the back of the leather sofa, stunned. Had she heard correctly? Did Cooper Sams just invite her aboard *Vanguard* for its first and possibly last flight? Was he serious, or was he battling doomsday stress with a little comic relief at her expense? Even more bizarre, did she just hear herself accept his invitation? Beth had done a lot of crazy things during her career to get a story, some of them dangerous. But she had never knowingly volunteered to go through certain disaster. She felt like she had just agreed to cover a force five hurricane by standing in its path with nothing between her and the storm but a camera and digital recorder.

Yes, Mr. Sams had offered and she had accepted—eventually. That much was clear. But why had he made the offer to her? And was he serious about it? Beth didn't know. Why had she so thoughtlessly accepted? Beth knew why. Because Sams was ready to jerk the interview out of her hands if she didn't. And Beth needed that interview to try to get inside Sams' head and find out how he intended to prove his faith in God on doomsday. She had to make sure that his leap of faith didn't result in a fatal fall for a planeload of gullible and unsuspecting passengers.

Would Beth be among those who might die on February 20? She didn't plan to be, especially if she turned up evidence that Sams intended to take the plane down. She had no twinges of conscience about saying yes to Sams' invitation to get the interview knowing she might have to back out at the last moment to save her skin.

On the other hand, if she could be assured that Cooper Sams planned to bring *Vanguard* back to earth safely when the rapture didn't happen, what better place to be for the story than on that plane? What an opportunity Sams had provided for her! She clearly had much more to learn about the doomsday flight before deciding whether or not to claim her seat.

She had to tell Libby and Rachel the good news about the interview. But first she had to call Reagan. She had only been away from him for two nights, but she missed him terribly. Ever since she bought this ranch-style home on Whidbey Island overlooking Skagit Bay seven years earlier, Beth had lived here alone and loved it. Now, having been married to Reagan Cole a grand total of fifty-one days, she hated being here alone. She felt incomplete. Flying up to Seattle on Saturday, she had assured herself that she could stay here alone for three months—until after the doomsday flight—if she had to. Now she couldn't wait to complete the interview and head home to her husband.

Beth checked the clock on the mantle: almost 5. Reagan would probably still be in his office or in a meeting at Parker Center. She should wait a couple hours until he got home to call him, but she couldn't do it. She tapped the memory code in her wireless phone and flipped her leg over the arm of the sofa as the call was processed.

"This is Reagan Cole."

"And this is a lady in distress. I need a sergeant right away."

"Yes ma'am," Cole replied, playing along. "I'm a sergeant. What can I do for you?"

"I'm being harassed by a bad case of the lonelies. Will you please come over and chase them away?"

"What's your location, ma'am?"

"East Silverlake Drive, Oak Harbor, Washington."

"I'm sorry, ma'am, but that's about 1,000 miles from my present location."

"What is your present location, Sergeant? It sounds a little noisy."

"Westbound on the Santa Monica Freeway, creeping along with rush hour traffic on my Kawasaki."

"You're on the way home already?" Beth said, breaking off her pouty little act. "Short day at the office, I'd say." She pictured him astride the bike talking to her on the headset in his helmet.

"Somebody has to be home to care for the poor babies. Their mother abandoned them to pursue fame and fortune in Seattle."

"Oh, how are the puppies?" she said with longing.

Cole laughed. "Just the same as you left them, except they're two days older and cuter."

A pang of loneliness turned in Beth's stomach. "I miss the babies.

And I miss you, Reagan."

"In that order?" he teased.

"I miss the babies a *little;* I miss you a *lot.*"

"I miss you too, Babe. When will you be finished up there?"

"Well, guess what?" Beth chirped, remembering her exciting news. Then without giving her husband a chance to guess, she said, "Rachel Sams introduced me to her husband today, and I have a personal interview with the two big mucky-mucks of the cult tomorrow morning."

"That's great!"

"Well, it's only a little great," Beth explained. "I got the interview on the condition that I won't publish anything until after February 20, and of course the world will be nothing but smoke and ash by then."

"Not till after the flight? That's too bad," Cole said.

"It's not *too* bad, because I think Cooper Sams will come to his senses after the flight and give me permission to do the book."

"Good, good," Cole affirmed.

"Yeah, but it's only good if he lands the plane after the bogus rapture instead of crashing it."

"So is this news good or bad? I'm getting confused."

"Bottom line: Right now everything is good. At least I get the interview tomorrow. I'll take the rest as it comes."

"OK, if you say so."

"And here's even better news," Beth continued. "I'm flying home tomorrow night."

Beth expected her husband to erupt with glee. Instead he said, "For how long?"

"It depends on how the interview goes. I may need to come up a couple of times between now and February 20. Maybe we can come up together over Christmas. I don't think I'm ready for another Christmas in L.A. yet."

"Christmas on the island? Sounds nice."

"Then I'll have to be here for several days before the doomsday flight."

"Why?"

"To finish the story, numb brain," Beth said playfully, overemphasizing the obvious.

"Oh, yeah, finish the story."

Beth laughed. "Sometimes I wonder if you're sucking too much carbon monoxide on those long motorcycle rides."

They talked for three minutes longer, mainly discussing where Cole would pick up his wife at LAX and confessing their mutual loneliness. They decided that if Beth was coming home as planned she would not call again. If her plans changed, which both she and Cole hoped wouldn't happen, she would call to tell him.

Beth tapped off the phone and went to the bedroom to change into jeans and boots. She had already decided that she would spend the evening decorating a small Christmas tree in the living room while she noodled on questions for the interview. She seemed to think better when her hands were busy. And doing the tree might help her get into the Christmas spirit. But first she had to go outside and cut down the tree, a four-foot noble fir she had spotted from the driveway when she arrived home.

While lacing up her boots, Beth finally admitted to herself that she had purposely avoided telling Cole about Cooper Sams' invitation to be a passenger on the doomsday flight. And she knew very well why she had not told him. He would have asked, "Did you accept the offer?" to which she would have felt obligated to answer truthfully, "Of course, I did. He would have cancelled the interview if I didn't."

At this point, Beth surmised, the conversation would have taken a sharp downward turn. Cole would have launched into a lecture on the dangers of getting involved with a religious nut. He would have insisted that an interview and a book were not worth the risk of such a crazy stunt. Beth would have stiffened in resistance and argued that she could take care of herself. The conversation would have degenerated to a fight, and perhaps one of them would have hung up on the other in a huff.

Beth felt rather noble for preventing a big brouhaha and spoiling their romantic reunion tomorrow night. Until she was ready to trade in her free ticket on Captain Sam's airplane she hoped to save her husband a lot of grief by keeping it to herself.

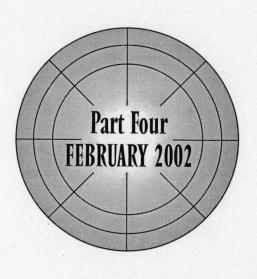

Part Four
FEBRUARY 2002

Forty-nine

"All right, people, sit down and pipe down." Mitchell Schetky wasn't used to raising his voice to control a meeting. The noisy audience of eight crowded into the small conference room was amused by his uncharacteristic brusqueness, and they took their seats around the table grousing about Mitchell being a tyrant. They were only joking, of course. The forty-two-year-old operations superintendent was normally even-tempered and quiet, conducting the day-to-day affairs of the Snohomish County Airport with the quiet efficiency and reliability of a digital timepiece. Mitchell Schetky usually stayed out of everyone's face and let people do their work. As such, he was respected and well-liked by the Paine Field staff, even when stress pushed him to bark at them.

Mitchell took a last slurp of lukewarm coffee from a paper cup while everyone got settled. He remained standing at the end of the conference table, as he did during all meetings he chaired. It was an unconscious compensation for his lack of commanding appearance: small stature and boyish, borderline nerdy face. Mitchell wore what he wore every day in the airport administration office: dark slacks, a short-sleeve, button-down shirt—white or pastel, never print or striped, and a dark tie—striped or solid, never floral or patterned. No one meeting Mitchell for the first time would guess that he was once a Navy F-16 top gun, decorated for service during Desert Storm.

"I'm sorry to drag all of you out so early on a Monday morning," Mitchell began. "But, as you know, we have only ten days left to get ready for the big circus coming to Paine Field, and we all have our real jobs to perform on top of it. So I thought if we get some things sorted out now . . ." Mitchell didn't need to finish his thought. His audience was already nodding agreement. No one liked the idea of the extra attention coming to Paine Field. But they liked even less being unprepared to deal with the kooks and the curious who would flock to such an event.

Not everyone on the airport staff had been invited to the meeting; only those whose departments would be directly effected by the hoopla surrounding the February 20 departure of the New Jesus Family. In addition to Schetky, there was Jo Ellen Case, airport manager and a former Boeing executive, Rogie Petrovic, assistant manager, Alton "Freddy" Frederickson, maintenance manager, and Weldon New Feather, chief of the Paine Field Fire Department and public safety supervisor for the airport.

The other three persons at the table were not airport staff but would certainly be involved in airport security when the crowds descended to applaud or protest or gawk as *Vanguard* took off. Kurt Nixon was acting sheriff for Snohomish County, and Lieutenant Pamela Yarrow represented the Everett police department. They looked Monday-morning spiffy in their fresh-pressed uniforms. Gil Isaacs, a relative newcomer to the group, represented the regional office of the Federal Aviation Administration. He wore a suit.

"Let me bring us all up to speed on this event," Mitchell Schetky said. "Then we can make sure everybody's concerns are addressed.

"The New Jesus people will be bussing up from their headquarters in Seattle a week from Wednesday. There are supposed to be 135 people on the plane. That probably means two big coaches. The passengers are having a private catered dinner in the hangar at 5 P.M., so I expect the buses to roll in a little before 5."

"The condemned get a last meal, eh?" Rogie Petrovic cut in wryly while doodling on a yellow pad in front of him.

"To hear them talk, those of us left behind are the ones condemned," Freddy Frederickson added, chuckling. "Maybe *we* deserve a big dinner."

Mitchell went on as if he hadn't heard the interruption. The doomsday jokes, which were plentiful, were wearing on him. He just wanted Paine Field to come through the ordeal without contributing to the comedy through ill-preparedness or ineptness. "Only the buses will be allowed access through the gate to the hangar. No relatives, press, or hangers-on."

"So there won't be any tearful good-byes on the ramp," Lieutenant Pam Yarrow speculated aloud.

"And no last-minute kidnappings by desperate loved ones or professional cult deprogrammers," Jo Ellen Case added. As airport manager, much of Jo Ellen's job entailed public relations and serving as liaison to the airport's most influential client, Boeing.

Mitchell said, "I was informed that the passengers will say their final good-byes before arriving at the Stouffer-Madison on Sunday, at least those passengers whose relatives even know they're planning to take this trip."

"You mean some of these cult people are getting on the plane without telling their relatives what they are doing?" Lieutenant Yarrow said disbelievingly.

Mitchell nodded. "No names of members have been officially released by the group. And about two or three dozen standbys have been selected to take the empty seats. Nobody knows who they are either."

"The better they keep those names under wraps, the easier it will be for us," Weldon New Feather emphasized. "It's going to be crazy enough as it is dealing with the people who are already making a stink about this flight." Several at the table nodded.

Frederickson, the maintenance manager, spoke up. "I still don't see what the big deal is. They're going to fly around for an hour or two, and when Jesus doesn't show up, they'll be back. I don't believe all this mass suicide garbage they're talking about on TV. Cooper Sams has a reputation for saving passengers, not killing them."

"But if he's going to bring the plane back, why doesn't he just say he's going to bring it back?" Petrovic challenged no one in particular. "Instead, he says nothing, so people get suspicious and we have to deal with a crowd of malcontents next Wednesday, not to mention the press."

Mitchell jumped in before anyone else could prolong the digression. "The passengers will board the plane inside the hangar. At about 6:45 they will open the hangar doors and a tug will pull the plane outside for engine start. The captain will take delta taxiway to alpha and alpha to the end of 16 right. He hopes to be airborne by 7:02, exactly one hour before the so-called Reunion."

"Good riddance," Petrovic breathed loudly enough for everyone to hear.

"Isn't there any way you can keep them from doing this?" Jo Ellen was looking at Gil Isaacs the FAA man when she spoke.

Isaacs shook his head slowly. "On paper, this airplane and its cockpit crew are solid. They've jumped through all the hoops. The 737 in the Tramco hangar is in better shape than most aircraft in commercial use today. And the cult has said nothing to make us suspect that they intend to crash the plane. The captain told me he would submit a flight plan for Juneau from his computer a couple hours before the flight. I tend to agree with Freddy. When things don't happen the way these people expect, they'll either go on to Juneau for the night or come back to Seattle."

Jo Ellen Case objected, "But all the scuttlebutt in the media about Sams putting the plane in jeopardy, planting a bomb—"

"Just scuttlebutt," Isaacs interrupted. "At this point, nothing more than rumor, hearsay, Earl Butcher's idea of a good story. If it will make you feel any better, we have someone in the hangar who assures us that there are no explosive devices on the plane right now. And there won't be any suitcase bombs since no one is taking a suitcase. Our man will scan the passengers as they board—"

"Surreptitiously?" Pamela Yarrow cut in.

"Of course, Lieutenant," Isaacs assured, just a little put off that the cop would think otherwise. Then he continued his thought. "If we pick up anything suspicious in a purse or Bible or anywhere, we'll pounce on it. But I don't think we'll find anything."

"Yeah, why would they mess with a bomb or something?" Frederickson put in. "Once they're airborne, Captain Sams can dump the plane into the Sound if he wants to, and no one down here can stop him."

"I really don't believe a professional flier can find it in his heart to destroy a refurbished 737 let alone 135 human beings," Isaacs continued. "I think these kooks are just out for a harmless little joy ride. They'll come flying home when their balloon pops."

Mitchell jumped in quickly again to steer the discussion back to his agenda. "Regardless of what the New Jesus Family does after they leave, we have to keep the airport in one piece *until* they leave. We're expecting relatives and friends of the passengers to show up, some of them very unhappy about this flight. And judging from the way the event has been hyped in the media, we will probably have right-to-die sympathizers on site to send them off and sanctity-of-life protesters to try and talk them out of going. That's like putting open beakers of nitric acid, sulfuric acid, and glycerin on the same table and wishing for an earthquake. We could have major crowd-control problems.

"We'll also have the press—pushy reporters, cameras, lights, microphones, cords, uplink vehicles. And we'll have the nosy public coming in like vultures at a hanging. I've heard that they're coming in from all over the West like this was the state fair or a UFO convention or a religious camp meeting. The ramps will be full of private aircraft, and we could have cars clogging Airport Road and 100th Street for miles. It baffles me that people don't have anything better to do than overrun a small county airport to watch a jetliner take off."

Mitchell turned to the fire chief with a weak smile. "Weldon, how are we going to keep from getting trampled next week?"

"Without giving the impression to the watching world that our *guests* are under martial rule," Jo Ellen Case added. She emphasized "guests" to remind everyone around the table that the taxpayers swooping in next Wednesday owned the airport.

Weldon New Feather was a stocky Native American in his mid-forties with a salt-and-pepper crew cut, no neck, and skin the color of burnt sienna. He had been with the airport fire department for eighteen years, serving as chief for the last six. Weldon remained seated to give his report, and Mitchell Schetky remained standing to listen.

"The goal, as always," Weldon began, "is to keep people out of the air operations areas—the ramps, the runways and taxiways, the surrounding turf—and keep them orderly within our limited public access areas. The trick is to do it decently, short of topping the fences with razor wire or bringing in a pack of Dobermans to patrol the perimeter. I think our best shot is to educate the masses and be proactive."

New Feather outlined a plan to post off-duty police and fire personnel, explorers, and police cadets at the main entrance and at strategic points on the east and south sides of the airport. These persons would greet every visitor and hand them a colored airport map, indicating restricted areas. Weldon held up one of the maps. "We'll give them a big smile and tell them that they are welcome in the white areas but they must stay out of the fenced yellow and green areas." When the small parking lot in the airport was full, Weldon explained, volunteers would direct cars to park along Airport Road and 100th Street and walk in.

A small complement of Snohomish County Sheriff's deputies would be on hand to enforce the directives, Weldon stated. If needed, additional crowd control would be supplied by additional deputies and Everett police. Weldon would coordinate the security staff from the communication center in the fire station. Also at his disposal in case of emergency was the Mukilteo Police and the Washington State Patrol. "I'll bring in people as we need them. Hopefully, we'll be able to avoid a repeat of the Yeltsin debacle."

Everyone at the table knew what Weldon meant. In 1994, then President Boris Yeltsin stopped by Everett during a U.S. visit to inspect the Boeing plant. A mob of curious citizens swarmed Paine Field to get a look at the Russian leader. They trampled fences and spilled out onto the ramps. Parents took their kids and strollers onto the grass alongside the runways like they were attending a picnic. Airport officials, including Weldon New Feather, were out on the grass in pickup trucks herding people back to the terminal with bull horns.

The airport manager asked, "What if the anti-cult protesters hop the fences and form a human chain around the plane to keep it from taking off?"

"The tarmac will be off limits to the public, and we'll have officers around the plane."

"The crowd could take over the tarmac," Jo Ellen postulated.

"We'll work hard to prevent it," Weldon said confidently, "but if we can't, we'll arrest the violators and haul them away one by one."

Gil Isaacs of the FAA offered the next challenge. "What if the protesters and sympathizers come to blows out there? You could have a small war on your hands."

"We're equipped with pepper gas, Tasers, and the like," acting sheriff Nixon informed. "We'll be ready for a small war." Lieutenant Yarrow agreed with a nod.

"Pepper gas and Tasers?" Jo Ellen moaned aloud. "Turning our airport into a battlefield like South Central L.A.?"

Weldon answered quickly, "We'll be as tolerant as we can for as long as we can. But if somebody wants to play hardball, we have to stop them."

"That might delay the flight, even past their magic moment of 8:02 P.M.," the airport manager considered aloud.

Weldon shrugged. "I can't do anything about that. Our job is to get the plane away as quickly and safely as possible."

Rogie Petrovic spoke next. "Somebody might be desperate enough to try to shoot out the plane's tires to keep it on the ground. Are you planning a weapons search?"

Weldon shook his head. "We don't have the manpower. Remember, folks: This isn't the Pope or the President on this plane. As Gil says, it's just a bunch of people going for a plane ride. We're not talking airtight security here. We'll do the best we can to deal with situations as they come up. If we see any weapons, of course, we'll grab those people and quietly lead them away."

Discomfited by the prospect of problems but satisfied that the fire chief and his staff would indeed do their best, the group asked New Feather no more questions.

Focus shifted to preparation of the physical property. Freddy Frederickson reported that his staff was working hard to rid the runways and taxiways of foreign object debris ahead of the projected influx of private aircraft. "The amount of F.O.D. has been increasing on runway 16L-34R and taxiways G and F," Freddy said. "We've found sheet metal screws, a fuel strainer, a quarter-inch ratchet and socket, small airplane parts, and garbage strewn around. Blown tires and chipped paint resulting from F.O.D. leaves a bad impression on visitors. If any of you see stuff laying around, please call me. We aim to have the place F.O.D. free for our company."

Mitchell Schetky hastily ticked off several minor items of concern surrounding the doomsday flight. Then he adjourned the meeting and the members quickly scattered to busy workdays which awaited them.

On the way back to their office, Rogie Petrovic asked his boss, "Will you be here when the doomsday flight takes off?"

Jo Ellen measured the question for a moment. Then she said, "If you mean will I be here to make sure the airport isn't destroyed by the tourists, yes. If you're talking about being here to see what a plane full of religious wackos looks like, no thank you, I'm not interested."

"You're not just a little bit curious about what makes these people tick?" Rogie pressed.

"No. I think what they're doing is stupid. If anything, I feel sorry for them. What about you? Do you get off on stuff like this?"

Rogie nodded. "Yeah, I think it's kind of entertaining, like going to the circus. I'm bringing the wife and kids down here next week. We're going to watch the whole thing while we eat a picnic dinner."

"You're kidding," Jo Ellen gasped with surprise.

"I kid you not. I'm trying to spend more time with the family, and this is cheaper than taking them to the circus. And it could be a lot more entertaining."

Fifty

"Captain, I have the final number."

Cooper Sams stood quickly as Lila Ruth Atkinson entered his office unannounced. She wore a midnight blue and white checked suit with gold jewelry accented with sapphires. She carried a single sheet of paper.

"Did we lose any more over the weekend?" Cooper asked as she approached his desk.

Lila Ruth's countenance conveyed the disappointment of a mother whose children had just run away from home. "Yes," she sighed, "five more. But that's the last of them."

"You have talked with the others?"

"Yes, I have interviewed each of them personally. And I'm sure that the New Jesus Family is now intact for Reunion." She held the sheet out to him.

Cooper received it and glanced over the printout. There were 91 names, down 18 from the original membership of 109. He felt a pang of loss, sadness, abandonment. "Where have they gone?"

"Most of them were talked out of participating in Reunion—in some cases coerced is a better word—by their unbelieving loved ones," Lila Ruth said, trying to veil her melancholy.

"Hm," Cooper inserted to fill the momentary silence.

Lila Ruth quickly regained a positive air. "However, we must accept the wisdom of Saint John the Divine: 'They went out from us because they did not belong to us. If they belonged to us, they would have remained with us.'"

"Yes, those who belong have remained," Cooper said, holding up the sheet.

"And that which our departed members have forfeited will be considered gain for the strangers and aliens in the land. Jesus-Brother is even more generous in mercy toward unbelievers than we first thought."

"Indeed. We have room aboard *Vanguard* or . . ." Cooper paused to figure in his head ". . . a total of forty-four guests, putting us well into our standby list."

Lila Ruth clasped her hands at her waist as she often did when teaching the glorious mysteries of Parent-God. "It is time to issue invitations and instructions to our additional eighteen guests. Send the gold coins at once, and prepare a final passenger list for me. Invite the last eight standbys to the hangar for the feast, but inform them that they will not be on board with us."

"Unless others of our confirmed passengers renege on their plans to be aboard," Cooper added quickly. He had hoped that his pragmatism wasn't an affront to Lila Ruth or Jesus-Brother. But his instincts told him that some of the strangers and aliens who had earlier accepted invitations might back out at the last moment.

Lila Ruth clearly did not want to think about additional defectors. But she finally concurred. Drawing a long breath, she said, "All right, inform the eight to come prepared to go up with us in the event places are available."

"I will have the packets ready to ship by overnight express before 4 P.M.," Cooper assured.

"Very good, Captain. Even so, come, Jesus-Brother."

"Even so, come," Cooper responded.

Lila Ruth turned and exited the office without another word.

Cooper's task was clear, and he commended himself for the advance preparation that would further expedite his task. In early December, he had personally contacted the twenty-six individuals whose applications Pathfinder had impressed him to select from those received in the office. Each of the applicants eagerly accepted the invitation. In the case of Robert Lamar, the cancer-ridden inmate in Texas, authorities in the federal prison asked for time to process the request through their superiors. The warden called Cooper eight days later and said they would transport Lamar to Seattle in shackles with two FBI agents, who would deliver him to Paine Field in time for the flight.

To each of the confirmed passengers, Cooper sent a packet of confidential instructions—the same instructions distributed to Family members. Each outsider was also sent something which Family members did not receive: two specially minted and numbered Reunion coins, one silver and one gold. Upon arrival at Paine Field, each applicant would be required to present the two coins in order to board. Such a procedure was unnecessary for the ninety-one Family members who were recognizable to the leaders.

Cooper urged the twenty-six guest passengers not to discuss Reunion or their participation in it with anyone in order to avoid family conflicts and unwanted attention. From the stories appearing in the *US Star* and other avenues of the media since December, a number of passengers had blatantly disregarded Cooper's request.

Next Cooper had contacted the twenty-six standbys, explained the procedure, and secured confirmation of their desire to be aboard. To each of the standbys he sent limited instructions and a numbered silver coin. He assured them that they would receive an identically numbered gold coin and full instructions if and when their seat became available. And he exhorted each to silence.

In accordance with Lila Ruth's dictum, Cooper simply had to ship a gold coin and full instructions to each of the first eighteen names on the standby list and qualified invitations to the remaining eight. His assistant Margaret Harold would put the packets together, and Raython Braggs, the eager volunteer with limited office skills, would deliver them to the express depot.

As Cooper sat down to begin the process, something curious about the pared-down list of New Jesus Family members made him turn his attention back to the sheet Lila Ruth had given him. He scanned the list of ninety-one names and recognized all of them—eighty-five adults and six minors. Then he realized what he was looking for and furrowed his brow. Two expected names were missing from the list: Kathy Keene, the Northstar flight attendant responsible for introducing him to Lila Ruth Atkinson, and her housemate, Bradley Smith. Cooper was immediately on his feet and headed for Lila Ruth's office. He walked in unannounced as she had done to him moments ago.

"Kathy Keene is not on the list," he said, approaching the desk.

Lila Ruth looked up from one of the open volumes of Eastern wisdom always on her desktop. She did not seem offended by the interruption. "That's correct. I'm sorry to say that Ms. Keene and Mr. Smith opted not to join us for Reunion."

"Did she say why? Did you talk to her?" Cooper felt a deeper sense of loss over Kathy than any of the others. The two of them had survived the Juneau wind shear together on February 20, 1995. They had both found Lila Ruth Atkinson and Jesus-Brother and their earthly destinies as a result. They were friends, not fast friends but soulmates of a sort because of their brush with death. Kathy had never once hinted that she would not be aboard *Vanguard*, nor had Cooper imagined she would not.

"Apparently it was Bradley's doing," Lila Ruth explained, revisiting the sense of abandonment by her children. "Jesus-Brother calls him Cautious, and the dark side of caution is doubt. He wavered and fell away. Kathy's faith is strong, but her love for Bradley is stronger. She decided to stay with him."

"And trade a glorious Reunion for a fiery baptism into the next world?" Cooper retorted on the verge of anger.

"I am of the same mind and soul as you, Captain," Lila Ruth consoled. "Such a choice sounds absurd. But Kathy and Bradley are out of our hands now. They have made their decision, and we must accept it."

Cooper studied his cherished spiritual leader's face. Lila Ruth was two months short of turning sixty-eight, yet she appeared even younger to him than when he met her. The woman's hair, which she claimed was natural in color, seemed as blonde as it did gray. Her skin was supple and smooth. Her eyes were bright and clear. And her aura of spiritual wisdom was as vibrant as her physical appearance. If Cooper had ever looked into the face of an angel of light, this was one.

But at this moment, Cooper disagreed with his wise mentor. Lila

Ruth might be able to accept Kathy's sudden desertion to a doubting boyfriend, but he could not, at least not without an explanation. He felt as if a plank in the solid platform of his faith was loose under his feet. He had to see about tacking it into place.

"Very well," he said confidently to mask his intentions, "I'll carry on then."

Lila Ruth nodded and forced a smile, then tacitly dismissed him by returning to her book.

Cooper was dialing Kathy Keene's number before he sat down at his desk. After three rings the machine answered. Kathy's recorded voice invited the caller to leave a message. She sounded uncommonly cheerful for someone who had just waived passage on the ark of deliverance to face the fires of judgment. He assumed that she was on a trip with Northstar. Cooper decided not to talk to her via the machine, and he did not want to talk to Bradley at all. He would try Kathy's number every day until she answered in person.

Cooper steeled himself to put thoughts of Kathy Keene behind him and center on the task at hand. He opened the passenger files on the computer and carefully updated the lists in three categories: members, guests, standbys. Cooper winced at each member name he removed from the list. It seemed that with each tap of the DELETE key he was condemning a friend to judgment. In his head he knew the individual had made the choice himself or herself—or was talked into it by well-meaning loved ones. But he grieved over the disintegration of the Family and the pain these brothers and sisters would suffer so needlessly.

Cooper had little trouble making Bradley Smith's name disappear from the list. He had suspected from the beginning that Kathy Keene's common-law husband was one of those whom Saint John claimed "did not belong to us." Bradley had always appeared guarded and withdrawn to Cooper, as if tolerating the activities of the New Jesus Family to humor Kathy. Bradley had the right, Cooper agreed, to take himself out of the Reunion picture. But he had no right to keep Kathy from fulfilling her destiny. The idea of such self-indulgence made Cooper mad.

When he scrolled down to Kathy's name on the monitor, he could not bring himself to delete it. A lot could happen in ten days. She could reconsider and change her hasty decision. He would certainly encourage her to do so when he talked to her. Yet in order to comply with Lila Ruth's directive, he had to remove her from the member list. So he highlighted her name and transferred it to the end of the standby list, which would be reduced to eight names when the reorganization was complete—nine counting hers. And if he convinced her to change her mind, he would make sure she was aboard when *Vanguard* rolled down runway 16R at Paine Field a week from Wednesday.

Before Cooper completed the final passenger list, Margaret announced that Walt Meisner was on the line. Cooper had spoken to his providentially supplied copilot only once since early December when he accepted Walt's offer to join him in the cockpit. There was no reason for them to interact more frequently. Cooper had no interest in fostering a friendship, and he was sure Walt didn't either. Furthermore, apart from the ultimate destination of *Vanguard*, there was nothing unusual about preparing for the flight. As a certified 737 pilot, Walt needed only to show up at the Stouffer-Madison in time to travel to Paine Field for the Reunion feast and departure.

"Good morning, Walt," Cooper said in a quasi-business tone.

Meisner replied in his familiar deep voice, "Cooper."

Aversive to small talk as he was, Cooper waited for his copilot to state the reason for his call.

"I'll be flying up to Seattle on Sunday," Meisner informed. "Can you secure a room for me in your hotel there until departure?"

"Can do, Walt. A room will be waiting for you on Sunday." Cooper scribbled a quick note to remind himself.

"Good, good." No more adept at small talk than Cooper, Meisner resorted to the mundane. "What kind of weather can we expect for next week?"

Meisner could locate detailed, two-week weather projections for any region in the country in any on-line service or daily newspaper, Cooper knew. He suspected that Meisner was biding his time to ask a more significant question.

"Standard late-winter fare for us, Walt. Plenty of precip, temps in the upper forties, low fifties. Nothing we can't fly in."

"Good. I like the rain. I should have stayed in the Northwest. The South hasn't been much fun."

Cooper hummed noncommitally. *You would still be here with Northstar now had you cleaned up your act on the flight deck*, he thought. *Don't give me any sob story about getting a lousy deal. If you had played it hard and tight, you would have earned your bars here.*

"Say, Coop, what are the chances we can take your airplane up for a shakedown flight early next week—maybe Monday sometime? I've been out of the cockpit for a couple of weeks, and I'm itching to get behind the yoke again."

So this is the question you've been working up to, Cooper mused. He would not grant Meisner's request, so he tried to make light of it. "It's just a garden variety Boeing 737 with a fancy paint job, Walt. It flies just like all the rest of them."

"Yeah, but this one is kind of special, what with its religious purpose and all. I'd just like to spend a little more time in it. What do you say?"

Cooper didn't have time to chat about it. "No can do, Walt. Paine Field is—"

"Just a quick circle over the San Juans, Coop, for old time's sake,"

Meisner cut in, sounding more insistent. Cooper identified with his request. Fliers love to fly. It's an addiction that never completely goes away. Cooper's former coworker was looking for one extra hit before the final flight.

"Sorry, Walt, but Paine Field is already crawling with people hoping to get a sneak peek at *Vanguard*. Who knows, one of them might be crazy enough to toss a grenade under it to keep us from going up. No, the airplane stays locked in the hangar until Wednesday evening."

Meisner was silent for a moment. "Well, yeah, I understand," he said at last, disappointed. "Just thought I'd ask."

"No problem," Cooper said. "We'll see you on Sunday. By the way, take a taxi to the hotel. It's a little difficult for us to get out these days with all the attention we're getting."

"Roger, Captain," he said, subdued. "Sunday, then."

Cooper didn't want his copilot to hang up moping. "Cheer up, Walt. You're going to be up front for the greatest flight in the history of aviation. You're flying right into heaven, man."

"Yeah," Meisner responded, sounding a little more upbeat, "and I'm planning to get this one right."

After signing off, Cooper completed the passenger lists and instructed Margaret Harold to ready the packets for shipping. Returning to his computer, he closed the file and exited to the main menu. It occurred to him that he had not changed the password yet this morning, something he had done every Monday morning since the New Jesus Family took up residence in the Stouffer-Madison. Cooper didn't seriously expect anyone to tamper with his computer, certainly no one in the office. But the thought of some practical joker hacking into his system to put a friend's name on the passenger list provoked him to take this one simple weekly precaution.

Cooper had used a series of easy-to-recall passwords related to his destiny: REUNION, VANGUARD, SAMS, PILOT, FAMILY, BROTHER, PATHFINDER. But he was running out of keywords, so he sat at the keyboard for several minutes trying to think of one. With only ten days remaining, one final password should do it. But he was stumped.

When the word finally came to him, he smiled at its simplicity. It was a word he had steadfastly avoided in any reference to Reunion, though the scoffers and unbelievers used it repeatedly. The term had been offensive to him because it described the event from the wrong side of the flames. Yet now it seemed comically appropriate. It was the perfect key word to leave in a computer that would be reduced to vapor at the moment of Reunion.

At the password prompt, Cooper typed it in: DOOMSDAY.

Fourteen hours later, Earl Butcher was hunched over his own computer keyboard chain-smoking through his last pack of Pall Malls.

Layers of cigarette smoke dominated the cramped, dimly lit apartment like a bad mood.

Butcher had come to rue Monday nights. Cooper Sams changed passwords on Mondays as predictably as some people do their laundry. Butcher usually had to spend a half hour or more in the middle of the night trying out new passwords to access the relatively defenseless New Jesus Family system. On the plus side, Cooper Sams wasn't clever enough to keep a crafty hacker like Butcher out. On the minus side, the passwords Sams selected were often so dumb that Butcher schemed right over them.

Tonight, Butcher had been at it for almost two hours, nearing the record two hours and twelve minutes it took him to discover COOP four weeks ago. He tried previously used passwords, all relating to Cooper Sams' spiritual hobby horse: VANGUARD, REUNION, CAPTAIN, FAMILY. He tried previously guessed passwords which had unlocked nothing: FEBRUARY, FLIGHT, PAINE, FAITH, BELIEVE, TWIN, TAKEOFF. He tried abbreviations, acronyms, even the old passwords spelled backward. And with each batch of failures he took another drag and released a curse with the cloud of smoke. Butcher had never been shut out on a Monday night yet. But he had only three cigarettes left, and when he was out of smokes he was no good for anything.

Snooping through Cooper Sams' files each week had yielded very little Butcher could turn into a story. In reality, the last three pieces he had submitted to the *Star* were rejected because they lacked something new, something juicy. What the *Star* wanted was the passenger list—the *final* passenger list—and they were ready to pay big money for it. The Scene editor told Butcher she wanted to publish all 135 names "as a public service to the unknowing families of the intended victims of this diabolical mass suicide."

Right, Butcher thought sardonically when Cleo first pitched him on the idea. *Don't kid yourself, because you're not kidding me. You want to publish the list for the same reason I want to find it for you: to make serious bucks. You want people running out to the newsstand by the millions to see if anyone they know is among the misguided souls secretly preparing to board the doomsday flight.*

But he had kept his tongue and kept prying through Cooper Sams' lists, which seemed to change weekly. The *Star* wasn't interested in partial lists or prospective lists or temporary lists. They even rejected Butcher's story on Gavin Cornell, the has-been actor whose name appeared on one of Cooper Sams' guest lists. The *Star* wanted *the* list, preferably about a week before the event, when hype and public curiosity were mounting to the climactic doomsday flight itself. And Butcher was determined to get it for them and go to the bank one more time on the demented New Jesus Family.

With a smoldering butt between his lips, he tried another burst of ideas: ENGINE, WING, TAIL, JET, JETLINER, AIRLINER. Each was rejected. After lighting up a fresh smoke, he tried another batch: NORTHSTAR, 737, 737-300, 2002, 20020220, 200202202002, COOP, COOPER, COOPSAMS, SAMS, HEAVEN, HELL, ETERNITY. Nothing.

Running out of cigarettes, ideas, and appropriate curses, Butcher worked one more string of ideas linked with Cooper Sams' close call: JUNEAU, WINDSHEAR, ROTOR, DIVE, CRASHLAND, MAYDAY. Each attempt brought up the same response that was burning an image on his screen: ACCESS DENIED.

Butcher slumped back in the old chrome and padded vinyl kitchen chair. "It's right in front of your nose, it always is," he told himself. "Sams always outsmarts himself and comes up with something dumb. What is it this time? What haven't I tried?" Butcher's questions were cut short by a coughing fit that doubled him over on the chair. Recovering, he snapped off the computer and ground his last butt to shreds of tobacco in the ashtray. *Tomorrow*, he thought, *I'm sure I'll get in tomorrow.*

Fifty-one

Beth Scibelli-Cole hated flying on Pacific Pride Airlines. PPA is a barebones, no-frills L.A.-based fleet of 737s linking Southern California with the Bay Area, Las Vegas, Reno, and the Pacific Northwest. Beth often referred to the carrier as "Pacific Prod" because of its cattle-car approach to passenger service. No assigned seats, no first class, no business class; just herd 'em in and pack 'em tight. No meal service; just a tiny bag of pretzels and a beverage—and they never leave the can. And no nonstops to the Northwest from L.A. Every trip to Seattle means a stop in San Francisco, San Jose, Las Vegas or Reno, *and* another stop in Eugene or Portland. And every flight was full to the doors.

Pacific Pride's 737s are painted ocean blue with a trademark gray dolphin leaping over the front cabin doors on either side. Beth considered the leaping dolphin a fitting symbol for an airline that doesn't stay in the air very long between stops. Normal people fly nonstop to Seattle in two and a half hours. Pacific Pride customers must cope with a four-hour, up-and-down milk run. Beth wondered how many people had fainted from hunger on their way north, hoping to subsist on only three tiny bags of pretzels.

But PPA was cheap: $99 one way and $198 round trip to Seattle, nearly half the bargain rate for United, Delta, and Northstar. And cheap was the operative word for this trip. Beth had asked her husband to fly up to Seattle later in the week and be with her until the doomsday flight fiasco was over. He had countered that it was too expensive for them both to go. So Beth had compromised. She offered to give up her $489 business-class seat on a United nonstop for two round trips on the pretzel flight if Cole would take a few days off work and come. He finally agreed. She would go today—Tuesday—as planned; he would fly up on Saturday. But now, as she jostled with the herd down the jetway, Beth feared the next four hours on this cattle car might sour her loving disposition for the whole trip.

At five feet, eleven inches, Beth's game plan on an open-seating flight was to go for leg-room first: bulkhead or window exit seats. But by the time she got inside, the window and aisle seats in those rows were already taken. Middle seats in leg-room rows were her third choice, just ahead of the dreaded middle seat with no leg room. She began to look for an aisle or window seat anywhere, but they were going fast.

Beth made a snap decision. She grabbed an aisle seat at row 8 that others ahead of her had passed up as a bad idea. In the window seat was a mother and infant, and in the middle seat was a squirmy four-year-old boy. Beth judged that a little noise and an occasional heel or elbow in the ribs was better than being sandwiched between two adults, especially if they were men trying to hit on her.

Beth stepped out of the aisle and dropped her briefcase in the seat as other passengers pushed by her. The four-year-old snapped, "This is our seat," then underscored his territorial defiance by flopping one leg across the briefcase. The mother scolded him and snatched his leg back, glancing at Beth apologetically. Beth flashed a smile to communicate "No problem," but thought about reconsidering her choice of seats. By now the coveted aisles and windows were nearly gone. She would have to be happy with 8C.

She slipped out of her fitted brown leather jacket and stowed it in the overhead. She was dressed in tan cotton slacks with a wide leather belt and a green print shirt. Her silky dark hair, which had been growing out since summer, was finally long enough to flip under and still touch her shoulders.

Beth had plenty of work to keep her occupied during the next four hours. But during taxi and takeoff she kept her computer in its case as instructed in the safety spiel. Instead, she tried to make friends with little Lucas in the middle seat. She showed him pictures from her wallet of Princess Di and her puppies, which had all been given away seven weeks after birth.

Occasionally Beth stole a glance at the young mother, who was nursing her two-month-old unashamedly without covering up. Having been through the birthing process with Princess Di, Beth's awe at the miracle of life was acute and her yearning to some day bear a child was increasing. But as she watched the innocent cherub nuzzle and root at her mother's breast, Beth wasn't sure she was quite ready for the drastic transition to parenthood—and the stretch marks that may come with it.

As the plane approached cruising altitude, Beth pulled the computer out of her case and set to work. The baby was asleep on the middle seat, and Lucas was being entertained on his mother's lap with kid-vid books she had brought along.

Beth had put very little time into her doomsday flight book over the last two and a half months, for two reasons. First, after writing up her interview with Cooper Sams and Lila Ruth Atkinson, there wasn't much else to do on the story. Information about the passengers on the flight, including the members of the New Jesus Family and the "guests" who would fill the empty seats, had been withheld from her and every one else. Cooper and Lila Ruth had been adamant that they would not compromise the privacy of those planning to be aboard. And without the human interest angle of the passengers, Beth didn't have much of a book.

Second, with a financial return contingent on securing Cooper Sams' permission to write the book after the Rapture failed to occur, there was no guarantee that the project would generate income. Beth and her husband agreed that it was not wise for her to invest all her time in a project that may eventually net them zilch. So when the National Basketball Association gambling scandal broke open in early December, Beth jumped on it. Her book, *Late Whistle*, documented the investigation of seventeen NBA players and officials for racketeering. It hit the streets four days after the indictments were handed down.

The project kept her occupied from mid-December to the first week of February, even though the dark specter of the doomsday flight was never far from her conscious thoughts. And her fee was sufficient to allow her to proceed with the doomsday flight—something she fully intended to do—even if it never paid off. In the meantime, the two coins of passage sent to her in December by Cooper Sams she kept hidden from her husband until she found the right time to tell him what she planned to do.

While working on *Late Whistle*, Beth flew to Seattle only once—with Cole for the week between Christmas and New Year's. At that time, her request for another interview with the New Jesus people was denied. So she spent several hours with Libby Carroll and Rachel Sams catching up on what they had learned, which wasn't much. Beth and Cole were back home in time to attend the Rose Bowl game, where Cole's alma mater, the UCLA Bruins, was upset by the University of Minnesota Golden Gophers, 24–21.

Even while working on the NBA scandal, Beth made some headway in her understanding of the motivation of the New Jesus Family. "How do intelligent people get sucked into this stuff?" Beth had asked Matt Dugan one night as the Coles and the Dugans ate pie at Posey's Pie House. "How can anyone with half a brain buy this line about Jesus-Brother, earth-sister, and the end of the world? Where do they get this drivel?"

Matt Dugan, twenty-seven, was the pastor of the little church in Santa Monica that Cole and Beth considered their spiritual home base. Matt and Cheryl had fostered a friendship with the newlyweds, which often included a visit to Posey's on Sunday nights for pie and conversation.

"It's hard to figure, isn't it?" Matt had said that night at the table, after a king-sized bite of coconut creme pie.

Beth nodded. "Yes, especially when these New Jesus people seem ready to follow their leaders off a cliff—or in this case, to follow them onto an airplane bound for nowhere."

"And not just this cult," Cole put in, loading up a forkful of peach à la mode. "What about the people who let their kids die of treatable illnesses because they don't believe in medical science? What about people who handle snakes in the name of religion? What about anti-abortion and anti-euthanasia activists who shoot doctors, saying God told them to do it?"

"And what's scary is that they really believe God told them to do it," Cheryl added emphatically. "They're convinced they're doing what God wants them to do, and you can't tell them otherwise."

"It's really awful how Satan blinds people, how he twists a lie so cleverly and skillfully that it looks like the truth to people who don't know any better," Matt said. "That's what we're talking about here, I think. When people ignore the truth, just blow off God's perspective about life and sin and salvation and righteousness, they're prime candidates to be duped by the devil."

"Kind of like that old saying," Cheryl said. "If you don't stand for something, you'll fall for anything."

Matt nodded agreement. "Exactly. If you don't know what the truth is, or if you know the truth but decide not to believe it, you're likely to believe anything that sounds good to you."

Beth said, "So even though the Bible says that the end of the world is something only God knows, Cooper Sams and Lila Ruth Atkinson and their followers ignore it and decide that the Rapture—or Reunion, as they call it—will happen on February 20. And they believe it will."

"*Firmly* believe it," Matt said. "They have quit their jobs and sold their property, just like many other doomsday cults before them. Even though every other prediction failed, they somehow believe they finally got the inside scoop, the true formula, that other groups missed. That's blindness."

Cole said, "How can they be so convinced about something that is so obviously false?"

Matt raised his fork to make a point. "It all goes back to a lie. The devil has tricked these people into believing a lie, and he's using the lie to control their lives and ultimately destroy them."

Beth wore an expression of puzzlement. "So how do they get out of this devilish black hole? Is it a life sentence? Is there any way to penetrate the thinking of people like Cooper Sams and wake them up before it's too late?"

Matt's return gaze telegraphed that he didn't have an easy answer. "I know you can't argue them out of their blindness. The door-to-door cult people aren't interested in dialoguing with you about the truth. Their minds are made up, and if you try to convince them they're wrong, they walk away. I know; I've tried to argue with them. I'll bet the New Jesus Family is the same way."

The words that penetrated Beth most deeply from the mid-January discussion at Posey's came from Cheryl Dugan. "Only Jesus can heal the blind and make them see. It was true in Palestine 2,000 years ago, and it's true today. We may not be able to convince people that they are deceived, but God can. Our job is to pray for these people, pray that God will give sight to their spiritual eyes so they can see the truth. Once they see the truth, the truth will set them free."

So Beth had prayed, during her morning run and sometimes while she was driving in the car alone when thoughts of Cooper Sams and Lila Ruth Atkinson came to mind. It had occurred to her that if God answered her prayers and opened the eyes of the cult leaders, her book about the doomsday flight may go down the drain. But she continued to pray and at the same time collect what little information she could find on the New Jesus Family and the proposed Reunion.

The long flight to Seattle gave her plenty of time to review what she had collected. She had downloaded to her computer every video clip and blurb from the print media she could find on the New Jesus Family, from Carlton Pigg to the "NBC Nightly News," from the *US Star* to *Christianity Today*. She noted that after coining "doomsday flight" and producing two major articles about it, Earl M. Butcher had disappeared from the pages of the *Star*. His byline did not appear in the thirty to thirty-five articles in her doomsday file. She wondered if the writer—someone she had never heard of before the two *Star* articles—had retired on his earnings or was holed up somewhere working on follow-up articles.

Watching video clips on her computer monitor as she munched on her first bag of pretzels, Beth thought about Cooper Sams' invitation to ride along on the doomsday flight. She had gone back and forth on the proposal for two and a half months. Sometimes she regarded it as a tremendous opportunity; sometimes it loomed darkly before her as a tremendous risk.

But the more she prayed for Cooper Sams' blindness to be removed, the less risky it seemed to her to take him up on his offer. After all, the man was going to come to his senses, wasn't he—if not before taking off, certainly before he implemented a diabolical urge to ditch the plane in the ocean? And if his spiritual awakening occurred at the last moment, what better place for Beth to observe it than on the plane?

At least once a week since her interview with the cult leaders, Beth had come within a breath of showing her husband the coins which guaranteed her a seat on the plane. But she couldn't bring herself to do it. Reagan Cole had a lot on his mind—chiefly his stress-filled work with the LAPD, and Beth didn't want him to worry about her. At least that's the logic she employed for remaining silent. What she did not want to admit to herself was the real reason she clammed up in front of Reagan: She knew he wasn't going to let her go, and Beth wasn't ready to take no for an answer.

Fifty-two

Cooper Sams sat down at the controls of *Vanguard*. The cockpit was in near darkness. It was 9:35 A.M., but inside the locked hangar it was black as night except for two security lamps, glowing like two small moons from the rafters high above the 737. The deserted hangar seemed enveloped in the still of night, which is why Cooper had come here. Only the buzzing drone of an occasional Cessna taking off outside disrupted the silence.

Cooper had been awakened at 4 A.M. by sirens in the streets outside the Stouffer-Madison Hotel. From his room he could see smoke boiling from the upper-floor windows of an old office building three blocks away. Unable to get back to sleep during the commotion, Cooper took advantage of the distraction to slip away from the hotel at 5 unnoticed in his black Lexus. He could use the time to think and seek the wisdom of Pathfinder.

He got on I-5 and drove all the way to Bellingham before stopping at a freewayside Denny's Restaurant. Content that he was not recognized, Cooper stayed in the booth alone after a breakfast of sausage and eggs, sipping coffee and watching the drizzle out the window. By 8 he was back on the freeway headed south to Everett for an impromptu visit with *Vanguard* at Paine Field.

Two women had been on his mind since he left the hotel early this morning. Kathy Keene's puzzling defection from the Reunion flight had kept him awake until past midnight, and her face was before him shortly after he awakened to the sirens. He had felt all morning that if he could not talk Kathy into boarding *Vanguard* on February 20, Reunion must somehow be postponed—something he knew was impossible. It didn't seem right to leave without her, any more than it was right for a father to escape a burning house without trying to rescue his daughter. Another call to Kathy's number as Cooper motored south connected him with her machine. Again, he did not leave a message.

The other woman on his mind was his wife, Rachel—or *estranged* wife, as people no doubt called her. He had given the woman plenty of reason to wash her hands of him and bid him good riddance. Pulling the Mercer Island house out from under her without saying anything was admittedly a cruel and cowardly act. His ongoing stubborn avoidance had embarrassed him at times, though he would never admit it.

Yet for the past three months, with Cooper wishing that Rachel would disappear so he was not reminded of his unkind treatment of her, she had seemed maddeningly devoted to him. She sent notes to him at the hotel, about one every couple of weeks. These were not flowery, mushy, sappy sentiments; Rachel knew Cooper gagged on them. But each brief note contained a message of admiration and appreciation, as if he were a model husband involved in the most noble of endeavors.

Rachel never mentioned his involvement with the New Jesus Family or Reunion or his abandonment in her notes. But she always recalled something about him that she appreciated: strength of conviction, pride in his work, diligence, gutsy individualism. Each note took Cooper back to early December in the Family's office and what Rachel told him the last time he saw her: *I don't agree with what you're doing, but I still love you.* And each note closed with the simple, disturbing words: *Yours forever, Rachel.*

In addition to the notes, a small sack of goodies was delivered to Cooper's hotel room every Sunday evening. The sacks contained no note, but the contents—different every week, all items that Rachel knew he liked—clearly identified her as the sender: navel oranges, bananas with plenty of green still on the ends, smoked salted almonds, Payday candy bars, sugarless cinnamon gum, bottles of flavored sparkling water. It had occurred to Cooper that if Rachel was trying to kill him with kindness, her aim was deadly. Every missile of thoughtfulness seared him with the awareness of his cruelty.

Arriving at Paine Field twenty minutes earlier, Cooper had dodged a handful of media people by driving directly to the old Tramco hangar, which was off limits to all visitors. Once inside, he circled *Vanguard* slowly in the dim light, stopping to admire the gleaming 737 from several vantage points. As he did, he realized why Pathfinder had brought him here: a solo rehearsal, a meditative visualization of what was to happen on the evening of February 20, culminating with glorious Reunion at 8:02. So he climbed the portable stairway and entered the cockpit as reverently as a cleric approaching the altar.

Cooper was prepared to sit at the controls in the captain's chair for an hour, as long as it used to take him to fly a nonstop from L.A. to San Francisco. Yet his journey in the cockpit today would be inward only, quietly seeking Pathfinder's approval for his flight plan and visualizing the execution of that plan as the final hour of earthly time ticked away.

Buckling in, Cooper pictured *Vanguard* sitting on the central ramp far enough from the hangar for engine start. He performed the standard captain's flow, moving left to right and top to bottom, touching each dark instrument and piece of equipment from the emergency strap above the side window to the rudder and aileron trim switches on the pedestal between the two chairs. He pretended to enter departure settings in the mode control panel and loaded the flight management computer to coordinate with the flight plan he would file to Juneau, Alaska, a flight he never intended to complete. It seemed only fitting to Cooper Sams that his final flight should head him toward the place where he intersected with his destiny seven years earlier.

Call for clearance, Walt. Cooper imagined Walt Meisner in the seat next to him contacting Paine Field tower. He heard the clearance figures coming through the dead headset nestled over his ears. *Before-start checklist.* He could hear Meisner's ultra-bass voice snap through the items, and he moved his lips soundlessly with each response. Every instrument, every piece of apparatus came to life in his mind's eye as he worked precisely through the steps of preparation.

Cooper continued through every stage of takeoff in his real-time simulation: before-push-back flow and checklist, start clearance, engine start, after-start flow and checklist, taxi clearance. He moved his left hand to the tiller and right hand to the thrust levers, then he saw himself accelerating away from the ramp to the taxiway. The revving of the engines and the exhilarating motion of an aircraft underway seemed almost real.

Turning right on delta taxiway, Cooper rolled past Paine Field's tiny main terminal to the alpha strip alongside the main runway, where he angled north. Rolling past the huge Boeing ramp on the right, he tested the flight controls—ailerons and rudder—as the copilot talked to ground control. He worked through the before-takeoff checklist and takeoff briefing from memory. He would call for a maximum power takeoff in order to enjoy one last time the thrill of hurtling down the runway at top speed. He imagined setting the bugs on the airspeed indicators. He revelled in Pathfinder's hovering presence in the empty cockpit, bringing an eerie sense of realism to the mock flight.

Minutes later he was sitting at the end of runway 16R ready to flip on the landing lights and power the 737-300 to 148 knots and lift her nose to the sky. Instead of the darkened hangar beyond the windshield, Cooper saw 9,000 feet of rubber-scarred tarmac stretched out before him and miles of open sky beyond it. Then he heard the takeoff clear- ance message, almost as clearly as if it had come through his headset: *"Vanguard,* you are cleared for takeoff on one-six right."

It was all there for Cooper Sams right inside the dark hangar. The rush of releasing the brake and feeling the auto throttles take over. The thrill of hearing the engines spool up and sinking back in the chair as the plane began its takeoff roll. The sense of power at drawing back the yoke at rotation speed and pointing his bird into the sky. The sense of godlike mastery at harnessing aerodynamics to conquer gravity and the elements. If regrets were allowed in Parent-God's new kingdom, Cooper knew that his greatest one would be never again flying a 737 after February 20, 2002.

After effecting a U-turn during climb-out to assume a northwest trajectory, Cooper compressed the next thirty minutes in his private simulation. Cruising northward at 35,000 feet along the coast of Brit- ish Columbia was more the airplane's job than his or Meisner's. Dur- ing the real flight, Cooper would likely spend some of this time in the main cabin celebrating the countdown to Reunion with his spiritual Family as Walt Meisner monitored the autopilot. It was for the final thirty minutes of the flight that Cooper would resume control.

Envisioning the aircraft at 35,000 feet at 7:30 P.M. Pacific Standard Time, Cooper disengaged the autopilot and began easing the thrust levers forward. Next Wednesday evening, this simple act would signify the beginning of the end of Cooper's seven-year pilgrimage to destiny. His pulse quickened as he sensed the invisible hand of Pathfinder on his. The two GE engines commenced a transition from monotonous hum to a slowly swelling roar. The readout on the digital mach air- speed indicator, steady at mach .72 — approximately 260 knots at this altitude, comparable to about 300 MPH — for the past half hour, began to climb. But Cooper's gaze was focused on twin EGT gauges in the center of the instrument panel between the pilots' seats. Though dark in the quiet cockpit, the digital gauges glowed brightly in Cooper's imagination.

EGT gauges monitor exhaust gas temperature in the aircraft's two jet engines. Normal cruising temperature for the engines is around 600 degrees centigrade. As Cooper moved the throttles slowly forward, the engines whined louder at the increased workload, and the numbers on the EGT gauges slowly began to rise: 630, 690, 740, 800. Within ten minutes engine temperature had surpassed the recommended maxi- mum — 895 degrees C — and was still climbing. Meanwhile, airspeed had also reached recommended maximum — mach .78 — more than three-fourths the speed of sound, tripping the automatic overspeed warning. An insistent electronic clack sounded in the cockpit, something like loud, rapid castanets. Cooper saw himself calmly open the circuit box and pull the breaker, terminating the clacker. But he resolutely pressed the thrust levers forward, and the numbers on the airspeed indicator and EGT gauges continued to climb toward dangerous levels.

The entire scenario Cooper Sams now imagined had materialized in his mind in late November, the night of the news conference at the Stouffer-Madison Hotel. And the audacity of that seedy *Star* writer, Earl Butcher, had provoked it. His final flight was the perfect way for Cooper to display his faith in Jesus-Brother, Reunion, and *Vanguard*. On February 20, 1995, he had survived a blown engine over Juneau and landed safely to accept his destiny as a leader in the New Jesus Family and the pilot of *Vanguard*. On February 20, 2002, he would wholeheartedly demonstrate the depth of his conviction.

Seconds before Jesus-Brother translated him and his spiritual family from *Vanguard*, Cooper would intentionally sacrifice both engines. What better place to complete the mission than on the way to Juneau where it began. And what better way to commit his life to his savior than to abandon all means of saving it himself.

After fifteen minutes the throttles were wide open. *Vanguard* cut through the thin air at mach .8, approaching critical mach. Exhaust gas temperature had increased to near 1,000 degrees C, 100 degrees beyond recommended maximum. And the roar in his ears, which Cooper remembered vividly from the last time he had fire-walled the engines over Juneau, was deafening.

At .82 mach or critical mach, a 737 begins to buffet. At .84–.86 mach, the buffeting becomes uncontrollable. Cooper was not interested in pushing the envelope to critical mach, transforming *Vanguard* into a vibrating, bone-jarring thrill ride for the last fifteen minutes. But he was interested in pushing the engines to the limit and driving the EGT numbers even higher. So he turned off the encoding altimeter, which transmits altitude readings to air traffic control, and gently pulled back the control wheel to effect a 2 degree climb. He imagined being contacted by ATC saying they had lost altitude reading and instructing Cooper to check the encoding altimeter. As prearranged, Walt Meisner replied that the altimeter was defective and that *Vanguard* was continuing to Juneau at 35,000 feet. In reality, the aircraft was climbing through 36,000 feet on its way to glory.

The more *Vanguard* climbed in the thin air, the harder the engines worked, driving engine temperature toward 1,100 degrees. Meanwhile, the outside temperature at the upper edge of the troposphere was about -58 degrees C. Cooper understood fully that, the moment he shut down the blazing engines, the icy air would flood the vulnerable turbines, which were suddenly without the protection of searing engine heat. The supple steel vanes would expand and harden too quickly, and the turbines would disintegrate in minutes if not seconds. It happened that way by accident to one of Cooper's engines on Flight 202 seven years earlier under much less engine stress.

Under normal circumstances, with two engines suddenly gone, the plane would be stranded aloft without power, doomed to plummet, break up, and crash. It was exactly what Cooper Sams planned in order to validate his certainty at Jesus-Brother's precise, instantaneous appearance in the heavens above the crippled jet. It would be his supreme act of faith.

As the simulation counted down to 8 P.M., Cooper dropped his right hand to the two fuel levers just below the fire-walled throttles. The silence of the cockpit was obliterated by the two engines howling thunderously in his head. The instruments above and below the window seemed surrealistically ablaze, as if every gauge and dial flashed a desperate warning, sensing the plane's impending doom. Cooper's heart raced at the realization that life on Planet Earth was ticking down to its final 120 seconds. Pathfinder seemed to envelop him as he awaited the final moment.

At 8:01.30, he simultaneously snapped both fuel levers to the off position. The thunder of the engines abruptly fell away to a dying whine which was replaced by the eerie whish of air rushing past the cockpit. The 737 was suddenly a giant glider. How long before one engine and then the other blew apart from the radical temperature change? Would they hold together thirty seconds until zero hour? There was no way to predict it, and Cooper knew it didn't matter. He turned his attention to the final ten seconds . . . then five, four, three, two, one.

He envisioned a blinding flash of light. He imagined weightlessness, his body released from the seat and passing through the safety belt and sheet metal of the plane as if through a thin sheet of water. He felt himself soaring without wings toward the brightness, not through subfreezing, oxygen-deprived atmosphere but through fragrant, moist, tropical warmth. *Vanguard* and the earth seemed light years behind him, and Cooper wasn't interested at all in looking back to see what had become of them. All he could see was the brilliance of a thousand suns ahead. All he could hear were the cheers of the New Jesus Family around him as they hurtled gleefully together into the light that was Jesus-Brother.

The splendor quickly disintegrated to reality when Cooper opened his eyes to the darkened cockpit and surrounding hangar. His stomach was in his mouth from the startlingly realistic simulation. He found his hands gripping the control wheel tightly, so he relaxed them and let go. It seemed that every inch of skin on his body was wet with perspiration. He thought he heard the voice of Pathfinder whispering, "Well done. The end is near, and you are ready for Reunion."

Thanks to Pathfinder's presence, the simulation had seemed more real than any virtual reality program Cooper had ever experienced. Then his pulse spiked again at an amazing thought: *Next week it will be no simulation. Next week I will really fly this plane into the light of Jesus-Brother's kingdom.*

Elated but drained of emotional strength, Cooper removed his headset, unsnapped his safety belt, and pulled himself out of the captain's chair. He exited the cockpit and gazed down the long, dark center aisle of the refurbished 737. Once again he flashed on the moment of translation. *One moment, these seats will be full of people. The next moment, the plane will be as empty as it is now.*

As he descended the stairs and walked toward the hangar door, two unanswered questions drifted between him and his joy like clouds dimming the light of the sun. He was not surprised that the questions centered on two women who had been in his thoughts so strongly. *What possessed Kathy Keene to give up her seat aboard* Vanguard? *What possesses Rachel Sams to overlook my faults and love me so devotedly?* Cooper didn't think he could fully enjoy the anticipation of Reunion until he knew the answers.

Fifty-three

"Are you sure you don't want me to stay? I can cancel my trip." Dimitri's blue eyes were intense with compassion.

"For the millionth time, no, Dimitri," Tommy said, tiring of his partner's incessant fawning. "What I want is for you to go knock 'em dead in Houston."

Dimitri winced. "But I hate to leave when you feel so poorly."

"I'm fine, I'm really fine," Tommy insisted. Both men knew that Tommy was *not* fine. Small-boned and slight to begin with at five-seven, in three months Tommy had dropped from 142 to 114 pounds. The purplish tumor, Kaposi's sarcoma, which first appeared the size of a collar button, had spread around to the side of his neck and up to the base of his chin. He never went out in public without a turtleneck shirt covering the tumor. New lesions were popping up weekly on his arms, legs, and torso. The rest of Tommy's skin was a sickly gray-yellow. The infection had also invaded his throat and tongue, making swallowing difficult.

To Dimitri's disappointment, Tommy had steadfastly refused chemotherapy for the tumor. Doctors measured his life in months. Tommy had a much shorter time frame in mind.

"There's beef barley soup in the fridge," Dimitri said, reluctantly picking up his suit bag at the door.

"Wonderful. I love your beef barley soup." In reality, Tommy was eating very little of anything these days.

"And bread. I baked a fresh loaf this morning while you were at the doctor."

"I smelled it coming in. Thank you."

"I'll call you when I get to the hotel," Dimitri promised, opening the door.

Tommy glanced at the watch strapped to his thin wrist. "Your plane gets in at about 9 our time?"

"Yes, 11:10 in Houston."

"By the time you pick up your car and get to the hotel, I'll be asleep. In fact, I'll probably be in bed by 9."

"All right, I'll call you before noon tomorrow—my time, before I go to the theater."

"If I'm out, I'll leave you a message," Tommy said. He already knew he would be out.

"I feel like I'm deserting you," Dimitri complained. "I should be here taking care of you instead of traipsing the country with my show."

"Nonsense. When I know you're doing a show, I feel better. Your success is a miracle drug." It was a lie, Tommy knew. He would miss Dimitri during this last week of his life. But it would be worse if he were around to spoil Tommy's final exit.

Dimitri nodded. Then he kissed Tommy on the cheek and stepped out the door, only to turn around again. "If you need anything—"

"I know, Mrs. McPhee is always home," Tommy finished for him. The widow two doors down had been a willing caretaker for Tommy before.

Dimitri nodded. "You won't do anything . . . foolish . . . will you?" he said softly, unable to look Tommy in the eyes. Dimitri had brought up the topic of suicide before. He was morally opposed to suicide and personally concerned that Tommy might consider it.

Tommy had lied steadfastly if not convincingly on this one. Tommy loved Dimitri, but how and when he departed from this life was his own business. He would make his departure as painless as possible for his partner, but he would not postpone it to protect the older man's beliefs or sentiments. "Nothing foolish, Dimitri," Tommy said, forcing a smile. "Trust me."

Dimitri nodded and left.

Tommy had much to do, but he wasn't about to start until he was sure Dimitri wouldn't walk in on him. So he nuked and ate a small cup of beef barley soup and a half-slice of homemade oatmeal bread for lunch, then rested for two hours. In his weakened condition, Tommy usually spent afternoons lying down, either sleeping or watching TV.

At quarter to three, hopeful that Dimitri was airborne on the first leg of his flight—a San Francisco-to-Kansas City nonstop—Tommy called. When Dimitri assured him that he was somewhere over Western Colorado, Tommy made up a question, something about a bill he wasn't sure Dimitri wanted him to pay. Dimitri told him to pay it. Then Tommy wished him a good flight and signed off.

Well-rested and free of concern about Dimitri, Tommy programmed the music master with three hours of classic tunes by Artie Shaw, Louie Armstrong, and Tommy Dorsey, then set to work. On his computer, he retrieved the farewell letter he had written to his lover and friend of over three years. Tommy wished he could have communicated his affection and appreciation for Dimitri more convincingly, but he didn't have any more energy to put into the letter. So he printed it, signed it, folded it, and propped it up on one of the throw pillows on Dimitri's side of the bed.

Tommy had written nothing about what he planned to do, just that he was going away "until the end." But he did remind Dimitri to follow through with the disbursal of his personal property as they had discussed it—once his death was confirmed.

Next, Tommy packed one small suitcase for his week in Seattle. The main article of clothing was his best suit, which he would wear with a turtleneck for the flight. Tommy had decided to travel light because he didn't have the physical strength to carry more. Anything else he needed could be purchased out of the $2,000 in cash he had withdrawn from the joint account.

Tommy dug out the padded envelope he had hidden deep in his closet, the envelope which was shipped to him from Seattle in early December. The envelope contained a gold and silver coin, each stamped with the same number, and a packet of instructions for arriving in Seattle and boarding *Vanguard*. A cover letter, signed by Captain Cooper Sams, informed him that he would be allowed to board the jetliner for Reunion after the members of the New Jesus Family were aboard. The letter closed with an admonition to confidentiality, an admonition Tommy had followed to the letter.

Tommy had been surprised to hear from Cooper Sams in December. He had been serious about wanting to ride Cooper's so-called doomsday flight, but he wasn't sure Cooper was completely serious about flying, or if he was, that the cops or the FAA or Northstar Airlines or his wife—if he had one by now—would let him pull it off. Furthermore, after his run-ins with rednecked, bigoted, anti-gay Coop the poop at Northstar in Seattle, Tommy was doubtful that Captain Sams would even let him on the plane.

Yet Cooper had called him personally and, with what sounded like a dash of genuine charity diluting his characteristic aloofness, informed

Tommy that he had been providentially selected for the flight. A few days later Tommy found the information packet and coins in a P.O. box Dimitri didn't know about. After reviewing the contents now, he put the envelope in his suitcase and zipped it closed.

Tommy had also hidden in the closet his Amtrak ticket to Seattle, which he had purchased two weeks earlier. For all the miles Tommy had logged in jet aircraft, he had never taken a ride on the train. It was one of the few things he wanted to do just once before he died. So he got the most expensive ticket available for the scenic journey up the Pacific Coast, including a private berth and bath. After checking the departure time, he took the ticket and the suitcase to the front door.

Raul Barrigan's neighbor, a Navajo graduate student at ASU, stuck her head out the door as Raul turned the key to let himself into the apartment. "Hey Raul." Jani always pronounced his name "roll," which Raul found humorous considering that his life for the time being was confined to a wheelchair. "This came for you today," Jani said, waving a brightly colored overnight delivery envelope as she walked toward him. "I told them you were at work, so they left it with me."

Raul received the envelope with curiosity. "Thanks, Jani." He added the envelope to a stack of stuff on his lap—sports jacket, tie, briefcase, mail, newspaper—and rolled through the door. When he saw the return address on the envelope, he quickly dumped everything else on the sofa, went to the dining room table, and switched on the light.

Spreading out the contents before him, Raul was awestruck and motionless for several seconds. The cover letter from Captain Cooper Sams announced that he, Raul Barrigan, had a confirmed seat aboard the New Jesus Family's *Vanguard* for its first and only passenger flight on February 20. The packet of instructions told him where and when to connect with the other passengers in Seattle and urged him to remain silent about his plans to be aboard. And a numbered gold coin bearing the imprint of a Boeing 737 flying into the sun assured Raul that God's call was authentic. Aside from the color, the coin perfectly matched the silver coin he had received in December identifying him as a standby passenger. He was now a space-positive passenger. He had indeed been ordained as possibly the final witness of the Gospel to the blind and misguided passengers of *Vanguard*.

Electric excitement and icy fear battled to rule Raul's suddenly queasy stomach. It was the same sensation he had experienced three months earlier when he received a phone call from the former airline captain in charge of *Vanguard*. After Cooper Sams mechanically explained that Raul had achieved standby status by reason of a random draw, the Phoenix detective almost declined the invitation to board the flight if given the opportunity. It was a crazy idea based on an emotional experience in an unguarded moment.

But in an instant Raul decided to throw out a safe, reasonable fleece. He was not on the passenger list at the time; he was only a standby. *If You want me on that flight,* he had prayed silently, *let me receive a final invitation and a gold coin. If this is a nutty idea I'm dreaming up on my own, don't let my name be selected as a confirmed passenger.*

In order to accommodate a possible positive response, Raul had put in for vacation the week of February 17–24. When asked, he explained that he was driving to L.A. to visit relatives and friends, something he fully intended on doing unless he was divinely directed to Seattle. But with only eight days until departure, he was increasingly doubtful that he would be included on the passenger list. He had begun to make plans to notify his uncle and aunt in Saugus that he was coming and to make contact with his friends Reagan and Beth Cole in Santa Monica.

Several feelings had surfaced, most of them negative, as Raul acknowledged that he might be excluded from the doomsday flight. One was relief at being let off the hook for such a staggering responsibility. Another was disappointment at not being chosen as God's emissary, precipitating a dismal self-doubt that he was not considered worthy of the task. Raul had sensed increasing anxiety that losing this opportunity to prove his faith might further delay his healing.

An even darker discouragement had surfaced over the last few days as Raul's exclusion from the doomsday flight loomed more probable. The life-threatening implications of the event had not been lost on him. And the possibility that he might lose his life in his noble evangelistic effort had become more welcomed than feared. Raul had not accepted the call because he wanted to die, at least he didn't think an inadvertent suicide was part of his motive. But the thought of not receiving his healing and remaining alive to deal with it was producing more disappointment in Raul than comfort.

So the sight of the gold coin on the table was guardedly uplifting. Raul had half a week to get ready to drive to Seattle. Preparations would include writing a will, which he had purposely put off, and writing a letter of explanation to his parents. As he thought about leaving on Saturday, excitement began to melt the remaining icicles of fear within him. Raul pushed away the thought that some of his anticipation was for the wrong reasons.

It was nearly 8, and Tommy Eggers was down to his final task, a telephone call he had been wanting to make—and at the same time dreading—for weeks. With the bubbly exuberance of his life having drained away to its final drops, Tommy's thoughts had turned in surprising new directions. It was one of these pressing thoughts that urged him to reconnect with someone who might be able to help him make sense of these thoughts. So he took the phone to the living room, eased down the volume on Artie Shaw's rendition of "Begin the Be-guine," and dialed.

"Hello." A woman was on the phone, a voice Tommy remembered with pleasantness.

"Mrs. Dukes?"

"Yes."

Tommy hesitated, wondering again if this was a good idea. "Mrs. Dukes, this is Tommy Eggers. I'm an old friend of your daughter, Evie. We were neighbors in—"

"Yes, Tommy," Nora Dukes sang with recognition. "How are you? We haven't heard about you in an age."

"Yeah, I've been . . . busy," Tommy said, purposely vague, "you know how it is."

Nora Dukes laughed. "Oh, yes, I know. Even us retired folks stay pretty busy."

Tommy said, "How is Evie these days?"

"You mean you haven't talked to her?"

"No, not since she moved away from the city."

"You wouldn't recognize her, Tommy," Nora said with an obvious glow in her voice. "She's back to teaching high school English. She's engaged to be married. And she's even singing in the church choir."

"Engaged? Evie Dukes? *My* Evie Dukes?" Tommy said, playing to her maternal pride.

"Yes, and she will hate me if I don't insist that you call her."

"You'll have to give me her number so I can get in touch with her," Tommy said, knowing that he wouldn't. He had tacitly terminated most of his relationships in preparation for his departure, helped in large measure by the fact that many of his friends were avoiding him in his declining health. He didn't want final words with anyone—except Marvin Dukes.

Nora rattled off a telephone number for Evie, and Tommy repeated it as if he were writing it down.

"Would you like to say hello to Marvin?"

Tommy was grateful that Nora spared him asking. "Yes, if he's not busy."

"You know Marvin, he's never too busy to talk," Nora said. "He's out in the shop. I'll buzz him."

Tommy was on hold for less than a minute before Marvin Dukes picked up the phone. In the background Tommy identified the sound of a table saw winding down. The men exchanged the normal pleasant-ries and recalled previous visits in San Francisco. Marvin sounded genuinely happy to hear from Tommy, which is what Tommy expected and hoped for.

Tommy got right to the point. "I wonder if I might talk to you in confidence—you know, kind of man to man." Tommy didn't mean it to be funny, and Marvin didn't take it that way.

"Mrs. Dukes and I don't generally keep secrets from one another, if that's what you mean."

Tommy thought about it a few seconds. "Well, you can tell your wife if you want to, I guess. But this is kind of personal. I just don't want it getting around; you know, to Evie and some of our old friends, at least not right now."

"I understand," Marvin said. "We'll keep it to ourselves. What's on your mind?"

Sparing Marvin the sordid details, Tommy described his history with HIV and AIDS and his rapidly failing health. He said nothing about the doomsday flight or his intention to be on it. He was prepared to be just as misleading with Marvin about taking his own life as he had been with Dimitri—if the subject came up at all.

Had Tommy suspected for a moment that Marvin would scorn him for his unholy, immoral behavior or rail on him as the self-appointed agent of God's righteous judgment, he never would have called. Marvin did not disappoint him. The older man listened respectfully and responded with words of unfeigned sympathy.

"I've never been a religious person, Marvin," Tommy said, concluding his story. "In fact, some people tell me I'm going to burn in hell for the way I've chosen to live my life. But something you used to say has been on my mind lately. I didn't understand it before, but I can't say I was very interested at the time. Now I'm wondering about it."

Marvin's silence invited Tommy to continue. "You used to say something like 'God loves the sinner but hates the sin.'"

"Yes, I still say that."

"Well, how can God do that? I mean, does He conveniently forget about the sin part and send the sinner to heaven, or does He change His mind about the love part and send the sinner to hell? It can't cut both ways."

Marvin Dukes laughed a friendly laugh. "Well put, Tommy. And you're right, it doesn't cut both ways."

"So which way is it? At this time in my life I could use a little advance warning." There was a hint of desperation in Tommy's voice.

"I guess you could say that this is one of those bad-news-good-news situations." Marvin Dukes still sounded rather lighthearted, intimating that he didn't judge the discussion to be as serious as Tommy was making it out to be. "The bad news is that all sinners go to hell. The Bible is pretty clear about that. The good news is that the sinner can be separated from his sin and go to heaven instead of hell."

"Separated?"

"Yes, that's the good news of the Bible, Tommy. The sinner and his sin can be parted by God's grace. At that moment, the sinner is transformed into a saint and his eternal destiny is changed."

"You make sin sound like a bad case of appendicitis," Tommy said with a doubting little laugh. "All you have to do is take out the infected appendix and the problem is solved."

Marvin sounded a little more serious now. "Sin is more complicated than appendicitis, Tommy. But getting rid of it and going to heaven is a lot easier than suffering through an appendectomy."

In fewer than ten sentences, Marvin recounted the simple story which has been heard around the world for over 2,000 years, a story about God and man, sin and separation, redemption and salvation. Tommy had heard the story before, but never more plainly or eloquently told than by Marvin Dukes, who seemed to know the hero intimately. Throughout the story, Marvin stressed that its application—salvation and sainthood—was available to anyone no matter how far they had strayed from God.

Tommy thanked Marvin for the information when it seemed that the man speaking to him on the phone was ready to make like a TV evangelist and call Tommy to the altar. Just before he signed off, Marvin promised Tommy that he and Nora would pray for him and check up on him occasionally. Tommy expressed his gratitude—which was genuine—and hung up. He was sure the Dukes would be sadly disappointed when they heard about his death, and the thought brought him a measure of comfort.

Tommy called for a cab. As he prepared to leave the apartment, Tommy had serious doubts about how he fit into the great story just related to him. Tommy knew that some Bible thumpers, unlike Marvin Dukes, considered his homosexual lifestyle unforgivable. He wondered with irony if his spiritual condition was more like AIDS than appendicitis: preventable but definitely incurable. If he cried out to God for mercy, would the Almighty respond, "Too bad, so sad. Gays pass heaven and go straight to hell."

Tommy reasoned that if he were God, he wouldn't open the door to eleventh-hour penitents. It didn't seem fair to hard-core religious giants like Marvin Dukes. Tommy wondered if he would change his mind on the issue in time to get God's attention before Cooper Sams' 737 reached its final destination.

Fifty-four

Myrna Valentine's envelope from Express Air Delivery arrived on Tuesday afternoon, but she didn't discover it until Thursday morning. The EAD driver was racing to finish his route in record time. When his customer didn't answer the doorbell, he had hurriedly slipped the envelope under the welcome mat, leaving a small corner showing.

But when Myrna and her son arrived home after dark, Guy, scuffing across the porch, inadvertently kicked the envelope fully under the mat and out of sight before Myrna reached the porch. Had the little boy not exposed the envelope on Thursday morning the same way he buried it—by kicking the mat on the way out to the car—perhaps Myrna wouldn't have seen it until she swept the porch in the spring.

"Look, Mommy, a present for me," Guy exclaimed, bending down to pick up the bright pink and green envelope. He gave up the treasure reluctantly at his mother's insistence. The contents of the envelope rocked Myrna emotionally. She was startled, as if suddenly confronted by a masked assassin, a killer she had invited to her home but didn't really expect to come. Myrna held herself together until she had delivered Guy to day care. Then she called her assistant from the car to cancel her morning classes and appointments. Returning home, she popped an extra Darvon and sat down to sort through her feelings about the notice confirming passage on the doomsday flight for herself and her three-year-old son.

It had been a stressful three months for Myrna. Guy Rossovich's deceit had devastated her. His venomous threat to take her son had both enraged her and petrified her with fear. She had quickly realized that her former lover possessed sufficient clout in Southern California to make good on his threat no matter what she did. Every letter from Guy's lawyer—he had sent four of them—about the hearing on March 4 seemed timed to scrape the scabs off the inner wounds and start the bleeding all over again.

Myrna's emotions, held in delicate balance in the best of times with drugs, seemed to spike higher and lower each day. She knew she should see her therapist to evaluate her condition and adjust her prescription. But instead Myrna took matters into her own hands, experimenting with various doses, often making things worse instead of better.

Her intentions about running away to Seattle with her son to hop on an airplane reportedly bound for oblivion changed as wildly as her moods, sometimes several times a week. On some days the idea of intentionally placing herself and her baby in mortal danger in the name of vengeance was abhorrent to her. She sympathized with Guy Rossovich and yearned to comfort him, ready to do anything to heal the rift between them.

But within a few days, when emotionally revisiting Guy Rossovich's heartless rejection and his malicious intent to steal her son, Myrna's attitude rushed hard to the side of revenge and punishment. In those darkest hours, a double suicide on the doomsday flight seemed a welcome means of repaying him for hurting her. A murder-suicide involving all three of them also held a morbid appeal. Myrna had been to the top and bottom so many times on these feelings that she had lost her bearings on what was right.

Unfortunately for Myrna, little Guy discovered the Express Air Delivery envelope from the New Jesus Family on a day when she was scraping the bottom emotionally. Today, the invitation to board the plane named *Vanguard* as a confirmed passenger seemed like the solution to all her problems. The two gold coins, counterparts to the silver coins which arrived three months earlier, gleamed like tokens promising to unlock a painless future for her and her fatherless son.

Ignoring her therapist's standing rule never to make important decisions on a downward swing, Myrna made her plans. It was Thursday, and the flight was scheduled for next Wednesday evening. She and Guy would spend the day with her parents in Astoria on Saturday without telling them anything about Seattle or Vanguard. If the subject came up as a topic of conversation, she would pass off the flight as a joke. It would be a happy day for little Guy's grandparents, constituting a pleasant, final memory of Myrna and Guy for Mark and Thuy Valentine.

On Sunday Myrna would lock up the loft, load her little boy into the Trooper, and leave for Seattle. They would enjoy three days alone together before boarding the airplane, something that would thrill Guy to no end. Myrna hoped and prayed that the rumors about the flight of *Vanguard* were well-founded. She and Guy would ride the plane into the ocean or the side of a mountain, and Guy Rossovich would pay for his hardheartedness and greed with remorse for the rest of his life.

But at the moment, that final vindictive act didn't seem quite enough. Myrna wanted to twist the knife and maximize the pain. So she sat down at her computer to compose a letter to Guy Rossovich, a letter which would be discovered in her apartment after she was gone. *My only regret*, Guy, she thought bitterly as she retrieved a blank sheet of paper to the screen, *is that I won't be here to see you crumble when you realize that you were the cause of your only son's death.*

Beth met Libby Carroll and Rachel Sams at Zelda's for lunch, but only one of the women was eating normally. Beth had postponed the meeting yesterday—their first time together since late December—because she woke up in her Whidbey Island home with a touch of the stomach flu. She was only a little better today, but she didn't want to miss out on an opportunity to touch base with Rachel about Cooper Sams and the doomsday flight. Unwilling to test her queasy stomach, Beth sipped warm lemon water as she talked.

Rachel's appetite hadn't been up to par for weeks, but she worked steadily on a small salad during the conversation. Trying to keep up a brave front, Rachel's perpetual anxiety over Cooper Sams' behavior had taken a toll. Already petite, Rachel had lost fifteen pounds, adding years to her normally youthful face. Libby Carroll, with whom Rachel still lived, had kept gentle pressure on Rachel to eat regularly and take sleep aids if necessary to assure plenty of rest. Rachel readily admitted that if it hadn't been for Libby, who doted on her like a sister and held her accountable like a parent, she would have collapsed in a heap long ago.

Beth warmed her hands by wrapping them around the mug of hot water. "Have you heard anything from Cooper?" she asked Rachel.

"Nothing at all," she replied sullenly. "I keep writing notes and dropping off treats at his hotel, but it's not doing any good."

"You don't know that, Rachel," Libby said, in between bites of Zelda's homemade vegetable and pasta soup. Libby's appetite for a full lunch of soup, salad, and bread did not reflect a lack of concern for her friend, nor was it interpreted as such by the two women sitting with her. "You're doing all that you know to do; we all are. You're remaining positive and doing the right things, even if your heart isn't 100-percent in it. And we're all praying with you that no harm will come to Cooper Sams or anyone on that plane. We don't see much hope yet, but we can't give up now."

As Libby took her next bite of soup, Beth said, "It's like a friend of mine in L.A. says. You may feel like you're tunneling through a mountain of problems all alone. All you have to work with is a puny pickax and shovel. Deep inside the mountain it's dark and hopeless. Your efforts seem so futile. You think you'll never get through."

Rachel nodded slightly, identifying with the scenario.

Beth continued, "What you don't see is that God is tunneling through from the other side, and He is doing the major share of the work. At any moment He may break through the tunnel and the struggle will be over. We have to hang in there and keep doing what we can do, even if it seems pointless."

Rachel nodded again. "I know," she said softly, "but it just hurts. Not only Cooper's aloofness but the telephone calls from the media, the embarrassment, the hate mail I receive simply because Cooper is my husband. I've been off work for over a month, and none of my friends at Northstar have called. I'm a social leper—a freak, and I've done nothing to deserve it."

Beth and Libby hummed sympathetically. Then Libby coaxed Rachel into another bite of salad.

Beth said, "Have you heard anything from anyone since we last talked that helps you believe *Vanguard* will come back safely when the supposed time of the Rapture comes and goes?"

Rachel shook her head.

"Have you heard anything to suggest that the FBI or the cops may ground the plane on suspicion of foul play?" Beth's questions were as much for herself as for Rachel. The gold and silver coins sent to her by Cooper Sams were still tucked away in her wallet. She had determined to say nothing to Rachel or Libby about her desire to be aboard *Vanguard.*

Rachel waited to answer until she had washed down a small bite of spinach, romaine, and tomato with a sip of water. "No. If anything, people seem to be bending over backward to make sure the plane gets off the ground."

"The right-to-die protesters in the city outnumber the right-to-live faction four to one," Libby interjected. "And I read that the FAA has found no cause to ground the plane at this time. Everything seems to be on the up and up."

"Which could be a good sign," Beth added, trying to encourage a positive drift to the conversation. "If the FAA thinks the airplane and crew are airworthy, maybe they're convinced nothing will happen."

"I'm not," Rachel snapped, foiling Beth's attempt. "If *Vanguard* is allowed to take off, I know something awful is going to happen." Beth began to object, but Rachel cut her off. "I believe that scrap of paper I saw the night I found the news releases in Cooper's office was his fanatical declaration of faith. He's going to fly to heaven or crash that plane. I know it. I can feel it."

"Maybe he'll snap out of it in time," Libby said. "It's what we're praying for."

"God can't stop him," Rachel countered. "He gave him a free will, didn't He?"

Beth and Libby looked at each other, then Libby answered. "Yes, I think we all have a free will. God doesn't make anyone do anything."

Rachel said, "Well, you don't know Cooper Sams like I do. Once he's made up his mind to do something, he does it. And believe me, he's not backing down on whatever he has planned for the flight of *Vanguard.*"

The three women were silent as Rachel's words penetrated. Finally Beth spoke. "Maybe God can't or won't change Cooper's mind directly—I don't know. But I think God knows what will influence him to change his mind, and I think He can use those influences if we keep praying."

Libby picked up the thought. "Maybe Cooper's stubborn will is already being eroded. Maybe those notes and candy bars you have been sending him are wearing down his resolve. Maybe the thought of a planeload of people dying in an instant is affecting him, and we just don't see it yet. Maybe he's going to wake up tomorrow morning and realize that the prophet he's been involved with doesn't know what she's talking about. Anything can happen in six days."

Rachel put down her fork, deciding that half a small salad was all she was going to be talked into. "I hope you're right," she said, sounding unconvinced.

"I do too," Beth echoed. At the moment she was thinking more about a gold and silver coin in her possession and what it meant than about Rachel Sams.

In his smoky, unkempt apartment, Earl Butcher began his nightly attempt to hack into Cooper Sams' computer at the Stouffer-Madison Hotel. Cleo Vance at the *Star* had called him again today dangling a nice fee in front of his nose in exchange for the passenger list. She wanted the story for the front page of the Scene section, Monday morning edition, and that meant she needed copy—including all the names—by Friday. Earl promised to come through for her, because he needed the money as badly as Cleo wanted the elusive list. So at 11:40 P.M. he sat down at the computer with a fresh carton of Pall Malls and a butane lighter on the table and a pot of strong coffee simmering in the coffee maker.

Every night had been more frustrating than the previous one. Earl always ran through the passwords he had already tried in case the New Jesus Family had made a change during the day. Naturally, the list of once-tried words grew increasingly longer because it included all the new attempts from the night before. He had over 200 words now which, up until tonight, had failed to unlock the magic passageway into Cooper Sams' hidden knowledge. At least Earl had programmed his computer to try these words automatically so he didn't have to enter each one separately.

Earl Butcher downed a cup and a half of coffee and smoked two cigarettes while the computer methodically tried the 200-plus words. Again, no luck. Earl hadn't expected success, but he cursed anyway when the display invited him to try another word. The blinking cursor was laughing at him, he imagined. "Betcha can't get in tonight either," it seemed to taunt.

Earl was beginning to wonder if he would ever crack the code. Cooper Sams had clearly avoided the obvious in his choice of a password. The possibilities were endless. The former pilot could be using the name of an old girlfriend or a little town in the Ozarks or a kitchen appliance or a song title. There were tens of thousands of parts on a 737, and any one of them could become a password. Or perhaps he simply made up a word: fernbock, zagtag, firepip, essoroo. Earl wasn't looking forward to spending another three hours only to get shut out again.

He typed in the word DOOMSDAY just to make the annoying cursor move. The word had been staring at him from a short stack of newspapers he had moved to a corner of the table during the day. He had discarded the idea that the New Jesus Family would consider for a moment using doomsday as a password. It was a dirty word to them. It would be like a fundamentalist Christian using the word "antichrist" for a computer password, or a Democrat using "Nixon," or an abortionist using "pro-life." Doomsday flight had been Earl Butcher's intentionally offensive tag for the flight of *Vanguard.* No way would the cult soil itself by embracing the word doomsday so personally.

Just for fun, Earl tapped ENTER, then stepped to the range to warm up his coffee. It took about four seconds for the computer to insert a key word, find it not to fit, and flash the message ACCESS DENIED. But when Earl returned to the table fifteen seconds later with a steaming mug in his hands and a fresh smoke between his lips, the flashing red words on the monitor's barren blue screen had been replaced by a white field and a brief main menu. Earl stared at the screen for a moment without sitting down, wondering if he had punched a wrong key and opened a different window. Then he saw the simple four-letter heading to the menu: SAMS.

He put the mug on the table and took a long drag on the Pall Mall. He exhaled a stream of expletives with the smoke before breaking into a hacking, rasping laugh. He had gone from the basement to the penthouse in mere seconds. He had cracked the code. He was inside Cooper Sams' computer.

"Doomsday," he said aloud, still standing and staring at the screen. "Nice try, Sams, you old son of a gun. But not good enough." Within five minutes Earl had found what he was looking for, downloaded it to his own computer, and slipped out of Sams' computer without a trace.

Fifty-five

Cooper Sams dialed Kathy Keene's number at 8 Saturday morning and finally got a live response instead of a recorded message. "Good morning," Kathy said, trying in vain to sound like the phone had not awakened her. Her voice was rough and low.

"Kathy, this is Cooper Sams."

"Cooper? What time—" Her voice broke up, so she stopped to clear her throat. "What time is it? What's going on?"

"I've been trying to get hold of you for days. Where have you been?" Kathy was still trying to clear her throat. Then Cooper heard muffled conversation in the background. He hoped Bradley wasn't going to take the phone. He didn't want to talk to Bradley, whom he knew was the major influence in Kathy's defection.

Kathy came back on and said, "Cooper, have you been drinking."

Cooper cursed silently. "You know I haven't been drinking, not for over three years," he insisted emphatically. "I'm just concerned about you, where you've been, what's happening to you."

The pause told Cooper that Kathy was putting things together. She knew what he was talking about. "Bradley and I have been . . . away. We kind of reached a crisis point in our relationship. We had a lot of stuff to sort through."

"You mean about the New Jesus Family and Reunion?" Cooper stated more than asked.

"Yes, mostly about that."

"So you dropped out of the Family. You decided to forsake your destiny and abandon Reunion."

Kathy sighed audibly. "Yes, that's what I decided. That's what *we* decided—Bradley and I."

"Why didn't you tell me?" Cooper said, unable to conceal his disappointment.

Kathy sighed again, wishing she had just let the phone ring. "It all came up rather suddenly, Cooper, at least the decision did. Actually, things have been bothering me for several weeks. For Bradley it's been even longer."

"What things?"

"Cooper, I don't think it's right to talk about this now," Kathy said. "We have some serious doubts about—"

"You mean *Bradley* has some serious doubts," Cooper cut in curtly. "He's the one who made the call on this, am I right? He's the one who said, 'If you get on that plane, you get on alone.' You backed down on your faith because he gave you an ultimatum—'It's me or the New Jesus Family.' "

Kathy's response was forceful. "Yes, Bradley has very strong feelings, and he made sure I was aware of them. But if you think he made up my mind for me, you don't know me very well. I made the call for myself. I decided that the New Jesus Family is . . . well, it's just not right for me."

"What's the problem?" Cooper insisted.

"I don't feel good about answering that question, Cooper."

"Why not?"

"I don't want my doubts to cause you to question what you believe."

Cooper forced a laugh that was devoid of humor. "If you think your doubts will affect my faith in Jesus-Brother and Reunion, you don't know *me* very well." Cooper was blind to the lie he had just uttered. Kathy's absence from the Family passenger list had affected him in ways he was as yet unable to acknowledge.

"I didn't mean to—"

Cooper talked right over the top of her attempted apology. "Remember, Kathy, I was in the cockpit seven years ago. I saw the miracle firsthand. I was there when the rotor shear took the controls right out of my hands. And I was Jesus-Brother's instrument in the salvation of Flight 202. I was clearly spared for Reunion—we both were. It's our destiny. Don't worry about me; my faith is intact. I just need to know what happened to yours."

Kathy was silent for almost a half minute. Cooper waited. When she spoke, Kathy sounded deliberate and cautious, still trying not to offend. "I'm just not convinced that the New Jesus Family is something God put together. And I'm not convinced that Lila Ruth is a genuine prophet."

"You think she's a fake?"

"I think Lila Ruth is sincere, kind, well-meaning . . . but . . . wrong."

"You think she fabricated everything about Jesus-Brother and earth-sister and Reunion?"

"Not exactly fabricated but—"

"Ms. Atkinson is a great religious scholar, Kathy. She knows the apostles, the church fathers, the mystics, and the sacred writings as well as I know a 737. How could she be wrong?"

"I agree that Lila Ruth is intelligent and well-read in the field of religion. And I believe in God and salvation and eternity like she teaches. I just don't think she has reached the right conclusions on these topics."

"Ms. Atkinson teaches eternal spiritual truth."

"If it's the truth, Cooper, why haven't more people recognized it? In seven years she has attracted and kept less than 100 people, and that number has been shrinking. Bradley and I aren't the only ones to leave recently."

Cooper saw Kathy slipping further away. She was obviously blind to the truth. He knew there was one body of proof she could not deny. "What about the signs?"

"Signs?" she echoed.

"Flight 202. Aircraft N122NS. All the other twos."

"I don't know, Cooper," Kathy answered, sounding unthreatened. "Coincidence maybe."

"Ms. Atkinson knew about my problem with alcohol. She knew that Rachel and I weren't getting along. And remember: You were the one who convinced me that she has a private line to God."

"That's what I believed at the time, Cooper. Right now I'm not sure where she gets her information. Maybe she's psychic. Maybe she has a very knowledgeable spirit guide. Or she's just a lucky guesser. But I don't believe she's a prophet. This Reunion stuff was just getting too weird for Bradley and me."

"But Kathy, what about our Reunion names? She knew I was Vanguard before I told her about the card I found in the blanket. She said, 'Jesus-Brother calls you Vanguard,' just like that, no clues. Nobody can do that with mirrors. She's every bit the prophet she claims to be."

After a moment of thought, Kathy Keene said, "I have two responses.

First, you're the only one in the Family with that experience. Lila Ruth predicted *your* Reunion name, but the rest of us dreamed up our own which she merely confirmed. Again, I don't know how she did it with you, but one lucky bull's-eye doesn't put her up there with Moses and Joseph Smith and Muhammad.

"Second, I hate to say so, Cooper, but your whole argument is centered on the Vanguard thing. It sounds like you're trying to convince yourself, not me, about Lila Ruth."

Kathy's brash statement stunned Cooper speechless for a moment. Then he retorted, "I'm not the one who needs convincing, Kathy. Like I said, my faith is diamond solid. I'm still planning to fly on Wednesday. So are 134 others. I just want you to be sure you know what you're doing."

"I'm following my convictions, Cooper, just like you are. And if you and Lila Ruth turn out to be right, I'll look you up in the great beyond and buy you a drink."

Cooper did not smile at Kathy's attempt to break the tension over their clashing viewpoints. Then he said, "For your information, we may still have some dropouts at the last minute. I'll save an empty seat for you just in case you come to your senses."

"Thanks, but no thanks, Cooper," Kathy said. Then she was serious again. "By the way, there's no truth to the media hype about you turning this into a suicide flight, is there?"

"Is that what Bradley is afraid of? Is that why he put the kibosh on your involvement with the Family?"

"No, Cooper. I told you, my problem is with Lila Ruth Atkinson. I don't think she's the spiritual leader she thinks she is. But I want to be sure that what I'm hearing is nothing but rumor. If Reunion doesn't happen as you think it will, I want to be sure you're bringing those people safely back to Seattle."

Cooper said, "You're underestimating my faith again, Kathy. Reunion will happen as Lila Ruth predicted, so I don't need a contingency plan. At 8:02 P.M., it will be all over."

"So you're not planning to booby trap the airplane or dump your fuel at the last minute?" Kathy's tone wasn't accusatory, but playfully inquisitive.

Cooper flashed back to his moving simulation of Reunion in the hangar on Tuesday. He remembered vividly the brightness of the first seconds of eternity and his total lack of concern for the crippled jet. "Rest assured, Kathy. I'm not going to do anything but point *Vanguard* toward heaven and fly into the arms of Jesus-Brother. And I'm just sorry that you're going to miss out on the most exciting flight of your career."

Beth wandered through her chilly, ranch-style Oak Harbor home as if in a daze. In twenty minutes she had to leave for the two-hour trip to

SeaTac to meet her husband's flight from L.A. But she was still dressed in her pajamas and an oversized sweatshirt. On her feet were two pairs of wool socks, substituting for the slippers she forgot to bring on this trip. Beth couldn't make herself hurry. She was still preoccupied with what she had discovered shortly after she got up.

She stopped at the kitchen sink and absently rearranged a couple of knickknacks on the window sill. She shuffled to the sliding glass door and pulled open the drapes, staring at the lush, wet ferns in the patio without seeing them. She moved to the utility room and started a small load of whites in the washer and watched the wash cycle through the open top-load door. Then it was back to the kitchen, into the guest room, back to the living room. At every stop in her pointless journey Beth seemed paralyzed for several minutes by two words that had changed her life this morning: "I'm pregnant."

When she finally put it together, it all made perfect sense: a queasy stomach—the "flu" that kept coming back every morning, her slightly overdue period, the memory of an intimate encounter with her husband in which they were a little careless. The simple self-test during her first trip to the bathroom this morning confirmed it. The pregnancy kit had been hidden away in the under-sink cabinet for almost three years following an anxious false alarm during a former relationship.

But this time the test strip was a different color. By Beth's calculations, the baby would be born in eight and a half months, around the first of November. *We're going to be parents! I'm going to be a mother! We're going to have a baby!* The realization had stunned Beth into instant lethargy as a web of implications and questions quickly spun around her brain.

It was while Beth was wondering how she would tell her husband the news that the time finally bored through her stupor and snapped her into action. She had to get to the airport. She hurriedly washed and dressed, grabbed her cosmetic kit, and left for the Mukilteo ferry in the old S-10 pickup she and Cole kept on the island for transportation. It wasn't the first time she had put her makeup on while sitting on the ferry.

Beth had less than an hour to make the 10:33 ferry. Racing down highway 525 toward the Clinton ferry dock, Beth sensed a ray of elation trying to penetrate the fog of uncertainty and mild panic which had swept in on her just over an hour ago. She wanted to have children someday, perhaps in two or three years when she felt better prepared, more mature. She remembered seeing the nursing infant on her flight from L.A. Tuesday and lecturing herself that she wasn't ready to assume the important role of someone's parent. But as she drove, somewhere deep inside her a little girl was jumping up and down at the prospect of cuddling a real live doll.

It wasn't until Beth was sitting in line ready to drive aboard the big green-and-white ferry that she considered the implications of her condition on her present assignment. Especially unnerving was the prospect of Cole's response when she hit him with both barrels at once: *I'm pregnant and, by the way, the kid and I will be checking into the Stouffer-Madison sometime on Sunday, and we will be on the doomsday flight Wednesday evening. What will he say? Will he get tough for the first time in our brief marriage and forbid me from boarding the plane? He's always liked my spunk, drive, and independence. Will he try to clip my wings? If he tries, shall I let him get away with it?*

Beth remained in the truck during the thirty-minute ferry crossing to put on her face and fix her hair. Before she reached the Mukilteo dock, she had decided that blasting away with both barrels wouldn't be fair to Cole. She couldn't *not* tell her husband about her morning discovery right away. That would be immoral. Besides, with every mile the excitement of being pregnant gradually overpowered her initial trepidation of being a parent and fitting a baby into her busy life, just as the relentless sun burns through the morning fog.

Yes, she had to tell Cole about the baby, and that would be plenty of news for him today. But the issue of her seat on the doomsday flight could wait a little longer, at least until she figured out how to counteract her husband's objections.

Making a quick stop at the Hallmark store in Burien put Beth a little behind schedule for meeting Cole at the gate. So instead of driving into the parking deck at SeaTac, she knifed between vehicles and pulled up to the curb in front of Pacific Pride baggage claim. She hoped that, since it was Saturday, the airport cops weren't ticketing curbside vehicles. Flipping on the truck's emergency blinkers, she climbed out, locked the doors, and hurried into the terminal building.

Beth found Cole walking down the concourse halfway between the gate and the security checkpoint. They peeled away from the river of foot traffic to enjoy a lengthy embrace.

"How did you enjoy your days of solitude at home?" Beth said after a long, delicious kiss.

"I hated it."

"Good. How did you sleep without me?"

"Lousy. I hate sleeping alone." Cole kissed his bride several times on the cheek.

"*Very* good. And how soon do you want me to go away again without you?"

"At least a jillion years; make that a megajillion."

Beth smiled, then kissed him lightly on the tip of the nose and on the lips. "Congratulations, Detective Cole. You just passed the newlyweds compatibility test with flying colors."

"What's my prize?" Cole teased. "There's got to be a prize for such a lofty achievement."

"How about a lifetime supply of love and tenderness," Beth cooed.

"Wow, that's a pretty good prize, especially since I've only been a newlywed for, er, 124 days."

"Oops, sorry, the correct answer is 125 days. You just lost first prize."

Cole screwed his face into a mock frown. "What's second prize?"

"It just happens to be two lifetimes of love and tenderness," Beth said, smiling.

Cole kissed her again. "Well, since I have a two-lifetime supply, I'd better get started. I don't want to waste any."

Beth giggled. "Plus, you have to—I mean, you get to—take me out to lunch on the way back to the island. That's part of the prize."

"Great idea," Cole said, picking up his carry-on bag and taking Beth's hand. "I've only had three dinky bags of pretzels all morning."

At Zelda's, Cole ordered a chili burger and Beth ordered a salad with no dressing. "No dressing?" Cole said after the server left. "You always have dressing. Lite Italian or honey dijon."

Beth didn't want to give away her secret quite yet. "You know, the stomach flu I told you about on the phone?" she said. Then she hid her smile behind a sip of ice water.

"Ah," Cole responded, nodding.

Then Beth pulled two greeting cards out of her handbag. She did a good job of suppressing a broad grin of excitement at her announcement. "I picked up a couple of cards today, one for your mom and one for my parents," she said, sliding them across the table to her husband. "What do you think?"

"Cards? What's the occasion?" Cole glanced at the cards without really seeing them.

"Reagan," she scolded playfully, "just read the cards and tell me if you think they're all right."

"I trust you, Babe," Cole said. "If you like them, I like them."

Beth glowered at him. "OK," he acquiesced, picking up the cards, "I get it. Another part of the newlywed test, right? Showing interest even when I'm not interested."

Beth said nothing as Cole studied the first card. "Mm, nice flowers," he said. Then he read the inside sentiment aloud. " 'Congratulations to the happy grandmother.' This must be for my mom."

"Yes, I picked that out for Jackie."

"So one of my sisters is having another baby," Cole postulated.

"Could be," Beth said vaguely. "Now look at the one for my parents."

Cole dutifully examined the second card. "Nice design, but I like the flowers on the other one better." He opened the card and read, " 'Sharing in your joy as new grandparents. Congratulations.' "

Beth watched him study the card as a lump of joy began to swell in her throat. She could almost read the progression of his thoughts: *Another grandparent card. Funny, Jack and Dona Scibelli don't have any grandchildren. In fact, they don't have any children except Beth. So this card is a joke because Beth isn't . . .*

When Cole snapped up his head to look at Beth, her expression blurted out the secret totally. Her eyes glistened with tears, and her mouth was formed into a broad, tight-lipped grin as she gamely held back a joyous emotional outburst.

"Beth, are you saying . . . I mean, are you . . . that is, are we . . ."

Beth just kept nodding her head until Cole was bug-eyed and speechless. "I just found out this morning," she said as small tears escaped both eyes and traced the contour of her cheeks to her chin. "I hope you're not disappointed."

"Are you sure? Could it be a mistake?"

Beth laughed a crying kind of laugh. "I guess I should have expected that from a detective. You want ironclad proof. Yes, Reagan, I'm sure. The test I took is 98.7 percent effective. I'll go to the doctor of course, but—"

Out of sheer happiness, Cole lunged across the table to embrace Beth. In the process he knocked over both glasses of ice water, drenching the two greeting cards.

"Disappointed? Babe, I'm thrilled. I can't believe it. I—" The joy choked off his words.

Beth felt the ice water cascading from the tabletop onto her jeans, and she was sure her husband was getting soaked too. But Cole wouldn't let her go. Beth knew this would be a laughable memory shared among family and friends for months: When Beth and Reagan found out they were going to have a baby, they both wet their pants!

Beth reveled in her husband's embrace. She hoped he could be only half this happy when she got up the courage to tell him her second big item of news.

Fifty-six

Delta's Sunday morning nonstop from Atlanta, a jumbo L1011 with only eighty-five passengers aboard, hit the runway hard at Seattle-Tacoma International Airport. The jolt awakened the first-class passenger in seat 6B, Walter Meisner. En route, Walt had survived three Jack Daniels doubles and a rum and Coke only to crash halfway through a double cognac an hour and a half out of Seattle. Assured that his passenger was zonked for the rest of the ride, the flight attendant had stowed 6B's service tray, reclined his seat, wedged a pillow between his head and seat 6A—which was unoccupied, and draped him with a blanket. Meisner never stirred. During final approach, the flight attendant pulled the man's seat forward and fastened his seat belt as required. Walt Meisner remained oblivious to the outside world until the abrupt touchdown.

Those who knew Walt would agree that the former A-6 pilot, former Northstar first officer, and current Dixie Air Services captain had let himself go over the last ten years. The large-boned, square-shouldered, hale-and-hearty Navy colonel of the '80s had entered the third millennium round and soft. His square, jutting chin now rested on a roll of fat. His once rugged physique was obscured by a layer of blubber and a beer belly. Thanks to the genetic kindness of his maternal grandfather, Walt still sported a full head of straight, gray-white hair. But he was at least a month overdue for a haircut, and this morning shocks of unkempt mane flopped over his forehead and ears.

Those who knew Walt would also agree that the man had given up on life in the last few years. The move from Federal Way to Atlanta had decimated his family. The advancement of Jeannie Meisner's MS had led to her being institutionalized shortly after the turn of the millennium, a financial burden Walt found difficult to bear. Jeannie's physical decline was exacerbated, the doctors said, by depression at being uprooted from her family home in the Northwest and transplanted to the humid, unfamiliar Southeast. Walt had succeeded in getting five children through college, only to see them all return to the West Coast, leaving him alone to care for Jeannie.

Walt Meisner had tried in vain to get back West. But his age and less-than-sterling performance record had all but condemned him to finish his flying career with Dixie Air Services, where he was at least tolerated. Meisner feared that his Navy pension and limited Dixie Air pension at forced retirement this year would be swallowed up by Jeannie's medical care. Nearing age sixty, Walt faced the bitter prospect of having to find a ground job to support Jeannie until she finally passed on.

He also found himself battling an ugly reality: The sooner his wife died, the sooner the burden would be lifted. The financial pressure added to the agony of watching Jeannie waste away had gradually eroded personal restraints between him and alcohol.

The serendipitous reconnection with an old coworker from Northstar had seemed a godsend to Walt Meisner. In his addled brain, the so-called doomsday flight promised a solution to his major problems and a fitting end to his miserable life. So, after leaving written instructions for Jeannie's care in his safety deposit box, Walt had splurged for a first-class upgrade on the discounted Delta industry ticket and headed for Seattle and a reunion with Cooper Sams.

Once Delta 806 was parked at the gate, Walt struggled into his rumpled suit coat, grabbed his flight bag and a small suitcase, and trudged up the jetway into the terminal, speaking to no one. After a few minutes in the restroom straightening his tie and brushing his hair back with his fingers, he found a cab.

"Take me to the corporate offices for Northstar Airlines, Military Road and 200th," Walt instructed the driver as he tossed his bags across the back seat and climbed in. His voice had the low droning quality of an old B-17 engine.

"This is Sunday, sir," replied the middle-aged Pakistani driver as he activated the meter. "The building will be closed."

"I know that," Walt rumbled. "I just want to see the place. Then I'm going into downtown Seattle."

"Yes sir," the driver sang happily at the prospect of a $30 fare.

The dinged-up, dark-green Ford station wagon exited the airport onto Pacific Highway, sped two miles south to 200th Avenue, and turned left. In less than a mile the driver turned into the deserted, rain-slicked parking lot of Northstar's corporate headquarters at the southwest corner of 200th and Military Road, overlooking the onramp to southbound Interstate Five.

"I just want a good look at the building," Walt said to the driver as he stared out the window. The Pakistani accommodated him by driving slowly across the parking lot, stopping occasionally when his passenger leaned toward the window for a closer look.

The modern building, built in 1999, was low-slung, sprawling, and bordered by towering conifers. Its unobtrusive design helped the structure blend into the surrounding residential neighborhood while at the same time conveying the feel of corporate pride and success. Walt identified the main entrance just south of an imposing representation of the Northstar name and logo. He assessed that the row of large windows across the uppermost third floor overlooking the parking lot and freeway comprised the offices of Northstar's chief executives. It was this brain trust, Walt knew well, who had repeatedly denied his application for captain.

As the cab rolled by the main entrance, Walt stopped the driver. "Wait right here for a second," he said as he stepped out. A steady mist was falling from the leaden sky, but the large man showed no concern about his suit getting wet. Hands in pockets, he ascended the broad steps to the oversized glass doors and peered inside. Then he strolled the paved walkway across the length of the building along beds of lush green shrubs.

Finally, Walt walked to the east end of the parking lot where it dropped off to the freeway onramp. He stood at the fence staring first toward the eastern horizon and then back to the west at the building. Meanwhile the cab's engine purred at idle, the meter continued to click, and the Pakistani driver beamed.

After about twenty minutes, Walt returned to the cab. His hair was matted wet, and the shoulders of his jacket were dark with moisture. Content that he had seen what he wanted to see, he instructed the driver, "Stouffer-Madison Hotel, downtown."

Six hours later, Raul Barrigan guided his big Chevy Caprice out of the Arco station at Fife, south of Tacoma, and back onto northbound I-5. He had hoped to be in Seattle before nightfall so he wouldn't have to find the hotel in the dark. But early this morning, the Siskiyous in Northern California had been treacherous with snow and ice, passable only with traction devices. It took him an hour Saturday night to locate a set of chains for his car in Redding, where he spent the night. Then he wasted an hour early Sunday morning alongside the freeway outside Dunsmuir trying to chain up the Caprice himself.

Finally Raul acknowledged that his inexperience at the task combined with his handicap was a definite hindrance to success. He finally allowed a helpful CHP officer to call in a tow truck driver to do the job, which ate up another hour. Then in Ashland he was delayed again stopping at a service station to remove the chains. So at just past 6 P.M. he was still almost an hour away from downtown Seattle at a time when he had hoped to be checked in at the Stouffer-Madison.

Raul consoled himself that he had still made the right choice of routes from Phoenix to Seattle. He would have preferred to take I-17 and I-15 north through Arizona and Utah to I-84, which angles northwest across Idaho into Oregon. But mid-February is not the time to take the scenic route if you're interested in making time. The chances of being delayed by winter weather are much greater via the higher elevation route than through California and Oregon—the often troublesome Siskiyous notwithstanding. So Raul had taken I-10 west to L.A. and I-5 north to Redding on Saturday. Even though he was behind schedule, he was grateful that the worst was behind him.

Raul switched on the wipers again. They had been needed almost constantly since he left Eugene, Oregon. Holding the steering wheel and combination accelerator and brake with his left hand, he began another search of the AM and FM radio bands for an inspirational program: a local Sunday evening church service, a syndicated Christian broadcast, a program of traditional or contemporary Christian music. The closer Raul drew to his destination, the more he sensed the need for inner strength. And for the past two days, the radio was his only outside source of inspiration.

Raul had not listened to the radio much since leaving Phoenix. He had spent most of his silent drive time thinking and praying about his assignment in Seattle. He was certain that he was supposed to board the doomsday flight along with its mislead passengers. The gut-wrenching vision at Echo Canyon Park three months earlier had convinced him that something had to be done to reach out to these lost souls. The packet from Captain Cooper Sams that arrived Tuesday was clear confirmation that he was the one to do it.

But was Raul the only one involved in this divine rescue attempt of souls? The question had come to him several times over the past five days, and he didn't know the answer. Perhaps God had miraculously prepared the way for other people like him to board the plane, like a band of spiritual guerrillas infiltrating the devil's death flight in order to bring the good news to the cult members.

If there are others, Raul found himself thinking yesterday somewhere between Sacramento and Red Bluff, *they may be like me: damaged merchandise, people no longer capable of fulfilling their primary calling, just as I can't be God's agent among the San Francisco Giants. God may be putting people on the plane who are blind or deaf or crippled or scarred in some way. Just in case the plane does crash, as many people seem to think it will, God won't lose His best players.*

Raul had rebuked himself sternly for such an unholy thought. He didn't want to believe God was putting him on the doomsday flight because he was of little use to anyone, yet he couldn't escape the logic of such a plan. He had thought about old war movies where the wounded soldier stays behind to hold off the enemy squad while his buddies make good their escape. It made sense. If the poor guy gets killed, no great loss; he is already half dead anyway and of little use to his fellow soldiers. In some of his darker moments since the accident, Raul had wondered if dying in some noble and dangerous endeavor wouldn't be better than spending the rest of his life in a wheelchair waiting for a recovery that might not come.

Or perhaps Raul was God's lone agent in this caper—like John the Baptist, the voice of one crying in the wilderness. He liked this idea best. It was a test of faith, he thought, an opportunity to prove that he was yet willing and capable of making a significant impact for God. In Raul's ideal scenario, he would singlehandedly succeed in turning many New Jesus Family members to God before the Rapture prediction failed and the plane returned to the airport. In response, God would touch him. Raul imagined himself walking off the plane under his own power, his legs restored to full strength. It was this mental image that had kept Raul motivated during the last thirty-six hours when doubts hovered near.

Whether Raul was the lone witness on the plane or one of a company of witnesses, he still was clueless as to what he was to do and when and how he was to do it. Having been in Sunday School and church since infancy and well trained as a member of the campus outreach ministry at Arizona State, Raul knew what to say to people about sin and salvation and getting ready for eternity. He knew the right Bible verses to read and the right questions to ask.

However, once Raul was out of his wheelchair and strapped into a seat, his access to passengers aboard the airplane would be limited. *Shall I request—or even demand—access to the public address system in flight?* he pondered for the umpteenth time during his journey north. *Shall I try to talk to as many passengers as possible in the hotel or in the terminal before boarding? Shall I recruit someone to pass out the leaflets I brought, then wait for people to come to me? Or shall I just take the experience as it comes and make the most of any and every opportunity?*

Raul still didn't have the answers. The only thing he knew for sure was that he would be at the hotel in about an hour and begin the most bizarre and unpredictable chapter to date in his young life. And his greatest hope was that his efforts be pleasing to the only one who could get him on his feet again.

Cooper Sams welcomed his copilot into his private suite with a warm handshake. Walt, who had changed into faded cords, a sweater, and loafers when he arrived, definitely looked like a junior officer next to Cooper, who wore expensive slacks, shirt, tie, and sweater vest.

"Did you have dinner?" Cooper asked, ushering Walt into the living room where two other guests sat waiting. They were as smartly dressed as their host.

Taking in the unexpected sight, Walt's look of chagrin exposed his sudden wish that he had worn his freshly pressed suit to the meeting. "Dinner? Yes, downstairs," he answered, not knowing what to do with his hands.

Nodding toward the elegantly dressed female guest sitting in a wing-back chair, Cooper said, "Walt, I'd like you to meet Ms. Lila Ruth Atkinson, our spiritual leader. Ms. Atkinson, Walt Meisner, my first officer."

Lila Ruth smiled and reached her hand toward Walt without standing. Walt approached and shook it. "It's a pleasure, ma'am."

Turning toward a gaunt, sallow-skinned, older gentleman on the sofa, Cooper said, "And this is Mr. Gavin Cornell. You probably remember him from the movies. I invited Mr. Cornell to ride the jump seat in the cockpit with us."

Cornell struggled to his feet and flashed a welcoming smile. "How do you do, Mr. Meisner," he said in polished stage diction. The hand he offered was gnarled and grotesquely swollen at the joints. "I'm thrilled to be riding up front with you fellows."

Walt took the hand lightly by the fingers for a quick shake. "Hello, sir. I've enjoyed your movies," he said, concealing his shock at seeing the once dashing screen hero in such ill health.

Cooper motioned his guests to be seated. "Can I get you anything,

Walt? Coffee? Tea?" A silver service set was on the buffet. Each of the guests had a china cup nearby.

"A brandy would be nice," Walt answered hopefully.

"I'm sorry, Walt," Cooper said. "I don't keep a bar in the room. You may want to visit the lounge later."

"No problem, Coop," Walt returned, looking a little embarrassed again. "Nothing for me, then."

"I'll join you in the lounge, my good man," Gavin Cornell piped up cheerily. Then he added with a wink, "It seems that our esteemed religious hosts are guilty of what we heathens call the unpardonable sin: temperance. We will have to seek the light on our own."

Walt joined Gavin in the laughter. Cooper and Lila Ruth smiled benignly.

After the perfunctory small talk about the hotel's accommodations and food and the growing number of gawkers populating the lobby, Lila Ruth took control of the conversation. "Why did you decide to join us, Mr. Meisner?"

Walt folded his arms across his protruding belly. "Well, Coop and I go back a few years. So I thought if he was involved with your organization, it had to be OK."

"Do you believe in Reunion?" Lila Ruth continued, appearing to look deep inside the man.

Walt shifted on the chair and glanced at Cooper to evade the penetrating gaze. "To be honest with you, ma'am, I don't know if it's going to happen like you people believe. But then again, it sure could. Like I say, I trust old Coop here, and I'll try anything once."

"My sentiments exactly, Mr. Meisner," Gavin Cornell cut in emphatically. "Whether we meet the Son of God in the air as they claim or some other glorious fate awaits us, I believe Captain Sams will do right by us, don't you?"

"Er, yes sir," Walt said, trying not to sound too enthusiastic.

Lila Ruth was not distracted by the interruption. Still boring in on Walt Meisner, she said, "Do you believe any of the nonsense in the media about our journey being some kind of suicide flight?"

Walt dropped his head as if contemplating a deep thought. After several seconds, he looked up and said, "Ms. Atkinson, I guess I don't believe or disbelieve what the media says about the trip any more than I believe or disbelieve what you say. But if Cooper Sams is ready to go, that's good enough for me. I'm ready to go."

Lila Ruth trained her next question on him like a gun, as if a wrong answer would provoke her to pull the trigger. "Mr. Meisner, do you have any reasons for wanting your life to end next Wednesday?"

Walt pondered again for several seconds, but this time he matched the woman's invasive gaze with one of his own. "Doesn't everybody?" he said at last.

The room was a vacuum of silence as each occupant regarded the exchange and anticipated the next comment. Finally Lila Ruth broke the tension by standing. The three men respectfully followed her up. Directing her words to Gavin Cornell, she said, "I'm sure Captain Sams and Mr. Meisner have much to discuss concerning their duties. Perhaps we should allow them to do so."

A professional at picking up cues, Gavin the actor chimed in, "Very good, my dear woman." The two of them moved toward the door, and the pilot and copilot followed.

Lila Ruth turned to Walt and gripped his hand firmly. "Thank you for being honest, Mr. Meisner," she said sincerely. "We're privileged to have you in the copilot's chair for Reunion." Walt nodded his thanks, and Lila Ruth left for her quarters.

Gavin Cornell said, "I'll save a table for us in the lounge, Mr. Meisner. Thank God these old hands of mine can still lift a martini glass." Walt smiled his acceptance of the invitation, and Cornell limped away down the hall.

"I guess I passed muster," Walt quipped as they returned to the living room. "That boss lady of yours asks tough questions."

"Ms. Atkinson was merely curious," Cooper responded. "Your place in the cockpit was never in doubt. You're under my supervision."

Seated again, the two men talked. Walt tried to loosen up the serious captain by recalling some of their adventures at Northstar. Cooper didn't seem interested in talking about the past. Nor did he have much to say about preparing for the flight. He explained that he would file a flight plan for Juneau, Alaska and that they would take off from Paine Field at about 7 P.M. on Wednesday. Then he quickly changed the subject, asking about Jeannie Meisner. Walt gave the dismal report.

The conversation lagged, and Walt realized that Cooper was ready for him to leave. Walt had not remembered Cooper to be a sparkling conversationalist, and he seemed even less so tonight. The copilot wasn't excited about joining Gavin Cornell in the bar, but it was time to go, and he was anxious for a drink.

Before he left, Walt posed two questions he had come to ask, even though he didn't expect to receive a satisfactory answer for either. "Level with me, Coop: Are you planning to dump this plane into the ocean or something if, you know, your savior doesn't show up? It doesn't matter to me, if you know what I mean. But I think I have a right to know."

Cooper's thoughts seemed to be elsewhere. It took him a few seconds to acknowledge the question and respond. "The only thing I'm planning, Walt, is to meet the savior in the air at 8:02 P.M. Pacific Standard Time. He promised to be there for us, and I promised to have the Family there for him. It's my destiny. I have no other plans." Cooper stood, clearly indicating he was done talking.

On the way to the door, Walt asked his second question. "I'd still like to take your airplane up for a spin tomorrow or Tuesday. It would mean a lot to me. How about it?"

"I understand your eagerness to fly, Walt," Cooper said, opening the door for his guest, "but it's out of the question. There are too many crazy people out there who would like to take a potshot at us. If it's any comfort, you'll have the controls for a while after takeoff. That will have to suffice."

"Well, you're the captain," Walt said with a sigh. "But if you change your mind, just say the word."

Cooper nodded. "Good night, Walt," he said, closing the door.

Walt moved his large frame hurriedly down the hall toward the elevator on a beeline to the lounge. *No, you* don't *understand my eagerness to fly, Coop,* he argued silently. *And when you do, it will be too late for all of us.*

Fifty-seven

Sales on February 18, 2002 began like any other Monday for the national satellite daily, *US Star*. But by 3 P.M. Pacific, every available copy in America had disappeared from the racks. It all started when several live morning talk shows across the country reported that the *Star* had swiped and printed in Monday's edition the entire passenger list for the much-maligned, often-ridiculed doomsday flight of Seattle's New Jesus Family.

News of the cult's proposed end-of-the-world antics had captured national media attention in late November when the *Star* ran two titillating stories by Earl Butcher. The public was morbidly enchanted by a group that, according to Butcher, allegedly planned to commit mass suicide aboard the doomsday flight if Jesus did not appear as they expected. But like every tantalizing news item, the cult became commonplace as the ears of the nation itched for something new. The New Jesus Family and the doomsday flight had faded to the back page of the print media and virtually disappeared from TV.

But with "doomsday" drawing near, the public's curiosity over the kooks in Seattle had begun to rekindle during the last two weeks. The article in Monday's *Star* was to America's curiosity what a lighted match is to a puddle of gasoline. Interest in the flight, which was again being sensationalized as a possible mass suicide, suddenly exploded with the unauthorized release of the names and ages of 135 confirmed passengers and 9 alternates.

Awareness of the article spread across the country from east to west like a range fire driven by high winds. Those aroused by such inflammatory topics rushed to the newspaper racks with one question in mind: Do I know anyone on the list: a celebrity? a coworker? a friend? a family member?

The story splashed across the entire front page of the Scene section. The headline was equal in size to the *Star's* front-page banner in November of 1998 reporting the assassination of three U.S. Supreme Court justices: "Secret cult list exposed: Former star, children included on doomsday flight." Photos on the page included Captain Cooper Sams, Lila Ruth Atkinson, actor Gavin Cornell, and a never-before published picture of *Vanguard,* the Boeing 737 many suspected would become the coffin for 135 sadly misinformed religious zealots.

There was no byline on the article, perhaps to shield Earl Butcher from a libel suit. But a sidebar statement by the newspaper's legal counsel strictly prohibited the copying, electronic transmission, or broadcast of anything but small excerpts from the article and list of names. Anyone driven to possess a copy of the complete list had to buy a paper or get the information illegally. Both options were abundantly employed.

However, to say that by Monday night *everyone* in the U.S. knew about the *Star* article or prized a copy of the celebrated passenger list or gave credence to the New Jesus Family event would be a gross misrepresentation. Large pockets of the population didn't hear about the article, or they heard but refused to rush to the news racks, or they bought papers but blew off the story as they would a report of the reincarnation of Elvis. Yet a sufficient number of people were captivated by the story or personally impacted by the names on the list to make some residents of Seattle and Everett, Washington wish they had sabotaged the *Star's* presses Sunday night.

Mitchell Schetky's home phone started ringing before 6 A.M. Monday. The operations supervisor for Paine Field was in the middle of his early morning workout on the power stairstepper when the first call came in. It was from an old Navy buddy in Baltimore, who had tipped Mitchell off about the previous *Star* articles. Robby figured Mitchell would want to know that the *Star* had struck again. Mitchell thanked him and hung up. But instead of going back to the stairstepper, he headed for the shower, cursing under his breath.

Mitchell's sleepy-eyed wife shuffled into the steam-clouded bathroom. "Who was on the phone? Why are you in the shower so early?"

"That was Robby Wenstadt," Mitchell called back from inside the stall. "He says the *US Star* printed the names of the *Vanguard* passengers. One of them is an old movie star—Gavin Cornell. It's all over local radio and TV back there."

"Which means it will be all over radio and TV here in a matter of hours," Jo Schetky said.

Mitchell's muttered curse was overpowered by the noisy shower spray. "Just what I need is more publicity. That list was supposed to remain a secret until the plane was gone. Now the world is waking up to read the names of the people invading my quiet little airport to board a suicide flight. Who knows how many distraught friends and family members are going to show up to rescue their loved ones from this screwball cult."

"Or try to get a last look at Gavin Cornell," Jo added.

"Yeah, or get a picture of that beautiful 737 while it's still in one piece."

"So you're going in early," Jo verbalized the obvious.

"Right. I have to huddle with Weldon and retool our security plan. I can see the crowds already, swarming the taxiways and runways."

"Can you call in more police?"

"I'll take anybody in uniform I can get: firemen, national guard, private security guards . . ."

"I know a few Cub Scout den mothers with uniforms," Jo injected with a laugh. She was good at helping her husband keep things in perspective with her humor.

"Ha! Send them down, and have them bring their little monsters—in uniform, of course."

Jo ran a brush through her hair. "When will you be home?"

Mitchell cursed again, the light side of his predicament suddenly buried under a cloud of responsibility. "If I'm lucky, midnight— Wednesday night."

At 5:25 A.M. Eastern, the usual twenty-four copies of the *US Star* were loaded into the coin-operated newspaper rack next door to the Garden View Care Center in Belvedere Park, Georgia, an Atlanta sub-urb. An orderly arriving for work just before 6 bought one, saw the article about the doomsday flight, and excitedly told the departing graveyard shift about it. Six more copies were bought by them before they went home. The rest of the morning shift took another four copies. By the time the afternoon aides arrived for work, the *Star* rack was empty.

Like so many of the patients in the care center, the bedridden wom-an in room 144 cared little about what was happening in the outside world. She read no newspapers and watched no television. Jeannie Meisner had been moved to Garden View from a smaller facility only two weeks earlier. Ironically, most of the staff members perused the list of names on the cover of the Scene section, and no one noticed that the first officer on the doomsday flight had the same last name as one of their newest patients.

Shortly after 10 on the West Coast, LeAnn Meisner, twenty-five, walked through the reception area of the Carlsbad, California bank where she worked as deputy loan officer. The youngest of Walt and Jeannie's offspring, LeAnn was on her way out to get coffee when she spied the bold *Star* headline about the doomsday flight. Intrigued by the story due to her father's background in the airline industry, she took the Scene section to scan as she walked to the 7-Eleven next door.

Halfway across the parking lot, LeAnn stopped abruptly. "O God, no!" she gasped when she saw the familiar name. Racing back to her desk, she called her older brother, Keith, in Santa Ana. He hadn't seen the paper. They tried to reach their father at home without success. Then they conference-called the other three siblings, all in California, and broke the news. They agreed that Dad must have snapped under the stress of caring for Mom. Each blamed the others and shouted and wept and finally confessed a measure of fault.

After thirty soul-baring minutes they came up with a plan. The two brothers, Keith and Warren, would fly to Seattle immediately to look for their father. LeAnn would catch the first plane to Atlanta to be with their mother, whom they agreed was as yet unaware. The other two daughters, at home with small children, would stand by the phone and pray that Walt Meisner would come to his senses and walk away from the crazy cult before something terrible happened.

Dimitri Arantes, still in Houston hovering over his production of *Guys and Dolls*, listened to the chatter about the *Star* article in the hotel restaurant while eating a late breakfast. When he overheard that a list of confirmed passengers for Wednesday's doomsday flight had been published, he had a chilling premonition. Leaving the restaurant immediately, he bought one of the last copies in the hotel lobby but retreated to his room before opening it.

Running his trembling finger down the list of names, Dimitri found what he knew would be there: THOMAS G. EGGERS, JR. The name appeared just as he expected it would—not Tommy or Tom or Thomas but Thomas G. with Jr. tagged on. Dimitri reached for the phone but began to cry before he could enter his home phone number. He dropped his head onto the newspaper and wept until the list of names was dotted with tears.

Finally getting a grip on his emotions, Dimitri again reached for the phone. "No, Dimitri," he said aloud, "you can't interfere. If Tommy had wanted to include you in this, he would have told you about it. The most loving thing to do is to let him go, let him face the end alone the way he wants."

After another siege of tears, Dimitri washed his face and went out to find Roland Richmond, a gay man in the Houston chorus who had been especially friendly. Dimitri hoped that Roland had a listening ear, a comforting touch, and a shoulder to cry on.

Guy Rossovich stopped by Francie's desk on his way in from lunch to check the electronic datebook she kept for him. His executive assistant was poring over the front page of the *US Star*'s Scene and eating a carton of low-fat strawberry-banana yogurt.

"You read the *Star?*" Guy said, disparaging the newspaper with his tone.

"Not usually, not unless there's something that catches my eye," said the matronly but attractive woman without looking up.

"What's so interesting today?" asked the California state senator from Beverly Hills as he scrolled through the hand-held calendar.

Francie looked up at him. "You don't read the *Star?*"

"Never."

"Never ever?"

"Never ever. It's shallow, it's slanted, it's . . . it's a tabloid—what more can I say." Guy made a couple of notations on the screen by tapping on the tiny keyboard.

"Then you haven't heard about this cult in Seattle that's flying to heaven in a 737?"

"The doomsday flight?" Guy said, still working on the hand-held calendar.

"Then you *have* read the *Star.*"

"No, Francie, I have never read the *Star,* I don't read the *Star* now, I never will read the *Star.* In fact, I wouldn't housebreak my dog on the *Star.*"

"Well, excuse me," Francie said, pretending to be offended.

"I think I heard about the cult on TV. Some people say the pilot is going to destroy the plane if their messiah doesn't appear on time."

Francie set her yogurt down and looked up at her boss. "Right. But today the plot thickens. Somehow the *Star* got into the cult's computer and stole the passenger list," she said excitedly. "The names are all here, right on the front page. I'll bet these people didn't want their names printed. The *Star* sure spoiled their deepest, darkest secrets."

"Mm-hm," Guy said, unimpressed.

"There's even a name on this list that you know," Francie said.

Guy looked away from the datebook for the first time. "Somebody I know is going to be on the doomsday flight?" he said disbelievingly.

"Yes, Mr. Rossovich. Look." Francie ran her fingers down the list of names, stopped below one, and tapped her index finger like a little signal light.

Guy bent down to look at the name. "Gavin Cornell, the actor?" he said.

"Yeah, but I bet he's doing it for the publicity. He can't work in the movies anymore because he's a lush and he's crippled. So he's playing this cult for a little attention, that's what I think. He'll get off the plane at the last minute and sign up for the talk-show circuit to tell his story for $20,000 a pop."

Guy didn't respond. He was huddled over the newspaper scanning the list of names. After a minute he said, "Well, there's nobody on that list I know personally. If they want to ride the hallelujah express to hell, it's OK by me."

Francie feigned alarm. "Senator Rossovich, some of these people may be our constituents," she scolded.

"That's all right, Francie," Guy said with a mischievous grin. He closed the datebook and returned it to the desk. "The fewer nut cases in my district the better." Then he wheeled and strode into his office.

Francie laughed and returned to the *Star* article. She picked up the yogurt container, which had been on the paper. The carton left a light ring of moi sture around a group of names. Had Guy Rossovich seen two of the names in this circle, his attitude toward the doomsday flight would have changed dramatically. Francie read them and thought nothing about them, except that a three-year-old boy, apparently traveling with his mother, had the same first name as her boss.

The phone rang in the deserted Phoenix apartment until the machine kicked in. After the beep, a tentative Latino female voice, clearly uncomfortable talking to a machine, spoke.

"Sugar Bear, this is Mama. I know . . . er, I think you told me you're on your vacation trip to California. But I want to talk to you, and your personal phone number doesn't go through, and your uncle in Saugus won't answer his phone either. Maybe you will hear me on this machine and call. I hope so."

Serena Barrigan hesitated as if uncertain how to broach a delicate subject. "Sugar, your sister-in-law Lisa told me that your name was in the *US Star* newspaper today. Except it must be someone else with the same name as yours. Lisa was upset because the people in the paper belonged to a cult, the devil's business. She said the Raul Barrigan in the paper is twenty-four, just like you, and she hopes it isn't you.

"I told her it isn't you because you serve Jesus and don't get involved with cults. I know you aren't the Raul Barrigan in the paper, but if you will call me I will feel better, and Lisa and the rest of the family will feel better. Please, this is your mother. God bless you my Sugar Bear." The machine clicked off.

Unknown to Serena Barrigan, the chip on which her plea had been digitally recorded contained six other messages of a similar nature from friends, former teammates, and a sports journalist named Marta Friesen.

Fifty-eight

The private half-mile gravel road winding away from Silverlake Drive served as a shared driveway for the six homes scattered among the trees off the main road. When visiting her home on Whidbey Island, Beth Scibelli-Cole used the driveway for a cool-down walk after running three–four miles along Silverlake. Today's run had been delayed a couple of hours by what Beth now knew was a mild case of morning sickness. But by 9:30 this cool, overcast Monday morning she had felt well enough to slip into tights and a hooded sweatshirt and strike out, leaving her husband to enjoy a well-deserved sleep in.

Trudging slowly along the gravel road back to the house with hands on hips, Beth considered the tiny life growing within her. She smiled as the picture of an infant wearing a sweat suit and tiny Nikes came to her. *Get used to it, kid,* she thought. *All that bouncing around means you have been assigned to a very athletic family. You and I will be doing this together about three times a week until the doctor tells me to stop. After you're born, I'll probably have to get you one of those three-wheel jogging strollers so we can run the Santa Monica Beach Promenade together.*

As soon as you're on your feet, Daddy will put a basketball in your hands. You will be a star, of course. The biggest argument in the Cole household will be over where you play college hoops: USC or UCLA. Since we will doubtless be living in the Northwest by then, you'll probably disappoint us both by accepting a scholarship to U Dub. Good for you. That's the kind of spunk and spirit this family is already famous for.

As she approached the house, Beth slipped off her headband and used the driest side to dab perspiration from her nose, cheeks, and chin. She reflected with pleasure on the what-shall-we-name-the-baby? conversation she and Cole enjoyed last night in bed, a conversation that at times had them both howling with laughter. Since they didn't yet know the baby's gender, all names were fair game. And the later it got, the more ludicrous the suggestions. There were basketball names— Scoop, Swish, Air, Stuff—and biblical names—Jehoshaphat (Jumping Jehoshaphat or Jehoshaphina—J.J.—combining basketball and the Bible, got a good laugh), Jezebel, Hezekiah—and Hollywood names— Keanu, Clint, Meryl, Madonna. The laughter and fun helped divert Beth from the mounting anxiety of the assignment awaiting her aboard the doomsday flight in two days.

Beth entered the house quietly in case Cole was still asleep. He wasn't. He was waiting for her in the living room, slouched on the sofa with his bare feet up on the coffee table. He had pulled on a pair of jeans and a T-shirt, but the bird's-nest disarray of his sandy hair told Beth that he hadn't been up for long. And Cole's body language—arms folded across his chest and furrowed brow—communicated that he was not starting the day in a good mood.

"Good morning, sleepyhead," Beth said cheerily, trying to chase away the funk hanging over her husband. She pulled the drapes open hoping a splash of daylight would help. "You figured out where I'd gone, right? J.J. and I took our first Silverlake run together, at least it's the first time I've run knowing she was in there."

Cole's serious expression and inhospitable posture were even more obvious in the light. "Will you sit down for a minute, please," he said without humor.

Beth came around to face him. "Are you all right?"

"Sit down please, Beth," Cole said coolly.

Hearing Reagan speak her name instead of the more intimate "Babe" led Beth to suspect that she must be implicated in whatever was bugging him at the moment. She lowered herself to the upholstered chair across the table from the sofa and sat on the edge to minimize the contact of her sweaty clothes with the fabric. "Are you upset that I left for my run without telling you?" she said, hoping that was it.

Cole glared at her without hearing her question. "When were you going to mention your seat on the doomsday flight, or were you planning to sneak away from me and get on the plane without saying anything at all?"

The perspiration on Beth's skin instantly turned to ice. She was shocked and mystified that Cole knew her secret, because she had told no one. And she was chilled to the bone by the realization that he had learned about her plans from someone other than herself. He was angry and hurt, and Beth knew she was clearly to blame. She should have told him. Her shoulders hunched forward, and she was speechless with guilt.

"Libby called about twenty minutes ago," Cole explained, maintaining his cold stare. "The *US Star* published the passenger list this morning. She wanted to know why your name was on it. I didn't know what to tell her."

"That list wasn't supposed to be made public," Beth said. "Somebody at the *Star* must have hacked into a computer. They could be in deep yogurt for that."

"I don't care about the *Star*. I just want to know how your name got on the list and why you didn't tell me."

"It wasn't my idea, Reagan," Beth said weakly. "When I interviewed Cooper Sams, he asked me if I wanted to go along and—"

"You knew about this clear back in December?" Cole pressed forcefully.

"I didn't decide to go back then," Beth defended. "I mean, I told Sams I would go because it sounded like a good opportunity and he wanted my decision right then. But I wasn't sure if I should go. So I didn't say anything because I didn't want you to worry for nothing, since there was a good chance I would cancel the reservation."

"When did you become sure you should go?"

"I'm not *sure* sure," Beth waffled, "just more sure."

"So you let the *Star* break the news for you."

"I was going to tell you, Reagan, I really was," Beth said. "I just didn't know how to say it."

Reagan flushed red with anger. "Geez, Beth, the whole country knows about your idiotic plans before I do."

"Just a minute, Reagan. It's not an idiotic plan," Beth retorted, sensing a little anger herself. "This is a journalist's gold mine. There will be 135 different stories on that airplane, and the public wants to read about what happens up there. Think about it: I have been granted exclusive coverage of an event of national attention."

"An event of national tragedy," Cole corrected insistently.

Beth felt defensive. "Reagan, the plane will come back down when the magic moment comes and goes, I'm sure of it."

"Are you *sure* sure or just more sure?" Cole snapped sarcastically.

Beth stood and began to pace in subtle defiance of Cole's hostility. "Reagan, I've talked to Cooper Sams; you haven't. He may be a nut case when it comes to religion, but he's not a Jim Jones or David Koresh. He's an intelligent, experienced, professional flier. When he realizes that the Jesus-Brother game is over, he'll land the plane. There's nothing to worry about." Beth wanted to sound right even though a few doubts leered at her from the fringes of her confidence.

Cole raked his hair with his fingers, then dropped his hands to his lap. He released a long breath and said, "Beth, I won't allow you to get on that plane."

Beth stopped in the middle of the living room and turned to face him. "I thought we were having a discussion," she said with hands on hips. "That sounded like a papal order."

"We could have had a discussion about this three months ago, but one of us independently decided not to bring up the topic. It's too late for discussion. I have to make the call on this, Beth. You're not going."

"But if I had told you about Cooper Sams' invitation back in December, and we had discussed it calmly and rationally then, you would have agreed that this is a great opportunity and given your blessing. Is that what you're saying?"

Cole stared at his wife while processing her words. "Yes, that's what I'm saying," he conceded, then added quickly, "but hearing you say it, I know that's not what I mean. Letting you get on the doomsday flight is a bad idea today; it would have been a bad idea three months ago.

It's just a bad idea, Beth. I can't let you go."

"But I gave my word," Beth objected. "It's the only way I will get a story out of Sams when this thing is over. I have to check into the hotel tonight to stay until Wednesday with the rest of the passengers. I'm already a day late."

"Tonight?" Cole snapped. "You really were waiting to the last minute to tell me, weren't you? Well, I'm sorry, but you're not going."

Beth resumed pacing, obviously agitated. "When you say, 'You're not going,' what do you mean exactly? Do you mean, 'I strongly advise you not to go, but as always I trust you to make the right decision'? Or do you mean, 'You're not smart enough to make the right call on your own, so I'm going to handcuff you to the front door until after Wednesday'?"

Cole stood now. "Babe, I think you're reading too much into what I'm saying." At this point in the argument, Beth was not comforted by Cole's use of his pet name for her. He continued, "The issue is not your personal freedom versus my responsibility as your husband. The issue is putting your life and the life of our unborn child into the hands of a religious nut who has at least intimated that he might put a 737 in a death dive to prove his faith. You are risking two human lives—the two most important people in the world to me—to gain a story. That's a very bad risk, and I won't let you take it."

"Meaning what exactly?" Beth pressed again, nearly shouting. "How are you going to stop me?"

Cole sighed and dropped his head. When he spoke again, his voice was subdued. "Beth, you know how I admire your drive and spirit and individualism. It's what attracted me to you in the first place—next to your body, of course. The downside of these qualities is that you sometimes take unnecessary chances. It's happened before, but I didn't have as much invested in us before. I'm your husband now, and I feel responsible to protect you. I don't think it's wise to trust Cooper Sams with your life. So I'm asking you, please, to give up your plans to be on that plane."

"And if I don't?" Beth challenged.

"I'm afraid for you and for our baby. I'll do anything I have to do to keep you from getting aboard."

"You're that serious."

"I'm that serious."

Beth stared at Cole for several seconds. Then, without relaxing her attitude, she said, "I'm going to take my shower."

Cole stayed in control. "Yeah, and I have some reading to do. Then I'm going to play racquetball."

They quickly left each other's sight.

Beth stayed under the pulsating water jets much longer than it took to get clean. She wished the hot water could penetrate deeply enough to wash away the grit she felt inside after her argument with Reagan. She had been wrong in not telling Reagan about her plans sooner. And she had been prideful and adversarial when responding to his demand to stay away from the doomsday flight. *I guess I need to apologize for being a little hardheaded, but I can't help it,* she rationalized. *I was on my own for thirty years before I married Reagan Cole. I'm not used to anyone telling me not to step over the line. Reagan should realize that by now.*

She ducked under the shower head and let the hard streams of water massage her scalp and neck. *Besides, you have to take risks to get good material; any journalist worth her salt knows that. If he's going to put the brakes on any project I undertake just because it's a little dangerous, I'm finished as a writer. I know Reagan feels responsible for me, and to a point I admire that. But does he really think I would seriously endanger myself and our child for a story? Does he really believe I don't know when to back off? I have a better grip on what Cooper Sams may or may not do. I'm the best qualified to make the call on the doomsday flight story. He just doesn't realize that yet. I'll apologize for being a little pushy, and Reagan will cool off and cut me some slack. He's probably reconsidering his hasty decision right now.*

But by the time Beth had dried off and dressed, Cole and the S-10 pickup were gone.

Fifty-nine

"Captain Sams, we have a problem." Eunice Carver, manager of the Stouffer-Madison Hotel, had called Cooper out of a meeting room. Members of the New Jesus Family and guests holding gold and silver coins were being briefed by Lila Ruth Atkinson on the glories of Reunion. Cooper had been standing in the back of the room savoring the moment.

Ms. Carver was about the same height as Cooper Sams—six feet—but nearly double his weight. However, the woman's weakness at weight management was amply compensated by superior skills in personal fashion, makeup, and hair styling. Cooper regarded her as a very attractive black woman.

Cooper knew what the problem was before Eunice stated it: Hotel security was stretched to the breaking point thanks to this morning's *Star* article. Word about the story had reached Cooper early. His best attempts to shield his flock from the news that their names had been made public failed. By 9 A.M. every *Vanguard* passenger and alternate checked into the hotel had heard about the story, and every copy of the *Star* in the hotel lobby had been snatched up.

Even before 9, calls began flooding the switchboard from irate and distressed loved ones demanding that the cult release its "brainwashed prisoners." And as the day wore on, the hotel lobby crowded with a throng of nosy spectators hoping to catch a glimpse of at least one crazy cult member.

"I am committed to the security of your party, Captain," Eunice Carver explained as Cooper listened, "but our resources are wearing thin. We have your meeting room and dining room well secured. But a few of the thrill-seekers out there have eluded us and made it up to the residence floors. We chase them out, of course, but like flies they seem to find new holes in the screen. The crowd in the lobby is getting loud, and the media people are pestering the employees for Mr. Cornell's room number. Our small security corps is maxed out, and I'm afraid the problem will be even worse tomorrow."

Cooper nodded and smiled beneficently. He was confident that Eunice Carver was doing the best she could under the circumstances. And he regretted the unconscionable action of the *US Star* which had complicated Eunice's job. He anticipated her purpose in the discussion, so he answered her bottom-line question before she could ask it. "Ms. Carver, we greatly appreciate your efforts. You have been very helpful, and I'm sorry that the newspaper article has made your work more difficult. Please hire any additional security staff you need—preferably off-duty policemen trained in crowd control—and charge it to our account. We want our group to feel safe here until we check out and board the buses on Wednesday."

"Thank you, Captain," Eunice Carver beamed. "Thank you for understanding. I'll make a few calls right now. We should have some extra security people on site in a couple of hours."

Cooper dismissed her with a pleasant handshake. He checked his watch: 5:45 P.M., almost time for Ms. Atkinson's session to break for dinner. He stepped quietly back into the rear of the large meeting room. Lila Ruth was completing her third plenary session of the day, reviewing Jesus-Brother's divine call to Reunion for New Jesus Family members and curious guests. As always, Lila Ruth held her audience spellbound with her gentle voice and wise words. Cooper expected that a few of the doubters would become believers before *Vanguard* left the hangar on Wednesday just from hearing Lila Ruth speak.

Surveying the group of 118 people from behind, Cooper noticed that a decent number of guest passengers had opted to attend today's meetings. The handsome young Latino man had been the most noticeable of the guests through the day. As the only person in the room in a wheelchair, he was hard to overlook. But he had also been quite gregarious, rolling his chair from group to group and introducing himself during the breaks.

Cooper had overheard the young man encouraging people to "prepare to meet God by confessing your sin and accepting Jesus Christ as your personal Savior." He had also passed out leaflets liberally. Most Family members listened politely and thanked him for his concern, citing that Lila Ruth Atkinson had already helped them prepare to die. Non-Family members offered a wider range of responses to the wheelchair evangelist, from brusque rejection to patient interest. Cooper was delighted at the diversity represented among the individuals who would be first to gaze into the face Jesus-Brother.

Cooper also took note of the non-Family guests who had checked into the hotel as requested but skipped the meetings with Lila Ruth Atkinson. A lovely Amerasian girl with a dark-haired little boy were absent, along with other parents who found it taxing to keep children quiet through the long meetings. Gavin Cornell and several others with serious illnesses had opted to remain in their rooms. Tommy Eggers, Cooper's former coworker, had come to the morning meeting but retired to his room before lunch, utterly fatigued. He looked like a skeleton compared to the last time Cooper had flown with him. The two men had enjoyed a brief but civil reunion upon Tommy's arrival at the hotel.

Walt Meisner was in his room drinking, Cooper knew, and perhaps sulking about not being allowed to test-fly the airplane. Cooper felt lucky that a copilot was little more than window dressing for this flight, a certified pilot on board to fulfill federal aviation requirements. In actuality, Meisner wasn't needed; under most circumstances a 737 pilot can manage the controls alone. Cooper only hoped to keep Walt Meisner sober enough to sit at the controls and watch the autopilot fly while he visited with his spiritual family in the cabin.

Three more of the guests originally selected by Pathfinder had reneged on their intentions to board *Vanguard*, so three of the remaining eight alternates—nine counting Kathy Keane—were awarded the open seats. Cooper feared that the pressure generated by shocked loved ones reading today's *Star* article might result in others leaving the hotel before Wednesday. They were free to do so, of course. And Cooper still had alternates ready to take any openings. He had an inkling that all remaining alternates would be on the plane, including his unwilling personal choice, Kathy Keene. It would be just like Pathfinder to arrange that for him.

One guest had been specifically prohibited from arriving in Seattle until a couple of hours before departure on Wednesday. Robert Lamar, the cancer-ridden prison inmate from Texas, would be delivered to Paine Field in shackles by two FBI agents, Cooper had been told by the warden. Lamar, wearing the standard orange prison uniform, would be strapped into one of the two jump seats in the aft galley, next to another passenger yet to be determined. The agents would be prepared to remain at Paine Field, the warden had said, until the plane returned, something Cooper assured him would not be necessary.

Beside Kathy Keene, only one passenger was unaccounted for. Cooper had been prompted by Pathfinder to offer a *Vanguard* seat to Rachel's friend Beth Cole. He suspected that Beth had accepted the offer only because he threatened to cancel the exclusive interview, which is what she really wanted. To date, the journalist had made good on her promise not to publish a word about the Family before *Vanguard*'s departure. But she had not arrived at the hotel with the other guests on Sunday. He figured she might be one of the last dropouts.

At five minutes to 6, Lila Ruth concluded the session by having Family members recite the Reunion prayer. Cooper spoke along softly from beside the back door. Then the group was dismissed to an elegant private dinner in the adjoining meeting room. As the congregation swept by him, many greeted him with the New Jesus Family greeting — "Even so come, Jesus-Brother." To each greeter he replied pleasantly, "Even so come."

He scanned the faces looking for Beth Cole. As he expected, she wasn't in the room. She had given her word to go, but Cooper knew he had no way to penalize her if she didn't follow through. There would be no article about the New Jesus Family either way. In just over fifty hours it would be all over.

Reagan Cole's racquetball game at the small club in Oak Harbor turned into a wildly competitive round-robin series with three guys from the Whidbey Island Naval Air Station. It was just what Cole needed to work out the tension from his conflict with Beth. After showers, the four men met at the Pizza Palace for calzone and salad. Still smarting from Beth's defiance, Cole punished her by not calling to let her know where he was. She apparently was doing the same, he concluded, by not calling to ask.

Not in a hurry to get home, Cole spent an hour in the public library browsing for books and replaying the heated exchange with Beth in his mind. Had he been too harsh? too domineering? By 3 o'clock he began to miss her, so he stopped by the market to pick up a half-gallon of their favorite ice cream — chocolate cherry cream — for a peace offering. Then he headed home to try to explain his feelings about her participation in the doomsday flight — which he was still firmly against — a little more compassionately.

It was almost dusk when he turned off the gravel road and nosed the S-10 up to the garage door. The kitchen light was on, but Beth was not home. Instead a handwritten message was waiting for Cole on the kitchen counter.

Reagan,

I'm sorry I got a little testy this morning. Please forgive.

   I promised to meet Cooper Sams at the Stouffer-Madison. Nancy gave me a lift to catch the air shuttle to King County Airport. I'll stay at the hotel to write and interview people until the airplane leaves. Call me if you want to talk.

Love you, Beth

Cole stared at the note trying to decipher it. *Is she telling me that she has changed her mind or that she is going ahead with her plan? Is she staying at the hotel when the cult leaves for Paine Field or is she going with them? Is this a rare case of unclear writing from Beth or is she being purposely vague?*

After several seconds he gave the note sheet a spin on the formica. Then he dished up a large bowl of chocolate cherry cream and sat down to think hard thoughts about how to provide protection for a wife who didn't want it and seldom needed it.

Beth navigated through the crowded lobby to the registration desk, using her briefcase as a prow and her small soft-side suitcase as a rear guard. She ignored the harassing comments and questions from the throng, who assumed anyone checking into the hotel under this kind of pressure must be with the party of heaven-bound fruitcakes. She also looked the part, dressed to the nines in her best tailored suit in compliance with Cooper Sams' written instructions.

Showing her gold and silver coins to the registrar, Beth was quickly assigned a hotel room and escorted to the ninth floor by a burly, uniformed bellhop. On the way, he informed her that the New Jesus Family dinner was already in progress in the Cascade Room. Beth asked him to wait outside her room for two minutes while she freshened her lipstick and then escort her down to the meeting room. He did, even though Beth didn't need him for protection, as it turned out. She gave him a ten-dollar bill, thinking she might need his services again.

Beth hoped to slip into the dining room and blend in with the crowd. But Cooper Sams was on his feet so quickly when she entered that she figured he had been watching for her. "Good evening, Ms. Cole," he said, shaking her hand. "I was beginning to wonder if you had forgotten about our little agreement."

Beth recognized the subtle insinuation that she would skip the flight, but she ignored it. "I'm sorry to be late, Captain, but I had some family matters to attend to."

"You have a room, then?"

"Yes, I'm checked in. I wasn't aware that your group was picking up the tab for the rest of us. Thank you."

Cooper smiled. "It's our Reunion gift to our guests."

Beth said, "While I'm here, I would like to sit down with you and Ms. Atkinson again and—"

"I'm afraid there's just no time for that," Cooper cut in. His demeanor was very pleasant, but there was no mistaking the message: No more interviews.

"I understand, sir," Beth yielded. "I'd also like to talk to as many passengers as I can—group members and guests. I'd like to get their impressions of the New Jesus Family, their thoughts as they approach the flight, and so on. Is *that* agreeable?"

"Hoping to convince a few to reconsider?" Cooper's tone was free of accusation but clearly inferred his view of her as an outsider.

"Not exactly. But I would like to ask some of them to explain their reasons for such an . . . unusual . . . choice."

"More material for the story you plan to write after Wednesday?" Cooper's little wink conveyed that the joke was on Beth.

"Only if there is an 'after Wednesday,' " Beth returned with a wink of her own.

"And you will be aboard when we take off Wednesday evening to find out, as we agreed?"

Beth swallowed hard, hoping her inner turmoil was not evident to the host. "Yes, I plan to be aboard."

Cooper studied the pretty face. "All right, Ms. Cole, you may talk to anyone you like, ask them anything you like, and tell them anything you like. Another one of our guest passengers is a rabid young evangelist seeking souls among my flock. I don't expect that either of you will be able to turn the heads of the elect, but you may certainly try if you wish."

"That's very broadminded of you, Captain."

Cooper shook his head slowly. "No, just realistic. The Family members in this room are here because they wholeheartedly believe the prophet's message that the world is down to its last two days. You won't change their minds. Most of our guests are here not because they think literal destruction is upon us but because the world outside these walls, if it were to survive, has nothing left to offer them. You'll be hard-pressed to find anyone in either group who will give up their hope for Reunion to return to a condemned planet."

Beth desperately wanted to ask Cooper the question which was on the mind of millions of readers of the *US Star*, a question he had sidestepped repeatedly in their December interview: Will you bring the plane safely back to earth if the world *does* survive Wednesday? And she felt Captain Sams had opened himself up for the question again. But before she could ask it, she was distracted by someone approaching in a hurry to join the conversation. Beth looked to see a handsome Latino dressed in suit and tie rolling up in a lightweight wheelchair. He was looking directly at her as he came, and his face was wan with surprise—a face she finally recognized.

Cooper followed her gaze to the young man. He said, "Here's the energetic young preacher I was telling you about. You two will have—"

"Beth Cole?" the young man blurted disbelievingly as he braked his chair beside Cooper Sams.

"Raul Barrigan?" Beth gasped.

Cooper's eyes flitted between the two, unable to tell who was the more surprised.

Beth and Raul, eyes locked on each other, spoke next in unison. "What are you doing here?"

Sixty

Beth wasn't going to sleep before talking to her husband. She had been expecting him to call—and hoping he would call—all day and all evening Tuesday. They had not spoken since their argument at the house yesterday morning. Beth wasn't angry with Reagan, and she didn't think he was angry with her. But they were in the middle of a serious disagreement over the doomsday flight, and Beth thought it was probably good that they had been apart for a while. But as the evening wore on, she missed him terribly.

At 10:30, just when Beth was ready to pick up the phone and dial, Cole called. "How is it going?" he said. His voice was devoid of chatty warmth, reflecting the strain of their two-day disagreement.

"It's going OK," Beth said in the same tone. "I've worked on the computer. I've talked to a lot of the passengers."

Cole responded without enthusiasm. "Good."

"What have you been doing?"

"Not much. Pruning the fruit trees."

Beth had wondered all day if Cole was as shocked as she was to learn that Raul Barrigan was on the passenger list—or if he knew at all. She couldn't blame him for avoiding the print and broadcast media on the event. Even if he saw the names in the paper, he may not have realized or suspected that the Raul Barrigan listed there was the quadriplegic police officer from Phoenix they met last fall. She expected her husband to be upset if he still didn't know and she failed to tell him right away.

She asked, "Have you seen the passenger list?"

"Yes, but only to see if your name was really on it."

Avoiding that part of the discussion for now, Beth said, "You didn't recognize any other names on the list?"

"No, I'm not really interested in anyone else on the list."

"Raul Barrigan is on the list. I ran into him last night."

"What? The cop from Phoenix? The guy in the wheelchair?" Cole was suddenly animated.

"Yes. He's one of the standby passengers. He said he applied because he felt compassion for the cult members and the others. His name was picked at random, so he believes God arranged it. He's been passing out leaflets and talking to people about Jesus since he's been here."

"Is he going with them? Is he actually getting on the airplane?" Beth read the subtle cynicism in his voice. It communicated, "Raul is certainly smart enough not to get on the plane, unlike a female journalist I know."

"Yes, he says he is going with them," Beth responded, trying not to mock him with her tone. "In his words, 'They need a witness all the way to the end of the flight.'"

Cole paused. "So Raul believes the plane is going down?"

Beth leaped at the chance to defend her position. "No, he doesn't think so. Raul just wants to be there with them no matter what happens. He sees himself as kind of a missionary to the New Jesus Family."

"Geez," Cole breathed in awe, "that's quite a commitment."

"Yes," Beth agreed. She decided not to relate a couple of comments Raul had made, leading her to suspect that he might regard a possible martyr's death as a blessing in disguise because of his disability.

Cole said, "What is Sams saying about the flight? Does he talk about proving his faith or anything like that?"

Beth knew Cole was fishing for more ammunition to keep her from getting on the plane. Despite their differences of opinion, she could not lie to him. At this point she wasn't even tempted. "Cooper Sams and Lila Ruth Atkinson are saying nothing. They have refused all my requests for additional interviews. Sams isn't talking to anyone about the flight."

"I say he's hiding something."

"I say he has nothing to hide."

Beth heard her husband sigh. "So you're still planning to get on his plane," he said.

Beth hated the prospect of locking horns again on this issue. She yearned for tenderness and support from Cole, not conflict—especially tonight. But she couldn't make herself bow to ask for it. "We've been over this already. I told Sams I would go. It was one of his conditions for allowing the interview."

"But you agreed before talking to me about it."

"Sams put me on the spot, Reagan. I had to put up or shut up."

"And there's another human life involved now who wasn't considered in your snap decision."

"I've already done the interview and written half the book. What am I supposed to do, give Sams the disks and walk away from the project?"

Cole said nothing for a moment. Then, speaking quietly, he said, "Yes, that's what I'd like you to do: Give it up."

"I've put a lot of hours into this book. That's money down the toilet."

"It's worth it to me. The risk to you and the baby is too great."

"In your opinion."

"I know you disagree, Babe, but I'm asking you please to trust me on this one."

"And if I don't?"

Again Cole paused thoughtfully before answering. "You mean, am I going to leave you if you go through with this?"

The question had crossed Beth's mind a couple of times since their heated exchange Monday morning, but she had blocked it out. She didn't want to think such a possibility was an option. Beth expected Cole to be angry with her for a week or two after the flight was over, and she could deal with that. Hearing her husband utter the L word brought her a chill. She didn't know what to say.

Thankfully, Cole answered his own question. "If that's what you're thinking, the answer is no. I love you, Beth. You're my wife. I'm committed to you. That's why I'm holding such a hard line on the doomsday flight. I don't want you to take unnecessary chances."

Again Beth was without a response.

"I'm never going to leave you, Babe," Cole continued. "But please do what I ask. I don't want to bury you either."

Myrna Valentine had not come to Seattle intending to participate in any of the rigamarole of the New Jesus Family at the Stouffer-Madison Hotel. *All that religious stuff—the prayers, the songs, the lectures—is for the kooks who really believe that the 737 named* Vanguard *is going up and not coming down,* she had told herself during her Sunday drive from Portland to Seattle. *Guy and I will eat with them since the meals are free, but that's all. I want to spend my last three days having a wonderful time with Guy in the city before we board the plane on Wednesday.*

But the mini-vacation with Guy in Seattle hadn't turned out the way Myrna had hoped. It started downhill fast with the shock of seeing her name in the *US Star* on Monday. People began buzzing around the hotel like flies around fresh garbage, making it difficult to get a taxi and impossible to walk to Pike's Market or the waterfront or anywhere else without being pestered.

Furthermore, Myrna feared that her parents or brothers might see the article in the paper and come to Seattle to get her. Worse yet, if Guy Rossovich found out, he might jet up the coast with a cadre of lawyers to seize their son. So on Monday afternoon she had locked herself and Guy in their room, leaving only to eat dinner with the cult group in the private Cascade Room.

By Tuesday evening, Myrna had been ready to snap. She had been cooped up in the hotel with her three year old for over thirty hours, trying to keep him occupied with interactive TV. She had ordered a room-service breakfast and lunch, and she let Guy have snacks and soda pop from the vending machines—something she rarely allowed. They left the ninth floor only to enjoy the sumptuous dinners with the rest of the passengers.

The forced confinement had darkened the cloud of depression hanging over Myrna and further confirmed her desire to end it all. The telephone became an adversary as the hours wore on. At first she was glad that it never rang. Then when it didn't, it meant to her either that nobody noticed her name in the *Star* or nobody cared she was involved with the doomsday flight. The fact that none of her family members or friends had missed her or tried to contact her deepened her inner pain. Not even Guy Rossovich had tried to call, either to talk her out of her folly or to say he was coming after the kid. The fact that Guy would eventually read her note and feel the remorse he should feel brought Myrna only small consolation.

When she joined the small congregation in the Cascade Room for dinner each night, Myrna was a stranger, embraced neither by the cult people nor the smaller group of guest passengers. However, two individuals in the entourage seemed unperturbed by the mounting flow of negativism rushing Myrna toward the precipice of Wednesday's waterfall. They were the two people with noticeably different agendas. They seemed as unconcerned about their potential destruction as two immense boulders unmoved by a river's torrent.

One was a tall, attractive writer named Beth Cole. Beth had spent several minutes with Myrna after the Monday evening meal, showing a friendly interest in her and admiring little Guy. Her questions about Myrna's involvement in the New Jesus Family and the flight of *Vanguard* did not come across as prying, and she was content with the shallow answers Myrna gave. Rather, the journalist seemed more concerned by how she felt about the event, stopping just short of encouraging her to reconsider her decision.

Beth had also sought out Myrna during the Tuesday evening meal. Myrna liked the woman and wondered how she got involved in this suicidal assignment.

The other bright spot in the deepening twilight of Myrna's life was a young man in a wheelchair. Myrna couldn't fault him for wanting to be aboard the doomsday flight, since he had been robbed of his strength and mobility well before his prime. Raul Barrigan had also approached Myrna and initiated conversation as she and Guy waited to be seated for dinner Monday night. Responding to the little boy's interest, Raul hoisted Guy onto his lap and gave him a wild ride up and down the hall. Guy laughed like Myrna had not heard him laugh in weeks, and the young quadriplegic was having just as much fun. "Faster, faster," the little boy urged, and Raul complied until his face was wet with perspiration.

Raul Barrigan had been more pointed about his agenda, but Myrna had not regarded him as offensive. The young man had told her that he didn't know what was going to happen at 8:02 P.M. on Wednesday evening—the end of the world, a tragedy of some kind, or a return to "life as we now know it." But he claimed to know a solution for any eventuality. He talked to her about Jesus Christ instead of Jesus-Brother and personal peace now instead of Reunion. He gave her a leaflet and encouraged her to read it. He said he would see her again before boarding on Wednesday. Then he rolled away to spread his message to others in the room.

Raul was outside the Cascade Room again Tuesday night to delight Guy with another wheelchair ride. He talked to Myrna again, asking if she had read the leaflet. She had not, but the young man wasn't insulted in the least. He told Myrna he was praying for her. She didn't know whether to thank him or ask him to stop. Prayer didn't seem to harmonize with her preponderant thoughts as the minutes ticked away to Wednesday.

Back in her room now with Guy sleeping soundly, Myrna sat in the dark, defenseless against the demons tormenting her. A feeble message played in the back of her head, one which had been ingrained through all her years of therapy: You're placing too much stock in your negative circumstances; you're allowing your feelings to control you; you're not monitoring your medication properly. But the wisdom of past counseling was overpowered by accusations of inadequacy and hopelessness goading her to follow through with her plan for vengeance.

In the darkness, Myrna's vision was filled with Guy Rossovich's face, twisted by the horror of his only son's death. She was counting on Captain Sams to make that horror a reality in less than twenty-four hours.

Tommy Eggers had thrown up every objection he could think of during his two-hour meeting with Raul Barrigan. Yet the enthusiastic self-styled preacher boy in the wheelchair had an answer for every one of them, not theological-sounding answers like a real minister might give, but down-to-earth, convincing answers nonetheless. Exhausted from the exchange, the frail AIDS victim allowed Raul to let himself out at almost 11:30 P.M. Then he dressed for bed and slipped wearily between the sheets. But sleep eluded him as he pondered the conversation just completed.

Tommy chuckled inwardly at the mental picture. As a flight attendant spending two or three nights a week in hotels, he had invited lots of men up to his room over the years, but never for a religious discussion. Tonight Raul Barrigan had rolled up to Tommy after dinner and introduced himself. Tommy had thought Raul might be hitting on him—he had been propositioned by a few wheelchair-bound men before—until Raul brought out the leaflet about Jesus and salvation and heaven. The conversation with Marvin Dukes was still fresh in Tommy's mind, so he listened to the cripple's brief "pitch," which turned out to be as clear and compassion-driven as Mr. Dukes' little talks about God. So when Raul asked him if he wanted to learn more about God's plan of salvation, Tommy agreed to a meeting in his room.

Staring at the ceiling in the darkness, Tommy recalled the highlights of the conversation. It had been the classic confrontation between an eager salesman and a reluctant prospect, Tommy mused. For each of Raul's selling points Tommy had a reason why the "product" wouldn't work for him. And for every reason he gave, Raul had a comeback that reduced the reason to a mere excuse. (Raul had emphasized that an excuse is the skin of a reason stuffed with a lie. He could deal with reasons but not excuses.)

The young evangelist's persistence to "close the deal" was fueled by the fact that the offer of salvation might expire at any time, possibly during the flight of *Vanguard*. But Raul Barrigan was clearly not motivated by profits or the size of his client base. Like Marvin Dukes, the young man seemed to have the best interests of his prospect at heart. Unlike Marvin Dukes, Raul was riding along on the doomsday flight to prove it.

"God can't be interested in saving me," Tommy had objected. "I've never been religious."

"God isn't looking for religious people," Raul had countered. "He's looking for sinners who are willing to receive His free gift of salvation."

"I'm not just your ordinary sinner. I'm kind of in the big leagues when it comes to doing stuff God doesn't approve of."

"Big or small, sin is sin to God. You're no worse than a shoplifter and no better than a mass murderer. And Christ's death paid for it all."

"I'm dying of AIDS, and you can probably figure out how I got it. God's on my case. He's already punishing me big-time for my sin."

"AIDS is a consequence, not a punishment. God isn't on your case. He loves you just as you are and He wants to save you."

"What for? Even if I survive the doomsday flight—God forbid, I have only a few months to live at best. Why would God want me?"

"He wants to spend eternity with you in heaven. In the meantime, God will transform your life and heal you of AIDS—at least He *can* heal you of AIDS. That's why Jesus was raised from the dead. His resurrection power will give you a new life."

In round after round of questions and objections, Raul Barrigan had proved unflappable. More than once he conceded, "I don't know the answer to that," only to quickly assert, "but Jesus knows, and He'll give you the answer if you wait on Him." Raul had attempted to get Tommy to "pray the sinner's prayer," but he backed off quickly at Tommy's refusal. When Tommy bid Raul good night, he was firmly convinced that this salesman was sold on his product. But Tommy himself was ambivalent about buying in.

In pain and weary beyond sleep, Tommy tossed in the bed and wrestled with words he wished he could blot out of his mind. He thought it ironic that his last night on earth would be so unsettling. "God, I wish I could relax," he muttered aloud. Forcing himself to lie still, he suddenly thought that Raul Barrigan was back in the room. The same sense of urgency and compassion seemed to surround the bed. Tommy dismissed the idea as nonsense. But his thoughts kept being funneled back to Raul's words about God, as if a silent whirlwind in the room was transporting him to heaven.

Tommy gasped, thinking he might be dying right now. But he was still here and still feeling lousy—except for a warm, welcoming presence that seemed very near, as if heaven had been brought down to him. After a few moments of breathless contemplation, Tommy began to ask some of the questions which had stumped Raul Barrigan, wondering if he had somehow gained the ear of the Man at the top of the organization.

Sixty-one

Wednesday morning dawned clear and bright over Paine Field. But barely half an hour after sunrise a weather system swooped in from the Gulf of Alaska and snuffed out the lights with boiling gray clouds and steady rain. The storm was no surprise to a region of the country where the TV meteorologist's rain icon is employed in the forecast more times than not during the winter.

Operations supervisor Mitchell Schetky and his airport staff were prepared for the foul weather and a very hectic day. Chief Weldon New Feather's special security team, decked out in yellow slickers, began patrolling the airport grounds at 8 A.M., with additional units scheduled for deployment every two hours. By 4 o'clock there would be a force of 120 off-duty police officers and firefighters on site to control the expected crowd of doomsday onlookers and keep them out of the air operations area. Two sheriff's patrol cars were already dedicated to the airport, with two more available at noon and the entire force on call by 4. New Feather also had the Everett Police, Mukilteo Police, and Washington State Patrol on alert.

As late as 9:45 A.M., the yellow-clad platoon policing the grounds looked like a case of precautionary overkill. Except for a few cars cruising through the airport every half hour to gawk and a couple dozen protesters staking out territory near the gate to the Tramco hangar, it looked like a normal, quiet Paine Field day. Mitchell Schetky gazed out at the small parking lot from an office window in the single-story administration building. Sipping coffee, he wondered if he had overestimated public interest in the doomsday flight—at great expense to the county. Then, right before his eyes, he was quickly convinced that he hadn't.

Two TV uplink trucks lumbered into view on 100th Street and turned into the parking area in front of the administration building. One truck was emblazoned with the logo of Satellite News Service. The other was from ABC. Each truck was tailed by one or two luxury-class rental sedans, and the classy cars were followed by more onlookers.

The news trucks had been stopped at the entrance and handed a folder describing the guidelines for being on airport grounds. They could not enter without passing the informal checkpoint. As they jockeyed for parking spaces in the lot—each truck took up four of them—the drivers were approached by a small squad of personnel in yellow slickers. Mitchell watched the scene play out.

Discussion ensued between the security staff and the people in the sedans, who quickly took over for the truck drivers. Mitchell assumed they were producer types, and as he watched the discussion appeared to heat up. From the hand gestures Mitchell discerned the point of conflict. The TV people wanted to set up shop for the day, and the security staff was saying "No way." Mitchell and Weldon New Feather had agreed not to allow oversized vehicles in the main lot—which could handle fewer than 100 cars—and not to waive the two-hour limit. The staff was dutifully attempting to carry out the directive.

Another TV truck appeared, and behind it were more cars, drawn to the parking lot as if the news trucks were magnetized. A few more yellow slickers gathered around to deal with the newcomers, but the security staff was quickly outnumbered. The SNS and ABC people were not budging, and the protesters across the street were getting interested in the argument. Mitchell didn't like the looks of it. He regarded the parking lot issue as a critical early battle. This was the responsibility of airport manager, Jo Ellen Case, and her assistant,

Rogie Petrovic. But they were at a meeting with the Tramco people at the south end of the airport. Realizing that Weldon New Feather probably had his hands full at the main entrance, Mitchell set down his mug, hurriedly donned his London Fog raincoat and broad-brimmed hat, and charged into the fray.

When he stepped up behind the small crowd, an SNS producer with Tom Selleck proportions and a decent-looking toupee was nose to nose with a female Snohomish County firefighter in a yellow slicker. The producer was waving an open checkbook in the rain. "I understand your problem, soldier," he said emphatically, "but I can solve it in a heartbeat. How much do you want for parking? I'll give you a $100 an hour in advance. I'll make it out to you. Take your whole crew to dinner tonight if you want." TV people from the other two trucks— with checkbooks at the ready—and security people pressed in to see who would prevail in the winner-take-all conflict.

The firefighter, whose plastic name badge read G. STICKLE, was a foot shorter and seventy pounds lighter than the producer. But she stood her ground unflinchingly. "Sir, listen to me again. You cannot park here. You cannot pay to park here. This lot is reserved for cars, vans, and small trucks only. There is a two-hour limit. You must move your truck. End of discussion."

"All right, $150 an hour. We're talking $1,200 here, and my friends at ABC and CNN can do at least that."

Mitchell feared that Stickle was not far from calling the guy a choice name or two and trying to punch his lights out. The last thing he wanted was a brawl. So he pulled her aside politely and stepped in to deal with the producer himself. "Mitchell Schetky, operations supervisor at Paine Field. How can I help you, sir?"

The noncombative approach took the producer aback. "Tony Franz, SNS," he said, moving the hand with the checkbook behind his back. "I'm just trying to set up our truck to cover the doomsday flight. It seems that your crew here doesn't appreciate the value of having an international news team on the premises."

"Well, Mr. Franz," Mitchell said with plastic buddy-buddy charm, "we can't allow you to do that for the reasons Ms.—" He stopped to read her badge "—Stickle stated. However, Snohomish County has graciously allowed parking along Airport Road. I happen to know that you can operate your equipment quite effectively from that distance. I suggest that you get your truck out there before too many others arrive and take all the good spaces. If you fail to leave the parking lot, I'll have you arrested and your truck will be impounded by the county. And covering the story from the county jail will be even more difficult than from Airport Road."

Tony Franz stared at him as the rain dripped from the curls of his expensive rug. He brought the checkbook into view again, but Mitchell cut him off before he could make an offer. He was more serious this time. "We're not cutting a business deal here, Mr. Franz. You're a guest at my party, and I'm just telling you where your seat is—take it or leave it."

Franz hesitated again, but his competitors didn't. The ABC and CNN crews scrambled into their trucks and cars and headed toward the street. Franz flipped his wet checkbook closed dramatically as if to say, "You missed your chance, chump." Then with a signal to his coworkers, Tony Franz and the SNS contingent mounted up and slowly retreated to Airport Road.

"Don't pussyfoot around with the media," Mitchell instructed the security people standing near him as the rain poured down on them. "If they don't play by the rules, use your com pack to call in the law—pronto. That goes for the spectators too." He gestured toward a growing stream of cars pulling into the available parking spaces. "When their two hours are up, get a tow truck in here." The yellow-plastic-draped band nodded assent and fanned out through the downpour and the puddles to do the job.

Mitchell Schetky retreated to the warm, dry office, but he didn't stay there for long. The crowd continued to swell, filling every available space in the parking lot within twenty minutes of his confrontation with Tony Franz. Carloads of nosy visitors streamed into the airport to ogle the terminal, circle the parking lot, and exit, urged along by the security staff. The more daring of the lookers tried to ditch their cars in the private lots leased by airport tenants. A steady stream of calls on Mitchell's pocket phone led him from hot spot to hot spot.

In the meantime, foot traffic into the airport swelled like the small rivers along the roadside as rain continued to fall. People crowded into the tiny terminal and any other dry corner they could find to wait for a glimpse of the celebrated 737 and its passengers. Conflicting rumors about when the buses would arrive from the hotel and when the plane would depart were rampant. Every time an engine roared—a private plane, a fuel truck, a Boeing test flight—necks craned toward the flight line.

At one bend in the road circling the small parking lot, about thirty scruffy-looking members of the Death with Dignity Coalition waved soggy cardboard placards and chanted in favor of those supposedly ending their lives on the doomsday flight. In the corner nearest the administration building, another small congregation exhorted the unseen *Vanguard* passengers, "End the strife, choose life! End the strife, choose life!" And the milling throng of watchers, media personnel, and even souvenir vendors grew larger.

When Jo Ellen Case and Rogie Petrovic returned from Tramco, they took over general supervision of the airport grounds, allowing Mitchell Schetky to zero in on the air operations area. As vehicles and pedestrians increased, so did air traffic in and out of the airport. By noon all available private aircraft parking and tie-down facilities were occupied, with subsequent visiting planes allowed only to drop off passengers or touch and go. Mitchell spent most of the late morning and early afternoon out on the terminal ramp shooing planes back out to the taxiway.

By 2 P.M. the perimeter security of the AOA was bending under the strain. Several screwballs had attempted to scale the chain-link fence separating them from the Tramco hangar. As soon as they dangled a foot over the top they were hauled down by the slicker brigade and handed over to a uniformed police officer for transport to the county jail. A couple of college kids from the DDC even made it all the way over and across the tarmac to the hangar while their cohorts staged a clever diversion. But the hangar was secure, and the intruders were apprehended before they could tag the bay door with spray paint. Mitchell and Weldon New Feather personally escorted the young daredevils to a waiting Washington State Patrol car.

Many other perimeter breaches occurred away from the terminal crowd where the fences were shorter or nonexistent and the security force more spread out. Luckily for Mitchell, it was difficult for the trespassers to hide for long in the wide open spaces of the AOA. State, county, and local police cars and vans queued up like taxis around terminal circle to cart away the offenders.

At close to 3 o'clock, Mitchell stood outside the FAA tower in the drizzle watching the cops escort another group of fence-climbers off his turf. The brim of his not-so-water-repellent hat drooped low around his head. His shoulders were cold from the rain soaking through his coat to the skin. His gut burned from too much anxiety, too much coffee, and no food. His rubber-soled wing tips were drenched.

What hole did you people crawl out of? he mused sourly as he scanned the masses clamoring loudly against the fence across the tarmac. *Why are you here trampling my airport and ruining my day? Why aren't you at work or at school or shopping or at home tending to your children like normal folks? What morbid thirst do you hope to quench out here? What do you hope to see: a plane blow up? a riot?*

Just then another young climber scampered up the fence only to be promptly pulled down by a security staffer. The violator was cheered and the law enforcer was booed by the crowd.

Mitchell cursed at the lot of them under his breath. *You people are the real freaks. You make the New Jesus cult look like Baptists on a Sunday School picnic.*

In downtown Seattle, Eunice Carver was thinking similar thoughts. The manager of the Stouffer-Madison Hotel had been up since 4:30 directing the work of her own security force and counting the minutes until the charter buses arrived to take her celebrity guests away. *When the garbage goes, the maggots will go,* she reminded herself as she surveyed the crowded lobby through the one-way glass of her office. *That's right, you people are maggots,* she groused silently to the loiterers and reporters cluttering her lobby. *You eat and sleep and breathe in the garbage. If there wasn't a freak show like this to feed on, you would wither up and crawl away. And that's what I'm just waiting for you to do in about an hour from now. Good riddance to bad garbage—and to all you maggots.*

Eunice's morning had been even more harrowing than Mitchell Schetky's. During the New Jesus Family's breakfast buffet in the Cascade Room, with Eunice present to assure good service, three men dressed like caterers burst into the room with automatic weapons. Moving with the skill of professional commandos, they kept security guards at bay while they subdued and carried away a young couple who had been in the New Jesus Family for less than a year. They made a clean escape through the underground service entrance. Police later told a shaken Eunice Carver that it was the work of militant cult deprogrammers, obviously hired by the families of the kidnap victims.

Seattle police officers and King County deputies swarmed into the hotel in force after the incident to bolster security. Opportunities for invading private territory were not as numerous as at Paine Field, but Eunice watched as a number of jokers were dragged off by the police for attempting to get to the congregation. Several of them were the frantic friends and relatives of cult members or guest passengers. Two of them claimed that the copilot was their father. Yet none of the protestors were as smart or as skilled as the commandos in their endeavors to rescue loved ones.

With little more than an hour until the group's departure, Eunice Carver had another major problem brewing. The two jumbo, eighty-passenger coaches rented for the trip to Paine Field were too big for the underground garage. The passengers would have to board at the main entrance curb, leaving them exposed to the public as they walked from the hotel to the bus. The police had assured her and the cult's leaders that they would form a human corridor to expedite boarding. But Eunice was afraid that desperate loved ones might try something dangerous to disrupt the process. And she didn't want anybody trampled or maimed in front of her hotel. As she thought about it, a way to minimize the trouble broke over her like sun through the clouds.

The New Jesus Family and guests were already checked out of their rooms and sequestered in the Cascade Room for their final religious meeting before departure. Cooper Sams and Lila Ruth Atkinson had asked that the group not be disturbed, so Eunice would have to act on her own to follow through with her idea. It took her five minutes to make the appropriate contacts. Satisfied that the end was near, she sat down to drink the Diet Coke she had opened two hours ago.

At 3:45, two blue and silver luxury coaches pulled up to the curb in front of the Stouffer-Madison. Uniformed police cordoned off the loudly idling buses, and the crowd swarmed restlessly outside the human barricade, jostling for a good observation point in the rain. At 3:50 another contingent of officers began evacuating the hotel lobby, from the elevators to the front doors. Reporters, cameramen, and gawkers spilling outside were bodily dispersed beyond the police barricade, grumbling all the way.

At 4 o'clock there wasn't a square inch of pavement within fifty yards of the entrance that wasn't occupied by someone hoisting a camera or straining for a look over the police barricade. Several had already been arrested for crowding the blue line too closely. Eunice stood in the liberated lobby watching the maggots squirm. Satisfied that her plan was working, she left for the Cascade Room to inform Captain Sams.

By 4:10 the throng crowding the hotel entrance began to get rowdy. People were getting soaked, feet were getting stepped on, diesel fumes were stinking up the air, and the cult members had not appeared. Angry cries erupted: "Where are they?" "What's the holdup?" "Let's get on with it." Yet the police remained stationed like statues and the lobby remained empty.

Soon another cry erupted at the fringe of the crowd. Those who heard it above the rattling of the two diesel engines turned and ran. Finally the alarm reached the front lines: "Side door!" But it was too late. Two silver and blue coaches, identical to the decoys parked out front, roared around the corner and down the street behind a police motorcycle escort toward the freeway. Only a handful from the crowd had spied the New Jesus Family hurrying through the side door and onto the waiting coaches. But another troop of officers easily kept them from interfering.

Having dispatched her guests out the side door, Eunice Carver and her staff gathered in the lobby to enjoy a good laugh watching the maggots scramble for their vehicles. The two empty buses pulled away, and the small army of police returned to their regular assignments. Cooper Sams had appreciated the decoy plan and gladly paid for the extra buses.

"All right, people," Eunice announced to her relieved coworkers, "let's get busy. We want this place put together before Jesus comes back." The crew enjoyed another good laugh.

Sixty-two

Captain Cooper Sams was elated to be on the road. He sat in the front aisle seat of the second coach with northbound I-5 stretched out before him through the massive windshield. Wipers four feet tall rhythmically swept the raindrops away. The meetings with Lila Ruth Atkinson at the Stouffer-Madison had been inspiring, but time moved too slowly. This is what he had been yearning for: activity. The acceleration of the powerful luxury coach on the rain-slick freeway could not compare to the takeoff roll of a 737. But at least he was finally moving. And the anticipation of being in the cockpit soon brought a rush he labored to contain.

He had purchased a new uniform for this occasion: black trousers and jacket sporting four gold bars on the sleeves, black cap with shiny brim trimmed with a captain's gold braid, short-sleeve white shirt, and black tie. Walt Meisner, sitting beside him, wore one of his Dixie Air Services uniforms devoid of ornamentation. It was a tad shiny in the seat but clean.

Their fellow passengers, quiet and pensive behind them, were also dressed in their finest apparel in keeping with Lila Ruth's request. Affluent members of the New Jesus Family were decked out in fine wool, silk, fur, gold, and precious stones. Most of the invited guests wore the best they had, from suits and dresses to pressed jeans and pullover sweaters. Even the most plainly attired were at ease, having been assured by Lila Ruth that beauty springs more from the inner life than from outer adornment.

All other clothes and possessions, including personal telephones, had been left with the luggage at the hotel to be disposed of at the end of the week as the management saw fit. Most of the women still carried their purses, and the journalist in the first bus also had a small computer. Cooper and Walt had their flight bags. But in less than four hours, Cooper mused, none of these prized items would be "necessities."

Cooper thought about the couple who was kidnapped from the hotel as he and the rest of the group watched in shock. He had not known the Henneseys well, but he was convinced they had not staged their own abduction. They had been devoted disciples of Lila Ruth. Cooper felt sorry for them, even though their sudden departure had allowed him to offer two of the last five alternates their vacant seats.

Cooper removed the computer from the bag at his feet and placed it on his knees. It took him less than five minutes to enter a flight plan from Paine Field to Juneau International Airport and submit it via a wireless phone in the bus' console. Two minutes later a weather and

notams package appeared on the screen. Disconnecting the phone, he
sent the data to the printer and two copies emerged from the slot
under the keyboard. He handed one copy of the package to Meisner,
even though the man didn't need it. Cooper was surprised to see his
copilot study the data so carefully. *Walt probably still hopes to take the
controls for longer than a token shift*, he thought.

"Weather might get exciting up the coast of B.C. tonight," Meisner
said in his low drone, still scanning the report.

Cooper was pleased that the smell of liquor was barely perceptible
on the man's breath. Meisner was virtually unnecessary to the operation of the plane, but Cooper didn't want him falling-down drunk in
front of any FAA inspectors who might pay them a visit in the hangar.
Booze on Meisner's breath wouldn't keep them out of the air, he knew.
To be guilty of an infraction, a member of the cockpit crew had to
actually operate the aircraft within eight hours of consumption of alcohol. Technically, a flight crew could take off drunk. They couldn't be
cited until they were in the air or after they landed. Since *Vanguard*
wouldn't be landing, Cooper was content to let Meisner have a drink
or two to keep him calm, as long as he looked and smelled presentable.

"Nothing up there we can't fly over," Cooper responded, unconcerned.

"*If* we get off the ground," Meisner said.

Cooper turned toward him. "What do you mean 'if'?"

"Didn't you see the stuff on TV about the crowds at Paine Field
today?"

"Oh, that," Cooper said with a shrug. "No problem. Schetky is a
Navy man. He'll get us out of there on time."

"The airport super?"

"Right."

"What about security?" Meisner worried aloud. "A nut with a rifle
and scope could ground us with a couple of well-placed shots."

Cooper's response was preempted by the voice of the bus driver.
"Mr. Sams, you have a call from the airport." The small man behind
the big wheel kept his eyes forward while stretching a phone behind
him toward the seat on the aisle.

Cooper took the phone, having anticipated the call. "Captain Sams."

"Captain, this is Mitchell Schetky at Paine Field." The man sounded
harried.

"Good afternoon, Lieutenant." Cooper figured the former naval officer would appreciate being identified by rank, just as he did.

Avoiding chitchat, Mitchell Schetky said, "We have a crowd situation here, Captain. Traffic is at a standstill. I need to give you a new
vector to the airport."

"I heard about your difficulties, Lieutenant. I'm sorry for the trouble."

Mitchell pressed on without acknowledging the sympathetic word.

"Plan to approach the field from the south on Airport Road. But instead of using the main entrance, turn off at 106th."

"I know where it is," Cooper assured.

"There may be some civilians hanging around the southeast entrance, but I'll have security there to let you in and keep them out."

"Roger."

"Then take Perimeter Road to the north end of the east ramp. Cross runway one-six-left at foxtrot one to the central ramp and drive directly to the hangar. The runway is closed, so you won't have any ground traffic to contend with."

"North end of east ramp to central ramp," Cooper repeated. "Got it."

"The spectators near the hangar are draped on the fence like ivy. But with a little luck you can run your buses inside and lock the doors behind you to disembark."

Cooper said, "I should send the buses out the same way then."

"Correct," Mitchell said, "unless they want to wait around until you depart."

"No, I'm sure they just want to get out of there."

"I don't blame them," Mitchell said. "And one more thing, Captain. Your prisoner is here, the guy they flew in from Texas."

"Lamar? He's a little early," Cooper said.

"Yeah, well two FBI agents showed up with him in shackles about half an hour ago. I got them into the hangar. They're waiting for you."

"Thank you, Lieutenant. And once again, sorry about the inconvenience."

"We're here to serve," Mitchell said without much conviction. "I'll talk to you in the hangar." Then he hung up before Cooper could say good-bye.

Cooper stepped up to describe the new route of travel to the driver, who in turn radioed the information to the bus ahead of them.

When the captain returned to his seat, Meisner was still absorbed in the flight plan and weather data as if boning up for an exam. Resting his head on the seat back for a minute, Cooper's thoughts turned unexpectedly—again—to Rachel. With all that was on his mind concerning departure, he had no time to think about her, and yet there she was. Cooper was relieved that Rachel was out of his life during the final hours, and yet she still haunted him. He did not want her with him aboard *Vanguard,* and yet he felt strangely incomplete without her. As much as Cooper resisted the idea, he sensed that she was still tied to him by some mystical force. It was a stupid time to wish he had treated her differently, but that's what he found himself wishing.

Beth had hoped to sit beside Raul Barrigan on the way to the airport. Bothered by her husband's lack of support, she needed a sympathetic ear. But when she boarded the lead coach, Raul was already seated next to another passenger, a dapper, elderly man from the New Jesus Family. And Raul was already into a conversation with the man, pointing to diagrams in a leaflet Raul held open for him. Beth could get no more than a quick glance and a "Hi" out of the Latino evangelist before the bus roared away from the hotel.

Instead, she sat down next to a skinny, sickly looking man she had seen only once in the Cascade Room and never talked to. "Hello, I'm Beth Cole," she said with a modicum of friendliness.

The man's arms were tightly folded across his chest, and his head leaned against the window as if his thin neck needed the rest. There was a slight grimace on his face. He clearly felt as bad as he looked or worse. "I'm Tommy," he said softly before closing his eyes and rolling his head toward the window. He would stay in that position all the way to Paine Field.

Across the aisle sat Myrna Valentine, with whom Beth had talked in the dining room for several minutes one evening. Her adorable three-year-old, Guy, knelt in the window seat staring up at the skyscrapers as the coach departed downtown Seattle. From their earlier conversation, Beth suspected that the statuesque Amerasian was disturbed and suicidal. Now she was moved by the model's face. It was so dark and distorted by gloom that it appeared deformed. Beth's heart went out to the beautiful girl so clouded with despair.

Beth reached her hand across the narrow aisle and touched Myrna's forearm. "Are you all right?" she asked.

Myrna recoiled at the unexpected contact. Measuring Beth from shadowy eyes, she muttered, "I just want to get this over with."

Beth did not remove her hand, and Myrna appeared to relax with the sustained contact. Beth said, "It might take us an hour to get to the airport in this traffic. Is there anything you want to talk about? I'll be happy to listen."

"I don't want to be in your story," Myrna said without looking up, adding sardonically, "if there even will be a story."

"This is strictly off the record, Myrna," Beth assured. "You look like you could use a sympathetic ear."

Myrna sighed, weighing Beth's offer and analyzing her sincerity. "Oh, what could it hurt?" she mused aloud. "It's all over anyway."

What tumbled out of Myrna's mouth during the next twenty minutes, with only a little prodding from Beth, was a disjointed self-history from a woman on the edge emotionally. At the center of the maelstrom, Beth discovered, was an affair with the little boy's father, who had spurned Myrna's attempts at reconciliation and threatened to sue for custody of their son. The model's problems were aggravated by personal negligence in the treatment of her depression. As she rambled on, cute little

Guy took pleasure in waving at the passengers in the cars beneath his large window.

Beth assessed that Myrna was adrift without a rudder, and that she was stepping aboard the doomsday flight to administer the ultimate punishment to herself and her former lover. "What will you do if nothing happens up there?" Beth gestured to the sky as she asked.

"I'm not expecting the Second Coming, if that's what you mean," Myrna said, almost mumbling. "I'm counting on the pilot ending it for all of us like the paper said he would."

"But what if he doesn't? What if you end up back on the ground later tonight? Where will you go?"

Myrna didn't answer. She simply dropped her head lower and shook it slowly. Beth was afraid she didn't want another option. If Cooper Sams wouldn't pull the trigger for her, she would find another way to get it done.

The idea came to Beth instantly and she offered it without pausing to evaluate it. "I know someone in Portland, Myrna; a dear friend named Shelby. She's been through a lot herself. I think you would like her."

Myrna showed barely a flicker of interest.

"In fact, you don't have to get on this plane. I can call her from the airport. You'll be home tonight. Guy can be in his own bed. And Shelby will help you get back to an even keel. She probably knows some good people in the legal system who can help you fight for your son. Isn't it worth a try?"

"I can't live without my baby," Myrna said flatly.

Beth leaned across the aisle and laid her hand on Myrna's arm again. "Yes you can, if you have to. Give it a chance. Even if you must share custody, at least your beautiful son will still be alive to enjoy."

Myrna slid her arm out from under Beth's hand. "Thank you for your concern," she said, suddenly distant. "But I need to spend the rest of my time with Guy." Then she turned toward the little boy and nuzzled him playfully as if they didn't have a care in the world.

Beth withdrew to her seat. Looking at Guy, she was instantly thankful that the child growing inside her now had a much brighter future than the little boy across the aisle with a divided family. Then it just as quickly occurred to Beth that her child's family was not exactly a model of unity at the moment. She and her husband were at odds over this assignment. They were still speaking, but they were in sharp disagreement when it came to Beth's participation in the doomsday flight.

Beth felt obligated to follow through with her agreement to fly with Cooper Sams in order to get the story she wanted. Cole was just as firmly opposed to it, stating that her first obligation was to her family. Beth felt that her freedom to do her work her way was being threatened. Cole intimated that Beth's independence had to be balanced by her commitment to him and to their relationship. Beth had asked Cole to be at the airport to see her off. He stated that he wasn't sure he wanted to be there when she took off or when she returned—if she returned. This wasn't Beth's idea of a happy family.

Is this the way it's going to be from now on? Beth pondered as the coach gradually escaped rush hour traffic and picked up speed. *Is Reagan going to contest me on every assignment? Are we going to be locked into a running feud that will eventually pull us apart? Is our child destined for the same sad, fragmented existence as cute little Guy Valentine?*

It was clear to Beth that her husband was entirely too stubborn and overprotective on this issue. She hadn't been able to convince him of the importance of her assignment and the seriousness of her promise to Cooper Sams. *If Reagan is going to change his perspective*, Beth thought, *God will have to do it, not me.* She concluded that the best way to spend the rest of the bus trip was to silently tell God what needed to happen and implore Him to get started.

Sixty-three

Mitchell Schetky's decision to bring the coaches into the airport via the east ramp proved to be a stroke of genius. About fifty spectators were waiting at 106th Street and Perimeter Road as the silver and blue coaches swept around the corner and were admitted onto the ramp through a temporary barricade manned by security personnel. Four of the more adventurous onlookers attempted to chase the vehicles across the ramp on foot, but they were quickly apprehended.

The two coaches traversed the east ramp, the short east runway 16L, and the private aircraft parking area to the central ramp without incident. As the coaches approached the Tramco hangar, a number of fence-climbers took courage from the inciting crowd and made a bold attempt to get over. Those who got past the guards waiting on the inside of the fence were easily corralled by a second wave of officers before they crossed much of the expanse between the fence and the hangar.

In the meantime, the massive bay doors opened and the coaches disappeared inside the cavernous structure, parking between the gleaming 737 on the south end and an elaborate banquet area set up on the north. The sight of the plane prompted a few more brave souls to test the security net on the wrong side of the fence. They were as unsuccessful as their predecessors. Many more of the bystanders lifted their cameras and zoomed in with telephoto lenses to record the event.

Other watchers from the fence waved homemade signs or cried out to their loved ones by name, begging them to renounce the cult and not to get on the plane. One woman screamed hysterically at the sight of her adult son stepping out of one of the coaches. The young man did not look her way, and the mother collapsed in grief. Others simply pressed themselves into the fence and wept and prayed in futile disbelief.

Having successfully delivered their cargo, the luxury coaches backed out of the hangar and departed the airport the same way they entered. The bay doors remained open only long enough for the diesel fumes to dissipate, then they were hastily closed to the accompaniment of raucous protests from the crowd lining the fence.

Inside the hangar, the grand departure banquet commenced immediately. Cooper Sams delayed taking his place at the head table in order to meet the one passenger he had not yet met. Mitchell Schetky led him to a small office in a corner of the hangar. Inside were two men in business suits. One of them partially leaned and partially sat on the corner of the desk. The other sat with legs crossed in a plush chair near the door browsing a copy of *Guns and Ammo* taken from a side table.

Sitting in a folding chair against the far wall was a man in faded, baggy orange coveralls. He was thin but not skinny as Cooper expected for a man dying of cancer. He looked to be around fifty with lined face, sunken, downcast eyes, and gray-brown hair in need of a cut. The man's hands were cuffed at his navel, and a chrome chain from the cuffs encircled his waist and dropped to shackles at both ankles.

Mitchell Schetky provided the introductions. "Captain, this is Agent Sutton and Agent Maggert with the FBI." Cooper initiated a handshake with both. Mitchell motioned to the man in the orange coveralls. "And that's your passenger, Robert Lamar." Having done his job, Mitchell excused himself.

When Cooper stepped close to shake the prisoner's hand, Agent Maggert moved in suspiciously. "Welcome aboard, Mr. Lamar," Cooper said. Robert Lamar did not stand. The chain jangled as Lamar accepted Cooper's hand tentatively. He did not make eye contact. "You are welcome to join us for the banquet." Looking up at the agents, he added, "And you gentlemen as well."

The agents declined politely. Robert Lamar grunted, "I ain't hungry."

Cooper studied the prisoner and his guardians. "It will be over an hour before we board. Can I get you people something to drink?" The agents shook their heads, but Robert Lamar mumbled, "A glass of water."

"But not in anything made of glass, Captain Sams," Agent Sutton interjected. "We don't want Robert to hurt himself just before his big field trip."

Cooper nodded. "You can join us out here if you'd like," he said, motioning to the tables where the *Vanguard* passengers were enjoying lobster bisque.

"Thank you, Captain, but we'll be fine right here," Agent Maggert responded. "Sutton and I have been baby-sitting Robert since 5:30 this morning, and we'll probably have him all day tomorrow on the way back to Texas. Another hour or so in here won't kill us."

"Isn't it unusual," Cooper said to the agents, "for the federal penitentiary to let a condemned man out for something like this?"

"A little unusual, yes," Agent Sutton answered. "But Lamar here is dying of cancer, and the warden has a soft spot for him. Like I say, it's a field trip for Robert at the government's expense. We figure he'll be back on death row tomorrow night."

Cooper wanted to hear Robert Lamar explain his view of the "field trip." But the prisoner didn't appear interested in saying much about anything, perhaps because of his ever-present chaperons.

"All right, I'll send someone for Mr. Lamar when we're ready to board," Cooper said, starting toward the door. "And I'll bring some water in."

Only after Cooper was gone did Robert Lamar look up. "Field trip— that's a good one," he said with a sly smile.

Reagan Cole had to park the S-10 nearly a mile from the entrance on Airport Road. He was grateful for the old brown cowboy hat that was stuffed behind the seat. It had been left in the truck when they bought it from a farmer in Mt. Vernon. The hat and Cole's leather jacket kept the top half of him dry as he walked along Airport Road in the drizzling rain. But his jeans and Nike high tops were damp by the time he passed the blue sign at the entrance to Paine Field at almost 5:30.

Vehicle traffic inside the airport was at a standstill. Unable to get anywhere, drivers left their cars where they were pinned in. Tow trucks had given up trying to drag them out, apparently conceding that in an hour or two it would be all over and the knot would untangle itself.

Crowds swirled through the parking lot and between stranded cars on the road. To Cole the atmosphere seemed part carnival, part sit-in, and part camp meeting revival. Some people obviously saw the doomsday flight as a lark, a joke. Bursts of laughter from around the grounds were numerous. Others were using the event as a platform to denounce someone else's cause and promote their own. Cole could hear the rhythmic chant rise and fall: "What do we want? *Dignity.* When do we want it? *Now!*" And there were a few self-promoted street-corner evangelists sprinkled throughout the crowd ranting about their own version of doomsday and salvation.

The concentration of the crowd was in the direction of the Tramco hangar, so Cole walked that way, knowing his wife was inside with the plane and the rest of the passengers. Broad-shouldered and six-foot-five, with a big hat casting a shadow of mystery across his face, Cole was an imposing figure. Large knots of the crowd relaxed to give him berth. Approaching the fence near the hangar, he found a place just out of the press of humanity to stand and watch. There was no shelter above, so he tugged the hat lower on his brow and nestled his hands into his pockets against the cold and rain.

Over the last forty-eight hours, Cole had considered a variety of responses to his wife's headstrong behavior. After only a little thought, he had eliminated the two extremes. Bodily removing her from the situation à la the commando raid at the Stouffer-Madison this morning might win this battle but leave him a bitter war to wage. Furthermore, fixing things by force seemed the least harmonious with his belief that God could solve this problem. Besides, he didn't have a commando team to employ anyway.

The other extreme, chucking it all to take the first plane back to L.A., would be a gross breach of his promise to "stand by you in whatever circumstances life may bring." Running out on stubborn Beth now was as wrong as trying to physically control her.

But the middle-ground options had proven toothless to Cole, futile. Reasoning with Beth had not worked, nor had laying down the law: "I won't permit you to go." Beth hadn't lost many contests where her will was pitted against another's, and Cole knew she intended to win this battle also. Cole had considered preaching at her about honoring her husband, but he didn't want to sour her against God's authority. He had also spurned the temptation to mount an emotional appeal, choosing to keep his tears to himself.

So in the last forty-eight hours Cole had resorted to a strategy he knew was the most effective but which left him feeling the least accomplished: prayer. Standing in the rain and staring at the hangar, he pleaded with God to pound some sense into his beautiful, obstinate wife.

Lila Ruth Atkinson had saved her most inspirational talk for last. Standing at the head table as her congregation finished dessert, she delivered a scintillating ten-minute devotional in which Reunion with Jesus-Brother loomed as real as the airplane sitting in their midst. Glowing in a floor-length white gown and diamond-studded tiara, Lila Ruth never looked more divine. As she concluded her final prayer, her faithful followers and many of the guest passengers stood to salute her with enthusiastic applause.

Boarding *Vanguard* commenced immediately. Having conducted his walkaround during dinner, Cooper Sams entered the plane first along with his first officer, Walt Meisner. Gavin Cornell, whom Cooper had chosen to ride in the cockpit jump seat, was allowed to remain comfortably seated in the hangar until the last minute due to his poor health.

The rest of the passengers were boarded by means of two portable stairways leading to two doors in the aircraft. Two FAA agents, dressed as airport ground crew, stood at the base of the stairs scanning the boarding passengers for weapons or explosives. Their scanners were hidden in their baggy gray coveralls.

Members of the New Jesus Family boarded first through the forward door behind the cockpit. Lila Ruth stood at the top of the stairway calling her flock individually by name, beginning with the most recent members of the Family and ending with those who had served as faithful disciples the entire seven years.

Each elegantly dressed Family member mounted the stairs alone and was warmly embraced by Lila Ruth. During the ceremony, the throng broke into a spontaneous melodic chant of their popular greeting: Even so, come Jesus-Brother. Family members were seated from row fifteen forward to the first-class cabin, where Lila Ruth, her elders, and their spouses took their places. Finally, Cooper Sams descended the stairs to escort Gavin Cornell to the cockpit. The actor played the role of honored passenger with a flourish.

The boarding of invited guests was conducted by the Family's uninspired administrator, Margaret Harold and her assistant, Raython Braggs, through the aft door. There was no ceremony and no singing for this group. There were no warm embraces. Margaret simply read the names of the twenty-six guests and eighteen confirmed standbys. They trudged silently up the stairs single file in no particular order, displayed their coins of identification to Raython, and took seats in the last seven rows.

Beth Cole, dressed in her burgundy suit, started several times to blend into the line leading to the stairway. But she found it difficult making her feet move. She kept waving others ahead of her until there were only a few left on the hangar floor, including Raul Barrigan in his wheelchair, two men who had volunteered to carry him up the stairs, and Robert Lamar, who was sandwiched between the two FBI agents. The last few standbys huddled at a distance in case of a last-minute defection.

Beth chided herself for the sudden reluctance. *This is the chance of a lifetime to witness a cult ritual and the impact on its members,* she coached herself. *I have to go through with this to finish the book. All my work up till now is worthless without this final, dramatic scene. And if I don't follow through, Cooper Sams has every right not to approve of me writing anything about this event when it's over.*

After each mental pep talk, Beth took a few more halting steps toward the stairway. But her feet and hands seemed to be pulling forward against an unseen force pulling her back. She saw herself as a marionette trying to break free from a puppeteer who was unwilling to let her go. And the person at the other end of the invisible strings, she knew, was Reagan Cole. He was the one trying to hold her back with his unfounded fears and the confining chauvinism of a domineering, overprotective husband. She had intended to show him once and for all that her judgment could be trusted. But it was proving to be more difficult than she had anticipated.

Raul Barrigan was lifted from his wheelchair by two other guest passengers and carried up the stairs. One of the FBI men gave the wheelchair a shove, and it rolled away toward the banquet area. Beth and Robert Lamar were the last to board. Margaret Harold spoke from the top of the stairway, "Ms. Cole, the only seat left is the aft jump seat next to Mr. Lamar. It's time for you to board."

It was a plus Beth had not counted on, and her hesitancy had secured it for her. Had she boarded earlier she would have been given a seat in row twenty or twenty-one. Now she would be able to spend the entire flight talking—or at least trying to talk—with the passenger about whom she knew the least: a death row inmate dying of cancer.

Agent Maggert, with a thin smile, gestured toward the stairway. "Ladies first." Beth gazed up the stairs at the jump seats anchored to the wall in the open doorway. Her sudden windfall spurred her to pull away from the annoying invisible strings and mount the stairway. Robert Lamar and his chaperons followed her.

Beth showed her coins to Raython Braggs, who stepped aside to let her inside. Standing in the cramped galley was the copilot, Walt Meisner, who had come back to close the aft door. The smell of liquor was on his breath. Beth stepped past him to get out of the way. The FBI men lowered the jump seat nearest the aisle and Robert Lamar sat down. Agent Maggert pulled the harness around him and snapped it in place. "Have a nice flight, Robert," Maggert said with a wry grin. "We'll see you a couple of hours." Lamar hung his head and said nothing.

Having fulfilled their responsibility, the agents descended the stairs. Having completed their jobs, Margaret Harold and Raython Braggs walked forward to take their seats.

Walt Meisner stepped around Robert Lamar to close the door so Beth could settle into the jump seat next to it. As the door swung around and covered the opening, Beth suddenly felt short of breath. When Meisner pulled the door secure and moved the handle to the locked position, she almost panicked, as if she were being locked inside a vacuum to suffocate.

It was instantly clear to her what was happening and what she now must do.

"Wait," she almost cried. "Open the door . . . please."

Meisner swung around to face her. "You change your mind, lady?"

"Yes, I'm not going."

Robert Lamar looked up with sullen eyes and a twisted smile. "I won't bite you, ma'am, if that's what you're worried about."

Beth didn't have time to answer him. To Meisner she said again, "Please open the door."

Meisner shrugged and did as she asked. Without waiting for the copilot to get out of the way, she squeezed between him and Robert Lamar to gulp the life-giving air and hurry down the stairway.

Beth was met at the base of the stairs by someone who seemed as much in a hurry as she was. Beth had seen the woman from a distance among the final few standbys. The petite figure was bundled in a leather coat, and a silk scarf covered part of her face.

The woman held out her hand. "May I have your coins please. I must get aboard."

In her haste to get away from the stairs, Beth almost didn't recognize the woman in front of her. When Beth *did* recognize her, she gasped, "What are *you* doing here?"

"I can't explain," the woman answered almost in tears. "If you're not going, I must go. Please, before the other standbys get suspicious." The woman's extended hand was trembling.

Beth wanted to protest, but she could not find the words. The pleading eyes looking up at her would not be denied. Beth quickly placed the coins in the open hand. Without a word of thanks or another second of delay, the woman hurried past her up the stairway and into the plane. The copilot glanced at the coins and let her in.

Beth turned to watch the woman disappear through the doorway. She thought about the passengers she knew: Raul Barrigan, a model named Myrna and her baby, the sickly looking man calling himself Tommy, and now someone else she never expected to join the *Vanguard* party. She hoped she would be able to write their stories, and she prayed they would be alive to read them.

Walt Meisner stepped out on the landing for a moment and looked down the stairs at Beth. "That was probably the smartest decision you've ever made, lady," he said with a quirky smile. Then he stepped inside and the big door closed behind him.

Sixty-four

When the diesel tug appeared from behind the Tramco hangar and approached the bay doors, the milling crowd stacked up at the fences eight deep in the rain to watch *Vanguard* emerge. Primed for the moment, the security force converged on the tarmac and formed a wall inside the fence. Cole took a position at the rear of the crowd where his height allowed him a decent view.

The bay doors opened, affording the waiting throng a view of the 737 bathed in bright hangar lights. A roar arose comprised of the cheers of the entertainment-seekers, the epithets of the scoffers, and the cries of the disheartened. Additional fence-climbers had been discouraged from the attempt by the imposing yellow line of defense beyond the chain-link barrier.

Cole could see that *Vanguard*'s doors were closed and her running lights were on. The aircraft was loaded, buttoned up, and ready to be towed out for engine start. It seemed smart to Cole that passengers were already on board with the doors locked before the bay doors were opened. Anyone rushing the plane now would have a difficult time getting to the passengers short of throwing a grenade or launching a rocket.

Then another jagged edge of anxiety scraped Cole's gut as he pictured Beth locked inside the plane, a willing captive of Cooper Sams' unknown intentions. The pain momentarily tempted him to scale the fence and try to stop the plane from taxiing himself. But logic assured him that attempting to break through the line of surly security troops would be a mistake. *She's in Your hands, the plane is in Your hands*, he breathed to calm himself.

The tug pulled into the dry hangar where the operator attached a boom to the nose wheel while his assistant plugged the service interphone into the cockpit jack. In the meantime, the two small trucks supporting the portable staircases emerged from the hangar and sped off toward the airport equipment garage. Apart from the two-member ground crew, Cole could see no one else around the airplane.

In a few minutes the tug surged slowly forward, pulling *Vanguard* out of the hangar's cover into the rain. At the sign of movement, crowd noise swelled again. One ground crew member walked beneath the nose of the plane maintaining contact with the cockpit via the headset. A short distance out of the hangar, the tug began a slow turn away from the fence and toward delta taxiway.

As *Vanguard* moved more into the darkness the glow of the cabin windows grew brighter, making silhouettes of the passengers sitting next to them. Cole strained to look for Beth or Raul in one of the windows as the plane gradually turned away from him. But he could identify no one from this distance.

At the sight of the airplane moving farther into the darkness, the crowd grew less vocal. People began extricating themselves from the horde to find their cars and head home. The security barricade relaxed, with a number of officers breaking rank and moving toward shelter. People still at the fence could see only the rear of the plane as it continued its wide turn to a northwest heading near the taxiway. The thrill-seekers in the crowd would soon be gone. Those who remained at Paine Field, like Cole, would wait apprehensively until *Vanguard* returned—if it returned.

Having completed a 180-degree turn taking *Vanguard* 200 yards from the fence, the tug stopped, released the nose wheel, and unplugged the interphone. With the ground crew well out of the way, *Vanguard*'s engines spooled up and roared to life, stirring up clouds of mist in their wake.

Another brief ripple of noise from the crowd around him drew Cole's attention back to the hangar. A cluster of people—three or four, Cole guessed at first from the silhouettes—had emerged from the bay doors and were hurrying across the tarmac toward the fence. The figures were hunched together, covering their heads against the rain with coats or newspapers. Straining to see over the crowd and between the loose line of security people, Cole studied the approaching group. It was a group of three, he determined: a man and two women. His heartbeat abruptly accelerated when he noticed that one of the women was taller than the other two persons.

Still unable to see clearly but filled with hope, Cole cried out Beth's name. But the heavy blanket of noise from *Vanguard's* engines and the crowd swallowed his attempt. Keeping his eyes riveted on the three figures, Cole pushed through the crowd toward the fence for a better look. People complaining about the jostling behind them quickly quieted and squeezed aside when they saw the big man coming through.

Catching sight of the group from the hangar, the security guards waved them toward the administration building near the end of the long fence. The trio broke off their course toward Cole and angled directly to the white building where they would be checked out. Reaching the front of the crowd at the fence, Cole groaned in frustration to see the woman he hoped was Beth headed away from him.

Desperate to catch up with the three figures walking quickly through the puddles on the tarmac, Cole resorted to a dirty trick. Pulling out his wallet and flashing his LAPD shield in front of him, he began pushing his way through the crowd along the fence. "Police officer coming through! Step aside please! Police officer coming through!" Like Moses at the Red Sea, the sea of humanity parted to let Cole squeeze through, but not fast enough for him to keep up with the trio heading for shelter.

Cole hailed the yellow-slicker brigade standing thirty feet on the other side of the fence. "Police officer! Stop that tall woman!" he said, waving his badge and jabbing his finger in the direction of his suspect. At the sight of a badge, the weary troops sprang into action. The cry went down the uneven line to those near enough to the trio to accost them. Meanwhile, Cole continued to blaze a trail through the curious mass at the fence.

Once the surprised trio from the hangar had been stopped and the "tall woman" turned in Cole's direction, he recognized her. Beth's lightweight raincoat and burgundy suit were stained from the downpour. She held her soft-sided case over her head with both hands. Rivulets of water ran down her arms into her sleeves. One of the off-duty cops gripped the upraised elbow of the woman he had been ordered to stop, unsure from the commotion if she was a fugitive he may have to subdue.

"Beth!" Cole cried as he started pushing through people again. "Move aside, please! Police officer coming through! Beth!"

Beth heard the familiar voice and quickly spotted the tall man in the big brown cowboy hat bobbing through the crowd. She dropped the case to her side and hurried to the fence to meet him, dragging the guy in the slicker with her.

Staring at Beth face to face through the chain-link, Cole was suddenly at a loss for words. Their last face-to-face conversation two days ago had been guardedly hostile. And their phone conversations since then had been cool and defensive. Cole didn't know if Beth's attitude had changed or if she had simply been bumped off the flight. But with the wide-eyed security man hanging onto her arm, he wasn't about to say anything personal. Cole flashed his badge at the man and said, "It's OK, buddy; she's my wife. Thanks." The guy returned an I-can't-believe-this smirk and walked away shaking his head.

Cole took a neutral approach, hoping Beth would explain. "You missed your flight."

Beth stepped closer and gripped the fence with her free hand. The rain sprinkled her face and ran in beads down her straight dark hair. She didn't seem to notice. "I . . . I couldn't do it, Reagan. I was inside, they were ready to go, but I couldn't do it."

Cole waited, studying her rain-streaked face, loving her deeply.

"When that door closed, I felt claustrophobic—cut off from my air supply. I knew instantly what was wrong: I was cut off from you. I had isolated myself and our baby from you."

Cole gripped as much of Beth's hand as he could through the holes in the fence. His throat swelled with emotion. "That's how I feel without you, Babe—cut off, helpless. I hate it."

Beth continued, "I've been acting like I'm on my own, but I'm not on my own. I think something really happened to us when we were married. Like Shelby said, we're not two anymore; we're one. That door closing—that awful feeling of being alone—brought it home to me. I can't operate like your feelings don't matter. I was wrong, Reagan, and I'm sorry."

There were no tears until the two were reunited minutes later in the narrow, crowded hallway of the airport administration building. They clung to each other in their wet clothes, weeping, apologizing, and forgiving each other. Once the air was clear between them, they went outside arm in arm to watch the takeoff while Beth told Cole about the last-minute passenger who had taken her seat.

The rear of the plane bounced lightly as it rolled along delta taxiway toward alpha. The prisoner wasn't really interested in talking to the woman strapped into the jump seat next to him, nor did she seem eager to chat with someone in handcuffs and shackles. But he had to keep up the small talk in order to distract her. They were isolated between the galley and the lavatories, and the galley lights had been left on. There wasn't much else for her to look at but him. He just didn't want her to look too closely.

He said, "I'm sorry you had to sit back here with me. I guess you got the last seat."

The woman kept her gaze straight ahead. "No problem."

"You're not afraid of me, are you—I mean, me being a felon?"

"No, I'm not afraid."

"I won't hurt you or anything. I'll be a gentleman."

"Thank you."

"Are you one of the New Jesus People?" he asked, trying to engage her eyes with his.

She turned her head only slightly toward him. "No," she said, clearly trying to avert a conversation. This and the next several responses she made were preceded by a pause, demonstrating that she was participating under mild protest.

"Then you don't really believe Jesus is going to meet us in the sky."

"No, I don't."

"Me neither," he retorted with a little laugh. "I don't believe in none of this Jesus stuff."

She said nothing this time. The prisoner decided he would have to prod her with questions if he was going to keep her engaged. "So why did you get on?"

"I have my reasons, just like you."

"Are you sick or something? That's why they let me come, you know. I'm *real* sick. Cancer."

"No, I'm not sick."

"Broke? Depressed?"

"No."

"Trouble with the law? Boyfriend problems?"

"I really don't care to discuss it."

The man searched his brain for another question. "So what do you think: Is this baby going to make it back in one piece?"

The woman turned to look him in the eye but did not reply. He finally had her full attention. He continued, "You know what I mean, don't you? Haven't you read all that stuff in the papers about this being a suicide flight?"

"Some of it."

"Well, do you think that guy up front is really going to do it?"

"What have you heard?" the woman asked with obvious interest.

The prisoner began to tell her everything he knew. He even threw in a few facts he made up, and she kept probing him with questions. The woman was now absorbed in the topic, freeing him to go to work.

The man's clasped hands, linked together by handcuffs, rested on his lap. Slowly, imperceptibly he began digging the nail of his right index finger into his left palm. In minutes the thick layer of skin-colored latex began to crumble and drop unseen between the folds of his pants to the seat and floor. He kept digging until his finger touched the small key which was hidden there.

In another minute he had the key secured in his right hand, and his seat partner was none the wiser. He judged that the aircraft was nearing the end of alpha taxiway and ready to turn onto the runway for takeoff. All he could do now was wait.

Sixty-five

"Before-takeoff checklist, Mr. Meisner," Cooper Sams announced as *Vanguard* approached the end of alpha taxiway. The regimentation and formality of an airline takeoff was not necessary on this flight, Cooper knew. But nestled into the familiar, cramped cockpit with the control wheel in his hand and an array of gauges and instruments glowing around him like stars in a beckoning heaven, he could not be otherwise.

Walt Meisner did not share his captain's penchant for precision and protocol. Indeed, the copilot's seeming indifference to the way things are done, Cooper recalled, had been a major cause of his departure from Northstar, despite his skill as a pilot. However, tonight Meisner had cooperated commendably—though without enthusiasm—during each series of standard checks. It pleased Cooper that his first officer was going by the numbers on his final flight.

"Recall," Meisner recited, referring to the list on his control wheel.

"Checked."

"Flight controls."

"Checked."

"Flaps."

"Flaps five, as required."

"Rudder, ailerons, and stabilizer trim."

"Zero, zero, and four-point-zero units."

"Cockpit door."

"Locked."

"Takeoff briefing."

"Twenty-two K max power takeoff. V-1 at 145. V-R at 148. V-2 at 155. Max speed, 170. Clean maneuvering speed, 220."

Even with 135 passengers and crew, a maximum power takeoff of 22,000 pounds of thrust was not necessary because there was no luggage or cargo in the plane's belly. But Cooper was not going to be cheated on his final takeoff, and he had no reason to spare the horses on *Vanguard*'s engines.

"Takeoff briefing reviewed," Meisner announced.

"Reviewed," Cooper echoed with satisfaction.

Watching the procedure silently and with interest from the jump seat mounted on the cockpit door was Gavin Cornell. The actor had to sit up straight to keep his knees from bumping the elbows of the pilots. The three men were so close in the compact space that each could touch the necktie of the other two without leaving his chair.

Cooper pulled the thrust levers back to idle as *Vanguard* reached alpha one leading to the main runway. "*Vanguard* two, you are cleared onto one-six right," came the voice from the tower. The message was no more or no less clipped and businesslike than for any other flight. Cooper wondered with an unseen smile what the controller really thought about giving final takeoff clearance to the plane known as the doomsday flight.

Cooper rotated the nose wheel control to affect a left turn onto alpha one. He stopped short of the runway. "Check for incoming, Mr. Meisner."

Walt Meisner dutifully peered out his side window into the rainy darkness to assure that no descending aircraft were approaching the runway. None had been reported, and there were none to be seen. "All clear, Captain," Meisner said. Cooper leaned forward to check for himself, as was his custom.

Cooper accelerated again, turned left onto runway 16R, and stopped. "Down to the lights, Mr. Meisner."

Meisner mechanically read through the cleared-for-takeoff checklist, and Cooper responded to each item short of switching on the brilliant landing lights in preparation for takeoff roll. As if on cue, the announcement from the tower came as soon as the checklist was complete: "*Vanguard* two, you are cleared for takeoff on one-six right. Wind is zero-five-zero at 12 knots."

Instead of reaching for the landing lights, Cooper switched on the cabin P.A. Normally his first officer would have made the takeoff announcement. But Cooper took pleasure in making this last one. "Brothers and sisters, we have been cleared for takeoff. Please make sure your seat belts are securely fastened. Just remember: In little more than an hour you won't need seat belts any longer. Even so, come Jesus-Brother."

Cooper did not hear the response from the cabin, which he presumed was joyous and full. But the weak, affected voice directly behind him spoke the familiar words clearly and with conviction: "Even so, come." Cooper smiled as he reached back to pat Gavin Cornell's knee. Then he flooded the runway ahead with the blaze of the landing lights and hit the throttles.

After a strong dose of medication with dinner, Tommy Eggers felt markedly better than he had on the bus. He felt so well, in fact, that he had finagled a trade with another passenger to get a seat on the plane next to Raul Barrigan. Tommy figured that he would be a lot better off seated beside a Bible-spouting Christian when the end came than beside one of the New-Age-pie-in-the-sky cult members. The crippled man's forthright message and accepting nature had affected him more than he was ready to admit. And he had one gnawing topic he wanted some answers on.

The plane was still taxiing when Tommy cut the seat exchange deal. "Well, don't this beat all," he quipped to Raul as he stepped over the man's unfeeling legs and settled into the middle seat. He was a little embarrassed about being so forward, so he covered it with humor. "All during my career with Northstar I ended up squeezed into the middle seat on standby flights. And now, my last hurrah, the most significant ride of my life, and I give up a choice window seat for this."

Surprised at the sudden change in seat partners, Raul could say no more than, "Tommy."

Tommy quickly picked up the slack. "I hope I didn't interrupt a poignant moment. I mean, did you have that guy on the verge of dropping to his knees?" Tommy gestured toward Raul's former seat mate who was now three rows in front of them next to the window.

Raul shook his head. "He was very clear: 'Don't hassle me with your religion.' He seemed pretty happy to move."

"And I thought he was just happy about getting a window seat," Tommy laughed. He marveled at how good he felt. He suspected that his revival of spirits had more to do with his psyche than with the six horse pills he swallowed during dinner. Part of it had to do with the imminent end of his life. There was no time left to maintain a false front. If he only had an hour left, he would spend it being himself. And part of it had to do with the man in the wheelchair who had seen the ugly side of him and didn't look away.

Tommy was interrupted by the voice of Captain Sams over the cabin speakers: "Brothers and sisters, we have been cleared for takeoff. Please make sure your seat belts are securely fastened. Just remember: In little more than one hour you won't need seat belts any longer. Even so, come Jesus-Brother."

The unison response in the forward half of the cabin was moderately enthusiastic: "Even so, come." Back where Tommy and Raul sat it was spotty at best.

The steady, swelling clamor of jet engines followed immediately. The 737 lunged from its standing start and eagerly dashed down the runway toward rotation speed. Tommy allowed the growing momentum to draw his head back to the headrest. He sensed the nose wheel leave the ground as the aircraft mocked gravity's domination and committed allegiance to the laws of aerodynamics. He felt the landing gear retract into the belly and relished the upward climb.

How is Cooper Sams going to ruin all this? he thought. *How does he plan to usher us all into the great beyond when Jesus-Brother stands us up?* Tommy had thought about the options discussed on the talk shows. He hoped for something quick, like hitting the ground nose first at 300 knots and being liquefied as the plane collapsed like an aluminum can. But he had even come to accept the prospect of water ditching and drowning as more merciful than allowing the AIDS worm to eat him alive over the next few months.

"Why are you doing this?" Tommy said to Raul almost a minute into takeoff.

Raul replied confidently, "In order to talk to people like you about God, to help you get ready to meet Him."

"Right, but that's not what I mean," Tommy said, shaking his head slightly. "Any number of preachers or evangelists or missionaries could be in your seat right now. How did *you* get elected?"

Raul nodded understanding. He hesitated, leading Tommy to suspect he was debating with himself over how to answer. "It was kind of a vision."

"A vision," Tommy echoed with interest. Raul related briefly the compelling scene of *Vanguard*'s demise he had witnessed as he sat in his car in front of Camelback Mountain three months earlier.

"So God told you that this plane is going to crash," Tommy said.

"No, that's not what I got from the vision," Raul contested.

"That may not be what *you* got, but it seems to me God wouldn't crash a plane in your vision if it wasn't going to happen."

Raul seemed only a little flustered by the objection. "I don't think God was telling me the plane was going to crash. After all, we're nowhere near Camelback Mountain, and that's where it appeared to crash. I think He was trying to impress on me the desperation facing the people on this flight, especially those who see a 'suicide flight' as a way to end their misery."

"But the plane could go down," Tommy said. "You know a lot of people think it will. I'm sure there are odds on it somewhere: Vegas, Atlantic City. There are people holding their breath to see what's going to happen to us in the next hour because they have a lot of money riding on it."

"I'm not God, Tommy. I don't know that the plane will crash."

"And you don't know that it *won't*," Tommy bored in.

Raul smiled at being cornered. "You're right. The plane could crash. The pilot may be a sadistic mass murderer. I just don't know."

Tommy smiled satisfaction. "Then let me get back to my original question. Why are you on board? You had three days in the hotel to preach to your flock, and I have to say you did a bang-up job. You got my attention, that's for sure. But why get on the plane? You're immobile. You can't march up and down the aisle and pass out your leaflets."

Raul looked away. "I hoped they would give me the opportunity to talk to everyone over the P.A."

"What would you say on the P.A. that you haven't already said to everyone in person? Nothing to risk your life for, that's my guess."

Raul was still averting his eyes. "I didn't want to miss an opportunity to speak to one more person."

"Well, the first guy sitting here wasn't very interested. That seems like poor planning on God's part."

"But you're here now," Raul said. "Maybe He wants me to talk to you about your soul and salvation."

"We already had that conversation. And we wouldn't be talking now if I hadn't arranged to swap seats. God didn't do that, I did."

Raul said nothing. *Vanguard* continued its steady ascent.

"Here's what I'm getting at. It's been on my mind since we talked at the hotel last night. Your opportunities up here are minimal compared to the potential risk." Tommy leaned closer. "I just want to know if you have another agenda, something to do with these." Raul looked to see Tommy's hand resting on his thin, motionless legs.

"What do you mean?" Raul shot back, unable to cover his defensiveness.

"I mean maybe you're on this plane because, like many of us back here, dying in a crash would put an end to *your* misery."

Raul remained statue-still, staring at Tommy, so Tommy continued. "I heard from your writer friend that you were a baseball star in college and that your big dream of playing professionally was wiped out in an instant. That's a disappointment that would make a lot of kids give up. And it must be hell for a handsome young buck like you to think about living the next fifty years without normal sex. I don't doubt your holy motives over the last three days. But somewhere in that saintly heart of yours I think there's a little demon telling you that going down with the plane won't be all bad. Am I right?"

Tommy had neither the time nor the inclination to mince words, and he hoped Raul Barrigan felt the same way. If the young Latino could not admit even a small temptation to escape a difficult life to go live with Jesus, Tommy would begin to doubt the credibility of his message—a message which appealed to him more with each passing minute.

Raul did not answer for several seconds. His eyes were on the ceiling and his lips were taut. Tommy heard the hum of the wing flaps retracting as *Vanguard* continued its climb toward cruising altitude. He waited.

Finally Raul turned to face him. "I have to be honest with you," he said softly. "You're right. Life for me without legs and without baseball is the pits. And no sex or children—yeah, that's the pits too. From the night I was injured almost four years ago, I've thought about suicide a lot. Maybe the devil sent a demon of self-destruction to be my constant companion. Maybe these thoughts are from my sinful flesh. Maybe both—I don't know. But almost every day I think about the Bible verse that says, 'To live is Christ, to die is gain.' I find myself willing to trade the rest of my life for the 'gain' part."

Raul looked away again as if summoning strength. Then he turned back and said, "But I would be less than honest if I let you believe that a little demon of suicide is responsible for me being on this plane today. Yes, it has occurred to me that I could die doing this, and I admit that the thought isn't totally unpleasant. But I came to Seattle because I believe God sent me here. I boarded this plane because I believe God wanted me on this flight. If I live through it, the greatest reward God could give me is my legs. But if my life ends tonight, it's my gain."

"What if you survive the flight and God *doesn't* give you back your legs?" Tommy pressed.

Raul nodded knowingly. "I think I've learned from the last few days that God can use me anyway—without legs, without a wife and children."

It was Tommy's turn to retreat into thoughtfulness. Then he said, "So the doomsday flight is a no-lose situation for you."

Raul savored the statement for a moment. "No lose—yes, I'd have to agree," he said.

Tommy's gaze dropped. "Funny, it's all coming up no-win for me." It wasn't funny to Tommy. But he knew he didn't have to explain to Raul his reference to the disease that would claim him if he survived the flight and the uncertainty of his eternal destiny if the plane went down.

"Then maybe that's the reason I'm sitting here right now," Raul countered confidently. "I think I can get you out of this with a big win."

Sixty-six

The elders of the New Jesus Family had boarded fifty chilled magnums of exquisite champagne and enough pieces of crystal stemware for everyone. Shortly after reaching cruising altitude, glasses were distributed and corks were popped. Those who chose to imbibe joined in a round of joyous toasts commemorating imminent translation into Jesus-Brother's kingdom. The less festive unbelievers in the rear third of the plane lifted their glasses to a number of less glorious causes or memories.

Having remained a virtual teetotaller for his four years in the New Jesus Family, Cooper Sams felt he deserved one last glass of the bubbly. And his appetite was keen for a drink. Walt Meisner had been nipping from a small flask of liquor in his flight bag since they got on the plane. The fragrance of alcohol, so foreign to the cockpit during his career, appealed to Cooper tonight. He felt reckless. After all, in about twenty minutes he would break all the rules he had so carefully observed at the controls over the years and initiate his plan to accelerate the engines to the breaking point. He certainly could afford one leisurely glass of champagne.

Wanting to fully enjoy his last flight, Cooper had operated *Vanguard* completely by hand, going from takeoff to cruising altitude without autopilot. Now, leveled off at 35,000 feet at .75 mach, the captain engaged autopilot with a touch to the mode control panel and put Meisner in charge. Meisner knew nothing yet about the deviation from the flight plan Cooper had in mind. *He'll love it,* Cooper had told himself, *especially if I let him help me inch the throttles forward. Until then all he has to do is watch the instruments while good old "Otto" flies the plane.* Cooper remembered how he and Meisner had joked about a nerdy, invisible third crew member always in the cockpit with them. They called him Otto Pilot.

Cooper donned his cap as he always did to cover his large bald spot, but he left his jacket in the closet. As Meisner and Otto worked, the captain and Gavin Cornell retired aft for a drink.

The forward galley and entry door area and the entire center aisle were jammed with people. Women in satin gowns, furs, and jewels and men in tuxedos and expensive tailored suits squeezed around each other to propose toasts. Magnums of champagne circulated freely and glasses were generously refilled. The noise of chatter and laughter was punctuated by the melodic ring of fine crystal. An informal, repeated litany dominated the sound of conversation: "Even so, come Jesus-Brother"; "Even so, come."

Filled glasses were thrust into the hands of Cooper and Gavin as they stepped outside the cockpit. Gavin moved ahead through the first class section to make his final public appearance in coach. Before Cooper could follow, he was enveloped by the Family elders in joyous celebration.

During Cooper's tenure as senior elder in the New Jesus Family, the relationship between himself, Lila Ruth Atkinson, Kimberley Bemari, Frank Woods, and Erich Dammasch was similar to that of the officers of a corporation. They worked hard together to achieve common goals while battling resistance from the outside. But socializing among the elders had been strictly platonic and limited to Family business functions. Yet tonight the mood in the first-class cabin, Cooper quickly determined, was far from businesslike.

First to greet him was Lila Ruth, who gathered him into her motherly embrace and kissed him on the cheek while trying not to spill her champagne on him. The embrace and kiss were the first in their four years together. "Your destiny is fulfilled, Cooper," she sang with unbounded joy. "I am so happy for you. I'm so happy for all of us." Cooper could not remember Lila Ruth calling him by his first name before.

Cooper had scarcely left Lila Ruth's arms before he was engulfed in the bear hug of Frank Woods. Frank was a former logging contractor who had left his wife and children five years earlier to join the Family. He had also donated a small fortune to Lila Ruth's ministry. Frank's second wife, Melba, had also left her family to follow her spiritual destiny. Frank and Melba were the first of several couples in the New Jesus Family united in marriage by Lila Ruth.

Frank Woods gripped Cooper for several seconds. When he pulled away, his face beamed with joy and his eyes were filled with tears. He could say nothing. Melba hugged Cooper too, even though the two of them had rarely spoken since they met.

Next to greet Cooper was Raython Braggs, who was chug-a-lugging champagne like it was Kool-Aid. Cooper edged two steps around Braggs only to find Kim Bemari waiting for him. Kim was a buxom, moderately attractive forty-something widow and socialite who looked especially alluring in her black evening gown. She had poured a significant portion of her late husband's estate into the New Jesus Family over the years of her membership.

Before Cooper could defend himself, Kim Bemari, with champagne glass in hand, wrapped her arms around his neck and drew him into an embrace that was anything but motherly. She pressed her body against his and covered his mouth with a long, moist kiss. Had her glass been filled, champagne would have trickled down the back of Cooper's neck.

Flowing with the streak of recklessness coursing through him since takeoff, Cooper responded impulsively. He wrapped his arms around the unlikely temptress and pressed her closer. When she finally released him, she said, "It's been a pleasure serving Jesus-Brother with you, Cooper." Kim's tone and eyes were overtly seductive, a side of the woman he had never imagined.

"Thank you, Ms. Bemari," Cooper said, trying to regain his objectivity. He was astonished at the sudden dissolution of restraint which he observed around him and discerned in himself. *These people sincerely believe the end is upon us,* he observed silently. *They have no reason to hold back, no reason to hide what they really feel, no reason to play out a role. Is this how everyone responds when they know death is only minutes away?*

Sliding away from Kim Bemari, Cooper took his first sip of champagne. It tasted bitter to him, not at all what he had expected. He tried another sip with the same result. Valerie Dammasch, Elder Erich's wife, was right there to fill his glass and embrace him before edging away with her half-full magnum in search of more empty glasses.

Cooper tried a third sip of the sparkling, pale-gold liquid but still didn't like it. But wedged into the center aisle between passengers, he didn't know how to get rid of it. Finally, reaching the bulkhead between first class and coach, he found enough room to stoop down and hide his glass behind the last row of first-class seats.

Before leaving the cockpit, Cooper had determined to walk the length of the center aisle and greet each of his passengers, if not with a handshake, at least with a smile, nod, or casual salute. He never did so during even one of the thousands of commercial flights during his career. But it seemed the right thing to do on this most significant journey. These people trusted him to deliver them into the hands of their spiritual Parent and Brother. Cooper felt an obligation to assure them that he would honor their trust.

As he inched through the crowd in the aisle, the normally sedate and dignified New Jesus congregation was as lively and familiar as their elders. Cooper was backslapped or glad-handed or embraced or kissed by most of the people he had called his spiritual family for four years. For many of them, their exuberance was greatly implemented by the effect of high altitude on too much alcohol. A few Family members Cooper encountered were already drunk and drinking still.

It occurred to him that these people were displaying an emotional release of pent-up pressures Cooper had heretofore failed to fully acknowledge. Nearly all of the eighty-nine individuals who comprised the final roster of the New Jesus Family (after the Hennesseys were abducted) had paid a stiff price to follow their convictions. Some had been disowned by family members, ostracized by coworkers, and abandoned by friends for their religious beliefs. Others had walked away from loving relationships at great personal pain to obey the call of Jesus-Brother. And all had been ridiculed and laughed at during the three months the New Jesus Family had been in the national fishbowl.

These eighty-nine had toughed it out and survived the harassment. They were on their way to glory while those who mocked them were destined for the flames. The New Jesus Family believed wholeheartedly in Lila Ruth Atkinson, Cooper Sams, Jesus-Brother, and Reunion. The reward for their faith and persistence was at hand. Wrapped in the security of the ark called *Vanguard*, they needed only a little champagne to spring the lid on their closely guarded emotions.

Cooper understood the phenomenon before him, but he could not fully identify with it. He had suffered very little as a result of his choice to follow Lila Ruth Atkinson. And though he believed in Reunion, he was too burdened with the responsibility of commanding the ark to completely uncork his emotions as fellow Family members had done. And there was the matter of his consummate, intimate act of faith at the controls of *Vanguard*. No, others may celebrate now, but he could not, perhaps not until the blinding light of Reunion finally drew him out of the cockpit and into the arms of his God.

Cooper felt restrained for another reason—two reasons, actually: Rachel Sams and Kathy Keene. As fully as he had prepared himself to leave the earth and enter heaven, these two emotional accounts were still open.

Cooper Sams could not rectify his strong faith against Kathy's desertion. He was the emperor regaled for Reunion; her decision not to participate was like the impudent child declaring that he had no clothes at all. Kathy could not be convinced otherwise, nor could Cooper produce sufficient empirical data to convince her. She had stayed behind, and he was perplexed by it.

Neither could Cooper rectify his commitment to Lila Ruth and Jesus-Brother and Reunion with Rachel's equally strong commitment to him. Try as he might—short of outright cruelty, which he would not countenance in himself, he had not succeeded in shaking her. Had she threatened him, sued him, cursed at him, or simply disappeared, he might feel that his departure was a favor to her. But for loving him unconditionally when he had done little to encourage it, Cooper had no explanation or defense—and that unsettled him as well. It was an enigma he would take with him into the next life.

The gaiety of the crowd began to diminish from the middle of the coach section aft. Fewer of the guest passengers crowded the aisle toasting each other and sipping champagne. More of them sat talking or idly watching or purposely drinking themselves into a stupor. And many of them leered at Cooper, asking with their eyes, "Are you going to pull the plug for us as we hope?" Some even posed the question aloud, to which Cooper gave his stock reply: "Jesus-Brother will answer your question at 8:02."

Cooper dutifully greeted everyone row by row except those who obviously did not want to be disturbed. Most of the seriously ill passengers had reclined their seats, draped themselves with blankets, and closed their eyes to wait for the end. To Cooper they looked like so many corpses already laid out for burial.

Tommy Eggers was an exception. When Cooper reached his row, the former flight attendant with waxy yellow-white skin was engrossed in conversation with the quadriplegic. A worn, leather-bound Bible sat open on the service tray in front of Tommy. Raul Barrigan was talking and Tommy was listening. They broke off their conversation only long enough to return Cooper's greeting.

Barrigan's pitch sounded familiar. Cooper had eavesdropped on him a few times at the hotel. God loves you, but sin looms between you and God like an impassable chasm. The cross of Christ fills the chasm like a bridge. Personal faith in Christ allows you to traverse the bridge and enter eternal life with God. Cooper admired the man for his faith and persistence, though he concluded it mattered little now, since everyone aboard *Vanguard* was about to cross the bridge to God together.

As Cooper continued to snake through the thinning crowd in the aisle, he reflected on the probability that Rachel had found religion — somewhere, somehow — during the last year. The loving devotion she displayed in place of bitter vengeance had to come from deep inner peace. Cooper wondered if he and Rachel would still be together if she had found her center in the New Jesus Family when he had.

Cooper had also seen Raul Barrigan talking to Myrna Valentine, the beautiful Amerasian model, during their stay at the Stouffer-Madison. Looking at her now, Cooper guessed that the Latino evangelist's message of hope and salvation didn't take with her. She sat in the window seat of row 18 while her little boy watched the activity wide-eyed from the middle seat. The model was not physically ill like so many in this section of the plane. But the death pall shadowing her face rivaled that of the shrouded bodies near her. Myrna accepted Cooper's handshake with no change of expression.

Cooper approached a knot of eight passengers jamming the aisle at row 22 just ahead of the galley. Sensing the need to return to the cockpit soon, he knifed into the clog with his put-on smile and hand of welcome. His last stop would be the aft jump seats where, according to Margaret Harold, Robert Lamar and Beth Cole were seated. Cooper imagined that the journalist was making the prisoner's last hour miserable with her incessant, ultimately meaningless questions.

The knot unraveled as Cooper pressed into it. The last two people stepped aside like a curtain parting, and the captain was suddenly face to face with his estranged wife. Rachel Sams stood under the arch of the aft bulkhead, having waited for him to work his way to the back. Her auburn hair was nicely styled. Her face was bright and confident, though unsmiling. She wore a conservative cobalt blue, long-sleeve party dress with a subtle splash of silver and topaz accessories.

Cooper was stunned breathless. As if anticipating his reaction, Rachel spoke right away. "I'm not here to interfere, Cooper. But I am still your wife. No matter what happens, my place is with you. I knew God wanted me here when Beth Cole decided at the last minute not to come. I convinced her to give me her place. Please don't be upset. I promise to stay out of your way."

The cluster of people around Cooper was oblivious to the confrontation. They didn't know the petite woman in the blue dress. And since they were not looking at her, neither could they understand her above the loud slipstream surrounding the aft cabin. Cooper and Rachel were effectively alone in a space the size of a phone booth.

A rush of conflicting feelings exploded in Cooper at the sight of Rachel, feelings that provoked expletives of shock rather than questions. But before he could utter a sound, Cooper and Rachel and everyone standing in the airplane were abruptly thrown sideways as *Vanguard* snapped into a hard, sustained turn.

Sixty-seven

Celebration turned to terror in a heartbeat for 134 men, women, and children inside the 737 called *Vanguard*. Laughter and conversation were overcome by cries of fear and pain. When the airplane flipped into a 50-degree right bank, everyone and everything flew to the left, toward the upraised wing. Those standing in the center aisle—over sixty people in all—toppled onto those seated in the A, B, and C seats to the left. Those who were not belted into the D, E, and F seats—and few were—tumbled toward the center aisle. Those whose equilibrium was already challenged by alcohol fell the hardest.

Flying crystal stemware smashed against the windows and walls or shattered between colliding bodies. Heavy, dark-green champagne bottles careened across the cabin like bowling pins, splitting a few scalps. Flailing hands and arms and legs, contacting shards of crystal, were sliced open. Blood sprang immediately from jagged wounds and mingled with foaming champagne, which sprayed in every direction.

With *Vanguard* frozen in a tight bank, people stayed where they had fallen, pinned down by 2 Gs of force. Some yelped in pain, unable to push off a smothering body or turn away from a piece of glass. A few became immediately sick, regurgitating dinner and champagne where they fell. The aircraft also complained under the maneuver with groans of materials under stress.

The force of the turn had thrown Rachel Sams against the galley wall beside the center aisle. Her training and experience in the air immediately took over. Spreading her feet and bracing herself against the wall with her hands, she was able to remain upright through the turn.

Even though he was standing within a foot of Rachel at the sudden turn, Cooper missed the galley wall and fell into row 22 on top of two passengers. He banged his thigh hard going over the armrest and scraped his right hand on the jagged stem of a champagne glass. The man standing nearest Cooper fell with him, bounced off, and slid down between the seats.

Cooper's thought during the first few seconds of the crisis was that Reunion had occurred earlier than expected, that Jesus-Brother had snatched the 737 out of midair. But with the pain he felt and the pandemonium around him, he quickly realized that this was not the work of God. His thoughts turned immediately to the man sitting at *Vanguard*'s controls.

The plane was in the middle of what Cooper assumed was a 180-degree turn—on a dime. But the fact that the contents of the cabin had flown to the high side of the bank was clear evidence that it was not a controlled turn. It is both possible and normal in a jet aircraft to effect a tight turn without disrupting the center of gravity. The yaw damper, when on, automatically stabilizes the aircraft and keeps it from skidding through the air during the turn. Everything and everyone aboard banks with the plane, just as a race car driver stays erect and in control in his car at 200 mph through a 45-degree banked turn. The yaw damper creates a stable artificial highway beneath the plane during the radical maneuver.

Meisner had not only overridden autopilot, Cooper realized. He had also overridden the yaw damper by depressing the right rudder pedal to effect the surprise turn. Without the yaw damper, the plane was skidding through the turn like a race car losing traction in a high-speed banked turn and skidding toward the high side. Chaos in the cabin was the result. And Cooper had to get back to the cockpit to find out why his copilot had allowed or induced such chaos.

At the first sign that the bank was abating, Cooper, minus his cap which disappeared in the fall, pushed himself out of the row to the aisle, gripping the armrest and seat back for balance. His right thigh stung with pain, and blood from the wound on his hand stained the fabric on the seat.

Cooper cautiously stood and immediately turned to look for Rachel. What he saw was a man in orange coveralls brusquely pushing the woman aside and charging toward him. The handcuffs and shackles were gone. The man had a small, black, semiautomatic pistol in his hand.

The prisoner moved cat quick from the galley into the cabin. In a blur of motion, he spun Cooper around by one arm and held him over a seat back. The man was too fast and too strong to be dying of cancer, Cooper knew. Out of the corner of his eye he saw that the pistol was aimed at the ceiling but ready for action. The people around them, including Rachel Sams, froze at the sight of the weapon.

"All right, Captain, what are you trying to do with this airplane?" the man demanded fiercely.

"Who are you? Why do you have a gun on my airplane?" Cooper demanded in return.

"Agent Ron Whiteside, FBI." The man almost growled his identity. "I'm sitting in for Robert Lamar, who never got his invitation, by the way. Federal pens don't allow field trips, even for cancer patients. I'm surprised you didn't figure that out."

"FBI?" Cooper said, astonished and puzzled.

"That's right. The feds want onboard insurance that this plane comes down as safely as it went up."

Vanguard had resumed a steady, level course, except Cooper knew they were headed away from Juneau now. The passengers were picking themselves up cautiously and trying to help the injured, keeping a wary eye on the scene playing out near the aft galley.

Cooper said. "We're not going to Juneau. We're—"

"I know you're not going to Juneau," Whiteside barked. "That was about a 180-degree swing tighter than I've ever flown one. And I want to know what you're doing with this airplane."

"I'm not doing anything," Cooper replied, keeping an eye on the gun. "My copilot is at the controls."

"You two are trying to take this plane down, aren't you, just like the papers said?" Whiteside said, pushing on the back of Cooper's neck for emphasis.

"I told you, *I'm* not doing anything," Cooper snapped. "The hard roll wasn't my idea. We're supposed to be on autopilot and heading north. I have to call up front and find out what the problem is."

Whiteside hesitated a couple of seconds, then he pulled Cooper upright by the back of his shirt then let him go. He waited to speak until Cooper turned around, boring into the captain as if to discern whether or not he was telling the truth. "All right, call him. But I'm watching and listening." The menacing tone was fading from his voice.

Before Cooper could move to the interphone in the galley, a man five rows ahead risked an interruption. "Captain Sams, this lady is bleeding badly. We need a first aid kit here." Cooper could only partially see the woman sitting on the floor in the aisle. The shoulder of her white sequined gown was stained red, and someone held a bloody blanket against the side of her neck.

Without consulting Whiteside, Cooper turned to Rachel, who was watching from the galley. He read the shock and fear on her face, and his heart suddenly went out to her. "Are you all right?" he said, genuinely sympathetic.

Rachel rubbed her left shoulder. "Yes, just a bump."

"Will you take over the first aid while I get the plane under control — and find someone to help you?"

"Of course," Rachel said eagerly. Then to Agent Whiteside she added, "May I get the first aid kit out of the overhead?" She pointed to the last bin over row 22.

Whiteside nodded and stepped aside to let her pass.

"Captain, I'll get the first-class kit and help up there." The voice came from a skinny man a few rows forward who looked too sick to help anyone. But at least he wasn't bleeding.

Cooper turned to look. "Thank you, Tommy," he said, "we can use your help. And keep everyone up there away from the cockpit door until we find out what's going on." Then the captain called out, "Everybody else, please try to get back to your seats and fasten your seat belts while we take care of this problem."

Tommy Eggers called to Rachel as he motioned toward the aisle seat next to him. "Mr. Barrigan here could use a bandage. He was hit on the head with a bottle."

"I'll be right there," Rachel said, removing from the overhead compartment the white metal box bearing the bold red cross. Assured that Raul Barrigan would be cared for, Tommy began stepping around and over people on his way to the first-class cabin.

Other passengers called out their need for help as general calm returned to the cabin. Passengers who were able moved back to their seats and buckled in, leaving a few in the aisle to tend to those who were more seriously injured.

Cooper stepped through the bulkhead to the aft entry area next to door 2L and the jump seats with Agent Whiteside right behind him. On the floor were the prisoner's chain and handcuffs with the key still in the lock. Cooper figured the FBI man had the compact polymer pistol strapped to his leg underneath the baggy pants. Whiteside still held the gun at his ear, pointed up.

Before picking up the phone, Cooper said, "Please put that thing away. You could blow out a window, causing serious depressurization problems. We could lose a passenger. Or a bullet could go through a wall and hit a hydraulic control line."

Whiteside, who was watching Cooper and the passengers in the aisle at the same time, finally relented. He slipped the weapon into the large pocket of his orange coveralls.

Cooper punched in the code for the cockpit, and Meisner picked up immediately. "This is the captain speaking."

"No, Walt," Cooper said angrily, *"this* is the captain speaking. What *are* you doing? That stunt of yours got some people hurt back here."

Meisner laughed. "Well, I'm sorry, Coop. But like the flight attendants always say, 'You are free to move about the cabin. But when seated, keep your seat belt fastened securely in case we encounter unexpected turbulence.'"

"That was not turbulence, Walt. You threw us into an uncontrolled turn. What are you trying to do?"

"I just wanted to stand this honey on its ear one time before the end. It wasn't as fun as an A-6, but I enjoyed it." Meisner laughed again.

"You're drunk, Walt."

"Not as drunk as I'd like to be. And not too drunk to fly this thing."

"Well, you're not flying anymore," Cooper said, eyeing the FBI man. "Just hold it steady until I get up there."

"Don't bother, Coop," Meisner said rather casually, "because the door is locked and I won't let you in. I have the crash axe up here. I'm going to take the controls from now on."

"What?" Cooper snapped.

"We're going back to Seattle. I have some unfinished business to take care of."

"What business?"

"With our former employer Northstar. They wouldn't give me my bars, Coop. In fact, you even joined the review board in voting me down a time or two. As a result, I had to move to Atlanta, and the move all but killed my Jeannie. I'm a good pilot, Coop, but Northstar screwed me over. It's payback time for you and them."

"What are you planning to do, Walt?" Cooper said, afraid that he already knew. Agent Whiteside asked "What's happening?" with his eyes, but Cooper ignored him.

"We're going to drop in on corporate headquarters—literally," Meisner said, seemingly proud of the way he phrased it.

Cooper's spine turned to ice as he envisioned *Vanguard* swooping low across Seattle and plowing into Northstar's new corporate buildings on Military Road. Choosing his words and tone carefully so as not to tip off the FBI man to the dilemma, he said casually, "But you have to think of the other passengers, Walt."

"I *did* think about them, my friend. Remember, I begged you for a shakedown flight, just you and me and your pretty 737. It would have been especially nice to drop in on headquarters during the day while all the brass were in their offices. But you didn't go for it. So now we have to take your whole charter group to the party."

Cooper remained calm and vague in his reply to keep Whiteside in the dark. "I don't think that's very considerate."

"Captain, don't joke around with me. Your people back there don't expect to live through the night anyway. You're taking them all to Jesus, remember? When He doesn't catch you in the sky you're going to plant this thing in a mountain or something, right? Well, I'm doing the same thing, just a different target."

Cooper glanced at his watch. It was 7:32. He should be in the cockpit right now getting ready to move the throttles forward to race into the light. *Why so many obstacles to my mission?* he wondered. *First, Rachel appears out of nowhere. Then Walt Meisner turns into a skyjacker. Pathfinder, what am I to make of this?* Cooper felt nothing inside, nor could he stand by and wait. If he didn't reclaim the cockpit, *Vanguard* had a good chance of hitting Northstar headquarters before Jesus-Brother appeared to rescue them. This was not how he and Pathfinder had planned it. But at the moment Cooper's inner guidance system was silent.

Cooper had to stall to come up with an idea. "Walt, ATC can see what you're doing and—"

"I may be a little drunk, old pal, but I'm not stupid," Meisner snarled. "I turned the radio and encoding altimeter off, and they will stay off. Air traffic control can see that we're headed back to Seattle. They tried to reach us, but unfortunately our radio is out—they think. They'll clear out Paine Field and Boeing Field and SeaTac for an emergency landing. They won't know we're headed for the Northstar complex until it's too late."

"Walt, let me come up so we can talk about—"

Meisner continued as if Cooper hadn't spoken. "And just for good measure, Coop, listen to this." What came through the earpiece next was the sound of destruction—metal crashing against metal, blows being struck.

Cooper could remain calm no longer, even though he knew his outburst would excite the FBI agent watching him. "Walt, no! Stop! Whatever you're doing, please stop!"

Whiteside's eyes widened and his nostrils flared. Without waiting for an explanation for the captain's outburst, he drew his pistol and started up the aisle toward the cockpit.

Sixty-eight

Raul Barrigan shook off the effects of being clubbed by a flying champagne bottle, thrown sideways in his seat, and sandwiched between Tommy Eggers and a large woman who had fallen on him. Dazed from the blow which left an inch-wide cut on his forehead, Raul had missed the excitement in the back of the plane. Someone—Raul didn't see who—had dropped off a butterfly bandage. Now, with all but a half dozen people back in their seats, he was holding steady while a woman in Tommy's vacant seat applied it to his wound.

When the wings suddenly went vertical—at least he felt like they were going vertical—and bodies and bottles started flying, Raul thought it was all over. He was sure the plane was banking into a death dive, and unwelcome terror rose in his throat like bile. Yet even in the first second of chaos he knew Cooper Sams wasn't the cause of it. He had greeted the captain briefly on his way to the rear of the plane and had not seen him return. Then the bottle conked Raul on the head, and he didn't think about anything until the plane was righted and he found a bloody handkerchief in his hand. Somebody—perhaps Tommy—had set him up again.

"Stop! Don't do it!" The authoritative cry came from the back of the cabin. Raul whirled his head around, saw what was happening, and reacted all in the same instant. What he saw was a man in prison garb starting hurriedly up the aisle with a gun drawn and raised high. Raul knew immediately that this had to be the prisoner who was flying with them. He also knew what was wrong with the picture: Prisoners are supposed to be in chains and they are *not* supposed to have guns.

In that fast-as-a-blink glimpse, Raul also saw Captain Cooper Sams crying after the prisoner from the aft galley. There was panic on the captain's face. Raul's snap conclusion was that the man in orange and someone in the cockpit were working together to sabotage the plane. And if the captain didn't want the man going up front, somebody had to stop him.

Using his powerful arms, Raul hurriedly launched himself into the aisle just as the man, who was breaking into to a run, reached his row. Raul's useless legs collapsed under him when he hit the floor. But the sudden human blockade clipped the surprised Whiteside at the knees and sent him cartwheeling over Raul, legs bent and splayed. Grabbing the man in flight by one arm, Raul pulled him hard to the floor and caught the gun in midair when it flew from the man's hand. The safety was still on.

Whiteside shook off the blow and scrambled to his hands and knees to retaliate. But he froze at the sight of the gun aimed at his heart with Raul's slightly deformed thumb releasing the safety. People in the nearby rows, at first curious to watch the confrontation, backed away at the sight of the gun.

"Police officer, Phoenix P.D.," Raul announced with authority. "Hold it right there."

"FBI agent," Whiteside replied in the same tone, smart enough not to move.

"He told me the same thing," Cooper Sams said to Raul, hurrying up behind him. "But I want to see ID."

"I have ID," Whiteside insisted, respecting the man with the gun.

Raul didn't move his eyes from his captive. "All right, FBI," he said to Whiteside. "Nice and easy."

Whiteside nodded. He slowly brought his right leg forward and began to pull up his pant leg, watching Raul and the gun closely. Strapped to the man's calf was the breakaway holster where the nine-millimeter polymer pistol had been hidden. Underneath the strap was a plastic card. Whiteside removed it with the care of someone disarming a bomb. Then he held it out so Raul and Cooper could see his holograph next to the FBI seal.

Satisfied, Raul snapped the safety in place with his thumb and moved the gun barrel from horizontal to vertical. Whiteside tried to cover a sigh of relief.

"What were you planning to do—kick in the cockpit door?" Cooper hissed at the FBI man.

Whiteside bit his lip but wouldn't comment.

"I'm missing something here," Raul said, slipping the pistol inside his belt for a moment. "What's going on? What was behind the sharp turn that made the sky fall in on us?"

"Yeah," chimed in Whiteside, "what did the guy up front tell you?"

Unwilling to divulge the contents of the interphone conversation with the passengers listening around them, Cooper motioned to Whiteside, and the two men lifted Raul off the floor and carried him back to the aft galley where they could talk. After strapping Raul into the jump seat, Cooper reported on Walt Meisner's intent to turn the airplane into a missile of revenge against his former employer.

"The last thing I heard on the phone," Cooper concluded, "was a hard banging noise. I'm guessing he smashed up the radio."

Whiteside cut in as soon as Cooper finished. "Is he armed?"

"He has the crash axe, a tool we use to hack into a panel to expose a hidden fire. That's probably what he was using to bust up stuff."

"Are there more axes on board?" Raul said.

"No, only one in the cockpit mounted on the wall behind the first officer's chair."

Whiteside stood up straight. "OK, I can take it from here," he announced in a cocky tone. "That's why I was assigned to this plane. I'll neutralize your skyjacker. I can even land this thing if I have to."

"You're a 737 pilot?" Cooper pressed skeptically.

"Close enough. I fly C-130's in the Guard. That's why I was assigned to this mission. Now give me the gun and I'll take out your copilot. If you cooperate, you can land the plane."

Cooper shot back, "What are you planning to do—kick down the door and shoot him?" Before Whiteside could answer, Cooper said, "Not on my airplane you're not. You should know that a gun is more trouble than it's worth up here, especially in the cockpit. No, I think Officer Barrigan will hold the gun for a while. There's got to be a safer way to get him out of there."

Whiteside saw that he was outnumbered and backed off.

"How much time do we have?" Raul said.

Cooper looked at his watch and shook his head. Meisner couldn't have timed it any worse. Impact with the Northstar buildings could occur within minutes of Reunion. "If he maintains normal cruising speed," Cooper said, "we'll be over downtown Seattle in twenty minutes—sometime around 8 o'clock."

"Is the cockpit door locked?" Raul asked.

"Yes, but I have the key. The problem is the crash axe and anything else he has in there."

"But we can't just sit around while he flies this thing into a building," Whiteside objected. "At some point we're going to rush him, axe or not."

Cooper flashed him a cold glance. "We can only get in the cockpit one at a time. Do you want to go first?"

Whiteside's stare was equally icy. "That's why I'm here, Captain."

"Without a gun?" Cooper pressed.

"I can take him out without a gun," Whiteside responded, his cockiness waning.

Cooper was suddenly struck by the incongruity of it all. Reunion was not supposed to happen this way. Pathfinder had given him the flight plan: Head for Juneau, then accelerate into the hands of Jesus-Brother. But unless Cooper returned to the controls soon, they would be descending over Seattle at the moment of Reunion. That was the opposite of what he and Pathfinder had planned. Cooper wasn't sure if the New Jesus Family would still qualify to be caught away under such conditions.

Worse yet, Walt Meisner might fly them into the Northstar complex before 8:02, and the New Jesus Family would be reduced to embers, destiny unfulfilled. All the while, the frightened and confused passengers sat trusting their leaders implicitly. Cooper had to get back up front and explain the predicament to Lila Ruth. Then he had to take over the controls and turn the plane around immediately.

But other cracks in the once flawless Reunion plan were glaringly evident to him. He gazed up the aisle to where Rachel was administering first aid to several passengers. She wasn't supposed to be here. She was an unbeliever who seemed hopelessly devoted to him. In return, she might die in a flaming plane crash on his account. It wasn't right.

Kathy Keene, who was supposed to be on board, had walked away. That wasn't right either. One of Cooper's models of faith had decided that the New Jesus Family was a bogus religion. What did she know that he didn't know? How could she bear to turn her back on her destiny? Where was she getting her revelation if not from Pathfinder?

To top it all off, the man in the cockpit, whom Cooper regarded as a Reunion gift from Jesus-Brother, had turned out to be the copilot from hell. Walt Meisner had obviously volunteered for the flight with a deadly ulterior motive in mind. He was the one plotting to turn this into a suicide flight. Why would Pathfinder allow such a desecration of Reunion? Surely He knew about it. Why hadn't Jesus-Brother stopped him long ago? The son of Parent-God was certainly powerful enough to control this misguided product of earth-sister. The fact that Cooper had unwittingly thwarted Meisner's attempts to do the deed during a proposed shakedown flight was of little consolation to him now. It disturbed Cooper that his control of the situation, entrusted to him by Jesus-Brother in the speaking of his Reunion name, seemed to be quickly unraveling.

The aft interphone sounded. Looking up the aisle to the forward galley, Cooper saw Tommy Eggers standing with Lila Ruth Atkinson, motioning that she wanted to talk. Cooper picked up the receiver.

"Are you hurt, Ms. Atkinson?" Cooper began.

"A little shaken, Captain, but unhurt. What is the problem? Why did we turn around?" Her speech was uncharacteristically slow and slurred.

Cooper explained the mutiny in the cockpit as concisely as possible without mentioning Meisner's intended destination, saying only that he was returning them to Seattle. Cooper hastened to assure Lila Ruth that he and the two law officers were working on a plan to regain control of the aircraft in time for Reunion. He urged her to keep everyone up front seated and away from the cockpit door.

Lila Ruth was silent as she processed his words. Then she said, "What will happen if you cannot turn the plane around in time?"

Cooper was puzzled. "I was about to ask you the same question," he said. "Will Reunion occur even if we are only 2,000 feet over Seattle? Do we have to be on our original flight plan?"

Again Lila Ruth was silent. "I don't know, Cooper," she said at last. "This is all so confusing. I . . . I don't know . . . I just don't know." Lila Ruth's voice trailed away, prompting another sledgehammer blow to Cooper's foundation. *How can you not know?* he demanded silently. *You're the prophet. Pathfinder tells you everything. You can't fail me now. Has Jesus-Brother given up on us? Shall we simply allow Walt Meisner to fly us into the ground? You must know!*

"Time is slipping away, Captain," Whiteside interrupted gruffly, sticking his face in front of Cooper's. "Let's get moving."

Cooper nodded agreement. Then to Lila Ruth he said, "I'll talk to you again when we come up with something."

"What should I do, Cooper?" Lila Ruth sounded lost, further muddling Cooper's brain over what was happening. But with *Vanguard* less than twenty minutes from impact, he had no time to ponder the spiritual questions harassing him. He had to get his hands on the yoke, then he could deal with Reunion. It bothered him that Lila Ruth may be of little help to him at that point.

"Just sit down and buckle up, dear," he said. "I'll talk to you in a few minutes." Then he returned the interphone to its recessed cradle.

Cooper had never addressed Lila Ruth Atkinson so informally before. "Dear" was the term he had used for his mother in the years before she died while Alzheimer's disease, like a blight, relentlessly turned the fertile garden of her mind into a wasteland. He didn't want to ponder why the term suddenly seemed to fit the beautiful, ageless spiritual leader he once revered as an angel.

Cooper turned to the two men that fate had sent him to solve the dilemma Jesus-Brother apparently had overlooked. They were an unlikely trio of heros, he thought. A police officer with useless legs. A trigger-happy FBI agent without a gun. And a displaced pilot whose faith seemed to be unraveling by the minute. But there was no time to look for a more competent crew. Whatever happened had to happen with these three men, and it had to happen now.

"All right, gentlemen," Cooper said, licking his dry lips, "how are we going to do this?"

Mitchell Schetky hurried down the stairs of the FAA tower and forced his way into the crowded passenger terminal. Most of the Paine Field crowd had disbursed shortly after *Vanguard* lifted off from runway 16R and tucked in its landing gear. But a small throng moved into the terminal building to wait and pray, in case their loved ones returned after the magic moment of 8:02 came and went. Mitchell hadn't asked for the job of public information officer. But when the tower crew heard about *Vanguard*'s course change from Vancouver Center, the operations super, who was watching with interest, was elected to break the news to the spectators.

Finding a chair to stand on, Mitchell quickly drew the crowd's attention. "Folks, I have some news." The room quieted to a hush. People waiting together gripped hands or held each other close, bracing for the worst: that *Vanguard* had disappeared from the radar screen somewhere over British Columbia, fulfilling Earl Butcher's prophecy of a suicide flight.

"Air traffic control informs me that, approximately ten minutes ago, *Vanguard* executed a 180-degree turn. It is presently headed toward the Seattle area." Mitchell's statement provoked a loud murmur of exclamations and questions. He waited until the response died away. "ATC reports that they have lost radio contact with the aircraft and that they are no longer receiving altitude readings, which means that the encoding altimeter is not operational."

"Do you know where they're going?" someone shouted out.

"Without a radio or phones up there, we have no way of knowing. At this point they're headed south and, according to radar, they are maintaining normal speed, suggesting that they still have both engines. All we can do is watch them."

"Can they land without a radio?" someone else wanted to know.

"Yes, the plane can land. But without a radio, they just can't tell us where. However, ATC is treating this as an emergency. Every airport along *Vanguard*'s projected route is being prepared for an emergency landing— including ours. All air traffic is being diverted."

"They're coming back!" an unseen listener exulted. "They've given up the Reunion gag, and they're coming back!" A small cheer erupted from those who desperately wanted to believe the speaker was a prophet.

Mitchell Schetky promised to keep the crowd informed. Then he excused himself and headed back toward the tower. A tall, handsome couple intercepted him in the hallway leading out of the administration building. They still bore evidence of having spent time waiting and watching in the rain.

"I'm Reagan Cole, Los Angeles police," the man said, hovering over the diminutive supervisor. He flashed his ID for good measure. "And this is my wife, Beth, who is writing a book about this religious group."

Mitchell stopped to listen to what the policeman had to say.

"Isn't it true that *Vanguard* was in excellent mechanical condition for this flight?" Cole asked.

Mitchell nodded. "The FAA people told me it was the most airworthy 737 they've seen in years."

"Then doesn't it seem odd to you that the radio and encoding altimeter are out of order? Could it mean that someone up there doesn't want to communicate with the ground about what's going to happen next?"

Mitchell looked around to assure that no one else was listening. Then he stepped close to the couple and kept his voice low. "Being in the line of work you are, you know as well as I do that something funny is going down. But we can't let these people believe that. So I'd appreciate it if you would keep your suspicions under your hats."

"Of course," Beth assured him. "But isn't there something we can do to get ready for this?"

Mitchell looked around again. "That's just the point. There's nothing we can do because whoever is running the show up there doesn't want us to know what's going on. But between you and me, I think we have a skyjacking on our hands. I don't see Cooper Sams pulling a stunt like this. But whoever is at the controls, God only knows what he or she has in mind and where it's going to happen."

Sixty-nine

Cooper Sams, Agent Whiteside, and Raul Barrigan quickly agreed that their best option was to try to talk Meisner out of the cockpit. Their worst option, Cooper maintained firmly, was using the gun. That left them with a total of two options, only one of them acceptable. Cooper picked up the interphone and rang the cockpit.

"Otto is dead, Coop. I killed him with the crash axe." Walt Meisner's first words were followed by a fiendish laugh that sent chills up Cooper's spine.

The captain covered the mouthpiece and whispered, "It sounds like he's disabled the mode control panel. No autopilot. He's taking us down manually."

"Planes were never meant to be flown by a computer," Meisner continued. "It's the man behind the yoke that counts. That's how it was in 'Nam, and that's how it's going to be tonight."

Cooper said, "Walt, let me come up and help you land at SeaTac. You can be the captain; I'll be the first officer. What do you say?"

"You're too late with the promotion," Meisner said cynically. "You should have said something when you had the chance—back when you were on the pilot review board."

"Let's talk about it now. I'll come up and—"

"No!" Meisner thundered. "And don't even try to open the door. I know you have the key, but anybody who comes through that door will get the same treatment Otto got."

"OK, OK," Cooper said quickly, detecting the twisted resolve in Meisner's voice, "I won't come in. Let's just talk."

"You're wasting your breath, Coop. I can see the lights of Campbell River below through the clouds. I'll begin normal descent in a few minutes over Victoria. Then about fifteen minutes after that, you and your amen brigade back there will be in the arms of sweet Jesus, just like you planned. You ought to spend this time singing your hymns or chanting or whatever you do."

Cooper checked his watch and winced. At this rate they would reach SeaTac several minutes before 8:02. Time was running out.

Meisner laughed. "How about that, Coop. My last stint at the controls and I'm getting my passengers to their destination ahead of schedule. My on-time arrival rating is going way up tonight. Northstar doesn't know what they're missing."

"It was politics, that's all, Walt," Cooper said, sensing panic as the clock in his brain ticked away almost audibly. "Northstar needs good pilots. I think they're hiring. I'll talk to the brass. I'll put in a good word for you. I'll—"

"Shove it, Coop," Meisner snarled. Then he cursed at Cooper, concluding, "You know they'll never do anything for me. It's over, my old friend. It's over."

Cooper quickly took another tack. "What about Jeannie? She needs you, Walt. What about your kids? Consider what they will have to live with if you crash this plane."

"What they will have to live with is about $1.4 million dollars in life insurance, a lot more than I can give them alive. That'll ease the pain for all of them."

Cooper countered, "But your insurance won't pay off for a suicide."

"Oh, they'll pay off, all right, Coop, because I'm not committing suicide—at least not in the eyes of the people below. You're the captain. You're the one they expect to fly this plane into the ground. I'm just an innocent victim of a religious fanatic."

Cooper was quickly running out of ideas. Before he could try another one, Meisner said, "I see Vancouver ahead to the east. Victoria is coming up. So I'm going to hang up now and pay attention to what I'm doing. I have only one chance at a pinpoint landing before your Jesus-Brother comes back to spoil my big finish."

Meisner laughed again. Then he added sternly, "Just stay away from the door, do you hear me? Or somebody is going to end up looking like poor Otto." He was laughing as he switched off the interphone.

Cooper stowed the receiver and turned to his comrades in the galley. Mounting anxiety was draining the color from his face. It was a stupid thought, but he wanted to be near Rachel. He could not give up trying to get to Meisner yet. But Cooper decided that if they failed altogether he wanted to be with Rachel when the end came—if she would have him.

During Cooper's interphone conversation, Raul had been studying a laminated safety folder he found in the rack next to the jump seat. Looking up at Cooper and Whiteside, he said, "I have an idea." He pointed to several items on the card and asked Cooper about their operation. Then in two sentences he sketched out a plan that would require all three of them to work together with split-second precision.

Raul's option sounded almost as dangerous to Cooper as using the gun. But with the failure of the first option and no time to brainstorm another, they quickly pieced together a strategy.

As they did, the engines slowed and the sensation of descent began. Cooper had flown this approach hundreds of times. They were over Victoria, British Columbia, at the south end of Vancouver Island. The plane would gradually descend from 35,000 feet to 12,000 feet, and from over 300 knots to close to 210, by the time the Hood Canal Bridge near Seattle was in sight. It would continue to descend over the heart of Elliott Bay to 3,000 feet at Boeing Field, about five miles north of SeaTac. At that point, the aircraft would be lined up for a normal

SeaTac landing. Cooper could only speculate how his disturbed copilot planned to finish off his stint at the controls once he got to that point. He only knew it wouldn't be good.

Cooper thought about the people in the tower at Paine Field. *You know we're up here,* he said silently to those he guessed were still at the field. *You're tracking us on radar and wondering what I'm doing. Even if you knew what was happening, there's not a thing you can do to help us—except pray. Dear God, I hope someone down there is praying.*

Myrna had been holding Guy tightly in her lap since the terrifying midair turn. The sudden maneuver had catapulted the child, who was not buckled in, into the passengers across the aisle. Myrna had followed him into the aisle involuntarily, bruising her ribs and elbows on the armrests. Guy was unhurt in his fall, but he had screamed in terror at the sudden upset. As soon as the plane returned to level, Myrna snatched him from the pile of humanity which had pillowed his fall, and mother and son returned to the window seat where they clung to each other for comfort.

It took several minutes for Guy to stop crying. The look of fear and betrayal in his eyes broke Myrna's heart. She had done this to him. She had put him in jeopardy. Seeing her little boy fly helplessly across the cabin opened her mind to what she might see when the plane crashed. Her final picture of Guy could be much more hideous than watching him sail across the aisle.

Would they die together instantly, or would her little boy burn or bleed to death before her eyes? Would he survive the crash only to find his mother mangled and lifeless beside him? The few seconds of crisis had jolted Myrna like an electric shock. She could do nothing but wrap the boy in her arms and pray that they were returning to Seattle.

Guy Valentine stayed on his mother's lap for another reason. The middle seat he had occupied was needed. Gavin Cornell had been in the center aisle nearby when *Vanguard* went up like a tilt-a-whirl. The aging, fragile, and slightly inebriated actor had taken a bad tumble in the upheaval and dislocated his right elbow. Since Cornell wasn't bleeding, the petite, auburn-haired woman in charge of triage ushered him to the middle seat next to Myrna to wait while she attended to the more seriously wounded. The man sat cradling his arm, grimacing and moaning with every small bounce of the plane.

The mood on the airplane had changed markedly since the incident, Myrna noted. The festive air had dissolved to quiet uneasiness. New Jesus Family members and guest passengers huddled together in their seats like sheep at the faint scent of a wolf. Appearances were no longer important. Expensive clothes were torn, spotted with blood, and stained by champagne. The odor of vomit was pervasive. Once elegant hairstyles were disheveled. Jewelry was broken. Faces and arms were marred by cuts, scrapes, and bandages.

The expressions Myrna saw reminded her of little Guy's queer looks when he transitioned from a dream state to reality after a nap. These people clearly didn't know how to interpret their circumstance or respond to it. So they sat and waited as they had been instructed.

Myrna also felt like *she* was waking up from a bad dream. Her wish for a sudden and terrible end for herself and Guy was now a shameful memory. She knew she had brought this predicament on herself by discounting the counsel of those committed to her mental and emotional health. Somewhere beyond the stormy thoughts and emotions buffeting her she and Guy had a life. She had to return to her moorings and salvage that life for Guy's sake. It would be difficult, but—

Myrna suddenly flashed on the conversation on the bus with the writer, Beth Cole. The woman had mentioned a friend in Portland, someone who might be able to help her take a firmer grip on her life and endure the custody hearings. Myrna wanted the name of this person. It occurred to her that she had not seen Beth during the flight. She determined to look for her as soon as they were safely on the ground. From the rate of descent, she assumed it wouldn't be much more than ten minutes until touchdown. From the view out her window, she guessed they were headed back to Paine Field.

Mitchell Schetky emerged from the door to the tower and was immediately besieged with questions. He ignored the badgering until he was back on his chair addressing everyone. His statement was brief: *"Vanguard* just passed over Paine Field. Radar shows it to be headed straight into Seattle, possibly to Boeing Field or SeaTac. That's all we know."

The crowd scattered quickly and noisily for their cars. Beth hurried outside to find Cole, who had located someone kind enough to retrieve Raul's wheelchair from the Tramco hangar. The rain had diminished to a dense mist that ignited into large glowing spheres around the outside lights. Beth spotted her husband returning from the gate to the hangar, which was now practically deserted. He was pushing the wheelchair in front of him.

"Seattle," she called out as she hurried toward him.

"Then let's motor," Cole answered. They took off at a trot toward Airport Road and the S-10 with Cole carrying the collapsed, lightweight wheelchair in one hand.

While still in the aft galley, Cooper contacted Tommy Eggers in the forward galley by interphone. He quickly explained the plan and enlisted his help. Tommy was assigned to find something to cover the fisheye peephole in the cockpit door. With Meisner flying manually, Cooper doubted that he would risk leaving the controls to check on his passengers. But if he did, the captain didn't want Meisner to see what they were preparing for him. Tommy commandeered a wad of used chewing gum from a teenager in row 6 and quietly spread it over the tiny window.

Next, Cooper instructed Tommy to pass through the cabin and tell the passengers to be ready to sing. When Cooper explained what they should sing and why, Tommy agreed and quietly spread the word from first class back. Tommy's Captain-Sams-says announcement came as a hopeful sign to the congregation, which had been patiently waiting for instructions from their leaders.

It took several precious minutes for Cooper and Whiteside to gather the supplies they would need from the overhead compartments and for Tommy to complete his assignment. A quick check out the window alarmed the captain. They had passed through 10,000 feet at about 230 knots. Elliott Bay was dead ahead. They had to get moving.

When Tommy reached the aft galley, he looked like a corpse from exhaustion. His dark, sunken eyes and taut yellow-white skin made his head appear to be little more than a bleached skull. He dropped into the jump seat next to Raul to catch his breath.

"Tommy, I need you to get these people singing at the right moment," Cooper said as he and Whiteside hovered over the two seated men. "Can you handle it?"

Tommy forced a brave smile. "Yes, I can handle it." Then he said with a glimmer of mischief in his eyes. "Captain, I got on your airplane tonight hoping we *wouldn't* come back. But I want to chicken out. So if you wouldn't mind saving my life one more time, I'd appreciate it."

Cooper gazed at the forlorn figure sitting before him looking as frail and careworn as Gavin Cornell, but only thirty-eight years old. Memories of how he had scorned the young man for his lifestyle and personality embarrassed him. There was no time for apologies now, but Cooper felt that he owed Tommy a big one. "If these gentlemen will give me the opportunity," Cooper said, forcing himself to retain eye contact, "I will be pleased to save your life again."

Raul had a last-minute question about his equipment. As Tommy answered him, Cooper knew now was the time to speak to Rachel. Having provided first-aid care for the passengers in the rear half of the plane and retrieving needed equipment, she had returned to the galley and kept out of the way by staying next to the door. Cooper stepped across the aisle to face her.

He ran his bandaged right hand over the white buzz cut surrounding his large bald spot. As much as he wanted to, he could not look her in the eye. Knowing he had to hurry up front, he tried to summarize his feelings in one sentence. "I think our life could have been better." His tone conveyed that he was the one who could have made it better.

Rachel also averted her eyes as she answered, "I'm hoping it still can be, Cooper." Another wave of humility broke over him at the realization of Rachel's unquenchable optimism.

Whiteside was at Cooper's elbow, abruptly ending the brief exchange. The FBI man had already hoisted Raul Barrigan up behind him piggyback style. "Let's do it, Captain."

Cooper and Tommy picked up the rest of the equipment and the four men hurried to the front single file. Rachel took her place alone in the aft jump seat.

Whiteside silently deposited Raul in the jump seat beside the cockpit door. Just as he did, *Vanguard* banked left, provoking a mild gasp among the passengers. Cooper looked out the window of the forward entry door. They were over Boeing Field and banking east at about 3,000 feet. Cooper knew exactly what Meisner was doing.

"The Northstar buildings face east. He's flying out to the east, probably six or seven miles, somewhere over Kent Valley. Then he's going to turn around and try to fly right in the front door. Hopefully he'll stay at 3,000. We have about seven minutes to make this work."

Raul, Whiteside, and Cooper silently armed themselves with the materials they had collected and took positions outside the door. Cooper cued Tommy to get on the P.A. and start the singing. From the panel next to door 1L, Cooper switched off all cabin lights and placed the critical interphone call to the cockpit.

Seventy

Walt Meisner allowed himself one last gulp of liquid courage from the flask in his flight bag. Any more alcohol and he knew it might impair his vision for making the final 180-degree turn and picking up the landmarks guiding him into the corporate headquarters of Northstar Airlines. Any less and he might think too long about the innocent people behind the cockpit who were inextricably involved in his personal vendetta against Cooper Sams and Northstar. Meisner kept reminding himself that these passengers didn't plan on being around past 8:02 anyway. What did it matter how they were dispatched into the next life as long as they reached their intended destination?

Meisner thought it odd to be flying over metropolitan Seattle without the constant stream of chatter coming at him through the radio. The instrument was in shambles after two blows from the crash axe. In fact, apart from the steady hum of the engine and whisper of the wind slipping by, the cockpit was silent. Without copilot, autopilot, and interference from the tower, Meisner was alone.

It also felt different flying by hand instead of on autopilot. Meisner had considered entering the longitude and latitude fixes into the flight management computer and letting Otto be the suicide pilot. The computer was completely capable of sticking the aircraft into the Northstar building without his help. The ultimate smart bomb, Meisner had mused. But somehow he didn't feel satisfied giving Otto the honors he had craved for so long. So he had smashed Otto in the head with the axe and taken the wheel himself.

The silence reminded him of night missions in Vietnam aboard his beloved A-6. Yet the grid of lights stretching out below in all directions took him back to promising days with Northstar when he was bucking for captain, days that had dwindled to one long night of disappointment and rejection. Tonight's final mission over the urban jungle would atone for everything.

While keeping his eyes on the terrain and the instruments, Meisner was keen to an assault on the cockpit from the cabin. In fact, he anticipated it. The passengers might sit by like unwitting sheep headed to slaughter, but Meisner didn't expect Cooper to go down without a fight. Meisner was ready for the captain. The crash axe was tucked between his left hip and the armrest of his chair. To allow for easy maneuverability in the first officer's chair, he had removed not only his crash strap and shoulder harness but his lap belt. And the lightweight communication headset connected to the dead radio had been discarded.

At the sound of the door being unlocked, Meisner could swing around and deliver a rain of slashing blows with the axe before anyone got two steps into the cramped cockpit. And if Cooper was not alone in his heroic attempt, the others would have to drag out his battered body before the next attacker could get in, and the same thing would happen to him. Since there were no other axes or weapons on board, Meisner was confident he could defend his position until impact.

Estimating that he was six miles east of his target over Kent Valley, Meisner turned the control wheel to the right, initiating the 180-degree bank that would bring *Vanguard* around for its final descent toward South Seattle and the Northstar complex. The turn was tight, but not like the one he had subjected the passengers to on the way to Juneau. The mental image of the chaos he caused in the cabin brought him a twisted smile.

The panorama greeting Meisner out the windshield as he completed the U-turn was magnificent, a view he had always loved. The illuminated skyline of downtown Seattle, with its trademark Space Needle, loomed off to the right. Tacoma was to the left. Seattle-Tacoma International Airport and its north-south runways were ahead and to the north. And somewhere short of the airport and a little to the south was the doomed Northstar building.

Meisner was well under the cloud layer, and his landmarks were clearly visible: the freeways, the major business complexes, the lights of SeaTac, and Interstate Five stretched out before him like a finish line. Impact would occur just beyond it at the corner of Military Road and 200th Street.

Meisner eased the yoke slightly forward to begin *Vanguard's* final descent from 3,000 feet. He would maintain a speed of 210 knots until impact, fast enough to keep the plane aloft without flaps and yet slow enough to allow him to hit the target. As the descent began, the interphone sounded. He debated about picking up. It was no doubt a last-minute plea for mercy from Cooper Sams or anyone he thought could deliver the message more convincingly.

Meisner had no more time for the others, so he ignored the tone at first. It continued to sound. After several seconds, he reasoned that having Cooper on the interphone might be better than not knowing exactly where he was or what he was doing.

When he picked up the instrument, Meisner heard music—singing. He recognized the tune of "Amazing Grace." It sounded like all the passengers were singing the hymn. The plane was going through 2,700 feet.

"Walt, we're preparing to meet our Maker," Cooper said. He was remarkably serene for a man about to die in a flaming crash. "And since you're going with us, I thought you might like to hear—"

The cockpit door clicked and flew open. Meisner knew immediately that the attack was upon him. In that instant he silently rejoiced in the opportunity to defend his mission. One thought exploded in his brain at that moment: *Clever diversion, Captain Sams, but not clever enough. I'm ready for you.*

Meisner dropped the interphone and let go of the control wheel. He began turning toward the open door and reaching for the axe in one motion. Before the interphone hit the floor, an ear-piercing, sustained *whoosh!* burst into the cockpit from the doorway at floor level. Simultaneously, a cloud of gas shot up into the dark cockpit and boiled around the man at the controls. Completely enveloped in cold fog, Meisner could not see and, for a moment, he could not breathe. He knew immediately what was upon him: a thundering flood of carbon dioxide—CO_2.

The jet stream of pressurized CO_2, roaring into the cockpit like the sound of a wind tunnel, was designed to displace oxygen and smother a fire. Only now Meisner was the target. The cold cloud was robbing him of oxygen. And the stuff just kept coming. Somebody was emptying one of the onboard fire extinguishers on him. Had Meisner had time to think about it, he would have cursed the Environmental Protection Agency for banning extinguishers containing invisible, odorless, tasteless Halon, requiring commercial aircraft to return to CO_2 for fire protection.

Meisner heard hasty footsteps behind him. Gasping for air in the fog and suddenly a little dizzy, Meisner fumbled for the axe at his side. He wished he had not taken that last drink from the flask. He found the weapon, but before he could lift and swing, sudden hard pain ripped across his chest. He heard the rattle of sturdy chain. Then the sensation on his chest slipped to his neck and closed in on him like a garrotte.

Instincts of human survival kicked in. Meisner's two hands flew to the chrome chain cinched around his bulging neck. He scrabbled frantically to pull it away but could not get his fingers around the links. His body stiffened to launch himself out of the attacker's grip, knocking the yoke forward and increasing *Vanguard*'s rate of descent and speed. Struggling to rise or turn around, Meisner pounded the rudder pedals with his feet, rocking the plane violently. In the sudden movement, his attacker slammed against the wall of the cabin and slipped to one knee. Meisner bounced against the side window and swayed toward the captain's chair. But the chain remained locked around his neck and pinned him to his seat.

In seconds, *Vanguard* dropped through 2,000 feet and continued its quick descent. Speed increased rapidly from 210 to 220 to 230. With every frantic convulsion, Meisner's feet hit the rudder pedals, flipping the wings up and down, throwing the nose of the plane toward the northwest and then to the southwest. Yet Meisner was oblivious to the sudden peril to the aircraft. An even more personal nightmare of peril had overtaken him in the form of a chain which gripped his neck like a hangman's noose.

Had the struggling Meisner been able to control his actions, he would have taken the axe at his side and swung it behind him, hoping to disable the strangler. Or he would have intentionally held a rudder pedal to the floor, forcing the plane into a death dive. But hysteria at being unable to breathe ruled him. He could not pull his hands away from the chain or force his legs to do anything but bang the pedals. Yet the steel noose was secure, and Meisner felt consciousness slipping away.

Somewhere during the melee, the roar of escaping CO_2 ceased and the cloud dissipated. The singing in the cabin had also stopped, replaced by cries of alarm through the open door at the sudden downward plunge of the aircraft. It had been less than fifteen seconds since the attack began.

His consciousness fading, Meisner heard a shout directly behind him—strangely muffled: "Go! Go! Now!" Someone squeezed by the unseen attacker and struggled into the captain's chair. It was Cooper Sams. Convulsing violently, Meisner screamed for help, but nothing came out. Then darkness closed over his eyes like a suffocating hood of black velvet, and he fell limp.

Vanguard's nose was 23 degrees down and the wings were wavering between 12 and 18 degrees above or below level when Cooper grasped the control wheel. The motion threw him against his side window and bounced him off the suddenly still mound of flesh in the copilot's chair. The altimeter displayed 1,400 feet and falling at a speed of nearly 260 knots. "Get his feet off the rudders!" Cooper shouted as he eased back the yoke.

Agent Whiteside relaxed the chrome chain around Meisner's neck, the same chain which the FBI man had worn aboard the plane during his ruse as Robert Lamar. Now he looked like something out of a low-budget space movie from the '50s. He wore a PBE—for protective breathing equipment, a firefighting hood with a view window. The PBE was equipped with tiny canisters of oxygen which enabled him to survive the CO_2 storm.

Whiteside's chest, back, and shoulders were layered with deflated yellow life jackets he had strapped on in hopes of minimizing the damage of an axe blow. Thanks to his quickness and luck hooking Meisner with the first toss of the chain in the fog, Whiteside's simple armor had not been tested.

Reaching around Meisner's large, unconscious body in the first officer's chair, Whiteside jerked at the pant legs until the feet were free of the pedals. Then he quickly pulled Meisner's limp arms behind the chair and secured them with the handcuffs. Without a moment's pause, he dropped the chain to his prisoner's ankles, encircled the base of the chair securely, and snugly attached the chain to the handcuffs. Then he further pinned the man to the first officer's chair by snapping his lap belt, crash strap, and safety harness in place. Walt Meisner would not touch the controls of the aircraft again.

In their planning, the three commandos had determined that, if they succeeded in neutralizing Meisner, they wouldn't waste valuable time trying to wrestle his ponderous frame out of the cockpit. Thanks to the chrome chain and handcuffs, Walt Meisner wasn't going anywhere when he came to—at least not until Agent Whiteside said so.

Meanwhile, just outside the doorway, Raul Barrigan lay flat beside a spent CO_2 canister, trying to keep from flopping around in the turbulence. Raul had been the "gunner," launching the noisy storm cloud of gas into the cockpit from his position on the floor the moment Whiteside pulled the door open. Following Raul's plan, the FBI man had stormed the skyjacker armed with the chain either to choke him or beat him into unconsciousness—whichever worked. Cooper Sams, who had dropped the interphone the moment Whiteside sprung the door open, had waited for Whiteside's command before hurrying in to reclaim the controls.

Raul and Whiteside had completed their assignments, but Cooper's critical task in the rescue mission had just begun. Assuming control of a plane almost out of control brought a sour knot of fear to his throat, just as it had seven years earlier in the black, turbulent skies above

Juneau. Yet it took only seconds for Cooper to assess that *Vanguard* was much better off than Flight 202 had been at the mercy of the wind shear.

And *Vanguard* was much better off than it might have been had Walt Meisner not been disabled so quickly. Cooper and his aircraft would not come within 250 feet of extinction this time. *Vanguard* would survive to fly again.

Using the control wheel, Cooper returned the wings to level. Keeping back pressure on the yoke at the same time, he pulled the nose up to level and beyond. He saw the altimeter bottom out at 980 feet before *Vanguard* started climbing again. Speed quickly decayed, so Cooper inched the throttles forward to encourage the climb. A quick check of the vital instruments showed that, apart from what Meisner had done with the crash axe, nothing had been damaged in the cockpit siege.

Scanning the ground for landmarks, Cooper saw that *Vanguard* was now heading northwest toward Boeing Field. The compass verified his observation. Meanwhile, with the aircraft finally stable, Agent Whiteside and Elder Wood assisted Raul Barrigan from the floor to the jump seat and made sure he was buckled in. Whiteside then closed the cockpit door and strapped himself into the jump seat to keep an eye on Meisner and Cooper.

"Is anyone hurt back there?" Cooper probed.

"Everybody looks OK—except maybe your beloved leader," Whiteside said. "She's blotto with her eyes open, like somebody moved out and left the lights on. Your people are talking to her, but she's not answering. I think her lines have come loose and she's drifting out to sea."

Cooper responded with a hum. The report jibed with his last impression of her from their brief interphone conversation. Cooper assessed that the trauma of the takeover was too much for Lila Ruth and she snapped, something he never imagined possible to the Family's seemingly invincible leader.

Whiteside turned his attention to the task at hand. "Let's get this thing on the ground ASAP, Sams." His brusque command intimated that he would be as quick and merciless on Cooper as he had been on Meisner if the captain did not immediately swing the plane into a landing pattern at SeaTac.

Cooper was confident—and grateful—that ATC had cleared the SeaTac area of air traffic until the silent blip on the radar screen either landed or flew off toward another airport. Emergency conditions meant that a number of jetliners were circling over eastern Washington or Puget Sound right now waiting for the emergency to be resolved. It also meant that SeaTac had been on alert for almost thirty minutes, probably with emergency vehicles lining the runways. Cooper kept *Vanguard*'s nose aimed at Boeing Field where he would swing south and land at Seattle-Tacoma Airport.

"Can I trust you to get us down, Captain?" Whiteside pressed, seeking a verbal commitment.

Before Cooper could respond to Whiteside, he was startled by a clear, familiar inner voice. It was Pathfinder. He was speaking to Cooper for the first time since *Vanguard* left Paine Field. *The glory of Jesus-Brother's appearance is not dimmed by the unbelieving copilot's actions. Let us now mount up to the heavens and soar into the light just as we planned. Jesus-Brother will meet you the moment your faith fully bursts forth. Even so, come Jesus-Brother!*

Normally Pathfinder's voice stirred Cooper Sams to excitement and immediate compliance. But after the events of the last thirty minutes, this message sounded hollow and strengthless, like the ravings of Oz after Dorothy discovered him to be merely a booming voice without any real authority.

Cooper checked his watch. When he saw the stark black numerals against the glowing background—8:04:43—the absurdity of the inner directive crashed over him. *This is ridiculous. What kind of God would change His appointment for the glorious, long-awaited climax of human history? What kind of God would allow a half-drunk, washed-up pilot on a mission of vengeance to thwart His timing? There will be no Reunion. The moment has come and gone. Jesus-Brother promised but failed to deliver. I've been duped.*

In seconds, the past four years flashed through Cooper's mind. The weaknesses and inconsistencies of his chosen faith, previously ignored or overlooked, were suddenly glaringly obvious. Every stark realization slammed into his consciousness with the force of a sledgehammer. And with every blow, another chunk of the foundation under his feet crumbled and fell away.

The inner light Cooper had followed had dimmed to that of a common 60-watt globe. In its place, a greater light suddenly fell over the years Cooper had invested in the New Jesus Family. And in the spotlight's brilliance every flaw was clearly visible.

Lila Ruth Atkinson is neither god nor angel nor prophet. Intelligent, resourceful, intuitive bordering on telepathic, inspiring—yes. Divine, omniscient, clairvoyant—no. Her name, Vision, is a sad joke. Lila Ruth's uncanny "insight" into my Reunion name must have been what Kathy Keene said it was: a lucky guess or knowledge from a spiritual power masquerading as the light of God she claimed to possess.

The New Jesus Family is not a handpicked welcoming committee for Reunion with the Son of God. At best it's a band of impressionable people whose careless thirst for the spiritual and the supernatural has plunged them into a current sweeping them away from common sense and truth. And I have been the most gullible of the lot! Kathy Keene awoke to the peril in time to make it to shore. In my stubborn blindness

I nearly took Lila Ruth's misguided flock over the falls.

I'm not Vanguard, the point man for Reunion with Jesus-Brother—if there even is a Jesus-Brother or ever will be a heavenly reunion. I'm a proud, inflexible man who has succeeded at my career and at squeezing the beauty and love out of my life in the name of what's expedient and self-satisfying. And in my bullheadedness I have neglected the one person who sees more in me than I see myself.

"What about it, Captain?" Whiteside interrupted. "Are you setting us down in Seattle or do I have to do it?"

Cooper had no doubts about what he would do. He pretended that he had not heard the disturbing inner command of moments ago. "I'm taking us in," he assured over his shoulder.

Cooper knew he must make an announcement to the passengers, explaining what had happened and where he was taking them. And, as uncomfortable as he was with the prospect, he knew he had to talk to Rachel before they landed, before she was swallowed up in the crowd of passengers and spectators. He decided to call Rachel first. Approaching Boeing Field at 3,000 feet in preparation for a turn toward SeaTac, he picked up the interphone and dialed the aft galley, hoping she was still in or near the jump seat.

Rachel answered immediately. "Yes."

Cooper felt embarrassed and humiliated, especially with the FBI agent near enough to hear much of what he was about to say. He was tempted to do again what he had learned to do well: run and hide. He was tempted to hang up and hope Rachel *did* get lost in the crowd. But he refused to put the phone down. "Did you . . . I mean, are you OK?"

"That was scary," Rachel said with an audible sigh. "But I'm all right now. And you?"

"OK," he said, wanting the words to apply to more than just his physical safety.

"And your copilot?"

"He's in custody, handcuffed in his chair."

"Are you taking us to SeaTac?" Rachel said.

"Yeah. We have no radio, so the sooner we get down and tell our story the better." He glanced over his shoulder. "And that's where the FBI wants us to land."

Short on time and determined to say what he had to say, Cooper took a deep breath and pressed on haltingly. "Rachel, I'm . . . I'm sorry. I'm sorry for . . . for everything. At the moment, I don't know how I got into this mess. I really don't. I've been . . . well, I really haven't been the kind of man I should be. I just . . . I mean, I . . ." Frustration at trying to put words together right only made him feel worse. Finally he said, "I'm just sorry, that's all I can say."

Cooper heard Rachel sniffing. Then she responded. Her voice quavered with emotion. "I need to know what you really mean, Cooper.

Are you saying, 'I'm sorry and good-bye,' or are you saying, 'I'm sorry and I hope we can work something out together'?"

Cooper wished he could put her off. But he knew that wasn't right, and he desperately wanted to stop doing to Rachel what wasn't right. So he sucked up his courage and pressed ahead. "I've been a first class fool, Rachel. I lost the house, I lost you, and I put all my money into this . . ." He couldn't find the right word to describe his last four years trapped in Lila Ruth's captivating web. "I'm going to be the laughing-stock of our industry . . . of the entire country. I can't expect you to stick with me through all that."

"Do you *want* me to stick with you?"

Cooper had to be honest. Rachel might throw his honesty back in his face and join the world in laughing at him. He couldn't blame her if she did. But he would tell her the truth now and take that chance. And if Rachel turned his back on him, at least he would know he did something right.

"Y—yes," he stammered, "I want you to stick with me. I *need* you to stick with me."

Rachel didn't speak for several seconds. Then she could only get out a few words. "That's what I want too." Ever the airline professional, she quickly composed herself and told him that she had to help pre-pare the cabin for arrival. Cooper said he would see her after they were on the ground.

The captain negotiated an easy turn over Boeing Field and drew a bead on the runway lights of Seattle-Tacoma Airport in the distance. Then he switched on the cabin P.A. Speaking like an airline captain instead of a spiritual leader, he gave the bare essentials of the attempt-ed skyjacking. He explained tersely and without emotion that he had been mistaken about Reunion. He was landing in Seattle, and they would all be going home. He assured them that those who needed a place to stay for the night would be accommodated at the Family's expense. He closed by promising to assist Lila Ruth and the other elders in moving on from here.

Switching off the P.A., Cooper realized he might face months of red tape and legal action as the New Jesus Family was dissolved and loved ones of members laid claim to its assets. If Lila Ruth Atkinson was indeed physically or mentally incapacitated as she seemed, he would bear the brunt of those actions. The prospect was staggering. But knowing that he would not face the music alone brought him an imme-diate sense of peace.

Shortly after straightening out the turn, Cooper dropped the landing gear. As he did, a familiar voice was in his mind once more. *You have one last chance to enter the glory for which you were appointed. You have a sacred obligation to deliver Jesus-Brother's chosen ones to his kingdom. One sudden, downward thrust of the yoke will send* Vanguard *plunging into the ground, a glorious display of devotion to Jesus-Brother.*

Cooper's jaw clenched and his hands trembled with rage at the audacious suggestion. He didn't know exactly whom he was addressing, but he had to say his piece. He also realized that he would have to explain himself to a startled FBI man as soon as he said it. But the pain and remorse of his years of listening to this devil in his mind boiled up and spewed out his reply aloud: "Get out of my face and stay out!"

Seventy-one

After a safe landing in front of a convoy of emergency vehicles decked with rotating beacons of red and amber, Cooper steered *Vanguard* off 16R onto a taxiway to await instructions. Walt Meisner came around just after touchdown. But apart from moaning hoarsely about his painful condition, he said nothing.

Within seconds, two white airport police vehicles raced up to the nose of the plane and stopped, lights flashing. One officer guardedly approached the panel under the nose with a service interphone headset while three others stood by with weapons showing. Cooper understood their caution. The world outside *Vanguard* knew only that the plane had abandoned its flight plan to Juneau and returned to Seattle unable—or unwilling—to communicate by radio. The erratic final ten minutes on the radar screen must have provoked suspicion of foul play. The contingent in front of the plane now had been sent to ascertain the status of the crew and passengers before allowing it to proceed.

Speaking to the officer through the interphone, Cooper succinctly reported the skyjacking, the disabling of the radio and mode control panel, and the eventual capture of the perpetrator. He requested a private hangar or terminal, secure from the public and media, where his passengers could make plans for the night. Cooper also asked the officer to roll a team of EMTs for the many on board who needed further medical attention.

At Whiteside's insistence, Cooper also asked the officer to contact the local FBI to take the skyjacker into custody. The man on the ground informed him in a tone of disdain that the FBI was already on site in force.

Following the lead police vehicle, a four-wheel-drive Explorer, Cooper taxied *Vanguard* to the private Weyerhauser hangar on the west side of the airport, on the opposite side of the runways from the commercial terminals. Apparently convinced that his prisoner was secure and the pilot was trustworthy, Whiteside exited the cockpit during taxi.

Cooper parked the nose near the closed hangar door so his passengers would have only a short walk to get inside. Rising slowly from his chair, he realized how sore he was from the rough flight. His thigh and bandaged hand ached, and he knew he would be more sore tomorrow. But one glance at dull-eyed Meisner assured him that it could have been worse.

It had occurred to Cooper when he shut down the engines that he might never sit at the controls of an airplane again. For a fleeting moment he realized he had no plans at all except to extricate himself from the New Jesus Family and survive the humiliation he had contributed to. He would have to talk to Rachel about where to go from here. He would have to talk to Rachel about a lot of things.

A portable stairway was dispatched to the forward door, which Cooper unlatched and swung open. The rain had stopped, but the smell of rain mixed with jet fumes was still in the air. The cold, moist breeze greeting Cooper as he stood in the open doorway felt good on his bare arms and head.

While Walt Meisner remained in the cockpit and FBI Agent Whiteside and Cooper stood in the forward galley, the passengers deplaned. Most of them looked morose, confused, defeated. Few made eye contact with Cooper as they passed. Fewer still spoke. Those more seriously hurt, including Gavin Cornell and Lila Ruth Atkinson, remained on board to await the EMTs. Both were then attended to and assisted off the plane.

The preliminary diagnosis for Lila Ruth was that she had suffered a stroke. She was awake but unable to communicate. For the first time since he had known her, Cooper saw the years lined on her face and a pitiful disorientation in her empty eyes. He had been blind to a lot of things over the past several years, he conceded.

Wheelchairs were needed for a few passengers, particularly Raul Barrigan. As the handsome young police officer was carried off the plane, Cooper thanked him for his part in saving the plane. Cooper admired the man for dealing with his disability and making so much of himself. It was obvious that Raul's faith and enthusiasm for life had not been dampened by his injury. There was surprising depth to this young man. Cooper remembered that he had accepted one of Raul's religious tracts in the hotel and stuffed it away in his flight bag unread. He thought he might want to read it when things settled down. He would also ask Rachel about her religious experience. She showed a measure of courage and devotion equal to Raul's.

Once all the passengers had been assisted into the terminal, a delegation from the FBI scampered up the stairway to deal with Walt

Meisner. As Cooper and Whiteside watched from the first-class cabin, the local agents released the prisoner from his bonds, assisted him out of the cockpit, cuffed him again, and led him down the stairs to a car waiting on the tarmac. Meisner's hair was tousled, his shirt was untucked, and the swollen, bloody ring around his neck looked like it might result in a permanent scar.

Meisner didn't look at Cooper as he was led away, and Cooper didn't speak as he watched the unlikely skyjacker trudge down the stairway under close guard. But he felt a twinge of compassion for the man just as he had for the others aboard *Vanguard*. *Had I not become involved with this group*, he thought as the first FBI car drove away, *maybe Walt wouldn't have gotten himself into such a mess*. Cooper knew better than to take responsibility for Meisner's actions. But he wondered if he should do anything to help him and his invalid wife. The idea of showing charity to the man who had almost killed him was foreign to Cooper. It was something he would ask Rachel about.

"Nice work, Captain," Whiteside said, using his official FBI tone. His job complete, he was ready to leave the plane. Cooper waited to shake the agent's hand, but it wasn't offered. "Tell you the truth," the man in the orange coveralls continued with a cocky smirk, "I thought I might have to take you down too."

Cooper surmised that the FBI man was still miffed about having his gun taken away. Whiteside exited the plane without waiting for a reply.

When Cooper turned for one last look down the aisle of the empty plane, Rachel was standing before him with his cap in her hands. Her lovely blue dress was soiled, but her lipstick was fresh and she had run a comb through her hair. The fragrance of her perfume, which Cooper had grown to appreciate during their years together, surrounded her like a warm log fire on a wintry day.

Unable to cover his surprise, Cooper said, "I thought you got off with the others."

Rachel cocked her head and smiled. "I'm sticking with you, remember?"

Cooper reckoned that he didn't have much to smile about after what he had been through and what he had discovered about himself. It might be months before he would look back on these four lost years and find any humor in his nightmare experience with the New Jesus Family. But at this moment, he couldn't keep a smile of deep gratitude for Rachel from brightening his face.

Cooper took the first hesitant step and Rachel took the next. They slipped gently and comfortably into each other's arms and stayed there for several minutes. No words were spoken. No words were needed.

Once off the plane and inside the spacious but cool hangar, the *Vanguard* passengers responded to their disillusionment in a variety of ways. A few of them left the building immediately, passing like zombies through an assembling cordon of security guards and a gathering crowd of media people and onlookers outside. They boarded cabs or limos or buses and disappeared into the night to make some sense out of what they had been through. A handful who needed hospital attention, such as Lila Ruth Atkinson and Gavin Cornell, were whisked away by the airport rescue unit.

Others lined up at the two telephones in the hangar. They contacted friends or relatives and arranged to be picked up. Some of them broke down as they talked on the phone about the failure of Reunion and the trauma of the last hour. But most remained stonefaced, stunned by the harrowing and disappointing turn of events.

The majority of the passengers sat down on the floor to wait for someone to help them take the next step. With Lila Ruth gone, they waited for Cooper Sams, who had promised during the landing to get them settled for the night if they needed help. They looked like stray puppies at the animal shelter, waiting with naive longing in their eyes for someone to come and claim them. Kim Bemari had the presence of mind to telephone the Stouffer-Madison Hotel and reserve a number of rooms for so many of the passengers who were far from home and without family or means.

Outside the hangar, many people from Paine Field, who had watched in grief as their loved ones departed, turned up with tears of joy to greet their surprise return. And with a ring of security people present to keep the hangar from being overrun with TV people and gawkers, a system was devised for getting people together. Security guards, like hotel pages, entered the hangar and called out the names given to them by loved ones outside. In response, people left in ones and twos—some expectantly, some reluctantly—to be reunited with those who had come for them.

Tommy Eggers sat exhausted and feeling ill on the floor in the hangar unsure of what he would do next. His fellow passengers had a new lease on life, but he did not. His hourglass was nearly empty, and the return of *Vanguard* could not turn the sand to the top for him as it had for others. Raul Barrigan had talked convincingly about forgiveness, a relationship with God, and eternal life. And Tommy had felt something very wonderful at the hotel after Raul had talked to him. But he had not yet come to terms with God as Raul had urged him to. Even if he did, Tommy mused, life—what little of it he had left—goes on. And he was still discomfited and afraid about facing it alone.

It wasn't as if Tommy felt he had many choices. He could try to contact Dimitri. Raul Barrigan had offered to drive him back to the Bay Area on his way home to Phoenix. But why would he want to go there? Why complicate Dimitri's life further—if indeed the man wanted him back at all after Tommy had left him so unkindly?

Tommy still had most of the $2,000 he had brought from home. He could hole up in Seattle until his money ran out. But then what? Who would take care of him when he could no longer take care of himself? The thought of dying friendless in a hospice made his blood run cold. Raul had challenged him to give the rest of his days to Jesus. But what if Jesus was as careless about taking care of him as He had been taking care of *Vanguard*? The image of the Golden Gate Bridge and other devices for a quick and painless escape again lurked at the perimeter of his thoughts.

"Is there a Tommy Eggers in here?"

Tommy snapped his head up, startled at hearing what he thought was his name being called. A uniformed airport security guard scanned the crowd waiting for a response. *It can't be my name he called,* Tommy objected. But the man in the uniform, seeing Tommy look his way, called out again. "Tommy Eggers?"

Tommy stood with difficulty, feeling bone weary. Constant activity with no time for rest had drained him. The drugs and adrenaline had worn off, leaving him weak. But he was curious to see who could be outside asking for him. *Could it be Dimitri?* he thought. *Did he see my name in the paper? Who else would know that I'm here? Who else would care?*

Following the guard through the executive waiting room adjacent to the hangar, Tommy was greeted by a noisy crowd and bright TV lights on the outside. The throng was kept back from the entrance by a nylon rope barricade. He stood shielding his eyes from the glare to search the collage of faces for Dimitri's familiar white hair. But Dimitri was not in sight.

"Tommy, over here!" The voice came from the right. He turned to see a young woman slip under the rope. Evie Dukes, his old neighbor from San Francisco, beamed with delight as she hurried to him and wrapped him in her arms.

"Evie. What . . . why. . . ?"

A disgruntled guard interrupted and pushed them toward the rope. "Outside the barricade, you two," he grumbled.

"We saw your name in the *Star,* and we had to come," Evie explained as they retreated. "We couldn't believe it. We were so concerned about you. Thank God nothing happened to you."

Slipping under the rope, Tommy came face to face with Evie's parents, Marvin and Nora Dukes, who also embraced the fragile man joyfully.

"We drove all day today, but we got to Paine Field too late," Marvin explained apologetically. "They wouldn't let us near the plane. We were on I-5 when the radio said the plane was headed to SeaTac."

Nora Dukes didn't give Tommy a moment to respond. "We don't know why you got on that plane, and we don't care. But we want you to come home with us to Redwood City. We have a big house, Tommy, with plenty of room. I've done some nursing in my day, and I can cook anything you need. You'll be comfortable with us until . . ." Nora did not need to state the obvious.

"We'll have plenty of time for some good, deep talks," Marvin put in, smiling warmly.

Tommy gazed on the expectant faces of his surprise benefactors. "You drove all the way from the Bay Area today?" he said, amazed.

Nora tried to explain. "We thought you might . . . need us. You know, the plane, the rumors about crashing. We thought you were . . . well . . ."

Tommy said it for her: "Flipped out."

"We didn't know what to think, Tommy," Evie said. "We just wanted to be here to help."

Tommy couldn't avoid thinking about the motives behind the Dukes' generous offer. To Evie he said, "I hear you made some changes in your life — getting back to your religious roots. I've been talking to a guy on the plane about that. But I don't know if I'm ready for that kind of change. I don't know if I *can* change."

"This isn't about changing you," Nora inserted quickly. "This is about making sure you are properly cared for — and loved — until . . . you don't need us anymore."

Marvin spoke next. "Tommy, you know what we stand for. And you know we don't push what we believe on others. We just want to be available to you, that's all."

Marvin pressed on before Tommy could answer. "Listen, let's get out of this crowd. You've had a big day, and so have we. We'll get a couple of rooms at the Red Lion. In the morning you can let us know what you need to do. We'll take you wherever you want to go."

Tommy nodded as if he had a choice. Marvin, Nora, and Evie began weaving through the throng toward the parking lot with Tommy in tow. He already knew what he wanted to do. He would be a bigger fool for turning down the Dukes' hospitality than he had been for getting involved with the doomsday flight. And after his soul-stirring talks with Raul Barrigan, he had many more questions he wanted to ask Marvin Dukes about the God who hates sin but loves the sinner.

Since entering the hangar, Raul Barrigan had been rolling the cumbersome borrowed wheelchair around saying good-bye and offering to pray for people. He was so busy that he didn't hear his name called. Nor did he ever *expect* his name to be called. He was prepared to take care of himself. He would see as many people as he could, then hitch a ride to the Stouffer-Madison where his car was waiting. He had offered a ride to Tommy Eggers, but the man he thought was on the verge of giving his life to God had been called out of the hangar ten minutes earlier and had not returned. So Raul continued around the room hoping to plant one last seed of hope with each fellow passenger who remained.

Someone tapped him on the shoulder. Raul turned from a conversation and looked up into the face of Myrna Valentine. "Our names were called," she said with a look of concern. Guy Valentine was in his mother's arms, clinging to her tightly.

"What?" Raul said, not understanding her message.

"That officer called our names, yours and mine." Myrna pointed to a woman in a blue uniform scanning the crowd. "Someone outside has come to see us. I was hoping you would go out with me." Her expression of concern darkened to one of pain.

Raul understood. Aware that innocent ears were listening, he said, "You think maybe it's the f-a-t-h-e-r?" Myrna had hinted enough about her situation during their conversations that Raul had a good picture.

Myrna bit her lip. "Maybe. Or it might be my parents. I would just appreciate having someone with me."

"Glad to help," Raul returned with a smile. Then, hoping to cheer up Guy, he said, "Would you like another ride in my chair, Cool Cat?" The little boy shook his head and strengthened his hold on Myrna.

"He's wiped out and scared," Myrna explained. "Maybe another time." Raul nodded.

Passing through the lounge and approaching the crowd, Raul saw Reagan and Beth Cole right away standing with his empty wheelchair. He waved to acknowledge them, then flashed a give-me-a-minute sign to buy some time. He turned to Myrna. "Do you see him? Do you see anyone you know?"

Myrna searched the faces watching from the other side of the nylon rope. "No," she said, "I don't recognize anyone but the writer. She was on the bus. Why wasn't she on the plane?"

"I heard she got off at the last minute," Raul replied, "but I don't know why. She missed quite a ride." Myrna didn't consider Raul's comment amusing.

Beth kept waving. "Raul, Myrna, come here," she called above the boisterous crowd. "We sent for both of you."

When the little group moved away from the crowd, Beth introduced Cole to Myrna and Guy and explained her decision not to go on the flight. The tall couple gripped hands and exchanged looks of affection as Beth confessed her commitment to keep her husband and family above her work. When she announced that she was pregnant, even Myrna's face flickered the brightness of joy for a moment.

Then Cole invited Raul, Myrna, and Guy to spend the night at their home on Whidbey Island. He added quickly, "We want to hear all the details of the flight. We still hope to talk Cooper Sams into giving Beth permission to write the story." Beth flashed a pleased smile at her husband.

"I'm grateful for the place to stay," Raul said, "as long as I can leave for home first thing in the morning. I have some explaining to do to my family in Arizona. And I'm itching to get back to work."

"Sounds like you have a law officer's blood in your veins," Cole said.

"Maybe I do. But the work I'm most anxious for relates to the people I met on this flight. I have a lot of conversations to follow up on. And my work in Arizona has a lot to do with the people in the department. A lot of them are just as desperate for peace as the people on the plane. God has shown me over the last three days that He can use me to help people like that, legs or no legs."

Turning to Myrna, Beth said, "We'd like you to stay with us too. I'll call my friend Shelby and introduce you to her by phone. Maybe you can set up a time to meet her in Portland. Would you like that?"

Myrna was overwhelmed at being the focus of kindness when she had expected to face the wrath of Guy Rossovich. She knew she would have to face him eventually, and she was already worried about the outcome. But the warm acceptance and hospitality of the three people surrounding her seemed like a good place to start preparing for the painful days ahead. Raul was a man she thought she might want to see again someday. His kindness to her and Guy was as attractive as his strong features, flashing eyes, and glowing smile. And perhaps Beth and her friend Shelby *could* help her find the peace which had eluded her.

Finally, Myrna said, "If it won't be too much trouble."

"No trouble at all," Beth answered, beaming with pleasure.

Libby Carroll appeared out of the crowd, her face masked with worry. Seeing Beth and Cole, she brightened immediately. They embraced and rejoiced together that the plane was safely on the ground. Then Beth provided the introductions.

Aghast when she heard that Rachel Sams was on the plane, Libby said, "Where is she now?"

"She hasn't come out yet," Beth said, "neither has Cooper." Then she explained how the guards were calling people out.

"Excuse me, but I have to see her," Libby said. "I have to find out what happened between her and Cooper." She said good-bye and started toward the rope barricade.

"Call us later and fill us in," Beth called after her. Libby signaled that she would.

Cole helped Raul transfer into his own chair. Then the five of them headed for the exit, debating lightheartedly about how they would get four adults and a child into the S-10 pickup. They had a half-hour ride to the Stouffer-Madison where Raul and Myrna had left their cars. Cole and Raul were bracing for a cold ride in the back.

Cooper Sams entered the hangar area knowing he would have to say something to the media. The thought of facing the public was burning a hole in his stomach, but he knew it was right. They would hound him until he spoke the truth about the flight, and in the meantime they would blow the story so far out of proportion that nobody would believe the truth when they heard it. So Cooper thought it best to tell them the facts right away, admit his incredible blindness, and promise to help his former Family members retrieve their investments and get on with their lives.

But first he felt an obligation to the lost souls still milling about the hangar with nowhere to go. He was able to hire a large coach to transport them back to the Stouffer-Madison for the night. He assured them that they would gather in the morning to talk about what had happened to Lila Ruth, Reunion, and the Family. Finally, when the coach arrived on the tarmac away from the crowd, Cooper sent them out to board and wait for him while he conducted an impromptu press conference.

Cooper and Rachel paused in the empty hangar while he straightened his tie, tucked in his shirt, and donned his jacket and cap to face the cameras. His lips were dry, and the bitter taste of anxiety and humiliation was on his tongue.

"Are you going to let Beth Cole write the story?" Rachel said as she brushed lint from the shoulders of Cooper's jacket. "You know she's going to ask you about it."

Cooper groaned. "And put this embarrassment in book form for all the world to read? I don't know if I can bear it."

"I know her, Cooper. Beth doesn't want to embarrass you. She wants to tell the positive side of what happened."

Cooper studied her thoughtfully. "I see you, and I see us, and that's positive. But I don't see much else that's good about the last four years." He put on his cap and adjusted it to a familiar position. "If she writes this story, it will have to be titled 'Crash and Burn' or 'Nosedive: The Story of My Life.' "

Rachel smiled at him. "I was thinking of something more like 'Flying Higher' or 'Phoenix Rising.' I just know a lot of good is going to come out all this."

"I'm sorry, Rachel, but I can't believe that yet," Cooper said with a look of consternation.

Undaunted, Rachel replied, "It's OK. Until you can, I'll believe for both of us."

She kissed him lightly on the mouth, and his frown dissipated. Then they walked into the bright lights of the waiting crowd together.

What does the future hold for
Sgt. Reagan Cole and Beth Scibelli?

The spellbinding adventure and intrigue that surrounds Reagan and Beth will have you racing through the pages of *Millennium's Eve*, *Millennium's Dawn*, and *Doomsday Flight*. Don't miss a single twist or turn as bestselling author, Ed Stewart, weaves his captivating stories.

Look for them at your local Christian bookstore.

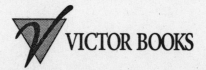

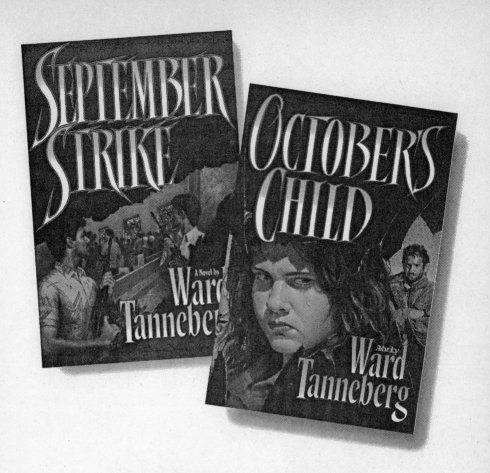

A ruthless world of terrorism threatens to tear the Cain family apart!

Life will never be the same for American pastor John Cain and his family. Unwittingly caught up in the high stakes game of international terrorism, the Cain family struggles for survival.

Look for *September Strike* and its sequel, *October's Child*, in your local Christian bookstore.

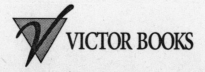